LEFT ON PARADISE

KIRK ADAMS

KIRK ADAMS BOOKS

Left on Paradise

This book was published in the United States of America.

ISBN 978-1-7356062-0-0

Kirk Adams Books

45497 Lost Trail Terrace

Sterling, Virginia 20164

Cover design by Reed Sprunger

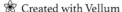 Created with Vellum

This book is dedicated to every American
who has contributed
to the greatest experiment in self-government
our world has ever known.

CONTENTS

And I saw a new heaven and a new earth:
for the first heaven and the first earth
were passed away;
and there was no more sea
—Revelation 21:1—

THE SECOND COMING OF OFFICERS AND GENTLEMEN

"Captain, Lieutenant Howard's on the radio."

A young Marine with a slim waist and a smooth face gave his handset to a squat, thick-necked captain dressed in desert-brown fatigues—who carried a holstered pistol on his hip and displayed twin bars across his shoulders.

The officer dropped his helmet to the ground as he put the receiver to his ear. "Captain Bradford here. What's that firing?"

A breathless voice came from the radio. "We've taken rounds, Capt'n. One man ambushed us. We took him out without taking casualties."

"Awww, crap," Captain Bradford muttered, but not into the radio. "Lieutenant, what's your situation?"

"We've taken up a position at the base of the hill," the breathless voice continued, "maybe a hundred meters inland from the LZ. I've sent a squad to secure our flank and deployed the rest of the platoon forward. What're your orders, sir?"

"Was the man alone?"

"Yes, sir. As best as I can tell, I've sent scouts forward."

"Lieutenant, hold your position and secure the beach. We're moving forward as planned. Recon reports no contact on the hill and

I'm approaching the north shore. We'll circle the island and be back to the LZ by dusk. Is that clear?"

The radio crackled. "Yes, sir."

"Lieutenant, you still there?"

Garbled speech came across the air.

"Don't let anyone get hurt," Captain Bradford ordered. "Or dehydrated."

The next reply sounded crisp.

"Roger."

A corporal packed the radio away as the captain turned toward a hard-muscled man with several stripes sewn to his sleeve and twenty years service stitched into his face.

"First Sergeant Rogers," Captain Bradford said, "have Lieutenant Diaz sent to me—and give the men a rest. Make sure they drink water. And keep scouts posted."

The sergeant hurried away to execute his orders.

A few minutes later, Captain Bradford and Lieutenant Diaz were seated on a fallen tree, drinking from canteens and nibbling food drawn from their fatigue pouches. A compass dangled from Bradford's neck as he studied an unfolded map. Though Lieutenant Diaz had only a single silver bar pinned to his shoulders, it was he who took the lead.

"Intelligence," Lieutenant Diaz said, "reported these people would be waiting on the beaches with outstretched arms."

"I haven't seen any parades," Captain Bradford said. "Have you?"

"I suppose not," the lieutenant said, grimacing. "We're going to be stuck here two days. Maybe longer."

"Most likely searching for stragglers and recovering remains."

"Looking at that beach near the LZ," Lieutenant Diaz said, "I'd like to get in some volleyball and a clambake. It'd be a shame to pass up a South Pacific paradise without a little rest and relaxation."

The captain gave a weak smile. "There aren't going to be too many native girls."

"And a shame it is, sir. A crying shame."

"To tell the truth," Captain Bradford said with a laugh, "I'd rather not see too many hula girls."

"Well," Lieutenant Diaz now raised his eyebrows, "I suppose times really are changing, so I won't ask if you don't tell."

"It's not that, you cretin. It's just that the wife's at Pendleton and I'm not. No use sniffing steak when you keep your teeth in a jar."

Both men laughed.

"Howard will secure a position," Captain Bradford said as he pointed to his map, "on the east side of the island while we move the company north, keeping a flank anchored to the shore and deploying a recon patrol inland to scout for unpleasant surprises. After we reach the north shore, we'll turn south down the west shore for the southern tip of the island and then complete the circle until we reach Howard's platoon at the LZ. It'll take the rest of the day to cover the outer perimeter of this god-forsaken place. We can wait till tomorrow to search inland. Since we're stuck here no matter what, we might as well do this right. Heck, we might even get the men a day on the beach out of this—and maybe that clambake you mentioned."

"There's no hurry," the lieutenant replied. "I'll post a squad forward—and I'll stay with them."

"Sounds good," the captain nodded as he folded his map.

"To tell the truth," Lieutenant Diaz said, "we're going to be boxed in that ship for the better part of six months, except for desert maneuvers. We need to exploit this opportunity."

"There's the making of a general," Captain Bradford said as he stood, shaking a leg that fell asleep while he crouched. "You bring clubs and a cart?"

The lieutenant said that he hadn't.

A few minutes later, both officers had secured their maps and now directed Marines into line. Sergeants slapped men on the back and jostled them into position, threatening extra duty if they didn't hurry—their brisk orders bringing sharp responses. Within minutes, every Marine moved forward at a steady, careful pace; not without noise, but with eyes trained ahead and weapon at the ready. The platoon made a broad sweep around the island, keeping one flank of the advancing line secured directly against the sea and the other extended inland. One man stayed near the lines of trees just off the shore while everyone else fanned out several feet apart. The captain remained with a reserve force stationed to the rear.

"Look, sir. There's another one behind the trees. That's not even a tough shot."

"Sergeant, hold your fire unless he shoots first. We're not savages."

"Yes, sir. I mean ... no, sir, we're Marines."

Lieutenant Howard lifted field glasses to his eyes and surveyed the tree line. Sergeant Abbott was right. There was someone in the trees, hiding behind a few broad-leaf palm bushes. But the man posed no immediate danger and orders were clear: to fire only in self-defense. This was former Russian territory and spilling blood could cause a stir for everyone; most of all, for a mere lieutenant exceeding his authority. He'd put in too many long days and sleepless nights at Annapolis to forfeit his commission now. The lieutenant dropped his glasses and searched among his men until he spotted a fair-faced Marine crouched behind a clump of palm trees twenty yards to his right.

"Corporal Michaels," the lieutenant said, "can you put a few rounds over that man's head? To keep him down."

"Yes, sir."

"Then do it. Over—I repeat—over his head. Don't hurt him."

The corporal, a thin youth with a boyish face, took aim from a sitting position. The stock of his rifle near a cheek, he closed an eye and squeezed the trigger. A single three-round burst exploded from his rifle and its bullets whizzed into the crown of the palm tree, striking a clump of coconuts—which burst open. From a distance it looked as though they exploded directly atop the half-hidden stranger—who immediately raised his hands and stood, shouting for the Marines to hold their fire.

Lieutenant Howard ordered his men to keep watch as he himself stepped into the clear. "What's your business?" he yelled to the stranger.

"I want to go home," came the distant reply.

"Then go."

"Not here," the man shouted. "Home. California."

The lieutenant looked through his binoculars before yelling out a short question. "You alone?"

"Yes," the man replied, cupping his hands over his mouth.

"Then move forward—slowly. Hands on your head. Drop the sack. It stays there. One false move and you're dead."

The lieutenant turned to Sergeant Abbott.

"Keep a bead on him," the officer ordered. "Don't make my fiancée a widow before I marry her, but don't get us court-martialed either. Fire only if he fires first or I give a direct order."

The sergeant aimed his rifle directly at the distant stranger's chest and held his position fast, his right forefinger resting against the frame of the weapon and his thumb posed to disengage the safety (as needed). Several others prepared to provide supporting fire. At less than two hundred yards, none would miss their target.

Lieutenant Howard watched as the stranger moved forward as ordered, hands raised high. It took the stranger a minute or so to cover the ground. Only at the last instant did Howard advance to frisk the stranger before leading the captive through the platoon's perimeter. There, the man stopped before a squad of gun-toting Marines—hands over his head and coconut shards sprinkled in his scraggly hair. Sticky coconut milk covered his unshaven whiskers.

Lieutenant Howard laughed a little. "Anyone for coconut?" he asked.

The captive fell to his knees. "Don't kill me," he cried out. "Have mercy."

Lieutenant Howard pulled the man to his feet. "No one," he said, "is going to kill you."

"Please don't hurt me," the man said as he dropped to his knees a second time to plead for his life.

"Get a grip," Lieutenant Howard answered as he pulled the man to his feet. "We're here to evacuate the island."

"Oh lord," the stranger said as he fell to his knees yet a third time, "don't lie to me. Tell me the truth."

This time the Marines just stared at him.

Only after the captive saw that not a single Marine fingered his trigger did he take a deep breath and relax.

"Finally," the man said as he stood up, "you've come."

"We were told there's a hundred Americans here," the lieutenant said, "but you're the first person we've seen. Other than the stupid bastard who took a shot at Sergeant Abbott—God rest his soul."

The stranger looked to the ground.

"They're crazy," the man said. "There's maybe half a dozen left. Radicals under the command of Father Donovan. We've fought 'em for days."

"How many guns," Sergeant Abbott now joined the interrogation, "do they have?"

"One they stole from a yacht."

"What kind?"

"A black one."

"This it?" Sergeant Abbott asked as he pulled a semi-automatic pistol from his belt and showed it to the stranger.

"I think so," the man replied.

"This was the only gun on the island? For a hundred people?"

A puzzled look came across the stranger's face. "We're pacifists and idealists, mostly. Even hunting was forbidden."

The sergeant moved his face within a foot of the stranger's, speaking with a growled whisper and pointing a finger to the stranger's face. "If you lie to us, I personally will ..."

"Sergeant," Lieutenant Howard said with quiet control, "let him speak."

Sergeant Abbott checked himself and considered his words before glancing at his officer and then looking straight at the captured stranger. "He'll stay with us. Any traps and it'll be his ass too."

The lieutenant nodded before again addressing the captive. "You mentioned a yacht. Whose yacht?"

"A good Samaritan's," the man whispered as he dropped his eyes and shuffled his feet.

The lieutenant's face tightened. "Captain James Strong?"

The prisoner nodded.

"Where is he?"

"Dead."

"And his wife?"

"All of them. His wife, her sister, his brother-in-law."

"You sons of ..." Now it was Lieutenant Howard who struggled to check his anger as he turned to his sergeant and spoke with a sharp voice. "I roomed with his son at Annapolis."

Sergeant Abbott said nothing.

"Sons of bitches," the lieutenant grabbed the man by the shoulders and growled through clenched teeth. "Where're all of your hippie friends? Where are they? Where?"

The prisoner dropped his eyes and turned white before choking out a quiet answer. "They're gone."

Howard let the man go and stepped back—his forehead furrowed and cheeks crinkled. "Where'd they go?"

"Gone," the stranger said, his voice high pitched and anxious. "There can't be more than a dozen of us left, plus the rebels. Maybe a few more on other islands. I don't know. Everyone's dead. Some are buried."

"Corporal," Lieutenant Howard gave orders to a clean-shaven youth waiting several feet away, "get Captain Bradford on the radio. Pronto."

The corporal just stared at the dirty stranger, shaking his head in disbelief and saying nothing.

"Now, Corporal Billington," Lieutenant Howard snapped. "Now!"

As the corporal reached for a handset, the lieutenant composed an operational plan that he briefed to Sergeant Abbott.

"Deploy recon teams," the lieutenant said, "to secure a base camp for the night. Looks like it'll take a couple days to clean this mess. I hope no one gets hurt in this operation."

"Yes, sir," Sergeant Abbott said as he glared at the stranger, "it'd be a waste to lose a good Marine to save a bunch of Clinton-loving liberals. These are probably the jackasses—I mean, Democrats—who got my vote thrown out."

"You have no idea," the stranger said, "how good it is to be insulted by an American military fasc"—the man looked at the line of Marines in their fatigues, rifles at hand, and came to the conclusion that some things are better left unsaid—"by an American fighting man."

The sergeant and lieutenant shook their heads before giving instructions to two privates and then leaving the captive with the two guards—at which time one of the Marines threw a folded knife and a food ration to the stranger.

"After you eat, use it to shave your head," the Marine said. "We don't need no fleas in our camp."

"Lice," the second Marine explained. "You need to shave your head to get rid of the lice. Sergeant Abbott is sending back some clothes too. They probably won't fit, but they'll be clean. You'll feel better after you wash up. Then I'll help you shave your head. It's not easy the first time. With a knife, I mean."

The stranger nodded.

"It's called a MRE," the Marine said as he pointed to plastic-wrapped block the size of a large brick. "That stands for Meal Ready to Eat. Instructions are on the plastic."

"I've had plenty," the captive said as he sliced the thick plastic open like a veteran. Ten minutes later the MRE was reduced to a pile of scraps and discarded remnants littering the ground. After he finished eating, the stranger approached the mannerly private to have his head shaved. Though the haircut wasn't one of the most stylish to have adorned the stranger's head, it did the job.

"Thanks," the prisoner said to the soft-spoken private, "for your kindness. It's been a long time since ... Well, what's your name, soldier?"

"Ron, sir. PFC Ronald Reagan Shoemaker."

AFTER CAPTAIN BRADFORD heard a prisoner was captured, he ordered Lieutenant Howard to hold his position until reinforced and to secure a base camp for the night. The subordinate did as told, though he soon radioed that Sergeant Abbott had detained a second prisoner—a Latino woman who surrendered without trouble. In the meantime, the captain pushed his troops forward as the whining scream and thumping blades of helicopters filled the tropical sky and forward observers scoured for signs of the missing Americans. Aircraft hovered over nearby islets looking for survivors and airlifted a group of refugees to an aircraft carrier. But on the main island, no movement was observed—with pilots reporting only smoldering flames, blackened ruins, and dead bodies.

Their observations were confirmed on the ground.

Lieutenant Diaz was leading First Squad when the Marines came to the rubble of a burned village along the north shore. A destroyed fiberglass boat had been dragged across the sand to the trees, holes burned through its hull and the motor also burned beyond repair. Two charred buildings and several torn tents were located west of a stream fifty yards inland and a wooden pole—little more than a sapling stripped of its bark and branches—was posted nearby. A crossbar was nailed to it and a middle-aged Latino woman was nailed to the bar, her shoulders and head slumped forward and her face covered by blood-caked strands of graying hair. The woman's stiffened hips and legs hung moribund above the ground, slightly bent at the knees, and her chest and back were scarred by the cuts of a lash. Her legs were chewed up and bloodied by some animal: the tendons of both legs chewed to the bone. All of the woman's toes were missing.

Nearby, the head of an open-eyed teenager—also Latino—was stuck on a stake. Her eye sockets were empty, face bruised, and torso altogether missing. Several feet away, a half-eaten light-skinned woman was lying close to the stiff carcasses of two dark-skinned aborigines who'd been dead for days.

The camp looked like a garbage dump. Worn clothing, pieces of wood, half-rotted books, and even rusted tools were scattered from one end to the other. The tents weren't much better inside. Several reeked of a penetrating, clinging stench and two Marines who peered inside were afterwards on their knees vomiting. The odor smelled of spoiled food, burnt flesh, and decaying refuse left to percolate in the tropical heat. Flies swarmed to the dead flesh and birds picked what was soft. An open latrine was no more than an infested cesspool, filled with piss and shit and every human waste—and thousands of vile-smelling maggots. The whole village was an environmental disaster. What stood was falling down, what fell was returning to earth, and what returned to dust was no more. Only what had been burned to ashes was no longer repulsive.

Lieutenant Diaz marked the position of the bodies with a bright tape wrapped around nearby trees and radioed to Captain Bradford for body bags. Then he left a squad to secure the position and sanitize the area while he marched the rest of the platoon around the northern tip of the island and then south for hours—the men burdened with sixty-pound backpacks and slowed by tactical formation, rough terrain, and the frequent need to rehydrate.

Three more villages were discovered during their sweep, none containing a living inhabitant. The bodies of a tall black woman and a short Asian man were found near a village on the west side, along with two white men—one of them still clutching a charred spear with burned fingers. The smell of singed flesh and burned gasoline was strong. Further south, shredded tents were discovered near a small grave likely dug for a child—the shallow grave only two feet long and marked with an uncut granite stone. A fourth village located on the east side of the island was scouted late in the afternoon, though every building in the village had been burned to the ground. The remains of one unidentifiable man and two Polynesian women were found along a path to this eastern village: one of them a girl whose spine was severed and the other an old woman missing her arms and eyes. What struck Captain Bradford about the natives was less their small stature than their tight lips and bad teeth. They looked starved—their paucity accentuated by the torn flesh and teeth marks left by some indigenous scavenger. The captain warned his men to watch for predators. Scouts also found four bodies washed ashore near ship wreckage consisting of bottles, clothes, coolers, and chairs. All four bodies were swollen and half-eaten by crabs.

After the Marines circled the island, they bedded down for the night, most of them sleeping atop bedrolls under open sky near the remnants of the village closest to the landing zone. Before retiring, some enlisted men bathed in the surf while others searched the trees for fresh fruit. A corporal found an old steel helmet lying near a main path and stuffed it in his backpack as a souvenir. Several Marines took their pictures atop a half-sunken World War Two-era LCVP landing craft washed ashore by the tide—the boat painted with a rainbow and political slogans and symbols and showing no sign of rust, though its ramp was dropped and its cab burned out. Lights out was ordered two hours before midnight and sentries were posted with loaded weapons.

THE MARINES WOKE before dawn and ate MREs for a cold breakfast. More fortunate Marines found their plastic-wrapped meals stocked with beef or pork while the timid or unlucky ate vegetarian meals smothered in Tabasco sauce. Only sergeants and officers didn't complain, though even they groaned as they opened their breakfast —most of them too young to console themselves with memories of C-rations. By first light, the company was on the march, backpacks stacked at the beach and Marines deployed with a day's rations stowed in their fatigues and full canteens clipped to their belts. Platoons moved in formation up the island's main hill, splitting the slopes to either side of its peak. A recon patrol reported activity near the summit, as well as a deserted fortress and mass casualties. There-after, the Marines marched even more cautiously, weapons at the ready. Scouts advanced to look for ambushes, but reported only dead bodies. The hill was a steep climb for Marines moving in tactical formation and weighed down with rucksacks and it was midmorning before the troops reached the top.

Lieutenant Howard was twenty yards to the rear when his point man stopped. He motioned to Sergeant Abbott.

"Sergeant. Find out why that man stopped."

"Moving now," Abbott said as he jumped over a fallen tree and trotted forward, his rifle carried barrel up.

When Sergeant Abbott arrived forward, his stomach turned. Eleven corpses, ash-colored and bloated, were lined in a row—some were men and others were women. There was one youth and a small baby. All of the dead rested side by side across a trail overgrown with foliage: its green vines already beginning to creep over the human remains. The baby's face was partially covered with an exotic white flower and a woman's bent and stiffened legs provided the mount for the fresh shoots of a climbing vine. And though the thick canopy had cloaked the site from overhead observation, wild animals had sniffed out their prey. Two of the bodies were partially eaten and all of the eye sockets of the dead were reduced to hollow indentations—presumed feasts for island birds. The breasts of one woman were gone, as were the arms of a small child. A middle-aged man with long hair was chewed open from kidney to crotch.

The sergeant signaled four men to follow as he advanced toward a rudimentary bunker. A wall of felled logs and bermed earth was near the hill's crest, though the logs didn't fit well and it was clear they'd been constructed in haste. After the squad maneuvered toward the fort, Sergeant Abbott himself entered—having positioned one team for fire support before motioning for a second team to follow. The Marines moved tactically toward defensive positions and it took them little time to secure the fort.

Inside, every man among them went pale. A hastily raised gibbet stood before them, its wood stained with dried blood, and a human head had been discarded a few feet away. One of the Marines rolled over the head with the tip of his rifle—only to find the dead eyes of a young girl staring through him. He gasped, turned his face away, and stepped back before finding himself compelled to take a second look at the straight teeth and long hair of the bodiless head. As soon as he did so, his stomach churned, bile came to his throat, and his face drained of blood. Swallowing the vomit that rose in his throat, the Marine struggled to retain his composure.

"Sergeant," the Marine said with dry voice that didn't carry far, "can you come over here?"

Sergeant Abbott jogged to the pale-faced Marine. "Private Shoemaker," the sergeant asked, "are you okay?"

"Look at this, Sergeant Abbott," the Marine said, waving his rifle toward the severed head.

Sergeant Abbott looked at the dead girl's face and turned white. "Damned barbarians," he whispered, his finger moving from the frame of his weapon before being pulled back by deliberate force of will and habit of training.

"Yeah," Shoemaker replied with a slow, deliberate choice of his words. "I ain't ever voting Democrat again. No matter what my granddad says."

The Marine's stomach quivered and he fell to his knees, throwing up until little more than a soupy, brown bile dripped down his chin. Afterwards, he wiped his mouth on a bared wrist and looked for the sergeant. He nodded without speaking when Sergeant Abbott told him to take point when he could.

Already, a dozen Marines passed by and it took Shoemaker a minute to weave though them as he jogged toward the point position.

2

IMAGINING PARADISE

A new world was conceived on December 13, 2000—as soon as the United States Supreme Court cast its lot with Republicans in the disputed presidential election. Ryan Godson's jaw dropped as reporters announced the Florida State Supreme Court's effort to secure an impartial election was suspended and the ballots of thousands of Democratic voters wouldn't be recounted. Ten minutes later, the actor told his wife—actress Kit Fairchild—that a whiff of fascism had been legalized and it was time to emigrate: just as he'd threatened throughout the campaign. Ryan refused to be played as another Hollywood liberal standing as a stooge on stage for whoever might come to power. He wouldn't play the part of court jester. For her part, Kit agreed to go with her husband of seven years, saying they could manage careers from abroad as well as from California. Ryan observed Roman Polanski did quite well from Europe—though Kit said she didn't want anything to do with the convicted rapist of a teenaged girl.

By midafternoon, Ryan contracted an apartment in Geneva and booked an international moving company to ship the couple's possessions. Thereafter, he and Kit spent the evening telephoning family and friends to explain their decision to leave the United States and even organized a farewell banquet for those who lived nearby—at which the couple announced that they planned an imminent departure. Ryan expressed his intent to move abroad long before Bush was sworn into office as the country's first illegitimate President.

Two days later, Ryan canceled the lease and forfeited his deposit. Having watched a public television documentary about Russian noble émigrés, he realized life abroad would be an endless parade of caviar and cigars, parties and affairs, love and leisure. Ryan had freed himself from the glamour of Hollywood by political activism during the Gore campaign and knew it wouldn't do to fall back into the spoils of pleasure while others suffered the ravages of conservatism. Mere escape wouldn't make an impact.

A better path was needed—a truer realization of the ideal. Acquiescence wouldn't suffice and neither would Hollywood grandstanding. Someone needed to effect change and Ryan wanted to be the one. Why else did he double major in political science and theater arts at USC and star in so many historical epics? What could he accomplish with his talents and resources? For what great purpose had he been given his good looks and fame?

A few days before Christmas, Ryan lounged beneath palm trees in his Beverly Hills backyard. There, an idea—a revelation—was given to him. As if inspired from heaven, he decided that he no longer would preach like a priest or lecture like a professor, but must plan like a politician and paint like an artist. He must make things that weren't become things that were and create a new society ex nihilo. Like-minded and good-willed people had labored under utterly impossible circumstances far too long. The intrigues and interests of slavery and racism, nationalism and militarism, capitalism and individualism, conservatism and pietism so distorted the body politic that every honest effort to implement social justice was doomed from the start. Shiny schools were built in urban slums too dangerous for gentrification and national parks carved from natural wastes too remote for exploitation (though even bare tundra was coveted by conservatives eager to squeeze every drop of profit from the earth). The welfare state served as little more than a sales tax on the leftovers of unrestrained greed and NRA gunmen shot up any effort to keep children from pistols and rifles alike. Even female suffrage often empowered narrow-minded housewives and miserly old women to outvote thoughtful feminists.

"How could we ever expect," Ryan explained to friend and family alike, "progressive ideas to work here? We're pouring new wine into recycled bottles capped with used corks and then act surprised when the wine leaks and spoils. Jesus had it right: we need to start from scratch. To lay a new foundation before we build. You can't construct skyscrapers on prairie sod."

Fortunately Ryan was between sets, so the next day he called his agent to search for land and sent Kit to visit family in Manhattan while he locked himself inside his Bel Air mansion for a fortnight: his phone line disconnected and cell coverage suspended. Security guards were given strict orders under pain of dismissal to let no one through the gate and even his mail was held at the post office. Two weeks later, Ryan emerged from his Hollywood manor—famished by his long fast on home-cooked meals and domestic wine—with a plan to make a new society. He reconnected his phones, picked up his mail, and told Kit to hurry home.

It didn't take Ryan long to work out the parameters of a new world. Population size and composition were easy to set, apportioned according to a generous relationship of square acreage to living humans. The technical arrangements also were easy to engineer: medical, mechanical, and educational demands for a modest number of emigrants. It was a little more difficult to calculate the little things: the nuts and bolts and tools and tonnage necessary to supply a population with its daily bread. But several excellent software programs and two cutting-edge computer simulations enabled the actor to calculate in a week what an ancient king might have needed a court of royal officials to decide. An upgrade of the popular game Simulation Civilization proved particularly helpful, showing Ryan what physical and social systems needed to be accommodated—even delineating some of the cultural and moral controversies that might come into play. Ryan also drew from his movie-making experience, extensive travels, and progressive education. In any event, he determined the types of goods needed for the first several months, then compiled a purchase list and estimated costs. A wholesaler promised to prepare the goods for shipping in a matter of weeks, assuming a new land was discovered—a task that was delegated to Joshua Steinberg, Ryan's long-time agent and confidante.

On New Year's Eve, Steinberg paged Ryan with an important message. He had spied land up for sale: a crescent-shaped South Pacific island southeast of the Marquesas Isles and north of Easter Island. The island was the dominant isle in a tiny archipelago too small and isolated to be of strategic value during the age of competition and possessed no navigable harbors to make it commercially productive even today. The main island was less than four miles long and two miles wide—while a spine of broken ridges over nine hundred feet high traversed the length of the island, sloping almost to the shores, except for a few isolated patches of flat ground. The island was ringed by a coral reef, though a dozen motu rose from the sea to its west—with the largest of these being no more than a block-sized covering of thin soil and coconut trees and the smaller ones little more than clumps of palms and pandanus fruit protruding from the lagoon. Islets east of the atoll were eroded by surf and tide and remained only as submerged reefs that rendered the archipelago too dangerous for deep-draughted ships. Like a submerged fortress, the reef protected the island from commercialization and exploitation.

What Ryan liked best was that the islands were claimed by Russia based on a landing by Siberian settlers who'd sailed south from Alaska to establish a permanent colony. Though some land was cleared for fruit and nut orchards, the colony became untenable after the sale of Alaska to the Republican Secretary of State William Seward in 1867 for millions of dollars that otherwise might have been spent on the Bureau of Refugees, Freedmen, and Abandoned Lands or similar poor relief efforts. Indeed, the Republican administration purchased the territory for nearly two cents per acre with the objective of profiting from the immoral and obscene seal fisheries. Recognizing both that their colony was even more isolated than a similar

Russian enterprise that previously had failed in Hawaii and that the liquidation of the Russian-American Company had disrupted financial backing for the colony, Russian settlers burned their cabins and sailed back to Vladivostok. Colonial records were lost at sea during a squall that sank one of two ships returning to Russia and the few colonists who survived the abortive expedition lived out their days as laborers and farmhands who left few records of life on the island they once called Novi Mir.

Now the island was unpopulated and available for purchase at twenty million American dollars. Godson hired an international property attorney to finalize the deal both in a Russian court and an international panel—both of which recognized the leasing of the island for ninety-nine years or as long as the atoll remained demilitarized. Keen to collect Hollywood cash without arousing domestic opposition, the Russians kept negotiations secret and a newly-established multinational corporation named New World Inc® was established to govern the island as an autonomous state entity recognized under international law and guaranteed its legitimacy as long as the provisions of its contract remained inviolate. In particular, it was stressed by Russian magistrates that the importation of any organized military force to the archipelago nullified the contract—with immediate forfeiture of the purchase price. Putin didn't want Godson's enterprise to function as a covert arm of American diplomacy.

The United States Department of State, which was eager to keep the islands from potential Chinese acquisition, surreptitiously approved the deal as Ryan sped negotiations through The Hague with well-placed gifts to Russian diplomats and well-timed phone calls to the White House. Even in his final days, President Clinton didn't forget his friends from Hollywood and sent the Secretary of State to negotiate terms. The contract was signed hours before George W. Bush was sworn in as the 43rd President of the United States of America (with Grover Cleveland counted twice)—somewhere between the pardoning of Marc Rich and the federalization of Utah's forests.

Six weeks later, Ryan and Kit began interviews and continued them through March as applicants sought the right to emigrate. Word was circulated discreetly through contacts in the progressive community that a hundred colonists were needed to establish an eco-colony dedicated to preserving a tract of Brazilian rainforest and implementing multicultural mores (somewhat like the Ecosphere 4 project in New Mexico). While Ryan sent his agent on a public trip to Rio de Janeiro to negotiate the down payment on a 65,000-acre preserve as a decoy, applicants flew to Los Angeles at their own expense (where they met Ryan and Kit in a Burbank high-rise office). Many were called, but few were chosen—and Ryan himself numbered the elect.

"Kit, who's next?"

Kit reclined against a blue velvet love seat, her legs crossed and hands folded at her knees. She wore a black satin dress with a slit that exposed her right thigh. The sparkle of diamonds gleamed from her ears and a garland of pearls graced her neck. Every word from her lips was articulated with propriety and polish, as if rehearsed.

"Alan and Steve Lovejoy."

Ryan watched from behind a large oak desk: a pile of marked manila folders stacked on it. He wore a brown sport jacket, his black hair combed behind his ears and lightly distinguished with gray streaks.

"Brothers?"

"Newlyweds," Kit said, "married in Vermont a couple months ago."

"That's right," Ryan said as he pushed a button on his intercom. "Miss Sayers, please send in the Lovejoys."

The door opened and a slender receptionist with short hair and dark glasses escorted two middle-aged men into the office and made introductions. The men were offered coffee after being led to a blue couch opposite Kit's love seat and made themselves comfortable without fanfare.

"So," Ryan began, "you were just married?"

"Yes," Steve said, "we're from Las Vegas, but we married in Vermont on vacation."

"It was a lovely wedding," Alan said, "just the two of us and a justice of the peace."

"Ours was a little bigger," Kit said with a smile.

"About a hundred grand bigger," Ryan laughed. "Eloping's not a bad idea."

"We didn't have much choice," Alan said. "Our ..."

"That," Ryan interrupted, "brings us to the topic at hand."

Alan fell silent.

"We want," Ryan said, "to make a world where love is never a controversy. We want to make a place where every family is free to decide its own rules. And we want to help create a society completely free of stereotypes and prejudices."

"Sounds great," Alan said.

Ryan pulled forms from a dark folder and glanced at a note card with a few handwritten notes before turning back to the two men.

"I see from your resumes," Ryan said, "you studied horticulture at the University of Nevada."

"We own a greenery near Las Vegas," Steve said. "We supply plants to thirty flower shops and two university labs."

"Very useful. Do you know anything about tropical plants?"

"We have plenty in our greenhouse, including fruit trees."

"Very, very good," Ryan said. "Your credentials are strong."

As Ryan shuffled through a few more papers, he turned slightly toward Kit and asked if she had any questions. Though she had none at present, she reserved the right to question the men later.

"Looking at your application," Ryan said after a moment, "I see you have no immediate family to speak of."

"That's not exactly what it says," Alan said. "It says that we have no one we're close to. Most of our relatives are bigots—I mean Baptists—and our recent marriage just made our situation worse."

"We're not going to miss the States," Steve added, "if that's what you want to know."

"What else can you add to our enterprise?"

"Here are our strengths," Alan said. "We're liberal and committed. We avoid every sort of stereotype and we've both voted Democrat since Dukakis. We have technical expertise with botany and we're both in great physical shape. We jog five miles every day and work out at the gym three days a week."

"Anything else?" Ryan asked.

"We don't have kids," Alan said. "Nothing against children, but you're going to need a few extra adults in this enterprise."

Ryan nodded and Kit motioned to speak.

"Are you ..." Kit asked, "I want to say this just right—are you ... I guess the best word is proselytizers."

Alan removed his arm from Steven's shoulder and leaned forward, his hands clasped together beneath his chin as he stared at Kit.

"I believe," Alan said, "we were born homosexual just as you apparently were born heterosexual. I chose Steve but I didn't choose the desire to marry a man. We can no more make other men homosexual than you can engineer the color of your hair. It's all genetics. You can't escape who or what you are. Even dye shows through after a few weeks."

"I'm a natural blonde," Kit said, now red-faced, "and I didn't mean to offend you. I ask the same question of everyone. We don't need zealots of any lifestyle choice. Tolerance is our strength."

"We're fine," Alan said, relaxing a little and falling back into the sofa. "All we want is to be left alone. We'll respect everyone else's choices, whatever they are. Freedom is what we're about."

"And public monogamy," Steve added. "We want to live as a couple just like everyone else: without prejudice or condemnation. 'Don't ask, don't tell' isn't enough for us."

Ryan laughed. "Clever."

"And appropriate," Alan said, "since Steve was discharged from the army under Dubya's dad."

Ryan's voice dropped. "You enlisted?"

"I needed college money and my parents couldn't help," Steve said. "I served three years before I went to school."

"That would be a decade ago," Ryan said. "Are you a Gulf War veteran?"

"I ran supplies," Steve replied with a nod, "to the front till my truck hit a mine. I sat the rest of the war out alongside the road, waiting for a lift. A year later, I came out of the closet and was drummed out of my country's army."

"Then you've shown courage twice over," Ryan said as he stood up. "Not bad at all. We won't need too many soldiers where we're going, but you can always help us beat swords into plowshares."

"Self-discipline," Steve said, "and a bit of courage are always useful."

Ryan looked at Kit and caught her eye before standing to extend his hand to the two men who likewise stood to receive Ryan's approach.

"Mostly," Ryan said, "I make my decision from the essays and application. This interview is used primarily to weed out imposters, crazies, and fanatics."

"Which are we?" Alan asked.

"You," Ryan replied, "are citizens of the new world. If you wish to be."

"Great," Alan said.

Steve said nothing.

Ryan shook the hand of both men and Kit extended the same courtesy before they told Alan and Steve to prepare for any contingency, not withstanding previous announcements that a Brazilian site was being considered.

Ten minutes later the two men found themselves in the adjacent office of a staff attorney—where they received legal advice regarding steps needed to protect their financial interests and order their legal affairs. Only after they had signed waivers and non-disclosure agreements were the applicants directed to a staff nurse to schedule physical examinations. The two men were sent from the office with a set of instructions, a pile of legal documents, and a full calendar.

.   .   .

A WHITE MALE in his late twenties sat on the blue couch. Short brown hair stood straight from his head and he wore a sweatshirt printed with the word Berkeley.

"I'll answer your question," the young man said with a grin, "after you answer mine. Why do you, of all people, want to leave this world?"

"Fair enough, " Ryan replied, setting a folder on the desk and leaning back in his swivel chair. "There's no doubt I've had a good career in Hollywood. And Kit, too, as far as that goes. But we're tired of the pretense. Not the movies and shows, mind you, but the politics. We bit our lips and pretended to love Tipper and Lieberman to support Al Gore and we pretended for eight years Clinton wasn't Arkansas trailer trash and his wife the Ice Queen. I'd personally nominate James Carville for an Academy Award for his public performance as the dogged defender of persecuted innocence. Every day, we sent emissaries and delegates across America to preach our message to the American people. And we gave. We gave mountains of money. I donated a million or two myself. And where did it end: with the Republicans stealing the Florida election and the Presidency. Now they'll control the White House, Congress, and the Supreme Court, as well as most governorships and state legislatures. It's getting hard for a liberal to be elected dogcatcher. He'd be accused of being soft on rabies if he decided to cage strays rather than hang 'em from the nearest tree. I want to live in a community where progressives speak freely, where they make a true democracy, and where they really live liberal values. And to be frank—I want to help create such a world. A city on the hill was how the Puritans saw themselves. We can do better than burning witches, swindling land, and fighting natives."

"I can live with that," the young man said.

"I'm glad," Ryan said, "my opinions please you, Mr. Kelly. Now what can you say to convince us of your value?"

Sean didn't flinch.

"Only that my father," Sean said, "was an anti-war protester during the sixties and my mother one of the first flower children. She knew Janis Joplin in '66. They lived in a commune for a while, but left after I came along. Afterwards, they remained active in the Sierra Club, which explains my love for nature. I suppose their lifestyle and my infancy in the commune explain my interest in reforming society. But America is beyond redemption. Mom and Dad knew it when they tuned in and dropped out and it's worse now. The idealists have sold out and the silent majority has become the moral majority. I want to go to a new land free from all prejudices to begin a new life. I suppose it's undeniable the drugs and orgies hurt the communes. Mom and Dad left their comrades because they didn't want to end like Charles Manson and his clan of renegade hippies shacked up down the street. Still, the deeper problem is America itself: militarist, sexist, racist. All of us on the left know society shapes the individual. Every one of our policies is predicated on that notion. The inverse of that truth, however, is even the blameless man or woman can be corrupted by a bad society. And all of us are and I no longer want to be."

"Bravo, bravo," Kit clapped her hands lightly. "You've given the best speech yet."

Sean shrugged. "Sorry."

"Don't be," Kit said with a smile. "It was very moving."

"We've already talked of your practical qualifications," Ryan said, "which are strong. You've worked construction and fishing. And you studied civil engineering as an undergrad. What about your love life? Are you leaving anyone behind?"

"I live with Ursula Gottlieb-Tate."

Ryan nodded. "She's the gypsy girl? I'm sorry. I meant to say the Roma woman."

"Afro-German," Sean answered as he shook his head. "Her father was an American soldier who got himself stationed in Berlin after Vietnam. He brought Ursula and her mom to Georgia when he returned, but Ms. Gottlieb used both names both for her feminism and because it wasn't politically correct for a white woman to marry a black man in those days. There weren't too many legs still broken over such sins when Ursula was born, but prejudice was real enough.

Eventually, they made their way to Chicago, but Ursula kept both names."

"That's what she said," Kit said.

"We interviewed her yesterday," Ryan explained.

"We made," Sean said, "a joint application but for some reason they're being processed separately."

"I apologize," Kit said. "It certainly wasn't intentional."

"No problem. We guessed a glitch in the paperwork."

The interview lasted another half hour, centering on plans for the community, the tools necessary for proper construction, and Sean's relationship with Ursula. At the end of the interview, Ryan and Kit shared notes and whispers while Sean sat on the sofa. Then they congratulated him on his acceptance and told him to schedule his appointments for the following day.

A few minutes later, Kit telephoned Ursula at her hotel and told her she too was chosen and her appointments were scheduled with Sean's.

"WHY DO you want to leave the United States at your age? Second year of grad school, is it?"

A petite woman with golden skin and dark hair pulled in a tight bun sat on the blue couch, her legs crossed at the knees and dress pulled over them. The woman's eyes flickered in the sunlight which streamed through half-drawn curtains and her hands moved in graceful cadence with her words, her fingers flowing from swaying wrists and brightly polished nails glimmering from reflected light. Kit watched her husband—her smile tight and eyes hard—as the young woman answered.

"Well, Mr. Godson ..."

"Call me Ryan, please," Ryan interrupted.

Kit bit her lip.

"Ryan," the woman said, "I study the humanities at UCLA. School's going well enough, but it's so bookish. I want to experience the world, to live in it, to love in it."

The young woman batted her eyes and smiled as Ryan locked his eyes on hers for an instant before fumbling through his notes.

"Wh-what's your major, Maria?"

"I'm studying Political Science."

"And what can you add to our enterprise?"

"Beyond my formal education," the young woman replied, "I suppose I can make a difference from my own experience. I've been a cross-cultural counselor and a day-care provider in the past. I've also helped to raise my three young sisters and tutored Spanish."

Ryan smiled and nodded.

"Also," Maria added after a pause, "I don't know if it's relevant, but I've been an aerobics instructor."

Ryan glanced at the young woman's toned arms, his eyes crossing her breasts and waist as Maria turned away—her cheeks flush.

"Good shape, as I tell Kit every day," Ryan said as he looked at his wife, "can never do a body any harm. Right dear?"

"Right," Kit said, her voice flat.

"I try to stay fit," Maria said, "and this new life will help—with plenty of physical exercise and few fattening foods."

"Only what you carry in yourself," Ryan said, "and I don't imagine too many people bringing cupcakes to the jungle."

"Or ice cream," Maria said, leaning forward as she laughed.

Ryan looked at Kit. "Any questions for her?"

Kit reviewed her notes.

"My question," Kit finally said, her voice still flat, "pertains to the rigors of camp life. Ryan and I have lived on remote sets for weeks on end and it can be difficult enough doing without the conveniences of life when someone's there to set your hair and groom your nails. This will be more spartan. How does that sit with you?"

"Don't let the aerobics and nails fool you," Maria answered. "One of my grandfathers was a migrant to the San Joaquin Valley and I've seen what it's like to do without. I dress as fashionably as I can afford, but I also go without food to watch my weight and work hard at every job I take. It was because I studied harder than my friends that I was admitted to grad school and it was because I looked under every rock for a scholarship that I found money to attend. I'm not giving it up for a vacation. This looks fun and I'll enjoy it as much as anyone, but I'll do my share of work. You needn't doubt that. I'm one of the most determined women you'll ever meet."

"You're also feisty," Kit said as she arched her eyebrows.

"Meekness isn't the virtue often supposed. The study of politics makes that clear."

"There's a chance," Kit said, "we could move to a coastal area. Would that suit you as well as the rainforest?"

"I've taken trips," Maria now perked up, "to the rainforests of Honduras and I've taken vacations to the beaches of Puerto Rico. I love both. But it's the community I'm interested in as much as the environment. My master's thesis was titled Darwinism and the Politics of Conflict in Reproduction and covered social ethics rather than more strictly biological and ecological forces."

Kit cleared her throat. "Do you," she asked, "have a problem with environmentalists?"

"Nothing like that," Maria said. "I only mean to say I'm interested in this enterprise whether it goes to the Arctic or Aruba. It's humanity that matter to me more than its habitat."

Maria glanced at Ryan while Kit jotted notes. After final questions regarding diet, she was dismissed to a waiting room where she waited until Ryan stepped out alone to congratulate her on her acceptance and send the young woman—like the others—to schedule medical examinations and legal consultations.

RYAN AND KIT celebrated with steak and lobster after having manifested one hundred handpicked pilgrims and twenty standby passengers (to replace last minute cancellations or be shipped to the colony after several months). When Ryan and Kit themselves were counted, the group equaled the one hundred and two pilgrims who landed at Plymouth Rock and also achieved an almost statistically perfect profile of race and gender for the new community—at least according to American demographics. Though Ryan originally hoped to reflect earth's population patterns, the purely practical difficulty of finding progressive Afrikaners, liberal Arabs, and multicultural Asians proved insurmountable, so it was decided to emulate American ethnic composition only. The Hollywood couple also was pleased that no more than one in three interviews culminated in rejection. The political, vocational, and personal questions on the applications were well considered and applicants proved both articulate and honest.

"It will be enough," Ryan said over champagne and hors d'oeuvres, "to show how a racial profile of American society can live in harmony."

Kit just smiled.

"We sail in a month," Ryan said. "A toast to progressives everywhere."

"Godspeed," Kit added.

Shortly, Ryan and Kit returned to their Beverly Hills estate and stayed up late—pressed to enjoy every moment left in the old world and make every preparation for the new one. When they awoke the next morning to finalize their plans for paradise, the first day of April already had arrived.

3

PILGRIMS SAIL WEST

The Flower of the First of May was secured to a long wharf with a dozen hemp ropes. Though the ship bobbed in the water, its gangplank remained a steady connection to the quays of San Francisco as groups of well-wishers escorted loved ones to the ship and details of sailors used cranes and hoists to stack cargo on the deck. There was no media, no crowds, no frenzy. A wisp of black smoke, dissipated inland by breezy harbor winds, billowed from the ship's soot-covered stacks and a weather-worn Russian flag fluttered over opened cargo holds—sometimes snapping in smart salute over the cluttered decks and rusting railings of the old ship. The transport pitched and rolled in the pull of the afternoon tide and its faded-red waterline flashed through the harbor's choppy waves— which splashed against the dulled and rusted hull that once had been a mainstay of the Soviet merchant marine and currently hired itself to whichever capitalist paid a few dollars more. The painted letters of the ship's name peeled in Russian and English alike.

The pilgrims boarded by ones and twos. Studious coeds weighed down with book-filled backpacks stumbled up the gangplank behind lanky young men carrying half-emptied haversacks holding little more than a few changes of clothing and a sleeping bag. Middle-age

couples followed teenaged children to the deck and young parents
shepherded toddlers up the gangway. Babies were carried at the hip
or held to the breast. One was brought in a shoulder sling. Blacks
walked with whites and Latinos with Asians. Asians walked with
blacks and Latinos with whites. Some emigrants arrived in formal
dress while others were dressed for a day at the beach. Men wore
khakis and denim and women wore khakis and denim. Men sported
shaved heads and shoulder-length hair and women styled close-
cropped cuts and shoulder-length hair. Sneakers and boots and
sandals—and even deerskin moccasins—paraded up the unan-
chored steps of the gangplank (where one of the ship's officers
checked faces and paperwork against a digitized log). At the wharf,
two uniformed security officers prevented arriving settlers from
congealing into attention-attracting groups and quietly admonished
new arrivals to keep to themselves until they'd reached the privacy
and protective custody of the The Flower of the First of May.

By dusk, the ship's deck was covered with the seeds of a new
world: backpacks were strewn across the decks as settlers searched
for assigned quarters, crates were stacked in two of the freighter's
largest cargo holds, and animal pens and feeders were secured in the
third. In addition, small boats were secured to the rails and a refur-
bished World War II-era LCVP landing craft was lashed to the aft
deck and covered with canvas. Still, the bark and bay of domesticated
animals locked in their cages was drowned by the deep rumbling of
diesel engines and the strong bite of sea salt in the evening air was
overpowered by the taste of burning fuel which settled on the deck
like a transparent fog. The final glow of the first day of May shone
from the west, casting the long shadows of stacks of cargo across the
deck until even they were blotted out by the dark.

RYAN WATCHED from the bridge as three sailors quick-stepped to sever
the ship's tenuous connection to American soil by slipping the
mooring lines. Smoke poured from the stacks as the rumble of the
engines grew louder.

"Now I really believe it'll happen," a middle-aged man who wore khakis pulled high and a green tee shirt half-tucked said. "You did it, Ryan."

"Correction, Doc," Ryan said. "We did it. And we still have plenty to do."

A blonde whose white shorts were long and mauve sweater tight snuggled behind Ryan—her breasts pressed his back as she wrapped arms around her husband's chest and nuzzled her face against his. Ryan leaned to a side and rubbed the unshaven stubble of his face against Kit's cheek, then unclasped his wife's hands and walked into the bridge—where he selected a bottle of champagne from an ice-filled bucket and grabbed the crystal necks of three long-stemmed champagne flutes. He offered glasses both to Kit and the doctor, then popped the champagne's cork and poured. All three savored the bouquet and sipped their toast with deliberation and delight as the clank of the engines grew even louder.

"When will you announce our destination?" Kit asked.

"After we leave the harbor," Ryan said. "When we're safely at sea. The press will search for us in Brazil or the Azores if Joshua does his work. They'll be lining up for the emigration ceremony in St. Augustine on Saturday and our decoys will have spread false rumors the night before—disinformation that'll be continued for several months. What they don't know is that we've decided to play hide and seek. Tag, they're it."

After pouring a second round, Ryan tapped his glass against that of his wife. "Let's make a toast to hope."

"Cheers," the doctor said.

Kit giggled.

A few minutes later, the three settlers watched the crew scurry around the bridge as the ship began to move. One officer and two sailors manned the wheel and radio as the orders of the port authority crackled over the airwaves and running lights flashed from the mast. A loud whistle sounded that the ship was underway. As the ship cleared its moorings, a tug nudged the freighter's bow toward the outer harbor and guided the ship toward open sea. As the deep reverberation of the ship's screws began to vibrate, the captain ordered his first officer to take the helm while he turned to Ryan and spoke with a heavy Brooklyn accent.

"Good evening, Ryan."

"Good evening, Captain Chappell."

"We're underway," the captain said.

"To a new land."

The captain put a hand on Ryan's shoulder. "You ready?"

"Never been more ready in my life."

"So's your ship. The crew's at quarters and the hold's full."

Kit smiled at Ryan. "You've pulled it off."

"Not me," Ryan said as he swept his arm across he deck. "It's all these people. This is their day. I'm just their grateful servant."

Ryan offered the captain a drink—which was declined.

"I'm driving tonight," the captain explained, "even if I'm not at the helm. We wouldn't want our journey to end like Exxon's Valdez. That wouldn't be politically correct, especially for this adventure."

As the captain returned to the bridge without a drink, the others laughed. Soon, noise and light emanating from the helm grew more noticeable and the churning of the ship's screws vibrated faster. The tug pierced the quiet of the night with an occasional blast of its horn as it steered the freighter past a line of mothballed destroyers. The retired warships appeared abandoned and obsolete in their stored state, as unsuited for modern existence as were the wars they'd won.

No one toasted the destroyers or the valor of their crews.

"THESE ROOMS AREN'T VERY BIG."

A lanky youth stood at the door to his berth. He threw a duffle bag toward the bed, but it fell short and crashed with a hollow thud. Afterwards, he emptied his pockets upon an adjoining nightstand while a dark-skinned girl threw herself belly down on a second bunk. The young woman's black hair parted at the neck as it fell across her shoulders and her coal-black eyes closed as she reached for a pillow and buried her face into it—her slender waist centered on the bed and her legs spread so her toes edged over both sides.

"Gawd," the young woman said, her voice muffled by the pillow, "I'm tired."

The man kicked off a sandal. "You going to bed this early?"

"I didn't say that," the girl mumbled, "I said I'm tired. There'll be plenty of time to sleep when we arrive."

"I heard there's a party on the main deck. Wine and eats."

The girl rolled over as the lanky youth took a place beside her and slipped his hand between her knees, stroking her thighs as she wiggled close and leaned her head against his shoulder.

"My parents," the young woman declared, "just don't understand what this means—especially me quitting law school to join up."

"They never understood us either," the man said. "I don't think your parents really liked the idea of white on black."

"They endured stereotypes longer than we've lived."

"Then they should understand."

"Daddy understands I'm his little girl. He just wants it nice for me. Like mom never had it. You can't really blame him for loving me."

"Times have changed."

"We've raised eyebrows."

"Not for the color of our skin."

The girl grinned as the man moved one hand toward her belly while his other hand pressed her breasts.

"I had to come," the girl said. "I ... we had to join. This is a once in a lifetime chance. Think of it. Only one hundred people were accepted and you and I both made it. If I weren't an agnostic, I'd call it providential."

The man didn't reply since he was busy unbuttoning her blouse.

"The ship's moving," the girl said as she grabbed the man's hand. "There's the horn."

"No need for this social conformity any more," the man said as he unhooked her bra and tossed it to the floor.

"We're free now," the girl whispered, "God only knows how free we are from bourgeois values. Whooo."

The girl jumped and the boy pressed home. Both warmed fast and moved quick and in minutes they lay naked—some of their clothes flung into the corridor through the berth's half-open door. Afterwards they dressed and left the room. Only a crumpled bedspread, a little spillage of love, and a wallet with a round bulge left on the nightstand attested to their passion.

JASON BREWER PINCHED a joint with his fingertips and took a deep drag of its acrid smoke. A moment later, he handed the home-rolled cigarette to a tall, freckled, and red-haired girl sitting beside him— her eyes bloodshot and head thrown back as she stared into the heavens. She took a drag, then passed it to a square-shouldered brunette beside her who took a hit and also passed it along. The joint made it around the circle only once, so Jason lit another.

"Man," Jason said, "the stars have never been so bright."

"Nature's so cool," the red-haired girl said, "if only we'd let her be. Stop polluting and exploiting."

Jason smiled as he listened to her talk.

"That's why I'm here," the girl continued, "to get away from exploitation and pollution. Imagine paradise. An entire archipelago almost free from human imprint is what Ryan said—a new world. Virgin beach and pristine forest for us to garden. Living in communion with nature. No factories, no pollution, no toxic waste."

"This," Jason said as he passed a joint, "is pure nature. Mountain high and ocean deep."

The young woman took a deep drag and coughed. "We'll do it," she said. "We'll show how it can be done."

"Peace," someone in the circle giggled.

"Freedom," another chimed in.

"Love," the red-haired girl declared.

"Legalized dope," Jason added and everyone laughed out loud.

Two joints later the dope ran out, except for a stub that Jason stashed for himself. A couple smokers stumbled toward their rooms and several others lay beneath the nearest roof, but Jason remained where he was—the red-haired girl now sleeping beside him, her lips stretched in an obvious smile. Jason laughed a little, for no particular reason except he felt at peace and the stars were bright. It was good to be alive and to be on this ship. Mostly, Jason thought, it was good to have a stash of Hawaiian Gold and a bag of unburned seeds.

The girl stirred as Jason watched. She was lying on her back still, the shallow slope of her chest lifting the image of Gaia on her tee shirt with each breath—her movements soft and slow. A moment later, she folded her hands across her belly and lifted her legs at the knees: her bare feet now flat against the deck. She pressed her legs together and lifted her head. Finally, she smiled at Jason, closed her eyes, and drifted into oblivion.

Jason lit one last stub and raised it to his lips. "A toast," he whispered, "to good crops and free love."

With his mind swimming in dreams and desires, Jason smoked the joint and watched the girl until he fell asleep.

HEATHER COULD SMELL the pungent aroma of marijuana. Someone was smoking dope down the deck and the slip of the vessel through the ocean was carrying her through the smoke's lingering odor, though not nearly enough to catch a buzz—for which she was thankful. She turned her head toward the stern and looked toward the black ocean, the foamy wake shimmering in moonlight—a magnificent sight for a first-time seafarer. Heather sensed The Flower of the First of May was only now reaching full speed as she herself looked east, where the dark silhouette of the California coast barely remained visible: now disappearing, now reappearing as the glint of moonlight broke through clouds.

Soon, the coast was gone.

The thin-faced teenager remembered the sights and sounds of the city, the vaulted climb of the skyscrapers and the grinding crush of New York traffic. She thought of the ragged people beneath the surface and the elegant ones strolling Fifth Avenue. Heather remembered friends from the Upper East Side and the sharp stench of a

Midtown alley percolating in the summer heat. She remembered the raised torch of Liberty and the crowds of gaudy tourists making perfunctory pilgrimage. She wondered where they came from and where they went. So many passed through.

Heather looked at her watch. It was nearly midnight. She'd told her parents she'd be out until eleven or so. Since she was bunking with them, it was mindful to give them a little privacy. After all, it was their dream being fulfilled. Now a memory of her parents came to mind—when she once heard them in the night—and she quickly suppressed it. It was unseemly to dwell on such things and Heather decided to wait outside another fifteen minutes. She sat on the deck for a time, then lay on her back. The clouds were breaking up and a half moon was clearly seen. The stars were indeed bright at sea and Heather remembered how ancient navigators crossed the oceans with little more than a sextant and an unclouded sky. Columbus and Vespuchi and ...

The Pilgrims.

She laughed a little to remember that she too was a pilgrim now. She closed her eyes and remembered grade school stories of idealistic ventures and misbegotten plans, of hard winters and failing crops, of friendly natives and grateful feasts, of difficulties endured and thanksgiving given, of potatoes and corn and turkey.

It had been a long day and Heather fell asleep to the soft pitch of the seas and the gentle caress of warm winds. An hour later, a Russian-speaking sailor woke her and pointed to his back and the hard wood deck, reminding the young woman of the backache to be suffered for a night off a bunk. Heather thanked him for his consideration and returned to her room. It was past midnight when she opened the door, only to discover that her parents remained out: their bed was empty and unmade and the lamp remained lit.

Heather kicked her shoes off, brushed her teeth, and went to bed without changing from shirt and shorts to nightgown. Just after she unfastened her bra and loosened her shorts, Heather set her alarm so she could shower before breakfast (since the Godsons had announced that a public meeting would follow the morning meal).

As the young woman dimmed the lights and closed her eyes, she wondered whether the young women on the Mayflower had gazed upon the same stars and dreamed the same desires as she—whether they too longed for undying love and hoped for a good life.

It wasn't long before she slept.

4

THE FLOWER OF THE FIRST OF MAY COMPACT

One hundred and two people, not all of them adults, crowded into the unadorned state room—which was little more than an improvised mess hall never intended to hold so many guests. Elbow pressed elbow and knee brushed knee—though babies remained in the back of the room while older children sat on the floor with books and writing tablets and younger children played in a corner with educational toys purchased by Kit at an upscale toy boutique. One of the babies nursed from her mother and three others were cradled in the arms of anxious-appearing men.

Ryan stood before a lectern at the front of the hall. A half-filled glass of orange juice sat on a stand beside the lectern and a cup of coffee was in his hand. He chewed the final bite from a breakfast roll as he surveyed his audience, then rubbed the crumbs from his fingers and spoke. His voice carried to the back of the room, so he switched off the microphone rigged to the lectern.

"Is everyone here?"

A few people clapped.

"Then it's time to begin," Ryan said. "For today, ladies and gentlemen, is the first day of a new calendar. In what promises to be a truly great society."

Several people cheered and a dozen others clapped.

"We're going to make a new world: a progressive one."

A score of voices rang out.

"And we're going to do it now."

Everyone clapped and cheers rang through the room. Even on the bridge, the crew heard the roar of excitement and wondered what was afoot. Only in the engine room did the pump and grind of the ship's great pistons prevent the crew from sharing in the moment. Only there did the fire and smoke of the world's work obfuscate the liberal acclamation.

As the cheers died down, Ryan stood before the lectern, grasping its sides with his hands, eyes staring straight ahead and shoulders pulled back. He panned the room slow and deliberate as he spoke.

"It was I," the actor declared, "who conceived this dream and it was I who purchased this island and gathered our provisions. It was I who posted announcements for this great enterprise and sorted your applications—all with Kit's help, I hasten to add. But it was each one of you who left your comforts and security to tame a jungle. It was each one of you who uprooted yourselves from the old world to begin a new one. It was each one of you who gave up father and mother and sister and brother for the sake of this adventure. You are the true hope and destiny of all mankind. There are doctors and nurses among you who left lucrative careers to heal without pay. There are university professors who resigned tenured positions to teach mankind to live in peace and engineers who've forsaken family and friend to build a new civilization. The new land is you. All of you. Give yourselves a hand."

The crowd cheered wildly for itself. Upraised hands clapped hard and lowered hands slapped together.

"Every one of you," Ryan continued, "has devoted your life to this enterprise. Some have given much and others even more, but now we stand as equals: each one of us ready to sacrifice prestige, honor, and our very lives for the good of humanity. None of us has held back. What is owned by one is owned by all. What is given to one is given to all. No one will lack what he needs and no one will need what he lacks."

Now the crowd roared so loud Ryan couldn't be heard. He waved several times for quiet, but each time failed to quell the enthusiasm. Finally, he stepped away from the podium and waited several minutes for the crowd to settle.

"We have business to tend to," Ryan said after a review of his notes. "As I explained in yesterday's letter, the government of this island will pass from Russia to the community itself only after we've ratified a formal charter. Did anyone not receive a copy of the hand-out? Raise your hand."

Two hands went up and Ryan asked Kit to pass copies to them.

"I'll summarize," Ryan announced, "the contents while you review. By international treaty, we need to submit a governing charter. Therefore, we intend—if you please, that is—to organize a basic charter while on this ship. A copy can be faxed to Geneva from the bridge and the captain himself will deliver the original when he returns to Russia. With that charter, we'll cease being a party of ideal-istic dreamers as they call us in the old world and become a legiti-mate government recognized by international law—with formal rights and obligations. We are a people and we will become a state."

Cheers broke out once more and Ryan was forced to wait several minutes for the noise to subside.

"And our government," Ryan continued, "truly shall be of the people, by the people, for the people. That's why we've been so careful to select only proven progressives and liberals who've marched against racism, campaigned against pollution, protested capital punishment, resisted militarism, and—I think that I can say it out loud in this room without fear—voted for Green and Democratic candidates. You weren't picked on the basis of equal opportunity laws, but on the basis of your commitments and your character. Having given yourselves completely to humankind, a state of paradise now is entrusted to you. Brothers and sisters, look around. These are your executives and your legislators and your judiciary. Here are the only princes and kings and emperors and presidents and justices and mayors and bosses and fathers and mothers you'll ever know again."

The crowd again broke into long applause while Ryan took a sip of coffee and exchanged a few words with his wife. When he returned to the podium and raised his arms for quiet, the cheers slowed.

"Once upon a time," Ryan said, "we tried to create a new society. In Selma and San Francisco. In Berkeley and Chicago. We knew no law in those days but love, as our artists and prophets sang. But politicians and lawyers and generals and bankers never could accept us. They wanted to keep their power, prestige, and profit. And they crushed us. We can be honest here: the sixties were a victory for conservatives and their silent majority. Nixon crushed our head even if we bruised his heel. And I'm not sure we did even that."

The crowd fell silent.

"They called us a counterculture," the speaker now dropped his voice so that many in the audience were forced to strain to hear his words, "as if freedom and equality could ever be mere dissent movements rather than the rightful inheritance of all humankind. They laughed at us, fought us, and even co-opted some of us. And now they've betrayed their own constitution to steal from us what is ours. They condemn the rise of illegitimate births in America. Well, we condemn the advent of illegitimate democracy. Dubya, Cheney, Powell, and the whole lot of them are bas ..."

Ryan stopped himself mid-sentence. "Well," he said with a smile, "they're illegitimate."

A few catcalls and a couple whistles sounded from the crowd.

"Still," Ryan continued, "our noble dream will become reality. There will be hard times, I'm sure. Many of us have left family and friend for the sake of this new colony and we'll certainly miss them. But, as I explain in the letter, we've made provision to rotate in additional inhabitants after six months and to allow vacations to the United States after a year. That's assuming, of course, that American authorities accept our passports. We'll need to endure a full year without seeing the mothers who birthed us or the loved ones we've left behind. Look to your left and to your right. These are your fathers and mothers and sisters and lovers. Together, we'll make a true paradise, so remember who you are and love the ones near you."

As Ryan concluded his remarks, he stepped from the podium and hugged his wife, afterwards stepping into the crowd to shake hands with the men and kiss several of the women. The audience also turned inward. Couples embraced and strangers shook hands. Men and women spoke words of good cheer to each other, then embraced and kissed. Everyone hugged the children. Not one person was left alone, neither the plain nor the pretty. Every woman was adored and every man admired. Yet their love remained almost untarnished—for this night brought the reunion of mother and daughter and father and son and brother and sister.

Several minutes passed as Ryan let the crowd settle before returning to the podium. When he did, he was professional and to the point.

"Now," Ryan said, moving his eyes over the assembly, "we have work to do. Hold your applause until the day's work is done."

The audience remained quiet.

"First," Ryan said, "by a show of hands, who wishes to establish a democracy?"

The actor scanned the crowd and saw two hundred hands raised. When he asked whether anyone opposed democracy, not one hand was raised.

"It's unanimous," Ryan declared. "We're a democracy."

Ryan sipped from his water before continuing.

"Next," Ryan said, "those who prefer parliamentary democracy after the European style gather to my left. Those who prefer a checks and balances system after the American pattern move to my right."

It took ten minutes for the crowd to separate in the crowded room, but after it did, the tally became clear. Every single citizen voted for parliamentary democracy, many shouting the Bush triumph was enabled by an archaic political system that thwarted the will of the people—a form of government originally constructed to line the pockets of Yankee capitalists and Southern slavers. It also was decided within the hour that all significant political decisions would be brought before the entire citizenry via direct democracy. Allowing every person to vote on critical decisions was judged the only way to ensure that all ethnic, gender, and even ideological distinctions were fairly represented. Moreover, the majority voted that everyone past puberty would be awarded the vote since the most crucial private and public interests come into being at the advent of sexual maturity. In short, the form of government was deliberated and determined before the first coffee break.

It took until noon to decide the legislative assembly also would serve as the judiciary. Trials of accused criminals were to be conducted before the assembled people—each of whom was to be instructed in matters of the law. In this way, political dominance by a legal class could be avoided. Several trial lawyers objected, but were outvoted and overruled. When the lawyers argued only legal experts could protect civil rights, majority spokespersons observed that a community of liberals wasn't likely to face much crime in the first place, and if it did, the political ideals of its citizenry would prevent the unconscionable abuses that law-and-order conservatives inflicted on the American judicial system.

"Where will we find," one young man articulated, "the poverty and prejudice that create crime? We need neither attorney nor judge. We must presume innocence, not guilt. For our judges and juries as well as the accused."

Neither was an independent executive branch established (from fear of a Nixon-like imperial presidency). Instead, the citizens decided to create an Executive Council of the People's Will—an executive and administrative body of five delegates slated to serve two-week terms of office beginning on the first and third Monday of each calendar month. Four delegates would be drawn from each of the four neighborhoods and the fifth representative selected from staff headquarters. The Small Council, as the Executive Council of the People's Will was nicknamed, was scheduled to meet weekly and submit a written report to each convocation of the entire electorate in a General Council of the People's Will. The General Will, as the communal assembly soon came to be called, was to meet as often as necessary to resolve legal, constitutional, and political issues by public deliberation and direct vote. It alone was considered the final guardian of democracy and interpreter of law. Following Ryan's recommendation, the assembly voted to name the new country the State of Paradise.

LUNCH WAS SERVED at noon and the rest of the day was spent dividing one hundred and two settlers into separate villages—or neighborhoods as they also were called. Though it had been decided to establish four twenty-four-person villages, considerable debate was needed to resolve the complexities of ethnic composition. Some voters thought racism best eradicated by integrating all peoples of whatever color while others thought is better to let each racial group live after its own fashion. A few even wanted the matter resolved by lot. After three hours of debate, it was agreed by a 68-20 vote (with fourteen under-aged children not voting) to integrate.

Ryan consoled the losers with remembrance that no minority would be oppressed within the wider community. He also reminded them that all inhabitants would be free to intermingle as they themselves chose. It also was decided that a neighborhood of professional staff would oversee and distribute a central store of critical and otherwise scarce supplies. This village would include: physician Dr. Marc Graves, nurse practitioner Cynthia Fallows, anthropologist Dr. Tomas Morales, psychologist Dr. Janine Erikson, sociologist Dr. Scott Law, and veterinarian Dr. Mary Vander Mare.

After organizing a framework for local communities, the people selected their neighborhoods. By voice vote it was decided to choose inhabitants by lottery rather than individual choice to guard against cliques and hurt feelings. Ryan loaded a laptop with a database that included every inhabitant's name, race, age, family status, and personal preferences and the assembly set parameters for neighborhoods during an hour-long discussion. After consensus was reached regarding selection criteria, Ryan clicked his mouse and the computer's screen flashed for an instant as the database configured several hundred possible neighborhoods—each one no more than fifty percent Caucasian and no less than fifty percent female. A kindergartner with blond cornrows and fair skin was asked to choose a number between one and six hundred twenty-four—and selected both of her favorite numbers: four and seventeen. Lucky twenty-one, as many called it, was used to select the actual inhabitants of villages from the many potential populations. The villages determined (as if by divine election), rosters then were printed and distributed to volunteers who called the neighborhoods into existence from the four corners of the room. During the next few minutes, most villagers introduced themselves in the cramped corners of the hall while the professional staff met in the middle of the room.

The day's final order of business was conducted just before a late dinner: the colonists needed to divide their territory among the four villages. Ryan used old Russian maps and commercial satellite imagery to divide the island into four quadrants: as equal in their share of land, water, and beach as could be achieved consistent with clearly delineated borders—with the headquarters staff assigned a portion of land large enough to meet its own needs. A copy of the map was cut along the boundaries of assigned districts and the quadrants folded and dropped into the emptied purse of one of the younger men. A representative of each neighborhood took a single share back to the corners of the hall for review by the newly formed villages. With their portions of paradise in hand, neighbors used laminated maps of the island (and felt-tipped marking pens) to plan where to pitch tents and plant fields. A cartographer and two agricultural specialists provided technical assistance in map reading to those whose experience was limited to tourist guides and road atlases.

After a meal of vegetarian burgers and tofu fries, Ryan asked the conclave to consider the drafting of a state charter—recommending that each neighborhood spend the evening formulating key principles by which the community would govern itself. Ryan hoped these could be discussed and ratified the following morning and a new charter then proposed. Following his recommendation, it was suggested that a succinct document along the lines of the French

Declaration of the Rights of Man and Citizen would prove a more useful document than an extensive constitution following the American model. This suggestion was seconded and ratified by unanimous vote of the assembly.

After the vote, everyone rose to applaud Ryan and Kit for their efforts before dispersing into neighborhoods for discussion and debate. Within the hour, casks of beer and cases of wine were opened and copies of political documents distributed for study, though many emigrants soon drifted toward the comfort and companionship of established acquaintances.

ASSEMBLY RECONVENED THE FOLLOWING DAY. Each of the five villages —four territorial and the staff neighborhood—provided ten planks to debate. There was nearly unanimous regard for the rights to reproductive freedom, freedom of association, freedom from religion, freedom of speech, and freedom of conscience—as well as for legal and social equality. A majority of the citizens also accepted that there should be freedom both from conscription and pollution. Proposals dealing with marriage, artistic expression, weapons ownership, drug legalization, and animal rights also were reviewed. Before lunch was served, each proposal was voted into law or removed from immediate consideration. A constitutional committee headed by Ryan was empowered to draft a charter. Though several citizens wished to debate the social theory underpinning the charter, the majority proved more interested in limiting debate to immediate political and legal realities. Thus authorized, the constituent assembly worked through lunch while the citizenry enjoyed leisure on deck. The framers grouped like-minded proposals together, then simplified these to core principles and necessary issues. Afterwards, a political scientist and former writer of campaign speeches for several Democratic Senators and progressive advocacy groups penned a draft of the charter (which was debated and amended within the committee). Finally, the speechwriter rewrote the draft—to which Ryan contributed several stylistic changes. The revision was read before the re-assembled convocation at dinner. Everyone listened with undistracted attention and even the children were unusually quiet.

The Flower of the First of May Compact, as the document was called, was accepted almost without amendment. The only real controversy regarded guns. Several activists wanted the possession of firearms explicitly outlawed, but majority spokespersons pointed out the fifth and sixth provisions of the charter were clearly anti-NRA in concept and intent—forbidding militia membership, private gun ownership, and hunting with firearms. Besides, Ryan argued that because no such weapons were to be brought on the island there was very little danger of mischief with guns. He questioned whether the technological know-how even existed for arms production since not a single gunsmith had been selected for citizenship—unless, he quipped, Kit secretly had invited members of the Smith and Wesson families. After loud laughter, the objectors accepted his arguments and didn't push a vote. Gun ownership was rendered a moot issue.

Of far more critical importance was a debate over Article I—which defined the members of state. Several women wanted confirmation that citizens needed to be born before inheriting political rights, thereby securing a woman's right to an elective abortion through all nine months of pregnancy. Nearly everyone agreed with their judgment and the assembly voted by voice that the women's interpretation of the clause was correct, though a few children of former Latino immigrants sought clarification regarding the rights of immigrants. Since the citizenship clause imitated the American Constitution in extending citizenship to the children of citizens and to soil-born immigrants, they feared a class of foreign-born immigrants might be excluded from citizenship on that basis—just as those born in Mexico or Haiti possessed no inherent right to vote in American elections. This modification was greeted with great celebration since it was the first time any government in human history had granted such comprehensive political rights: anyone living among them would be counted a citizen and anyone not living among them would not.

After this final amendment, the charter was voted upon. Everyone eligible to vote (only a few of the younger children were unable to exercise that right) ratified the charter. The constitution read:

The Flower of the First of May Compact

Being willingly gathered together to create a new society, we the undersigned declare that the citizens of the State of Paradise confirm the following principles to be our governing charter:

1. The political community is composed of nothing more and nothing less than free individuals. All persons living in our realm shall enjoy the privileges and exercise the responsibilities of citizenship. No restrictions shall be placed on the right of a woman to terminate pregnancy.
2. No person shall be restricted in the exercise of her or his own choices except to secure the freedom of others.
3. No distinction shall be made between persons before the law.
4. The right to freedom of conscience, speech, sexual preference, artistic expression, public and private association, and due process under the law shall not be curtailed.
5. The public authority shall possess the right to safeguard domestic tranquility and public safety and to regulate all armed and police forces. However, it shall possess no right to suspend, infringe, or otherwise abrogate individual freedoms and rights. There is no right to possess or use any weapon or tool except as authorized by public authority. Military service shall not be made compulsory.
6. Every person possesses an equal share of nature that is to be used and preserved. The harvesting of natural resources and the taking of animal life shall be regulated by public authority.
7. This compact shall be sworn at the commencement of every public meeting and may not be abridged.

After ratifying the new charter, everyone signed the document with commemorative pens and official copies thereafter were sent to the ship's captain for delivery to officials in Geneva and Moscow. Unsigned copies were provided to every member of the state and the original draft was safeguarded by the professional staff for permanent archiving.

With a government formed and its ideals established, the community decided it was proper to celebrate—and a party was decreed by unanimous vote. Cases of Napa Valley's finest wine were pried open and served with hors d'oeuvres. The staff psychologist—a petite blonde in her thirties with narrow hips and perky hair named Janine Erikson—lectured as Chardonnay and Chianti were poured into commemorative goblets. After every glass was filled, she led the toast.

"To our teachers for their wisdom," Dr. Erikson said. "To Ryan for his vision. To all of us for the courage of our convictions. Cheers!"

"Cheers," the audience thundered.

Celebrations continued well through the night.

5

POST-CALIFORNIA DREAMING

Most emigrants gathered to party in a decorated cargo hold, except for several groups congregated for private celebrations on deck and a few couples who remained in their own cabins or nearby passageways. Among the former were a wiry Asian and his wife—who sipped sodas where the passageway to their room opened to the deck. They stood hidden in the shadows as they spoke in unbroken and unaccented English and occasionally checked into their cabin.

"They still sleeping?" the man asked his wife as she returned from one of her forays into the room.

"They're still pretending to sleep," the woman said with a laugh, "but they're listening to the party. I heard them giggling when I opened the door."

"I dread the teenage years," the man replied.

"They're not here yet."

"Soon enough."

"Do you think this will be a good place for them to grow up?"

"Better here," the man said, "than Inglewood."

"Or Michigan."

"You're right about that, Linh."

"I always am."

Now the woman pointed toward the stern. "It's loud down there." Her husband nodded.

"I like the smell of the sea," the woman said just before she pointed across the deck to a canvas-covered boat nearly as long and wide as a freight car. "Is that an imperialist landing craft?"

"That it is," Viet said with a laugh. "It's called an LCVP. They used them at Normandy. And in the Pacific."

"Vietnam?"

"I read about a couple landings. Not often, though. They had helicopters to use against us."

The woman rolled her eyes. "Us?"

"Well," her husband said, "against my father."

"He died an American ally. Like my father."

"It's ironic," Viet said after a pause.

"How's that?"

"My father fought the Americans and became a boat person to get to the United States. He brought me to Los Angeles and now I'm sailing into the Pacific to escape America."

"It's worth a chance," Linh said. "There's still too much racism back home. I want our daughters to escape every kind of prejudice: rioters who burn our shops and administrators who stereotype our students and embittered veterans who call us slopes."

"You're right," Viet said after considering his answer several seconds. "I couldn't get into law school even with straight A's. Not in California. And it's the most progressive state in the union."

"That won't happen to our daughters."

"It won't," Viet said. "My parents worked themselves to early deaths trying to make a new life for us. They thought they could escape oppression and poverty by coming to a new land."

"Mine thought they could live the good life in the Midwest," the woman added, "but all they got was bored. And unemployed."

"We're going to do it right for our children. With these people."

Now Linh said as she pointed toward canvas-covered stacks of crates sitting beside the LCVP. "Are those ours too?"

"And everything," Viet said, "stored in the two cargo holds, along with everything on the boat. Except for the captain and the crew."

The woman said nothing as she sat beside her husband, holding his hand. Low-moving clouds obscured the moon and a strong head-wind occasionally sprayed a mist of salt-water across the deck as the couple enjoyed the peace. Both husband and wife looked to the sea and their own thoughts as they held hands without talking.

Only after several minutes did the woman break the silence. "What do you expect?" she asked.

"Good people," her husband answered, "who want to do the right thing. Who live moral lives and care for the world around them."

"Do you know what I want?"

Viet shook his head.

"I want a life," Linh said, "where race is never mentioned."

"We all have eyes."

"And," Linh said with a nod, "we all have hearts and minds too. I want to live with people who'd rather read a book than its cover."

"You have your wish. These people are such a mix of nationalities and races and religions that it'd be impossible to fix a stereotype. If diversity is enough to make a good society, we'll have the world we've always wanted."

"I'm glad we came," Linh said, "to a truly new world."

A few minutes later, the couple retired. As their two daughters finally slept, Linh slipped into a nightgown and lay beside one of them as Viet removed his shirt and took a place on a narrow cot across the room.

A BARREL-CHESTED MAN WITH THINNING, gray hair sat on stacked crates in a decorated hold, sipping a bottle of imported lager. A black-haired woman with high cheekbones and narrow eyes sat beside him as rap music played across the room and dozens of people added to the din with loud talk and raucous laughter. The man focused his attention on the narrow-hipped woman.

"It's really paradoxical," the man said, "when it's considered."

The narrow-hipped woman laughed. "It is."

"We have a Russian crew commanded by an American captain being paid in Eurodollars to deliver a hundred benefactors of Anglo-European industrial capitalism to a socialist tropical paradise."

"One hundred and two," the woman said.

"Lenin must be rolling over in his tomb."

"I thought it was Beethoven who rolled in his grave. I'd pay uninflated rubles to see Lenin turn in that glass coffin."

"Very witty."

Both laughed as the man drank from his dark bottle of lager and the woman sipped white wine.

"Incidentally," the man said, "I'm Charles Marks. That's my wife across the room. In the red dress."

The woman extended her hand. A small diamond glittered from her left hand.

"I'm Deidra Smith."

"Children?"

"Someday, I hope," the woman answered. "How about you?"

"One daughter," Charles replied. "She's a high-school senior. Probably sitting in her cabin right now contemplating Plato's eternal forms or Kant's transcendent categories. She's not much for parties."

"I've haven't talked to you for ten minutes," Deidra said, "and you've already brought up Marx, Hegel, and Rousseau. Not to mention Plato and Kant. I'm guessing she's her father's daughter."

"More like the antithesis spawned by my thesis. I'm a materialist and she seeks transcendence. I'm a realist and she's a romantic. She's a wonderful daughter but her mother and I thought it best to bring her to a new environment. She was running with a bad crowd."

"My sister," Deidra said, "lost a stepson who got tied up with gangs."

"Heather was hanging with Young Republicans."

Deidra shuddered.

"And," Charles continued, "she threatened to apply to Big Ten schools. Said she wanted to live in the Midwest. Iowa was her top choice. Refused even to consider Berkeley."

"That is serious."

"She was likely to end up worse than a neocon."

"At least," Deidra said, "there won't be any of those throwbacks on this island. It'll be a safe place to come of age."

"I guess," Charles said with a laugh, "she'll come of age in paradise. I should rename her Margaret Meade."

Both laughed and the conversation wound down. After a time, they wished each other good night and the woman returned to her cabin while the man remained in his chair.

Only when his wife stole behind and brushed the back of his neck with a forefinger did Charles stand.

"There you are, Joan. Ready for bed?"

"It's late," Joan said with a smile. "What'd you do all evening?"

"Drank a couple beers, talked some politics, met some neighbors."

Joan took her husband's hand. "That reminds me," she said. "I forgot to pack alcohol. Could you see to buying some? On ship?"

"They're Russian sailors," Charles said with a grin. "For certain, there'll be both booze and a black market."

Joan nodded as she reached for the cabin door and turned the handle. Tiptoeing into the room, they fell into bed without lighting a lamp or changing to nightclothes since it was late and their daughter already slept.

"She's so grown up," Joan whispered.

"She is," Charles replied. "We've done our job. Now she's a woman and can choose her own values."

Joan kissed her husband on the side of the cheek and pulled the sheet to her shoulders. Both soon slept as silent as their daughter.

. . .

A SHARP-FACED Caucasian with hard limbs was lying on a bunk, sheets pulled to his shoulders. A light-skinned and dark-haired woman—her curls frosted with gray—reclined beside him, propped on an elbow as she looked at the man. She, too, was draped with a thin sheet. Neither wore clothing and the woman talked loud.

"Does it bother you," the women giggled, "that ... that I'm Protestant?"

Father Donovan shook his head and smiled. "Not at all," he said. "I'm ecumenical. Served three years as a consultant to the Board of Trustees of the World Council of Churches."

"What'd you consult?"

"Mostly efforts to reach out to Islamic countries."

The woman raised her eyebrows. "Did you devote yourself to good works there too?"

"I brought paradise itself," Father Donovan answered, "to the daughters of Muslims and freed them from their burkas—at least for a few minutes."

"That sounds fun."

"And it is, too. At least until the first Iranian girl confesses fornication to her father, the ayatollah. Then it's all fatwas and threats and resignations. That's when I went to Nicaragua to minister to the proletariat. I spent three years as spiritual advisor to troops trying to flush out Contras. They needed comfort and strength for the tough work at hand."

Now the woman sat up, her countenance serious and voice soft. Her breasts slipped from behind the sheet and fell forward, though she made no effort to veil them.

"I remember that battle," the woman said, "back in the States we were trying to prosecute Casey and Reagan."

"And you just about won," Father Donovan said, "till fascist public opinion turned in favor of Colonel North. Then it was just a matter of time till the U.S. did to Ortega what it did to Castro and Mao and Lenin."

"Lenin? What did the Americans do to him? I was taught that

Herbert Hoover saved Lenin's government by sending food supplies that averted starvation."

"There are U.S. soldiers buried in Archangel."

"How did that happen?"

"The Bolsheviks killed them."

"I mean, why were Americans in Russia?"

"Don't you remember that Churchill wanted to strangle the baby Bolshevism—as he himself phrased it—in its cradle? Fortunately for all of us, the child grew to be a man despite the attempted infanticide."

The woman pressed herself against the man. "I've never met a priest like you," she said.

"I take religion to the streets."

"Watch yourself," the woman said with a laugh. "You didn't find me on the streets."

"I meant that I bring religious experience to the people."

"Bring it to me. Give me some sins to confess."

"Socialization isn't sin," Father Donovan said as he pulled the woman to his side, "and in the spirit of Vatican II, I define my own communion. An ecumenical approach to religion."

The woman climbed atop the man and pressed closer yet, until the two nearly became one. After they were finished, they slept with their backs touching until they were awakened by sunlight and the sounds of bartering.

THE DINING ROOM WAS NOISY. Nearly every colonist seemed excited about the nature of the new government and several former scholars and journalists were conducting interviews so that posterity might have a full record of those first few days of paradise. Breakfast added to the excitement as it included croissants and fruit cups served with coffee and tea: the last real breakfast likely to be enjoyed for several months. Young people loitered about the halls and children played on the ship's deck—where sailors mixed with settlers as smooth-faced deck hands used universally recognized signs to flirt with progressive girls and weather-beaten sailors negotiated trades of cigarettes and booze. Sometimes they bought and other times they sold; either way, the Russians turned a profit.

Inside a main corridor, two men haggled over a bottle. A dark-haired sailor with pocked cheeks and greasy hair shook his head at a pale-faced American who held out a fistful of rubles—which the sailor pushed away.

"Nyet."

"I don't understand," Charles Marks protested. "This isn't U.S. currency. I bought these from your purser. They're as Russian as you are."

The Russian's eyes flashed and he shook his head vigorously. "Nyet ruble. Nein marks."

Charles spoke with a lift to his voice. "Nine marks? German?"

"Nyet," the Russian grew more animated, now waving his arms and speaking with irritation: his words deliberate and broken. "Nyet mark. Nyet ruble. Doe-lar."

"Dollars?"

"Da," the sailor said as he raised ten grease-stained fingers. "Doe-lars."

Charles pulled a handful of change from his front pocket and handed the sailor ten quarter-sized coins imprinted with the bust of middle-aged matron—the woman's hair fixed in a dour bun.

The man shook his head again. "Nyet. Doe-lars."

"They are dollars," Charles said as he pointed to an inscription stamped on the back of one of the clad coins.

The Russian pushed his hand away again.

"Giorgi," the sailor said. "Toylko Giorgi."

Charles shrugged his shoulders. "I don't speak Russian. I read Lenin in German translation."

"Giorgi," the sailor repeated, this time more slowly. "Gi-or-gi Vosh-een-ton."

"You mean George Washington?"

"Da," the Russian said with an exasperated nod. "Giorgi Vosheenton."

Now the American reached into his billfold and pulled out seven Giorgi Washingtons, two Abraham Lincolns, and two Andrew Jacksons before holding out six fingers for the Russian to see. The sailor slipped into a nearby cabin and quickly returned with six bottles of clear liquor: cheap Russian vodka. The smile on his face was broad as the exchange was made and grew even wider when Charles unscrewed the cap from one of the bottles.

"A toast, comrade," Charles said as he took a sip, "to a great society in a new world."

After drinking, Charles handed the bottle to the Russian—who grabbed it and took a long swig.

"T-t-to," the sailor stuttered, "t-to Amerika. Kh mnoga Giorgi Vasheenton."

Charles shook his head in dismay as the Russian took another gulp, but still reached into his wallet to give the Russian all of his remaining bills—as well as a pocketful of coins. There would be very little need for the trappings of commerce in the new world.

Tears welled in the Russian's eyes as he stuffed the money into a pocket, embraced his socialist comrade, and God blessed America while racing down the hallway praising the profits of capitalism in a Russian dialect.

Charles took a long drink from the open bottle.

THE NEXT FEW days brought one mild storm (that caused dozens of emigrants to suffer severe seasickness until Doctor Graves prescribed anti-emetics) and boredom after the bad weather cleared. Because it proved difficult to navigate the narrow corridors of the ship without encountering some ill-tempered and quick-moving sailor who cursed settlers in brusque Russian for impeding his movement, many settlers endured the monotony from their rooms while the long days passed—though some sat on deck chairs and watched for the first glimpse of the new world.

On the tenth day of the voyage, one such lookout spotted land. "Land ho! To the west. The new world."

It was a young brunette who jumped up and down on the ship's bow and shouted for others to come quick—which they did. Within minutes, passengers knocked at cabin doors and called down passageways. Ten days of slow sailing had proved tedious since most planning had been completed in the first days. Now, there was something to see and within a half hour, nearly every emigrant stood on deck—straining for a good glimpse of the promised land. Still, even as the crowd bustled with energy and desire, no one was pressed too hard and every citizen took a turn looking from the forward positions.

Nothing more promising could have been imagined. By the time the pilgrims gathered, the ship neared its destination: an atoll of small islets and submerged reefs ringing a central island, the largest of the surrounding motu no more than a suburban block and the smallest little more than a few palm trees, a bit of broken coral, and a coating of bird droppings. The islets rose from a barrier reef that protected the island, punctured only by a leeward current that opened several gaps. The main island sat in the center of the atoll, its lush hills and dark shores framing a pristine lagoon whose turquoise waters were protected between a barrier reef and the beach. The island's largest hill rose over three hundred yards at the peak, its steep slopes streaming to the sea where stretches of white sand ringed the shoreline like the glimmer of glass. Colonists with binoculars saw coconuts hanging ripe for harvest and sea turtles lumbering ever so slow across the beach. Even those who looked with the naked eye saw flocks of gulls fly overhead, some circling the ship and others diving into the lagoon for fish. A smooth-skinned and saw-toothed whale twice broke the surface near the ship before it slipped into the sanctuary of the sea and disappeared.

Now the ship was nearly stopped, its wake churning all the more for being slowed and the crew scampering across the deck as they relayed orders, shifted gear, and weighed anchor. The captain instructed passengers to prepare cabins for departure and Ryan told them to finish breakfast. Cooked meals, he announced, wouldn't be available for several days. Settlers were told to fill canteens and draw military rations from the commissar. Every inhabitant was allotted four MREs—more than enough to cover three expected days of encampment. Water purification tablets were distributed by the handful as settlers gathered into their respective neighborhoods and sent delegations to collect tents, medicine boxes, cooking utensils, farming tools, food supplies, and water jugs. The process was completed before noon.

In the meantime, the ship's crew secured anchor and lowered the landing craft using cables and a crane. The flat-bottomed LCVP then moved entire neighborhoods in a single trip—taking less than two hours to load, thread its way through a reef channel, and disembark its cargo. Each neighborhood moved with tents, camping gear, medicine boxes, cooking utensils, water rations, and personal effects while the ship's crew both helped settlers climb down netting into the vintage landing craft and unloaded heavier cargo with a light crane. The first trip commenced at noon and the final landing was concluded at dusk. Russian sailors worked fast, though they took little care with their more urbane passengers—carelessly casting man and material alike on the sand so they could finish the day's work as fast as possible. In their haste, they even dropped one crate of supplies into the sea (where it sank) and damaged two others. Disembarkation timetables and incentive bonuses required citizens to be ashore by day's end.

After reaching shore, colonists moved materials to an open field previously designated a recreational area and base camp. Maps were checked for campsite markings and cargo was moved beyond the reach of the tide. As time permitted, tents were pitched and sleeping bags unrolled—and when each group completed its assigned tasks, members returned to the beach to assist new arrivals. Willing hands raised tent poles, built campfires, and warmed dinner packets. Groups of men equipped with axes cut firewood from fallen trees while older children scoured forests for kindling.

It was nearly dark when the last boat was unloaded and the final tent was pitched. The new land had been peopled and only a few settlers remained on the freighter to tend heavy cargo, feed hungry livestock, and water those plants which hadn't been hauled ashore. For those settlers already ashore, there was both gratitude and relief for having escaped the inconveniences of life at sea—though not a single person, man or woman alike, was observed kneeling on the soft sands of a tropical beach to give God glory for delivering them from the perils and rigors of their ten-day journey.

6

THE SANDS OF NEW PLYMOUTH

"We came for them."

A dark-skinned man who looked to be in his early thirties and sat before a dying fire spoke out loud. Only a few flames flickered in the cool night air, dimly lighting the shadows of his dark flesh. The fire had burned down long ago and now was little more than white-hot coals covered with gray ash. Only after the man threw another log into the coals did it flare into flames as the green wood quickly dried—steam pouring from the pores of the bark and sap sizzling from every crack. Within minutes, the log blazed bright as it began to burn to soot and coals.

Watching both the fire and the man, an ebony-skinned woman, dressed in a sleeveless shirt and cutoff shorts—and who looked to be the same age as her mate—smiled.

"Remember," the woman said, "how I didn't want kids."

"Only because of society," the man replied, "and I never really blamed you."

"Maybe we were right. But all the same, I'm glad we had them."

"I guess accidents aren't always bad."

The woman smiled.

"I wonder," the man continued, "how our parents are doing? They weren't prepared to lose both grandchildren so young."

"It's only been four years since they were born."

"It seems longer. The work's been awful—twins for our first pregnancy—but it also seems that we've ... I mean, you've only just had them."

The woman took a drink from her canteen and ate a bit of coconut. "We had to come, Brent," she said. "We didn't have a choice."

"For them, Tiff."

"Imagine," the man said, "no racism, no pollution, no war."

The woman nodded her agreement.

"And," the man added, "no Republicans."

"Do you suppose they're as bad as racism and war?"

"Is there a difference?"

Both laughed.

"Seriously," the man said, "think of all the temptations in the world: capitalism, commercialism, racism, sexism, militarism, classism. That's what scared me about life back there. And our parents would've entangled our children in the world's snares as surely as we're sitting in sand. We had to come. Not for our sake, but theirs."

"I agree," Tiffany said. "Your father already gave the boys plastic soldiers and toy guns and mindless computer games. And both our moms would've forever drilled stereotypes into our boys."

"Mine," Brent said, "already did. Remember when she yelled at Theodore for crying like a girl. What a Texas sexist!"

"I wanted to slap her. If she weren't your mother, I would've too."

"Well, we won't need to now. Not among these people. We've got a great neighborhood."

The woman nodded and the man stood. Brent threw a little trash into the fire and secured a few rocks around its perimeter while Tiffany placed a bucket of water near their tent's entrance twenty feet away before taking her husband's hand and pointing to the beach.

"It's taken millions of years," Tiffany said, "to prepare this island —the eruptions of volcanoes, the cooling of land, the seeding of soil, and the erosion of surf. Millions of years to make this garden for us. It almost makes one believe in God."

The man moved his arm around the woman's waist and pulled her near.

"It's our Eden now," Brent said, "and our children's."

Tiffany zipped open the tent's flap and slipped in as her husband followed. Just inside the tent, she stretched her hand to stop him.

"Look at them," Tiffany whispered. "They're so sweet."

"Your best work, Tiff."

The woman leaned against her husband and whispered something. He smiled and reached past two little boys sleeping back-to-back as he collected two sleeping rolls. After quietly zipping the tent flap, husband and wife together spread their sleeping bags across grassless sand. When the fires of nearby encampments flickered out, the couple embraced and afterwards enjoyed a long swim while their children slept.

ON THE SECOND DAY, a malfunctioning crane slowed the unloading process and it wasn't until dusk that the beach showed its full complement of two hundred crates and boxes, each marked for a specific neighborhood or general storage. Supplies were moved beyond the reach of the tide and draped with plastic in the event of rain. Particular care was taken to roll twenty casks of wine away from the shore to the protective shade of thick-leafed trees. With the day's work completed, half of the pilgrims slept in tents and half beneath the stars. Only one of them—a young woman who'd never visited a beach—woke to find her feet soaked by the rising tide before she could drag her blankets to the safety of higher ground.

On the third day, the landing craft delivered its last five loads. The first two cargoes included potted vegetables and fruits, most of them mere shoots. The next two loads included treated timber, bags of cement, steel piping, iron grating, and even a pallet of red bricks. The final batch transported domesticated livestock—fifteen goats brought for their milk, cheese, and wool—as well as a brood of speckled chickens and several roosters. Each goat was fitted with a collared bell so strays could be tracked. Chickens, in a like manner, had their wings clipped and were restricted to cages until real coops could be built. No domesticated animals were to be allowed to roam free or feed from island vegetation. By lunch, bags of animal feed were stacked in the sand and a herd of leashed goats shaded beneath the palms. Several children, including the daughters of Linh and Viet, fetched buckets of water to quench the thirst of bird and beast. The children also gave names to the animals.

Each inhabitant worked as he or she pleased during disembarkation. Some unloaded crates while others tended camp. A dozen people helped the professional staff prepare ground for a permanent base a hundred yards inland—just beyond the crest of a shallow rise thought to provide sufficient protection against the most vigorous swells of the sea. The site encompassed a sloped meadow half the size of a youth soccer field and was comprised of three nearly equal sections: personal tents in loose lines along the northern edge of the meadow, public meeting tents in a circular encampment on the eastern side of the field, and supply tents (to include three large military tents and three smaller pup tents) set in rows to the west. A small library was constructed from a self-assembly shed (made of hard plastic able to endure the worst weather) and quickly filled with an assortment of books suitable for life and leisure on a remote island. Finally, a ready-made animal pen holding the goats was built within a grove of coconut palms opposite the human quarters.

The base camp was designed to serve both as a permanent settlement for the professional staff and a public shelter during emergencies. Therefore, its supply tents also housed a large emergency generator and a crated desalination system—as well as radios and batteries, spare tools, extra utensils, bags of flour and rice, tins of meat, cans of condensed milk, tubs of freeze-dried vegetables, assorted tents, medicines, blankets, hardware, and various provisions. Outside of the tents were stacks of bricks, treated wood, rolled wire, iron grills, and a dozen bags of concrete mix. A bermed storage area with a collapsible shelter enclosed the site's supply of fuel: three hundred gallons of gasoline and diesel fuel stored in double-walled plastic drums (stacked in tarp-lined pits for additional protection). Indeed, the base camp resembled a construction site, though most settlers maintained stringent standards of environmental concern and kept their supplies in neat stacks. Drainage ditches were dug and reinforced revetments built around toxic materials.

Tents to the east of the supply yard served as an office area for the professional staff and consisted of six military staff tents, one hospital tent (designed for refugee camps), two six-person medical tents, and an enormous company-sized military dining tent. The square-shaped staff shelters stood eight foot tall, possessed vented windows, and were assigned to the doctor, veterinarian, nurse practitioner, sociologist, psychologist, and anthropologist. Each professional possessed an office tent complete with necessary supplies, including: bookshelves, desks, laptop computers (whose batteries were charged on the generator), and office supplies. The hospital tent stood no higher than the staff tents, though it was twice as long, having been chosen to accommodate two rows of four beds each. Two smaller tents flanked the large hospital tent (one a sanitized surgical tent and the other a small dispensary) and a potable water purification facility and a large medicinal refrigerator were colocated in a shed erected behind the hospital tent—their equipment powered by six large batteries charged by a prudent combination of wind power and solar energy. A self-enclosed and sanitized portable toilet (like those used at state fairs and political rallies) sat outside the hospital tent as the only industrially produced toilet on the island. Finally, the enormous dining tent in the village consisted of a single room that rose fifteen feet in the center and eight feet at the sides, with room for the entire community to sit inside. One hundred folding chairs were stacked in ten rows of ten seats each—with additional chairs kept on either side of a small lectern that faced the entire assembly.

"GOD? He's just another social conservative—the absolute absolutist."

A middle-aged woman donning professorial spectacles and clenching a bound-leather edition of Das Capital spoke to a man nearly her age—who carried a single-bladed ax by the head, his thick fingers securing the steel on its dull side.

"Sorry ma'am," the man said, a consternated look on his face, "but all I said was thank God we've arrived safely."

"That statement," the woman lectured, "implies the existence of a transcendent being, his providential government of the world, and the necessity of human obeisance—both individual and corporate. That simple sentence is a veritable theological lesson that blurs the separation of church and state and has no place in a progressive community."

"I didn't intend," the man apologized, "to sacrifice virgins to the gods. I wasn't thinking of religion at all."

"I'm sorry," the woman said. "I suppose I'm a little touchy about divinity. Because of the tight academic job market back in the States, I was forced to work at a Congregationalist seminary as the only confessing atheist on staff."

"It's Joan," the woman said as she extended her hand, "if you remember."

The man clasped her hand and shook lightly. "And I'm John Smith," he responded. "We talked a little on the boat. Just chitchat. No theology."

"Sorry, John. This wasn't very neighborly of me."

Now the man slid his free hand down the ax handle and let the head drop to the ground, though breaking its fall before the tool struck earth. Turning the ax blade away from his own booted foot and the sandal-clad foot of the middle-aged theologian, John Smith tried to make peace.

"I bet you have stories to tell."

The woman let her shoulders fall a little and breathed deep. "The most interesting," Joan said, "was when I was called—as the head of the theology department, mind you—to present the graduation invocation. Hundreds of families were present and many of them were influential donors. One wrong slip and I'd not only be out of the theological closet, but out the divinity door as well—straight to the veritable hell of looking for a religious studies position at a secular university. Given my beliefs, I mean my ideology, I walked on eggshells until I was tenured. It was only then that I was able to throw a coming-out-as-an-atheist party."

The man leaned forward, his hands curled around the base of the ax handle—the head of which now rested secure on the ground.

"So," John asked, "the dean was after you?"

"Heavens, no. The only thing he was after was coeds. He and I got along quite well. He was a pantheist himself, but he respected my atheism. No, the problem was the audience. They expected me to be a true believer. Some kind of religious fanatic simply because I taught church dogmatics."

"So what happened?"

"I told the audience," Joan said, "I'd be reciting one of the great prayers of the Western tradition. And so I did: a paean originally addressed to Jupiter by a Roman pagan. Late third century if I remember. A literal translation from the Latin. I didn't change a word."

"How'd they react?"

"The simpletons loved it. The dolts thought it Christian. Athanasius would have excommunicated the whole lot of them and they applauded me. The irony is simply delightful. Absolutely delightful."

John wiped his hand across his shirt and extended it. "Peace?"

"Peace," Joan said as she clasped his hand with her own, then pointed to a stacked cord of firewood. "How long have you been cutting?"

"A couple hours."

"Let me give you a hand carrying this to camp."

"That's not necessary."

A frown crossed Joan's face before she collected her thoughts and forced a smile. "John Smith," she declared, "religious fanaticism was bad enough. We don't need to resort to gender stereotypes as well, do we?"

"I suppose not," John said as he set down his ax and walked to the woodpile—where he grabbed a few logs and gave them to the woman.

"More. A man's load."

John picked up three more logs. He placed them atop the others, balanced the theologian's copy of Das Kapital atop the wood, and returned to his own work.

Joan thanked John for his assistance before she stumbled back to the beach—reaching camp without taking a rest, only a little short of breath.

A LATINO WOMAN sunbathed at the beach, her eyes shaded with dark glasses as she lay on her back—the curves and contours of her slender hips and flattened breasts covered by a white bikini drawn smooth against her oil-glistened skin. She spoke to a Latino man in his mid-twenties (with a slight build and unexceptional height) who lingered near her and who wore a yellow Dodgers sports cap that covered his close-cropped hair and shaded his clean-shaven face. The young man wore blue shorts and a yellow polo shirt as morning light shined like a halo around his head and caused Maria to blink and squint as she looked into his face.

"I haven't seen you since the ship," Maria said.

Jose glanced down, his eyes flitting over Maria's flat belly and curved chest. He stepped backwards and sat down, now looking at Maria's face.

"I helped," the young man said, "with animals and cargo."

Maria opened her eyes wider now that the sun no longer silhouetted Jose's face like a halo. She brushed hair behind an ear with a single sweep of her hand.

"Is everything unloaded?" Maria asked.

"For now. Ryan took my spot on the landing craft."

"Ryan? What's he doing now? Where's he at?"

"Checking some paperwork, I think."

"When's he coming back?"

Jose shrugged and Maria dropped her eyes.

A moment later they heard the sounds of war play as children began to shout from nearby trees. Young boys aimed sticks at the water and cried from mock pain. High voices mimicked machine gun fire, bomb explosions, and the screams of the wounded and dying.

"It's ironic," Jose said with a grimace.

Though Maria furrowed her brow, Jose took no notice.

"Me landing in the Pacific on an invasion craft, I mean," Jose continued. "My grandfather landed in one at Iwo Jima and Okinawa. He knew one of the soldiers who raised the flag at Mount Suribachi. Not the Native American."

"I don't understand your point."

"I'm a strict pacifist," Jose explained, "and I used to argue with grandpa and dad about war and ethics. Grandpa served in the Pacific during World War II and Dad was a B-52 mechanic on Okinawa during Vietnam. He even approved of the Christmas bombings over Hanoi. I didn't."

"What of your grandfather?" Maria asked as she looked straight at Jose. "What about his service?"

"I didn't debate as much with him."

"Did he do the right thing fighting the fascists?"

"War never accomplishes any good."

"Wasn't it good to bring down Hitler and Mussolini and Tojo?"

"One violent imperialist state defeated another."

"You don't mean to say the Americans were as bad as the Germans?"

"They also had concentration camps."

"Forced resettlement camps."

"Same thing."

"Without gas chambers."

"The Soviets murdered as many as Hitler."

"Stalin was no Hitler."

"As a point of fact," Jose protested, "though he didn't murder as many Jews, he utterly liquidated the kulaks and committed genocide against the Baltic countries. Still, I'll concede your point for debate. Because even if the Allies did less evil to their own civilians, they still murdered millions of Germans to stop the killing of millions of Jews. Quid pro quo."

"Killing the guilty isn't murder."

"Killing some German father conscripted to fight against his will is."

"He shouldn't have taken up arms."

"His motives weren't much different than my grandfather's."

"Your grandfather was on the right side."

"Who can make that determination?"

Maria drew a deep breath. "The Allied effort was good," she declared. "It was a just cause."

"A great cause," Jose replied with noticeable disdain. "Such a great thing my grandfather did—ordering his men to use flamethrowers against caves filled with Japanese soldiers too scared to surrender."

"What was he supposed to do? Let them to come out shooting?"

"You sound like my father," Jose said with a laugh. "Did you attend West Point?"

"No," Maria said as her eyes flashed, "but I studied enough political science and history to understand a little more than Neville Chamberlain ever did. You can't let evil men destroy the weak and innocent."

"Do the weak remain innocent once they've picked up the warmonger's weapons?"

"I'm no militarist," Maria said, "but some wars have to be fought in self-defense."

"Better to be killed than to kill."

Maria lifted her shades and looked straight at Jose. "Would you," she asked, "die rather than kill?"

"I hope I'd be brave enough."

"You're telling me that the world is better off with good men dead and bad ones in power?"

"The world is better off," Jose explained, "with every good man refusing to kill so warmongers can't organize armies."

"What about your own family?"

"I'm single."

"When you have a family, will you let a madman assault your wife or strangle your children while you stand aside?"

Jose blushed. "I don't know if I'd have the bravery, but I hope so. It's the right thing to do."

"The father of my children will fight for his family."

"I'd die for them," Jose said, "but I won't turn them into militarists or warmongers. Not to save their lives. My way takes more courage."

"At least you've come to the right place," Maria said. "It's safe enough here for strict pacifism."

The screech of a distant whistle indicated it was time to return to work. Jose turned toward the shoreline as Maria stepped into a pair of loose shorts and pulled a sleeveless blouse over her arms while Jose stole a couple glances. Though they walked together down the beach, their path separated at base camp.

The children's mock crusade in the Pacific continued until dusk.

FIVE DAYS after the first pilgrim landed, the construction of the base camp was complete. Land was surveyed, plants and animals unloaded, prefabricated buildings raised, and equipment tested. On the sixth day, colonists cleaned the landing zone and collected litter, except for a few people who polished tools and packed gear. Later that day, supplies were distributed to the neighborhoods and assigned crates were marked for transport. Near dusk, the entire assembly gathered in the main hall to receive final instructions from the staff. At Ryan's suggestion, the base camp was christened New Plymouth—after which Kit read the charter as inhabitants repeated their pledge of allegiance.

The state of Paradise legally constituted, The Flower of the First of May was given permission to depart for the cold waters of the Bering Sea—its crew only a little sad to leave the tropical island. The captain carried with him letters addressed to American lawyers with instructions to pay every sailor a generous bounty in U.S. dollars if the location of the new state was left undiscovered for six months.

The hardscrabble Russian crew assured Ryan that no man among them would throw away the much-needed reward, not if he wished to live the full measure of his days.

The first hard rain erased every footprint showing that the shoreline had served as a beachhead for the landing party. Nor was even one plank of a wooden crate or a single spent cigarette butt left behind. In fact, the only visible reminders of human civilization were a flagpole with a newly sewn banner and a bright green storage tent pitched near the tree line which contained snorkeling gear, swimming goggles, life jackets, surfboards, and beach towels. The community's kayak, sailboats, rowboats, and six-person motorized launch were stored between inland trees and the LCVP (now decorated with a large rainbow and peace signs painted by the island's children) was anchored south of the beach nearest the base camp. No one wanted the pristine beaches of Paradise spoiled by the bulky invasion craft, however necessary it had proved for disembarkation.

Atop the flagpole, a banner fluttered and folded in the tropical breeze. The flag was divided between two equal-sized horizontal stripes (one green and the other red) that represented environmental purity and social justice. Atop the stripes was a large blue circle representing earth—which was adorned with brown and green continents, the most prominent among them being the Eurasia landmass. The flag waved from a thirty-foot steel flagpole anchored in a concrete foundation. More than a mere decoration, the banner served as a marker for nearby ships and indicated state sovereignty over the island. Every time the flag fluttered or snapped, it declared that a State of Paradise now numbered among the nations.

7

A STATE OF NATURE

The first emigrants arrived at dawn. A crate of MREs was opened and each settler collected four of the brick-sized rations, with parents choosing suitable meals for younger children. The morning was warm and it wasn't long before every tent was dried and every bedroll stowed. All four neighborhoods assembled at prearranged staging points that led to the four corners of the island. One group planned to move a short distance north along the eastern shore and another expected to hike southwest into a large forest. A third group positioned themselves to move along the coast to the northernmost point of the island while the fourth neighborhood planned to cross the island's nine-hundred foot hill to encamp themselves near the western shores of Paradise.

Ryan and Kit Godson were assigned to the fourth neighborhood and were among the first residents to rise. Kit prepared breakfast from a MRE while Ryan folded their tent. When they were ready to move, Ryan pulled a laminated map from a nylon pouch and worked with several neighbors to plot the easiest route to their destination: a meadow located near an inland bay. The hikers decided it best to flank the steeper segments of the hill by circling northwest to the lowest point of the ridge—from which they could turn south to their allotted land. After mapping their route, Ryan returned the map to its pouch and prepared to depart. Neighbors helped one another buckle into backpacks, shifting awkward weight and redistributing uncomfortable objects or handing tools to those posed to move. Only one or two neighbors failed to offer assistance.

Ryan was the first hiker saddled up. His backpack was stuffed full (every compartment bulging with possessions and a sleeping bag tied atop). Both a compass and binoculars dangled from his neck and a canteen was strapped to his side. He wore loose-fitting khakis, drab hiking boots, and an olive tee shirt—and held a machete.

Kit stood beside him, dressed in stylish green hiking shorts and a brown cotton shirt, and shielding her eyes with wrap-around sunglasses and her hair with a pink sports cap embroidered with the name Angels. She covered her calves with red wool-blend socks and her ankles with green canvas-nylon boots—which Ryan helped lace while Kit steadied the unwieldy bundle on his back as he kneeled to pull her bootlaces tight. Kit's own backpack was smaller than Ryan's and less bulky. Indeed, several pouches remained empty and her ultra-light sleeping roll was tucked almost by itself deep into the main compartment. After tightening her bootlaces, Kit adjusted her backpack to distribute its weight and balanced her step with a shovel doubling as a walking stick. Finally, she took a long drink from a bottle of spring water secured to her belt.

Others neighbors gathered nearby. Every adult wore boots (only children were indulged sneakers) as colonists prepared to cut their way through vines and thickets of unpenetrated forest. All adults carried backpacks and most also brought crates, water jugs, shovels, picks, or axes. Ryan and John wielded machetes and two mothers tended children rather than supplies. Tarps, tools, pots, pans, and other common-use items were stuffed into already heavy packs (though a few of the larger items were secured for later collection). One of the younger men carried brick-sized bundles in his hands— each of the double-wrapped and waterproofed packages tucked beneath an arm for additional protection. Both packets looked to be composed of dried weeds.

"Hilary," Ryan called to a thick-shouldered brunette with thin hair and a square face, "you have a minute?"

When Hilary asked what he needed, Ryan displayed his map.

"Compare these trails," Ryan said as he used a grease pencil to trace routes across a laminated map. "It's four times as long if we circle around the beach, so we've decided to cross that hill. We'll probably top it about right ... here."

Hilary ran her forefinger over several breaks in the hills. "That's not a bad place to cross," she said. "The hill's a little lower there and it's not too far from our destination. But it might be better to climb a little further south, closer to the stream."

Ryan looked puzzled.

"I know what you're going to say," Hilary said. "It's a higher point and a steeper climb. I agree. Still, if we climb alongside the creek, we assure ourselves of a steady water supply, a sure reference point, and a direct climb. It'll be steeper going up, but we won't get lost in the forests—and we won't need to cut through as many thickets and vines. Remember, there aren't any paths on this island. We cut as we move."

Ryan nodded. "It'll be faster?"

"Half the time," Hilary said. "Believe me, I've cut through the forests of Costa Rica. It's always better to stay near a stream. You can never have too much water."

Ryan presented both options to the neighborhood and Hilary's plan won unanimous consent. A few minutes later, loose items were secured and scraps of litter stored in trash bags as the pilgrims began their trek toward a stream that emptied into the lagoon close to New Plymouth. When they reached the stream—which was several feet wide at its final run into the sea—they stepped into several inches of cool water. John Smith was the first to splash upstream as he used one arm to pull vines from his path and the other to cut away every branch that impeded progress. Logs were pushed to one side and rocks kicked away. Ryan stayed to the rear, helping compatriots step safely into the water. Often, he fell behind while checking for fallen equipment or collecting scraps of discarded litter.

The hikers soon found that the creek bed required careful navigation. Large stones were staggered up the stream, often carpeted with thick layers of velvet moss from which red-leafed plants also climbed upward. A thick woven canopy of green vines hung overhead—knotted between trees by the twisting and climbing of new shoots—and flat leaves thick as banana peels pushed away by slow-moving settlers sprang back like waving palms in an Easter processional. White-blossomed orchids fell away when brushed, their fragrance clinging for a moment to man, woman, and child as the brightness of the tropical morning lighted the stream and the glimmer of splashing water recreated the first joys of Eden. Bright-feathered tropical birds startled by the first sounds of human laughter and the first splashes of human feet fluttered into the skies or perched themselves high atop the trees to observe the penetration of human civilization into the thick of their forest.

Indeed, the overgrowth was dense and the column soon disintegrated into separate bands. Four trailblazers opened the path—severing vines and moving logs as fast as they could—while three other hikers lingered a short distance behind. Two additional groups of three persons each paced themselves perhaps twenty and forty yards behind the leaders and a larger group of stragglers fell behind another forty yards, increasingly out of step and behind schedule. This staggered column included one woman and one man whose packs proved difficult taskmasters, as well as two sets of parents struggling with the complaining of older children and the delays of younger ones. Ryan fell to the rear of the procession so he could help the slow of foot, collect dropped possessions, and (whenever possible) restore nature to its pristine state.

HILARY HIKED behind the foremost trailblazers, keeping company with Alan and Steve Lovejoy. The young woman wore khaki shorts, a sleeveless shirt, and canvas boots fitted to muscular legs. She chewed jerky and sloshed upstream with a canteen strapped to her right hip and a binocular case secured to her side. Her ears were tanned from days on the beach and her close-cut hair already had been lightened by the sun's bleaching. Hilary's backpack was fuller than those of most settlers (woman and man alike), though its weight seemed to flatten her walk as she moved bow-legged uphill. Occasionally she looked at the two men following behind, but mostly kept her eyes fixed forward and moved at a steady pace, seldom lagging too long.

A few steps behind her, Steve and Alan dressed in jeans with work shirts and wore black-laced camping boots. Steve supported himself with a staff as he waded upstream while Alan carried a hoe that he frequently planted in the stream to steady his step.

Thirty minutes after setting foot in the stream, Hilary and the two men turned a bend and saw a great hill rising before them.

Hilary stopped in her tracks. "My God," she said, "it's beautiful."

"A shrine," Steve declared.

"Mount Zion," Hilary said as she turned toward the men. "The voice of nature, the holy of holies."

Alan cupped his hands and shouted toward the rear. "Ryan, has this hill been named?"

A distant shout came forward. "Hill 1. On the map."

Hearing this, Alan again cupped hands to his mouth, stepped to a side of the stream, and yelled even louder than before. "Hilary," he shouted, "called it Mount Zion. Any objections?"

"None here," came the distant reply, "that ought to goad the religious right."

Now Alan shouted the same message to the front, asking if there were objections to the new name. There weren't and several voices soon agreed that Hilary's suggestion should be adopted. A moment later, the column restarted its trek upstream, having stopped for less than two minutes to name a mountain. Soon, the water flowed faster and the channel narrowed as banks became somewhat steeper and rocks more numerous. Slips and falls became more frequent, especially for the children—with one boy managing to bruise a knee and scrape an elbow when a stone slipped from underfoot. He delayed several hikers for ten minutes while his mother bandaged the wound.

Hilary and the two men, however, continued sure-footed uphill.

An hour after naming Mount Zion, water splashed their calves in pools where the cold water occasionally brought a momentary chill. As Hilary stretched her socks above her knees to stay warm, she heard the cry of young children down the stream.

"Those little boys must be walking in knee-deep water," she said after one particularly loud yelp.

Alan shook his head. "Did you hear what Steve said a minute ago?"

"Something about Ryan?"

"He said the waters aren't parting for Ryan's chosen people."

"I suppose," Hilary said with a smile, "it's miracle enough to be here, but my boots are drenched with holy water. Feels like a Baptist full immersion. Hope this doesn't make me a social conservative like John the Baptizer or next thing you know I'll be preaching against a man marrying his brother's wife and getting my head cut off for preaching without a permit."

Alan laughed and relayed the quip to Steve, who kneeled to fill his canteen. It didn't take long to tighten its cap and close the distance to husband and neighbor.

"Besides," Hilary noted as she rested her backpack on a bank and stooped to fill her canteen from the stream, "if this is the Jordan River, there must be Canaanites nearby."

"According to the religious right," Alan said, "we're the Canaanites."

"I plan," Hilary said with a smirk, "to worship an idol at sunset. Or maybe just the sun itself."

"We'll need a child to sacrifice," Steve said.

Hilary nodded toward the yelping. "I think Theodore will do just fine."

"Was he the firstborn," Alan asked, "or the other brat?"

"I wouldn't know."

"Then," Alan said a little less loud, "we'll have to roast them both. Just to be sure."

Hilary laughed out loud. "If he doesn't stop crying," she said, "he's going to be left on the short side of the Jordan. Like Moses."

All three laughed and Hilary reached into her pocket for some caramels. The melted candy stuck to its wrapper when opened, but she prevailed over the heat and soon put one of the pliable candies into her mouth. Alan and Steve declined her offer to share treats, so she stuffed the spares into a pouch on her backpack. With Steve's help, she stood to her feet and shifted the weight of her worldly possessions so the pack again set square to her shoulders. It didn't take long to close the distance with the trailblazers and to leave the sound of Theodore's crying far behind.

Others also stopped to take drinks. Two men fished plastic-wrapped protein bars from their pockets to replenish fading energy and another man slipped behind the trees to urinate—not far from two women doing the same. Five minutes later the hikers again moved as the two dozen immigrants (nineteen adults, one teenager, and four children) threaded through underbrush, waded upstream, and climbed uphill. As John Smith cut his way through vines (stopping every few minutes to catch his breath and rest his arms), the other trailblazers pushed fallen logs to shore and kicked rocks aside.

Still, the pace slowed as the bed narrowed and the hill steepened. Indeed, as the sun burned through the tops of the trees with the passing hours of morning, the pilgrims increasingly were covered in sweat and sapped of strength. Arms grew weary and backs sore. Legs ached and feet hurt. Canteens dried more quickly, only to be refilled from a stream that grew ever more shallow. Rapids appeared more frequently and waterfalls hindered passage.

It was at one of these—a three-foot waterfall amounting to little more than a drop over eroded rock—that lunch was eaten, sore legs rested, and water-soaked blisters gently rubbed.

"How're your feet?"

Ryan looked at his wife's toes soaking in the shallow rush of cool water. Her boots stood paired atop a flat rock to her right as her husband sat to her left, his own boots dangling from a bush.

"A little sore, but no blisters," Kit replied. "How much further?"

"Not far," Ryan said. "We're nearly at the ridge. If my map is right, this stream flows from the crest. We'll cross over a few trees at the hilltop and start down the other side. It's a straight shot to our campsite."

"It's been three hours already."

"We could've taken this hike in an hour or two if we weren't so weighed down with people and packs. And children."

Kit pointed at the waterfall. "But look at them," she said. "They're adorable."

Ryan didn't smile. "For children, I suppose."

Now Kit walked near the waterfall to watch the four children playing. Brent and Tiffany ate while their twin boys splashed along the bank and Viet and Linh lay in the grass—their eyes shut—as their elementary school-aged daughters soaked their feet in a shallow pool. When Tiffany waded into the water, her sons squealed with delight and soon she splashed both boys as they returned fire. She even dunked one of the boys, though she remained careful not to keep his head under water for longer than a couple seconds.

Kit watched for a time, then turned to Brent—who reclined in the grass, his knees raised and eyes open as he listened to family play.

"Don't they ever need naps?" Kit asked.

Brent laughed out loud. "In my dreams."

"They're good boys."

"Yeah," Brent said, "but I'm discovering they aren't the best hikers in the world."

"They're only little boys," Kit replied.

"It's hard," Brent said as he sat up, "not to fall into the trap of toughening them the way I was raised."

"This isn't boot camp."

"Right now, it feels awfully close."

"At least wet boots camp," Kit said with a smile as she turned to watch the boys play. Now their mother tossed them into the water. One boy went under briefly and came up crying. His twin laughed as Tiffany shrugged—not exactly overwhelmed with remorse. Brent closed his eyes and reclined for a short nap as Kit returned to Ryan.

Ten minutes later, all four children were refreshed and dressed with dry socks and wet shoes. Soon, the neighborhood waded upstream and it took less than thirty minutes even for stragglers to reach the crest—where settlers scrambled the final few steps before disappearing over the top. A few weary travelers needed a helping hand to finish their journey.

"There's our portion of Paradise," Sean said, pointing to a distant break in the forest. The meadow wasn't big, stretching little more than the size of a youth soccer field—and filled with tall grass and the charred remains of several ironwood trees. Likely, a lightning fire had cleared the land and the western settlers now received a meadow large enough to pitch tents even before timber was cut and farmland cleared.

Lisa Greenwood waved her arms across the horizon. "Look at the wonder of this place," she said as she turned toward a man a few yards from her. "So lush and alive. So exotic and exciting. To think this island has never been seen by human eye. What d'you think? Did you ever imagine?"

"Virgin forest," Sean said. "Unknown and untouched and ..."

"And," Lisa interrupted, "we're not going to gang rape her like prairie homesteaders. We'll protect her and nourish her just as she protects and nourishes us. Tit for tat."

A cry echoed from below the ridge that help was needed, so Lisa dropped her pack and started for the crest. Sean followed in her steps as the cries for help continued and they soon saw it was Tiffany who needed assistance as she stumbled up the hill, dragging a small water jug and two young boys. Behind her, Brent was loaded like a mule—every pouch of his backpack bulkily protruding outward with an overabundance of household goods—as he pulled a second pack by its strap while crawling up the ridge.

"What in creation," Lisa said with a quiet voice and raised eyebrows, "does he have?"

"What he has," Sean answered a little less quietly, "are two kids.

And now he has his wife's pack so she can help the boys. We can't go fifteen minutes without a break and still they're stumbling up that hill. Look at 'em."

One boy tripped over his brother on the slope and both fell face down in the grass. From the crest, neither Sean nor Lisa could tell whether they were crying or laughing. Their mother struggled to pull them to their feet.

"I think," Lisa said, now dropping her voice, "they're exhausted."

"Just our luck to get them," Sean muttered.

As Lisa and Sean talked, John passed them as he hurried down-hill—where he lifted one boy over a shoulder and pulled the other by an arm to the crest while Tiffany held the back of his shirt for balance. Soon all four stood atop Mount Zion and John returned to help Brent with his double load of gear. Ryan arrived a few minutes later, carrying a bag of discarded plastic wrappers, lost toys, and even a wet shoe dropped by one of the boys.

As the rest of the neighborhood reached the summit, the emigrants took a break. Hikers stopped to catch breath, eat a snack, or rest sore legs. Canteens were shared and Ryan reminded everyone to drink a full tin to avoid dehydration since the sun was reaching its peak. After a short rest, garbage was collected for recycling and stored in a bag tied to Ryan's pack.

Then the descent began.

This time John Smith led one boy and Brent the other. Sean and Jose worked together to carry Tiffany's pack since she was too tired to shoulder it any longer. Everyone else completed the journey with the equipment they carried at the day's beginning. Within the hour, the first campers reached the meadow and others soon followed as tall grass was trampled flat, tents pitched, and a fire started. Hot coffee and tea were served with a box of chocolate bars and a tin of cookies that Linh had brought. Several colonists napped. The afternoon was spent pitching tents and unpacking possessions.

All four children were sent to an early bed and immediately fell asleep in tents pitched far enough from the firepit that floating sparks burned themselves out before reaching the thin nylon of the tents. A short time later, a village meeting was called to order and several settlers stuffed their backpacks with bedrolls to use as improvised lawn chairs. Two emigrants unpacked portable canvas sports chairs —which they shared in gestures of good will.

After several minutes of idle chat, Lisa called the meeting to order by clearing her voice. "Friends, neighbors, and countrymen," she said with a loud voice, "lend me your ear."

A few whispers soon faded as Lisa stood before her compatriots, her arms crossed and her weight shifted to one hip.

It was time to build a village.

8

A GARDEN NEAR PISHON

Lisa unfolded both arms from across her chest and shifted her weight to the other hip. A sleeveless green tee shirt bared her shoulders and light gray jogging shorts covered her muscular legs to the knees. Her long red hair looked aflame against the flickering of a small fire behind her. She cleared her throat.

"The first order of business," Lisa declared, "is to elect village officers. Kit, can you please distribute pens and paper?"

As Kit walked around the group, handing each inhabitant a torn sheet of paper and a ballpoint pen, Lisa continued the meeting.

"Do we," Lisa asked, "want to select by lottery or election? The bylaws allow us to choose."

No one stirred.

"Speak up," Lisa said. "I know it's been a long day, but we need to get organized for tomorrow and we can't assign work duties until leaders have been selected."

"I vote we use a lottery," John said. "That way we won't be pulled into cliques or popularity contests."

His wife Deidra disagreed and said so.

"Around the neighborhood," Lisa said, "everyone speak."

Brent and Tiffany said they didn't particularly care either way and neither did Viet and Linh. Deidra, Hilary, Maria, Jason, and Jose preferred voting, along with Steve and Alan. Charles and Joan also cast their ballots for voting—though their daughter, Heather, opted for the lottery. Others who also favored the lottery included: John, Lisa, Ursula, and Sean. Ryan spoke last, noting that the majority already had chosen to vote, so his own opinion was inconsequential. Kit nodded her agreement with her husband, leaning her head on Ryan's shoulder as he spoke.

Elections were held to fill two posts: Chief Neighbor and Executive Councilperson. The Chief Neighbor was authorized to administer community rules for a two-week period while the Councilperson was called to represent the village in the Executive Council of the People—or Small Council—for a similar two-week term as specified in the bylaws of Paradise. Lisa was elected Chief Neighbor and Charles sent to the Executive Council. After a twenty-minute break in which Kit and Heather served pineapple juice, sliced mangos, imported cheese, and wheat crackers, Lisa took charge of the meeting and organized a proper division of work details. As soon as she stepped to the front of the assembly, idle chatter ceased.

"To begin with," Lisa announced, "let me thank all of you for this great honor. I never expected this, though I must admit I'm very, very excited by the opportunity it provides to make a real difference in a completely new world."

There was a round of light applause as Lisa reviewed a few handwritten notes. One of the men rolled a log into the fire while the neighborhood waited for their newly elected leader to speak. Soon, wood crackled and conversation continued.

"First," Lisa said, "we need to schedule our work week. We have to decide how much we'll do and when we'll do it."

Ursula raised her hand. "I think we need a forty-hour week."

"Let's make it," Jose said, "the four-day work schedule that European labor is seeking. Why follow the American model by working ourselves to death?"

Several neighbors applauded his suggestion and a few joked they preferred a three-day week while Jason proposed a one-day schedule for himself—though he volunteered to work an extra day tending his marijuana garden.

Ryan was still laughing when he raised his hand to talk.

"Let's be serious," Ryan said, "this enterprise will be hard work and every one of you were chosen for your ability to perform. Not one of you is a slacker. Each one of you has accomplished something significant through school, activism, or work. Even Jason here put in eighty-hour weeks working to open medicinal access to marijuana during last year's California elections."

Jason nodded as everyone laughed.

"There's plenty to do," Ryan continued. "We need to clear land, plant crops, build shelters, cut trails, gather food, and make tools. And we have two months to complete our work or we'll be eating nothing but flour and fish by the end of the year. Remember, we brought limited stores with us and aren't getting outside shipments for at least six months. Now let's get serious tonight since tomorrow we need to get to work."

After Ryan sat down, the newly elected chief neighbor again addressed the village.

"What I suggest," Lisa said, "is the following: every person should be required to put in a fifty-hour week of their own choosing. The Chief Neighbor can keep daily logs to track hours. Once quotas are met, the weekend starts—except for a rotation of weekend workers. Weekend shifts will be used to cook and clean, but we'll rest from heavy labor so we don't wear ourselves out. Firewood stocks can be built up during the week."

Tiffany jumped to her feet and took the floor almost before Lisa finished speaking.

"Flex-time," Tiffany said, "is a great idea. Ten hours per day should get the work done and give us a little siesta. I haven't seen a ten-hour day since I gave birth."

Jose agreed the plan provided both American productivity and European flexibility and Heather observed that it allowed for vacations by accumulating overtime hours. When Sean asked whether the proposal accounted for genuine sick days (since someone stricken with the flu couldn't possibly make up lost hours), Lisa suggested that genuine sickness—certified by a physician or neighborhood consensus—would be a valid excuse from work. Her proposal was ratified less than ten minutes later. When the division of labor had been both addressed and resolved, discussion returned to the workload itself.

"I've figured out four major tasks," Lisa said. "Wood needs cut, fields cleared, food gathered, and trails laid. Is there anything else?"

"What about environmental protection?" Hilary asked. "Litter pickup and pollution control?"

"Excellent," Lisa noted. "I hadn't really given that work an official status. My mistake."

A light round of applause sounded.

Tiffany stood to speak two words before returning to her seat.

"Child care."

"I hadn't thought of that either," Lisa said as she jotted the two words to her list of tasks.

"Won't children just stay with their parents?" Alan shouted from the back of the assembly.

"Not with heavy chores and dangerous tools," Tiffany answered, half-rising from her seat as she spoke.

"An important part of this experiment," Lisa said, "is the understanding that children are held in common. We're not social conservatives or bourgeois householders. Every one of us knows that it takes a village to raise the children. No more double-duty for mothers. Not unless they get double-hours for their work."

"Sorry," Alan recanted, "I was just trying to be practical. Besides, I thought children prefer to be near their parents."

"You also," Lisa said with a smile, "thought child-rearing is a part-time job?"

Everyone laughed except Alan.

"What I suggest," Lisa announced, "is we appoint Alan to the part-time task of child-care provider for the first shift."

Alan opened his mouth to speak, but before a full word was

uttered, Hilary seconded the motion and a dozen hands voted for the proposal.

"I've just run some numbers," Lisa explained after the vote was taken, "and subtracting four children, the Chief Neighbor, and the Councilperson from the roster, we have eighteen able-bodied adults. Since we need to work as two-person teams for the sake of safety, we have more work than teams. I figure that we need sections to gather food, preserve food, lay down trails, cut trees and chop wood, plant fields, clean litter, tend children, construct buildings, fish, and cook. Some of this will vary week-to-week, but it looks as if the child-care providers will also need to gather some food if we're going to make a solid start. Are there any objections?"

No one objected, so Lisa continued.

"Since the Councilperson," Lisa said, "will be absent only four or five days per month, he or she can also help with heavy labor. Likewise, the Chief Neighbor will resolve problems and also help with clean up."

"What kind of schooling will there be?" Tiffany asked. "Won't we need teachers?"

"Can we wait to set up a schooling schedule in a few weeks?" Lisa replied. "We'll take an early summer break."

Tiffany nodded. "But how many teachers?"

Lisa looked at her notes. "One should be enough," she said. "We can set a tent aside with the books since there are only four children. Once the land is cleared and crops planted, I'd think that we could even pull a couple people from manual labor to help teach the children later this summer or early in the fall. Maybe we can build a schoolhouse before rainy season."

"That'd be great," Tiffany said.

Lisa then proposed that work assignments be delegated—with weekly rotations of the various responsibilities to insure that every neighbor mastered every job. It also was decided that the Chief Neighbor should select work details in accord with immediate needs and the state charter, only insuring everyone be rotated through the full range of partners and opportunities without racial or sexual discrimination.

Next, Lisa prepared to assign the first week's jobs. "Alan," she said with a grin, "we'll let you gather food and watch the kids this week. Can you keep an eye upon four children while picking coconuts, breadfruit, and pineapples?"

Alan shrugged and everyone laughed a little.

"Don't worry," Lisa continued. "Everyone gets a turn. And you can pick your own assistant."

Alan turned toward Tiffany until Lisa cut him short.

"No parents," Lisa said.

Alan faked a grimace and everyone laughed. He panned the crowd until he fixed his sight on one particularly able-looking young woman.

"Her," Alan said, pointing at the girl.

"Any objections, Heather?" Lisa asked.

Heather had none, so she was assigned food gathering and child-care duties with Alan.

Land clearing was assigned to Ryan and Maria and chopping wood to Jose and Linh. Sean and Deidra were told to construct trails and explore the district while Steve and Kit were given cooking responsibilities. Hilary and John volunteered to prepare seeds and plants for sowing and Viet chose to work with Ursula to clean the camp and dig sewage pits. Jason and Sean were given construction duties: first for a rope-lashed wood bridge over the stream and then a storage barn. This left Brent and Jason to fish and Charles to help Lisa develop a town plan after his return from Executive Council. The older children would tend the few animals held by the village. It was a productive session and at the end of the hour, almost everyone was pleased with initial assignments.

Villagers also agreed the first few days of work should be approached with caution—to avoid making irreversible mistakes. Since Lisa didn't want the forest torn up haphazardly, she directed several neighbors to survey resources and make maps so she and Charles could approach both village planning and forest management most effectively. Trails, she noted, needed to be both as direct as practical and as far from old growth forest as possible. The neighborhood also decided that half of the community would return the next morning to New Plymouth to collect remaining provisions, livestock, and plants while those who remained were to gather food and organize the camp. And because it was already Sunday evening, it was voted to start work the next morning. Both wood and food were needed immediately and a bridge had to be built before anyone could take a day off.

Several days later, crates of tools and boxes of supplies were stacked in the center of the meadow and a flock of goats was penned near a water trough filled from the Pishon River (as it was named) via tile irrigation pipes. After surveying the district, Lisa decided (with the consent of her neighbors) that the meadow where they first arrived remained the most suitable site for encampment since it was located near the stream, centered between fruit orchards and the beach, and situated amidst a ready supply of harvestable wood. A main path was routed toward the sea: with separate forks leading to the beach and a grove of coconut palms located where the stream flowed into a small inland bay. A second pathway was slated to cross the Pishon River over a ten-foot bridge and eventually to cross Mount Zion. A narrow trail was planned to link the camp with its latrine (and recycling area) in the south woods while an old-growth forest located upstream was designated for permanent conservation. Several young forests were marked for harvesting—though only after forest reclamation was factored into the production cycle. Lisa assessed that a properly managed planting and harvest of trees would permit settlers to leave virgin forests untouched as long as human populations didn't outstrip available resources.

RYAN WORE khaki shorts and tall boots as he sweltered in the sun. Before him an ironwood tree (more than a foot wide at the trunk) had been chopped up: chips of wood scattered every direction. The tree hadn't fallen as Ryan intended, but had crashed atop a young beech tree and the latter also required trimming. Bundles of cut cord were stacked nearby: the wood's sap congealing in the heat as Ryan wiped sweat from his brow and motioned to Maria.

"What d'you say? How about a break?"

Maria pushed aside branches she was trimming and dropped a wide-toothed saw. She took a long drink from her canteen and wiped sweat from her brow.

"I do need some water."

Ryan said he'd go with her and soon they walked toward the stream—where they filled their canteens and started back for their untrimmed trees. When they came to a fork in the trail—one path leading to the beach and the other toward their work—Ryan asked Maria if she felt like swimming.

Maria nodded.

"But first," the young woman said, "I've got to eat something. I'm famished."

"I have bread in my sack," Ryan replied, "and we can crack a coconut. Maybe I can find a mango for dessert."

"A little siesta does sound nice."

It took them a few minutes to reach the bay where the Pishon River reached the sea. There, Ryan picked up a coconut from the ground and shook it. Hearing sloshing, he cracked the nut with a stone and let Maria take the first drink. When she dribbled a bit of coconut water on her chin, Ryan wiped it off with a forefinger.

"You promised me a swim," Ryan said as he pointed to the lagoon. "We'd better take it before the noon whistle. Lisa's a stickler with her schedules."

Maria untied her boots, then emptied her pockets and started for the water in her tee shirt and shorts—though stopping just as her knees splashed in the lagoon.

"I just remembered," the young woman said, "this is salt water. Our clothes will be sticky when they dry—and we still have to sweat in the sun."

Ryan also had removed his boots, stripped his shirt, and waded knee-deep into the lagoon. "But it feels good now. What should we do?"

Maria smiled. "We have two options: we can swim nude or we can rinse off in the stream afterwards."

"There is," Ryan said, "a bucket near the stream which ..."

"Which," Maria said with a laugh, "Kit would prefer we use."

When Ryan turned his back toward shore and took a step into deeper water, Maria followed until the water lapped at her hips. For a second time, she hesitated.

"I don't want to ruin this bra," Maria said. "Turn around."

As Ryan turned his back, Maria lifted her shirt, slipped through her shoulder straps, and unsnapped her bra. After pulling it through her sleeve, she threw the bra to shore and slipped under the surface. When she came up, she saw Ryan glance at the tee shirt clinging to her breasts. As she tugged to separate the wet shirt from her chest, Ryan blushed and turned away.

The two neighbors swam an hour before returning to work.

ALAN CLIMBED to the crown of the coconut tree and looked down. Panic struck and he twisted around the crown—his arms and legs secured to the foot-thick trunk with braided rope—to survey forest and beach, but saw nothing.

The twins were gone.

"Boys, get back here!" the caretaker shouted into the forest. "Keep away from the water!"

No one answered as Alan scanned the area a third time and saw nothing. He shimmied down the tree, soon touching earth. It was at that very moment that he saw skin flash through the bushes: a shirtless boy in hiding. As the boy darted toward the beach, Alan started to chase before he suddenly stopped to look for the twin—immediately seeing that the second twin was running toward camp.

Alan froze.

One boy was headed into forest and the other for water. Only when he heard the squawk of a gull did the beleaguered babysitter sprint for the sea, turning his head to yell for Theodore to stop where he was. Theodore kept running and so did Alan.

Wham!

Alan smashed into a tree. The impact was violent and he bounced back hard, landing on his back. He felt his head spin, the world go black, and his body go limp—waking a moment later as one boy tapped his forehead with a stick and a second giggled out loud.

"Agghh ... What ... Where ... Give me that damned stick."

The boy wasn't particularly quick and Alan seized the stick without much trouble, shaking the stick at Theodore and Tyrone before breaking it against a tree and hurling both halves into the forest.

"Sit down," Alan ordered with a snarl—and both boys did as they were told while the injured man sat up slowly, blood dripping down his cheek and his bruised eye already swollen shut. Blood flowed from his forehead and his cheek was dark purple, with bits of bark smashed into torn skin. When he checked his teeth, he noticed that while none of them were loose, his lip felt fat.

Now Alan staggered to his feet and picked up a burlap bag half-filled with coconuts while wiping blood from his face and flinging it to the earth.

"You little sh ... boys better follow me home or I won't be the only one hit with a stick."

The boys followed close, afraid to talk as they walked behind the bruised and bloodied adult. Only when they reached the safety of camp did they sprint past their ill-tempered guardian to romp. For his part, Alan found a bottle of aspirin in the medicine box to mitigate a headache that had begun well before he ran into the tree. Afterwards, he told Heather he'd failed to pick his quota of fruit and asked if she'd help.

While Heather called for Linh's daughters and started toward the lagoon with a wood crate and canvas bags, Alan confined the boys to their parent's tent (where they played pirates on their sleeping bags). When the boys finally slipped from the tent, they sat near the kitchen area and made jokes about Alan—eventually deciding he should be called a cracked coconut head.

The injured adult found no amusement in their antics and several times warned the boys to leave him alone.

By THE FIRST full week's end, the village showed signs of good order and Lisa and Charles had drafted an urban development plan adopted almost verbatim by the rest of the village—especially proposals to establish a recycling center and raise a storage barn. Indeed, based on their push for a central village with planned development, tents were rearranged into a square: sixteen tents in four rows (each one fifteen feet apart) and eleven were zoned residential. Tiffany and Brent shared a tent with their twins and Viet and Linh with their daughters. Five additional tents were assigned to married and cohabiting couples. Of the single villagers, Hilary and Lisa a shared a female dormitory while Jose, Jason, Maria, and Heather each chose to live alone.

Residential tents mostly were nylon and stood between five and seven feet. Many were single-room homes (though family tents included nylon partitions that provided a veneer of privacy). As for the larger storage tents, they were made of canvas—flaps tied open on both sides for airflow—and pitched in rows near the commons. One contained a firewood reserve, loose piles of kindling, and waterproof tins of matches. Another housed bottled water and emergency rations (mostly unopened MREs and decades-old C-rations) while a bright orange tent beside them stored camp records and the nucleus of a library. A hospital tent was pitched nearby and a tool tent behind —with the hospital tent including medical emergency kits and cabinets of medicinal supplies while the tool tent stored little more than a tool chest, boxes of hardware goods (such as nails and screws), and sawhorses on which shovels and axes were stored safely above the dew-drenched floor.

The village's public layout also was simple. The four rows of residential tents were pitched on the north side of the camp and cords of firewood stacked to the west. On the south side was the cooking and dining area and in the center was an open lot for public meetings and children's play. Cooking facilities included two fire pits twenty feet apart—one a small rock-filled pit for grilling and the other a bonfire emplacement used for warming toes and drying clothes (both fire pits were equipped with canvas tarps and poles that could be stretched as cover in the event of rain). Dining facilities were limited to a twenty-foot dining fly covering a picnic table (made from a self-assembly kit) surrounded by log stumps used as chairs. Nylon mesh fell to its sides, allowing air to circulate while keeping tropical insects out. Even in Paradise, insect bites itched.

Cords of firewood stacked beneath the umbrage of a beech tree west of the village were not counted among emergency stores kept in the canvas tent, but were considered the deadwood, driftwood, and drying logs slated for everyday consumption. An east-leading path led to a bridge across the Pishon River—from which perishable goods were submerged in the cool water of the stream in a plastic crate. Indeed, an assortment of food and other goods stored in the water included a case of wine, two canned hams, and a sealed tub of medicines. Further south of the commons and dining area (separated by a long walk that kept its odor at bay), there was a sewage and recycling center where waste products were transformed into compost and mulch. Between the dining areas and the bridge a nature preserve was situated—where several trees already had been trimmed for children's play. To its south stood an old growth forest officially constituted as an environmental sanctuary. Open pasture and farmland were being cleared to the north of the residences. To the west, the main trail split into separate paths to the beach or lagoon not far from where the Pishon River emptied into the sea.

A cold breakfast was served late Saturday morning—the first day of rest after eight days of uninterrupted work. Alan's child-watching troubles not withstanding, the staff had doubled their efforts Friday and even baked an extra batch of flat bread and prepared a vat of vegetable soup for reheating. Several gallons of the soup were poured into glass jars and sealed with wax, then wrapped in plastic bags for refrigeration in the stream while a smaller pot of the soup was reheated for Saturday's lunch. While several villagers promised to gather food or carry supplies to a planned dinner party, nothing really needed to be worked until later in the afternoon and most inhabitants spent the day resting, exploring, or playing. Some read books and others took hikes. Lisa jogged twice around the entire island, though she proved to be the only westerner who hurried to do anything that day.

9

THE FIRST HOLIDAY

"Hey guys, what's going on?"

Ryan walked toward Kit—who sat on a log at camp's edge, her legs crossed at the ankles and a summer skirt pulled to her knees. Two children played beside her, each one digging into a shallow hole with a stick. Both answered with the high-pitched voices of very young boys.

"I'm making a stick hole," one said.

"I'm digging dirt," his brother added as both returned to their play, not long distracted by the irrelevance of adults.

Ryan looked at his wife. "What're you doing here, Kit?"

"Alan had a headache."

"Where's Heather?"

"With the girls."

"So you're stuck babysitting on a Saturday? This is our time. Alan can do his own work."

Kit stretched her legs, toes pointed outward and lifted a few inches from the ground before lowering them as she answered. "I wanted to take them for a walk."

Ryan folded his arms as he stared at the boys. One flung dirt into his brother's hair and giggled. Almost on cue, both threw dirt as fast as they could—at least until Kit called to them.

"Settle down," Kit said. "Do you want a hurt eye like Alan?"

The boys laughed.

"He looks like a coconut eye," one boy declared.

"Yeah," his twin said, "he's a coconut head."

After Kit warned the boys to be nice, they returned to their digging and the older soon found a worm curled around his improvised shovel, squealing with glee at the size of his captive. His brother dug frantically to find his own prize, though he settled for a large beetle following several minutes of fruitless searching. As Kit watched the boys play, she leaned forward—her hands folded and eyes sparkling. She paid little attention to her husband.

"Kit," Ryan said after a time, "let's take a walk. By ourselves."

Kit didn't turn her eyes from the boys.

"In a while."

"Let's go now. You are one beautiful pilgrim, so ..."

"Ryan Godson," Kit said as she put a forefinger to her lips, "stop that talk. These children have ears."

"I mean it, Kit. Maybe we can take a swim. By ourselves."

"In a bit. I told Alan I'd watch the twins till dinner."

"Alan can fend for himself," Ryan said with a voice both pained and sharp. "You're my wife and it's been a long week. I'd really like to be alone for a while. Abstinence isn't exactly the paradise I'd planned."

Kit brushed her fingers across Ryan's shoulders. "You're right," she whispered, "but I did promise and I never had a chance to be with young children before. It was always nannies and formals. Can't you wait just a bit?"

"I suppose I'll have to. I wouldn't want to impose upon Alan."

Kit forced a smile. "Sit down, Ryan. Beside me."

Ryan took a seat beside his wife, but looked to the forest—sullen and unspeaking. Only after Kit nestled against his shoulder did he relax.

"It's been a long week," Ryan whispered.

"We'll make it up," Kit replied. "Maybe we can camp by ourselves on the beach. Somewhere secluded."

Ryan moved an arm around Kit's waist as the boys remained engrossed with their growing menagerie of insects and annelids. Most of the bugs were dead, although some worms still thrashed and wriggled about as they tried to burrow underground.

"You know, Ryan. Sometimes ..." Kit cut herself short.

"Sometimes what?"

"You'll think it silly."

"I never would."

"It's just sometimes I wish I could have a baby."

Ryan turned red. "We talked about it beforehand, Kit. We both agreed. It wasn't only my choice."

"No, Ryan, I'm not saying it was. Or even that we made a mistake. I guess the world really is overpopulated and children do require more than we're able to give. I'm just saying once in a while I wish ... I mean, I envy Tiffany. They're so sweet and they really do love her."

"Maybe they do," Ryan replied, "but remember all the troubles and tribulations."

"Not in Paradise."

Ryan looked to the clouds for a few seconds before turning back to his wife. After looking at her for a long while, he spoke.

"Maybe," Ryan whispered, "it'd be nice, but we made our choice."

"Some choices can be reversed."

"Not here. Not now."

"Maybe down the road we ..."

"I understand your regrets," Ryan said, "but you're almost thirty-seven. It's getting a little late for changes."

"I just wonder sometimes," Kit said as she dug her toes into the dirt. "That's all."

"Think of it this way," Ryan explained, "you're their mother now. From each according to her ability and to each according to her needs."

Kit forced another smile and turned to the children as Ryan stroked the back of her neck. She didn't stir when he stood to leave.

"I'll catch you tonight, Kit. You stay with the boys."

"It's all right?"

"Yeah, but you belong to me tonight. Agreed?"

Kit kissed her husband on the cheek before he left, then spent the rest of the afternoon making mud pies while Ryan changed to swimming trunks and started for the beach.

THE SUN HAD RISEN to its zenith as four hikers waded through the Pishon River. Vines that once thwarted passage through the stream had been cut away and the teenaged girl leading the way brushed aside the few that remained—the other hikers following at her heels as she sloshed upstream.

It was Heather who led, with her parents and Dr. Morales following close behind. Soon after the party reached a bend, they came to a small waterfall. Though it was only ten feet tall and a yard wide, its water dropped vertical into a shallow pool that overflowed into rock-strewn rapids. Brush grew thick on either side of the stream.

"We're there," Heather said, a little short of breath. The last twenty yards to the falls were steeper than before.

"About time," her mother said, "You're killing me and I haven't written my will. The state would get everything."

Heather rolled her eyes.

"Mother," the young woman said, "you've already given me paradise. What more can there be?"

"The will won't be for you, but for your father. How would he ever function without a wife?"

Mother and daughter alike laughed out loud as the two men smiled.

Dr. Morales hurried to catch up with Heather—who now pointed at the cliff over which the small stream cascaded.

"To the right of the water," the teenaged girl said, "do you see them?"

The anthropologist walked toward scratches in the rock. They weren't much, just simple etchings. Most marks were straight lines—

several ran parallel to one another and others crossed at right angles —while a few carvings were perfectly formed circles. The scratches were easily identified as human cuts into the weather-worn stone. It was clear that men (or women) had carved their marks into the rock, perhaps hundreds of years ago.

Dr. Morales grew excited. "What a discovery," he shouted. "How did you find these etchings?"

Heather blushed.

"To tell the truth," she whispered, glancing at her parents, "I come here to shower. It's a little more private and ... You won't tell anyone will you? Good. I wash my clothes while I bathe. It's like a cold shower. Anyway, I dropped my dress near this wall of rock and showered. Afterwards, I noticed these indentations. At first I thought that someone had vandalized the island—till I realized the marks looked old."

"Quite perceptive, Heather. These petroglyphs are older than you are. They must be at least fifty and maybe hundreds of years old. There's not much thawing and freezing in the tropics, but there is plenty of rain, so any markings eventually fade. These aren't fresh, but they're not too weather-worn either."

"Unlike," Heather said with a smile, "my cotton clothes."

Dr. Morales paid no heed to the teenaged girl's fashion concerns, but turned to his academic peers.

"Look at these marks," the anthropologist said as he rubbed the stone. "Aboriginal scratching of one sort or another. This island was once inhabited—or at least visited."

Heather's parents stepped forward to examine their daughter's discovery, rubbing the marks and asking pertinent questions of the anthropologist while Heather listened in silence. Only when it appeared their discussion was concluding did the girl speak.

"What does it mean, professor?" Heather asked. "Are other people close?"

"That," Dr. Morales said, "is precisely the issue. And it's a question I intend to answer. When you told me of this place, I expected to find cracked rocks or vandalism. Or maybe something from the Russians who inhabited the island for a few months. I didn't expect to find marks showing an ancient human presence. But now that we've found petroglyphs, we have to search for their makers. Or at least more marks. I'll put together an expedition to search beyond the horizon for other islands."

"That'd be cool," Heather said. "I'd love to see other places. If I ever return to civilization, I hope to study anthropology."

"I didn't know," the anthropologist replied. "Is that a serious plan?"

"Oh yes," Charles said, "she's studied different cultures since she was in elementary school. We've always tried to teach her about cultural diversity and social relativism—as well as about indigenous peoples and social mores."

"Really?" Dr. Morales said as he turned to Heather. "It looks like I have an intern. If you want the job."

"I'd love it."

"What's the work schedule for your neighborhood?"

"We operate on a fifty-hour week," Joan said. "We select free time ourselves."

"That's good," the anthropologist said. "Maybe we can get together for study and exploration."

"I'd really love that," Heather replied. "It'd be so much fun. And good for my education too."

"If that doesn't get her into a good anthropology program," Charles said, "I don't know what will."

"Coming here," Joan said, "is working out even better than we had hoped."

Heather reached into her backpack for a loaf of bread, which she broke into equal shares for a quick meal. After they returned to the neighborhood, Heather went to the beach while her parents took an afternoon nap, anticipating a late night party.

As for Dr. Morales, the anthropologist declined an invitation to stay for the beach party since he wanted to return to New Plymouth to consider the petroglyphs and begin preparations for a voyage of discovery. He drafted his proposal while the westerners soaked up the last rays of the day.

A BONFIRE BURNED on the beach, its flames consuming thick logs and its smoke rising heavenward—where it was dispersed by a gentle breeze into the nothingness of the dark. The green palm wood hissed, crackled, and exploded as it burned. No sooner would the fire fall than someone threw another log into the flames so the inferno again blazed. Red-hot coals filled the shallow pit and were insulated by glowing ash.

Several yards away, an improvised tarp was drawn tight across a crude wooden frame and secured to the sand with two-foot stakes. A table was set beneath the stretched canvas and spread with baked fish and boiled shellfish, as well as bread, crackers, and fruits. Three bottles of wine and a liter of Russian vodka sat on the table: the wine wrapped in wet rags and the vodka nearly gone. Cracked coconut husks and piles of fish bones were scattered near the table, along with a dozen dirty forks and a pile of personal effects. A biodegradable garbage bag overflowed with waste.

Villagers had separated into several groups. The largest party was located at the north edge of the beach and consisted of those villagers still in their twenties. Nearby, two women talked at the water's edge, their feet lapped by the surging tide. Further away, Tiffany and Brent lounged in lawn chairs while their boys played down the beach under Alan's supervision. Viet and Linh played cards with their daughters and were joined by Steve after a time. Other couples talked over drinks, sat quiet on the beach, or strolled back to camp.

An hour after supper was finished, Alan marched the twins to their parents. "Here they are."

A quizzical look crossed Brent's face as Tiffany explained that she didn't understand.

Alan answered her with a deliberate tone to his voice and raised eyebrows. "My duty time is up," he said.

"Ours too—it's your weekend for domestic duties."

"That's dishes and cooking. Not babysitting."

"I'm afraid," Tiffany said, staring straight into Alan's eyes, "you're quite mistaken. Domestic duty involves the whole household."

Alan kicked the sand.

"You're the one mistaken," Alan said. "I've watched your kids all week and suffered for it every day. Now it's my night off and I'm planning to take a walk with my partner as you did with yours. And these boys aren't coming with us."

Turning toward the two girls playing cards with Steve and their parents, Alan spoke out loud.

"Viet and Linh," Alan declared, "are with their daughters; they apparently enjoy their children."

"So do we," Tiffany snapped as she stood to her feet and brushed sand from her hips, "but we haven't had a night out for weeks and we aren't likely to get another one for months. This is our night. Tend your chores, please."

Alan told the boys to sit fast and started to walk away, but Tiffany cut him off—shouting to Lisa as she did so. As Alan also called out for help, Lisa staggered from the circle of singles to the place where Tiffany and Alan were quarreling. Though the chief neighbor's eyes were red and her smile unceasing, neither of them heeded her condition.

"Lisa," Tiffany asked, "what are the childcare rules for the weekend?"

"Domestic duty. Parents are off till bedtime. Why?"

"Alan doesn't want to finish his shift."

"You," Lisa turned toward Alan, "don't have a choice. No one enslaved by parenthood. Remember? But don't worry, when you've got kids it'll help you too. It's for everyone."

Lisa giggled and wandered in the direction of her friends, balancing herself with outstretched arms and wiggling her fingers as she tiptoed across the sand while Alan and Tiffany disputed several minutes more. She had reached her own circle of friends long before Alan finally returned the boys to the village as Viet and Linh taught Steve to play three-handed euchre.

. . .

TWO WOMEN SAT with toes in the tide. One was a slender Latino wearing white shorts and an unbuttoned shirt (a white bikini underneath) and the other was a thin African-American woman sporting a yellow tube top and gray jogging sweats. Maria and Ursula talked quietly—far from the bonfire down the beach.

"There weren't any tampons in the medical tent," Ursula said, "and I'm almost out."

"I need more for next month," Maria said, "I've only got a couple left."

"My period's due soon," Ursula groaned. "Hence the pants."

"Afraid to swim?"

"I can't waste tampons and I'm not risking an accident."

"I'm low too. We need to pick up a box or two at New Plymouth."

"You want to walk for supplies tomorrow?"

"Sounds good," Maria said. "I need the pill too. I left a pack on the ship and I'm down to my last week."

"I've got a box of condoms," Ursula said. "Want a few?"

"Not for me."

"Why not?"

"Paradise hasn't exactly been filled with romance."

"Just in case?"

"That's why I'm on the pill. Besides, I don't like them."

"Why's that?"

"It's not really a man."

"Maybe not," Ursula said, "but the pill makes me bloat."

"Dieting," Maria replied, "takes care of that."

"So does carrying logs."

Maria looked toward her toes. "Tell me about it," she said. "I was on tree duty all week. With Ryan."

"He's got that Hollywood look," Ursula said. "The best catch on the island."

"You do remember Sean, your boyfriend?"

Ursula scooted from the tide, which now lapped her ankles. "I remember we're not married."

"Ryan is."

"But he's so hot."

"He's more than that," Maria said as she dropped her voice. "He's sweet and has a great sense of humor. And he listens when I talk. He's the prize."

"Yeah," Ursula said as her teasing suddenly ceased and she looked straight at her friend, "and Kit won him."

Maria nodded.

"She's very nice," Ursula said as she continued to look at Maria. "She'd never hurt a flea."

Maria said nothing.

"You ever sleep with a married man?" Ursula asked.

"It's not right," Maria said as she shook her head. "I'd never do it."

"Me neither. I don't know about the rightness of it, but it brings too many complications: like babies and carriages as little girls sing. And more often than not, baby carriages without marriages."

Both women laughed as they stood. Maria flicked wet sand from her toes and Ursula tugged at her tube top.

"I'm going to the party," Ursula said. "How about you?"

"I'd rather get some sleep. It's been a long week."

"Suit yourself."

While Ursula walked toward her friends, Maria picked up her shoes and started home. On the way she passed several of the couples sitting in the sand. When she came to Ryan and Kit holding hands and talking in whispers, she kept her face forward and hastened her step until she passed into shadows.

"What is marriage?"

It was Hilary who spoke. She sat cross-legged amidst a ragged line of the younger neighbors. Jason handed her a joint and she drew deep before passing it to Lisa—who took a hit before handing it to

Jose and Sean. Only Heather (sitting on folded legs at the end of the line) refused the joint.

"Slavery," Lisa giggled.

"Sex," Jason said.

"I'm serious," Hilary said. "It's more than sex and slavery, even if it includes them. What is marriage?"

"The love of a man and woman for each other," Jose replied. "That's what I think."

"Boo," Lisa cried out. "Homophobe."

"Yeah," Jason noted, pointing to several shadows silhouetted in the sand down the shoreline, "think of Steve and Alan. What do they lack that Tiff and Brent have?"

Jose pulled the joint from his lips. "Children," he declared, raising his eyebrows and cocking his head as he spoke.

"Ooooo, point scored," Sean said as he reclined to his back, knees up and head lying on the sand.

Hilary shook her head. "That's pure catechism," she said. "Almost papal."

"Maybe," Jose said with a shrug, "the Popes had it right."

"Not in a thousand years," Hilary said. "They're mere men—and males at that. Do you actually believe traditional religion can get anything right?"

"I was born Catholic," Jose said, "so I suppose I have doubts about the doctrine of complete Papal fallibility. Even Popes have to be right every century or two."

Hilary groaned.

Sean now asked a serious question. "What about Deidra and John? They don't have kids."

"Yeah," Jason smirked, "tell us how Deidra and John differ from Alan and Steve?"

"Deidra has bigger breasts?" Jose said with a shrug.

"But what if Deidra was a 32A?" Hilary asked.

"Are you blind?"

"What if?" Hilary pressed the point.

"It's not what you see," Jose said, "but what can't be seen."

"Like what?"

"Milk-making mammary glands."

"She's dry as any man," Hilary quipped.

"There are other differences," Jose replied.

"Such as?"

"Didn't your parents tell you about the facts of life: complementary equipment and all that?"

Everyone laughed.

"Don't be crass," Hilary scowled. "The real issue is whether or not marriage should even exist on this island."

"To be, or not to be ... married," Sean shouted as he jumped to his feet and waved his arms, "is that the question?"

Everyone laughed and another joint was lit. Again, everyone but Heather took a hit and Jason took two.

"I think people should marry," Heather said after she sipped from a glass of red wine, "if they want to. Why not? As long as they choose freely. Freedom of choice. Isn't that our motto?"

"And exactly why marriage must be abolished," Hilary said. "It forbids choice. Even getting beyond Jose's homophobia."

"I don't think it forbids anything," Jose said, "as long as it's between consenting adults."

"Look at the couples," Hilary replied with a scowl. "What are they doing but drawing into themselves? There's Ryan and Kit sitting alone and Tiffany and Brent. Viet and Linh are with Steve, but that's only because Alan is tied up with the kids. And look at us. Not one of us is married, so we're all here together. Marriage divides the neighborhood. For the sake of one decision, every other choice—all choosing—is forbidden. For the love of one, many are left unloved."

Heather thought about Hilary's words before answering. "You can't make people share love," she eventually observed. "That's rape."

"Freedom and love are our only law," Hilary said, "and that's why marriage must be abolished. Let every relationship test love with freedom. It'd mean more too."

"I'd like to test Kit if she weren't married," Sean said a little too loud. When no one laughed, he just shrugged.

"You wouldn't be talking like that," Jose said after a short pause, "if Ursula was here."

"She's neither my wife," Sean replied, "nor my mother."

"She'll scold you like a mother," Jose said, "till you cry like a baby."

"Well," Sean smirked, "then she would be a wife. My mother never yelled at me."

This time laughter was loud and Hilary stood up to speak.

"Sex is only part of the equation," Hilary said. "We're also talking about love. I think almost everyone on this island agrees social conservatism needs to be abolished. We don't practice the traditional virtues of chastity and monogamy, yet we still marry. Why? Because we want to lock someone else up like a slave. Because we want to control them with the old-fashioned fears of adultery or infidelity."

Heather shook her head—the scarlet ribbon tied into her hair waving like a banner.

"Don't you think," the teenager asked, "that marriage protects our deepest feelings? That there's something in us that truly desires marriage? One man for the rest of my life? That's what I hope for."

"Ahhh," Hilary sighed, "the girl is a true romantic."

"What she is," Sean said out loud, "is one vow from a nun."

"Maybe," Heather laughed.

"What you need," Hilary said with a laugh, "is some good sex. That'll clear fantasies from your mind."

"What I want is deeper than sex," Heather said, looking first to her toes and then toward the stars.

No one spoke for a time.

"What can be deeper than sex?" Hilary said after a pause, realizing a moment too late that she'd set herself up for a series of raucous jokes that followed.

"This is getting vile," Hilary said after several minutes of distraction. "Back to the subject. You have to admit it's our nature to want many rather than few."

"I don't think that's true at all," Heather protested. "Most women desire one husband."

"I'll bet," Hilary pressed her argument, "even you've desired more than a single man since we came to this island."

"So, you think she wants a married man or a single woman?" Sean asked and everybody catcalled while Heather blushed.

"I'm speaking of love that's more than a tumble," Heather said.

"You don't deny," Hilary asked, "you've wanted more than one of the men on this island, at least for a moment?"

"If you mean to say there are attractive men among us, I guess I admit to having eyes," Heather replied. "But seeing isn't willing. Desire isn't love."

"What is love?" Hilary asked.

"I don't know for sure," Heather said, "but my parents have it. And I want it too. Someday. With one man—the right man."

"Or woman," Lisa added.

"I don't know about that. I want a man to love me all my life."

"Fine," Hilary noted. "Let's agree love is more than sex, though that's far from proven. Don't you admit infatuation—or romantic love if you will—is polygamous? We fall in love with many men. Or women."

"I'm not so sure," Heather said. "Just as we sleep with one man at a time, so we desire one man at a time. When I crushed on three guys in the fifth grade, I thought of them one at a time, not all at once. I dreamed of which one I'd marry—and never once thought about marrying all three. I mean, don't our hearts hate the orgy?"

"Mine doesn't," Jason declared, "who wants to play?"

"You're sick," Lisa said as she punched him in the shoulder.

"It's been that way, I'll admit," Hilary replied, "in a monogamous, conservative culture. But not here. Why should it be? If we abolish marriage, won't each of us love many rather than one? Won't everyone be included? Wouldn't that be the best way to build a truly loving community? Why should some people be left out of the celebrations?"

"And why should everyone be included in private moments?" Heather objected. "Does love have to be a public thing?"

"Right now," Jason quipped, "I feel left out by Lisa: both publicly and privately."

"Philosophy doesn't pertain to perverts," Lisa responded and everyone laughed hard.

"Can a woman love five men," Heather asked after the laughter died down, "as well as she loves one man or can five men love her as well as one is able to?"

Hilary thought about her answer while Jason rolled another joint.

"Maybe each love burns a little less passionate," Hilary observed, "but each man can fulfill different needs at different times. And she'd never be faced with the inconsolable grief of the monogamous widow or the loneliness of an unloved wife—or the fury of a jealous lover."

"I'd take that risk," Heather observed, "for a good man. Better one man known well than several strangers in my bed."

"Right now," Lisa rejoined the discussion, "you haven't even got one man—known or not—in the sack, unless there's some secret you're not sharing."

"What's going on, people?"

It was a woman's voice not yet heard that now sounded.

"We're talking about true love," Lisa answered, "and the abolition of marriage."

"Hand me that joint," Ursula said as she sat beside Jason. "You can count Maria's vote for abolishing marriage."

"Why's that?" Jose said as he sat up.

"I'm pretty sure she's got the hots for Ryan and she's frustrated by his marriage vows. She's torn between sexual frustration and self-respect."

"Don't you see?" Hilary said jumping to her feet. "This is exactly what I mean. Even now, the letter of the law thwarts love. All I want is to free love from every barrier."

"Down with the monopoly of marriage," Jason shouted.

"That sounds," Sean said with a loud laugh, "like laissez-faire morality."

Lisa groaned in pretended anguish.

"Besides," Sean continued, "it's a moot point. Maria's got nice hips, but she'd never compete with Kit's breasts. Or legs."

Ursula glared at her boyfriend. "What about my legs?" she snapped. "Tell me what they look like."

"Like feet," Sean said with a shrug of his shoulders, "in my mouth. They look like well-shaped ankles in my mouth, I should say."

"You better say that," Ursula scowled, "or my ankles are all you'll be seeing for a long, long time."

Soon, the conversation died as food and drink were distributed and it was decided to take a swim. Hilary and Lisa already wore bikinis beneath their shirts and shorts, so they simply stripped outer garments and plunged into the surf. Heather and Sean changed behind separate bushes while Ursula filled her hands with food and sat down on the wet sand. Lisa and Jason hadn't brought suits, so they waded into knee-deep water before stripping to their underwear and diving into the deep. Most partiers swam until their buzz burned off and sluggishness sent them home in groups of two or three.

The bonfire burned down as night passed and by the time its hot coals were covered with ash, not a living soul remained at the beach. Children and caregivers were long gone and most couples had made their way back to the village or toward some private place along the shore. A few celebrants laughed and shouted as they stumbled home while others followed more quietly.

By the time the last couple emerged from the sea to douse the warm embers with buckets of seawater, even the birds had retired for the night. Brent and Tiffany walked home hand in hand and crept into their tent, careful not to disturb their two sons tucked under sheets across the tent. With their short goodnight kiss, a great party came to its end.

10

FLESH OF FLESH

T he twins woke at sunrise, so Tiffany crawled from the tent with them—barefoot and dressed in day-old clothes. She gave Brent a parting kiss before following her sons into camp, having volunteered for a day of childcare. As she stepped into daylight, the boys ran ahead, unwilling to wait for their slow-moving mother.

"Good morning," Kit said as Tiffany neared the dining tent where the former actress was laying out plates of sliced fruit on an imported picnic table. "You and Brent get in late?"

"The beach," Tiffany said, "was beautiful last night. This is a wonderful place."

Kit pointed to Tiffany's blouse. "It looks," she whispered, "like you enjoyed a little romance."

Tiffany looked down and blushed: her blouse was inside out and she wasn't wearing a bra. "Whoops," she said, "it was dark and late and ..."

"I'll watch the boys while you fix yourself."

Kit called the boys to sit on a trimmed tree trunk and sliced several pieces of flatbread and kiwi—along with a bowl of oatmeal flavored with banana and sugar and a glass of goat milk—while she told stories of filming Sesame Street. It wasn't long before Tiffany returned.

"Thanks, Kit. And for fixing them breakfast."

"Do you mind if I take them for a walk?"

"Maybe this afternoon," Tiffany said, "if that works for you. We have family time planned this morning."

Kit said it was fine and Tiffany swept her sons into her arms with a suffocating hug and told them how much she'd missed them. The boys returned their mother's affection before scampering into the wooded park as Tiffany shouted for them to stay within sight and Kit poured coffee.

"They do love you," Kit said.

"They're the sweetest boys I know," Tiffany replied.

"I never saw boys who were kinder to their mom. Most of the ones I knew back home were brats."

"In New York?"

"Hollywood," Kit said. "I guess my nieces in New York weren't so bad, but I was only there for holidays. The kids I worked with were spoiled and mean–spirited little stars and starlets. Almost every one."

"We teach the boys progressive values," Tiffany said, "but our methods are a little more traditional. Mind you, we've never actually spanked ... I mean, hit ... the kids, but we do believe there's some-thing to the idea that children must be forced to be tolerant and kind. Of course, they're still boys. Snips and snails and puppy dog tails, that's what they're made of."

Kit laughed.

"They're not perfect," Tiffany continued. "They fight and whine too much and they don't listen very well, but we don't expect them to be flawless. All we want is a little respect and affection. And I think we get that."

"You do," Kit said. "They're sweet boys and if I ever had children, I'd like them to be like yours."

Tiffany nodded her gratitude and Kit refreshed the coffee. After finishing breakfast, both women cleaned dishes.

. . .

TWO WOMEN ANNOUNCED themselves with a polite greeting before entering the doctor's tent. They had started for base camp early that morning, but the climb up Mount Zion proved difficult and the descent down the eastern slope even worse—and they didn't arrive until lunch. Ursula was covered with sweat and felt ill (having stopped to relieve herself several times) while Maria clutched her side. The doctor's attention remained fixed on his computer screen even after the young women entered his office.

Dr. Graves wasn't a young man. His hair was streaked with gray and there was a paunch to his belly. His arms were spindly and his legs skinny—and he was dressed in plaid shorts with a button down shirt, along with sagging tube socks and open sandals. Even in Paradise, doctors dressed unfashionably. They also made patients wait. The doctor ignored the two patients as he scanned medical files.

After several minutes, Ursula cleared her throat and asked if the doctor had some time, but the physician dismissed the question with a wave of his hand. Not until he perused two last files did he turn toward the visitors.

Observing their flushed faces and sweaty shirts, Doctor Graves asked if they'd been jogging.

Ursula laughed. "Who needs to?" she asked. "You're going to end up with a ward of anorexics the way our calorie counts are falling."

The doctor chuckled. "You're from which neighborhood?"

"West."

"Over Mount Zion," Maria added.

"I just remembered something I have to do," the doctor interrupted. "I'll be with you in a moment."

Maria and Ursula continued to wait as the doctor again hunched over his computer. This time it took him only a minute to modify and save a file. Meanwhile, Ursula reached into a pouch in her khakis for a packet of saltines—over which she spread peanut butter—while Maria sat down. Ursula offered to share the crackers, but Maria declined her offer, having filled herself with day-old flatbread during the walk over Mt. Zion. Indeed, Ursula had just begun to chew when the doctor again addressed his patients.

"What brings the two of you to New Plymouth?" the doctor asked.

"Medical supplies," Maria said.

"Is someone ill?"

"Nothing like that," Maria said. "We need girl stuff."

The doctor winced. "Which products?"

"I need tampons," Ursula said, "and she needs the pill."

"Are you completely out?"

"I am," Ursula said.

"Almost," Maria added.

"That's bad," the doctor replied with a grimace.

The two women eyed each other.

"What's wrong?" Ursula asked.

"We lost only one crate when we unloaded," the doctor said, "but it was filled with women's supplies."

"I don't understand." Ursula looked confused.

"What I mean to say," the doctor said with a loud voice, "is our tampons, sanitary napkins, PMS pills, sponges, and birth control pills are gone. You could say they're sunk beneath the sea."

"What does that mean—sunk beneath the sea?" Ursula said, her tone agitated and voice loud.

"I mean sunk beneath the sea," the doctor said, "literally."

Neither woman spoke.

"Remember the crate," the doctor explained, "the Russians dropped that first day? Well, it included all of our female supplies."

No one spoke for a full minute, while the two women assessed the impact of the loss and the doctor waited for their reaction.

It was Ursula who finally broke the silence. "What are we supposed to do?" she asked, her voice curt.

"I've ordered replacements," Doctor Graves said with a shrug, "for the six-month resupply."

"But," Maria now joined the conversation, her voice also noticeably sharp, "what are we supposed to do now?"

"To begin with," the doctor said, "you can calm down. We have backup plans and homegrown remedies."

The women let him talk.

"I doubt," Dr. Graves said, "you'll find any of the pill to share. Not only are there differing prescriptions, but most women brought only a temporary supply—as we most unfortunately advised."

"What kind of solution is that?" Maria snapped. "Pope Paul VI's solution to world depopulation?"

"It's not the solution," Dr. Graves said. "The solution is that the men's supplies are intact. I have thousands of condoms, two boxes of fifty for every man on the island. That gives you and your boyfriend at least a hundred. Just for a few months. Probably more, since some couples won't use any at all. I suppose your appetite isn't much stronger than that. Even at your age."

"My appetite," Maria said with a scowl, "isn't for condoms."

Dr. Graves walked to a cabinet. "Perhaps," he said, "you can trade them to a friend with the pill. If not, it'll be unprotected sex, safe sex, or no sex at all. Of course, you can always take your chances with natural family planning."

"Unbelievable," Maria said. "Simply unbelievable. This is supposed to be the twenty-first century."

"Nevertheless, it's all we have," Dr. Graves said as he pulled a box of condoms from a cabinet. "One box or two?"

"I just want an emergency supply," Maria said as she took a few of the prophylactics. "These are enough."

"I have plenty for now," Ursula said, "but my period's due soon and I'll need tampons."

"As I said," Dr. Graves now shook his head, "they were lost. And I don't have enough to hand out. We have a limited supply for medical emergencies. Can you borrow from friends?"

Ursula flared in anger. "Do you think," she said loud and irritated, "we filled our backpacks with damned tampons to hike through the jungle? They weren't on the list of items to bring and they were on your list of products available, so I'd guess that any of us with any sense brought a one-month supply. At most."

"Oh," the doctor said as he sat at his desk to type notes into a computer, ignoring the impatient tapping of Ursula's fingers. Only after a couple minutes passed did he turn toward the young woman.

"I've made a note for spares," Dr. Graves said, "they'll be here with the replacements."

"What am I supposed to do in the meanwhile? Drip down my leg?"

The doctor folded his right arm across his lap and propped his left elbow on his right wrist, his chin resting in the palm of his left hand until he arrived at a solution after several seconds.

"In the past," the doctor eventually whispered, "women used old rags. Literally."

Ursula's jaw dropped.

"You'll," Dr. Graves explained, " just have to find clean cloth, cut and fold it, then ... I don't need to go into details, do I?"

Ursula shook her head in disbelief.

"Just make sure," the doctor advised, "you wash the rags between use. Probably ought to be boiled clean."

"Unbelievable," Ursula said. "Just unbelievable."

"I'm really sorry," the doctor replied, "but there's nothing more I can do."

A minute later both women stood outside the medical tent— where they grumbled several minutes before heading for the nurse's station to lament their plight to Nurse Fallows. While the nurse was far more understanding, even she could do no more than provide Ursula with a roll of gauze and suggest to Maria infertile means of sexual experimentation.

After picking up a bottle of aspirin, the western women took lunch at the base camp, then made their way to the supply center to collect a sewing kit, steel pots, and sets of snorkels and flippers. Ursula grabbed a roll of bleached-white cotton cloth and the women returned home via a scenic route around the coast, stopping near the south village for a midafternoon snack.

They reached their own village as dinner was being served.

LISA SAT ALONE by a beech tree whose roots dug deep into the soil underneath the Pishon River, upstream of the bridge—though not as far as the waterfall. Here the din of camp life was inaudible as she enjoyed the quiet of her thoughts. Her eyes were closed and she couldn't see that her freckled cheeks were browned as she reclined against an aged beach tree—whose canopy stretched to the heights of the forest. Lisa closed her eyes and yawned, her back arched and chest thrust into a gentle breeze. She wore no shirt and her red hair waved in the wind such that the split ends brushed the pink of her breasts.

Lisa let the wind blow where it may.

The young woman reclined against the tree and tucked a folded shirt beneath the small of her back before closing her eyes to enjoy the whisper of the woods as birds flitted through the trees—chirping to reveal themselves—and the creak of jungle insects echoed from the leaves. Mostly, Lisa listened to the soft whisper of the breeze across treetops and the noisy trickle of the brook streaming through rocks. Peace stilled her thoughts and nature quieted her soul. Her spirit grew drowsy and her flesh languid; her hair fluttered. She felt the sun caress her eyelids and massage her breasts, its shafts penetrating the membranous clouds of the South Pacific and warming her thighs. She smiled as she hoped for another touch. It came soon and it wasn't long before her legs felt aglow and her chest afire. Lisa opened her eyes and noticed that her breasts were freckled and legs tanned, even though the canopy of high trees had softened the sun's hard touch, and wondered whether she could spend the whole day in this place and decided to stay until dusk. Indeed, she so loved the touch of heaven and earth that she swore to remain faithful to nature until the parting of death.

After some time, a bird sang out and Lisa whistled a response, singing her own song for several minutes: giddy from excitement and pleasure. Taking precautions against burning, Lisa squirted herbal sunscreen into the palm of her hands and spread it from chest to thigh, careful to massage the lotion into flesh virgin to the sun's burning passion. She wiped the excess of the organic lotion into tall grass and then lay on her back. Following several minutes of agitated movement, she rolled to her belly (using the folded shirt as a pillow), stretched her legs, and pressed her forearms against earth. When she was comfortable, she sighed and relaxed. Soon enough, she slept— her breasts pressed to the earth, hips nestled into grass, and thighs hugged close. Her dreams were of love and nature as the sun pressed close until late in the afternoon.

BRENT WORE FLIP-FLOPS and a dirty apron as he pulled the lid from a large iron pot simmering over hot coals to sample an early taste of dinner. His face didn't show what he thought of the stew, but he did laugh out loud when he saw Sean's lips curl after doing the same.

"Like it?" Brent asked.

"Like the plague," Sean answered. "What is this shit?"

"Fish and vegetable stew."

"What else is in there?"

"Diced gords and canned corn."

"Anything good?"

"Linh's making bread."

"Any fresh fruit?" Sean groaned. "Something she hasn't touched?"

Brent pointed to a table filled with peeled bananas—already blackened from an afternoon in the sun. "She put them out early."

"Can't someone," Sean growled, "teach her to cook?"

"You can lead a horse to water ..." Brent said, "but you can't make him drink. Especially if Linh filled the trough."

Both men laughed.

Sean said he wasn't hungry after all and jogged toward the orchard. Linh returned a moment later and with her the first of the villagers hungry to eat. As Brent ladled generous helpings of stew, Linh pulled burned rolls from the fire pit—though several villagers declined the burned bread and what was rumored to be dead fish stew. Even those who actually tried to eat some of the soup left half-filled bowls beside the dirty dishes, politely apologizing that they'd eaten heavy lunches. Brent dumped the leftovers into a compost bucket while Linh scrubbed empty bowls with handfuls of sand and fresh water.

After the dishes were stacked, Brent announced he planned to construct a real oven. Instead of baking bread on a cooking stone, he hoped to use brick and mortar to make an oven that could be used to bake loaves and cakes. He asked only for help moving materials. When Linh promised to do all the cooking if he could find volunteers to haul construction materials from New Plymouth, Brent approached several villagers chatting around the campfire and requested help to bring bricks from New Plymouth. When no one volunteered, he singled out candidates.

"Jose and Ryan," Brent asked, "can you give me a hand?"

Before the two men could answer, Hilary protested. "Why just the guys?" she asked.

"We're carrying bricks and iron over the hill."

"And so it begins."

"I don't understand."

"Patriarchy."

"I don't understand."

"Then I'll explain," Hilary said, "because the minute you categorize women's bodies as physically weaker, you set in motion the whole range of patronizing platitudes that inevitably lead to male dominance. Men are made soldiers while women are made mothers. Men are made kings while women are perceived as princesses. Men ..."

Brent cut her short. "What d'you propose?"

"We women," Hilary declared, "will get the bricks while you men tend domestic duties."

"Fine by me," Brent said. "My shoulders still ache from carrying crates up the mountain. I'm all for equal rights."

After Brent told her what tools and supplies he needed, Hilary turned to the women for help.

"I need volunteers," she said, "to get supplies."

Linh walked from the dining tent to the fire and asked what kind of supplies were needed.

"Bricks and an iron grill," Hilary replied.

"Ask Viet," Linh said as she pointed to her tent. "He's strong."

Hilary told her not to be such a chauvinist.

"Chauvinist, my aching bones," Linh said. "It's physics, not politics. He can carry twice the weight I can."

"That's not the point."

"Getting the bricks isn't the point?"

"Exactly," Hilary said. "If we base our economy upon natural efficiency, we'll end up capitalists and chauvinists for sure. We need to organize ourselves to overcome appearances and prejudices."

"How?" Linh asked.

"In the States," Hilary said, "we'd use technology."

Linh rolled her eyes. "We're not in the States and I'm not lugging bricks up that hill."

"I'm perfectly aware of our present state. Anyway, I have a solution: water power."

Linh waited for an explanation.

"We'll use the boats," Hilary said.

"Up the stream?"

"Around the lagoon."

"The launch," Linh said with a frown, "can't be fired up except for emergencies."

"The rowboat can."

"And?"

"And we'll load the bricks into the rowboat and push it along the shore."

Linh's face relaxed. "That's not a bad idea."

"Or maybe we can hoist a sail."

"Maybe we can," Linh said, "but it'd still be easier to make the men lug the things."

Hilary shook her head and Linh laughed before conscripting Joan and Deidra as volunteers. When villagers realized Linh would be removed from kitchen duty for the day, the majority applauded the proposal to send the women to New Plymouth for supplies.

. . .

HEATHER CRAWLED from her own tent and walked to an adjacent one. She had fallen asleep after an early dinner and now the sun was setting and the forest quieting for the night. The teenager shook the front flap.

"Mom. Dad. Are you home?"

When there was no answer, Heather unzipped the door and looked in. Two bedrolls were neatly rolled and a plastic jug of water sat in the corner, still capped. Several books were stacked atop an otherwise empty rucksack and grooming items were set neatly beside the books. When her eyes fixed on a nylon brush and hand-held mirror, Heather stepped in to retrieve them and soon walked toward the stream.

The grass on the path was trampled and the trail already was two feet wide: vines cut back and every blocking limb removed. The track threaded around a grove of beech trees before it reached the bridge over the Pishon River—where Heather now sat down. To her right, the village was marked by a thin column of smoke dissipating into the tropical dusk and a few indistinct shouts echoing from the forest. To her left, a trail cut through the forests on the slopes of Mount Zion. Water streamed beneath the bridge.

Heather thought about wading toward the falls, then looked at the descending sun and decided against it. With her feet dangling into the stream and toiletries beside her, the young woman reached into the water and lapped water over her legs, careful not to splash her shorts. After she washed her face and arms, she pulled a toothbrush from her pocket and brushed her teeth. When this too was done, she slurped from an open hand to rinse and pulled a can of shaving cream from her bag. While lathering her legs, she inspected a used razor—only to judge it too dull for further use after a single swipe. Replacing the worn blade with a new one, she shaved the stubble from her legs with long strokes toward her hips. It took five minutes to clear her legs and several more to remove the stubble under her arms.

Afterwards, the teenager rinsed the shaving cream and whisker cuts away with handfuls of water before cleaning her razor—being careful to cover the blade with its removable lid; razors weren't replaceable in the jungle. With her shaving finished, Heather spent several minutes brushing her hair—stroking it from forehead to neck to untangle the worst knots. When every strand was separated, she watched the sun descend below the trees before retiring to early bed.

Dawn would bring a full week of work.

11

AND THEY KNEW NO SHAME

Ursula lay in Sean's arms, her head resting on his shoulder. When Sean pulled a sheet over both of them, the dark-skinned woman snuggled even closer. Already the dawn of life stirred: birds sang, insects chirped, and early risers stoked the village fire. Ursula spoke with a quiet voice and Sean answered the same. The indiscernible rustle of their touches drew no notice beyond their nylon-walled enclave.

"That was paradise," Ursula said as she smacked her lips and pressed close. "I hope we didn't wake anyone."

"It is a little early," Sean said, "for a work day."

"You've already put in your quota," Ursula giggled. "Take the rest of the day off on me."

"I'll be on you," Sean said, "the rest of the day. And the night too."

"I guess it's been a couple days."

"I'm glad you're feeling a little better."

Ursula pulled Sean closer still—wrapping her arms tight around his neck. "Is this all you need from me?" she asked.

"That a trick question?" Sean lifted Ursula's chin with a forefinger as he looked at her face.

Ursula just batted her eyes.

"What I need," Sean continued, "is you and no one else. You're the best thing I've ever had and I don't want anyone to interfere with us. Or anything."

"I like that answer."

"It's even better between us here than in the States. No bills, no politics, no worries. Just you and I together."

"No more bigots saying we're black and white."

"Here we're only man and woman and no one can keep us apart now. No prejudice or hatred."

"Nothing between us," Ursula said. "Ever."

"Promise?"

"I swear it."

"That's what I like about you," Sean said. "No agenda. Too many women want a man's whole life. You're happy with the day. With us."

"Live for each day they used to sing."

"It's not day yet," Sean said. "There's a little more dark to enjoy."

Ursula's dark flesh grew warm as Sean slid fair-skinned hands down her belly. A moment later he pressed his lips against hers and passion stirred. Half an hour later they emerged to take breakfast and prepare for daily chores. Sean was asked to build a box for gathering sea salt (a wooden frame to be filled with seawater left to evaporate, leaving dried salt behind) while Ursula was sent to fish.

LISA HAD SET out early to inspect the district. Carrying a day's rations and a shovel, she slipped from her tent before the sun broke over the horizon. As a courtesy, she threw logs into the remaining coals and built a stack of kindling around them. It didn't take the wood long to ignite and soon a fire burned. When the wind blew smoke into her face, she wondered what effect air pollution might have on the flora and fauna: especially birds whose nests were choked by the acrid smoke. Before she started east, Lisa wrote a few lines in a notebook that the day hadn't begun well since she herself was an air polluter and likely to become a repeat offender—at least if she desired hot food or boiled water.

When Lisa reached the bridge, she removed her boots and waded barefoot downstream, looking for signs of human habitation. She saw only smooth stones worn by steady erosion and unsevered vines knotted across the streambed when she first stepped across the stones and crouched beneath the vines—careful to do no harm. It was with considerable disgust, however, that she soon came to a logjam fifty yards downstream: an obstructing dam comprised of cut branches and trimmed foliage. After she broke the dam and pulled the man-made clippings to shore (leaving natural fallen logs to flow on), she made a note to collect the cuttings and continued her walk to the sea—scouring every bend of the stream for pollution. She found only two MRE wrappers trapped between large rocks and a rum bottle sunk in a shallow pool, which she stowed in her backpack for recycling. Lisa wasn't completely displeased with the state of the stream: several long weeks of human habitation left only a few scraps of pollution. She collected more trash from her front lawn in Connecticut every Sunday morning.

As the sound of falling water came to ear, Lisa picked up her pace. Each step was a little more difficult than the previous one as she waded through knee-deep water. At the three-foot drop of the stream to the sea, Lisa dropped her backpack and removed her outer garments—circling the shore looking for trash and then swimming the narrow channel to do the same across the bay.

It was on the far side of the bay where Lisa first found death: two fish floating in the shallows, their vacant eyes showing blank, uncomprehending stares as the sun flashed from silver bellies and seawater lapped into rigid, unmoving gills. Lisa lifted the larger of the dead fish by a dorsal fin to examine it. When she saw that the other fish bore no obvious marks of parasites or an aggressor, she double-bagged both carcasses and stowed them in her knapsack for additional analysis. Once her inspection was completed, Lisa slipped into her shorts and headed for the main beach, where she found the leftovers of Saturday's party: a bit of boiled crab, a pile of fish bones, and several cigarette butts. She also came across a used condom and a torn pair of panties—at which she shook her head in despair at human sloppiness while fitting herself with rubber gloves to move the debris into the ever-filling trash bag slung over her shoulder.

Ashes from the bonfire were thrown into the grass as fertilizer and the fire pit was filled with clean sand, though even Lisa thought it pointless to wipe every smudge of soot since rains would sift ashes through sand far better than any human hand. When the mess was cleaned, Lisa sat amongst the trees to eat—only to discover her lunch ruined by the stench of dead fish. The outer bag had worked itself open and death's reek had penetrated the knapsack: a problem discovered too late to correct. Hungry and disgusted, Lisa disposed her bread and soup into the waste bag and started home. Along the way, she picked up cigarette butts, an empty water jug, and three coconut husks. It didn't take her long to reach the recycling center where she sorted an overflowing trash bag held at arm's length as her face and stomach alike turned.

The recycling center, which Lisa herself had designed, was fifty yards beyond the village perimeter and consisted of three distinct components: recyclables, slow decomposables, and compost piles. The recycling area stored non-compostable goods like wire bands from cargo crates, torn plastic jugs, MRE wrappers, empty medical containers, and old cans. Most supplies brought to the island were environmentally friendly, so the recycling area wasn't allotted much ground. Slow decomposables included combustible materials like coconuts husks, pieces of wood, shards of cloth, and scraps of paper which could be buried or burned and were kept together for aesthetic and environmental reasons. The compost piles were knee-high mounds of dirt into which unneeded fish guts and food scraps were covered with layers of mulch. Because bacteria and other microorganisms flourished in the tropical sun, compost could be reduced to organic material in days and weeks. Compost piles also included inflow from sewage trenches through which rains carried human sludge flowing from the public toilets—which were located closer to camp, atop a shallow rise where men relieved themselves beyond a wood wall at the end of the trenches and women sat on hand carved toilets shaded beneath canvas. Several buckets of fresh water for rinsing the toilet permitted at least tolerable hygiene and were replenished every morning.

Now Lisa swatted flies while she sorted her trash into its proper components, then performed an autopsy of the dead fish—discovering that the larger fish had a hook in its throat and the smaller one did not (though she assessed both likely killed by human malfeasance). Lisa disposed of the dead fish and surveyed the sewage lines to insure that daily rains continued to wash waste down the trenches for dispersal into the forest.

What the young woman noticed, however, was that sewage pits were emptying far slower than planned—with the drainage ditches proving too narrow to allow proper flow of fecal waste into compostable sewage treatment. Several sewage lines were stopped up and required Lisa to poke them open with a stick. When examining the toilets, she also noticed that one smelled of urine, so she splashed two buckets of salt water on it and a third on herself. Even in Paradise, men proved unable to hit a large hole with a small stream. The sun blazed overhead and the young woman's clothes dried by the time she returned to the village a few minutes later.

When she reached camp, Lisa saw Jason smoking a cigarette—that is, tobacco—near the fire pit and hurried to him.

"Those things will kill you," Lisa said as she pointed at the cigarette.

Jason said nothing.

"I said those things are going to kill you."

"I can wait."

"Not," Lisa scowled, "if I find another butt on my beach, you won't. You'll wish for the slow death of lung cancer."

"It's just one butt."

"I found six today," Lisa said as she glared at Jason. "If I find anymore thrown about the woods, we'll have a tobacco bonfire. Get it?"

"They weren't mine."

"Don't blow smoke in my eyes. You're the only one in the village who smokes."

Jason flicked a smoked cigarette into the fire. "That work for you?" he said with a smirk.

"Burn the butts or I'll burn your ass."

"You look stressed today," Jason said as he flipped a half-full pack of unfiltered cigarettes at the young woman. "You need a smoke?"

Lisa took a cigarette and flung it into the fire, then returned to the village to collect a spare lunch and a clean trash bag before hurrying into the old growth forest where she'd sunbathed two days earlier.

JOAN STUCK her shovel into loose earth, then untucked and unbuttoned her blouse, letting it hang loose across her hips. She pulled out a bottle of tanning lotion from her knapsack and rubbed some on her neck and chest, being particularly careful to oil the skin near the frayed lining of her bra before returning to her work. Several times she smiled at the young man who worked with her and whose glances often flitted toward her chest. Twice, she caught his eyes with her own. The third time, she stopped working.

"Would you like me to button my shirt?"

Jose turned red. "They're ... you're fine."

"You think so?" Joan asked as she looked at her own cleavage. "You want me to lose the blouse? Or just loose it?"

"You can't talk like that," Jose said as he blushed. "You're married."

"You've noticed that too, have you? You certainly are an observant young man."

"I ..." Jose stammered, "I wasn't looking at you."

"I agree. You're doing more stalking than looking."

"I'm the one being stalked."

Joan reached over to tussle Jose's hair. "If I were stalking," the middle-aged woman declared, "you'd already be mine, but I'd have to get my husband's approval first. He's particular about the company I keep and you are a close neighbor."

Jose looked perplexed.

"Besides that, young man," Joan continued, "I've decided on you for my daughter and she doesn't seem amendable to time-sharing. She sees love more as some type of private property."

Jose stopped laughing. "Heather's just a girl."

"You really are an observant young man."

"Who's too old for your daughter."

"I think not," Joan said with a shake of her head.

"She's in high school."

"Already a senior and very mature. You do have eyes to see?"

"I graduated six years ago," Jose replied. "She's my little sister's age."

"I was only a little older when I met her father at Berkeley—I was a freshman and he was in grad school."

"I see the plan," Jose said as he forced a laugh, "to rope the single guy into marriage."

"Don't be so old-fashioned," Joan scowled. "I'd make a terrible mother-in-law."

"Good. Because I have no plans to be a son-in-law anytime soon."

"See how soon our minds met. Heather's even more accommodating."

"Ms. Ingalls," Jose said with a blush, "that's your daughter."

"Now don't get your hopes up," Joan said, "since she's a bit old-fashioned. I only meant to say she's deferential."

"That's different."

"Don't be in such a hurry," Joan said with a sober tone. "Spend some time with her and get to know her. If you like her, you have our approval. We brought her to this island to meet the right sort of people and to have a safe environment to grow up. Better to learn about love here than in the clubs of Manhattan or churches of Des Moines."

Again, Jose blushed.

"She can't remain a virgin forever," Joan continued. "For goodness sake, someone has to go first. What do you learn at school these days? Maybe the conservatives are right about the ineffectiveness of sex classes. We figured out the passion and physics of it without any instruction at all."

While Jose stood red-faced, Joan buttoned her shirt—though neither said much more as they continued their work.

RYAN STOOD BEFORE HIS TENT—HIS shadow stretched longer than his six-foot frame—and rolled his eyes as he looked at his torn, muddy clothes. Another shirt was ruined and another pair of pants was filthy. Crawling inside, he found clean clothes, collected toiletries, and walked toward the bridge. Passing Maria's empty tent, he called out, though he didn't stop when he received no answer. Finding the bridge occupied by Joan and Deidra, who were shaving their legs with disposable razors and lathered soap, Ryan waded upstream, thinking the waterfall a suitable destination—having heard some neighbors used it to shower. He walked upstream with clean clothes draped around his neck and a bag of toiletries clutched in his right hand. A comb was slid into his pants pocket.

Ryan's head was bowed and face drawn tight as he sloshed ahead. Kit had been difficult the previous night and the aftereffects of their spirited discussion hung over like a headache. And though fights were becoming a bad habit, last night was the first time in their marriage Kit had denied him sex from spite. Ryan relived the argument as he moved north and it was several minutes before his thoughts cooled—and he remembered he and Kit weren't newlyweds and this wasn't their first quarrel. The bickering would end soon enough, he supposed. It'd just take a little time.

Looking upstream, Ryan saw a woman who sat hidden in the shadows of an old beech tree. She looked slender and Ryan wondered whether it might be Maria, so he moved quietly to surprise her—keeping his feet from sloshing to keep noise down. It didn't take him long to reach her.

"Maria, is that you? It's me ..."

It wasn't Maria and Ryan cut himself short as he looked at Lisa. "You're not wearing a shirt."

"Oh ... Ryan," Lisa said, arching her back and thrusting her chest forward in a long yawn.

Ryan watched as her breasts rolled. They weren't as full as Kit's but flatter and firmer. Though he tried to look away, his eyes were drawn back to the woman's nakedness.

"I-I'm sorry," Ryan said. "I didn't know it was you."

Lisa yawned a second time and stood. Her breasts dangled earthward for an instant as she lost her step and stumbled until Ryan caught her by the wrists and steadied her balance. The young woman remained nonplussed despite having almost fallen chest-first into her neighbor.

"What's going on?" Lisa asked.

Ryan turned red and Lisa looked at her own freckled chest.

"They're just breasts," the young woman said. "I imagine you've seen a few before today. Kit has a full set."

Ryan looked away. "W-what," he stuttered, "in th-the world are you doing?"

"Don't worry," Lisa said with a shrug. "I'll put in overtime by the end of the day. I don't shortchange hours."

"I mean, what are you doing here?"

"Yoga and some sunbathing."

"Without a shirt?"

"No hang-ups, remember? Besides, Hilary tore two shirts this week. Clothing needs to be conserved."

Ryan looked to the stream. The water rushed through his legs and the blood through his face. When Lisa scratched one of her breasts, he gasped.

"Sorry," Lisa said. "Bad manners. The itch instinct got me."

"I know the feeling," Ryan blurted.

Now it was Lisa who blushed as she reached to the ground for a towel while Ryan took a step back toward the village.

"Weren't you headed upstream?" Lisa asked as she draped the towel over her shoulders and chest.

"I need to return to camp. Kit's probably looking for me."

"Probably."

As Ryan turned and hurried back to camp, Lisa slipped deeper into the woods.

. . .

KIT FINISHED her chores by midafternoon, so she strolled to the beach, eating green bananas for early supper and resting beneath the shade of a palm tree. Later, she bathed in the sun, her back warmed by the sand and ankles splashed by the tide. She let out a yelp when someone tapped her forehead from behind.

"Ehhhh."

"Sorry, Kit."

It was John Smith—carrying a fishing pole, a folded net, and a bucket of chum—who startled her. He asked if Kit was feeling well.

"I'm okay," Kit answered, glint shining from tears in the corners of her eyes.

"You sure?"

Kit nodded. "What're you doing here?" she asked.

"Fishing. I didn't catch much up north so I decided to move."

"Isn't Ursula helping you?"

"She was," John answered, "till the smell of fish made her sick. She went to rest."

"Weak stomach?"

"A little indigestion."

"I've never fished before."

"You want to try?"

"Sure," Kit said, wiping sweat from her face and tears from her eyes with the back of her wrist. "Here?"

"We'll use this net."

"I've never done this before. I grew up in Manhattan. I wouldn't even touch the iced trout at the market."

Kit unbuttoned her blouse and climbed from her shorts, revealing a two-piece bathing suit almost old-fashioned in its modesty, while John threw his shirt into the sand and kicked his sandals aside before unfolding his nets. Soon, he handed a corner to Kit—who walked into the lagoon until the water lapped at her waist.

John distanced himself from her as he pulled a fifty-foot nylon net. "Drop the net," he called out as he pulled the line tight, "when I say so, run for shore. Angle in as you move and we'll bag some dinner. Ready, set, go!"

Kit ran for shore. At first, she moved slowly through the water, though she gained speed as the water grew shallow. Twice, she staggered and once she nearly fell. John moved faster and angled in sharper and by the time Kit reached calf-deep water, he stood on dry ground pulling in the net even as Kit groaned and tugged as she tried to pull the net—now heavy with fish—to shore. Though several fish thrashed through the shallows to escape the trap, more were caught in the webbing. When Kit finally reached the sand, she grew excited as she surveyed the catch.

"Those are big fish!" she cried out.

Indeed, a couple large fish were caught along with several smaller ones. John untangled the strands of nylon as he threw fish inland, where Kit picked them up and dropped them into buckets—though one slipped from her hands and flopped all the way to the sea before she could get it. The rest of their catch secured, they made a second try. On her second attempt, Kit slipped in the surf and nearly all of the fish escaped.

Before Kit's aching arms ended the workday, another half-dozen casts were made—with most attempts catching at least a few fish. Then the day's catch was set on stringers and taken to the bay for cleaning. After completing the gruesome task of killing and cleaning their catch, John and Kit wiped their tools and washed their hands. The afternoon sun had dropped and only a few gulls circled over-head—the beach quiet and the trails still.

"John, can I ask you something personal?" Kit said as she shook the sand from her shirt.

"It depends, I suppose, on what you ask."

"Do you ever wish for children?" Kit asked with a somber voice.

"I did," John said after a pause, "but ... well, there's no reason to go into details. We just can't have them."

"I'm sorry."

"Don't be. It's not your fault. Just one of life's twists."

"Did you ever consider surgery or adoption?"

"Surgery and in-vitro were useless. Adoption, yes. Until Deidra decided against it. She wants her own."

"What about you?"

"I'm not sure I understand."

"You have needs too."

"She's suffered worse. And I'm her husband in sickness and health—as they used to say."

Kit turned her back as she climbed into her shorts and slipped her blouse over her bikini. When she turned around, Kit saw that John had covered himself with a shirt and shorts.

"Why do you ask?" John said. "Does Ryan want them?"

"Neither of us did really," Kit said. "In the States, we decided to forego children, so I had my tubes tied. It was my choice as much as Ryan's. Sometimes in Hollywood, I had doubts. Here I have nothing but them. It's so different."

"How?"

"The bustle of the world isn't here. It's peaceful and perfect and a place made for living. I'm learning that life's more than a career."

"The twins have inspired you."

"Yes," Kit said, "they have. And the girls. There weren't many children in Hollywood. Except for a few really obnoxious stars who weren't exactly Shirley Temples. Unless you mean the drink."

"Has Ryan changed too?"

"We quarreled about it last night and again this morning. He insists we did the right thing and doesn't want me to return to the States for a corrective operation. He thinks I'm too old to bear a baby."

John looked surprised. "You're ..."

"Thirty-seven in a few months."

"Thirty-six now?"

Kit nodded.

"I was born when my mother passed forty," John said. "You've got a little time, at least."

"There's more risk at my age."

"Maybe a little more risk," John said, "but also greater gain. A woman your age has much to offer a child."

"You're the first man," Kit's eyes lit up as she spoke, "I've ever heard say anything like that."

"To tell the truth, if Deidra would have it, I'd adopt a child today. I'd love to have a son. Or a daughter."

"Can you speak to Ryan for me?"

"I'd rather grab a shark by the fins," John said as he nodded toward the sea. "We've talked too much already."

Only after a long pause did Kit mention how beautiful the lagoon looked and John observe they needed to cook the fish as soon as possible. As Kit grabbed a tackle box and a bucket of cleaned fish, John collected the net and poles before walking beside Kit on the trail to the village. Just before they reached the village, Kit tapped John's shoulder.

"What if he never agrees to it?" Kit whispered.

"He's your husband."

Kit said nothing.

"Do you love him?" John said.

"I do."

"Then you live with disappointment. We can't have everything we want. That's something I've come to grips with."

"I suppose you're right."

The two villagers entered camp with their catch. Kit found Ryan at their tent (already waiting undressed and anxious for his wife) while John took the cleaned fish to the grill—where he replaced Linh as chef and organized a fish fry with vegetable side dishes and brown rice. Everyone praised the meal and even Linh didn't disagree since her mouth was filled with fish.

12

PARADISE LOST

I t took Charles most of Tuesday morning to hike to New Plymouth—where Small Council had been scheduled to meet midafternoon and was to be followed by a state dinner. Because he traveled alone and planned to remain overnight, Charles hiked along the shoreline, thinking it folly to risk twisting an ankle in the uninhabited hills where it'd be a day or two before he was missed. As a result of taking the longer route, he didn't reach New Plymouth until lunch. There, he collected a few raw vegetables from a food table and headed for a noisy tent. The last to arrive, he took his chair without fanfare as delegates administered oaths of allegiance to open the session.

Only members of the Executive Council attended: these being the four village and one professional staff delegates. Charles represented the west neighborhood and Dr. Graves the professional village. The other neighborhoods sent women as councilors: a soft-faced brunette in her thirties from the east, a twentyish blonde from the north, and a gray-haired matron from the south. The brunette was made moderator by unanimous vote, then entertained proposals for a calendar of future meetings and an agenda for the present one. Proposals and priorities were penciled in and it was decided the first session would discuss supply shortages, native markings, marriage laws, and several lesser concerns. No one objected to the agenda and the meeting began in earnest.

Dr. Graves spoke first, briefing fellow councilors on the loss of feminine supplies and explaining how rationing was being conducted until a resupply vessel could arrive. The doctor also reported that he'd used an emergency satellite connection to arrange an early drop of required goods with a retired green energy investor —a former neighbor and casual acquaintance—who planned to sail the South Pacific during coming weeks. The yachtsman had promised to bring tampons, sanitary napkins, PMS tablets, and birth control pills to replace what had been lost. Everyone applauded the doctor's initiative and the council sanctioned his efforts ex post facto. Executive Council also authorized overnight docking of the yacht for resupply and mail pick-up and also voted to honor its crew with a luau. At the eastern brunette's suggestion, it was decided not to request additional supplies beyond the replacement order. Since no one wanted to repeat the unfortunate inability of Jamestown to support itself without outside intervention and capitalist speculation, all additional resupply was limited to the scheduled six-month restocking. Only an emergency as dire as loss of birth control pills and sanitary napkins had justified outside intervention.

Subsequent agenda items concerned the issues of pollution, militarism, and capitalism. When the southern delegate requested guidance regarding the proper disposal of non-biodegradable materials, Charles explained how MRE wrappers were used as sandbags in the west and other councilors shared useful suggestions as the southern delegate—a gray-haired woman wearing faded jeans and a sleeveless tee shirt—recorded the better ideas and promised to implement them upon her return home.

Next, the southern woman asked whether children should be allowed to play with toy weapons, noting that two boys in her neighborhood had smuggled plastic soldiers into Paradise. Though the council considered this an egregious violation of charter rules, it was decided to make a mild rebuke and discreetly dispose of the offensive items without public censure. Charles suggested the soldiers be recycled as melted plastic rather than burned or buried (with the effect of polluting either the atmosphere with the acrid smoke of burnt plastic or the earth with non-biodegradable plastic), but the majority deemed it best to purify themselves from militarism and industrial plastics alike by sacrificing the toys to fire. There would be no beating of plowshares from swords since it was feared this might implicitly encourage making swords (or molding soldiers). Executive Council voted to ban all manufacture or use of toy arms, weapons, games, or simulations. Finally, an issue was discussed dealing with concerns raised by the east village after the soft-faced brunette explained how workload disputes were paralyzing her neighborhood. After a short discussion, it was voted that the staff psychologist, Dr. Erikson, be authorized to arbitrate differences—with her decisions possessing full regulatory power.

After a short recess, Dr. Morales petitioned to launch an archaeological expedition over the horizon. He briefed the council on the cultural significance of Heather's petroglyphs and requested permission to draw a week of rations and use of a sailboat to search for archaeological remains and artifacts. Though he assessed the discovery of anything larger than rock etchings unlikely, the anthropologist explained it was imperative that he make an attempt to contribute to substantive scholarship and cultural preservation as much as humanly possible. His request was granted, the councilors asking only that any finds be kept intact rather than looted or moved to museums—a request Dr. Morales accepted without reservation. As soon as his petition was granted, the anthropologist excused himself to begin preparations.

The northern representative—a tall blonde wearing a halter top and cutoff shorts—spoke next.

"Our only real issue," the woman declared, "has been litter. Several people have been careless with their trash. The neighborhood has assigned them cleanup detail and we hope the situation will be self-correcting."

Everyone applauded the northern success.

"Good effort," Charles said. "Anything else?"

"I guess we also had a dispute over our work schedule," the northern blonde said. "We were working a five-day week with flex hours and the early risers resented the late-birds arriving midmorning and then taking a long lunch to escape the sun. It got so bad both groups were threatening to unionize."

"How'd you address the issue?" Karla, the brunette delegate from the east, asked.

"We rewrote our rules," the blonde continued, "so breaks can be taken anytime after four hours of work. Now our late risers come in earlier to put in four honest hours before lunch. No one wants to be working at noon."

Another round of applause went out.

"Anything else?"

"One last issue. A bit more serious," the northern blonde said, panning the group to draw their attention.

"What's that?" Charles asked.

"A little jealousy. Apparently, one of our women is polyerotic by nature and two guys are bickering over her. We're not really sure how to handle arrangements since she left the boyfriend she came with. It's a little bit ..."

"If you don't mind, may I say something," Charles interjected, turning from the northern woman to the moderator, "that bears on this concern?"

The northern blonde yielded the table.

"We have similar issues," Charles explained. "There are hints of tension between those who choose strict monogamy and those who delight in their freedom more completely. In fact, some of my neighborhood have asked for an explanation of the laws of marriage and love so that ground rules can be set from the start."

Everyone now gave full attention.

"What is marriage?" Charles asked. "Is it a relationship or a promise, a signature or a decree of state? Who can marry? When? How? What makes a divorce? What are the implications of the right to sexual association? All of these questions require review, not for academic discourse, but for the practical government of this island. I suggest we draft a platform that can be sent to the whole people for deliberation before necessity forces the issue. Since none of us expects our relationships to remain static, we need to get on top of this issue early."

"Does everyone else," Karla asked, "believe this discussion necessary?"

Every hand was raised.

"Then let's divide," Karla declared, "the issue into components and break for the day. Everyone can reflect on the debate through the evening and provide talking points for discussion. If you can give these to me by, say ... nine in the morning, I'll prepare a final agenda by noon. Then we'll meet tomorrow after lunch to continue our discussion. Agreed?"

Karla's motion carried and delegates soon filed from the tent to study the issue. The stern-faced southerner found an anthology of feminist theory at the library and disappeared into the woods while the northern blonde took a notepad and a single pencil to a shady tree. Dr. Graves worked from his computer. Charles stuffed his knapsack with food, books, and sunscreen, then started walking toward the beach as Karla (the brown-eyed brunette from the east neighborhood) followed at his heels.

"Charles," she called.

"What's going on, Karla?"

"Going to the beach?"

"To do my homework," Charles said, nodding toward the sea.

"You mind if I join you?"

Charles eyed the woman from ankle to breast. "I'd like that. Where're your things?"

The woman picked up a half-filled knapsack and said she had everything. Then the couple walked side by side to the beach—where they found empty lawn chairs beneath a palm tree and set to work. Charles copied passages from his books while Karla worked from memory. Occasionally, they exchanged ideas or debated texts and soon were condensing notes into outlines. When they finished, they reclined into beach chairs and ate unwrapped MREs (along with flat bread and fruit punch) as they enjoyed the sunset.

After they were done eating, Karla retrieved a dark-colored bottle from her backpack. "I'll freshen that juice a little," she said.

Charles held his glass out as Karla unscrewed the cap from a bottle of rum and spiked their drinks.

"This is the best punch," Charles said, "I've drank in a month. We're down to two bottles of vodka we're rationing. And I think the village has a case of wine or champagne."

"Ryan and Kit?"

Charles laughed. "Hollywood in the jungle."

"I brought whiskey and rum," Karla said. "A full case. Much bigger bang for the buck."

"I agree," Charles said, clinking his glass against Karla's before throwing his head back and chugging the drink.

"More?" Karla asked and Charles took the bottle from her hand, taking a long swig of rum while Karla sipped her share. Indeed, they talked and drank until both the conversation and the rum ran dry, then rolled out sleeping bags and slept beneath the stars. They woke the next morning in each other's arms—their clothing draped over a chair and sand clinging to every fold of flesh.

THREE WOMEN SAT side by side at the campfire. Behind them, the dark contour of Mount Zion shadowed the eastern sky and before them the flames had burned down to coals. Two of the women sat hands folded over knees as they whispered and occasionally laughed out loud. The third woman's face dropped toward her lap, her hands clutched tight. She said nothing.

"Don't even start about labor," Linh said. "I spent twelve hours in labor with both girls. No second time discount for me."

Tiffany nodded. "I had twins. Eight hours of labor followed by a C-section."

"That hurts," Linh said, "even to think of it. They never cut me open."

"It took me six months to recover," Tiffany said with a groan.

"Six months?"

"I could walk in a few days, but it was six months before I had my strength."

"That's horrible."

"That's why I had Brent fixed afterwards. No more of that nonsense."

"Good for him," Linh said. "More men should have it done."

Ursula joined the conversation. "I wish Sean had."

Both women asked Ursula what was troubling her and she explained that her period was late.

"How late?" Tiffany asked.

"A day or two."

Tiffany smiled. "That's nothing."

"Plus a week," Ursula added.

Tiffany said no more.

"I'm sometimes a week late," Linh said.

"I'm never," Ursula said, "more than a day early or late and ..."

Tiffany and Linh waited for her to finish.

"My stomach's queasy and my breasts hurt."

"I'm sure it's just the sun," Linh said.

"No," Ursula said, "this is different."

"Then it has to be nerves," Linh said, "it's too early for much else and you're on the pill, right? I didn't feel anything at all till the third month."

"It's not nerves," Ursula said. "Today I almost vomited brushing my teeth and I've had to pee all day. Besides, I don't use the pill."

Linh looked startled. "That's a surprise."

"It seemed sensible till now," Tiffany said. "The pill doesn't stop diseases and it makes me bloat. Condoms are better protection."

"You use them properly?" Tiffany asked.

"Yeah, usually," Ursula paused, "but ... there was one time on the ship I couldn't remember whether we used one or not. There was so much going on that day and we partied all night. I was hung over all morning."

"How can you not know whether he was wearing a condom?"

"Occasionally we swap out for spermicide. I just can't remember using either that first day on the ship."

"Have you checked? To be sure?"

"No," Ursula said. "I couldn't walk to the clinic today. Not in this sun. I'm really not feeling very well."

"We have a test in the medical supplies."

"Really?"

"Stay put," Linh said. "I'll get it."

Tiffany waited with Ursula as Linh disappeared into the dark.

"Have you told Sean?" Tiffany asked.

"I need to be sure first."

"Have you decided what to do if ..." Tiffany's voice trailed off.

"It's not the States and I'm not about to take the morning-after pills they brought—even if they're not lost at sea. They're too experimental for me—I don't want to bleed to death in the middle of nowhere."

"They're safe. Or they wouldn't be here."

"No," Ursula. "I've done a fair amount of reading. Besides, there are far worse fates than raising my child in Paradise."

"That's," Tiffany nodded, "why I'm here."

Linh returned with a small box in hand. The square-shaped carton was torn open and its instructions scanned before being tossed into the fire. Ursula walked behind the mess tent and urinated directly on a plastic container, then returned to her seat as the chemicals processed. As Tiffany placed her arm around Ursula's shoulders and Linh held her by the hand, the women endured a long wait of three minutes. When Ursula finally held the test to the light of the fire, the women saw a blue cross—a positive reading—in the middle of the device.

"Oh my ... I'm having a baby."

"Congratulations," Linh said, "if you want them."

Tiffany gave Ursula a gentle hug.

"You have your own life to live and choices to make," Tiffany said, "but let me say one thing. Motherhood is better than marriage, though you have to swear never to tell that to Brent. Men can't stand the truth."

"Yeah," Linh said, "no man is completely good, but babies are never bad."

"You never regret giving birth," Tiffany continued, "and we'll always be here with you."

"We would be honored," Linh added, "to share motherhood with you."

Ursula forced a smile as tears welled into her eyes, then shuffled to her own tent as Tiffany and Linh lingered another twenty minutes —both women reminiscing about their firstborn and how their husbands responded. Only after the fire burned out and a night chill brought goose pimples to bared arms did they return to the warmth of their husbands and nearness of their children.

CHARLES SAT beside Karla at the reconvening of the Executive Council. He was dressed in green bathing trunks with a yellow tee shirt while Karla wore a blue bikini. Neither wore shoes.

"Charlie?" Karla asked when the last delegate arrived. "You ready?"

"Bring it on."

"Executive Meeting is in session."

The other members sat at the table, two whispering and two remaining silent.

"Charlie ... I mean, Charles and I," Karla said, "have reviewed your suggestions. It's remarkable how much we hold in common. We've sorted out your opinions and divided today's agenda into four topics: the intrinsic nature of marriage, making and dissolving marriage, codes of sexual morality, and the problem of effectively reforming marital law. I think everyone of us understands this matter is filled with theoretical difficulty and emotional volatility since the marital bond affects us in our most intimate concerns. This debate will have to be handled rather delicately—even in a progressive community like ours—or it may trigger a cultural reaction as it has in the United States."

Opening remarks were well received and the discussion soon began—with Charles speaking first.

"I propose," Charles said, "we entertain debate in the four areas and propose motions after suitable periods of discussion. We can draft a platform that'll be sent to the entire community for ratification."

His proposal was unanimously accepted and discussion began.

"First things first," Karla said. "We need to decide whether we want marriage to exist among us. To decide whether it's relevant to our experience and this island. After all, Jesus himself said there'd be no marriage in paradise. Who are we to doubt the foremost social conservative?"

Everyone laughed.

"Let's start." Charles said, "by listing its advantages and disadvantages."

Two hands were raised.

"First," Karla said, "I suggest we use one or two word descriptions so as to avoid boring speeches and senseless discussions. Let's cut to the chase."

Her idea was applauded.

"Domination," the gray-haired delegate said.

"Convenient sex," the northern blonde noted.

"Responsible parenthood," someone observed.

"Patriarchy," another delegate said.

"Love."

"Loyalty."

"Expectations."

"Quarrels."

"Trust."

"More sex," the blonde said.

"Housework."

"Continuity."

"Tradition."

"Freedom."

"Slavery."

"Happiness."

"Despair."

"Comfort."

"Reproach."

"Honor."

"Sacrifice."

"Shame."

"Adultery."

"Divorce."

"Enough," the eastern moderator said. "My point is proved perfectly: marriage is all things to all people. It's an individual arrangement, not a social consensus. Every one of us chooses if and how to marry based on our own predispositions."

"Agreed," Charles added. "For instance, Joan and I made certain arrangements in our married life others might not select for themselves. And others have taken on obligations we could never endure."

"So," the gray-haired delegate said, "you're saying marriage is an individual contract?"

"Exactly," Karla answered. "Nothing more. And there's no general obligation to marry, to procreate, or even to love."

"Or divorce," Charles added.

"Or anything," Karla said. "There are no obligations whatsoever regarding marriage. No natural roles of the sexes. No innate morality. No fundamental responsibilities beyond the will of two people made together. Do we agree on that?"

Everyone did.

"Traditional monogamy," Karla continued, "assumed marriage was an institution ordained—by God, man, nature, or whatever—for exclusive sexual gratification, protective child custody, and obligatory assistance. Isn't that true?"

The councilpersons agreed it was.

"But," Karla said, sitting up straighter in her chair and leaning forward ever so slight as she spoke with a studied voice, "such purposes have no place among us. Not one of us restricts sexual activity to marriage; we all believe children should be communally raised; and every one of us lives by a social egalitarianism that condemns the stockpiling of provisions in the capitalist household. To be frank, marriage—that is, the real marriage of the past—is a type of bondage as historically obsolete as indentured servitude. So why continue the hypocrisy?"

The northern blonde raised her hand. "What about love?" she asked.

"Are you proposing marriage and love are inseparable?" Charles asked.

"No," the woman said, "only that love leads to marriage as kisses lead to sexual intercourse."

"I agree with the latter," Charles said, "but not the former. Is love less real for remaining free? Don't couples fall in love before they speak of marrying and don't they part ways when they fall out of love?"

"Doesn't love crave marriage like sex demands climax?" the blond northerner asked.

"Ask your typical housewife about either one of those propositions," the gray-haired delegate from the south village said with a laugh, "and you'd be surprised at her answer."

Everyone laughed.

"Love," Karla said, "does desire completion. You're right to say sex started needs to be finished or it leads to frustration. But do you mean to say couples should never break up? Do you mean to restrict divorce? Do you think that love without marriage is romantic frustration?"

"No," the blonde said, "I mean only that the desire for marriage is as real as the desire for sex."

"I've never wanted to marry and I'm no virgin," the gray-haired woman said, "and I haven't been since I turned fourteen."

"Even if your point is granted," Karla said, ignoring the interruption, "I don't know what good marriage does. Isn't love the goal of the relationship?"

The blonde pushed her chair from the table. "Doesn't marriage prove love?"

"What kind of love can be proved by marriage?" Charles objected.

"A love that gives itself totally," the blonde said. "That surrenders itself for the other. That promises loyalty in sickness and health, good and bad, thick and thin."

"But now," Karla said, a more insistent tone to her voice, "you're making marriage obligatory."

"And pretentious," Charles said, "since marriage is a promise, not a power. A man can pretend to swear fidelity or loyalty or even to lasso the moon, but he can't really do it. Love lives only as long as a couple chooses to love. If they change their minds, old oaths become irrelevant."

"I understand," the blonde persisted, "that a lifetime isn't lived in a day. Children know that. What I'm saying is that it's worth promising to try."

"To try what?" Karla asked.

"To try to love."

"But what exactly is love?"

"Kindness and goodness and loyalty."

"No," the gray-haired delegate now said. "This takes us back to character. Back to morality and obligation. It's unconstitutional."

For the first time, Dr. Graves entered the conversation. "I'm not sure I understand the unconstitutionality of love as a self-chosen obligation."

"Article II of the charter," the gray-haired councilor said, "mandates the exercising of individual free choices and Article IV guarantees the right to free association and sexual preference."

"Yes," the doctor said, "but ..."

"But," the gray-hair cut him short, "you want to deny our constitutional rights?"

"No," the doctor now said, his voice now a little louder, "but the freedom of association includes the right to marry."

"As long as it's freely made," the gray hair continued, "and doesn't restrict other freedoms such as sexual preference and conscience."

"Granted."

"Which marriage does if it becomes a legal obligation. Authority is transferred from the wishes and desires of the individual man or woman to a so-called covenant made between two people that brings sanctions if broken."

"But what if they freely made their promises?" the doctor asked.

"And what if they promise to eat their children?" the southern woman said. "Or what if a black woman willingly sells herself as a slave?"

"That's ridiculous."

"As is every illegal promise."

"Enough! Stop it!" Karla now stood. "Everyone take a breath and settle down. We're not so far apart. No one wants to impose Christian monogamy and no one wants to prohibit couples from calling themselves married if they so choose. Agreed?"

Most of the councilpersons nodded—though the gray-haired southern delegate sat stone-faced.

"In any case," Karla said, "we'll never get complete consensus here or anywhere else. Maggie, what's the minimum we have to achieve?"

Karla turned to Maggie, the gray-haired woman, who thought about the matter for a minute before answering.

"Women," Maggie said, "must not be enslaved by marriage. There must be freedom for every woman to decide whether to marry and how to be married. No social pressure, no moral restraints, no legal persecution. Marriage can't be a type of living death in which a woman gives her life for the sake of someone else."

Karla turned to the blonde. "Naomi?"

"Marriage," the tall blonde from the north replied, "should be permitted if desired. Individuals must be free to choose. And although the law places no bonds upon them, they must be allowed to make their own rules—even to swear loyalty and fidelity till death do us part."

Karla went around the room, asking each delegate the same question. Charles asked that the rules of marriage made by couples be respected even when unorthodox and the twice-divorced Dr. Graves demanded that ending a marriage be uncomplicated and inexpensive. The northern blonde also requested marriage be clearly defined by law and its rules be self-evident. For the next hour, everyone shared thoughts regarding which individual rights to safeguard and how to do so. There was little disagreement among them regarding fundamental principles—though discussion was more heated regarding implementation.

During afternoon recess, Karla and Charles worked out a new agenda and new proposals, reconvening Executive Council after dinner as Karla opened the late session with a word of thanks.

"I know," Karla said, "tempers flared earlier today. They ought to. This is a tough issue that lays bare the human heart. Yet, Charles and I have drafted a law that we believe should withstand constitutional scrutiny, the public will, and your approval."

Charles pushed several copies of a short memo to the middle of the table. Each councilperson took a copy and read it silently. Five minutes later, the gray-hair proposed the new law be sent to the neighborhoods as drafted and brought to a General Will of the People as soon as possible. The blonde seconded the proposal and the motion unanimously passed after another ten minutes of amplification and clarification. The text of the first proposed amendment to the charter read:

Proposed Amendment to The Flower of the First of May Compact

The Executive Council of the People proposes the following ordinances of marriage and sexual freedom: Inhabitants of this community will be permitted to marry as they so choose as long as marriage is freely made and be unrestricting of individual and social freedom. To that end, the following amendment to the charter is proposed:

1. Marital and sexual relationships shall be permitted to all consenting adults of either sex. Only the public authority shall retain the right to set the age of sexual emancipation.

2. The contract of marriage is strictly a private association made between two individuals for as long as both desire to continue in the relationship.

3. Every citizen has a right to her or his own body, and shall not be obligated either to unite with or separate from another person, except by his or her own choice.

4. No legal or social discrimination shall be attached to any person on the basis of marital status, gender self-construction, or sexual orientation.

5. No individual may privately contract a marriage in such a fashion as to subvert the aforesaid public principles of marital and sexual union.

6. Marriages made in the old world are hereby considered unbinding and undone following the fourteenth day after the ratification of this amendment—unless explicitly and publicly confirmed via remarriage ceremony, declaration, or vows. No person freed from a previous marriage shall suffer any penalty or restriction.

7. Violators of this law of marriage will be brought before the Executive Council for appropriate action.

8. This amendment shall be put into immediate and full legal effect upon ratification by the General Will of the People of the State of Paradise.

9. Existing marriages annulled by this decree shall not be permitted renewal until another twenty-eight days have passed after dissolution.

10. The General Will of the People is hereby called together the second Sunday following nomination of this proposal to vote whether or not to ratify this ordinance of marriage.

A round of applause went up for Karla and Charles after the final vote polled. Delegates were especially pleased that the proposed public nature of marriage completely preserved the private realm of choice without creating burdensome obligations such as the duty to maintain a spouse or uphold chastity. Dr. Graves expressed doubts about annulling previous marriages (pointing out that international law upheld the legality of marriages made in foreign lands), but other delegates soon convinced him that requiring couples to remarry was the most effective way to preserve existing marriages by placing them under the direct authority of the State of Paradise; the northern blonde even thought the renewing of vows seemed romantic. Charles clinched the debate by noting such laws were absolutely necessary since there were presently no courts to uphold or void previous contracts. That is, without the new law there could be neither marriage nor divorce on the island.

Karla made a few formatting corrections before printing copies of the proposed amendment for delegates to distribute in their home villages. Afterwards, pineapple sour whiskeys were served in coconut husks and all five delegates drank late into the night—soon joined by New Plymouth's entire professional staff. The gray-haired woman retired to an empty storage tent and the northern blonde shared a sleeping bag with one of the staff. Dr. Graves passed out beneath a palm tree after becoming too drunk to walk home and Charles sat at the campfire with his arm around Karla's shoulder, his hand nestled around her breast. After everyone else retired, Karla stood.

"I have something to show you," Karla said as she led Charles to a hospital tent. "I need a doctor."

"Will a Doctor of Sociology do?"

"You tell me."

Charles smiled as soon as he stepped inside and saw the full-size mattress set square on a steel-framed bed. An hour later, both he and Karla finally fell asleep—smelling of whiskey and covered with a dirty blanket.

13

MORNING AND SICKNESS

U rsula woke at dawn, her stomach queasy and thoughts swimming. When she nudged Sean, he just pulled the sheet over his shoulders, so she tried to sit up—despite the fact that movement made her stomach churn. Turning in search of a bucket, she saw a plastic bag and reached over Sean to grab it just as her stomach exploded.

Most of the camp heard the shouting from the tent.

"Aaaaahhhhh," Sean yelled. "Ursula, what the hell? Nasty."

Warm vomit dripped from the back of Sean's neck as he scampered outside. After a moment of shock, he flung a sticky handful of brown bile from his hair and turned toward the tent in noticeable anger—unhinged and undressed alike.

"Damn it, Ursula," Sean yelled toward Ursula, who remained in the nylon tent. "This shit is disgusting. I'm going to shower."

While Sean found a dried towel and damp shorts hanging from a tent guideline and jogged to the stream, Tiffany hurried to the tent—where she grabbed a torn rag strung from one of the tent's guidelines and crawled inside to sop up the watery vomit. Though the stench of the morning's sickness threatened to overwhelm her for a moment, she regained composure with a breath of fresh air and soon finished the task (it wasn't her first experience cleaning vomit)—even pulling Sean's sleeping roll from the tent and blotting up remaining bits of half-digested banana strewn across the nylon floor. Twenty minutes later, she filled an empty bucket with soapy water, scrubbed the last traces of Ursula's morning sickness, and wiped Sean's sleeping bag.

After a spray of perfume deodorized the tent, Tiffany sat beside Ursula—whose eyes were swollen from crying and cheeks were covered with tears and snot.

"I'm a pig. I'm so disgusting. I'm ..."

Tiffany finished the sentence. "Pregnant."

"I am," Ursula said as she again wailed—her lips curled and her cheeks dimpled as she sobbed. "Where'd Sean go?"

"To shower."

"He hates me," Ursula said.

"What he hates is the taste of vomit. I suppose ..."—Tiffany stopped in mid-sentence, putting her hand over her mouth and biting her cheeks—"I'm sorry, but you should've seen him. Brent and I were returning from the mess tent with glasses of goat milk for the boys when we heard this hideous shriek and saw Sean come flying from your tent with bile dripping down the side of his face. I suppose Brent's still laughing."

Ursula stopped crying.

"Serves him right," the pregnant woman said. "He did this to me."

"I've seen men," Tiffany said, "suffer sleep deprivation and I've heard of them fainting during delivery—and there are plenty of stories of sympathetic labor pains—but I've never even imagined one getting his due for morning sickness. You've just scored a point for the women's team."

Ursula laughed and burst into tears at the same time. "Don't make me laugh," she groaned. "It makes me sick."

Tiffany fluffed the pillow beneath Ursula's head, then replaced the bucket of dirty water with clean and walked to the mess tent to stuff a few bits of food into her pockets and retrieve a fresh towel (and leave dirty sheets for Linh to clean). Soon, she returned to Ursula's tent to comfort the young woman with a wet rag for the pregnant woman's forehead and pulled a packet of American-made crackers from her pocket—placing the saltines in Ursula's hand.

"Welcome," Tiffany said, "to the wonderful world of pregnancy."

Ursula nibbled a single cracker for fifteen minutes.

SOON AFTER RECEIVING vomit-stained linen from Tiffany, Linh washed them in the Pishon River just a short distance downstream of the bridge. After hanging sheets and towels to dry, she returned to the mess tent and explained to Kit and Alan that Ursula was too sick to work.

Alan asked why.

"She's nauseous," Linh said.

"If she's hung over," Alan said with a scowl, "she can drag her sorry ass out to pitch in."

"Chill," Linh retorted, "she's sick with female problems. She couldn't look at beer, let alone drink it."

"I'll bet," Alan said.

Linh didn't respond and Kit remained quiet.

"Who's going to take her place?" Alan asked after a moment.

"Ask Lisa," Linh answered, "she's in charge."

"Where's she at?"

Linh shrugged.

"She needs to fix this now," Alan said.

"For goodness sake," Linh shook her head, "find her yourself. My children wouldn't whine so much."

Alan steeled his eyes, but said nothing as he stomped toward the beach. Only when he was beyond earshot did Linh pick up a slice of bread and move closer to Kit as she lowered her voice.

"What a crybaby."

Kit said nothing.

"Alan, I mean," Linh explained.

"He's nice enough to me."

"Then you're the only one."

"What's the problem?"

"He's too hard with Ursula."

"I haven't noticed it," Kit said.

"It's just been since she's become ill."

"She's been down a lot," Kit said. "What's wrong?"

"She can't clear wood from the fields," Linh replied. "She can't even stand up."

"Should we send for a doctor?"

"Maybe a gynecologist," Linh said, "or an obstetrician."

"That's wonderful news," Kit said with a smile. "Will she and Sean marry? I assume Sean ..."

"He is and I don't know if they will," Linh said. "In fact he doesn't know his good fortune. Ursula needs to tell him. I guess I shouldn't have said anything, so please don't spread the news yet."

"It's good news in any case," Kit said. "A baby to the village. I'm already excited."

Linh looked at Kit—who was dressed in an oversized shirt and torn shorts. The material was worn thin, stretched from wear and loose from the loss of weight. It looked almost like a maternity blouse as it ballooned around Kit's chest and waist.

"Don't be too excited," Linh said. "Things can go wrong and nine months is a long wait. We may be in Paradise, but we don't exactly have modern medical facilities."

"I suppose you're right about that."

Linh tore a piece of bread from a hard loaf even as Kit handed her a slice of coconut meat and a glass of milk.

"Does she need milk?" Kit asked.

"All she can keep down is crackers, but a sip of coconut juice wouldn't hurt. And prenatal vitamins."

"We don't have any in the village. They're kept at the base infirmary."

"Oh."

"Maybe I'll walk to camp tomorrow to fetch a bottle."

"That'd be helpful," Linh answered. "You're so nice."

Kit dropped her eyes and spoke only after a long pause. "I wanted five children when I was a girl."

Linh looked surprised. "Really?"

"When I grew up," Kit said, "and became an actress, I realized I'd been dreaming—as if the world was no more than a little house on the prairie."

Linh laughed.

"The trouble is," Kit continued, "I'm no longer sure which is less real: old books or the glitterati. What I once lived seems like a performance compared to this place. Everything feels so different now. Nature rains on my head and earth oozes between my toes. Motherhood seems so ... so natural. So real."

"Someday," Linh said as she brushed her friend's arm, "your time will come."

"No, it won't. Ryan and I made our choice and it's virtually irreversible. We're not having children."

Linh looked toward the shadows of the trees. Though dawn streamed over the canopy of the forest, the jungle remained indistinct in the morning haze. After a moment she smiled.

"Did you know I was adopted?" the Vietnamese woman asked.

"No, I didn't."

"I was raised in Michigan," Linh said, "but I'm told that my parents were killed in Saigon after the war ended. My birth father was an army officer and after he was arrested one of his soldiers—my adoptive father—took me into his home. We fled to a refugee camp in Thailand and eventually relocated to Grand Rapids."

Kit remained silent.

"You still can be a mother," Linh said, "if you really want to."

"Where would I find a baby?"

"Life brings them."

"Death," Kit whispered, "brings them."

"That's not how I see it," Linh objected with a quiet tone. "Death took my original parents, but life brought me new ones."

"I'm sorry," Kit said, "about your birth parents."

"I don't remember them," Linh said with a hushed voice, "only my adoptive ones. My real ones."

Kit let the conversation die and the two women returned to breakfast without further talk. A moment later, they were joined by Lisa and talk shifted to Alan's complaints and the day's work.

IT WAS MIDMORNING when Lisa approached Alan as he worked alone in a half-cleared field close to the main path leading to the bridge. Alan's eyes passed over the young woman's gentle-sloped chest without interest, fixing on her face. When Lisa asked where his work partner was, Alan scowled.

"We need to talk," Alan said.

Lisa asked what he wanted.

"Ursula's sick again," Alan complained.

"I can't heal her."

"Then get me some help with these trees."

"Have you made quota?"

"Not by a long shot."

Lisa turned her eyes from the sun, arched her back, and slipped from her backpack—letting it drop before she reached into a side pocket and felt for a pair of sunglasses. Putting the shades on, she looked at Alan.

"Why not?" Lisa asked.

"Because Ursula's a deadbeat."

"That's slander."

"If it's untrue."

"Did she put in all her hours?"

"If you can call it that."

"I don't understand."

"She was here," Alan said, "but she didn't finish a single tree. We were told to clear a strip near the trail. We counted out trees and divided sixteen between us. I've busted my ass all week and I'm down to my last tree. Mind you, the trees are cut and stacked. Ursula managed to cut one tree down, but it's not even stripped, let alone cut or stacked. She moves as slow as sap."

"I see."

"I gave her," Alan continued, "the choice on which side of the lot to clear but she didn't do anything."

"I'll find you some help for today."

"I'm not staying late." Alan now sounded angry.

Lisa stood straight, pulling her shoulders back and sucking in her stomach. "You owe the camp a full forty hours."

"And it's up by noon," Alan said, "then I'm done. The rest of her quota isn't my responsibility."

"All for one and one for all."

"And one isn't doing anything at all," Alan said. "Whether or not you find someone to do her work, I don't care. Just don't expect to see me after lunch. I have plans."

"Then go," Lisa snapped, "and stop complaining about it."

"Tell her work before play or we're going to starve."

"From each according to his ability and to each according to her need," Lisa replied.

Alan scowled as he walked away while muttering curses under his breath and Lisa returned to the village to summon help, finding Steve just as he finished lunch. When she brought Steve to the clearing, Alan was stacking wood—his saw lying in tall grass and ax driven into a large stump.

"What's that saw," Lisa pointed at the tools, "doing on the ground?"

"Taking a break," Alan said, "like Ursula."

"The grass will rust the blades."

"It hasn't rained all day."

"We can't afford to take the chance. Tools can't be replaced."

Lisa asked Alan to pick it up, but it was Steve who retrieved and wiped the blade before setting it atop a stump as he explained that he'd volunteered to help out.

"This isn't going to work at all," Alan objected. "We had plans."

"It was Steve's choice," Lisa said.

Alan turned to his husband and asked why he'd changed plans without asking.

"Let's chop some trees," Steve said, "then we can leave. These palms go fast."

"Not me. I'm at quota for the week," Alan growled as he dropped his tools and stomped off toward the village.

"Don't mind him," Steve said. "He's just tired."

"I'm not married to him," Lisa said, "he doesn't bother me."

Steve helped Lisa until dusk, by which time only one tree remained uncut. Several others had been trimmed—and one palm even stripped of its bark. After the two shared a quick supper, Lisa retired to her tent to read a book while Steve searched for Alan.

Four women set out for New Plymouth after eating breakfast. Hilary and Deidra walked to the front while Joan and Linh lagged behind, their legs short and steps slow as they ascended Mount Zion. By midmorning, all four western women arrived at base camp and moved bricks to the beach with a wheelbarrow. After loading the bricks into a rowboat, the women carried treated limber to the beach —with Hilary refusing several offers of male help, though she did allow Janine Erikson to take a turn pushing a half-filled wheelbarrow. After a quick lunch drawn from stored rations, the women collected an iron grate, a box of nails, and cement mix. An hour later, these too were secured in the rowboat and the return trip begun.

During the walk home, Joan and Deidra waded near the beach— pulling fifteen-foot lengths of rope over their shoulders as they trudged through shallow water while Linh and Hilary pulled shorter ropes with which they steered the raft through the surf. It didn't take the women long to move north when the wind was to their backs, but their pace slowed after they neared the north village and faced cross-winds and crosscurrents alike. By then, their arms ached and tempers flared and Joan and Deidra were arguing about religion.

The quarrel started when Joan damned the load in the name of the gods and Deidra responded that no honest work could be "gods-damned" since there were no gods. Though Deidra initially took the attack to be against her native heritage, she was somewhat mollified when she realized that Joan was cursing every faith equally. Still, as Joan argued that religious blessings and curses implied unscientific presuppositions, Deidra pressed her faith in the reality of her gods and customs of her forefathers. In any event, by the time the women rounded the north shore and reached Turtle Beach, they argued so hard that they had ceased complaining of their load and no longer pulled the boat at all.

"No," Joan said just after they stopped working to debate religion, "I chose my words carefully. I didn't say I objected to native religion, only that I didn't believe its tenets."

"Almost," Deidra scowled, "the same thing."

"Tell me why you chant."

"To honor the traditions of my people and to enjoy the achievements of my culture."

"And I respect that," Joan replied, "just as I enjoy Irish clog dancers and ghetto rap. Diversity must be encouraged. That's an absolute."

"That's not what you said. You implied native American religion is superstition. That it's untrue. If that's so, then our dancers are like little children pretending to be cowboys and Indians—our whole culture is make-believe."

"Those aren't my words."

"Close enough," Deidra said with a grimace. "Native American culture isn't singing and dancing and whooping in war paint around an open fire. It's not selling arrowheads at tourist traps or wearing feathers—just as Scotland is more than haggis and plaid kilts. It takes more than bagpipes to make Glasgow. Either the inner logic of the culture is tenable or it's no more than a charade."

"I disagree," Joan protested, "I'm more or less a Marxist and I believe that class consciousness and economic modes of production are the deciding forces of civilization, but I'm no monist. We don't need to pattern our lives by the trappings of Bolshevist Russia. Within the form of economic determinism, we are allowed the freedom of cultural expression."

"You're mixing," Deidra argued, "both your metaphors and your metaphysics."

"And you postmodernists," Joan said, "allow everyone to tell their cultural stories to the degree no one makes any effort to distinguish true from false, myth from history, or the plausible from the absurd. You think that everyone has a valid story and none of it can be disproved."

"I'm no post-modernist," Deidra said, "which is exactly my point. To reduce Native American culture to a self-actualizing narrative is to accept it only within the terms of post-Enlightened literary interpretation. According to the cynicism of the heirs of Voltaire and Comte."

Joan looked confused. "I don't understand."

"You published books on literary theory," Deidra said. "What don't you understand?"

"I understand the theory. It's you I don't get."

"What I'm trying to say is this," Deidra explained, "the only genuine Native American culture is that which perceives the world with the same eyes as Geronimo and Sitting Bull and Little Turtle. Apaches and Navajos were neither modernists nor materialists. They believed. And only if we believe are we their true sons or daughters. Anything else is a pretense. Just a show."

Deidra paused to catch breath.

"In fact," Deidra continued, "it's cultural treason to accept the white man's ways. Squanto and Pocahontas were traitors. Can't you see how they betrayed their own people by accepting the suppositions of European culture? They were even worse than the little whore who led Cortés to Montezuma. You want me to do the same? To commit cultural genocide against my own people? To defile myself in the bed of the white man?"

"Don't look at me," Joan laughed. "I'm not the one who married John Smith."

Deidra turned red.

"But," Joan continued, "I still want to know exactly what you believe. Are you arguing for a modernist or a post-modernist understanding of Native American religious culture?"

"Neither," Deidra objected, "I'm arguing within the framework and terms of the religion itself."

"Which is?"

"Faith."

"Faith in what?"

"In the power of the gods."

Joan rolled her eyes.

"But what exactly," Joan asked, "is represented by this so-called faith? What's its ideological meaning? I'm trying to see how your cultural theory relates to social organization."

"What I'm trying to say," Deidra objected, "is that it doesn't. It relates to the Earth Mother and the Sky God."

"Symbolizing?"

"Symbolizing," Deidra groaned, "nothing at all."

"Then," Joan pressed her point, "you're an existentialist? Or maybe a nihilist?"

"The gods," Deidra snapped with a loud voice and angry tone, "aren't symbols. They're gods."

"You mean real gods?"

"Yes."

"That exist?"

"Yes."

"Like Jesus?"

"That," Joan said as she shook her head, "would make me a Christian, not a Native American. My people are loyal to their own gods, not narrow-minded Jewish carpenters."

"What do these gods do?"

"Whatever they wish."

"Where do they live?" Joan asked as she grinned.

"In the spirit world."

"Can they see us now?"

"Yes."

"Can we see them?"

"In visions and dreams."

"So they're like Jung's archetypes."

"You're being stubborn," Deidra scowled. "You can't understand the gods through theory and scholarship. They're not a philosophy. They're spirits. Deities. Souls of the earth. As alive and real as you and I."

"You can't really believe this."

"If I don't, I'm no true Native American. So for the sake of my people and their sacred ways, I will believe it. I do believe it, the gods helping me."

Joan shook her head as Deidra took up the slack in the rope and pulled the boat. Soon they pulled the barge of bricks and timber through the shallows and it wasn't long before they saw the western beach—where John and Sean were fishing. After the women pulled the rowboat ashore and secured it to a tree, all four of them collapsed into the grass exhausted. Even Hilary didn't object when the two men dragged the barge to the trees and unloaded it. The women had done their share and were worn out with blistered hands and sore backs.

All four women arrived home shortly after Charles—who had spent the day with Karla at New Plymouth. After dinner, Charles assembled the village and summarized the council's actions to a few neighbors while suggesting a Saturday morning session to share further details. The villagers thought it a good idea and agreed to the meeting. Deidra, Hilary, and Linh retired early that night while Joan remained at the campfire talking with her husband: her face sober and voice hushed. Charles and Joan talked long after the fire burned down.

14

PRIVATE CHOICES AND PUBLIC TALK

As John opened his eyes to the first glimpse of dawn, he reached for his wife—only to touch an empty bedroll. Deidra was awake earlier than usual. Reaching for a shirt and shorts, John quickly dressed and left the tent. Outside, he stretched before walking toward cold fire pits and an empty mess tent —his shirt unbuttoned and boots slung over a shoulder. Though the chill of morning was warming, the camp remained quiet and lifeless, so he arranged several logs into the pit over kindling and struck a match. Soon, a fire blazed and children, accompanied by bleary-eyed parents, rose from their tents as John started toward the beach.

At the edge of the village, a spiderweb stretched across the path, indicating no one had passed west, so John doubled back to the Pishon River. Seeing no one at the bridge, he scoured the woods for signs of life. There, he observed the bright light of a new day burning like a disc through the heavens and thought about the life supported by the burning star: plankton, plants, fish, birds, animals, and people. He remembered myths about divine chariots and sun gods and smiled a little. Still, even if the sun was no more than one of billions of stars, it was part of a cosmos supposedly self-created from nothing at all. John wondered whether there indeed might be a ...

It was at this moment a distant chant echoed from the forest—the singing of a woman. John moved quietly into the old growth forest, his boots still dangling from his shoulders and his bare-footed steps noiseless. The singing grew louder as he drew closer and it wasn't long before he came to a cluster of ironwood trees where he found a dark-haired woman kneeling in prayer. She bowed before the tallest tree, her hands lifted to the heavens. Then she chanted, worshipping until her forehead pressed mud and her mouth kissed moss.

John stepped into the open. "Deidra," he called to his wife. "What are you doing here?"

Deidra glanced back only for an instant before returning to her ritual. A moment later, she stood—now chanting louder than before and dancing around the chosen tree: knees lifted high and arms over her head. John remembered how he once teased that dancing Native Americans looked to be playing drunken hopscotch, but now he didn't find it funny.

"Deidra," John said, "that's enough."

Deidra danced faster as John moved closer. She circled the old tree, shuffling from one leg to the other, moving her hands down her hips and whirling her black hair in a full circle. She paid the white man no heed as her pace quickened—her chanting almost frenzied.

"Heh-heh-heh-heh. Heh-heh-heh-heh-heh."

"For God's sake," John said, "get hold of yourself."

Deidra ignored her husband as she made two passes around the tree. As John watched, she fell to her knees, clasped her hands in prayer, and kissed the earth. Only when she'd completed her ritual did she turn around to face the earthly distraction.

"What," John growled, "in the name of heaven are you doing?"

"I'm praying," Deidra said as she stood upright and unembarrassed, "to the gods of this place."

"You're praying to a tree."

"It's the supreme god of this forest. Look how it towers above the others. It's older than you and I."

"So are the sea turtles."

"Wise aged creatures."

"Good soup, too."

"Don't mock the gods."

John shook his head. "Don't tell me you actually believe in your grandpa's mumbo jumbo?"

"Grandfather," Deidra scowled, "was a wise man."

"He was a witch doctor."

"Who had the power to heal."

"He couldn't cure cancer."

"The gods didn't will it."

"So they let their last true believer waste away?"

"I'm not going to debate theology with you."

"For goodness sake, Deidra," John said, "you have a Master's Degree from Arizona State. You know this superstition is a fraud."

"You follow the ways of your ancestors," Deidra replied, "so why shouldn't I?"

"My ancestors were miners and cavalry officers."

"And mine heeded the gods."

"A lot of good it did them."

"No wonder," Deidra replied with a scowl, "grandfather cursed me for marrying a white man."

"Now I'm a bad luck charm?"

"He cursed you too in case you've forgotten."

"Deidra," John said, "I've been damned in God's name by plenty of men and I'm still here."

"In any case," Deidra replied, "I intend to worship my ancestors and their gods and you'll just have to accept my beliefs."

"You used to poke fun at native religions more than I ever thought to."

"I was younger."

"And wiser."

"Wisdom is the blessing of the gods. They give it for ..."

"For what?"

"For lineage."

"I figured as much," John now said as he shook his head. "No dance around this tree is going to put a baby in your belly."

"Can you really say that? Don't your people claim God performs miracles?"

"My people don't snort mescaline and pray to the spirits of dead coyotes."

"Don't blaspheme," Deidra said.

"You know how I've always stood beside you," John said. "I've done everything a man can do. I came to this damned island just to please you. But I swear I don't know what to do about this kind of craziness."

"You haven't prayed to the gods of my people."

"It's nonsense."

"Was it nonsense that grandfather made me barren for marrying you?"

"I don't remember," John growled, "the tests registering positive for curses."

Deidra showed no embarrassment. "Science," she declared, "doesn't see everything."

"Well," John said, "science certainly can't see the non-existent, so it won't see me praying to wood—and neither will you or anyone else."

"If you scorn the gods," Deidra growled, "they won't bless your seed. Or any woman who sleeps with you."

"I won't participate in this nonsense."

"Then you're no husband of mine"—Deidra stomped her foot once—"if you won't pray to the gods of my house."

"I'll burn your damned gods if you bring them into my tent."

"Just like a Presbyterian," Deidra retorted as she walked away.

John watched her leave before he himself returned to the village —where he picked at his breakfast as he sat beneath a palm at the edge of camp. After eating, he found his work partner and started on his assigned duties, saying nothing of what troubled him.

It wasn't long after John lit a breakfast fire that the village stirred— many of the neighbors awakened by the aroma of burning wood.

Breakfast was served after a time, children eating before adults. Sean was the last one to arrive at the mess tent and collected breakfast for himself and Ursula as everyone else finished. Filling two mugs with coffee and two bowls with lukewarm oatmeal, he took the food home to serve Ursula breakfast in bed to make amends for yesterday's bad behavior. He propped the bowls filled with oatmeal against his ribs and held the cups of coffee in his fingers to unzip his tent fly—though he wasn't welcomed as he had hoped.

As soon as Ursula smelled the food, she clutched her stomach. "Uggghh," she screamed. "Get out! Now!"

Sean's eyes opened wide as he jumped backwards. He set the food on the ground outside the tent before sticking his head back inside. "You okay?"

"Of course not," Ursula groaned, "you jackass."

"What's wrong? You have the flu or something?"

Ursula turned from her stomach to her side and propped herself up with one arm. Her eyes were red and puffy, almost swollen shut, and her lower lip quivered when she talked.

"Explain how," Ursula growled, "someone gets the flu on a tropical island where there's no contact with the outside world?"

"Oh yeah. Then what do you have?"

"What I have," the young woman said, "is the firstborn child of the village idiot."

Sean froze where he stood. Only after a long pause did he step into the tent and sit, asking if she was sure.

"Don't I look sure?" Ursula replied.

"Did you go to the doctor?"

"Bastard," Ursula whispered, "maybe I should call for a medevac to fly me to base camp? Or maybe I should just jog there?"

"Oh yeah. You can't really hike, can you?"

"Like I said, the village idiot."

"How do you know?"

"Anyone who has met you knows."

"Knows what?"

"That you're the village fool."

"I meant the baby," Sean said. "How do you know you're pregnant?"

"The test was positive."

"When did you take it?"

"Two days ago."

"Take another to be sure."

Ursula looked at Sean with disgust. "You don't get," she said, "any more pregnant, you ass."

"I just thought," Sean said as he shook his head, "there might have been a mistake. Maybe we'll get lucky."

"I thought," Ursula growled through clenched teeth, "you'd be real excited."

Sean ran his hand through his hair as he asked how it happened.

"That first night on the ship," Ursula said. "I don't remember disposing of a condom. Or using spermicide."

"Aww shit," Sean said out loud, slapping his hand into his leg, "you're right."

Ursula reached for a nearby cracker sitting on a box and began to nibble.

"What will you do?" Sean asked.

"It's my choice," Ursula said. "My choice. Understand?"

"I know."

"I don't want a baby and I don't want to be pregnant ..."

"I agree," Sean interrupted.

"And," Ursula continued, "I was going to say I don't want to bleed to death on this island."

Sean looked confused.

"The morning after pill," Ursula said, "isn't a finished product. Everyone knows it. They just hurried the thing through before the Republicans got control of the FDA. And I think it's all we have here."

"Oh."

"I'm either leaving this island or having this baby."

"You could come back later," Sean said.

"Bastard," Ursula muttered. "I'm not leaving the island—daddy."

"Are you ... are we ready for a baby?"

"No," Ursula said, "as a matter of fact, we're not, especially you. But we have nine months to get ready. I've always known I'd be a mom. Just not this soon. But I've decided now's as good a time as any to begin. Linh and Tiff are here to help me—and you."

"I'm here for you. Just give me a little time to sort this out."

"You have about nine months."

Sean turned away.

"In the United States," Ursula said, "you'd be gone in a heartbeat. But from here, you're not going anywhere. Too much ocean and too few boats."

Ursula fell back into bed and Sean took a long walk. Neither one worked full hours that day.

KIT LOOSENED her bandana and ran fingers through her blond hair, then brushed her forelocks back and tied the scarf tight. A bird called from a bush and she whistled to it as she adjusted her bra—her last untorn one—to tighten its stretched straps before fastening a shirt button and tugging the cotton blouse away from her chest. She looked back to insure she wasn't being watched as she unbuttoned her shorts to tuck the shirt and afterwards retrieved a box of food and walked to the beach along the main trail.

Originally planned for a single hiker, the trail already was double-wide from heavy traffic and Kit wondered whether Lisa might try to narrow the path to its authorized size. Little permanent damage was done thus far—only the trampling of a little grass and the breaking of a few boughs, but Lisa was a stickler for sticks. Still, the widening had taken place naturally enough, without forethought or plan. Now Kit kept to the center of the path, looking into the forest's canopy and listening to the rush of wind through trees. It didn't take long to reach a narrow trail that veered from the main path and snaked through a glade of fruit trees near the lagoon. Just as she turned down the narrow trail, she heard the sound of play: the high-pitched scream of a young woman.

Kit wondered who it was and picked up her pace. Within seconds, she emerged from the trees and saw a man and woman swimming. Squinting, she saw Maria splashing a wet-headed man whose back was to the shore—recognizing the young woman by her bunched hair and olive skin.

As Maria looked at Kit, Ryan turned and waved, addressing his wife with a tone almost too pleasing.

"There you are. I was looking for you," Ryan said as he forced a smile to Kit. "You interested in a swim?"

"There's your lunch," Kit said as she dropped the lunch box to the ground. When the box broke open, flatbread flipped into the grass and breadfruit rolled toward the lagoon.

Ryan looked at Kit's face rather than his spilled lunch and said nothing. Instead, he swam for shore as Maria followed in his wake. Though Kit paid little attention as Ryan emerged from the lagoon with shorts soaked and feet bare, her jaw dropped when she saw Maria emerge from the water in a wet lace bra and beige jockey shorts—both garments nearly transparent. Kit threw the girl's dry clothes to her and spoke in a tone that wasn't gentle.

"Maybe you should cover yourself."

Maria caught the shirt, but the shorts slipped from her hand.

Ryan eyed the young woman as she bent over before catching himself and turning his eyes toward his wife—who glared at her husband. The couple stared at each other while Maria turned her back and slipped into her clothes before announcing she planned to help Heather pick fruit.

Kit didn't wait until the girl was beyond earshot before she scolded her husband. "I'd appreciate if you didn't skinny-dip with that girl."

"She was dressed."

"Dressed? She was wearing underwear."

"She didn't bring a suit."

Kit raised her voice. "Then don't swim."

"I didn't think ..."

"Didn't think. At least we're in agreement about that."

"We were just swimming," Ryan said as his face turned red.

"Everything was appropriate. Heather's right here." He pointed across the bay where Heather picked breadfruit and bananas.

"Heather's over there," Kit said as she too pointed across the bay, "and I heard your so-called swimming half-way back to camp."

"A ray startled her."

"She wasn't the only one startled, was she?"

"Don't be a housefrau."

"No married man," Kit said, her tone both angry and matter-of-fact, "has any business swimming with pretty girls dressed in underwear."

"And if she were ugly?"

"She isn't."

"It meant nothing."

"So respect for me means less than nothing?"

"That's not what I meant. I meant it was innocent fun."

"Would it be innocent fun," Kit said, "for me to take a swim with Sean in my bra?"

"Suit yourself," Ryan muttered.

"I'd rather Maria suit herself. Suit herself decently around married men. Someone needs to remind her you have a wife. I'll tell her myself."

Kit turned toward the fruit grove until her husband grabbed her arm.

"Your quarrel," Ryan said, "is with me."

"Let go of me."

"Let her be."

"She needs to let you be my husband."

Ryan relaxed his grip even as he stepped between his wife and her target and dropped his voice to a whisper.

"You're acting," Ryan said, "like a schoolgirl."

"And she," Kit said as she pointed to Maria, "has had a schoolgirl crush on you since the interview."

"Don't be crazy. She's half my age. Just another star struck girl. Every guy on the island sees you the same way."

"That possibility is why I don't parade myself in my underwear."

"Maybe you're right," Ryan said after several seconds. "I guess I should've used better judgment."

Kit's shoulders dropped as Ryan took her by the hand.

"It won't happen again," Ryan said. "No more swimming in underwear."

"With anyone?"

"Except you."

"Promise?"

"I already did. When you became my wife."

Tension eased and the couple talked several minutes more as they circled the lagoon to help the younger women pick fruit. Within minutes, three canvas bags were filled with breadfruit and bananas— and Heather climbed down a fruit tree now picked clean. Ryan threw full bags over each shoulder and followed the women home while Heather and Maria carried the third by its corners and Kit brought their tools. Both Ryan and Kit retired shortly after supper while Maria lounged near a bonfire and Heather strolled to the beach.

IT WASN'T long after dark when Charles and Joan found Heather sitting at the edge of shore, just beyond the tide—which already washed away the shallow imprints of human steps. The moon shined through the dusk's haze as they approached their daughter, both parents solemn and unsmiling.

Heather stood to greet them.

"You two look serious," she said. "Something wrong?"

"Neither wrong nor right," Joan said, "but your father and I do wish to speak with you."

"What about?"

"Life in this camp," Charles said.

"Men," Joan said.

"Which one?" Heather asked.

"Both," Joan said, "have you seen any men on this island?"

"I've noticed a few," Heather said, "aren't they the ones with hair on their faces and backs?"

"That proves," Joan said with a grin, "you're not altogether blind. Just closing your eyes."

"Noticing men," Charles added, "is only the first step."

Heather looked puzzled. "Is there something I'm missing?"

"I should say," her father answered.

"Life is so short," Joan said as she took her daughter by the wrists, "and you're so serious. You need to date around, to try different men."

"Urrhh ... or women," Charles added.

"Yes. We're not here to judge."

Heather tried to step back, but her mother grabbed her wrists. The girl's face went white and her jaw dropped.

"I don't think we ..."

Joan held her daughter's wrists fast. "Sit still and listen."

Now Joan turned to her husband and asked that he fetch drinks before she squared to face the teenaged girl.

"Listen, Heather," Joan said as she released Heather's wrists, "you don't have to be so serious about dating. This island's a girl's paradise. There's no HIV or herpes or syphilis. Everyone was tested before they were cleared. It's not that we wanted to discriminate against anyone who might be infected with a sexually transmitted disease, but proper experiments require controlled conditions. Only a stupid scientist would use an unsanitized petri dish in his lab. I suppose it's the same with social experiments."

Heather stared at her mother without speaking.

"What I mean to say," Joan continued, "is that I wish I could've been in your bed when I was your age. So many men and so little risk —and not one disapproving word from a judgmental mother. You're still on the pill. Right? That's good. At least you don't openly defy us. Now listen, you don't have to be in love to date a guy. Or a woman. Your father is right. To be truthful, sex is better when you're not married or in love. It's more exciting. Almost more sinful."

"Mother," Heather covered her face with her hands, "I don't want to hear this."

"You need to. People are talking. For God's sake, you're still a virgin."

"That's none of your business."

"What's wrong with Jose? He's a good-looking boy."

"Mother, he's not even asked me out."

"Ask him."

"I don't beg for dates."

"Who do you want to date? I'll set it up."

Heather didn't answer.

"Listen, Heather," Joan said, now with a stern edge to her voice, "we've provided you a solid progressive upbringing. You have to take some ownership in your life. We hope to be on this island the rest of our lives. If so, you'll need to fit in and it's just plain stingy for you to keep such nice legs for yourself. What good can they do you? It's not like you can wrap them around yourself. And you have rather nice breasts. More than one of your father's students has said as much. There's so much pleasure waiting for you once you open yourself to love. That is, if you'll stop being so soulful and self-absorbed. You do know your selfishness can be mistaken for social conservatism or even religious orthodoxy? I never knew a virgin who wasn't a faithful Catholic or a pious evangelical. I guess there was a Hindu girl from Mumbai in one of my seminars, but she didn't really have much choice in the matter. In any event, there are far too many people unwillingly sleeping alone for you to be cloistered in self-chosen chastity."

Heather started to speak but broke down after a single malformed syllable, so Joan pressed her point, moving beside her daughter and placing an arm around the teenager.

"Heather," Joan said, "your father says a new law of marriage has been proposed."

Heather said nothing; her face was pale and eyes misted.

"He'll tell us about it tomorrow," Joan continued, "but between the new law and our lifestyle here, it's become necessary for your father and I to tell you a little more about our marriage. The real facts of our life."

Heather remained mute as her mother talked.

"What I mean to say," Joan continued, "is that it's time you were told your father isn't the only man I've known and I'm not his only woman."

After Heather turned completely white, Joan paused for her daughter to regain her composure.

"The truth," Joan eventually said, "is both of us experimented in college—and rather enjoyed doing so. Even now, we've made ... er ... arrangements. We kept it quiet while you were growing up, so you wouldn't be alienated in a socially oppressive society that refuses to accept open marriage. But you need to know now, both because it's right and because it's becoming impossible to hide the truth on this little island—and we wanted to be the ones to tell you. Except that your father is so shy he's made me do it."

Heather's knees buckled and she staggered backward before sitting on the sand while Joan kneeled beside her just as Charles returned with two glasses of tea.

"Here we go, ladies," Charles said, "fresh tea spiked with a squeeze of lemon."

"Wonderful," Joan said.

"Did you tell her?" Charles asked.

"Most of it."

Heather looked at her parents, her chin quivering and her eyes tearing up as she asked how many affairs they'd had.

"Only two affairs," Joan answered, "and perhaps ten flings."

"I've been a bit more active," Charles added. "One long term affair and about twenty flings, plus a number of coeds for a night or two. I just spent a couple days with Karla from the east village. A memorable woman."

"Oh," Charles said, turning to his wife, "did I tell you that we used the bed in the infirmary Wednesday night? I'd forgotten how much nicer a mattress is than sand."

"I envy you," Joan said. "Maybe you can take me there sometime."

"I promise."

"Till death do us part," Joan said with a giggle.

Heather crawled to a nearby bush and vomited. A moment later she blacked out and collapsed face-first into the ground.

15

SELF-GOVERNMENT AND NEW LIFE

B rent and John rose early to start a fire and collect food while Kit and Tiffany prepared breakfast. It wasn't long before the aroma of eggs permeated the camp and everyone in the village—Lisa excepted—gathered at the mess tent as the cooks served orange juice, cane-flavored oatmeal, waffled breadfruit, pineapple, plantains, kiwi, coffee, tea, and eggs: scrambled or fried to order. The eggs were an enormous hit, being eaten for the first time. Helpings were generous, seconds begged, and plates cleaned. Indeed, a full hour was spent eating. Linh served mint tea and plain toast to Ursula—who remained too nauseous to move, let alone eat. Following breakfast, Kit and Tiffany were applauded and awarded the day off work for their memorable meal while several volunteers tidied the kitchen and washed dishes.

The meeting of the village assembly was scheduled for midmorning, though it was delayed a few minutes because Lisa was late in returning from her inspections. Dishes already were put away and the lingering odor of breakfast dispersed when she finally hurried to her tent. As the neighbors assembled for their meeting, Jose served coffee and Linh poured tea that was sweetened with granulated sugar and sealed packets of creamer brought from the mainland. After everyone was served, Jose and Linh took their places at their chairs and joined the small talk in the canvas tent as they awaited Lisa's return—who soon came into the tent breathless and called the meeting to order.

"Sorry, I'm late," Lisa stammered, "but there's a problem on the beach. One minute while I catch my breath ..."

Everyone stilled as they waited for Lisa to speak.

"But first," Lisa began after a pause, "the agenda. Today I scheduled four tasks: elect new officers, discuss economic productivity, consider environmental impact, and discuss proposed legislation to be voted on next week by the General Will of the People. There'll be time for new business at the end. Any questions?"

Every hand remained propped on a chair or folded in a lap.

"To begin with," Lisa said, "we need to elect new officers. Let's start with nominations for Chief Neighbor. My position."

Maria stood. "I'd like to nominate Ryan."

"Who else?"

"Put Kit's name on the list," a man shouted out loud. "Breakfast was fantastic."

Most villagers applauded Sean's suggestion.

"One vote for Chef Kit," Lisa said. "Who else?"

Kit raised her hand to speak. "I'd like to nominate John," she said. "He's done a lot of work behind the scenes to make things work. Just don't vote for me."

"Hold your campaign speeches," Lisa said. "We don't want to start down that trail. We'll end up with commercials carved into coconuts."

Kit laughed.

"Any others?" Lisa asked.

No other neighbors were nominated.

"Since we have three nominations," Lisa said. "Let's run a parliamentary system. Vote by hand for one of the three. The leading two candidates will conduct a run-off."

The vote was called and hands were raised. John received five votes while Ryan and Kit each received seven. In the second round,

Kit beat her husband by a single vote. Mostly the ballot was split on gender lines, with men voting for Kit and women for Ryan. Hilary was the only woman to vote for Kit and Alan the only man to vote for Ryan. The nominees voted for each other in what was applauded as a gracious show of affection. After the ballot, Ryan called for a recount, having lost by such a narrow margin, but Kit declared there were no absentee votes or hanging chads and told him to park himself— which he did after giving his wife a congratulatory kiss.

"No, no, no," Lisa laughed, "despite that Oscar winning performance, your work just begins. Now you're the moderator."

Kit walked to the front of the room and took the agenda from Lisa, thanking the younger woman for work well done as she herself took control of the meeting.

"It looks like," Kit began, "we need to elect a new Councilperson. Any nominations?"

"I'd like to nominate Alan," Steve said.

"Who else?" Kit asked.

Tiffany nominated Linh.

"Linh and Alan are on the ballot," Kit said. "Anyone else?"

"I'd like to nominate my wife," Charles said.

Kit scanned the neighborhood before soliciting one last nomination.

"Well," Jose said, "I'd suggest Maria."

"That's enough," Kit said, "now we'll vote for the run-off."

This time Alan collected seven votes and the three women were evenly divided with four apiece. Maria offered to drop from the race, but the villagers instead elected to canvass a vote from Ursula. There was good-natured teasing about whether she could enter the electoral process midstream, but the majority determined that every vote should count—unlike Florida's contested election—and Heather was sent with a slip of paper on which all four names were written. One was to be circled.

The teenager returned five minutes later with the ballot folded into quarters. She handed it to Kit who unfolded the sheet, looked at it with a frown, and gave her verdict.

"She wrote in Sean."

Laughter swept the assembly and it was finally decided to hold a run-off between the three runners-up. Maria won the run-off with seven votes (the two others losing by a single ballot each) before winning the final election against Alan, 12-7. Because the elections ran over schedule, Kit adjourned for a light lunch of bread and soup and only after the neighborhood had reassembled did she stand before them gavel in hand.

"To begin with," Kit declared as her neighbors returned to their seats, "I'd like to propose a beach party for tonight."

Cheers sounded.

"Now quickly," Kit continued as she passed around a list of party needs, "let's assign tasks. We need fish, shellfish, fruit, wood, drinks, and side dishes. Pass this card around and sign up. We'll eat before dark."

As neighbors reviewed the signup sheet, Lisa stepped forward to report on current economic conditions.

"To be brief," Lisa said, "we're on target. We've gathered almost everything we wanted."

"What remains?" Kit asked.

"We could use a little more salt for drying fish and some more dried fruit. And we need to build a barn this week."

"Any problems?"

"There are two. First, we need a little more flexibility from some of you. I know for a fact that I worked seventy hours last week and I don't want to hear groaning from those who did less. Second, we need to cover for the sick so that productivity doesn't fall behind our goals."

Kit asked if she was speaking of Ursula.

"Yeah," Lisa said. "It's not her fault and I'm sure she'll be up again in a day or two, but our process failed to get Alan the help he needed."

"Who," Kit asked, "was supposed to cover illnesses?"

"Charles and myself—the officers."

"What happened?"

"I was busy with environmental efforts and Charles was gone three days for Executive Council."

Charles stood up from the rear of the tent. "You'll see why," he announced, "soon enough. It was a tough meeting that kept several of us busy."

"Fine," Lisa said, "no one says you spent the time sipping daiquiris on the beach. We just need to cover our bases."

"I agree," Charles said, "but plan more time for Small Council meetings. They're going to be long."

Tiffany raised her hand. "I have something to announce," she declared. "Ursula's not getting better. Not for another nine months."

"Nice work, Sean," Viet shouted across the room.

"She can't prove anything," Sean yelled back.

Nervous laughter mixed with a few loud gasps echoed through the tent. The faces of several women turned red.

"Bad joke," Sean said. "Apparently I'll be the father of the first baby born in Paradise."

Now a mix of congratulations and sighs sounded.

"Don't worry," Lisa said, "she just finished her first month and morning sickness hit her hard. First pregnancies are rough, but she'll be on her feet soon enough."

"Cutting trees?" Alan said. "I doubt it. Not without a doctor's slip."

"No," Lisa said with a scowl, "she won't be cutting trees or she'll lose her baby."

"Her fetus," Alan interrupted.

"A woman's choice on what to call it. Not yours."

Alan glared, but said nothing.

"In any case," Linh continued, her eyes moving across those of fellow villagers, "she'll be able to work again, but she needs restricted duty. Nothing heavy and no climbing."

"May I?" Alan asked as he stood.

Linh sat down.

"We need," Alan said, "to decide how to deal with pregnancy. I agree Ursula will be less productive for a few months and ..."

"You ought to try producing a baby," Tiffany shouted.

"What I mean to say," Alan said, "is we need to decide how to pick up the slack. One person can't do the work of two. It's simple math."

"What d'you propose?" Kit asked.

"It's Sean's baby. He should cover for her."

Sean's jaw dropped. His mouth hung open and his eyes widened —though he said nothing.

Hilary wasn't so quiet.

"Patriarch!" Hilary shouted as she jumped to her feet. "Bourgeois moralist! Children are held in common. We reject social conservatism with its moral expectations and gender differentiations. Even America enacted liberal parental leave. Can we do less?"

"If you think," Alan growled, "she's going to stroll around this island picking flowers for nine months, you're crazy. Nothing will get done. The whole lot of you will be pregnant within the week."

The women exploded. Catcalls and shouts rose from angry neighbors. Only Kit and Heather didn't join the chorus.

"I'm sorry," Kit said after the crowd stilled, "but this is uncalled for. Alan, I want you to apologize for that remark."

Alan folded his arms.

"Alan," Kit said, "you have a legitimate point but it'll be debated in a civil manner. That goes for all of you and whoever refuses to cooperate will be cleaning sewer trenches as long as I'm in charge."

"Hilary," Kit said as she turned to the young woman, "tell Alan you're sorry. You were too harsh."

After Hilary apologized, Kit turned to Alan until he choked out what was considered an acceptable apology.

"Now," Kit said, "I'll lead this meeting and we'll behave like reasonable people. And we'll do so democratically—by the vote. Alan, give me three reasons fathers should bear the burden of parenthood."

Alan thought for a moment before answering.

"First," Alan said, "fathers choose—explicitly or implicitly—to make babies while others among us who don't want that responsibility choose other lifestyles. Second, love requires husbands or boyfriends or whoever to care for the women they get pregnant. It also demands that parents and children maintain a close relationship. Third, it's dangerous to let the burden of work fall on the community as a whole as some of the communists did. Everything falls apart when duties aren't specific and personal."

"Well done, Alan," Kit said. "Your turn Hilary. Three reasons only."

"First," Hilary said, "we're a community, not divided by household but united in everything. Second, we're all brothers and sisters and love should flow from each of us as husband to wife and wife to husband. Third, no one person can cover for another, just as Alan apparently found out ..."

"Keep it neutral, Hilary," Kit interrupted.

"Sorry," Hilary said. "What I mean is that necessity requires us to pitch in. We all benefit from the children and we all must pitch in to raise them. And this isn't just for pregnant women. The time will come when depression or disease or death will render some of us less productive. What will we do, send the useless eaters to sea on one-way ice flow cruises like old Eskimos?"

"Ice sounds so good," Sean said from the back of the room, though no one laughed.

"Very good," Kit said. "Let's vote. Who wishes for fathers to bear the burden of pregnancy by themselves?"

Few hands were raised, so Kit asked who wished for the community to be responsible for providing adequate childcare. When the vote was tallied, Hilary's position won 15-3.

"Now," Kit said, "we must decide what to do with the workloads of pregnant women. Suggestions?"

"Having given birth to two babies," Linh said, "I suggest we go case by case. Alan is right that broad rules can be abused. Sometimes a pregnant woman can work; sometimes she can't. It's all relative."

This suggestion brought light applause and even Alan unfolded his arms.

"That seems acceptable," Kit said. "What about Ursula?"

"I'd suggest," Linh said, "letting her take a week off to catch her breath. In the worst case, she could take care of my daughters and they can take care of her."

"I like that idea," Alan said with a grin. "Babymakers for babysitting."

"Yes," Linh said, "and she can cook once the sickness passes. Eventually she may be able to tend all four children and do a little food gathering; but no climbing coconut palms if you please."

Everyone laughed as tension eased.

"This," Kit said, "ruins Lisa's proposed work schedule. I'll have to refigure the workloads and give assignments this evening. Any objections?"

"Do I still get the sewage pits?" Alan asked.

"You behaved yourself," Kit answered, "so I'll take them myself. Or give them to my husband if he doesn't get his act together."

Ryan raised both hands in mock surrender.

"Charles," Kit continued, "will lead us in the last segment of this meeting, though I'd like to address new business first. Are there any new concerns?"

Lisa stood to speak.

"There's a serious problem," the young woman said after waiting until every citizen had stilled. "Someone poached the sea turtle nests."

"What do you mean, poached?" Kit said as she blushed.

"What I mean," Lisa said, "is the nests have been dug up and the eggs stolen. The sea turtle eggs have been poached."

"Mine were scrambled," a man's voice called out.

"Sunny side up for me," a second voice declared.

Lisa turned pale.

"I'm sorry," Kit said, "you weren't at breakfast. We had eggs today. We sent Brent and John to collect them. We're not getting many eggs from the hens. Barely enough for baking."

Lisa looked stunned. "Those turtles," she whispered, "are protected by federal law."

"We don't have federal laws," Kit whispered, more than a little shame-faced.

"We shouldn't need them," Lisa said, "we're better than that."

"But hungrier," a man shouted.

"You killed sea turtles. You killed baby turtles in their shells."

"I didn't think," Kit said with dropped eyes, "about them being sea turtles. They were just eggs."

"They weren't," Lisa said as she wiped away a tear, "going to hatch into chickens."

"I'm really sorry," Kit said as she looked away. "I'm really sorry I cooked them. I'd never kill a turtle, but I really didn't think much about their eggs. You couldn't see a turtle inside when I cracked them. Just yolk."

"But they were going to be turtles someday."

"We didn't take too many. The guys only brought a few dozen. There are hundreds—maybe thousands—of eggs at the beach."

"Every egg is precious," Lisa said, her eyes filled with tears.

Kit dropped her chin as she admitted this to be true and the room grew quiet as Lisa struggled to control her emotions.

"I propose," Kit said after a long pause, "we outlaw the killing of sea turtles or taking their eggs. At least in our district—where we have control."

"I second the motion," Jose said, "and I propose we make the beach a protected sanctuary."

The rest of the village joined the chorus and no more than fifteen minutes passed before Turtle Beach had been named and dedicated as a wildlife preserve. It also was proposed that egg-hunting be restricted to the nests of gulls and other common birds and Hilary suggested conservation laws be proposed to the Executive Council for island-wide adoption. Each proposal was ratified before the villagers turned toward what promised to be the most contentious topic of the meeting.

Charles led that discussion.

"This has been a difficult day," the former university professor began, "and we need to draw this meeting to a close. What I intend to do is to read a declaration from the Executive Council. You can discuss it on your own time. A week from tomorrow we're scheduled to vote the legislation up or down at an assembly of the General Will of the People. Any questions?"

There were none, so Charles proceeded to read the proposed marriage legislation and distribute printed copies for further review. He gave the assembly several minutes to consider the implications of the law.

Tiffany was the first to ask a question.

"I don't understand," Tiffany asked, "why this is being proposed. Are we abolishing marriage?"

"No," Charles answered, "just the opposite."

Tiffany's face went blank.

"We have no laws of marriage," Charles explained. "No one can marry here or divorce. Every marriage was made in the States under what is essentially the metaphysics and morality of social conservatives: of Puritans and Pilgrims and their legal descendants and cultural heirs. We need to reconcile the restraints imposed on the household in the old order with the freedoms allowed in our new society."

"Still," Tiffany said, "is it necessary to annul my marriage?"

"A mere formality," Charles said, "like second vows. Consider the alternative: if Brent decides to leave you, our laws provide no protection whatsoever. How can we uphold the laws of the American states —even if we choose to?"

"Don't worry, Tiff," Brent said, "I'll propose tonight."

"Of course you will," Tiffany said, not at all humored, "or you'll sleep on the beach. Alone. For a long, long time."

Laughter was sparse.

"Let me explain our objective," Charles said. "We propose marriage be freely made between consenting adults. Men and women alike should be free to marry or not as they see fit. Man can marry man and woman may marry woman. No duties will be imposed by marriage and the household won't be considered a law unto itself—exactly as we ruled this afternoon for pregnancy and work. Our goal is to insure that the law of love rather than the letter of the law be the real force to bind couples, married or otherwise.

The opinion of Small Council is that this is already the case, given the liberality of divorce and freedom to arrange one's own domestic affairs. All we wish to insure is every lifestyle be provided a firm legal grounding and marriage—as understood by progressives and liberals —be adequately defined before any mistakes are made or misunderstandings arise. Besides, this proposal will be publicly debated in open forum next week. We're not forced by the propaganda of conservatives to sneak it through the courts with our tails between our legs."

Tiffany said nothing more and Charles stopped taking questions. Kit gave final instructions regarding dinner preparations and the meeting was adjourned as villagers left the assembly in animated discussion. Some argued and others questioned; two or three kept their opinions to themselves.

Supper was served early. Ursula felt well enough to walk to the beach—though she ate little. Tiffany and Linh catered to her every whim and Kit kept herself available as well. Charles strummed a guitar for several songs, before being replaced by a boom box from which rock and roll blasted over the surge and splash of the surf. A few couples danced and others talked. Sean partied with Jason and Jose—his friends teasing him about the inevitable domestication he'd soon suffer.

"From stallion and stud to plow horse," Jason uttered in one particularly cutting remark, "you, my man, are shoed and collared and your main squeeze is now mare and master."

"Do you realize," Jose added, "you're going to be married to a woman whose belly won't zip into her sleeping bag, let alone fit into a bikini?"

"Maybe she can send for a bigger bedroll," Jason added, "and a maternity thong."

Sean groaned.

"Or," Jason quipped, "she can zip Sean's bedroll to her own. She'll have a double-wide."

"My man, " Jose pointed at Sean as he spoke, "you will be pushed naked into the rain."

"At least," Jason said. "Ursula was hot while she lasted. You always have her memory."

"Now she's just," Jose laughed loud as he made one last crack, "a goat belly in a bikini."

"Baaaaaa. Maaaaaa. Baaaaaa."

Jason and Jose broke into a chorus of goat calls. Sean took the teasing well, though he drank liberally from the bottle of vodka in his hand. Long after Ursula inched home, he staggered toward his nylon house—running into only one tree along the trail.

16

THE GENERAL WILL OF THE PEOPLE

Sunday brought deliberation and discussion as villagers debated the advantages and disadvantages of the marriage proposal. In the beginning, the mood was against the legislation—with support limited to Charles, Joan, Hilary, Lisa and Jason. But as neighbor after neighbor concluded some form of law necessary, more of them came to accept the decree—especially after it was observed the proposal codified progressive ideals and guarded against customs that punished adultery, chastised premarital sex, and upheld gender stereotypes. By evening, most neighbors rallied to the legislation and a majority was openly excited by it. Some couples even began to plan second weddings. Only John publicly dissented, arguing it dangerous to rework years of labor and affection—as if life had been a blank slate before Paradise. Kit and Heather abstained from voting. Several villagers debated late into the night.

Discussion came to an abrupt halt Monday morning after Kit delegated work assignments and declared her intent to build a barn by week's end. With more regard for efficiency than equality, she tasked men to saw lumber and women to cut grass. She assigned herself to help with bedridden Ursula, as well as to watch all four children—with Linh's daughters asked to help with the twins. Kit also agreed to assist Maria and Ryan in the kitchen and help Linh gather fresh fruit. Everyone else was assigned to construction duty: thatching roofs, digging foundations, and sawing boards. Whenever a neighbor slowed down or otherwise showed signs of weariness, Kit offered to trade duties for a time—though her offers generally were refused and, more often than not, inspired her compatriots to pick up their pace to prove themselves.

Deadlines were met and the barn built by the end of the week. Materials were collected and prepared Monday; the concrete foundation was poured on Tuesday; the frame was raised and a timber roof begun on Wednesday; and wood walls and a thatched roof were added on Thursday. Indeed, by Friday morning, a barn approximately the size of a two-car garage had been completed—along with a root cellar for dry food storage. Villagers also built storage shelving and policed the construction site for trash and debris. Throughout the week, teams were chosen well and worked efficiently as each neighbor labored where he or she was best suited and most inclined to contribute.

Doctor Graves visited Ursula Friday morning, providing a clean bill of health and a jar of prenatal vitamins—and prescribing rest and a double ration of goat milk. Afterwards, he inspected the village's sewage treatment system, gave the twins a routine examination, lanced a boil on John's back, chatted with Heather about gynecological irregularities, and sutured a cut to Sean's forehead. Following an early dinner, he restocked the medicine cabinet and started south upon hearing from a messenger that two young children had fallen ill from damp tents. The doctor wrote a prescription for vitamins and antibiotics and sent the courier to New Plymouth at a run. Indeed, the boy sprinted hard for the slopes of Mount Zion since it was his baby sister who was the sicker of the two. As soon as the courier departed, Dr. Graves hurried south, declining Lisa's offer to escort him over the hill (since he intended to follow the coast and had little fear of twisting an ankle or becoming lost).

Kit called for a voluntary workday on Saturday to fill stores for the coming week. Her request was answered by all except a handful of neighbors (who had previous plans) as fish were caught, fruit gathered, herbs stored, and salt dried. Ursula minded children from her tent while villagers worked through the day. Citrus fruit was harvested from the slopes of Mount Zion and coconuts and breadfruit picked from the beachfront. Clams were gathered and fish netted. By day's end, the barn was stocked with food and supplies alike and Kit applauded village crews for work well done.

THE GENERAL WILL of the People met at noon on Sunday in the assembly tent at New Plymouth. Nearly every islander rose early for the trek and most arrived midmorning. In the west, Ursula stayed at home since she was too nauseous to hike over the slopes of Mount Zion. Other villages also left a person or two behind: a middle-aged northern woman with food poisoning, an east villager with a sprained ankle, and a southern woman whose baby remained stricken with dysentery. Precisely at noon, the assembly recited the charter and reaffirmed their oath of allegiance and aspiration. Afterwards, delegates elected to the Executive Council took seats at the front while the lot was cast to select officiating representatives for the current meeting—one from each village. Four men (two white and two black) and one woman (namely, Maria) were chosen and subsequently conferred among themselves to establish meeting protocols. Only after they had come to agreement after several minutes did Maria step to the podium as the four men took seats behind her.

"Good afternoon," Maria greeted the assembly. "We have before us ..."

"Louder," someone shouted from the back.

"We have before us," Maria said louder, "a proposal to establish laws of marriage. Has everyone had a chance to examine the bill?"

Scattered applause sounded.

"Has anyone not seen it?"

No one raised a hand.

"Then let's start off," Maria declared, "with question and answer. Raise your hands to speak and please be polite."

A middle-aged woman stood from the middle of the tent.

"My neighborhood," the woman said, "didn't understand how marriages were to be celebrated. We don't have county clerks and no one's proposing the use of clergymen. Hell, we don't even have clergymen."

"I'm a theologian," Joan yelled across the crowd, "and an atheist. I can marry you."

"I already have a husband," the woman replied, "but I'll certainly keep you in mind if I need to upgrade."

"Any suggestions," Maria now spoke over subsequent laughter, "from the Executive Council?"

"We didn't discuss it," Charles said as he stood, "but the matter clearly falls under the Articles Two, Five, and Six of the proposed amendment. Article Two makes marriage a strictly private matter; Article Five forbids the making of any marriage under any other terms; and Article Six undoes all old world marriages."

Charles cleared his throat as the audience stilled.

"The new laws of marriage," Charles said, "as far as I can determine, allow couples to make or celebrate a marriage however they themselves see fit. It's prohibited only to do so under illegal auspices. That is, no one can establish binding private agreements as part of a marriage ceremony. No one can be made to promise to bear children or forsake divorce. Such obligations can't be slipped into a private contract as a way of subverting public law."

The woman raised her hand again. "Since we're free to do as we please, why the worry?"

"In a single word," Charles said, "Louisiana."

The woman looked puzzled.

"Was it four years already?" Charles said as he looked to Karla—who sat beside him.

"At least," Karla said as she rose. "Do any of you remember when the fundamentalists of Louisiana set up a two-tiered marriage code to allow so-called covenant marriages? These entailed more solemn vows and more serious consequences for adultery or abandonment and included legally binding private contracts that upheld almost puritanical laws of marriage. It was a means for the religious right to legally circumvent secular marriage by appealing to tort law."

"I'm from New Orleans," the middle-aged woman who had asked the question nodded, "and I remember loss of custody and property and even determination of fault in divorce."

"Exactly," Karla said, "the only things missing were stockades and stakes."

Karla took a seat and so did the woman.

When Maria asked the assembled community if there were additional concerns, a young African-Islander woman spoke up.

"I still don't understand," the young woman said, "how a marriage will begin. How will it be ..."—she paused several seconds before continuing—"how will it be registered?"

"Couples," Karla explained, "will announce their own nuptials just as they do engagements. Article Two seems to rule out signing contracts, so I'd suggest a simple ceremony be performed, if desired."

"Can couples marry without a ceremony?"

"If they choose."

"If I may," a gray-haired man interrupted, "we need to remember that the only real law of marriage is the law of love. Our camp considered this carefully and we don't believe that weddings create couples as much as couples plan weddings."

"Agreed," the black woman said, "but it seems to me we need to know exactly when a marriage has taken place."

"Why get hung up on documents and dates?"

"To know whether a man or woman is married, I guess."

"Ask her. Or him."

"I once dated a man for a month before he bothered to mention he had a wife and two daughters," the black woman said. "I guarantee I'd never have given him a glance if I'd known. I sure as hell wouldn't have slept with him."

"We don't have such men here."

"Tell that to Monica Lewinsky."

Several women told similar stories and it wasn't long before the assembly was debating the competing needs of public honesty and private vows. The assembly was almost evenly divided, with men and women equally favoring opposing arguments. After forty-five minutes of pressed debate, a middle-aged brunette sitting near the front addressed the crowd.

"As I've listened," the brunette said, "for the past hour, it's become clear we all agree love is the law of marriage. Right?"

No one dissented.

"It's also become evident we don't intend to set up a marriage court or even a clerkship. Right?"

No one objected.

"And it also seems that we want to distinguish between the married and the unmarried? Am I correct?"

A few voices expressed agreement.

"Then there is," the brunette concluded, "a very simple solution: we need to allow individual couples to chose how to become married as long as they do so in an unambiguous manner. Some may choose to publish vows; others may hold receptions or make private promises. It's like a dance. Everyone dances differently to the same music, but it's still easy to see who's dancing and who's standing on the side."

The brunette sat down to scattered applause.

"I'd add only," Karla noted as she stood to speak, "that divorce should be made the same way and it too must be made subordinate to the law of love. No one intends to force couples who don't love each other to stay married or to punish so-called adulterers and adulteresses for so-called sins of the flesh. Marriage doesn't create any new obligations that didn't exist before vows were taken. It's only a sign of love."

"Venus frothing from the foam," Joan shouted out, "we're getting tangled up with baptistic and eucharistic controversies: theological and philosophical sophistry. Someone tell me I'm not back in purgatory—I mean, seminary."

The crowd laughed.

"Not tangled," Karla said, "but untangled. Every one of us agrees love is the substance and marriage is the sign. We marry from love, to love, and as long as we love."

"What is love?"

A young woman's voice rose from the west village; it was Heather who had stood up and now spoke.

"That," Karla said, "is left to the couple to define. I mean, the individual. For couples are made of two distinct persons who retain complete freedom."

"People may be different," Heather said, "but isn't love the same for everyone?"

"Is it?" Karla asked. "How can we know?"

"We talk of it and try to find it together."

"Are we all really seeking the same thing?"

"Why else do men and women come together?"

"That," Karla said, "proves my point. Some believe men find love in the pelvis and women find it in the heart."

"Are you saying," someone shouted, "women don't like sex?"

"Not at all," Karla answered. "I'm saying that while men and women alike enjoy a roll in the hay and call it making love, most women ultimately want something different from love than most men do. Same word, different meanings."

"If couples," Heather said as she frowned, "don't mean the same thing when they hope for love, how can they ever come together? How can they even talk?"

"Maybe we can't," Karla said. "Maybe that's why they say women are from Venus and men are from ..."

Several women's voices rang from the hall.

"A black hole."

"Pluto."

"Brooklyn."

"My joke is ruined," Karla said, "but the point remains: love may not last forever, but arguments about it do. We could debate love for eternity and we'll never come to agreement. Not only man-to-woman, but woman-to-woman and man-to-man. This young woman may be an old-fashioned romantic, but many of us are not. In any case, our goal is not to define the obscurities of love, but to allow men and women to love. As they themselves see fit."

There was more applause.

"What does it matter to us," Karla continued, her voice now deeper and louder than before, "how love is defined in the dictionaries? Our concern is to love and to be loved. If you ..."

A voice from the podium interrupted the speech. "If I may take the floor back," Maria said, "we need to draw this to a close."

Both Karla and Heather sat down as Maria reclaimed the floor.

"Does anyone disagree," Maria asked, "that this bill allows couples the freedom to make marriage in whatever fashion they choose? Good. However we may define love, at least we can agree upon the interpretation of this particular law of love. Are there other concerns?"

Now an older man from the audience spoke—who stood with two big-toothed, blond-haired teenagers at his side: one boy and one girl.

"Nothing in the law prohibits the marrying of cousins."

A few groans were uttered and both teenagers blushed.

"Not like that," the man explained with a look of utter disgust furrowed into his face. "These two are brother and sister and their cousins live across the ocean. It's just that there aren't any laws to prohibit incest—if that's the right word to use for cousin marriages. And presumably we'll be here a long time, with plenty of cousins within a generation."

"Why should we stop cousins from marrying?" someone shouted —it was Alan who had objected.

"Don't you think it's a bit scandalous?" the father of the big-toothed teenagers said. "I mean, we're not in Arkansas."

A red-haired woman from the south stood to her feet. "As a point of fact," she declared, "marriage to a first cousin is prohibited in Arkansas."

"Well, then," the father of the big-toothed teenagers said, "I meant to say Kentucky."

"Prohibited there too."

"Utah?"

"Criminal offense."

"Where is it allowed?"

"California, Colorado, Massachusetts, New Jersey, Rhode Island
..."

"That can't be true."

"I did the legal research," the red-haired woman said, "for a civil
liberties group. We were looking for wedge issues to dismantle Christian influence on public policy, but decided that suing redneck—I
mean, red—states to allow first cousins to marry might look bad in
the press."

"Well," the father of the teenagers said as the red-haired southern
woman sat down, "wherever it's allowed, I still think it's scandalous."

"Gays," Alan now declared, "were once burned as scandalous."

"It's unnatural."

"Natural law," Alan objected, "is the handmaiden of social
conservatism."

"Do you mean to say," the man stammered, his jaw clenched and
face crimson, "my son should be free to marry his cousin or—heaven
forbid I should even say this—I'm free to sleep with my daughter? Or
my son?"

The big-toothed girl blushed and her brother turned away as he
struggled to restrain a smirk.

The assembly quieted.

"I'm not saying it's ideal," Alan said, "but I don't intend to burn
anyone at the stake. Do you?"

"No," the father said, "but we've got to uphold some kind of standard, whatever it might be."

In an instant, a dozen people sprang to their feet to object to any
hint of moral absolutism, pointing out that the creation of standards
of sexual propriety would inevitably lead to monogamy: unbending
and unbroken. Some even chided Alan for indicating that incest
might not be ideal—protesting that his choice of words implied a
standard of morally ideal behavior.

After some discussion, Dr. Scott Law settled the crowd.

"Dr. Morales," the sociologist said, "as many of you are aware, currently is on an expedition. He's been gone for a couple weeks and we're not sure when he's coming back—and it's really too bad he's away since this is a situation he could address. Still, if you don't mind, I'll depart from my own area of expertise and speak from his scholarship since he's written extensively upon sexual mores and I've studied his work."

No one objected.

"To begin with," Dr. Law declared, "even in Anthropology 101 we learn ethics are based on something more tangible than transcendent ideals and absolute precepts. It's from the needs of social organization and the development of a cultural ethos that morality rises. The reason we don't want to marry brothers and sisters is because of the development of progressive mores in a modern economy. That's anchor enough to avoid any scandal. Surely no one believes we've all managed to escape marrying our aunts and uncles from obedience to the laws of Moses or the theology of St. Augustine? Who studies Thomas Aquinas's defense of natural law? Or feels bound by the ethics of Paul or the precepts of Jesus? Who studies the decrees of Charlemagne and Justinian? To be honest, which of us ever read the legal codes of any of the fifty states against incestuous marriages?"

No one raised a hand.

"Now," Dr. Law continued, "it's evident that cultural mores govern conduct and are reflected in religion and philosophy and codes of law. That is, it's the social situation that makes ethical ideals, not vice versa. We don't need to delve into the structural forces leading to the establishment of cultural mores: primarily class organization and power relationships. That'd require Morales himself to lecture. What matters today is that we recognize the establishment of new laws as superfluous. Not only do they portend a return to puritanical legalism, but they're redundant and unnecessary. It's because this man's household has been organized as an exogamous social unit in a neo-capitalist society requiring sustained economic and social interaction between consumptive household units that his son feels shamed to sleep with a cousin, no matter how attractive she might be. And it's because the wider society is socially and economically exogamous that many of us are uncomfortable with the thought of him doing so. What could be a deeper drive than the social mores which we imbibe from infancy? Than our entire way of organizing culture? And I won't even touch on those who root the incest taboo in biological imperative, except to say that their arguments render it even less likely that individuals will sleep with parents, children, brothers and sisters."

The speaker paused one moment as he surveyed his audience— which remained hushed and attentive.

"In fact," Dr. Law concluded, "I believe we will prove ourselves most liberal and most progressive if we leave such laws unpassed—to show the rest of the world that their prisons and prejudices and whips are far less effective than they imagine. Let our cousins—when we have them—play together without strictures and threats and we'll prove to the whole world the presuppositions of Paradise."

The professor's speech carried the day as the assembly erupted into spontaneous applause and Maria waited several minutes for their enthusiasm to subside before she continued the session.

"Well spoken," Maria said as clapping finally faded. "Well spoken. By voice vote, who sides with the speaker?"

The assembly thundered its approval.

"Then I suggest," Maria continued, "we vote on the marriage laws. We've already opened them for discussion and found two points of controversy. The first was the issue of making marriage, which has been resolved by permitting freedom to couples to make their own nuptials. The second regarded the regulation of marital partners and we've decided the law permits all consenting adults to marry as they see fit. Ethnic and gender distinctions don't matter. Nor does age, except that marriage is permitted only to adults. We shouldn't pass laws explicitly forbidding incest, but mostly because it's understood such taboos are based in drives stronger than legislation; they're rooted in the very laws of human nature and social interaction."

"Any final comments?" Maria asked as she took a step backwards.

"This law is so pro-family," the gray-haired delegate who had helped compose the draft at Executive Council now stood to speak, "it almost could've been written by the Family Research Council. But as much as I wish we could live without any regulations or laws, we need some kind of public policy to protect ourselves. For those of you who think like me, it's important to remember this law maximizes freedom and choice and experimentation. In fact, it codifies alternative lifestyles and provides them a legal underpinning they lack right now. I can well imagine this code being used more often to extend our rights than to restrict them. My fellow delegates to Small Council know I was uncomfortable with this discussion in the beginning, but now I'd like to go on record in favor of the law. It's modern and individualistic."

As the woman sat to mild applause, Maria raised her hand to get the assembly's attention. "Are we ready to vote?"

The four men behind her signaled their readiness.

"Let's vote," Maria said, "then we can party."

The crowd cheered.

"By hands," Maria announced, "cast your votes. Those in favor of the proposal raise your right hand."

A sea of hands stretched toward the canvas ceiling as Maria and the other leaders counted seventy-seven votes for the legislation.

"Those opposed?"

Not a single hand was raised, though a handful of islanders shrugged shoulders or shook heads.

"The motion is carried seventy-seven to nothing."

Now one of the male moderators stepped forward and took Maria's place.

"Remember," the man said, "those of you already married—whether heterosexual, homosexual, or otherwise—you have fourteen days to renew your vows or present marriages will be dissolved and you'll become eligible bachelors, straight and gay alike. Understood?"

The crowd demonstrated its understanding with shouts and cheers.

"After the final reading of the charter," the moderator continued, "the beach will be opened for a party. The east camp has brought a mountain of food to celebrate this historic day and New Plymouth has fueled the generator to power a stereo for some dancing."

The islanders cheered one final time before the charter was read and the oath of allegiance retaken. After the meeting concluded, the crowd dispersed where it willed.

AN HOUR LATER, islanders gathered at the beach. Several swam and most ate. Nearly everyone drank. The party centered on a table of smoked fish, boiled lobster, and baked breadfruit that also was garnished with a spread of sauces and snacks. As islanders ate, Tiffany pushed through the crowd of partiers, dragging Brent by the hand and calling for witnesses. At first she merely talked over the din of conversation, but when that didn't get everyone's attention, she shouted so loud that the entire assembly quieted.

"Brent has something to say. Don't you, honey?"

Brent laughed. "Tiffany wants ..."

Tiffany elbowed her husband.

"I want," Brent corrected himself, "to affirm Tiffany and I'd like to marry."

Tiffany elbowed him a second time and Brent rubbed his ribs.

"Right now, I mean," Brent said.

Those who watched laughed.

"Is this a marriage freely made?" someone shouted.

"With all the freedom of an already married man," another voice cried out.

Brent sucked in his stomach, pulled back his shoulders, and covered his ribs with an arm.

"Yes," Brent announced. "She's the mother of my children and the love of my life and I want to marry her again. I give my consent. Now."

Joan stepped forward.

"Then," Joan declared, "I now pronounce you man and wife— again. Your wedding banquet awaits on the beaches of Paradise."

"And I'll take the kids for your honeymoon," Kit offered.

Tiffany wrapped her arms around her husband's neck as he leaned to kiss her and several women threw broken bits of coconut and unripened grains of wild rice at the newlyweds—though one girl lamented that she was unable to toss real birdseed in accord with modern custom.

The party was boisterous as husbands and wives teased about remarriage—many pretending to negotiate for better terms. Husbands called themselves freedmen and so did their wives; single girls danced close to married men and unmarried men flirted with women who wore diamond rings. Bowls smoking with marijuana and bottles filled with California wine, Jamaican rum, or Scotch whiskey circulated as dancing continued past midnight. When the night finally burned itself out, easterners and southerners staggered home while westerners and northerners bedded down at the beach —using blankets and bedrolls pulled from storage.

Most rose late and started the hike home before breakfast. A few who tried to eat breakfast threw up, still feeling the effects of the night before.

Morning was slow to warm.

17

NOTHING NEW UNDER THE SUN

K it woke at dawn. When she saw the empty bedroll beside her, she remembered that she'd walked home with Heather since Ryan was too drunk to stumble through the dark. She picked out a fresh set of clothes and emerged from her tent into a nearly empty camp where John and Heather talked over coffee.

"Anyone making breakfast?" Kit asked.

"I will," John said.

"Thanks. It's Jason's turn, but ..."

Heather cleared her throat. "Most of the neighborhood," she interrupted, "is still at base camp."

"How about Ryan?" Kit asked.

"Sean came back a few minutes ago and said everyone else was still there."

"Maria?"

Heather forced a nervous smile as Kit shook her head and sighed.

"We can start work after lunch," Kit said after a time. "Does that work for you?"

"Easy," Heather replied. "I'd like to clean up this morning."

"I'm planting crops after breakfast," John said.

"I'll help," Kit said.

John said there was no need and then asked whether Linh might help with child-care duties since Small Council wasn't meeting for several days. Kit hadn't yet answered when both she and John stopped talking and looked toward the tents—where Ursula now emerged. The pregnant woman's hair hadn't been combed in a week, her face was drawn pale, and her step uncertain—but she was out of bed and now inched toward a stool near the campfire.

"I feel like shit."

Kit put a finger to her lips.

"Not," Kit whispered, "in front of the children."

"Sorry," Ursula said as she looked around. "I didn't see them."

"I mean yours."

"Most likely," Ursula said as she smiled a little, "she'll have a potty mouth like her mother."

John called from the mess tent, asking Ursula what she wanted for breakfast. After the pregnant woman requested crackers and fruit, he served a plate of sliced fruit and hard bread before returning to the fire to stir oatmeal and warm coffee. As the three women talked, a breeze swept the aroma of cooking food toward the tents and it wasn't long before all four children lined up to beg food—with their parents soon in line behind them. The food tasted good and even Ursula decided to chance a second helping, this time trying a bowl of oatmeal sprinkled with sugar and diced pineapple.

Following breakfast, John gathered an armload of tools and bags of seeds and went to the fields—where Viet joined him while Heather and Kit washed dishes and Linh walked the children to Turtle Beach. After dishes were done, Heather and Kit collected their toiletries and escorted Ursula to the waterfall. By midmorning, not a living soul remained in the camp except Sean—who remained in bed with a hangover.

URSULA GATHERED strength as the sun rose. Color returned to her cheeks as the morning warmed and her step grew steadier as she followed Kit and Heather to bathe. She spoke louder and even joked about her misery. All three women removed their clothes after arriving at the waterfall.

Kit unfastened her bra and tossed it atop a small bush with a theatrical fling while the others laughed.

"It's my last decent bra," Kit said. "I made the mistake of swimming in the other and the salt water destroyed it. The elastic is ruined."

"That's what you get for filling it so full," Heather said after a glance at Kit's chest. "I'd offer you my spare but it wouldn't snap shut. I'm not sure it'd cover one side."

"Thanks," Kit said with a smile, "for such generosity."

"I just realized," Ursula groaned, "my bras won't fit if my chest grows."

Heather raised her hand.

"Dibs," the teenager called out, "on any you outgrow."

"We can adjust them," Kit said, "with needles and thread."

"Do you realize," Ursula asked, "my boobs will be stretched to my knees if I nurse out here? There's not a good support bra within a thousand miles. I'll look like some cannibal's mother from National Geographic."

"As a near-vegetarian," Heather cried out, "I protest that allusion."

All three women laughed.

One after another they showered in the cool water of the waterfall —though they paid scant attention to Heather's petroglyphs, being far more interested in the bar of soap and bottle of shampoo that the teenager had brought with her. Indeed, the women talked little as they soaked, scrubbed, and rinsed for nearly half an hour.

"Now I feel human," Ursula said as she dried herself.

"Cleaned with soap instead of sand," Kit said. "My skin feels smooth."

"You sound like a commercial," Heather said as she bunched and tied her hair with a dark blue ribbon.

"Commercial capitalism returns," Ursula said. "Charles and Joan wouldn't be pleased."

"Pleased or not," Kit said, "I'd die for an hour in Macy's lingerie department."

"I'd die for a banana split," Ursula said, then looked at a nearby banana tree, "without the bananas. Never another damned banana."

"Remember the baby," Kit said as she winced.

"You're right," Ursula said. "I'd share the ice cream with my baby, but neither of us want any damned bananas."

"You're right about ice cream," Kit said. "We'll get dessert before we shop for lingerie."

"I also want a potato with sour cream," Ursula said, leading all three women to place orders for their favorite foods.

"Order me one too."

"And chocolate cake."

"Me too."

"And real Chinese takeout."

"Same here."

"Don't forget the pizza pie."

"I want pizza and pie."

"And finally," Ursula said. "A steak. I'm dying for a slab of beef."

"Your kingdom for a cow?" Kit asked.

Ursula pointed toward Heather, who wore only a cotton towel wrapped loose around her hips. "She looks good enough to grill."

"She's almost Midwest corn fed," Kit said. "No mad cow disease from her."

"Halfsies?"

Kit started to grab Heather's arm, but missed when Heather jumped back and squared a fist, clasping her towel with the other.

"I'm a vegetarian," she said, "not a pacifist."

All three women laughed as they sat near the waterfall. Heather soon stretched her legs.

"I need a good shave," Heather said.

The others saw the long wet hairs, nearly a half-inch long, lying flat across tanned legs.

"That's nothing," Ursula said, lifting an arm. "I've got more hair under my arms than Sean does. I could curl it."

Both Heather and Kit grimaced.

"I haven't shaved in a month," Ursula continued. "I brought a jumbo pack of refills—and lost it the first week."

"That's lost treasure," Kit said.

"Tell me."

"I shave once a week," Heather said.

"So do I," Kit said, "but I'm still down to my last two blades."

"I have three," Heather laughed, "but my legs are a bit stubbly."

"As a progressive," Kit said with a shudder, "I'm against regress—especially to the fashions of yesteryear: like those of hair-covered cavewomen. I can hardly stand unshaved legs, at least on me. Too many years in the beauty parlors."

"Lisa," Ursula said, "is sporting a European style. She hasn't shaved since we arrived."

"I don't judge her," Kit said, "but I'd be wearing long pants if my legs were as fuzzy as hers. No matter how hot it might be."

"Long pants are unlikely," Ursula said. "She also told me she's going native."

Both Kit and Heather looked confused.

"Au natural," Ursula explained, "says she's tired of tearing her shirts."

"I won't be much different in a few weeks," Kit said, "I only have two decent ones left. The rest are rags."

"Save 'em," Ursula said, "for your period since we're out of tampons."

Heather and Kit nodded.

"I'm not about to run around this island topless," Heather said. "Not with Jason so close."

"Doesn't he give you the creeps?" Ursula said.

"He needs a wife," Heather said.

"That's premarital wife abuse," Ursula retorted. "I think it might be a mortal sin."

The conversation died a few minutes later when Kit found a pole to knock down some coconuts; her strike was hard and two nuts soon fell to the ground.

Heather cut through one with a machete and bore into the nut with an auger—handing it to Ursula.

"For your baby."

Ursula drank, then Kit and Heather finished what remained before they cracked the nut and used pocketknives to pry fruit from the shell. After they'd eaten, all three women lay in the shade. No one spoke until Kit tapped Ursula on the shoulder.

"Are you excited yet?" Kit asked.

"I'm getting there," Ursula said. "I've had time to think and I know I really want to keep the baby. No adoptions or anything."

"What about Sean?"

"He's a jerk," Ursula said, "but I suppose I'll have to keep him too."

"Will he help?"

"He says so."

"How?" Kit asked.

Ursula shrugged.

"What do you want from him?"

"I guess I'd expect marriage," Ursula said. "I'd rather not do single motherhood in Paradise."

"You," Kit said as she forced a smile, "have motherhood without marriage and I have marriage without motherhood."

"I haven't even got a boyfriend," Heather declared.

"Jason's available," Ursula said.

"I'll pass."

"What about Jose?" Kit asked.

"As far as I can tell, he's chasing Maria."

"I wish he'd catch her," Kit said as the women returned to the water's edge to shave.

Only after they rinsed arms and legs did Heather ask when Kit planned to renew her vows.

"We haven't had time to talk yet," Kit answered. "Tiffany probably did it the right way—public and to the point."

"Ask her to give me some advice about Sean," Ursula said.

"She is good at it," Kit said. "Not at all timid."

Heather and Ursula agreed and a few minutes later, the women packed their toiletries and each returned to her work. Heather climbed for coconuts while Ursula and Kit collected bananas and breadfruit. Ursula's strength soon was sapped by sun and sweat and she returned to camp with just two bunches of bananas slung over her shoulders while Heather and Kit returned much later with bags full of fruit.

AFTER URSULA RETIRED EARLY, Sean ate dinner with Joan and Deidra, then bathed and washed dirty laundry. After hanging the clothes to dry, he returned to his tent and lay down next to Ursula—whose eyes followed his arrival, but whose lips didn't move. When he scooted closer, she turned away, both hands beneath a pillow and sleeping bag drawn tight. Sean caressed the pregnant woman's neck until Ursula shook herself free.

"Don't."

"Why not?"

"I don't feel like it."

"You haven't felt like it for weeks."

"I'm pregnant."

"Only a little."

"Don't be a jerk."

"This isn't," Sean sat up as he spoke, "about morning sickness or whatever it's called this time of day, is it?"

Ursula said nothing.

"What's it about?" Sean said, with evident irritation to his voice.

Ursula still didn't speak, so Sean rolled her over.

"You're a jerk," the young woman said with a scowl.

"What'd I do?"

"Viet helped me cross Mount Zion last night. While you were partying it up at the beach."

"I asked you whether I should go or could stay a little longer."

"You shouldn't have to ask."

"I should read your mind?"

"You should be kind."

"I thought you liked your independence."

"I like compassion too."

"You have to tell me what you need."

"I don't know what I need," Ursula said. "I never carried a baby before."

"And," Sean said, "I've never done without sex for two whole weeks."

"Welcome to fatherhood."

"What a harpy."

"I've laid in this bed," Ursula growled, "for two weeks, wrenching my guts, and I'm a harpy because you can't have a little fun?"

Sean said nothing.

"Do you," Ursula continued, "really want me to vomit on you again?"

"You don't look sick now."

"Just sick of you."

"And this," Sean said, his voice trembling, "is why I don't want kids. Everything changes. Women mutate into mothers."

Ursula's face drew tight, her eyes wide and breathing labored. "You don't have any intention of marrying me, do you?"

"I said I'd support you."

"Meaning?"

"I'll be there for you and the baby."

Ursula began to sob.

"We never talked of marrying," Sean whispered.

"We never talked of babies either."

"It's your choice. Live with it."

"You selfish son of a ..." Ursula's words died in mid-sentence as she threw herself at Sean. She struck him across the cheek with the palm of one hand, but he grabbed the other and pushed her away and fell atop her, pinning her by the wrists.

"I didn't mean to say that," Sean said.

"You meant to think it," Ursula said as she went limp.

"It's been hard," Sean said as he backed away, "neither one of us are accepting this very gracefully."

"I want to know," Ursula said as she continued crying, "what you're going to do."

"I told you I'd be there for you."

"How?"

"You tell me what you want."

"I want," Ursula said as tears ran down her cheeks and her voice cracked, "a man who will love me when pregnancy stretches my figure and who'll accept me when it makes me crazy. I want a man who will be there during morning sickness."

"You never asked."

"Do you have any idea how embarrassed I am that Linh and Tiffany clean my messes while daddy parties?"

"Do you know what I want?" Sean said. "I want a woman who will sleep with me once in a while."

"I'm pregnant."

"Isn't that just convenient?"

Ursula wiped away her tears as she glared at the father of her unborn child.

"Ursula, when?" Sean continued. "I can't wait a year."

"I guess," Ursula said as her eyes flashed and lips tightened, "you'll wait as long as I do."

"You want a man to be there?" Sean replied. "I want a woman to be there with. How long, Ursula?"

"It depends on my body."

Sean muttered curses under his breath, then pulled on a pair of shorts and grabbed a shirt and a pair of dirty boots with socks stuffed in them as he started for the door.

"You're not," Sean growled, "the only woman on this island."

"I'm the only one who'd put up with you."

"And I won't be putting up with you if you don't start putting out."

As Sean started to leave, Ursula hit him across the back of the head with a shoe and he screamed—more from surprise than pain—

as he stumbled outside. Still, he was careful to aim far from Ursula when he tossed the shoe to the rear of their tent.

TWO TENTS OVER, Ryan and Kit lay on their backs and stared through a ventilation window into the dusk. Ryan tapped a toe on Kit's ankle.

"Sounds like," Ryan said, "Ursula and Sean are having it out."

"He's a jerk," Kit said.

"He's young."

"Old enough to be a father."

"She was there too."

"I didn't say she was a virgin."

"She should have been careful. It's her body."

"He doesn't help her," Kit said after a pause.

Ryan moved closer to his wife. "I didn't nominate him for father of the year."

"No, you didn't."

"But it's her body and she needs to take care."

Kit rolled away, her back turned to Ryan—who inched closer and kissed his wife on the neck, though she didn't respond.

"They'll work it out," Ryan said. "What's Sean to you and me?"

Ryan kissed Kit's neck a second time and ran his hands down her hips. "Turn around, Kit."

When Kit didn't move, Ryan leaned over his wife and asked what was troubling her.

"It's always the woman," Kit said, "who has to be careful. She has to endure pregnancy for nine months by herself and ..."

"And what?"

"And she has to give up children if the man doesn't want them."

"Not this again."

"I'm sorry, Ryan," Kit said. "Maybe we shouldn't have come here. I never thought of them in Hollywood, but this island makes me feel things I never imagined. I can't stop myself."

"It'll pass," Ryan whispered.

"I don't want it to pass."

"I don't understand."

"It seems better to feel childless here than happy in Hollywood."

Ryan took Kit by the hand.

"You want," Ryan asked with confusion in his voice, "to be moody and miserable?"

Kit closed her eyes for a long while.

"I'm happier and unhappier than before," Kit said after a time. "Only I need a baby someday. Or at least the chance—no, the hope—for a baby. I no longer dream of films and awards. I remember my mother and grandmother and hope for a child. Those are my ambition now."

"We made our choice," Ryan said. "Maybe it wasn't the best option as things are turning out. I don't know. But we both agreed it was sensible at the time."

"We did."

"And it can't be reversed."

"Not really."

"What exactly do you want me to do?"

"You can try understanding."

"I want to empathize," Ryan said, "but to be honest, I've never wanted kids."

"You could consider adoption."

"If it was possible, I'd consider it. For you."

"But you're saying it's not possible here?"

"I don't see a way," Ryan said. "Not unless Brent and Tiffany meet some grisly fate. And even then it's not a baby."

"Don't talk like that, Ryan."

"Sorry."

"If we're really to be a country, don't we need children?"

"We have four in this village alone."

"I mean we need to reproduce. How can we survive past a single generation if we don't have children to inherit our ideals? Won't all our dreams die with us?"

"We can grow through immigration."

"Maybe," Kit said, "but that won't help us transmit our way of life to the next generation."

"We can publish our story."

"Who'll read it?"

"The whole world."

"And if every woman tied her tubes?"

"They won't."

Kit said nothing.

"Moreover," Ryan said, "are you saying you want children for the good of society? That seems rather loveless."

"Was it more loving," Kit whispered, "to choose childlessness for the good of society?"

Ryan shrugged.

Kit took a long pause before she renewed the discussion. "Didn't you ever desire children?"

Ryan considered his reply for a minute. "Not that I can ever remember," he said. "Certainly not after college. Not after I learned about the population explosion and the drain on resources and the difficulty of raising children in the modern world."

Kit fell silent for a time. When she spoke, there was a tremor to her voice and her hands quivered.

"You know what I think?" Kit said. "I think I was too taken with my own glamour to want to share the spotlight."

"I don't remember it that way," Ryan said as he tried to hug his wife—though Kit turned away as Ryan moved closer.

"We can't change the past," Ryan said. "We have to make the best of it. Come closer."

Kit didn't move.

Now a shout sounded from outside—Sean had yelped a little from surprise or pain.

"Wow," Ryan said, "they're making it public."

"I don't know what Ursula sees in him," Kit said.

"He's not a bad kid. He just needs to grow up."

"He has eight months."

"That's an interesting point."

"I don't like his attitude."

"I like him being around," Ryan said.

"I'm beginning," Kit said, "to fear he was a bad selection."

"Just remember you pressed for him."

"I made a couple choices I may live to regret."

When Ryan asked for an explanation, Kit said she meant Maria.

"She does her work," Ryan noted, "and unlike Ursula, she's not pregnant. She doesn't even have a boyfriend. At least none I know of."

Kit turned around. "I'd be glad," she said with a sharp tone, "to hear someone put a baby in her belly too."

"That's not nice."

"It'd keep her away from you—with your aversion to pregnancy."

"We've been over this a dozen times," Ryan said. "She's a friend. We're all friends. I can no more keep away from her than you can keep away from the men of this neighborhood. We aren't in little white houses in suburbia."

"Three cheers for the suburbs," Kit said.

Ryan rested his head on a feather pillow as the two moved apart —now putting distance between the backs of their hips and the bottoms of their heels. Long after Kit slept, Ryan lay in bed awake, thinking all sorts of things.

18

THE RAINS OF EDEN

Most rains were brief in Paradise, just long enough to water the streams and green the vegetation. A cloudburst provided a moment's respite from the heat before the sky reclaimed lost moisture and breezes blew humidity seaward. Tuesday morning, however, brought storms. Heavy rain fell at dawn and continued into the night, repeating the same cycle on Wednesday. By Thursday, the heavy rains had flooded tents and washed out the bridge. Even after tarps were pitched over fire pits, the deep-dug holes flooded from below, forcing a profligate burning of logs to keep the campfire ablaze. Nylon cords strung beneath the tarp and near the fire were draped with shirts and pants (as well as shoes and socks and underwear and bras), yet drew scant attention from the close-pressed huddle of men and women desperate to stay dry. Occasionally, winds shifted and blew smoke into the eyes and mouths of the villagers—who coughed and turned eyes away without stepping into the downpour. A few inhabitants with dry tents stayed inside: snuggled in sleeping bags or warmed against a companion. Now and then one of them braved the rain to gather fruit or fill a bowl with tasteless mash, though such forays proved brief and infrequent.

Scheduled work stopped with the rains since wood couldn't be cut, trees couldn't be climbed, and fish couldn't be caught. Yet work parties continued to deploy: some to gather food and others to repair the damage caused by the storms. Extended stakes were driven deep into wet earth to anchor tents after the tool tent was blown over by winds that pulled its six-inch spikes from paste-like mud. Shifting occurred as the barn settled in the softening earth—with the new storage barn saved only by thick ropes and long spikes. Injuries also increased; Jose sprained his ankle with a fall from the barn and Ryan was fortunate to escape with a lump on the head when a coconut was blown from a tree. All four children caught colds and were confined to their tents—to the agitation of their stir-crazed parents and the relief of many others.

Now the rain pounded against a mud-soaked tent whose poles quivered from bursts of wind—though additional stakes had shored the tent's frame and allowed the nylon shelter to withstand the strain. Inside, Sean and Ursula lay on a shared sleeping bag and covered themselves with another. Their lunch had been pushed to a corner of the tent, insipid and uneaten.

It was Sean who stirred from the warmth of the sleeping bag. "Do you feel a little better, Ursula?" he whispered.

Ursula opened her eyes. She lay on her side, face toward Sean, her hands tucked between her knees and her body turned inward, curled into a fetal position.

"A little."

Sean moved closer. He wrapped his arm around the small of her back and pulled her close. "This give you any ideas?"

"Not good ones," Ursula said, an irritated tone to her voice.

"You said you're better."

"It's the middle of the day and I'm not going to have people imagine you on your pregnant wife. It's indecent."

"Who cares what they think? It never stopped us before."

"We need to set an example."

"An example for who? Jason?"

"For our child," Ursula said.

"Sex hasn't exactly done wrong to the fetus," Sean said. "It won't care one way or another what we do."

"It's he or she."

"Whatever."

"Whoever."

"Whichever."

"Maybe tonight," Ursula said, "after everyone's sleeping."

Sean rubbed his hand over the side of his hair. Inches of thick hair ran between his fingers.

Ursula softened her voice. "You could get me some more coconut water and toast if you have so much energy."

Sean crawled from the tent and walked barefooted to the mess tent where he found a green coconut in the mess tent and bore two holes through its eyes with a screwdriver, smashing the tool into the coconut with so much force that the fruit cracked and most of its juice drained away. He placed the nut in a plastic bowl and set it aside, then fetched a thick plantain (its peel already streaked dark brown) and a bit of sliced pineapple—along with some dried bread he warmed over the fire.

After gathering the food, Sean returned to Ursula. "This enough?" he asked.

Ursula took the food from Sean's hand and ate.

"I need a haircut," Sean said. "You have scissors?"

Ursula shook her head.

"Who does?" Sean asked.

"I borrowed a pair from Linh once. Deidra has some too."

"Will you at least cut my hair if I get 'em?"

Ursula nodded, her mouth too full to talk.

Sean looked at her stuffed cheeks and scowled as he said that he'd return in a few minutes, then hurried through the downpour through a row of tents until he came to a blue nylon dwelling near the back of the village.

"Is anyone home?" Sean said loud enough to be heard inside.

A woman's voice shouted out. "Is that Sean?"

"I need to borrow scissors."

"Come in from the rain."

Sean unzipped the tent and scooted in.

Deidra was alone, a short knife in one hand and a block of wood in the other. Whittled flakes were strewn all around her and a pool of water had accumulated in the corner of the tent. She didn't look up.

"One minute," Deidra said.

"I'm not going anywhere," Sean answered. "Not in this rain."

Deidra cut into the wood several more times before setting it aside. "Sorry. I was finishing the nose."

Now Deidra looked at her guest. "You need a towel?" she asked.

Sean nodded and Deidra handed him a towel from a dry corner of the tent with which he dried his face.

"Ursula sent me for scissors," Sean said.

"One minute."

While Deidra rummaged through a wooden box, Sean eyed the flat of her belly and the curve of her hips, then stared unflinching at her bronzed legs.

"Where's John?" Sean asked.

"He hiked to base camp," Deidra replied as she searched for scissors.

"In this downpour?"

"He said he might as well make something of the day."

"He does know it rains over the whole island?"

"He wanted to use the library."

Sean said nothing.

"I guess it's one way," Deidra faced her guest as she rolled her eyes, "to make use of the day."

Sean just shrugged.

A moment later Deidra found the scissors. "Be careful," she said as she handed them to Sean. "These are barber's scissors. They're very sharp."

Sean asked if she cut hair.

"A little," Deidra answered. "I took a class."

"What's it cost?"

"For you, it's free."

"Do you mind?"

"My pleasure," Deidra said. "Have a seat."

Deidra unfolded a sheet over her bedroll and Sean sat on it cross-legged and asked Deidra to trim his hair short since it now covered his ears and he wanted it cropped close. Deidra kneeled behind him and towel-dried his hair, then picked up a comb and worked over Sean's head while he moved his eyes around the tent.

After a minute or so, Sean looked at the half-cut block of wood. "What're you carving?"

"A tiki."

"The decoration?"

"The god."

"How long to make a god?"

"Keep your head still," Deidra said as she trimmed the hair around Sean's left ear. "Another week to finish the tiki and consecrate it as a god. Unless John has his way. He can be irrational when it comes to native cultures. Did you know that his great-grandfather helped capture Geronimo?"

"No."

"My family hated him from the beginning and his shunned me. They're Presbyterian and I'm not."

"What good's religion if you fight over it," Sean said.

"Let every house have their own god, I always say."

Sean nodded.

"Whoops," Deidra said, "don't move or this could end with a scalping."

"Sorry."

Sean straightened himself. "What kind of god is it?" he asked.

"A fertility goddess."

"Can you carve me a sterility god?"

Deidra slapped him light across the cheek from behind. "He who does the rain dance," she said, "should carry an umbrella."

"But we always did the sun dance—except one time."

Deidra's scissors snapped shut. "She got pregnant on one try?"

"Except we weren't trying. I guess I forgot to use a condom."

"Quite the stud."

"A lot of good it does me," Sean said. "Over two weeks out to pasture and still grazing alone."

"That's a long time for a guy your age."

Sean glanced back and answered with a quieter voice than before. "You look younger than I do."

"Flatterer."

Sean shrugged as Deidra leaned forward from her kneeling position, her breasts brushing the back of his shoulders. She inched forward until both breasts flattened against Sean's back. When she ran her fingers through his hair, Sean neither protested nor moved.

"It's warm in here," Deidra whispered.

"Warmer than before," Sean said.

Deidra used one hand to steady Sean's face, grasping the bottom of his chin and aiming his eyes straight ahead while she unbuttoned her blouse. When she leaned forward, Sean felt warm flesh against his back and turned just as Deidra's weight fell on him—her lips touching his, her flesh pressing his, her legs straddling his.

"O my great tiki," Deidra cried out, "give me your blessing."

"Whatever," Sean replied.

A woman's cries soon echoed through the camp.

RAIN FELL as Linh crawled from her tent and splashed through the mud—wet earth oozing between her toes and splattering against her ankles as she walked toward the mess tent. Linh kept her face down and couldn't see who remained at home, though she knew from the pungent smoke of burning dope that Jason was in his tent. She held her breath as she hurried through his cloud of euphoria since it wouldn't do for her to stumble into her tent too stoned to warn her daughters against drug use. A thousand talks would be discredited by sight of one red-eyed mother.

When she came to the center of the village, Linh waved to Tiffany (who sat with Alan at the fire) before entering the mess tent. After filling a nylon pouch with dry food, Linh sprinted through open air to the cover of the tarp pitched over the firepit. Wind cleared the smoke as the women talked.

"Hi, Tiff."

"Hi, Linh."

Tiffany hugged her friend while Alan watched without emotion or comment.

"How're your boys doing?" Linh asked.

"Better now," Tiffany said. "Teddy had a fever but it broke. And Tyrone was a bear till his father read him stories. What about your girls?"

"About the same. Bad colds. Nothing serious."

"Except to parents trapped in tents."

Both women laughed.

Tiffany then asked Linh to stay for coffee. Linh was pleased with the offer and took a seat as Tiffany filled two mugs from an iron pot simmering with fresh brew. For a time, they enjoyed companionship without talk.

"Viet," Linh said when her cup was half-empty, "is afraid we won't get crops down if the rain doesn't break."

"Brent says the same," Tiffany said before turning toward Alan. "What does your husband think?"

Alan stared at her.

"Sorry. I was just asking," Tiffany said. "I didn't mean any offense. I wasn't sure whether to call him a husband or a wife."

"Just don't call him some chattering hausfrau," Alan replied, "and we'll be fine."

Tiffany held her tongue and the two women sipped coffee as Alan warmed his feet at the fire even as rain continued to pour from the edges of the covering tarp, flowing down opposite sides like rival waterfalls. When the wind died for a moment and the smoke backed up, all three neighbors turned away coughing until the breeze returned and the smoke dissipated. No one spoke as they waited for the smoke to clear.

A woman's ecstasy broke the silence.

"Sheesh," Linh said, "can't they keep it to themselves?"

Tiffany glanced at Alan before facing her friend.

"Some people," Tiffany said, "forget there are children here. Toleration's a virtue, but so is good breeding."

"Nice pun," Linh laughed.

"Still," Tiffany smiled, "some people forget nylon walls don't keep sound out."

"Especially," Linh said, "during the day. There she goes again. That's twice."

Both women blushed.

Alan didn't.

"We ought to pitch a privacy tent outside camp," Tiffany said with a roll of her eyes, "so couples won't feel so inhibited."

"The only inhibited ones," Alan growled as he stood up, "are you two cackling hens."

Though Tiffany's eyes flashed, it was Linh who spoke.

"Alan, that's not very nice," Linh said. "Privacy is a two-way street and ..."

"Freedom in the walls of their own house," Alan interrupted.

"Within the walls," Linh said. "Not sounding from the streets. Nylon is a little less soundproof than brick."

"Then why don't we just build little farmsteads on the prairie and adopt Midwest decorum?"

"Have you ever thought," Tiffany said, "how delicate it is to discuss sex with children?"

"Once kids are old enough to know," Alan said, "they should be told. Before that they don't understand what they hear."

"Really?" Tiffany snapped, sarcasm evident in her voice. "I'm glad you've got it all worked out. Daddy."

Alan threw his coffee into the fire; it steamed away, the acrid stench of burnt beans lingering in the damp air.

"Don't tell me," the man said, "you've never made love in your tent."

"They've never heard us," Tiffany said. "We find another place if we're that amorous. Or energetic."

"If," Alan replied, "they can't hear you in the tent, they sure can't hear anyone else."

"You woke my family last night," Tiffany whispered.

Alan turned red.

"So don't tell me," Tiffany continued, "how to raise my children. It'll be awkward enough to tell them about the birds and the bees when they're old enough. I have no intention of discussing Alan and Steve this soon."

"Not only are you a bigot," Alan sneered, "but you're also against sex education."

"Sex education uses science books," Tiffany said. "It's pornography that uses live models."

"I think," Linh said, picking up her dinner bag and standing up, "the idea of a privacy tent would be useful. A sort of couple's motel."

"Maybe," Tiffany said, "but courtesy would also be nice."

"Let's pitch that tent," Alan said, "and let's set up a children's hospital on the other side of the camp. A place where mothers can stay with sick children."

Tiffany said nothing.

"What," Alan said, "is a few minutes pleasure to a whole night's misery? Suppose someone did wake your children. Is that any reason for them to whimper and cry till dawn?"

"They're sick," Tiffany said, "and they're small. They can't help themselves."

"They're not that sick and they're not that small. No one needs to whine all night over a sore throat."

Tiffany glared at Alan, her expression hard and eyes steeled. "They don't whine," she snarled, "half as much as you do."

"Maybe if I got some sleep, I'd be a little less uptight."

"You woke them up, not me."

Alan muttered a few curses before he left and Tiffany and Linh soon changed the subject, talking another hour—mostly about the private wedding that Viet and Linh planned for the coming weekend. Tiffany volunteered to watch their children for the honeymoon until

Linh explained she'd made no plans. After they finished talking, each woman returned to her own tent.

HEATHER WAS LYING ALONE, a candle lit to supplement the rainy day's dim light. A yellowed copy of The Swiss Family Robinson with a broken spine lay on the tent's nylon floor and the young woman—now snuggled in her sleeping bag—enjoyed the warmth of the down-filled sleeping roll on such a miserable day. Her lunch plate, mostly eaten, sat on an upturned crate that served as a table and the young woman turned to one side, snuggling with her pillow—breathing out and letting her mind drift. Thoughts of high-school friends and childhood memories came to mind. She wondered if ...

A woman's shout pierced the air.

Heather sat up, cocking her head to the right. The shout was close and it didn't sound like pain.

A moment later, the woman shouted again and Heather giggled. It was a neighbor making love. The woman moaned several times and the man groaned once. Heather triangulated the distance and figured it was Deidra—maybe she and John were getting along better than before.

When the woman began to moan rhythmically, Heather turned her ear to listen, rolling a little closer to the nylon wall. A few minutes later, the woman shouted again, this time not quite so loud.

"Quiet, for heaven's sake," the man said a little too loud, "or she's going to hear."

Heather couldn't make out Deidra's reply.

"Heather," the man said even louder.

Then the man stopped talking and love returned. Mostly it was Deidra who made noise and the man only occasionally sounded. Still, as Deidra's giggling and squealing grew louder and louder—increasingly abandoned and unrestrained—Heather began to feel uncomfortable. She rolled to the far side of her tent and covered her ears with pillows, but the noise grew louder and soon she felt flush. When the man let out a loud cry, Heather went weak at the knees. As silence returned (and with it, embarrassment), the virgin turned on her belly and made herself sleep—though it took a very long time.

SEAN SCOOTED into his own tent and sat near the front door, only glancing at Ursula—who remained covered by her bedroll.

"That took a while," the pregnant woman said.

"I decided to let Deidra cut my hair to spare you the trouble."

"She didn't mind?"

"I don't think so."

Ursula sat up, her sleeping bag drawn to her shoulders. "I've been difficult, Sean," she said. "I don't know what comes over me sometimes. I feel like a different person with this baby."

Sean looked away. "We all have weak moments," he whispered.

"And you really have been patient."

"I could do better."

"Did you hear a woman shout across the camp?"

"Was that a shout?" Sean stuttered. "I thought I heard something."

"It put ideas in my head. It reminded me of your work."

Sean didn't reply.

"Come over here," Ursula said, dropping the bedroll to reveal her naked body, slender and toned. Even her belly remained flat and smooth.

Sean gasped as Ursula climbed out of the sleeping bag and crawled forward.

"If you won't come to me," Ursula said, "I'll come to you."

Sean didn't move.

Only when Ursula had moved within reach of her prey did she stop. At first she smiled as her eyes moved from one side of Sean's head to the other; then she reached forward, turned his face to the left and to the right.

"Why did she only cut one side of your hair? How could ..." Ursula's face filled with blood and anger. "Those were her shouts."

"N-no," Sean started to say until Ursula cut him short.

"Get out!" Ursula screamed. "Get out!"

"But I ..."

Ursula hurled herself at Sean, her elbows tucked against her sides and her arms upright—fists pounding at Sean's shoulders. The stance was ineffective and Sean parried the blows, grabbing the young woman by the wrists and holding fast. Even when Ursula twisted to drive a knee into his groin, he turned his hip and blocked the blow with a thigh before pushing her across the tent, snatching a dirty sweatshirt, and jumping through the half-zipped entrance of the tent.

Ursula followed him into the rain. "Adulterer! Cheater! Bastard!" she screamed, following as Sean hurried toward the mess tent. Only after she took a dozen steps did Ursula realize she was naked and return weeping to her tent.

It was dusk when John returned from base camp. He had met with staff professionals during the day and used both online and book libraries for his research. As soon as he came home, he went to the fire to find both dinner and his wife. Deidra was carving her tiki and talking with Sean under the tarp while Jose and Lisa maintained an uncomfortable silence just a few feet away and Heather roasted breadfruit over an open flame. All four children played cards with their parents under the light of an oil lantern and cover of a canvas tarp.

When John broke a piece of bread and sat between Deidra and Sean, everyone fell quiet—with several villagers retiring through the light rain to their tents.

"You find anything?" Deidra spoke with a matter-of-fact tone to her voice.

"Medicine still can't make any promises."

"There's your science for you," Deidra said as she raised a glass of whiskey in a mock toast. "It means less than faith."

John watched as his wife downed a swig of whiskey and handed the bottle to Sean (who screwed the cap on the flat-sided bottle and left), then eyed Deidra's whittled block of wood. Already it took the square-shouldered appearance of a god.

"Faith in a totem pole?" John asked.

"No," Deidra snarled, "as a point of fact, totem poles are not native to this region and I need to honor the gods of this island. The tiki. This will be the goddess of fertility for my house."

"It's not," John spoke through clenched teeth, "staying in my house."

"I never said it would."

"I'll throw the damned thing in the fire."

"You're an ethnocentric bigot."

John glanced at the other neighbors. "These people," he whispered, "don't need to know all about our problems."

"I'm sure they're not naïve. Or deaf."

Deidra burst into laughter, laughing so hard tears streamed down her cheeks and she held her stomach from pain. Most villagers turned away.

John appeared perplexed as he asked for an explanation from his wife—though she broke into laughter every time she tried to talk. When he finally threw his hands in despair and started home, Heather rose to follow him, braving the rain without an umbrella. She quickly caught John from behind and tapped his shoulder. Even in the dark and the rain, the tears in her eyes were evident.

"John, you have a minute?" Heather asked.

"What's wrong, Heather?"

"Not here. Follow me."

Heather led John not to her tent, but Kit's—where they found Kit dressed in sweats and reading a book by lamp light. She explained Ryan was playing poker with the singles.

John asked what was wrong.

"We've terrible news," Heather said, "but I didn't think I should tell you. Since I'm not married."

"Is this about Deidra?"

Kit said that it was.

"Is she cheating?"

Kit nodded.

"Who?"

"Sean."

"How long?"

"I don't know," Kit said, "they were together today. Ask Heather. She heard. The whole neighborhood heard."

John's shoulders dropped. "I'm not surprised," he said.

"I'm so sorry," Kit said.

"I should've stayed," John said as his lip quivered. "I've tried to be there for her and I even went to camp to see if any new approaches were available."

"The sad part," Kit said with a quiet voice as she tapped John's shoulder with a single finger, "is that you're a good man. Not like Sean."

"It's been hard from the start," John said. "Did you know she dual-majored in Native American Culture and Forestry? That's how she ended up as a park ranger at the Grand Canyon. But she always wanted a son. She used to say she'd name him Geronimo to spite my dead ancestors. It was a joke at first. Not later."

"Can't doctors do anything?" Heather asked.

"No, and we shouldn't go into details. It's not a public matter."

"I'm sorry," Heather said.

"It's not your fault."

Both Kit and Heather nodded without speaking.

"I thought," John continued, "taking her away from her family would remove the pressure to bear a son. I failed and now she's whittling a totem. Her answer to medical failure is superstition. And adultery, I guess."

Heather dropped her eyes and Kit looked away.

"You said everyone heard?" John asked.

Both women blushed.

"Please," John said. "She's my wife."

"She moaned and hollered," Heather said.

"Loud enough for the whole camp to hear," Kit whispered.

John said nothing for a long while and the two women also remained silent.

"I can't go home," John finally said, "so I guess I need to find a place until I can make other arrangements."

"Use my tent tonight," Heather said.

"That wouldn't look right," John replied. "I guess I'll stay in the storage tent."

"Take my tent," Heather insisted. "I'll stay with my parents."

John consented with a nod, then returned to the campfire to speak a few quiet words to Deidra—who dropped her head and didn't reply. Afterwards, he returned to his tent and packed his bags before proceeding to Heather's tent for a sleepless night even as Sean moved his clothes into John's empty place. Both men packed light and it didn't take them long to move.

Even as the men changed tents, Heather packed her sleeping roll and a few toiletries before she walked through drizzling rain until she found herself at a dark and noiseless tent. When she called out, no one answered, so she unzipped the fly and looked in, grimacing as the sound of light snoring filled her ears. She squeezed through a partially opened door with her sleeping bag and looked into the darkness at the dark form of her father—who was cloaked in shadows at the far end of the tent, his head upon her mother's breast and covered with a single sheet. The tent reeked of sweat and gin.

Heather cleared a space near the door as far from her parents as possible—and unrolled her bedroll as the fall of rain on the nylon muted her bedtime preparations. She crawled into her sleeping bag fully clothed, her bra loosened and her shoes paired at the doorway. Her back turned to her parents, she scooted as close to the side of the tent as she could.

"Lord," Heather whispered as her eyelids grew heavy and her thoughts wavered between day and night, "please let them be too drunk for anything but sleep."

A moment later she was fast asleep.

19

THE SEWAGE BACKS UP

The rain was still falling when Heather woke: a steady patter of noise showering the tent. The rustle of sheets caused her eyes to open—her parents were making love.

"For heaven's sake," Heather shouted as she squeezed her eyes shut, "haven't you two any shame at all?"

Surprised that Heather was in the tent, Joan shouted her daughter's name—which caused the latter to bolt upright as she instinctively opened her eyes and turned to her mother's voice. But this wasn't what Joan intended and she screamed a second time on seeing her daughter's wide-eyed face as the virgin stared at her mother's bed: the older woman's breasts flattened against the chest of a thick-haired middle-aged man whose legs stirred beneath the sheets.

Now Heather's face turned white and her voice rose to a frantic pitch. "That's not dad," she shouted.

"Get out!" Joan screamed.

Heather jumped to her feet and tugged at the tent's door—though the zipper moved only a couple inches before snagging. Though she tried to pull the zipper back, it wouldn't budge.

"Heather, get out!" Joan screamed yet again. "Get out of here!"

"Stop it, Mother! Stop it!"

"Not in front of my daughter," Joan shouted out loud as she pushed the man away while reaching for a sheet.

"I can't stop," the man cried out.

"Get off," Joan yelled as she pushed harder at the man.

"Almost."

"Now. Dammit. Now."

"There," the man cried out as he rolled away from Joan—who immediately pulled up the sheet to hide her nakedness.

"Lord," Heather screamed even as she kept her eyes locked on the stuck zipper, "save me from these people."

Heather yanked at the zipper twice more, but still it remained stuck. When the girl heard the sound of rustling from her mother's bed and the voice of the strange man offering to help, she clenched her teeth.

"Let me help," the man said as he stirred from bed.

"Don't bother," Heather cried out, turning to speak just as the man stood to his feet without cover of clothes or blanket, plainly exposing to the daughter the nakedness her mother had just known.

Closing her eyes, Heather spun toward the flap, grabbed the zipper with both hands, and yanked as hard as she could. This time, cloth ripped, tent tore, and Heather fell forward—splashing face-first in the mud with yet another scream, more from surprise than pain.

Heather didn't remain in the mud long. Pushing herself to her knees, she wiped her muddy face with a muddier hand. When Joan emerged from the tent covered with a sheet and calling to her daughter, the girl scampered to her feet—splashing mud as she ran to her own tent, and looking neither left nor right as she left her mother behind. She quickly reached her own tent.

"John, are you up yet?" Heather shouted a few feet from the front flap.

"Yeah." It was a man's voice that answered.

"Can I come in?"

"I'm up."

"Are you dressed?"

"I am," the voice said.

"Head to toe?"

"I guess I don't have socks on. Otherwise I'm all covered up."

"Promise?"

"Come in, Heather," John said. "What's wrong?"

Heather entered the tent and looked at John—her face muddied and hair uncombed. Her shoulders were slumped and chin dropped.

"That's how I feel," John said as he handed the girl a towel. "Take this."

Heather caught the towel and wiped the mud as best she could, then explained—without divulging too much detail—how she'd caught her mother in bed with a stranger. Afterwards, she buried her face against John's shoulder and wept as he consoled her with soft hugs and kind words. Tears washed away the covering of dirt on the young woman's face as she sobbed until her voice shook and her breath gasped; then she wept another spell. Only after she calmed down did John retrieve breakfast for the girl before packing his bags and leaving Heather to the privacy of her tent.

THE RAIN FELL HARDER as the morning passed. As villagers drank coffee and made small talk beneath the shelter of a tarp and near the warmth of a fire, Alan and Kit worked through the morning's chores. As he mixed bread, Alan talked to Steve while Kit stood beneath the shelter of a canvas tarp. After a time, Alan pointed at the fire—which had burned down to its last log.

"Kit," Alan said, "we need firewood. Can you get it? I'm still kneading this bread. It's been slow to rise."

Kit didn't reply.

"You might as well move the whole stack," Alan said. "We're burning the stuff like it grows on trees."

Kit looked at the covered stack of cord twenty yards away. It'd be a wet walk to move so much wood. She looked back at Alan standing beneath a dry tarp. Slowly shaking her head, she stepped into the rain. The ground was soaked and mud filled her canvas shoes while the rain chilled her like a cold shower. By the time she reached the woodpile, Kit's hair hung limp over her shoulders and goose bumps pimpled her arms. She picked out an armful of wood and returned, stacking the logs neatly beneath the overhead tarp that protected the campfire. Then she went for a second load.

Four times Kit made the trip, each effort more labored than the previous try. Twice she took breaks to catch her breath, warm her hands, and nurse scratches across her wrists. Twenty minutes later only a single piece of wood remained: a misshapen stump dug from the earth that appeared to weigh twenty or thirty pounds. Kit rubbed her sore arms and took a long look at the mess tent before she called to Alan—who still was kneading dough.

"There's one piece left," Kit asked, irritation evident in her voice. "Can you get it?"

"You're almost done."

"It's too heavy."

"We'll get it later," Alan said. "This bread's giving me trouble. Working dough in this humidity is tough."

"So is hauling wood," Kit said as she glared at Alan. "It's a man's job."

"I'll get it later."

"We need to get it under cover."

"I'll get it as soon as I can."

Kit scowled as she looked again at the goose pimples on her arms and the mud on her legs. Her hair was drenched and she'd torn her shirt at the collar.

"Now," Kit snapped, her tone far more insistent than before. "Don't be so selfish."

"What's that supposed to mean?"

"You get wet and I'll bake bread for a while."

"Sorry you're wet," Alan said, "but I'm busy right now. We'll get the wood when we can. You've already brought plenty. What's the hurry?"

"The hurry," Kit said, her voice sharp and lips curled, "is to keep the wood dry and prove you're a gentleman."

Steve joined the conversation while Kit waited in the rain and Alan turned back to his dough.

"C'mon Kit," Steve said, "you're not the type to slur. We don't discriminate on the basis of gender roles here and Alan has as much right to bake bread as you. Go warm yourself at the fire and I'll get the log in a minute."

Kit kicked her foot into the mud and stomped the few steps back to the stump before Steve could wipe dough from his hands. She bent down to grab the log, turning deep red and groaning from the strain. Struggling to pull the stump to one hip, she stumbled two or three steps forward before slipping in the mud. As the log landed on her ankle, she let out a sharp scream: her shout of pain unmistakable.

Several neighbors immediately sprang to assist—with Steve arriving first, Ryan at his heels, and Brent a few seconds later. The men helped her to her own tent: where Ryan removed her shoe and Brent rotated the swollen ankle as he prodded at a dark bruise.

Kit fought back her tears.

"How does it feel when I wiggle it?" Brent asked.

Kit answered with a groan.

"At least you're not screaming," Brent said, "so I doubt it's broke."

"Should we send for the doctor?" Ryan asked.

Kit shook her head.

"Well, it's off to your tent for a day of rest," Brent said. "Maybe two or three."

Kit wiped the tears from her eyes with the back of her hand as she explained that the next meal was hers to prepare.

"You've put in your day's work," Brent said before retrieving aspirin for the injured woman. "Alan can cook by himself."

AFTER KIT WAS LEFT in her tent to recover, Brent moved the stump before joining Ryan and Jose for a round of euchre in Maria's tent. Alan and Steve were left alone in the mess tent, waiting for bread to rise.

"They're no different here," Alan said. "Just more homophobes.

I'm beginning to think it's a genetic flaw of heterosexuals to see us as different than themselves. Only if we don't tell will they not ask."

"She didn't mean anything," Steve replied. "She was cold and wet."

"Out of the mouth speaks the heart."

Steve said nothing.

"She's a feminist," Alan said, "for equal rights and equal work. Right? No chivalry, no patriarchal daintiness. And the men have no right to judge me. I was doing my assigned work. It was her turn for firewood. Why should I get soaked for her? Would she come into the rain to help me? She's not in Hollywood now. None of us are."

Steve shook his head and Alan muttered a few obscenities.

"I was going to help," Alan said, "as soon as I finished cooking. There was plenty of wood and the bread couldn't wait. Just like my mother—had to have it done right when she said. No patience at all. Women make me crazy."

Steve shrugged.

"And I'll tell you something else," Alan continued, "they're no different here than over there. Only here you can't ..."

Crash! A large bowl filled with slow-rising bread dough fell from the table. Alan spun and looked down to see the entire day's work covered with dust and mud and a few dead bugs. Theodore and Tyrone stood an arm's length away, one pushing and the other pulling at his twin.

Alan lunged for the boys—who jumped away just in the nick of time—then watched as the twins sprinted to opposite sides of the tent.

"Not that trick again," Alan said as a grim smile crossed his face and he vaulted over the table, blocking the sole exit just as the boys circled to reach it. The twins ran straight into his arms and he subdued them, dragging each one by the wrist toward the dough.

"Pick it up," Alan ordered.

The boys didn't move.

"Pick it up," the man growled louder.

Still the boys didn't move.

"I'm telling you boys to pick it up or I'm going to beat you a ..."

"Alan," Steve interrupted, "patience."

Alan shoved a morsel of dirty dough into Tyrone's mouth. "Here's your dinner," he barked. "You helped make it, so you get the first bite."

Tyrone gagged, spit the dough out, and bawled as Alan turned toward his twin and asked whether that boy also wished to eat a mud pie, but Theodore didn't want a mud pie and kicked Alan hard in the leg to prove it.

Alan grabbed the defiant boy, forced his mouth open with one hand as he stuffed a bit of dough into his mouth with the other.

Theodore spit the dough into Alan's face, wiggled free, and ran home with his brother following in his footsteps—both boys running straight to their mother to tattle on their older neighbor.

IT ALREADY WAS afternoon when Linh walked barefoot beyond the perimeter, dressed in a torn sweatshirt and grungy shorts. The cold rain streamed down her legs as she inched forward, her flip-flops sinking deep into puddles which filled every hole in the earth. Mud oozed over her toes, only partially washed by rain.

"At least," Linh told herself with a smile, "the toilet will be clean."

Now the woman frowned—a shallow pond had flooded the trail. Splashing through the water, she soon came to a canvas wall that separated private necessities from public exposure. The mud between her toes seemed grittier than before and the puddle looked off-color ...

Linh gasped.

A large strand of toilet paper was stuck to her foot. Shaking it off with a yelp, she looked toward the drainage ditch—from which the overflow backed up. Something solid drifted into her foot. With a groan, Linh shook off the shit now stuck between her toes, but her kick was so sharp that the sewage disintegrated into small bits that sprinkled across her calves. She shook her legs until the biggest chunks fell away, then maneuvered to dry land, trying not to splash as she waded through open sewage. Reaching solid ground, she first jogged and then sprinted for help. Breathless and winded, she sounded the alarm as soon as she reached the village.

Her cries didn't go unheeded. The risk to public health was immediately recognized and everyone who could work—which exempted only Ursula, Kit, and the children—dressed in their worst clothes. Boots were left in tents and torn shirts donned. Ten minutes later the camp was assembled, axes and saws collected, and hazardous waste bags drawn from emergency stores. Villagers marched to the recycling area to begin cleanup. One work party felled trees to dam the rising water while a second detail placed sandbags in an improvised levy to contain the overflow. A third group waded directly into the sewage—shovels in hand—to clear fouled drainage ditches. While the first two parties built a foot-high berm to block the rising tide of sewage, the diggers spent two hours working through the clogged drainage trenches. When they finally snaked through the final plug, water swirled around their feet and drained into the woods, taking with it whatever waste could be carried away. A few minutes later, the rain stopped, the sun came out, and the woods warmed.

Cleanup required the rest of the day. Shovels were used to clear the upper layer of contaminated soil from the path leading to camp, as well as to dig pits and trenches for draining puddles of raw sewage. Sandbagged berms were fortified to form permanent redoubts against future overflows and the toilets themselves were reengineered to better separate human flesh from its waste products. The sun burned brighter by the minute and even the wettest jeans soon grew stiff in the heat. Perspiration added to the itch of dried urine and crusted dung and soon everyone reeked of all three. Villagers cussed each other for every slop of sewage and the sun for every drop of sweat. Feet slipped in the gritty earth and hands shriveled from urine-polluted water.

Only at dusk was it decided to stop work—and even then only after Ryan announced a need for more salt-water and sand before cleanup efforts could continue. Soon a ragged column of ill-smelling idealists returned to their village. The cleanest among them was covered with muck from toe to thigh while the dirtiest was utterly polluted. A few laughed at themselves while the less cheerful cursed their ill fortune.

Lisa was in the worst shape. She was covered from head to toe with muck and mud. Soiled bits of toilet paper clung to her bare legs and her clothes smelled like warm piss. The red hair that reached the small of her back looked shit brown wherever it had been left uncovered by an old bandana used to keep hair away from the young woman's face. Looking at her arms and legs, Lisa suggested villagers make the best of good weather and a bad situation by taking a swim. Within fifteen minutes, the villagers were in various stages of undress at the beach. Some peeled their clothes on shore while others waded into the water before stripping. Most left their undergarments on, though a couple men and one woman swam naked. Heather alone bathed in shorts and shirt. There was little talk and no play—only a serious effort to scrub and rinse. When they were done, a bonfire was lit and nearly every piece of sewage-soiled clothing thrown into it. A few naked villagers, along with a dozen others clothed in stained rags, straggled to the village in search of clean clothes and cooked food.

Meanwhile, Ursula and Kit—whose ankle could bear a little weight—had remained at camp to boil soup and bake bread for dinner and now served their fellow villagers as the latter arrived in the commons with clean clothes and hungry stomachs. A short time after dinner, children were sent to bed as an emergency meeting of the village was called. It already was Friday night and there were issues to be cleared before the weekend began.

ALL EYES WERE on Kit as she called the meeting to order. She wore a baggy sweatshirt and faded jeans hung loose around her hips. Her feet were covered with sandals and her hair fell straight to her shoulders. She wore no makeup and also spoke without adornment. While she favored one leg and steadied herself with an improvised crutch cut from green bamboo, she was able to stand while speaking.

"We have issues," Kit said. "Lisa first."

Lisa had burned her clothes and not fetched others. She wrapped only a towel around her hips and wore no shirt—showing to everyone that her breasts had shriveled from the cold and wet. The young woman was short with words and curt in tone.

"We had an environmental disaster today," Lisa said. "It's contained now, but there's a week of cleanup ahead so the sewage doesn't contaminate the environment. We've managed to pollute virgin forest."

"I'd say we fertilized the forest," Ryan said.

"The dung will enrich the earth," Lisa said, "but it'll also bring disease and the littering of the woods with used toilet paper. I doubt anyone noticed, but the rains washed away the compost heap and recyclable trash—and even the non-recyclables. I found disposable razors as far as the trail. If anyone stepped on one of them, they'll need a tetanus booster. Immediately."

"Where can I find those razors?" Maria said and several women nodded in agreement.

"Have you forgotten," Lisa continued, "that any animal who steps on an old razor or takes one between its teeth will be cut and possibly infected. We have to find the razors and bury them. It'll take two of us working a week to gather trash. And another two to rake the lost compost."

"Just let it fertilize the woods," Jason said.

"Fine. Then you can squat on your dope seeds if you want anything to grow. The manure is gone and we didn't bring artificial fertilizer."

"Like I said," Jason said, "give me tall boots and a short shovel. My weed has a need to feed."

"We need four committed environmentalists," Lisa continued. "The work will be messy and hard. Who wants to help me?"

"Our first superfund cleanup," someone muttered and a couple people laughed.

"I will," Jose said.

"Me too," Brent said.

John raised his hand and the work detail was filled.

"Next issue," Kit said.

Charles raised his hand. "Joan and I," he said, "would like to announce our plan to remarry."

"When?"

"Now."

"Why bother?" Heather said out loud.

"What did you say?" Joan asked.

"Why bother?" Heather continued. "Why don't you just live together? There's a sin you haven't committed."

"There is no sin in Eden," Charles replied with suppressed irritation, "and we did live together for a few months—long before it was fashionable. When it was an act of protest as much as love."

"Seriously," Heather said as she rolled her eyes, "I don't understand the point."

"Your father and I married for life," Joan said, scarcely able to restrain her exasperation, "and we intend to keep our vows. We're monogamous."

"That's news."

"What's that supposed to mean?"

"How," Heather said with evident scorn, "did you ever teach ethics with a straight face?"

"Listen daughter," Joan growled, "I still remember the night when you were little more than sperm dripping down my thigh. Don't lecture me about ethics or tell me about marriage when you haven't had the slightest feel of a man between your legs."

Heather gasped and tears welled in her eyes, but she said no more as her parents exchanged truncated vows before a crowd of cheerless witnesses. Only after a quiet pause following the impromptu ceremony did Ryan break the awkward silence.

"I also plan to marry," Ryan said.

"Congratulations," Kit replied. "Now?"

"Not yet," Ryan answered. "I'd like to give you a proper wedding and we haven't had time to talk for five minutes all week. We'll send invitations later. Does that work for everyone?"

Kit nodded as the neighborhood's mood lightened as neighbors talked and teased while she took control of the meeting and Linh fetched coffee.

"What's next on the agenda?"

"John and I," Deidra announced, "don't intend to renew our vows. At least I don't."

No one objected.

"And Sean has moved into my tent," Deidra added.

John just glared at his ex-wife (to whom he was married only a moment earlier) while Ursula jumped to her feet—pointing at Sean with a shaking finger and shouting at him with quivering lips.

"Bastard," Ursula screamed. "You're not deserting me like this."

Sean dropped his eyes.

"I'm pressing a paternity suit," Ursula said.

"I sympathize," Charles now stood to speak, "with your plight, but the marriage laws are quite clear. No one can be forced to marry."

Ursula started straight at Charles.

"Then," the pregnant woman said, "he can take care of his baby. I'm giving him joint custody. He'll watch the baby every other day."

Sean jumped to his feet. "It's your choice," he protested, "to have a baby."

"And it's my choice to let you feed him every other night."

"I can't make milk."

"Get a goat."

Sean whispered into Deidra's ear and she nodded just before he stood to his feet and addressed the village.

"Deidra and I," Sean said, "would like to announce our engagement. We want to marry right now."

A groan of disgust sounded from the crowd and John walked away, soon followed by Ursula. Linh and Tiffany joined them for several minutes before eventually returning for a debate about supplies in which Maria complained she was down to her last razor and Hilary said the village supply of decent clothing was almost gone

—the discussion ending only when villagers voted to petition Executive Council for guidance. With the supply issue tabled, Kit asked for other issues of concern and Alan brought yet another matter to the table.

"I'm sick of rude children," he said. "Those brats ruined my bread after hours of work and their mother never even apologized."

"You threatened my children," Tiffany raised her voice. "You owe them an apology."

"What they are owed," Alan said, "is some old-fashioned discipline."

"They're not your children," Tiffany declared.

"That's where you're wrong," Alan said, "they're the village's children. If I have to help take care of them, I have the right to punish them."

"If you as much as sit one of my twins in a corner," Tiffany snarled, "I swear I'll hurt you in ways you've never imagined."

"She threatened me."

"You laid hands on my children. That dough could have choked them. It could have killed them."

"It was just a little dough," Alan replied. "Just as little as the manners of your kids."

"Chill out," Brent said, pressing his wife's shoulders until she sat down. "They're our children and we'll raise them. As we see fit."

"That's where you're wrong. They belong to us all. Just as I was told when all of you made me babysit the brats."

"That's just figurative language."

"No," Alan said, "they're brats. Literally."

"I meant," Brent growled, his nostrils flared and face red, "the village parenting idea. It only means that we care for each other in a spirit of true cooperation."

"My black eye wasn't figurative," Alan retorted, "nor my wasted work. Nor the pain of caring for those human miscreants and unbaptized demonstrations of original sin. In fact, I don't even remember myself being particularly cooperative. I was forced to help against my will. Compulsion made me help, not freedom."

"The point is," Kit said as she joined the dispute with evident agitation in her voice, "we need to insure bad children are properly disciplined. Right?"

"Socialized," Hilary said.

"The issue is to correct bad behavior," Kit said. "True or false?"

"That's PTA window-dressing," Hilary said. "The problem isn't to insure good boys and girls, but to address fundamental social obligations. Alan is right about the core issue: if the community can force him to watch other people's offspring, then the community holds the power to enforce social conformity against those same children whose interests it secures. Either it takes parents or a village, but someone has to be in charge."

"My sentiments exactly," Alan said.

Hilary panned her audience. "Since we're all progressives," she declared, "and believe it does take a village to raise a child, the only real debate regards the rules and regulations we'll adopt as a village. As I see it, the first debate is how we'll supplement timeouts."

"I vote for capital ... I mean, corporal punishment," Alan shouted.

The two mothers jumped to their feet and sprang forward, along with their husbands.

"Never," Linh yelled. "You have no right."

"You're assuming you've won the argument," Viet said a little less loud, "before it's been made. There's no way you can get eleven votes from this neighborhood to end parental rights. To abolish the traditional family."

For the next hour, Hilary argued her point and Viet spoke for parental authority. Hilary stressed authority was social in nature, proceeding from the general will of the people to individual households. She also noted that parental rights and parental responsibilities were codified in public law and unfit parents could have children forcibly removed. Viet claimed it was parents who gave birth and nourished life who were responsible for their offspring, even if their authority was less than absolute. He also insisted the natural rights of parents could be amended only when the needs of children were no longer being met—just as step-parents were needed only when natural ones died or departed.

Both perspectives proved persuasive and the final vote was taken only after the entire neighborhood had spoken its peace. At first the ballot seemed to go in favor of Hilary. That is, Lisa, Jose, Jason, Sean, Deidra, Charles, Joan, Alan, and Steve joined her in voting for a more communal government of children while Ryan, Kit, Viet, Linh, Brent, Tiffany, Heather, and Maria voted for parental government of children. Linh, however, requested John and Ursula be offered absentee ballots and sent Tiffany with slips of paper and pens. It took her only five minutes to return with two marked ballots.

John voted with a simple X in favor of parental rights while Ursula wrote: "I'll be damned if Sean and Deidra will have a say over my baby after I've suffered nine months to bring her into the world."

The two absentee ballots deadlocked the vote and traditional parental rights remained the custom. Lisa thought to ask for another round of debate until Linh and Tiffany threatened to bring their four children to vote—noting that most advocates of communal households also wished to establish voting rights for children. Knowing the children would vote as instructed by their parents, Hilary spoke privately with Alan and then appealed to Executive Council for redress. The necessary eight votes to bring the matter to the higher authority were garnered and the issue was sent to the adjudication of the central government.

In the meantime, Kit asked that Alan not be assigned childcare obligations given his impatience and Ryan suggested the staff psychologist be brought to the village to address simmering tensions. Kit announced that work details would be assigned at breakfast and scheduled the next village election for Sunday. After the meeting adjourned, Steve spoke to Ryan for an hour.

20

OLD CUTS AND FRESH BLOOMS

Saturday was spent cleaning the forest and rebuilding latrines. Almost everyone helped with the messy work and it wasn't long before recycling and sewage areas were tidier than before and the vegetation thicker and greener from the flood of fertilizer. Sunday was devoted to a half-day of rest and the holding of elections in which Heather was voted Chief Neighbor and Ryan appointed to the Executive Council. By Monday, the village mostly had recovered from its environmental disaster and returned to normal production.

Heather assigned villagers their work details early Monday morning, selecting Charles and Jose for woodcutting detail and Jason and John for fishing. She gave Lisa and Hilary food collection responsibilities and Joan and Deidra environmental cleanup. When Lisa protested what she claimed was a sexist arrangement of duty stations, Heather switched some of the responsibilities—with Lisa and Hilary consequently tasked to cut trees (which pleased both women). For their part, Kit and Linh didn't object to washing and sewing. Nor did Steve and Alan complain about gardening and planting. Sean was made to shovel compost while Maria cleared trails. Tiffany cooked meals and Ursula watched children. Since villagers had come to realize that mere tents wouldn't suffice year-round, they decided to start building permanent shelters—with Brent and Viet assigned construction duties.

Work started well. Lisa and Hilary felled three large palms along the village's south perimeter while Charles and Jose gathered bags of half-ripened fruit and pistachio nuts from trees growing on the slopes of Mount Zion (enough food, in fact, to help feed the village for weeks). Jason and John built salt flats along the beach, made racks for drying fish, and filleted a few dozen ill-fated perch. Kit and Linh scrubbed and mended dirty laundry while Steve and Alan planted a field of corn—placing generous scoops of compost around each valuable seed. As for construction, Brent and Viet rebuilt the bridge, then sawed palm trees as timber for the frame and siding of a mess hall. Maria cleared two trails of vine overgrowth and Heather explored the forests, discovering fruit trees along the northern territorial border, including three lemon, two kiwi, two pomegranate, three lime, and two banana trees. Ursula helped the children milk goats and deliver boxed lunches of roasted breadfruit, homemade jam, fresh pistachio nuts, and peanut butter toast to villagers working outside the main camp. In the evening, she taught the girls how to roast kebobs made from useful portions of an unproductive hen.

Nearly everyone rose at dawn and retired after dinner, not simply because Heather mercilessly woke everyone at first light, but also because villagers understood that the rains had set back production quotas such that lost hours required repayment—especially since the sewage backflow cleanup also had made for a short day and little overtime. As a result of the redoubled effort, storage tents soon filled with dried fruit and bagged salt to supplement existing stores of flour, spices, and dried goods. Heather even discovered a small gull nesting ground on Mount Zion and collected twenty-four eggs—being careful to leave a few eggs in each nest in order to conserve the bird population. Culled eggs were sealed in plastic bags and stored in the stream for next week's wedding brunch. Even Lisa didn't object to Heather's judicious harvesting of natural resources.

· · ·

EXECUTIVE COUNCIL MET Monday afternoon in New Plymouth as prescribed by law. It was a short meeting with little discussion and even less controversy. Hilary's concerns about village parenting were presented by Ryan, but voted down by a committee staffed with two middle-aged mothers, a wrinkled grandmother with bleached blond hair, and staff sociologist Dr. Scott Law. It was, however, decided to advise villages to adopt socially acceptable codes of conduct for the education and discipline of the young. Dr. Law petitioned to bring the matter before the General Will of the People, but couldn't garner the requisite two votes from his fellow councilors to do so. Consequently, the communal government of children was judged a politically dead issue (since charter regulations specified that defeated proposals must be tabled three months before being revisited). Laws to mandate vegetarian diets and reorganize neighborhoods by racial criteria likewise were tabled for future consideration. Executive Council spent a full hour discussing supply shortages before deciding to conduct an inventory of public and private property.

Late in the afternoon, Ryan made a final motion.

"We have," Ryan said, "a homosexual couple—married—who are in need of social support. One husband is widely liked, but the other feels isolated in what is a mostly heterosexual community, not that we sought such a lifestyle or seek to impose it. But the two men have petitioned to move to the east village."

The delegate from the east neighborhood sat up—a wide-featured Latino woman not quite forty years old, with dark hair and white teeth.

It was, however, Dr. Law who spoke first. "That raises," he said, "the same issues we just voted down regarding racial segregation."

"Not quite," Ryan replied. "Not only is this not a racial issue, but it's a private request rather than public policy. Alan and Steve understand they have no right to redress the situation, but simply ask for the clemency of this body in accord with their constitutional right to free association."

"That seems inconsistent," the sociologist said.

"It's like private education," Ryan explained. "Al Gore sent his kids to private schools while opposing vouchers for the country as a whole. As long as the public policy is clear, private whims can be indulged."

Dr. Law nodded.

"Ryan," the Latino woman said, "if I may?"

Ryan gave up the floor and the woman spoke.

"I agree," the Latino woman said, "with our friend from the east that Alan's request normally should be denied. Changing neighborhoods will open a Pandora's box of petitions and protests. We'd need moving vans to make all the switches that'd follow. There'd be integrated and segregated neighborhoods: white, black, brown, red, yellow, male, female, straight, and gay. Divisions and subdivisions and blocks and parties. Soon, we'd all be living in cliques of two or three—each house a home unto itself. But I have a personal problem whose resolution would assist your neighbors."

Ryan leaned forward.

"The trouble is," the woman said, "I have a fifteen-year old daughter who hasn't a single friend in our village. She's the only child in the neighborhood. Moving west would provide her with friends nearer her age and bring her closer to the teenagers of the north. The only kids even close are the Epstein twins in the south village and they play only with each other. We could justify the move for Ilyana's sake—something no one would object to. My daughter and I could move west while the two gay men moved east. To a camp that already has four gay couples and several singles."

"I'd vote for that," Ryan said.

"So would I," the north village's delegate said—a fortyish single mother who was raising two teenaged sons.

The southern grandmother with blond hair also voted yes. Dr. Law at first objected that the decision appeared to play favorites, but eventually he was persuaded to vote with the majority to present a unanimous ruling. After the meeting adjourned, the customary dinner was served and Ryan spent the night alone in one of the hospital's unoccupied beds while other delegates returned home.

The next morning, Ryan rose early and hiked to the east village—

where he helped Olivia (the Latino councilor) and Ilyana (her daughter) collect their personal possessions and a day's provisions. The three of them carried the belongings along the eastern shore until they rounded the north shore and turned south to Turtle Beach. After arriving at the west village, Olivia and Ilyana ate a late lunch while Ryan announced the swap to Steve and Alan. While the gay couple packed their belongings and said farewell, Ryan provided the new arrivals with a tour of the west neighborhood.

Later that evening, while the newcomers pitched their tent on the lot vacated by Alan and Steve, Heather discussed work schedules with them—placing Olivia on environmental detail and assigning Ilyana to childcare.

MARIA SAT ON THE BRIDGE, her feet dangling in the cool rush of the stream as she watched the sun's last rays shining through treetops. It was dusk and the heat of the day had dissipated as she pressed a hand to her side. Her tee shirt remained moist: the sweat of the day's hard toil still soaked into the cotton.

When the sound of boots echoed from the trail, Maria turned to see Ryan walking toward her.

"Early dinner tonight," Ryan announced as he approached.

Maria nodded.

"You look tired," Ryan said.

"I worked hard today."

"I counted supplies."

Maria said nothing, but stretched her arms in a long yawn, her back arched and chest thrust out as her legs straightened and toes curled.

"That's quite a yawn," Ryan said.

"I'll bet Kit stretches better."

"Married people," Ryan said with a grin, "don't discuss their physical exercises."

"You're not married."

"Close enough."

"When exactly," Maria asked, "do you plan to get around to remarrying your wife?"

"We've decided upon Sunday, but to tell the truth, I haven't had much time to think about it. The whole village has been playing catch-up for a week."

"Marriage is worth considering."

"I already did," Ryan said. "Long before we moved to this island. And I've never changed my mind."

"I was thinking of washing off in the falls," Maria said as she stood. "You up for a swim?"

"Do you have a suit with you?"

"I'm wearing things beneath. Like before. Does it matter?"

"Not to me."

Maria raised her eyebrows.

"Kit doesn't like it," Ryan explained.

"What's the difference," Maria said as she blushed a little, "between a bikini and a bra?"

"Respectability."

"That's nothing you can see."

"Kit can."

"That's silly."

"That's marriage."

"Some women," Maria said as she put her hands to her hips, "swim topless."

"Those women aren't you."

"I haven't that much to behold."

"I don't know about that," Ryan said. "Besides, it's not what's being held as much as who be holding it."

Maria glanced at her chest and shrugged. "Why does she hate me?"

"Kit doesn't hate anyone."

"She doesn't like me."

"She fears you."

"Why?"

"Maybe because you're just as pretty as she is—and ten years younger."

"She isn't competing for men, is she?"

Ryan said nothing.

"You should tell her," Maria continued, "I don't do married men. I never have. Not once. That's a line I choose not to cross. For myself."

"I respect that," Ryan said.

"So," Maria said after a time, "we can't swim any more?"

"Not quite," Ryan said. "I just can't swim with you dressed in underwear."

Maria tossed her hair behind her shoulders with a flick of her neck.

"What if," she said as she started to pull the tee shirt over her head, "I'm not wearing a bra?"

Ryan grabbed her wrists. "You are."

"I can take it off."

"I don't think skinny-dipping is exactly what she intended."

"Like I said," Maria said with a laugh, "I respect marriage. But I had you worried."

"You had me," Ryan said, letting her wrists fall away as he stepped back and Maria inched forward.

"But if you weren't married?"

"If I weren't married, what?"

"Would you take a skinny-dip with me?"

Ryan let his eyes fall to Maria's ankles.

"It'd be hard to just say no," Ryan said after a long pause, "if I were still single."

"Is that a promise?"

"I'm not sure what it is," Ryan whispered.

"If Kit doesn't marry you," Maria said, "maybe I'll make you father my children."

Ryan glanced toward camp, then turned back toward Maria.

"Don't even joke," Ryan said with an exaggerated grimace to his face, "like that or Kit will castrate me herself."

Maria laughed.

"She'd leave me for an affair," Ryan continued, "but a baby ... well, you can be sure I'd make only one."

"Can't she have babies?" Maria asked.

"Not any more," Ryan said, "and the brood of children on this island has stirred up regrets."

"I see that," Maria said, "when she plays with the twins."

Ryan said nothing.

"I won't make jokes," Maria said, "that'll cost you anything a woman might want ... if you swear to keep your promise."

"I guess I do," Ryan said, "but it's a promise I'm not likely to honor. I'm married for the rest of the week by the old law and Sunday by the new one. Kit's a loving wife and we've been through much tougher times than this. Anyway, I'm hungry and dinner's being served. You returning to camp?"

"No," Maria said. "Save me a bite of supper. I have things to do."

Ryan put a hand on Maria's shoulder. "You're a good argument for polygamy," he said, "and since we're almost Mormon already, making due without cigarettes and cola ..."

Maria blushed as she looked at her own toes. "And you're almost justification for doing married men."

Ryan touched the side of Maria's face with a finger before returning to the path from which he came and Maria threw her head back while sitting in the falling dark—her weight resting on outstretched arms as she splashed her feet in the water and enjoyed the rush of the stream.

Several minutes later she bolted upright and counted her fingers. Three times she counted them. When she'd finished, she jumped to her feet and smiled. Dark was falling and it was time to go home.

WEDNESDAY BROUGHT perfect weather as the sky burned bright and a gentle breeze drove every trace of humidity to sea. It was early when Heather directed villagers toward appointed tasks and by midmorning the work pace slowed as laborers took breaks or refreshed themselves with snacks. After lunch, she pushed even harder, asking several people to work extra hours. Her demanding supervision continued on Thursday and Friday. Only on Friday did she relax—since west villagers had replaced their lost hours and lost supplies alike. Indeed, most villagers already had begun to celebrate their hard-earned weekend, particularly after Ryan announced he and Kit planned to renew their vows Sunday at noon. Only a few villagers continued to work and even they moved at a more leisurely pace—John and Jason fished while Kit helped Linh and Tiffany with laundry.

Now the sun blazed overhead as Heather emerged from the woods barefoot, her boots dangling over her shoulders and empty buckets held in her hands. She headed straight for John and Jason, who worked beside a rack holding dozens of gutted and salted fish— the glassy eyes of dead perch looking everywhere but seeing nothing. John rolled a cleaned fish in a bucket of salt while Jason ran twisted vines through the gills of three others. Both men waved when the teenager approached.

"They need fish guts at the village," Heather announced.

"I can't eat another of Linh's horrible concoctions," Jason said with a groan. "Don't send them to her."

"That's cruel," Heather said with a smile. "Her cooking isn't that bad."

"I don't see you lining up for seconds."

"I'm watching my weight."

"Watching it plummet from Linh-induced starvation."

"They're planting corn in the new field," Heather said, "and they've run low on compost. The New England pilgrims apparently buried dead fish with their corn seeds and Deidra suggested we do the same. An old Indian trick. I mean, a traditional Native American technique."

"Not a bad idea," Jason observed.

John said nothing.

"I didn't think so either," Heather said as she handed Jason the buckets that she carried. "Can you fill these with some Linh leftovers?"

Jason kneeled to scoop fish guts. "Anyway," he said, "I was tired of fishing."

"Well," John said as he started to kneel beside Jason, "I can't fish alone."

"I can help fish," Heather said, "though I'm not very good."

"I'll teach you," John said.

"I'm about done with my hours for the week," Jason said. "A couple buckets and I'm at quota."

"Do what you can and I'll finish the job," Heather said as she looked to Jason. "Better yet, take Deidra and Joan two buckets so they can plant, then tell Sean to bring the rest. Between these guts and the sh ..."

"I mean," Heather paused to rephrase her sentence. "between these guts and the dung in the woods, he can finish his makeup hours."

"That's a lot of malice," Jason said with a frown, "from such a gentle lamb."

"Beware the wrath of the lamb."

"Can I take a bucketful to my garden?"

"Do the food fields first," Heather said, "then feed your weed."

"Thanks," Jason said. "I owe you a bag."

"You know I've never touched the stuff," the teenager said, shaking her finger in front of Jason's face.

"But it was a genuinely insincere offer," Jason said as he picked up a dirty towel and started for the west village while Heather and John continued to work their fishing nets—catching nearly a hundred fish during the next two hours. It was a good run and only when the lengthening shadows cooled the water did the nets come up empty. Only then did John dump all remaining buckets of flopping fish into live storage traps for killing and cleaning the next morning.

It was as Heather and John folded nets and stored bait that Sean arrived to fill four empty buckets from fish guts heaped in the grass. As Sean departed carrying a full load of stirred offal (whose stench drifted toward the beach), Heather held her nose and shook her head.

"What he did to you stinks," Heather said after Sean was gone. "You must hate him."

"I don't hate him."

"I would," Heather said.

"Deidra's no innocent," John said. "She's more to blame than him. She's the married one."

"I hate what he's done to Ursula."

"I agree he's been heartless to her."

Heather looked at John. "Do you hate her?"

"Deidra?"

Heather nodded.

"I don't understand her," John said.

"Some women get desperate over children."

"She knew a long time ago she'll never give birth. I'm not the problem and Sean's not the solution."

John moved to a palm tree and Heather sat beside him. It was the young woman who broke a long silence.

"Would you take her back?"

"If it'd work," John said, "I'd try. But it won't."

"You seem calm," Heather said. "I was worse when I found out my parents were having affairs."

"Only because ..."

John let his words die out and Heather didn't press the point. There was silence between them—only birds chirped and gulls squawked.

A minute later John spoke.

"This isn't the first time," John said. "She cheated our second year of marriage. That was really tough; it killed something that never really came back. Everyone told me to give her another chance. It was a hard time for us from the first. Her family rejected her for marrying a white man and mine were upset I hadn't married Presbyterian."

After a long silence, Heather asked how they'd met.

"We were seniors," John answered, "at a National Park Service internship. We lived together a few months to make sure, then married after grad school"—John wiped his face with outstretched hands as Heather put a hand on his shoulder—"but trouble came soon enough."

"I'm sorry for that," Heather whispered.

"You're a nice girl, Heather. Maybe we should've adopted someone like you."

"There are times when I'd like to be adopted. Can you divorce parents in Paradise?"

"You can't escape your own flesh and blood."

"Sometimes I wish I'd never been ..."

John cut her off mid-sentence. "None of us have been conceived in ideal circumstances or perfect families."

"But I hate that ..."

John put a finger to Heather's lips. "Hush," he whispered, "or you'll wilt before you bloom."

Heather said no more as she watched John stow nets—his thick neck and thinning hair showing that a number of years had passed since he was a young man. She looked to her young breasts and narrow hips and blushed. She wasn't old enough for him, good as he might be. When John told her to return to the village and keep peace with her parents, Heather did as she was told.

KIT DROPPED a bundle of grass sheaves and picked up what was left of her Saturday morning breakfast—a half-filled cup of coffee and a misshapen fruit pastry—as she watched Linh scoop hot coals into an antique iron. Linh blew away some ashes and latched the lid before putting the iron on a towel-covered oak plank sitting atop two stumps.

"I found it at an antique shop."

"Very Amish," Kit said.

"The Amish use cutting edge technology compared to us."

"It is clever."

"And it works well. I prefer permanent press but this'll do for a wedding."

"Just don't burn a hole in the skirt," Kit said with a laugh. "It's my only one."

Linh ironed out the wrinkles in a white skirt, then traded it to Kit for a blue blouse—which she ironed while Kit folded the white skirt over an improvised hangar made of a whittled stick and corded vine.

"Now for the honeymoon," Linh said, setting the iron to the ground.

"Two expense-paid days," Kit said, "on Big Motu Island. Only two hundred yards from Paradise."

Both women searched through the bundle of loose grass.

"Find the thickest strips," Linh said, "at least an inch wide."

Kit and Linh each selected strips of grass and folded them over a cord of twisted green vines, each woman working from an opposite end. The grass was tied to the cord of vines and cut so that it stretched no more than the length of a forearm. Both women worked without talk until the final strips of grass had been joined.

When Linh asked Kit to try it on, the latter slipped behind a tree and soon returned wearing both the grass skirt and a sheepish grin— her left thigh was exposed. The skirt sat low on Kit's hips, slipping below her belly button and dangling down her thighs.

"We need to add a few more strips," Kit said.

"Turn around," Linh replied.

Kit turned.

"It covers your hips completely," Linh observed.

Kit faced Linh.

"Look," Kit said, "at the opening on my left side. I'm able to tie the belt, but the grass falls a little short."

"It looks like a slit dress," Linh said. "I like it."

"I don't," Kit said as she looked at the grass skirt. "I wore gowns to the Academy Awards that showed more skin than this, but it seems indecent here. In front of our neighbors and their children instead of strangers and cameras."

"You've changed."

"Or the style has. I've always been a slave to fashion."

"Swing your hips."

Kit rolled her hips and the grass swished around her thighs. Linh adjusted some of the grass strips before giving further instructions.

"Raise," Linh said, "your arms over your head. Now do it again."

This time Kit moved more rhythmically and let the skirt dance around her hips before asking how it looked.

"If Ryan jumps the altar," Linh declared, "I might marry you myself."

"Stop it, Linh!" Kit screamed a little. "Don't say that!"

"Don't worry," Linh laughed. "I like men. Especially Viet."

"I should hope so. He's given you two children."

"But it does look good. You look good. I wish I had your shape. Viet wishes I had your shape."

"He ought to be pleased with who he has. Your hips haven't an inch on mine—and you've given birth. Twice."

"Still," Linh said, "even nursing I've only half the bust you do."

Kit turned red.

"The blushing bride," Linh teased. "That ought to tempt Ryan long enough for a renewal of vows."

Kit looked away.

"What's wrong?" Linh asked.

"Nothing."

"You're a bad liar," Linh said. "Lies don't suit you."

"Ryan's eyes," Kit whispered as she crossed her arms across her breasts, "aren't on me."

"Viet's are," Linh said. "I guess they all look around too much."

"Does Viet flirt?"

"Not if he wants to live to see our girls grow an inch taller."

"There's yet another reason to have children."

Now Linh put her arm around Kit and asked what was wrong—though the former actress spoke only after a long while.

"It's as if," Kit said, "I'm not beautiful enough for him out here."

"You're the most beautiful of all," Linh said, "even if every one of us could use a long day at the spa. Every woman on the island is poorly dressed and in desperate need of a perm. And a few need a shave."

"Not me. I've got razors left."

"For goodness sake, give one to Lisa. She has more hair under her arms than my husband."

"Maria doesn't."

Linh said nothing.

"Ryan flirts with her too much," Kit said.

"Have you talked to him?"

"He said," Kit replied with a nod, "he'd tone it down, but he doesn't really see the problem."

When Linh asked what really was the matter, Kit observed her friend was more perceptive than Ryan—and Linh replied that mothers learn to prod for information while husbands strive not to notice anything amiss.

"I wouldn't know," Kit said with a shrug, "anything about mothers."

"You're still bickering with Ryan over a family, aren't you?"

"He just won't admit," Kit said as her eyes tightened, "I've a right to my own children. I was as much to blame for what we did, but I wish he could see how much it hurts."

"He's not a woman."

"That shouldn't matter."

"We all know it does," Linh said, "and it's silly to pretend otherwise. How can they know about the need for babies? For sons and daughters born of our own womb? They're only men. The whole lot of them don't share a single ovary. I've never met a single man who wanted to give birth."

Linh gave Kit a hug before the actress slipped behind the tree to change back to work clothes. The women then added two strips to the grass skirt and set it aside before designing a matching grass top and a bridal wreath of shells and feathers. When their work was done, they collected their tools and returned to the supply tent— where they chose food rations and a bottle of liquor to stock the honeymoon tent that Viet had pitched between the camp and the beach. After carrying the food and clothing to the tent, they took a break that involved several swigs of peach schnapps.

When she returned home, Kit made Ryan promise to keep from the tent until they'd married since she didn't want him to see her dress before the wedding—only two days away.

21

LOVE LOST—AND FOUND

On Sunday morning, several neighbors sat in the mess hall watching Tiffany prepare a breakfast of pancakes and omelets—served with juice and biscuits dripping with toppings from the remaining bottles of honey and maple syrup. After first helpings were eaten, villagers hurried back for seconds. Even Ursula had a healthy appetite and drank an extra glass of goat milk. While their wives assisted Kit with wedding preparations, Brent and Viet talked with Ryan. Only Maria sat alone, frequently looking toward Ryan as she sipped her coffee and listened to the men talk.

"My second wedding," Brent said, "was over before it began. No exaggeration. I said I do before I knew what I'd done."

"Kit wanted the same," Ryan said, "a quick fix she called it. But I insisted on giving her a proper wedding; it's the only theater available on the island."

"You ready for the big day?"

"I've got my best clothes pressed and Deidra's giving me a haircut and shave after I finish here. Sean said he'd fetch my last bottle of champagne."

"One bottle for all of us?" Brent groaned. "Is Paradise a dry county? We might as well be in the Bible Belt."

"Not to worry," Ryan said. "The champagne's for me and Kit. We've saved vodka and rum for the rest of you. Along with half a bottle of good scotch. From my personal supply."

"That's more like it," Brent said. "By the way, Tiff says Kit's honeymoon dress is stunning. She says you're marrying a goddess."

"It won't be the first time."

"Are you taking a honeymoon?" Viet asked.

"John's gone to bring a sailboat so we can cross to one of the motu for a little surf and sun."

"How long?"

"A couple days. We can use the rest. And the privacy."

"Very nice," Brent said.

Ryan sipped his coffee—as did Brent and Viet.

"You nervous?" Viet asked after a time.

"Not really. I'm marrying my own wife."

"Good point," Viet said with a grin. "It's like kissing a pregnant girl."

Now Maria moved a little closer to the men.

"Technically," Maria said as she looked at Ryan, "you're not marrying your own wife."

"Whose wife is she?" Ryan asked with a laugh.

"She's single," Maria answered, "and so are you. Your marriage is already dissolved."

"No," Ryan looked puzzled. "Today is the last day for renewals."

"Actually," Maria said, "yesterday was."

"Kit and I went over this twice," Ryan said, his voice a little strained, "and the decree was ratified Sunday afternoon. The fourteenth day comes between lunch and dinner today. That's why we're marrying before noon. To be sure."

Maria turned to a circle of neighbors scattered around the campfire, most of them eating. She motioned toward two women. "Come here, Hilary," she shouted. "Lisa, you too."

Now the two single women joined the conversation.

"We're talking," Maria said, "about the marriage decree. To decide whether or not Ryan and Kit are making new vows or renewing old ones."

"Of course they're married," Lisa said. "The renewal period is still in effect."

"Is it?" Maria said. "That's the point."

"Let's see," Hilary said, "counting calendar days ... Sunday was the first day ... and Saturday makes day seven ... times two is fourteen."

Hilary let out a little shriek.

"She's right," Hilary said, looking at Ryan. "I'm afraid you've been living in sin since midnight."

Several villagers laughed, though Ryan wasn't one of them.

"No," Ryan said. "We passed the law Sunday afternoon and it's still Sunday morning."

Hilary shook her head. "Don't you remember the by-law vote on committee service? We agreed to use calendar days for enforcing laws. That's how we send delegates to committees. We couldn't really have terms of service end at 2:58 p.m. on the mark, could we?"

Ryan's eyes opened wide.

"Legally," Hilary said, "your marriage dissolved at midnight. Last night."

"That means we can't marry for a month."

The laughter stopped.

"Kit will be heart-broken," Tiffany said.

"I've already announced we're married," Ryan said as his face reddened. "This wedding is just the celebration."

"You announced," Hilary noted, "your intent to marry. You made future promises, not present vows."

Ryan threw his drink to the ground. Hot coffee hissed as it splashed against cool earth.

"Everyone," Ryan declared, "knows our intent. We can't get tripped up on a technicality."

"The will of the people is not a technicality," Hilary protested.

"But you don't understand?" Ryan said. "Kit refused to live with me before we married. Some damned promise to her dying grandma."

"She'll understand," Maria said, "we all know you're married in the States and you'll be married here in a month. No one's going to judge her."

Perspiration beaded on Ryan's face and he ran his hands through his hair. He looked panicked.

"If we don't tell her," Ryan said, "she won't know. I'll have a month to explain. We have to go through the ceremony today. Nobody says a word."

"Secret adultery with your own wife?" Hilary said with a scowl. "I don't think so. You're free to do anything you wish with her. Nobody cares. But the law is binding—you can't call yourself married for the next thirty days."

"And what if we do?" Ryan said.

"Probably nothing," Hilary said with an edge to her voice, "but it'd need to go to Executive Council for adjudication."

"And perhaps the General Will of the People," Lisa added.

"You helped to set the rules," Hilary continued, "and you need to be a good model of sticking with them even when they're inconvenient. If you of all people don't, who will? The rules have to be played out. No changing horses midstream."

"Listen to the girl," Lisa said. "She's become Katherine Harris."

Almost everyone laughed.

Ryan took a straw poll of those at breakfast and found that the majority accepted Hilary's interpretation of the law. Leaving an uneaten omelet at the table, he set out for his own tent.

"Wish me well," Ryan said with a wince, "or I'll be sleeping with one of you. I mean, in one of your tents."

A couple men told him it'd go well, though none of the women spoke. Maria folded her hands in her lap and said nothing.

It didn't go well. Within ten minutes, anger echoed through the camp. Neither Ryan nor Kit shouted too loud, but both pressed their case without fear of being overheard. Kit complained Ryan was stalling and Ryan protested his only motive was to provide a nice ceremony. His now ex-wife wasn't placated and the distraught ex-husband soon returned to the campfire alone, announcing Kit intended to go away for a couple days and asking for help pitching a spare tent since he couldn't live with her until they remarried. Sean volunteered to help, though he also asked if the party was still on. When Ryan agreed the food shouldn't be wasted, Sean quipped that he'd sponsor Ryan's bachelor party that night—though he was the only one to laugh at his joke.

Within the hour, Tiffany and John had loaded Kit's sailboat with a few day's supplies and pushed the craft seaward. The canvas filled with a mild breeze and Kit tacked toward an islet less than five minutes away. Her friends watched from afar as she landed along a strip of sand and pulled the craft ashore. Though Tiffany begged Ryan to pay his wife an early morning visit to make amends—even if he had to swim through sharks to do so—Ryan believed it best to wait.

AFTER BRUNCH, Jason slipped into his tent to check his stash of weed, sorting through a dozen brick-sized blocks of marijuana and a pouch of loose leaves. He even unwrapped several packets to taste the dope and eventually chose a brick of Columbia Gold for the party. Pinching two ounces of the dope into a plastic bag, he also picked through the weed to save several dozen seeds for future planting. After choosing his favorite pipe and finding a packet of rolling papers, Jason set his party favors to the front of his tent, restacked the bricks of marijuana beside his bed, and covered them with canvas. It wasn't possible to be too careful. There were no connections on the island and he alone had an abundant supply of dope. Jason shook his head at the lack of foresight of those who came without necessities and meditated on the benefits his stash already had provided. Northern women were especially appreciative of his tangible wealth in commodities and futures.

Now Jason lay on his bed to rest, pushing a pile of mud-covered laundry to one side and tossing a blackened banana peel out his front door. When he tried to drink from his dry canteen, he struggled to decide whether to walk to the stream to quench his thirst or stay in bed to rest his eyes. He chose the latter and an hour passed before he rose from his nap—at which time he collected his bag of dope and moved toward the mess area, where he found both a loaf of stale bread and a jug of warm water. After eating and drinking, Jason walked to a field located near the lagoon: a trailer-sized patch of flat ground on which was staked the entire legalized drug industry of the west village. There, Jason sowed the seeds he'd selected into a shallow trench running across the field and found a hand shovel to fill in the trench. After covering the seeds with dirt and mulch, he watered the seeds with a spouted canister and surveyed his garden. He also secured several dozen seeds he planned to use to plant in the forest as a reserve.

Already, most plants stood several inches high and had been secured to five-foot stakes. The plants were circled by wet rings of overturned earth from which fish guts, scraps of toilet paper, and bits of bone protruded—and one fish head lay atop the fresh earth, a single eye staring heavenward, without life and without hope. Jason spent several minutes deciding whether the scene was more reminiscent of Bosch or Dali, but couldn't make up his mind, so he opened his dope pouch and rolled a joint. Within a few minutes, he stood at the dope garden, a smile on his face and a smoking joint pinched between his forefinger and thumb. While he still couldn't decide which artist was more likely to have painted the scene, he no longer really cared.

"Can I have a hit?"

Jason turned around and saw that Ilyana now stood behind him wearing a tan halter top that blended with her olive-toned chest and black shorts that draped the narrow hips of a girl still in her puberty.

Jason handed her the joint.

"I didn't know you partied," Jason said. "I thought you still played with dolls."

"I babysit," Ilyana said, "but this is more fun."

Ilyana took a drag of the dope—and coughed as she exhaled—while Jason did the same without coughing.

"A day with those kids makes me tense," Ilyana said. "Do you have a stash of this stuff?"

"Enough," Jason said.

Ilyana drew more smoke.

"This," Ilyana said after she exhaled, "would get you a couple years for contributing to the delinquency of a minor back in the States."

"But you were delinquent before you ever came here. Right?"

"Maybe."

"Then I've contributed nothing but the dope."

"My mama would have your hide."

"She doesn't know?"

"She knows I party," Ilyana said, "but I promised to keep it to our own tent till I graduate."

"Why so strict?"

"She doesn't trust anyone."

"How long have you smoked?"

"Maybe a year. A couple times a week when I can get the stuff. We ran out in Sodom."

"Sodom?"

"That's what the east village calls itself. It's majority gay."

"That's really funny," Jason said.

"You got anything to eat? I missed dinner."

"There's bread and jelly over there," Jason said, pointing to a shadowed area near the trail.

As Ilyana walked toward the food, Jason warned her to be careful not to step on his plants—so the girl tiptoed around the tender shoots, though she caught one with her foot and uprooted it a little. Jason immediately cut back a broken branch and marked the spot for fertilization before sharing with Ilyana the pleasures of good dope and good food—feasting from a loaf of flat bread and a jar of pineapple jelly. After the dope was burned and the food eaten, Jason napped near his garden while Ilyana sauntered home to an empty tent (where a note explained Olivia had gone to curl Maria's hair).

. . .

RYAN ATE alone at his bachelor party. Several partiers offered condolences and Sean congratulated him for a narrow escape, but the actor said little. After an hour of polite conversation, Ryan took a bottle of champagne and an empty flute monogrammed with two sets of initials and an anniversary date and walked down the beach toward a quiet place beside some coconut palms. He had stared at the horizon for an hour when a voice sounded from the dark.

"Is that champagne for show or drink?"

Maria had quietly crossed the sand and stood nearby—her auburn hair set in a bun, long dangling curls falling in front of her ears. She wore a satin sweater and a white skirt wrapped tight around her hips and golden earrings that jingled when she moved. Her face shined from cosmetics and sun lotion and the fragrance of perfume drifted before her.

"You smell nice," Ryan said. "You look nice."

"It was supposed to be for your wedding, but I decided to throw it on for the party. It's been a while since I've had an excuse to dress up."

Ryan offered Maria his flute.

"We'll have to share," Ryan said. "The match is at the tent."

"That's fine."

They sat in the sand, well beyond earshot of the party.

Ryan pointed to a flickering light in the dark of the sea. "I can see her campfire," he observed, "through the brush."

"Do you miss her?"

"It'll do us good to have some time away from each other. We've done nothing but bicker for weeks. Ever since the decree."

When Maria asked if he was glad to have come to this place, Ryan blushed and asked where exactly she meant.

"This island," Maria said.

"It's been a challenge," Ryan answered after a pause, "but I've learned a lot. About myself, about life, about Kit."

"So have I," Maria said. "Thank you so much for bringing us here. For bringing me here. This really is paradise, especially tonight. The sway of the palms and the cool of the breeze are perfect."

Ryan poured a glass of champagne and took a sip. After Maria finished what remained, he refilled the glass.

"The party's breaking up early," Maria observed after she took a sip of the champagne.

"Tomorrow's a work day," Ryan said.

Maria sipped a little more champagne and Ryan followed suit. As slow-gliding gulls soared overhead and fast-moving clouds eclipsed a crescent moon, the young woman nodded toward the heavens.

"It's peaceful here," Maria said.

"We call it Paradise."

Maria took a long drink of champagne that drained the glass, so Ryan poured another.

"Cheers," Ryan said. "To the first day of my month as a bachelor."

"Cheers."

The two sat still for several minutes. One last group of neighbors left the party, making noisy farewells that echoed down the shore. As their shouts and laughter faded, the beach fell silent and Maria continued to look at Ryan: her eyes fastened on his. After several seconds, she batted her eyes.

"What?" Ryan said as the young woman stood to her feet.

"Stand up and turn around," she said.

"Why?"

"Turn around. I've brought a gift for your bachelor party."

"I didn't see any gift."

"You will."

A puzzled look came across Ryan's face as he did what he was told, taking the champagne flute from Maria's hand. He heard a little shuffling behind him, but didn't turn around until told.

"Now what is this sup ..."

Ryan choked on his words when he saw that Maria stood in front of him undressed, her skirt dropped to the sand and her breasts bare and belly uncovered—her unbuttoned blouse slipped behind her shoulders. As the young woman inched forward, he himself took a step back, though his eyes remained fixed on Maria's breasts.

"You promised me a swim," Maria whispered.

Ryan turned deep red.

"I never ..."

"Yes," Maria whispered as she stepped closer, "you did. You promised me a skinny-dip if you were ever single."

"But I'm not ..."

"But you are," Maria said as she closed the distance to Ryan, her breasts now pressing his chest. She reached with one hand to pull Ryan's face toward her lips while taking one of his hands with the other.

Ryan felt the young woman's breasts warm through his shirt and her hips snuggle against his own. As desire stirred, he dropped the glass and the couple slid to the sand in an unbroken embrace.

Several minutes later they sat up and retrieved their clothing.

"You still owe me a swim," Maria said.

"Now?"

Maria's eyes flashed from pleasure. "Maybe another time," she said, twirling her bra with a forefinger. "I have to work tomorrow."

After dressing, the couple walked hand in hand until they reached the village, where muffled sounds emanated from several of the village's tents as Ryan and Maria embraced one last time before separating for the night.

22

BROKEN HEARTS AND A HONEYMOON

Ryan didn't sleep. Aflame with passion, he spent the night remembering Maria's touch, craving more, and fretting over the implications of an affair. At first light, he crept toward an orange tent pitched at the end of a row. It didn't take long to reach his destination.

"Maria! Maria!" Ryan whispered as he unzipped the door. "Wake up, Maria."

Maria rolled out of bed and smiled. "Back so soon?"

"We need to talk."

"Talk is cheap," Maria said as she sat up and pulled Ryan close.

"Not now," Ryan whispered as he grabbed the young woman's hands. "John gets up early—and he's cooking today."

"Two cook hotter than one."

"Be serious. We need to talk while we can."

The smile left Maria's face as she fell back to her bed and told Ryan to speak his mind.

"I don't want Kit to know," Ryan said. "Not yet."

"How can we keep it from her?"

"I don't plan to have an affair."

"What do you call this?"

"I'm not married, so it's not an affair."

"Where does that leave us?" Maria said. "I'm not a one-night stand."

"You won't be," Ryan replied. "Let's enjoy the whole month."

"Till you marry her?" Maria said with a scowl.

"If I marry her."

Maria looked Ryan in the eyes and asked what he meant.

"What I mean," Ryan said, "is I'm pretty confused right now. I didn't sleep a wink all night. I love Kit and I ..."

Ryan looked at Maria. "Well," he said, "I'm rather taken with you and I realized last night I have been for quite a while."

"Then why marry her?"

"I need to figure out what's right for you and for Kit. And for me. Give me a few weeks."

"Then what?"

"I don't know," Ryan said, "but if you and I are meant to be, it'll at least buy me a little time to let her down gently."

Maria said nothing.

"She is my wife," Ryan whispered.

"Was your wife," Maria replied.

"As a favor," Ryan said as he looked away, "I'm asking you to let me tell her."

"Will you?"

"Yes," Ryan said, "I have to. We've had no lies between us. I never cheated on her and I never will."

"Will she want you when she finds out?"

Ryan shrugged.

"You don't belong to her any longer," Maria said, "but I'll do as you ask. Provided two things."

"Anything," Ryan said, his face a little less tense.

"First, you don't live with her until you decide for sure which of us you want."

"And second?"

"I sleep with you whenever I want."

"But privately," Ryan said.

Maria nodded.

"Fine," Ryan said, "but if Kit and I stay together, you and I are done. No married men, remember?"

Maria didn't answer. Already she had slipped from her sleeping shirt and nestled against Ryan. They shared a warm kiss, then a hot bed. When they were finished, Maria signaled the coast was clear as Ryan stole away.

KIT LEANED AGAINST A COCONUT TREE. The morning sun was shaded by palm fronds as she listened to the flow of wind through a chorus of branches. A bird flitted before her, hopping around a scrap of dropped food while looking about nervously. Kit whistled to it, but the bird took wing and left a day's meal behind.

"Sorry, little one."

Now Kit stood, yawning as she rose. Her arms tensed, her back arched, and her ankles extended as she stretched. She wiped the sleep from her dark-ringed eyes and relaxed, then adjusted her cotton blouse—insuring its straps were secured across her shoulders and its flaps tucked into her shorts. She collected her sandals and a bag of food before walking to the beach, where soon the surf splashed her ankles and the sun radiated warmth from every direction.

At the beach, Kit heard the sound of a distant cry and looked to sea where the fin of a small whale flashed across the surface before slipping beneath the water. She watched for its return, but saw nothing and after a long wait returned to the shade of the palms where she knocked a coconut from a low-lying branch and cracked its hull with a machete. She ate, drank, and slept—then napped all morning.

At noon, Kit started a fire in a shallow pit that she dug with a stick and baked flat bread mixed from flour, salt, and yeast. While the bread baked, she took a swim in the nude—though careful to insure no one watched from afar. With the sun beating down, she decided not to risk burning what hadn't been tanned and retreated into shade to rinse herself with fresh water (brought in plastic jugs) and slip into clean clothes. Soon, she pulled the bread from the fire, brewed some tea, and spent an hour doodling in the sand with a broken stick as she ate. Several times she stroked the unstretched skin of her belly and gave long looks to her own narrow hips. She cried once and laughed twice. Thoughts came to mind of children, neighbors, Ryan ...

Kit remembered her years with Ryan: the promises and compromises, the hopes and disappointments. She remembered girls who'd propositioned him and how he'd always turned from temptation—a few times after a moment's hesitation. So many of his friends took mistresses, but never Ryan. He was a flirt, but a faithful one who returned to his own bed each night; he even used doubles for love scenes at her request. Kit wondered how their marriage could be made to work.

"We're tired and torn," she said out loud, as if to convince herself, "but he's my husband and we have to keep our love strong. Maybe a month to ourselves will be good. It'll be like starting over."

Kit remembered her promise to her grandmother and debated whether it remained obligatory. After all, Ryan was a husband on her grandmother's terms and remained so under American law. Still, she wasn't in America and decided she'd have to sleep alone until they could sort the rules out. Though she wondered whether solitude was a good idea, she thought it necessary for her own self-respect and that of Ryan. He'd be patient, she told herself, as he had been before. It was only solitude she asked of him, not celibacy.

Already, Kit sensed her anger dissipating and concern for Ryan returning. She remembered how the same confusion often tried her whenever they'd been stressed on film sets. As always, a day away had softened her heart.

"Another day alone," Kit said, "and I'll go home. Then we can work on our marriage. Or whatever it is now."

Kit lay down on the grass and slept. The sun was hot and she tossed and turned the entire nap, dreaming of Ryan and babies and faithless girls.

.   .   .

ON MONDAY, the villagers rose early and worked hard. When the temperature grew hot and tempers flared, Heather asked everyone to break early since quotas had been exceeded. Linh suggested a picnic and most neighbors agreed that a barbecue sounded nice. By late afternoon, tables were moved to the beach and food brought by the armful: star fruit, kiwi, lemons, mangos, breadfruit, coconuts, bananas, pineapples, rice, bread, cheese, milk, clams, crab, lobster, perch, and even a cask of palm wine. Sean traded the smallest of the neighborhood's she-goats to southerners for a dozen chickens— which allowed Tiffany to grill four unproductive hens.

While Tiffany and Heather cooked, Linh watched the children play. Two northern boys with big teeth and skinny arms joined them; the boys carrying homemade bows strung with vines and quivers filled with bone-tipped arrows. Linh's daughters joined the visitors as boy and girl alike practiced shooting into a chalk-marked palm tree. Theodore and Ted spied on them from behind a panandu bush. Occasionally, the girls waved at the twins, sending the little boys face-first into the dust, laughing like fools.

Adults played volleyball. Sean retrieved a net from New Plymouth's recreation tent and set it up (with Jose's help) while teams were picked. Ryan, Maria, Jose, Linh, Tiffany, Viet, Olivia, and Ilyana played against Charles, Joan, Deidra, Sean, Brent, Hilary, Lisa, and Heather. John left after a quick dinner while Jason played only a single match before walking north. Ursula tallied score as she sipped tea from a lawn chair.

The first game went to Ryan's team by a six-point margin and the second game by eight points. But after two games on the hot sand, most players perspired and Charles removed his shirt. Sean and Brent did the same. Lisa soon declared their team the Skins and told her teammates to strip their shirts. Everyone did so except Heather— who held fast to her tee shirt and propriety alike even when Joan tugged at the former and declared her daughter had plenty to show. Ryan and Viet also wanted to play shirtless, but the Skins insisted the Shirts remain clothed. With the changed uniforms, momentum shifted toward the bare-chested team, their opponents worn down by the heat and distracted by the sight of so much flesh. Jose, in particular, played poorly, spending most of the game eyeing anything but the volleyball. The shirted team lost the next two games (by three and six points respectively) and were skunked in the game match.

After volleyball was finished and the party broke into small groups, Linh and Tiffany—with their husbands and children—walked down the beach to enjoy the sunset. Ryan and Maria retired early (walking home just a couple minutes apart) and Charles and Joan joined a circle of pot smokers. Olivia told her Ilyana to insure the northern boys reached home before dark while Heather directed the western children to collect trash. It was just after the children disappeared into the forest to collect litter that Jose tapped Heather's shoulder.

"Enjoy the game?"

"It was fun," Heather said. "You?"

"It was interesting, to say the least."

"Sorry I didn't entertain you like the others."

Jose blushed. "You have your standards."

"So do they," Heather said, "just not the same ones."

"To each his own, they say."

"Who says that?"

"Either Cicero or Hugh Hefner: one of the great philosophers of human friendship."

Heather forced a smile as Jose dropped his eyes, glancing at her legs before staring into sand.

"I was wondering," the young man said, "if you'd like to take a walk."

Heather didn't take too long to answer. "That'd be nice, I guess."

"Great."

"First let me finish here. Can we meet in a few minutes?"

"Fine by me."

"Half an hour?" Heather asked.

Jose didn't object and the two soon parted—with Jose hurrying to the stream to wash and Heather marching four children single file toward the west village.

Ilyana had more trouble with the northern boys—who left under protest and only then after stuffing their pockets with dried bread and sun-warmed fruit while complaining that they were being starved by their own village. Ilyana let them take as much as they could carry, then filled a bag with fresh citrus, found an unlit torch, and started north.

AN HOUR after she agreed to take a walk, Heather returned to the beach dressed in a sleeveless summer dress. Her hair was braided and her feet shod with leather sandals.

Jose also wore clean clothes: a cotton shirt and tan shorts.

Heather smiled at him.

"I didn't know," Heather said, "we were going so formal."

"I'm in rags next to you."

"Where to?"

"What'd you want to do?"

"A movie sounds good. Do you have the listings?"

Jose shook his head.

"Well," Heather continued, "a walk down the beach would be nice too."

"That I can do," Jose said. "Panoramic vision and widescreen. 360-degree sound and 3-D vision."

Heather walked toward the shore as Jose moved beside her. He kept close enough occasionally to brush her hand, but not so close that he did so often. At the shore, they removed sandals in the shallows and let the tide lap their ankles. At first they talked of the day's activities, but conversation abruptly ended when Jose made a joke about Heather's shirtless teammates. Only after several minutes did they again converse. An hour into their date, they found themselves on a somewhat unfamiliar stretch of beach, well past the northern border.

"I don't remember this place," Heather said.

"I've been here before," Jose answered, "but the rocks look different under the moon."

Heather sat on a weatherworn rock and Jose sat beside her. The rock wasn't more than a yard wide and their hips were only a few inches apart, despite the fact they'd edged as far apart as possible. Both looked to sea for several minutes.

Heather spoke first. "Sometimes," she said, "I miss New York."

Jose said he was from Los Angeles.

"New York," Heather mused, "had so many different things to do."

"And," Jose countered, "so many different types of crime and poverty and prejudice. The whole thing was predicated upon oppression and distinction and police brutality."

Heather shrugged. "Not Central Park."

"No?" Jose said. "I visited it in junior high. The crackheads sat in their waste and dealers sold drugs in the open. They even offered dope to me, even though I was only twelve."

"It's worth another visit since Giuliani cleaned it up."

"Since he turned it into a prison ward."

"I don't know about that. Even my mother felt safer the last few years."

"Thousands of convicts and jaywalkers might disagree."

"I suppose so," Heather said, "but they chose which streets to walk and which corners to cut."

"Chose?"—Jose grew somewhat agitated—"Between poverty and prison? That's a dilemma or a tragedy, not a choice."

Heather didn't reply and several minutes passed without conversation.

"Are you staying long?" Jose finally asked. "On the island, I mean."

"I haven't decided," Heather answered. "My parents claim they're here for good, but I'd like to go to college."

"Where?"

"Dad says I should consider Columbia, but I prefer Fordham if they make me stay in New York. To tell the truth, I've always dreamed of a Big Ten school. But I don't know if we have the money any longer. They gave away everything when they came here—except for their retirement."

"Public schools are cheap. At least in-state tuition is."

"Except I'm not sure if I'm even a U.S. citizen or a resident of New York since my parents surrendered their citizenship when we moved."

"I hadn't thought of that."

"I have," Heather said. "Who knows? Maybe I'll stay here a while."

"No one would mind."

"You see," Heather said with a smile, "the irony, don't you?"

Jose shook his head not.

"The twist," the young woman explained, "is the egalitarian ideals my parents preached in the university were cosmopolitan and urbane; but it's here that we have real equality, though not always a progressive lifestyle. If I'd announced in New York I wanted to be a housewife, my mother would've sent me to a boarding school. Now I wonder if I even have another choice. I'm certainly not going to take up the family business of teaching college."

"You have quite the wit," Jose said with a laugh. "Perhaps you can develop your writing skills. I hear the east village will be doing plays this winter."

"Maybe," Heather said, "if we make it through the first winter like the pilgrims did at Plymouth. Of course, I'm still too young for them to take me all that seriously."

"You look old enough to me."

Heather dropped her eyes to her lap as Jose moved nearer and pulled her close. When she didn't respond, he scooted closer yet and leaned forward, his face nearing hers until Heather gently stopped him—her fingertips pushing back his chest.

"I'd rather not."

"It's not wrong," Jose said after a moment. "Especially on this island. You're legal."

"There's more than the law."

"It's okay with your parents."

"What isn't?"

"Why not? What are you saving yourself for?"

"Love."

"You can share a little companionship while you wait."

"I'd rather wait alone."

"You're not," Jose said, "going to find romance in a convent. You have to make love to find love."

"Love," Heather said in an almost inaudible voice, "isn't what Ursula found in Sean's bed."

Now Jose drew back. "I'm sorry."

"Don't be," Heather answered. "It's only our first date."

Jose's eyes brightened. "Do you want to go out again?"

"I don't know. Let's not be in a hurry."

After a long pause, Jose said it was getting late and perhaps they needed to leave and Heather agreed. It didn't take the unpaired couple long to reach the beach (where a log still smoldered in the main campfire) and then the trail to their own village. They moved quietly in the night, a flashlight in Jose's hand to direct their feet past marijuana fields, cornfields, and an empty honeymoon tent. At Heather's tent, they parted without a kiss.

ILYANA ESCORTED the two northern boys within sight of their own village before shouting through the dark for their parents. When a woman's voice said she didn't know the boys ever had left, Ilyana turned around and hurried south. Just a minute later she heard the sound of fast moving feet and looked back to see the shadow of a man jogging toward her. She asked who it was and breathed easy when she heard Jason's voice. After Jason caught his breath, he pulled a thick joint and a thin lighter from his pocket, offering Ilyana the first toke.

The two walked slow as they smoked the joint and stopped altogether for a second one. When they finally started home, their steps were unsteady and it took the better part of a laughter-filled hour before they reached the beach (after being lost twice). The fire pit was reduced to embers and already the tide neared it. Jason rummaged through scraps of food, but found only a single brown banana—which they split. When he cursed a bite of cold crab leg as inedible,

Ilyana burst into laughter, thinking even her own ravenous hunger quite hilarious.

Jason pointed to the moon. "What I wouldn't give," he declared, "for a block of good cheese. Even half a block. Or a quarter."

"We can't reach it. It's too high."

"We need to get even higher."

Ilyana smiled, her eyes bloodshot and glassy and told Jason to find her a cow to jump over the moon.

"Or," Jason said, "a dish to run off with the spoon."

"Sounds likes drugs," Ilyana said with a giggle. "And munchies."

Jason found a second banana, divided it into equal portions, and ate. He threw its peel into the brush.

"I'm still hungry."

"Let's find food," Ilyana said.

Jason pulled a bag of dope from his pocket. "Man does not live by bread alone," he observed.

Ilyana shrugged and said she needed a bite to eat as she started down the trail.

"One for the road?" Jason asked as he followed the girl.

"Let's hurry," Ilyana said, "or the best food will be gone."

Ilyana walked down the trail and Jason moved beside her. He lit the joint anyway and Ilyana gave in. Not withstanding her hunger, she took several hits. As they finished it, they came to a clearing between the beach and village where a tent stood pitched near the trail.

"It's the honeymoonless suite," Ilyana said. "Maybe there's food."

Now the stoned teenager unzipped the front flap to the six-foot tent and stepped in. Jason followed and struck a match, lighting several candles already arranged on the floor. Using the flickering candlelight, Ilyana opened a basket in which she discovered crackers, jelly, and over-ripe fruit—and even a wide bar of Belgian chocolate.

"Paydirt!" Ilyana announced.

"Here we go," Jason said as he unscrewed the cap from a half-full bottle of peach schnapps.

Ilyana ate chocolate and Jason drank liquor; then they traded and

Ilyana drank while Jason ate. Indeed, they ate until they licked the last taste of chocolate from their fingers and stuffed the last crumbs of cracker into their mouths. When the schnapps was gone, Ilyana fell to the grass-stuffed mattress.

"I can't walk me to home," the girl said. "Tell me mother not worry."

As Ilyana folded her hands and closed her eyes, neither saying her prayers nor crossing herself that night, Jason stared through the flickering light of the burning candle at the narrow hips and slender legs of the teenager. After a few minutes, he snuffed the wick with a pinch of his fingers and told Ilyana her mother would just have to worry.

Ilyana didn't protest since she already was passed out.

23

CRIME AND ITS PUNISHMENT

A dozen villagers drank coffee and ate breakfast rolls as Olivia approached, still dressed in the oversized jersey she'd worn to bed. Her eyes were bloodshot and her voice concerned as she squinted into the early morning sun.

"Anyone seen Ilyana?"

Several neighbors shook their heads.

"That girl," Olivia said, "is always running off. Probably to the north camp this time."

Heather pointed north. "She was taking those boys home."

"When?"

"Near dusk."

"Well," Olivia said, "I need to go find her. I suppose she's with those people."

Viet looked to Brent—who rose from his seat.

"I could use a walk," Brent said as he followed Olivia into the woods. While everyone else speculated about possible explanations, Hilary brewed another pot of coffee and Heather served a tray of rolls.

Conversation continued until the sharp sound of a woman's scream sounded from the forest, followed in a breath by a second scream—this one more girlish and more anguished than the first. Jose and Viet jumped to their feet and sprinted toward the commotion, though fleet-footed Lisa passed them before they'd reached the woods. Hilary also chased after them, lagging only a little behind. All four arrived within seconds of each other at the privacy tent—where Jason stood stark naked as Brent held his wrists fast and Olivia pulled someone from the tent. The other person resisted as Olivia slipped and was dragged inside. A few seconds later yet another scream sounded—this one quite clearly from pain—and a red-faced Olivia stumbled from the tent while pulling her half-dressed daughter by the hair.

Ilyana cried for her mother to let go, but Olivia paid no heed.

"Shut up, slut!" Olivia screamed, "We're going home."

"Leave me alone!" Ilyana yelled back.

When Olivia raised the back of her hand to strike, Jason grabbed her wrist until the enraged mother broke free and directed a well-aimed kick to his unprotected groin. Though Jason tried to evade, Brent's grip had immobilized him and the kick struck square and hard. Jason screamed in pain and buckled at the knees, his wrist twisting from Brent's grasp as he fell to the ground.

Only then did Lisa interpose herself between Jason and his attacker. "No more," she shouted to Olivia, "let's sort this out."

"That bastard," Olivia pointed at Jason—who was clenching his groin with both hands while sobbing, "that bastard defiled my daughter."

Olivia pushed Lisa aside and aimed a second kick to Jason's groin, but this time the latter was able to roll away and the kick caught only his thigh. Though he screamed again, his shout was not as loud as before. Brent jumped over him and grabbed Olivia—who struggled only briefly before relenting. Her fight was elsewhere.

Now Olivia glared at her daughter, hunched in front of the tent, tears welling in the girl's eyes—one hand pulling an undersized tee shirt past her bellybutton and the other covering a thin veil of pubic hair.

"He's twice your age," Olivia said, her teeth clenched and voice low.

"I didn't do anything," Ilyana cried, breaking into a childish sob. "I didn't do anything."

"Don't lie to me," Olivia shouted. "How could you give yourself to this creep?"

"I swear ..."

Lisa stepped between the young girl and the men, shielding the girl's naked hips with her own body.

"Not here," Lisa told Olivia before turning to Ilyana. "Get yourself dressed so we can deal with this at home."

Ilyana went into the tent as Lisa followed. The flap fell shut and the others soon heard whispering and weeping. When Lisa emerged, her face was grimmer than before as she pointed straight at Jason—who'd finally stopped moaning and had sat up, though his cheeks remained tight from pain and eyes red from tears.

"We have a problem," Lisa said.

Olivia clenched her teeth and asked what she meant.

"Ilyana says," Lisa explained, "she passed out. From drinking and dope. She didn't wake up till you screamed at her—and she saw a naked man beside her. She remembers a bad dream about Jason and her having ... but she insists it was only a nightmare."

Olivia wept.

Brent turned on Jason. "Did you do her?"

"Yeah," Jason said as looked away. "We did it."

Olivia groaned.

"Did you rape her?" Brent growled.

"It wasn't like that," Jason said. "She wanted it."

"Was she drunk?"

"Smell her breath."

"Don't be a smart ass," Brent said.

"We both were. And high. I didn't mean ..."

Olivia sprang for him, her fists clenched. "She's fifteen."

Lisa grabbed Olivia by the hair and jerked the frenzied mother to a stop. "Not that way," she said. "The people will have their say in this."

Olivia shook herself free, slipped into the tent, and returned with her daughter—whose nakedness now was covered with rumpled shorts stinking of schnapps and smoke.

"I'm sorry," Olivia cried as she held her daughter fast. "I'm sorry. I'm so sorry."

Ilyana and Olivia both wailed and sobbed as they slowly returned to camp while their neighbors turned away in shame-faced silence.

Only after the two women were gone did Brent speak. "What do we do with him?" he asked.

"He goes to trial," Lisa answered. "I'll call for a jury of his peers."

"I suppose," Brent said, "that'll do—though what we really need is a good old-fashioned lynch mob."

Lisa sprinted to camp and called for an emergency meeting while Brent pushed Jason toward camp.

THE HEARING BEGAN SHORTLY after Kit returned to the island in early afternoon. Ilyana remained in her tent, nursed by her mother—with Lisa speaking for the teenaged girl and Jason conducting his own defense. There was little debate regarding matters of fact. While both sides agreed the pair stumbled to the tent after partying and spent the night, Jason insisted the sex was consensual—claiming he laid down alone, but the girl had crawled to him after he blew out the candles. Too stoned to resist temptation, he slept with her. He wept as he testified and swore to make amends—including a promise of marriage if Ilyana and her mother would have him.

Lisa testified otherwise. She said Ilyana admitted being too stoned to return home and remembered an erotic dream (possibly with Jason), but was shocked when she woke to find Jason undressed beside her. She claimed Ilyana didn't realize she was partially naked until after she had been dragged outside the tent—clear evidence that the girl hadn't willingly disrobed. Finally, Lisa testified that

Olivia wished to charge Jason with sexual assault and intoxicating a minor with intent to seduce.

After debating facts of law and intent, villagers indicted Jason on three counts of rape: statutory, date, and forcible. He was remanded to the General Will of the People for criminal trial and confined to the privacy tent and supervised work detail until his hearing. When Lisa was told to summon the rest of the island to New Plymouth for the coming Sunday, she stripped to olympiad essentials of running shoes and jogging shorts and sprinted toward the beach—returning only after notifying each of the other villages of the summons and successfully organizing a trial in New Plymouth for Sunday. By the time Lisa returned, it was nearly dark and most villagers already had retired: it proving too shameful to face each other around the campfire in light of the tragedy that had befallen Paradise. Residents simply wanted to put an early end to a day that had turned their dreams into nightmares. They wanted to start a new day as soon as possible.

But though the villagers retired early, few slept well. The wailing despair of Ilyana's persistent weeping unnerved everyone, her sobs and cries penetrating every nylon wall. Breakfast was served early and most islanders drank three or four cups of coffee to recover from sleeplessness and shock. Ursula served Ilyana breakfast in bed and Kit took all four children—the only ones to sleep well—for a day hike. Work details were completed with little chatter and supper served early. Jason faced grim remarks about hanging, especially by Tiffany and Ursula, and word came after supper that staff psychologist Dr. Erikson planned to visit the next morning. No one talked around the fire and lamps were extinguished early for a second night. And once again, neither the whispering of companionship nor the rustling of love was heard.

EARLY MORNING SHADOWS hadn't yet dissipated when Heather opened her eyes. Though the day was just dawning, the pungent stench of burning marijuana already drifted into her tent. The air was so foul she coughed.

"Doesn't he ever learn?" Heather said as she pulled yesterday's shirt over her bare shoulders and reached for shoes and socks set neatly beside her pillow. As the smoke grew thicker, she shouted out loud to Jason.

"Put it out. That stuff makes me sick."

No one answered.

Heather sat up. She hadn't noticed the stench of pot so thick before. Sometimes Jason's smoke drifted her way but it was seldom more than a strong odor, like the burning of leaves in a neighbor's yard. Something seemed wrong, so Heather unzipped her tent to take a look. When she stuck her head outside she saw smoke billowing from Jason's tent.

"Fire!"

Heather's scream was shrill and instinctive as she jumped outside and darted toward the burning tent before stopping to cry out a second time.

"Tent fire! Tent fire!"

Alerted neighbors scrambled from their tents. Within the minute, several villagers helped with the fire. Linh and Deidra evacuated their children while others raced toward the tool shed to get shovels and axes as Lisa took charge.

"Pull the stakes up!" Lisa commanded.

Ryan and Maria pulled stakes from one side while Hilary and Jose pulled them from the other. The tent collapsed inward: smoke and fire pouring through the nylon walls, opened vents, and front flap.

"Drag it," Lisa shouted, "by the lines."

Volunteer firepersons grabbed the four corners of the tent while Lisa seized the front flap. Heather stayed behind to deal with a grass fire as the others pulled the tent toward an open field. As flames blazed heavenward and smoke burned their eyes, the volunteers each held breath as long as able and moved as fast as possible. Still, by the time they reached the edge of camp, the tent and everything in it—Jason's sleeping bag, clothing, personal effects, stash—were ablaze and all five volunteer firepersons had inhaled considerable amounts of smoke. A few yards more and the villagers dropped their corners to escape the burning heat and gasp for fresh air. All five emerged from the smoke coughing.

Help arrived as Joan and Sean brought shovels and axes while John and Charles carried buckets of water. Brent and Viet brought bags of sand to the original tent site—where Heather had beat down burning grass with a worn blouse retrieved from her tent.

"Jason's tent caught fire," Heather shouted as she pointed toward the tent now burning outside camp—still obscured by smoke that hung heavy and thick in the air.

John scowled. "How much dope did he bring?"

"Apparently not enough," Brent said.

Everyone smiled just a little. Viet and Brent used his shovel to stamp out burning bits of tent marking where the flaming tent had been dragged while John and Charles returned their buckets of water to the storage shed and Heather walked toward the smoke rising from the edge of camp. The laughter of the volunteer firepersons was growing more raucous, so Heather picked up her pace. By the time she reached the burned out tent, the five volunteers were standing around a pile of smoldering ashes. The gray smoke rolling from the ashes smelled of dope.

Ryan stuck his face into the gray smoke and took a deep breath as the others watched. "Talk about the mother of all doobies," he said. "The smoldering flames of hell."

"Jason's hell," Hilary said.

"Jason's heaven," Lisa countered.

"Now it's just a big roach," Jose said.

"Anyone got a clip?" Maria said.

"You look like one big roach yourself," Hilary said, pointing at soot covering Ryan's face.

Ryan laughed and a series of inane jokes began—which grew more ridiculous by the word, even as laughter grew less restrained. Within minutes, Jose and Hilary rolled in the dirt holding their sides and Lisa wandered glassy-eyed into the forest while Ryan and Maria sprinted toward the bridge, peeling clothes as they ran.

Heather looked into the woods and took one step to follow them, but decided otherwise before returning to her tent. After inspecting it for damage, she retrieved a tent patching kit to plug several holes burned through the thin nylon of the tent by flying sparks and burning embers.

LUNCH CONSISTED of chicken noodle soup with rice (made from freeze-dried reserves), flatbread, and fruit salad mixed with pineapple, kiwi, and mangos. Juice and coffee were served too. Sean was finishing his soup just as Heather approached.

"Waitress," Sean said, "I'd like to order a hamburger."

"Would you like that priority mail or express delivery?"

"Which keeps the fries hotter?"

"That would be priority," Heather said and everyone laughed, "but express and dry ice work better for soft-serve ice cream."

"Tell me why," Kit asked as she raised her hands in mock disgust, "we didn't bring cattle."

"Ask your husband," Jose said. "He's the genius in charge of this enterprise."

Kit looked around. "Where," she asked, "is the genius? I haven't seen him all morning."

"He helped extinguish the fire," John said. "I'd guess he went to clean up afterwards."

Kit turned toward Heather. "Have you seen him?"

"Not since the fire," the young woman said, looking to the ground.

"You're acting," Sean said, "like a wife."

"I am ..." Kit stopped herself. "Well, an actress acts and we're not exactly divorced."

Now there was a lull in the conversation as Kit looked away and Sean said nothing more.

"Anyway," Jose said after a moment, "even I'd wage war for a glass of milk."

"I'd sell myself into slavery for a bite of cheese," Ursula said and Charles added he'd vote with the bourgeoisie for a bagel. The jokes opened a floodgate and a dozen different acts of self-abnegation were tied to a dozen different meals. Linh and Viet agreed to trade future children for Chinese takeout, though Tiffany and Brent disagreed between themselves which boy to trade for filet mignon—and their boys seemed eager to exchange both parents for sodas and fries. John offered a toe for a leg of lamb and Hilary said she'd trade her next boyfriend for a cola. Ursula offered to serve Sean for dinner.

"He's gamey," Ursula declared, "but if we spit roast him with plenty of sauce and stuff a pineapple up his ... into his mouth, we'd all get our fill."

Everyone laughed except Sean and Deidra whose groans brought an end to the laughter. Indeed, there was a long pause until wild shrieks of laughter punctured the silence. Olivia had returned to the public square and now threw uprooted plants into the fire, dancing and shouting as she fed the flames. When Linh asked what she was doing, Olivia laughed out loud. Other arrived only after the last plant was aflame.

"That's the end of it," Olivia announced.

Kit asked if she was okay.

"I'm better now that this village is drug free. That is his last dope plant. Correction. Was his last dope plant."

Everyone looked as a plant—perhaps a foot high with roots—burning as its smoke spiraled toward the sky and Deidra grabbed Olivia by the arm and asked if she'd set the tent on fire. Olivia said it was the first time she had ever lit dope and thought her effort good for a beginner. When Sean observed that someone might have been hurt, Olivia retorted someone already had been.

"We could've," Sean said, "lost everything if the winds were stronger."

"They weren't," Olivia said, "and you didn't. Ilyana lost more than a few possessions."

"What you did was dangerous."

"Tolerating his bad habits was dangerous."

"It's his life."

"And Ilyana's too." Olivia turned deep red and stared at Sean— who continued to dispute with her.

"No one knew he was capable of such things."

"Really?" Olivia said as she scanned the village's women. "How many of you would kiss him? Or a man like him before you married?"

None of the women stirred.

"I didn't think so. One look is enough to tell."

"You're her mother and we …"

Deidra began to speak, but Olivia turned her back and walked away just as Lisa emerged from the woods and hurried to the mess hall. After filling her face with handfuls of food, she staggered back into the forest announcing she needed a nap. Jose and Hilary followed on her heels and also took naps after eating. Neither Ryan nor Maria returned for lunch.

24

THE WAY OF ALL FLESH

Nearly an hour after lunch, Heather returned the tent repair kit to the supply shed and was proceeding to the mess hall to prepare food for dry storage in the barn when a petite blonde in her mid-thirties, dripping wet from the waist down and carrying an armful of clothes, headed straight to her—though the visitor didn't speak a word until she stood only a few feet from Heather.

"What in heaven's name is going on here?" the woman whispered. Her face was flush and voice somber. She didn't smile.

"We had a fire."

"These," the woman said as she thrust the pile of clothes toward Heather's face, "aren't burned—and I'd advise you to save them for the lunatics running naked through the woods."

Heather looked puzzled. "I don't understand."

"First," the woman said, "I ran across a woman hugging a tree. Mind you, embracing the thing, her legs wrapped tight around it. And not wearing a shirt as far as I could see from the back. Then I encountered a couple making love on a bridge. They were so hot and heavy they didn't even notice me and I had to wade through the creek to pass around them."

"Who was it?" Heather asked as she looked toward the woods.

"I tried hard not to look, but these are probably their clothes. You know the owners?"

"Those're Ryan's shorts," Heather said, "and Maria's shirt."

"Ryan our founding father?"

Heather nodded.

"Who's this Maria?" the woman asked.

"A village girl."

"Well, store these in your tent and I'll talk to Ryan later. He's still married to Kit, isn't he?"

"They missed the deadline."

The woman thought about Heather's words for a moment, then extended her hand. "Dr. Janine Erikson," she said. "I'm not sure we've met."

"Heather Marks-Ingalls."

"Nice to meet you, Heather."

Heather started to speak, but the woman's face grew concerned and she turned around.

"That smell in your camp," the psychologist said, "is that marijuana?"

"We had a fire, but only one tent burned—with pounds of dope, which they tell me is a lot. Several neighbors got stoned putting it out. Those were the lunatics you referred to."

"Very dangerous. Very dangerous."

"It could've been."

"How'd it start?"

"Arson. Olivia burned Jason's tent to the ground."

"Jason the rapist? I mean, the alleged rapist."

"Yeah."

"Curious," Dr. Erikson said with a frown. "But he's not my first problem. I need to find the girl. Where's her tent?"

"Ilyana's in the blue one," Heather said as she pointed down the row of tents.

Dr. Erikson thanked Heather for her assistance and started for the blue tent as Heather tucked Ryan and Maria's clothing inside

Maria's tent before walking to the mess tent to finish the day's work. Only when she'd set fifty peeled lemons out to dry and sealed another fifty in glass jars did she retrieve a canvas bag filled with dirty laundry and walk toward the stream.

THEIR LOVE SPENT, Maria and Ryan embraced one last time before falling apart. The rush of the dope and sex exhausted their bodies and they soon slept, waking only when the afternoon sun warmed their unclothed flesh. Ryan woke sweating, then touched Maria on the cheek.

"That was good," Maria said as she opened her eyes. "Even better than before."

"It was good dope too," Ryan said with a nod. "We should remember to thank Jason."

When Ryan asked where his clothes were, Maria giggled and pointed toward the bridge. Ryan stood and yawned—and so did Maria. Ryan watched as the young woman stretched her arms and arched her back, then desire stirred and he fell on her again. This time they didn't sleep afterwards, but immediately rose to find their clothes. When they found none on the bridge, they walked east and looked on the trail, but found nothing on the trail either. Only when they neared the glade of trees close to the village did they stop.

"They're gone," Ryan said.

Maria laughed. "Let's go get more."

Ryan didn't laugh.

"Stand back," he said, "here comes Heather."

Maria and Ryan retreated across the bridge and sprinted barefoot and bareback along the stream until they reached a ford. There, they crossed through the water into an old growth forest and slipped through the woods until they came to several citrus trees along the north edge of the village—within twenty treeless yards of Maria's tent—where Ryan crawled through bushes as Maria followed. They were especially careful to avoid thorns and nettles.

"Damn," Ryan whispered. "Look."

Maria looked and saw that Kit sat between the trees and the village, threading vine through half-dried fruit. Near her stood two poles with twine strung between them: from which hung several sliced mangos. Beside one of the poles sat a two-foot heap of mangos, limes, and kiwi. Kit evidently planned to be at the spot for a long while. Maria backed up as Ryan followed, though she waited until she was beyond earshot before laughing.

"We could tell her," Maria said, "our clothes washed to sea while we were skinny-dipping."

Ryan forced a smile before noting he had an idea and circled west toward the privacy tent—which stood empty. Ryan and Maria ignored the stench of stale dope and hurried inside, where Maria draped herself with a grass skirt and its matching top while Ryan put on a pair of Jason's dirty shorts. After dressing, Ryan stepped away to eye the grass skirt.

"Dance a little," Ryan said.

Maria rotated her hips and the grass swung from thigh to thigh.

"That's paradise," Ryan said. "That's what I dreamed of when I came here. Not a lot of talk about babies."

"Maybe I'll make you beg for my baby," Maria said as she stepped forward.

Ryan kept her at arm's reach. "Not here," he said. "We've been lucky twice today. I doubt the third time would be so charmed."

"You promised me love whenever I want it."

"And you promised me a private relationship."

"For a time," Maria said with a laugh, "but you'll be publicly exposed before I'm done with you."

"Just not today," Ryan said. "It's getting late."

They left the tent together but separated on the trail. Ryan reached his tent unnoticed and came out a few minutes later in clean clothes, having hidden Jason's shorts in his dirty laundry.

For her part, Maria wasn't so lucky; she almost had reached the privacy of her own tent when Kit saw her.

"That skirt looks like mine," Kit said.

Maria fingered the grass sheaves. "I found it in the tent out of camp. Is it yours?"

"I made it for my honeymoon," Kit said without a smile.

"I'm sorry," Maria said, "I didn't know. I stepped into the tent to take a rest when I saw it. It looked so authentic I just had to try it on. I hope I didn't ruin any surprises."

"Not if Ryan didn't see."

"I was alone."

"May I have it back?"

Kit waited for Maria to change and took the skirt back to her own tent, hiding it behind her clothes. A little while later, Kit found Ryan eating a midafternoon snack at the mess hall—where he explained how he'd staggered into the woods after being sickened and stoned by the burning marijuana and spent the day sleeping off the drug's effects. Kit thought the story funny and repeated it to Heather, though the teenager just forced a smile.

HILARY STARED AT SEAN, her face taut and eyes fixed, the late afternoon sun burning behind her like a torch. The woman didn't smile and her voice growled as she clenched breadfruit in her hands and glared at Sean—who reached to the lower branches of a fruit-filled tree to twist breadfruit free before handing each one to his coworker.

"You're a pig, Sean."

"All I said was that it's not real rape. I agree he needs to be punished for not respecting her. But you can't tell me he wasn't as stoned as she was—maybe more as much as he smokes. If the pot excuses her, why not him?"

"She's a girl."

"What if she were twenty?"

"She'd be old enough to know better."

"So," Sean said, stretching to reach a large breadfruit that he twisted from its stem and tossed to Hilary, "you wouldn't prosecute if she were twenty?"

"It depends on the circumstances."

"You mean," Sean replied, "it depends upon the girl's mood the next morning. If she calls it rape, it is."

"I didn't say that."

"No, but you meant it. If the sex is good and the man sends flowers, all is well. Otherwise, regret becomes rape."

"Nonsense," Hilary said. "It's a matter of consent."

"Fine. Give me the rules. I'll play by whatever set you choose. But they can't be changed after the fact."

"Respect."

"I thought you considered respectability bourgeois."

"Respect isn't respectability."

Sean just smirked.

"When respect is shown," Hilary continued with a frown, "rules aren't necessary."

"That's where you're naive," Sean said. "The people on this island are no different than the ones across the ocean. The point is to get the rules straightened out properly."

"No," Hilary said, "rules are for lawyers. Character endures."

"You sound more like Bill Bennett than brother Bob. More Republican than progressive. Are you certain you voted Democrat?"

"As a point of fact," Hilary answered, "I voted for Nader."

Sean cursed and asked which state.

"Florida."

"Thanks."

"Jeb," Hilary said, "was going to steal that election in any case. I'd have been just another voter to disqualify. Another chad to hang."

Sean pulled another breadfruit from the tree and then several more while Hilary carefully stowed each fruit in a storage bag.

After a time, Hilary renewed the debate. "Would you do it?" she asked.

"Do what?"

"Take a fifteen-year old girl stoned out of her mind?"

"Who's to say I haven't?"

When Hilary didn't laugh, Sean grimaced.

"Sorry," Sean said. "That was tasteless. And no, I wouldn't do a girl like that. Not even when I was fifteen myself. I guess I've chosen an existentialist morality; there may be no essential difference between right and wrong, but there is a difference between taking responsibility and avoiding it. You can't sleep with a girl who can't understand the consequences. It's like seducing the simple and slow —it'd be very poor sportsmanship. No matter how nice her hips might be."

"And which morality does Ursula preach?"

"The old-time religion," Sean said, "the way she hounded me for marriage."

"Marriage? She'd rather see you sent into the open seas on a burning boat."

"And to think," Sean smirked, "I fathered her only child. She's not a particularly grateful person."

"Back to our point," Hilary said with a scowl. "How is Jason wronged?"

"I didn't say he is. But there's a mob mentality at work and he won't stand a chance at trial."

"And rightly so."

"What if," Sean chose his words carefully, "Deidra and I chose to down a fifth of whiskey figuring the night would end with sex? Should I be punished because she willingly surrendered control of herself and only decided the next morning she wished she hadn't taken me?"

"No one would punish that."

"Why not?"

"Your relationship is already known."

"What if it were our first date?"

"It would depend on circumstances."

"How?"

"I don't know."

"Then you tell me," Sean pressed his point, "when I'm not allowed to take a woman."

Hilary didn't hesitate to answer. "When she's drunk or stoned. Or if she just says no."

"How drunk?"

"Too drunk."

"Are we going," Sean again smirked, "to set up breathalyzers and blood tests for sex? Maybe prosecute SUI: Sex Under the Influence?"

"Don't be a jackass."

Sean climbed from the tree, still talking as he reached the ground. "Give me a standard."

"It's relative to the situation."

"And the girl," Sean said, "and that's not fair to men. I'm as progressive as the next guy—more than most—but I can't live my life by the moods of women whose expectations don't line up with mine. We need a shared standard. Good sportsmanship requires known rules. Even hockey has referees and boxing has regulations."

"Then I'd say," Hilary observed after a moment's consideration, "that any woman too drunk or too high to prepare for sex should be left alone. So should girls too young to understand the full consequences of their actions."

"What do you mean by full?"

"I don't expect her to be either omniscient or as celibate as a nun, if that's what you're getting at. She just needs to have enough maturity and sobriety to weigh risks."

"That's it?" Sean asked. "Nothing more?"

"I don't think so."

"So I could sleep with a woman on our first date, as long as we drank two glasses of wine instead of four."

"That seems reasonable."

"What if we drank three? Is a man a rapist for one glass of wine?"

"Be practical."

Sean stopped laughing. "I am being practical," he said with an irritated voice. "One of my college buddies went to jail for drunk driving because his girlfriend was paralyzed in a car accident. The wreck wasn't even his fault, but he was .001 percent over the legal limit. He only drank three beers. If he'd crashed fifteen minutes later or even drank one swig less, he'd be a free man instead of a felon. To be honest, if he'd pissed before he left the bar, he'd be out of jail."

"And the girl would still be paralyzed."

"What if," Sean continued, "a woman consented in the evening after two glasses of wine but changed her mind with the hangover?"

"That'd be her fault," Hilary said.

"But how could it be judged if she swore otherwise. Your standards rely on the wisdom of Solomon to sort out every lover's quarrel."

"And yours," Hilary said, "are no standards at all."

"There are no real standards," Sean said, "beyond the choices of individuals."

"Which society must sometimes arbitrate."

"Why? It's a personal matter."

"Not always," Hilary said, "just ask the baby in Ursula's belly."

"She knew what she was doing."

"How many drinks did she have?"

"No more than two."

"So you're off the hook," Hilary said, "because she had no more than two drinks. Meanwhile, she has a baby for life. That's the attitude women hate—that I hate."

"It's her body and her choice," Sean said, "she can no more make me raise a child than I can force her to have one. Unless you'd rather give men a say over abortion?"

"Pig," Hilary said.

"The problem," Sean said, "is that you're one of those who can't imagine a woman might lie about rape. Or be mistaken."

"And your problem," Hilary countered, "is that you're one of those who doubt men exploit women."

"You've too much faith in honesty," Sean replied.

"And you've too much faith in hormones," Hilary retorted.

The debate ended as Sean took his pole to another breadfruit tree a short walk away. He used bare hands and bare feet to climb into the thick tree, its trunk sagging only a little from his weight. Standing among the branches, he used a pole with a sharpened blade (which Hilary handed to him) to cut breadfruit loose. Hilary tried to catch the falling fruit with a net and missed only two. They worked hard the rest of the day and returned several full bags of fruit to the store-house. The produce was much needed since breadfruit reserves had been reduced to a dozen withered fruit and a couple bags of flour.

THE NEXT FEW days stretched long. Jason mostly worked compost duty while a dozen villagers constructed a kitchen. Brent built an oven from brick and mortar while others raised a high-roofed building over it. Once finished, the building included a rear entrance near the firepits and an underground storage bin—as well as a dining room with a twenty-foot table constructed of treated lumber and surrounded by twenty stools of all shapes and sizes (each one brought by its user). A Saturday morning christening was held at the new oven, though Jason and John didn't attend since the former had fled to the north village while the latter disappeared before lunch and didn't return until dinner. Few talked, except a couple villagers who mentioned they'd be glad to get the coming trial over.

On Sunday representatives from all five neighborhoods assembled for the meeting of the General Will of the People. Attendance was sufficient to establish a quorum—which was down from the previous General Will of the People (since nearly thirty residents claimed to be too ill or too busy to attend). In any case, the session started at noon with the traditional swearing of the oath shortly after Jason and several compatriots arrived from the north village.

The trial was underway.

Dr. Erikson spoke on behalf of the assaulted girl—despite Jason's objections—as she recounted Ilyana's story and corroborating details provided by other westerners, testifying for nearly an hour. Jason spoke on his own behalf regarding the mutual intoxication of the couple, his lack of malice, and the unforeseen circumstances in which he found himself. He insisted Ilyana initiated sex while he was too stoned to resist and also swore she claimed to be seventeen. After Jason's testimony was complete, Olivia gave her account and though Ilyana asked to take the stand, her mother insisted otherwise—unwilling to subject her daughter to public shame. There was some discussion whether she possessed such authority, but no one wanted to force rape victims to testify publicly, so Olivia's decision was left unchallenged.

Jason made a good witness. His sobs and sorrow kept the crowd quiet and won sympathy. Olivia, on the other hand, behaved miserably. Her accusations were spiteful and her handling of evidence obscure. She cried a few times and screamed several others. She demanded vengeance and swore defiance when rebuked for burning Jason's tent. And though her daughter's sexual history wasn't reviewed, Olivia didn't bother to deny that her daughter potentially had demonstrated interest in a man with whom she smoked dope on more than one occasion. As for Ilyana, she was deposed and questioned in private by members of the Executive Council—and her testimony was relayed to the assembly only through a moderator. Witnesses were cross-examined by the contesting parties and final statements made late in the day.

No one doubted Jason had slept with the girl. What was disputed was the legality of the sexual union, as well as the proper punishment for illicit sexual intercourse. Olivia insisted her daughter was the victim of date rape, statutory rape, and sexual assault—and demanded Jason be punished harshly as a deterrence to sexual predators. Jason, on the other hand, admitted only to having been as stoned as Ilyana and to having shown judgment as poor as hers. He insisted he'd neither broken a law nor intended harm and offered to marry (or otherwise cohabit with) the girl if deemed best by the public assembly. He promised to submit to an intoxication management course—though he reminded his fellow citizens that drug use was a right of Paradise and that he'd provided marijuana to many of them. He publicly forgave Olivia the destruction of his property and renounced any right to restitution.

Dr. Erikson closed testimony by making a few comments about the gravity of the case, observing that important public safety considerations were at stake, along with the need to outlaw sexploitation and uphold acceptable standards for inebriated conduct. Though it was her personal opinion that statutory rape wasn't grounds for prosecution (since the recently adopted marriage laws permitted both sexual union and marriage to anyone old enough to consent), she did allow that the power differential of the couple might make date rape demonstrable on the grounds of Ilyana's youth—as long as the judicial interpretation wasn't taken to forbid all May-December (or even April-October) unions. Dr. Erikson also publicly rebuked Olivia for lawlessness and vigilantism which had endangered an entire neighborhood. After the psychologist finished speaking, a recess was declared so the judicial assembly might deliberate its judgment. Subsequent discussions were loud and sometimes frenzied as the assembly disputed and debated the island's first criminal case. Meanwhile, Olivia took Ilyana to the beach to get away from the commotion and Jason stepped into a storage tent to smoke a joint.

Three hours later, a vote was taken and Jason was acquitted of sexual assault, but convicted of inappropriate sexual contact. The sense of the community was that while Dr. Erikson was correct in arguing that statutory rape technically was not against the law (since no such prohibition had been legislated), the majority also believed that the state of Paradise needed to use this unfortunate event to establish and enforce gender equality: an essential element of the constitution itself. Several feminists protested tacit consent was no consent at all, though even they admitted this was a case of one word against another and it couldn't be proved Ilyana had withheld permission to be touched either by tacit or explicit denial—especially since Jason had testified so convincingly and Ilyana apparently had been too stoned to remember many details. Though the teenaged girl's erotic dream was taken by some to be evidence that she'd been aroused enough to enjoy the lovemaking (with arousal being judged the ultimate proof of consent since rape was deemed utterly incompatible with sexual pleasure), others noted that the girl's shirt hadn't been removed (suggesting she hadn't been particularly interested in foreplay). In any event, it was decided inappropriate sexual contact— or date rape in common parlance—was the appropriate charge and Jason was convicted thereof. Following Jason's conviction, a motion was made to indict Olivia for arson and her subsequent conviction was secured in minutes since she'd already confessed as much during her testimony.

Both sentences were considered severe. Jason was stripped of all rights as a citizen and forbidden to serve as a public official or vote in public assembly. He also was sentenced to a full week of exile on a motu to contemplate his rehabilitation back into society—though he was provided a sufficient supply of food and water to maintain his comfort and health. It also was decided he should write a letter of apology and undergo sexual predator counseling on Sunday mornings for the next two months and be transferred to the north village to reduce friction within the western village. Olivia was given a similar sentence, though without the loss of citizenship or transfer of residence. Her crimes were classified as hate crimes and punished accordingly. Though most members of the assembly sympathized with her motives, the majority decided vigilantism merited discipline and sentenced Olivia to a full week of internal exile after she absolutely refused to renounce her sins and beg clemency—though the original demand for external exile was mitigated in deference to Ilyana's needs.

Following the assembly's refusal to hear Jason's final appeal on the grounds that the case was closed and dusk was near, the governing charter was recited and the assembly dismissed. While several citizens of Paradise found flashlights and others lit improvised torches, most islanders stumbled home in the dark. Before they started home, a delegation of westerners met with Dr. Erikson to schedule a visit for Tuesday evening.

25

THE CHILDREN OF AQUARIUS

Work began at dawn with a communal breakfast during which proposals were made for village improvements. Since the new kitchen lacked both design and decorations, several women requested that New Plymouth be petitioned to import exterior primer and all-weather paint to adorn windows and doors originally built more to survive tropical storms than please the eye. It also was decided that leftover construction materials were sufficient to build a school at an undetermined time in the near future. However, despite several planned improvements in physical surroundings, many villagers remained dispirited and the session soon devolved into murmuring and complaining. Dissent ended only when Ryan called for July elections—it already being the second day of the month. This time, everyone agreed that a lottery was required to avoid favoritism and factionalism. To the dismay of many villagers, Sean's marker was selected for Chief Neighbor and Deidra's for the Executive Council.

Without much deliberation, Sean assigned Ryan and Kit to the fishing nets and John to sewage treatment. He made Jose work with Heather to cook meals while tasking Hilary, Linh, and Tiffany to clear land, plant crops, and cut wood. Brent and Viet were told to collect fruits, vegetables, and herbs—as was Lisa. Ursula was asked to tend children and animals and Charles to build food pantries. Joan was assigned food preparation (for storage) and Maria was given trail clearing. Ilyana was told to help with younger children and animals. Sean decided to rotate between assisting with trail clearing and food collection—staying near Lisa and Maria. Only Olivia wasn't given an immediate assignment due to her detention. Sean also requested a censure of John (who had missed the meeting), but counted only two votes in favor of his motion.

After breakfast was finished and the meeting adjourned, villagers began their assigned tasks. While the weather was perfect—a warm sun cooled by ocean breezes—life in the village wasn't nearly as nice as the climate. Most villagers remained irritable or despondent and their despair was reflected in sloppy work and quarrelsome attitudes. Following a sharp dispute regarding the portions served for lunch, Sean finally suggested a work suspension until tempers cooled. His proposal was accepted and several neighbors walked to the beach and others splashed with their children in the Pishon River. A few even passed the time napping. When the day was spent, nearly everyone retired early.

WHEN JOHN EMERGED from the forest well after dark carrying a rough-hewn piece of furniture, Kit was alone at the low-burning campfire as she sipped coffee and reflected on the day's events. She waved when she saw John.

"Hi, John."

"Where's everyone at?"

"Early bed. It was a rough day."

"I figured so. That's why I took off."

"I wondered where you were."

"I lost track of time," John said as he sat on a smooth-planed stump near Kit. "The battery died last week. On my watch."

"What're you carrying?" Kit asked.

"A cradle."

Kit's eyes brightened. "Really?"

"It's for Ursula," John said. "I carved it from a hollow trunk. See how it rocks. And these stabilizer bars will prevent it from flipping once they're screwed in."

"What if they fall out? Will the cradle roll?"

"They won't slip out. I'll soak the wood before I screw it in. When the wood dries, it creates a seal."

"Without glue?"

"Yeah. I once visited a log cabin in Kentucky recreated from the time of the Revolution. Ladder rungs to the loft were made this way: rods were soaked in water and pounded into holes. They were decades old and still could bear the weight of a grown man. This cradle will hold."

"It's perfect."

"It's not much to look at, but it'll work for a newborn. This was a quick job, but I'll make a real crib when there's more time."

"Why so early? She isn't due for months."

"We don't have time to waste," John replied, "though I'm not sure everyone realizes it."

"I must be one of the blind," Kit said. "Things seem to be going well as far as our work is concerned."

"I'm not convinced," John explained with a shake of his head. "We'll have our wood supply built up before the rainy season—and our food stores as best as I can tell. But these tents are a problem."

"Don't we plan to live in them for a year?"

"We flooded after a few day's rain. Imagine what it'll be like after a month."

Kit grimaced. "Uhhhh."

"Besides," John said, "our plan was to have a kitchen built for food preparation and a communal house for sleeping and schooling. Right?"

"That's right," Kit said, "and both buildings should be finished ahead of schedule."

"I don't intend," John continued, "to sleep in the same room as Deidra and Sean. Not for one night and not for three months."

"I hadn't really thought through the implications."

"I have."

"Oh, goodness," Kit said, "that means Maria will be sleeping near Ryan and me."

"And the other couples."

"Sean and Jose will see us when we dress."

"They'll see everything," John said, "and winters here aren't cold. All those bodies in one room will heat up. Blankets will be packed away and clothes removed."

"What can we do?"

"The communal house," John said, "will exist for those who want it. But I plan to build my own place and I'll help you build a home too. If Ryan and I work together, we can work nights to cut timber while you thatch grass. It'll only take a week or two to raise two houses if we work in tandem. See this drawing. It's a thatched roof hut: with a lifted floor and a storage loft and ventilation windows. If we want, we can even soften the floor with sand or use hot coals for indoor heating on damp nights."

Kit looked at a folded paper that John slipped from his shirt pocket and volunteered Ryan's help, then walked to the mess tent and poured two cups of coffee. John took his coffee black while Kit sweetened hers with lumps of processed sugar as she waited for him to renew the conversation.

"I'm concerned about Ursula," John said after his cup was half-empty, "and her baby."

"Why?"

"The rainy season will be dangerous for a newborn."

"I hadn't thought of that."

"A damp tent," John said, "could kill a baby."

"Maybe she can stay in the schoolhouse?"

"The others won't be thrilled to share a room with a baby."

"Maybe," Kit said as she looked at John, "Sean can build her a house?"

"He won't."

"The neighborhood can insist."

"We won't."

"What can she do?" Kit asked.

"I was thinking," John answered, "Ursula could stay with me. Do you think she'd be offended if I invited her?"

"Do you mean," Kit looked down, her eyes crossing her own legs as she blushed, that you ..."

"That's not what I mean at all," John said stone-faced. "I'm giving a cradle, not robbing one. Have you seen any women near my tent?"

"She is pretty," Kit said.

"She's a pretty girl," John said, "whose baby shouldn't suffer for its father's sin."

"Are there sins in Eden?"

John took a drink of his coffee. "Either a crime or a sin," he said. "I don't see any other way of describing the mess Sean's managed to make."

"Dr. Morales," Kit replied, "would say it's a question of social ethos and Dr. Erikson would call it a lifestyle choice."

John finished his coffee before he spoke again and Kit sipped from her cup as she waited for him to do so.

"Did I ever tell you," John eventually said, "my grandfather was forced to marry, more-or-less at gunpoint, after getting my grandmother pregnant?"

"That's horrible."

"They were married fifty years," John answered, "and he became a deacon in the church. I mean, a really conservative Presbyterian church. They left seven children and thirty grandchildren, most of them good enough."

"I'm sorry," Kit now finished her coffee. "I'm sorry about Deidra."

"It's not your fault."

Neither spoke for several minutes—until John yawned and stood.

"Time to go to bed."

"Me too," Kit said. "Sometimes I'm too restless to sleep. I'm used to having a husband."

"I know. Sometimes I think even a bad marriage is better than none at all."

"I'm not so sure of that."

"Neither am I," John whispered, "but I liked marriage. Usually. It was good to me and even bad years were better than the ones before. Better an imperfect good than absolutely nothing."

"That sounds profound."

"Almost Augustinian. Evil as the negation of good and absolute evil as nothing good at all."

"Maybe that's true," Kit whispered as she pressed the flat of her belly.

"You have Ryan," John replied as he pulled Kit's hand away from her waist.

"I wonder if I do."

"You also have honor," John said. "Keeping a promise to a grandmother even when she'll never know it. I admire that."

"My grandmother," Kit said as she looked straight at John, "was very traditional. She helped raise me when my mother traveled. When I was fifteen, she sat me down and told me bluntly that while it wasn't her business what I did in private—she didn't want to know one way or the other—she didn't want me living with any man until I was married. And she made me promise not to. She said I couldn't date until I promised."

"You're keeping a promise made under duress?"

"A promise is a promise, after all."

"You're a good person."

"She passed away," Kit said with a shrug, "before I met Ryan, but it was nice to know I'd have pleased her. She was a good grandma."

Neither spoke for a minute.

"Another week or so," John said, "then you and Ryan are back to normal."

"I wonder if it really is."

John didn't press the point, but thanked Kit for the coffee and took the cradle back to his tent. The fire had burned itself to ashes and it wasn't necessary for Kit to douse the coals with water before she retired.

.   .   .

TUESDAY WAS BUSY. Most villagers rose early to make up hours lost the previous day—though dinner wasn't served until late in the afternoon and the dishes cleaned only at dusk. Children were sent to bed early and improvised chairs lined up before a bonfire. Dr. Erikson was scheduled as a dinner guest, arriving late after having been detained by a counseling session with the northerners about their drug use and work habits. In fact, she remained noticeably flustered when she reached the west village and managed to settle down only after eating a plate of cold food. Then she collected her thoughts, rose before the assembled village, and spoke—not far from the campfire. Now and then, a villager threw a log into the fire and the flames would rise into the evening sky. At such moments, Dr. Erikson's face grew clear and her features sharp, but as the flames fell, her image became dark and dim.

"To begin with," Dr. Erikson opened the discussion, "you must remember—every one of you—that you're the chosen ones. You're the truest progressives and broadest-minded liberals drawn from the old world. Every one of you must remember how you lived your life to this very day and how you'll make a difference for all humankind for generations to come. Children yet unborn—though not to say unborn children—will live in peace and harmony based on how each of you chooses to behave on this island."

Dr. Erikson took a sip of water.

"You are—that is to say, we are—the rainbow coalition," the psychologist continued. "Look to your left and to your right. Black and white and brown and red and yellow. There are gays and straights, liberals and progressives, Marxists and libertarians on this island. Ryan left the accolades of Hollywood to begin this colony. He sold his home and left his fans. And each of you has done the same. You've given up father and mother and sister and brother for our peaceful republic of humankind. And now you've toiled and suffered and ached and endured a hundred trials. Yet look at what already has been accomplished. We've begun to feed ourselves from the fruits of nature: catching fish from the sea and collecting eggs from nests. Our hands and those of our compatriots plant crops and milk goats and one neighborhood even made its first cake of cheese. You yourselves have set a good example by raising this magnificent storehouse—with enough room to store several months of provisions. Haven't you already proven wrong the conservatives who mocked us—who always insisted the New Left hadn't the hardiness or the heart of the religious zealots who first built Boston? Haven't you given the lie to those who insist political progressives are capable only of expropriating wealth manufactured by capitalism and enjoying neighborliness engendered by social conservatives? As if none of us was any better than a Bolshevik profiteer or the rust that ruins an automobile. As if we are only social parasites best flung into this fire like leeches and ticks."

The crowd stilled as the speaker pressed her point.

"Even more," the psychologist said, "we've yet to endure a single racial incident or even the mere accusation of ethnic prejudice or sexual discrimination. Not even one slur. We've proven the prejudices of the past can be exorcized. That they've been exorcized. We've also shown direct democracy actually works. This whole people has come together to rule ourselves. There are no kings among us, nor prime ministers, nor presidents. Each one of us is equal to the other."

Dr. Erikson paused and the audience didn't stir.

"Yes, there've been problems," Dr. Erikson continued. "Some complain of monotonous food and others are in despair over Jason's crime. Still others are tired from all the toil. But we mustn't grow weary in our good works. The Pilgrims submitted to a winter of death for their dead Christ and Jamestown endured a year of hunger for its living king. Will we do less for mankind? If liberalism can't triumph here—with its own chosen people and the fruits of paradise—can it triumph anywhere? If we can't make a true community in this Eden, how can we expect our political kinsmen to do so in America? If we can't harvest the bounties of a tropical island, what have we to say to Russians and Chinese and Ethiopians and Indonesians?"

Neighbors sat up straighter and a few placed arms around friends or took the hand of a loved one.

"Now," Dr. Erikson concluded, "in a positive and productive

manner, let's deal with issues and set this community back to order. Each one of you was given a sheet of paper and a sharpened pencil. I want you to write upon it three things that you need and three things that you need to do. Take ten minutes while I pass out refreshments. Fold the paper and pass it forward when you've finished."

The staff psychologist handed out chocolate bars brought from the camp reserves, along with other sweets. Kit hurried through the assignment, then helped serve drinks. Both women popped corn over hot coals and filled serving dishes while villagers worked through their answers. Once the surveys filtered in, Dr. Erikson returned to her duties while Heather helped Kit with refreshments. Completed forms were returned to the staff psychologist—who transferred the answers to a separate notebook. Once she had finished her review, snacks were set aside and the meeting returned to order.

"There are several common themes," Dr. Erikson began as she pointed at the tallied stack of answers. "First, many of you are worried about supplies of perishable goods: especially razors, clothes, and wine. Is that fair to say?"

Heads nodded and voices assented.

"What choices do we have?" Dr. Erikson asked.

"To be more frugal," Heather suggested.

"What else?"

"To import additional supplies at the next shipment," Kit added.

"That can be done in a few months. What can we do now?"

"Manufacture our own," a man shouted.

"Very good. We'll come back to that. What else?"

"Do without," Lisa said.

"Free ourselves from consumerism," Dr. Erikson said. "Live more simply. Can you give us an example?"

Lisa pointed to the long hairs on her legs.

"I'm not shaving anymore," Lisa explained. "Why should I nick my legs with dull razors just to defer to the Western canon of beauty?"

"Live more naturally," Dr. Erikson said. "Excellent. Any other ideas?"

"Clothes are a real issue," Lisa continued. "This is my last untorn shirt. Other than one dress blouse I'm saving for special occasions."

"And how can we resolve this problem?"

"Open a boutique," a woman's voice said from the rear of the room.

Everyone laughed.

"Very funny," Dr. Erikson said. "But seriously. What can we do?"

"A couple of us," Kit said, "sewed a grass skirt. It didn't take too long and it seems durable enough."

"Perfect. Use the resources of this island."

"We can also do without," Lisa repeated. "It's not really necessary to wear clothing on a warm day. Native peoples in the South Pacific go topless, why couldn't we conserve our clothing the same way?"

The speaker panned her audience. "What," the psychologist asked, "do you think of that suggestion?"

A few men grinned and most women groaned.

"I'm not sure I like the idea at all," Linh said. "I've been married several years and I'm accustomed to my privacy. It just wouldn't seem right. I definitely don't want my daughters leered at after puberty. Or before."

"It does," Dr. Erikson said, "seem somewhat improper by Western standards. But would it be possible to adapt over time, as we became used to the idea? Remember that bikinis once were considered shocking and leg-covering bathing suits were a scandal a century ago. Not to speak of thongs. In a like manner, I ran around without any shirt at all in the Iowa town where I grew up till I was seven years old. And there was no scandal at all."

"Maybe we'd get used to it," Linh replied, "but I'm not sure I'd like to try."

"You can," the psychologist advised, "decide this among yourselves since it's your neighborhood. The only thing that really matters is you come to an agreement that everyone can live with. Remember, it's not whether someone dresses like a pilgrim or a hippie that counts. It's by our tolerance and our love we'll be remembered."

The crowd stirred and residents smiled.

"A second issue," Dr. Erikson continued, "many of you mentioned was Jason's crime. By the way, let me interject that Jason has been sent to the motu. I helped him to settle in and he sends his regrets. Now to the point. I should tell you that few of us were completely happy with the trial. The process was messy and the hearings unruly. By involving the entire assembly in the decision, debates of fact aggravated differences of opinion and the entire community was politicized. Still, it worked. The right result came from the trial: the protection of innocent women and the punishment of a guilty man. The people acted successfully as their own judge and jury and jailer. What else matters but the attainment of the right end?"

Some neighbors nodded, but not everyone.

"There aren't any complaints," Dr. Erikson continued to expound, "about work in this village. That's very good. The northerners are struggling with their use of free time. Several of their people don't help pull the wagon and others want to throw them off. I'll return to them tomorrow for more counseling. Dr. Law will go with me to speak on the rights and obligations of welfare capitalism and incentive socialism."

Ryan now threw two logs on the fire and the flames burned brighter for a time.

"Let's see," Dr. Erikson said, "You've had one divorce and ..."—she paused to consider her choice of words—"and one couple didn't renew their vows?"

"There was a technical problem," Ryan said as he blushed after glancing both at Kit and Maria, "at the time."

Dr. Erikson nodded and asked whether anyone else had trouble with the new law of marriage.

"It worked," Deidra said as she stood, "for Sean and I."

The psychologist looked pleased.

"Those who wanted to remarry did and those who didn't, didn't," Deidra said. "Ryan and Kit just proved that actors really do need agents since they can't count fingers and toes without the help of an accountant."

Everyone laughed except Heather and Maria.

"So far," Dr. Erikson said, "the professional staff has been pleased with its implementation. There have been a few unfortunate incidents, but in general it's working to uphold freedom and choice. And even the divorces were caused less by the new law than by psychological necessity. It's not likely that any law can hold a marriage together when choice can't. If love itself won't bind two people together, what can?"

"Fear."

It was Tiffany who had spoken with a deep, declarative voice.

"Fear," Tiffany continued, "of the pain he'll suffer if I ever catch him with his neighbor's wife or daughter or sister or any woman at all. Or her husband. I'm an unbigoted avenger."

Most neighbors laughed and Dr. Erikson smiled.

"Didn't," the psychologist asked, "one of the very apostles of social conservatism say perfect love drives out fear?"

"Exactly," Tiffany said, "if his love is perfect, he has nothing to fear."

Everyone laughed and the discussion returned to more mundane matters such as toilet paper substitutes and building code. When it became clear that at least rudimentary supplies would last until resupply and that Jason wasn't returning to the village after completion of his sentence, the public mood finally relaxed.

The other major complaint was that of singles who believed that an island-wide happy hour needed to be established so they could mingle with peers from other neighborhoods. Dr. Erikson thought it a good idea and promised to do what she could to arrange a dance or to set up a weekend rendezvous site. She also suggested the following day be declared a village holiday to cement the renewed camaraderie now circulating through the neighborhood. When a vote was taken, it was decided to picnic near New Plymouth for a village outing. Dr. Erikson promised to provide a cask of wine from New Plymouth—and the mere mention of wine brought cheers from most inhabitants.

Following the meeting, several village women approached Tiffany to tease that they found Brent utterly intolerable and absolutely undesirable—though Brent protested he couldn't be completely unattractive since Tiffany herself had married him twice. Linh claimed Tiffany only picked Brent from charity and Viet called their marriage a misbegotten social experiment, but Brent just brushed off the ribbing with a shrug.

THE WEATHER WAS perfect for a holiday and the westerners rose early for a Wednesday picnic, filling backpacks and loading coolers for the trek toward New Plymouth and crossing Mount Zion on cleared trails to reach familiar ground in little more than an hour. When they reached a wide path maintained by the east village, the west villagers took it straight toward the coast and soon came to a picturesque town of thatched-roof houses and large-framed barns. The settlement even included public baths and private saunas fed from a pristine stream and a public park now under construction. Most notably, a large greenhouse stood near the edge of the village—sheets of clear visqueen stretched tight and stapled to its timbers and rows of vegetables planted within (many of them already bearing fruit). The westerners were awed.

Alan was far more relaxed than before, even pleasant, as he took his former neighbors on a short tour of his new house (a cabin with a fenced yard and a small garden) and Steve showed off the foundation for a tree nursery. In return, the westerners invited Alan and Steve to picnic with them, though their former neighbors declined the offer since work requirements were very strict in their new neighborhood. Nevertheless, Alan and Steve chatted with their old neighbors for nearly an hour, until summoned to construction duties by an east villager with a shaved head and shaved legs—who pressed her fellow villagers that a new bathhouse wouldn't build itself.

After farewells were exchanged, the westerners hurried to New Plymouth where they collected a promised cask of red wine from the depot and invited the professional staff to their picnic. Most accepted and it wasn't long before a quarter of the residents of Paradise found themselves sailing, snorkeling, or sunning at the beach. A light lunch of bread and fruit was followed by a heavy dinner of broiled fish and boiled lobsters. Parents with children started home before dusk—along with Ursula and Heather—while those who remained at the party drank wine and played music on a portable stereo. Kit sang in tune with the disc player and Maria proved to be one of the best dancers in the village—and Ryan with her. A few couples slipped into the woods or vacant hospital beds for quick love, only to return refreshed and eager to party longer. Not until the second cask of wine ran dry several hours later did the evening draw to a close.

Most of the westerners returned along the road to east village while using moonlight and torch—though a group consisting of Ryan, Kit, Maria, and Jose decided to take a more scenic route along the beach, moving into the southern district after an hour's slow walk. Only after they rounded the southern tip of the island did they rest. Maria soaked her feet and Kit enjoyed the reflection of the full moon across the sand. Ryan sat himself upon a weatherworn boulder (thick with salt and crud) while Jose lay down in a patch of grass along the shore. After a time, Maria waded to Ryan's rock and asked if there was room. Ryan scooted to one side.

"You're always so sweet," Maria said. "Kit's lucky."

Kit stood several yards away, looking out to sea as the surf lapped against her knees, and now turned around. "Did I hear my name?" she called out.

"I was saying how lucky you are to find the man you want to marry."

"Maybe twice."

"That's twice as lucky," Maria said, looking more at Ryan than at Kit—who turned and walked toward her ex-husband and the young woman near him.

When Kit stumbled and slipped in the surf, Ryan jumped up and splashed through the waves to pull his former wife from the water with one hand.

"Are you all right?" Ryan asked.

"Hands off in public," Kit slurred her words just a little, "Mr. Ryan Godson."

Ryan grinned. "You're ..."

"I'm not."

"How much wine did you drink?"

"Just two glasses," Kit said, "and one for the road. I'm not driving ..."

Now Kit took Ryan's arm to steady herself.

"My head's spinning," Kit said. "I need to sit. It's all this walking."

"And," Ryan said, "the fact you haven't drank this much for months. It always hits you hard."

Kit giggled as Ryan led her to the large rock where he was sitting. As Maria edged to one side, Kit took a place on the other while looking at Ryan and patting the rock.

"Sit between us," Kit said.

As Ryan did so, Kit draped her arms around his neck and rested her head on his shoulder. "This was a nice day. The best in weeks."

"It's been something else recently"—Ryan glanced at Maria —"not exactly what I'd planned."

"No," Kit said, "not exactly."

"But," Maria said, "it's also been exciting, wouldn't you say?"

Ryan nodded.

"We've learned a lot about each other," Maria continued, "and freedom and love."

Ryan looked to the sea as Kit touched his cheek.

"It won't be long," Kit said, "till we're married again."

"I guess so," Ryan whispered, taking another glance at Maria— who turned away.

A moment later, Kit stretched and stood, saying that tomorrow was a scheduled workday and they needed to leave. However, when Ryan and Maria stood to join her, Kit sat back down.

"I'm too dizzy," Kit said, "I'd like to rest here. This is beautiful. It's so quiet. You go home with Maria and Jose."

Ryan looked at his ex-wife. "We can't," he said, "leave you here."

"I'll be fine."

"Have you forgotten Jason?"

"He's not even on the island."

"I'm not so sure he's the only bad seed."

When Kit said she'd take her chances, Ryan looked at Maria and shrugged, telling her that he'd catch up later.

Maria abruptly rose and started for the west village, quickly followed by Jose. After several seconds of walking, the young woman called for Ryan—who jogged toward her and exchanged a few quiet words. Thereafter, Maria and Jose disappeared into the dark while Ryan returned to Kit.

"What'd she want?" Kit asked.

"Just a timetable. To know when we were expected home."

Kit wrinkled her nose.

"In case," Ryan explained, "I need help getting you to bed."

"You've always managed before."

Ryan laughed a little.

"I'm not sure it's me," Kit said, "she wants to tuck into bed."

Ryan fell silent.

Kit looked at him a long minute before talking.

"She's very pretty," Kit observed.

"She has nothing on you," Ryan said.

"I have fifteen years on her."

"Only thirteen."

"Is that my unlucky number?"

"What's her age matter?" Ryan replied. "You're not that old. There's certainly no lack of men looking at you."

"Then why," Kit asked with a hollow voice, "did your Hollywood friends leave wives my age for girls no older than her?"

"Perhaps," Ryan said as he looked away, "they were fools."

"Are you a fool?" Kit asked. "Am I a middle-age woman whose time to go has come?"

"Maria," Ryan said as he dropped his eyes, "doesn't do married men."

"You're no married man."

"I'm tired of bickering with you."

Kit took Ryan's hand. "You know what I miss?" she asked after a time.

"What's that?"

"Holding you on nights like this. Why don't you want to love me?"

"We're not married," Ryan said, "and I've wanted to respect your promise."

"I never promised," Kit said, "grandmother to be a nun with my own husband. Maybe we need more love. Maybe that's why we're not so close these days."

Kit drew near to Ryan and he didn't resist. Desire stirred when Kit threw her arms around Ryan's neck and a few minutes later, they moved to the sands beneath the sway of palms and spray of surf. Only once did Ryan look toward the trail on which Maria had disappeared into darkness. When they were finished, both slept an hour before bathing in the surf and starting for home.

IT WAS past midnight when Ryan and Kit stumbled into camp. After they said goodnight, Ryan walked toward the mess hall and Kit returned to her tent. As Ryan ate a few morsels of unspoiled food and took a drink of fruit juice, Maria soon approached—wearing a long tee shirt that only half-covered her thighs.

"Is she okay?"

"A little tipsy," Ryan said. "She needs a rest."

Maria stepped toward Ryan. "I've been waiting for hours."

"There was nothing I could do."

"I suppose not," Maria said as she moved close to Ryan. She threw her arms around his neck and pulled him close. When their faces fell apart after a long kiss, Maria looked into Ryan's eyes.

"I miss you when you're gone," Maria whispered.

"Me too."

Maria took his hand.

"Where're we going?" Ryan asked.

"You can stay with me tonight."

"I can't."

"Why not?"

"Kit."

"You're a free man."

"Not right in front of her. It'd kill her."

"And it kills me to see you treat her like a wife. When she's not."

"Give me one more week."

"No," Maria said, "resolve it now. You've told me you're not going to marry her again. So tell her. It's only common decency."

"I will. Just give me some time."

"No," Maria snapped. "I'm not going to be strung along as if you're a married man. That's why I've avoided affairs."

"I understand, but this is a sticky situation."

"Till the end of the week," Maria said with a flat tone, "or I'll tell her myself. I swear it."

"I guess the end of the week it is," Ryan said.

Maria nestled herself against Ryan, her hips pressed to his. "Come to bed," she cooed. "My engine's been revved for hours."

"No," Ryan protested. "I can't. Not tonight."

"I've given you time to tell her, but I'm not playing the saint while I wait"—Maria now pulled the tee shirt over her head and threw it into the hot coals where the shirt burst into flames and burned to ashes—"either you come to my tent or every strip of my clothes will burn in this fire and I'll stand here naked till dawn. She may be yours in public, but in private you belong to me and I'll not be denied what you promised."

Ryan dropped his head and followed Maria to her tent, returning to his own bed after they were done.

26

USED SUPPLIES AND NEW DEMANDS

The early morning sun remained eclipsed by treetops as a trim, bare-chested Euro-Islander with red hair and dark freckles sat on the bridge: her legs stretched into the flowing stream and a razor in hand. She wore nothing but jogging shorts and a matching headband. A dark-haired woman wrapped in a towel sat beside her, rinsing shampoo from her hair as suds streamed down her olive-skinned back. Both women upheld an invisible partition of privacy and only when the fair-skinned woman jumped a little did they talk.

"Ouch," Lisa cried out when the worn edge of a dull razor caught soft flesh beneath her arm. "I've gouged myself again. This razor's too dull and my hair's too thick. You have a spare razor?"

"I pluck hairs out, with tweezers," Deidra said. "It was the custom of my people long before we traded the Ohio Valley for a few straight razors. Before all you white women came along."

"I've never been to Ohio."

"Maybe your grandparents robbed a different tribe. Ever been to Oklahoma? Or Montana?"

"I don't consider myself," Lisa said with a smile, "to be Custer's long-lost granddaughter."

"The way your legs are looking," Deidra quipped, "you might consider yourself his long-lost grandson."

Lisa looked at her thighs. "I suppose," she said, "I am sporting a more European flair. As fashionable as the French, or maybe the Italians and Greeks."

"All of them white women. Hairy white women."

"Better that than plucking five thousand hairs."

"I thought you gave up shaving."

"I tried," Lisa said, "but they're starting to itch. And feel fuzzy. You sure you don't have a spare?"

"I heard," Deidra replied with a grin, "the south camp has spares. There's a guy with an old-fashioned straight razor, so they've pooled their disposables for trade."

"What's the price?"

"Mostly, booze and drugs. I hear it's a bag of pot for one razor. Or a bottle of booze."

"I'm down to one bottle of rum," Lisa said, "and the village dope burned with Jason's tent. Whatever else is true about him, he was generous with the weed. I smoked my stash a week after we arrived."

Deidra looked at Lisa before speaking.

"Rumor also has it," Deidra said with a low voice, "there are guys there who give shaves ... to friendly women."

"For sex?"

"It's not said up front," Deidra said, "but it's understood. Like prom or taking a vacation with a guy."

"I've never given myself either way. I choose for myself when I want a man."

"That's good," Deidra replied, "because I'm not so sure many men will be choosing those legs of yours."

"I have nice legs from my running."

"Too bad no one can see them."

Lisa pointed to a particularly dense patch above one knee. "They don't look so bad," she said. "Call it an eco-friendly look."

Deidra laughed.

After she finished shaving, Lisa slipped out of her shorts and waded upstream where she slowly sat down (the cool of water almost too cold to endure), then washed her hair and splashed her back. She watched Deidra drop her towel and wade downstream—where the bronze-skinned woman rinsed with her back turned toward the younger woman, picked up her towel and clothing, and walked behind trees. Lisa herself climbed from the pond with far less circumspection and pulled her shorts over her hips from the middle of the main path. Looking carefully at her dirty underwear and ragged bra, she rolled them up for cleaning and pulled a torn shirt over her shoulders—laughing when a breast protruded through a frayed hole.

"I need to find a needle and thread after supper," Lisa said. "This is my best work shirt."

Deidra didn't reply. She had started down the path for the village and was beyond earshot as Lisa secured her toiletries into a canvas bag after tightening every lid and snapping every cap. Afterwards, Lisa splashed the stubble and soap from the bridge and erased every sign of human habitation before returning to camp for a breakfast of bread and fruit.

THE REST of the week went well. Balmy skies and fresh breezes provided ideal weather for the work of Paradise. Ursula and Ilyana watched children and tended livestock while Ryan and Kit fished: netting several dozen fish, twenty crabs, and two lobsters. Charles dug large pits near the storehouse, then sealed them with rocks and banana leaves according to Polynesian techniques and plastic tarps according to Western technology—the pits serving as breadfruit storage bins, each one able to hold dozens of breadfruit (the island's best source of starch) until the fruit could be milled into flour. Lisa gathered the much-needed fruit while Joan boiled jelly from pineapple and mango, preserving it in half-gallon jars sealed with paraffin and lowered into underground pantries (where temperatures were cooler). Viet and Brent scoured the western district for food and spices, bringing home canvas bags filled with fruits and flowers from the furthest outreaches of western territory. They even found some pistachio trees that they picked clean. Lisa gathered fruit for the day's eating from nearby orchards while Hilary cut down trees subsequently stripped and stacked by Linh. Sean spent the week working with Maria to blaze trails toward Mount Zion and Jose ran the kitchen by himself, turning out to be a fair hand with food preparations.

The pace was such that almost every neighbor put in overtime every day through the end of the week. Saturday was declared a day of rest: with most villagers spending the morning relaxing and recovering. Several men washed clothes in the stream and a few women swept the week's dirt from their tents. Parents played with their children and children chased each other. Later, Heather took the children to the beach while Ryan called the village to an informal meeting to review construction plans. Only Olivia (who remained in detention) and John (who disappeared for the day) were absent. In particular, Ryan relayed plans that he and John had drafted to build private houses for their families—using carpentry skills that John had honed while working boathouse construction and renovation jobs near the outskirts of Phoenix.

When Ryan finished speaking, Charles—who initially remained stone-faced at the back of the mess hall—went to the front of the tent to address the village.

"To begin with," Charles said, "you don't have the right to build a private residence. If we need houses, why not use cooperative housing? Why allow the beginning of private property? If Rousseau and Marx are to be believed, the roots of inequality and exploitation are found in private property. The very thought of a permanent home smacks of bourgeois capitalism. Imagine the beginning of land speculation. And resale values. Next, we'll have suburbs and slums. Maybe we should plant private gardens and set up a new economic policy with cash crops while we're at it."

Ryan didn't reply until Charles sat down.

"I'm as progressive," Ryan said, "as a man can be without joining the Comintern, but we haven't much time to prepare for the rainy season. There's no way we can build an apartment complex. Nor is there any need to cut down so many trees—a point Lisa will appreciate. Whoever wishes to stay in the communal building can do so. I'm just asking a few houses be allowed."

"Apart from the matter of private property," Lisa said as she stood, "is the question of common lands. The trees of the forest belong to the whole village. By whose authority can you cut down even a single one for private use?"

"Do we need permission to use what's already ours?"

"Yes, you do," Lisa said. "We're not ecological entrepreneurs."

"Do we seek permission to crack coconuts?" Ryan pressed his point. "Do we seek permission to pick every banana?"

"A seed is not a tree. We're not prolife fanatics."

"We're not deer either, so we can't eat bark. At harvest, every wasted coconut will mean a lot more than a few chopped trees."

"I don't want to debate," Lisa said. "Let's just vote."

"Fine," Ryan said, "but first tell me this: if the village permits only communal housing, who determines where people live?"

"To each according to his need," Charles said.

"Which needs?" Ryan asked.

"Human needs," Charles said.

"Will the neighborhood," Ryan said, "give John his own place because he doesn't want to watch his ex-wife sleep with Sean? Will we favor Ursula because she has a newborn baby?"

"I don't know," Lisa said, "what'll happen."

"I do," Ryan replied. "It'll be musical beds."

"Private property," Lisa said with a shake of her head, "breeds inequality. You'll end up with chateaux and slums."

"Won't even the poorest among us own a house rather than a tent?"

"Very clever. A rising tide raises all houses."

"Besides," Ryan said, "I've filmed in Bucharest and I've seen what state-run housing amounts to: cement and cinder block."

"That's one socialist vision. Take a look at San Francisco for another."

"Overpriced housing and homelessness?"

Lisa scowled.

"You also have to admit," Ryan continued, "that communal control requires everyone to work longer hours. We'll need to work sixty hours a week for the rest of the summer to build an apartment. Maybe more. Private control of housing, on the other hand, means more work only for those who freely choose to build a place for themselves."

When Charles asked that the matter be put to a vote, Ryan turned to his compatriots.

"How many think," Ryan asked, "that John and I are free to build houses for ourselves?"

No one raised a hand.

"Seriously," Ryan said, "those in favor of drafting housing codes remain seated. Those who wish for laissez-faire housing, stand up."

Brent and Tiffany stood up—as did Ryan and Kit. Heather and Ursula also voted for economic liberalism. That left Charles, Joan, Hilary, Maria, Deidra, Sean, and Jose to vote with Lisa to establish a zoning ordinance (with Viet and Linh abstaining). Ryan conceded the loss before debating Lisa regarding the advantages and disadvantages of public versus private housing.

Lisa argued the establishment of private property would lead to the rape of the environment, the creation of material inequities, and even the first step into urban sprawl. She also insisted the charter itself forbade laissez-faire capitalism as well as the unnecessary destruction of environmental resources. It was her opinion that a second communal house should be constructed, allowing individuals to choose the residence where they preferred to live. Regulations could be drafted regarding clothing, lovemaking, and cleanliness—and residents not suited for close residency could be separated. Lisa also thought it prudent to construct a permanent medical hut (with indoor heating) in which young children and sick adults could find shelter from the cold and damp. When pressed, she admitted she preferred not to sleep near Ursula's expected baby and couldn't name anyone who wished otherwise.

Ryan argued to the contrary. He claimed that Lisa's proposal required more lumber than four or five private cottages might—which conceivably could shelter most of the village. He also noted the construction of private housing could be done on private time, keeping public stores intact and permitting more rapid completion of work quotas. As for the charter, Ryan pointed out that the homes of the east village were all privately built and that the charter itself granted freedom of association. He argued private homes allowed greater privacy and were little more than the regularization of their present establishment of private tents. Both freedom of association and human relationships, he noted, flourish better in private places than public ones. His arguments won over both Maria and Jose and the building of private housing was authorized when the final vote was tallied. Lisa and Charles conceded gracefully—asking only that houses be single-story structures measuring no more than 225-square-feet of floor space to conserve resources and preserve equality and that land plots remain public property. Their proposal was ratified and codified as law.

When the village delegated to Lisa the right to organize planning for urban development, she promised to submit at least tentative plans for expansion within two days. The meeting ended with hugs and handshakes and everyone pleased with its conciliatory tone. When a few neighbors pointed out that the creation of houses might also work to reduce consumption of trees in the bonfire since wood walls would mitigate night chills, Lisa seemed mollified regarding the building proposals. Previously, she hadn't considered private housing as a way both to save trees and prevent smoke pollution.

Later in the day, those interested in building private homes met with Ryan. Among them was John—who had skipped the earlier meeting to search for suitable timber (not really expecting such a close vote). Linh and Tiffany decided to share a duplex and instructed their husbands to make proper plans while Sean considered building a home for Deidra until his new wife pointed out that the building would likely be expropriated by Ursula's baby and that she preferred a tepee or a wigwam. Even Maria decided to build a house and asked whether Ryan might help her to raise one and he agreed to do so. Everyone else chose to remain in communal housing, though arrangements hadn't yet been finalized when a commotion from the beach interrupted the meeting as Viet's and Linh's daughters emerged from the woods shouting for their parents.

"PAPA! PAPA!" shouted the older of the girls as she ran to her parents. "A boat's coming. From the sea."

Her sister said the same and everyone jumped from their seat and hurried down the trail. Only Ursula and Kit lagged behind. Even though the distance was short, the two stragglers arrived before the sailboat was dragged ashore.

Most neighbors recognized Dr. Morales before he struck sand and greeted him with shouts across the surf. After the anthropologist ran aground, Brent and Viet pulled his boat beyond the tide's reach while Morales stumbled on the sand with unsteady legs—looking sunburned, dehydrated, and several pounds lighter.

Kit offered fresh water and the anthropologist took both it and several green bananas Ryan picked from a nearby tree.

"That's better," Dr. Morales said after his thirst was quenched and hunger somewhat satisfied. "I'll need a place to stay. Till I can return the boat tomorrow."

"We have a guest tent," Kit said.

"I'll take it. And more supper."

"I'll roast some fish and breadfruit."

"Good."

Kit started back to camp as Dr. Morales followed.

"I have much to say," the anthropologist said to the crowd, "after I eat. Someone bring my backpack."

Sean picked up the backpack and followed, as did the entire village. Forty-five minutes later, Dr. Morales's hunger was completely satisfied and Linh collected his dirty dishes. Inhabitants previously dispersed to their tents reassembled (even John now was numbered among them). Parents sent children to bed early so they could listen uninterrupted. Only after the entire village gathered around the campfire did Dr. Morales stand to speak: a cup of coffee in his hand and a pipe dangling from his mouth.

"Sorry," Dr. Morales aid, "if this pipe offends anyone, but my matches got wet and I haven't had a smoke in four days."

No one objected.

"In any case, I was fortunate to make it home. The winds died and I had to paddle all day. I only caught a light breeze this afternoon. Who knows what might have happened if I'd been at sea another day. I was out of water and food."

"What's the news?" Jose asked.

"Patience," Dr. Morales said as he struck a match and put it to the end of his pipe as he drew the flame into the bowl to burn tobacco. Only after he exhaled did he speak. "I've discovered an indigenous people."

Mouths dropped and gasps sounded.

"Indians," Sean said.

"Native Americans," Jose corrected him.

Deidra shook her head. "If this weren't such good news at the end of a nice day," she said, "I'd call you both the dolts that you are."

"Exactly," Dr. Morales aid, "the people look to be of Polynesian ancestry—maybe Tahitian, except that some have blue eyes and light hair."

"Maybe you've found the lost colony of Roanoke Island," Sean joked and several neighbors smiled. "It's been missing four hundred years."

"What's it mean?" Hilary asked.

"I'm not sure. Maybe they have blood ties to Pitcairn Island— where Christian Fletcher and his Bounty mutineers took their Tahitian women to escape the British fleet."

"That's hundreds of miles from here," Deidra said. "Maybe a thousand."

"Polynesians have traveled further," Dr. Morales responded.

Deidra nodded.

"Besides," the anthropologist said, "there are other possibilities.

Perhaps a marooned sailor or an abandoned pirate fell upon a native girl. Or may be a GI. There were plenty of ships and planes lost in the Pacific during the Second World War."

"That seems speculative," Jose said.

"This isn't"—Morales opened the backpack lying at his feet and pulled a steel helmet from inside—"It's a gunner's helmet. American issue, I believe."

Everyone fell silent.

"It was preserved at a shrine outside their main camp. I gather that the owner of this steel hat was washed to the island."

"Did he have a name?" Deidra asked.

"They called him," Dr. Morales paused to translate, "goddess-gift."

"I mean a Christian name. In English."

"I don't know it."

"Did he have dog tags?"

Dr. Morales thought for a long minute.

"I didn't see any," the anthropologist said, "and I didn't see a grave or any markings either. We can call him M.I.A."

"Where do they live?" Deidra asked.

"There's an atoll maybe three or four hours east, a little beyond the horizon."

"I arrived," the doctor moved his hands as he spoke, waving his pipe between puffs, "on the third day of sailing. The first two atolls were nothing but coral rings around submerged islands. Finally, I came upon a small atoll of about twenty islands (only one of them larger than a couple acres) enclosed within a coral-ringed lagoon. A village of indigenous peoples was there—surviving on coconuts, panandu, and a few fish. They also eat some birds and an occasional turtle."

The speaker paused to remember the sequence of events.

"I came upon their island near dusk," Dr. Morales continued as he rubbed his hands together from excitement, "and anchored the first night offshore, certain the island was inhabited by the sight of a small fire on what I later determined to be their sacred island. First thing in the morning, I gathered my courage and ran the boat aground where I saw some locals. When the people kept their distance, I used bait and nets to catch a couple fish that I grilled on the beach while the inhabitants watched from afar. After a couple hours, I picked out their chief—who was partially hidden in some brush."

No one stirred while Dr. Morales added tobacco to his pipe.

"Where was I?" the anthropologist asked. "Well, I steadied my nerves and approached him—the old patriarch, I mean. He lived on the island with a young wife. She's in her mid-twenties and they have three kids: two girls and one little boy. And a couple young men, maybe sixteen or so, live with them. There was also an old woman. Maybe some others too."

"Were they dangerous?" Linh asked.

"I didn't know, but I decided it was better to die and be eaten for dinner than live never knowing. This was the professional opportunity of the century. Far better than Margaret Meade being tricked by Samoan teenagers."

Only those who knew that the renowned anthropologist Margaret Meade had built her academic reputation on badly translated interviews with Samoan teenaged girls—who had played an elaborate powder room prank on the scholar by boasting of fabricated sexual experiences that Meade naively accepted as cultural norms—laughed at the quip.

"They offered me a bit of food," Morales said, "and one of the girls. I didn't want to take her but it seemed to be a matter of custom, so I did. Just some half-starved teenager with bad teeth. Maybe seventeen. Don't be shocked. We need to judge cultures from their own perspective, not ours. When in Rome ..."

Ilyana stood and walked away and Kit followed her. So did Linh and Tiffany. Heather stirred, but stayed.

"Did I say something?" Dr. Morales asked.

"I'll explain later," Charles said with a somber voice.

The anthropologist frowned.

"The girl," Dr. Morales said, "wasn't any younger than the

teenager who loved Paul Gauguin. And I'm no older than he was. Younger, in fact, since I don't turn forty-three for a full year. When in Tahiti, do as the ..."

Charles cut him off with a wave of the hand. "This isn't the place or time. We'll talk later."

Dr. Morales shrugged.

"In any case," the anthropologist said, "I only had to take her a couple times. Then she stopped coming and I was left alone to my work. They sleep in hammocks held together by matted coconut threads. Their beds sit a foot from the ground, covered by green leaves. The hammocks keep them dry enough when rains come. Of course, they have to raise a new roof whenever the leaves crumble. In any case, I was given a hammock and they made some urchin of a child sleep in the grass. The next day I helped with fishing. We used my nets to catch a sand shark and a few small fish. They were very excited."

Dr. Morales took a moment to relight his pipe.

"Most of the islanders," the anthropologist continued, "seem to live in polygamous families—some on separate islands. Every household has a man and usually two or three wives. Sometimes I saw a teenager or a few children, but childbirth and infant mortality appear to take high tolls. There weren't too many young people."

Now Dr. Morales changed subjects.

"They don't eat well and it shows," the scholar said. "Their teeth are rotted and their legs are bowed. Not one citrus tree on the whole atoll and only a handful of pineapple plants. They live on coconut and fish and turtle. Not much else as far as I can tell. Maybe an occasional gull or rodent. Of course, they're not very tall. Maybe five foot or so for the men and several inches shorter for women."

Dr. Morales took yet another puff from his pipe.

"The aborigines," Dr. Morales said after blowing out tobacco smoke, "don't wear much because there isn't much to wear. Banana leaves covering the genitals is about it. The women grow hair to their waists, then cut it in long clumps with sharpened clam shells. I saw them do it with my own eyes. The long hair is used for thread. It was fascinating to observe."

A few people rustled as Dr. Morales paused.

"I worked alongside them for ... what was it, four weeks?"

A couple heads nodded.

"And I picked up a good deal of their language during that time. They have a simple vocabulary and direct grammar. Not much in the way of subjunctive tense. Easy to learn."

Everyone laughed.

"I have a good ear for languages," Dr. Morales explained. "My second doctorate was in dialects of the Pacific, so it wasn't hard to catch the tongue. At least enough to function like a tourist. A few words, like fish and chief and sun came straight from Polynesian. But by the end of my stay, I could also identify most meals, name a majority of the natives, and even list a few of their gods."

"What kind of totem do they worship?" Deidra asked.

"A goddess called Ra'ankyi. They've cut a palm into her totem pole. It's filled with images of life: coconuts, birds, fish, turtles, sharks. A woman's face and body are carved at the top of what otherwise seems a rather textbook phallic-shaped totem pole: a thick, tall palm trunk with a shallow sway."

"Is she a fertility goddess?" Heather asked.

"That's what I think," Dr. Morales said. "Locked in that terrible little atoll, they can see only that food keeps them alive and women produce life. It's very crude, but also very intriguing. Imagine trying to make sense of life isolated on some small atoll. I'm not sure they fully appreciate the male role in procreation."

"I know the feeling," Sean said, though none of his neighbors laughed.

"Anyway," Dr. Morales continued, "I left three days ago but hit a storm which washed most of my supplies overboard. I had only a canteen around my waist, a MRE in my pocket, and a compass around my neck. It feels good to stand on solid land. It'll be even better to be in my own bed tomorrow."

The whole neighborhood broke into extended applause and Dr. Morales bowed several times.

"This is so exciting," Deidra said as the clapping finally died down, "real aborigines unspoiled by civilization. Just like my people once were. Will we have the chance to meet them someday?"

"That," Dr. Morales said, "brings me to my plans. I told the chief when I left I would return with food and drink. He seemed very excited. Said that his forefathers long told of the coming of sea-men and raft-men. I guess we might fulfill his prophecy."

"This sounds a little too familiar," Deidra said with a grimace. "We're not supposed to come as conquering gods are we? As Cortés and his conquistadors?"

Dr. Morales laughed out loud. "Nothing like that. They treated me more like a dinner guest than a divine prophecy. Very formal and very polite, but not overly deferential. They saved that for their own chief."

"Because I wouldn't want to play the role of Quetzalcoatl."

"I swear to the God in whom I don't believe," Dr. Morales said with a broad smile, "that I won't claim the atoll in the name of the Lord Jesus Christ or King Juan Carlos of Spain."

"We need to be careful," Deidra said, "not to wreck what they've created over the centuries."

"It was because," Dr. Morales said, "I didn't want to infringe on an ancient culture that I decided not to share our technology with the islanders. Still, it might be useful to send a load of food to them."

"Can't they come here for food?"

"I forgot to tell you," Dr. Morales answered, "they apparently don't sail. Damndest Polynesians I ever heard of. It makes me think that whatever originally put them on that island is buried deep enough in their collective psyche to keep them from the seas. A few men float shallow rafts around the atoll to spear fish and all of them play some type of scrimmage sport in the lagoon shallows, but they never touch the high seas. It seems to be more than fear—almost a taboo."

"You ought to be afraid to head into the open seas in that sailboat again," Deidra said, "that ought to be taboo."

"I agree," Dr. Morales said, "the island's close enough for the launch and I hope to petition the Executive Council for permission to take a look at these people with some of the professional staff—and send supplies. Once everything checks out, I'd like to initiate some visits. All of you should have the opportunity to observe the atoll. There's nothing like it on earth"—he looked at Charles and Joan —"and with your permission, I'd like to take Heather on one of the first trips. Before anything changes. It'd be the internship of a lifetime."

Heather seemed eager, so her parents gave their approval (though insisting she was old enough to make her own choices). When Charles updated Dr. Morales on recent crimes (both rape and arson), the anthropologist didn't comment, but just asked when Executive Council was scheduled to meet. He was excited to learn a session was scheduled for the coming Monday, less than two days away. Dr. Morales departed for New Plymouth before breakfast, leaving behind only the steel gunner's helmet—which Viet stored in his tent.

27

SHARING THE WEALTH OF NATIONS

Deidra sat beside Dr. Morales and Karla (who had been reappointed to her post by the east village) at Executive Council. Across the table sat Cynthia Fallows representing New Plymouth and two middle-aged men representing the north and south villages. Before the meeting commenced, Dr. Morales spoke informally about his voyage during a lunch of fish and fruit. Only after the meal was completed did Deidra administer the oath to begin the session. Now the anthropologist presented his findings to those who were properly constituted public authorities: briefing that his discovery could change not only the State of Paradise, but the very manner of political and cultural interaction practiced throughout the world.

"What I suggest," Dr. Morales said, "is a delegation that meets the needs of scholarship and the native peoples rather than the interests of our own state. I'll return to the natives with a few of our people—a type of diplomatic entourage. We can take the motorized launch since it's seaworthy in calm water and we can stock provisions in the empty seats. I calculate we can load maybe four hundred pounds of goods as long as our human cargo isn't too bulky. I'm slight of frame and Deidra is medium sized. We can take a large man and another woman without any real danger. Four of us should suffice."

"What kind of supplies?" Karla asked.

"Fish, coconuts, breadfruit, mangos, salt."

"Why not send tins of rice and jars of jelly?" another delegate suggested, a middle-aged southerner (with gray-streaked hair and an untrimmed beard) who spoke with a heavy Boston accent. "They'd be a treat and we have plenty of both."

"The humanitarian," Dr. Morales said, "in me wants to give them help, as well as to send a doctor with a vaccination kit. But the anthropologist says let the native culture live out its own drama. Only the author should rewrite the script."

"God?" the southerner asked.

"No," the anthropologist replied. "God is also part of the script: the mythical introduction."

"Then who is this author you speak of?" the southerner asked with a quizzical look.

"Nature. History. Culture."

"I don't know about that," Deidra said, "but I agree we should only send more of what they have. We'll increase the quantity of their supplies without changing the structure of their daily life or the economic underpinnings of their social organization."

"I served ten years," the southerner said, "in the Peace Corps to Ethiopia and I can tell you that hashing out more of the same isn't enough. We can feed these people all the flour paste in the world, but they need to be taught self-sufficiency."

Dr. Morales raised a hand to speak. "At the price of their cultural integrity?"

"At the price of ending the malnutrition you've described."

"Man does not live by bread alone," Dr. Morales said.

"Well, he doesn't live long without it."

"He can eat breadfruit."

"Or cake, some say."

Dr. Morales smiled at the riposte.

"To the point," the southerner continued, "every one of us would wish the same for ourselves."

"There's no need to bring religion into the discussion."

"Not religion, but ethics."

"You paraphrased Jesus."

"And?"

"And do unto others is at the core of Christian belief."

"Sorry."

"What if we hadn't known any better?" Deidra asked. "Technology may work miracles, but it kills nature. Were my people better for having used the white man's tools and eating his food? A whole continent was stolen from us in the name of progress."

"So ignorance is bliss?"

"It's better," Deidra said, "than the knowledge of supposedly good white people and their social evils."

"No one's going to steal the little atoll of the aborigines," the southerner said. "This time the white man pays the bills."

Dr. Morales cleared his throat.

"We may not," the scholar said, "steal their land, but we could steal their essence. First we'll give them training and technology, then we'll conclude that the atoll can't feed them, and finally we'll end up transferring them to our island: a trail of tears drowning out the lives willed to them by their own fathers."

Deidra started to raise her hand.

"And mothers," Dr. Morales immediately added.

Deidra nodded.

"From your description," the southerner remained uncowed, "the only reason they didn't beat us to this island was their fear of water and inability to navigate the seas."

"And?"

"We'll help them to correct a weakness."

"You're assuming," Dr. Morales said, "aquaphobia is a weakness, as if swimming were a universal norm."

"Even cats swim when they have to."

"But don't you see?" Dr. Morales said. "A culture consists of all sorts of characteristics: fear and courage, right and wrong, nature and spirit. Anything we change destroys what they themselves have become."

"Surely," the southerner said, "you're not arguing that means of production never change and that human communities should remain as static as Buddhist monasteries? Or as eternal as the Christian God? Can't a few improvements be made?"

"Yes," Dr. Morales said, "but change must flow from the inside as indigenous peoples live out the logic and limitations of their chosen existence. No imperialism can be tolerated, no matter how well-intentioned or selfless."

"I agree," the southerner said, "and that's why we didn't try to make the Ethiopians into Americans or franchise fast food in refugee camps. We simply used our technology to permit the survival of local culture when the ravages of man and nature might have dictated otherwise."

Dr. Morales said nothing.

"What do you propose?" Deidra said as she fixed her eyes on the southerner.

"To insure their survival."

"That's what the Seventh Cavalry said when Custer ordered the Sioux to reservations."

"Let me say something," Karla now joined the conversation. "We ourselves fled Western capitalism and industrialism and I suppose there's not a person on this island who wishes to expose traditional peoples to their corrupting influence."

Everyone nodded.

"And what's been said today makes sense on both sides. Agreed?"

Everyone nodded again.

"We have to send food," Karla continued, "since hunger doesn't enhance the survival of any way of life and Dr. Morales has clearly described a level of malnutrition that can curtail fertility and cause starvation. Right?"

For the third time every head nodded.

"We also agree," Karla said, "that we ought to send only foods the natives are accustomed to eating, though in larger quantities and with a nutritional balance that Cynthia and Dr. Graves can recommend. After all, even the Red Cross doesn't send beef to India or pork to Somalia."

"Making them wards of our state is no solution," the southerner objected. "We might as well set up a Bureau of Indian Affairs—and then build bingo parlors and gaming casinos."

Deidra answered with a forced smile and a sharp voice. "You've never been the governor of Wisconsin, have you?"

"I'm not Tommy Thompson and I'm more interested in working for their welfare than working them off welfare."

Everyone laughed.

"Just as the study of anthropology," the southern delegate said with a sober tone, "has rules like non-interference, so too the improvement of humanity has its codes. One of our first lessons is to teach people to help themselves. As we all know, it was foolish to hope the American government would or could sponsor humanitarian efforts indefinitely. Look at what happened to the Peace Corps under Reagan and Bush; just imagine how little Dubya will do for poverty and disease in the Third World. I doubt he can name five countries in sub-Sahara Africa, let alone the diseases that afflict them."

"Hear! Hear!" another man said.

"What these people need are tools to make their work more productive. They fish, so we give them nets and line. They burn wood, so why not give them axes? And since they already dig holes, what harm would a few shovels do?"

"No Westernization?" Dr. Morales asked. "No vaccinations? No literacy?"

"Only a few tools," the southerner said as he shook his head, "and a lesson on how to use them. I've seen it make a difference."

Dr. Morales solicited additional feedback from the Executive Council before requesting a vote in which Deidra's literal interpretation of multi-culturalism was rejected four votes to one. A second vote was taken which required the natives to be treated as equals and encouraged to trade for their supplies rather than be given handouts —even if the aborigines could offer little more than island visitation rights.

Afterwards, both Deidra and Karla volunteered to accompany Dr. Morales on a journey scheduled for the coming Saturday. Karla promised to find a man from her village to fill the open slot (it being decided that a man was required to balance out the gender ratio) since no one else from the Executive Council wished to travel. It also was decided all five villages should be levied a charitable contribution to the natives. The east village volunteered five crates of citrus fruit and the northern delegate promised a hundred coconuts. The base camp offered ten pounds of sea salt and the south neighborhood was assessed one hundred breadfruit—as well as enough banana leaves to line a storage pit. Deidra volunteered two hundred dried fish from the west. When applauded for her generosity, even she admitted that it felt better to be generous than culturally pure.

Dr. Morales left shortly after voluntary contributions were levied and the Executive Council had commended his efforts. Next, the council discussed the inventory of material possession—with Karla tabulating results and filling in the account books. The northern delegate, a tall man with a shoulder-length ponytail and a ragged beard, spoke first.

"We're out of everything," the northerner said. "Most of us are on our last set of decent clothes and some are wearing rags. Our food supply is low—down to a week's provisions after today's tax—and our disposable goods are completely gone. We're rationing everything. The only provisions we have left are our condom supply, five pounds of grass, and a marijuana field that could be harvested early in the event of shortages. And we have a few razors left."

"It says here you have wood for six months," Karla noted.

"Wood grows on trees," the northerner said, "and we have plenty. Who doesn't? In fact, one of our people cut down a whole forest. I have no problem with a good buzz to make you whistle while you work, but we found out dope doesn't mix well with saws. We lost thirty fruit trees that week."

No one laughed.

"We're low," the southern delegate with a Boston accent spoke, "on wood and marijuana, but we have extra clothing since we've been wearing grass skirts for several weeks. We made them mandatory as a rationing measure."

A couple delegates nodded.

"We've traded most of our razors," the southerner continued, "except for a few allotted to our women for their legs. Our barber uses a straight razor on men's faces. We can continue our routine another year or so."

"That's good planning," Karla said.

"We've run a planned economy from the first day. Not one scrap can be used without permission. As a result, we've built a reserve."

"But," the northerner said, "your inventory says you're living in tents."

"That's right," the southerner said, "our rule has been two-thirds vote for any construction or planting since none of us wanted to risk overcrowding. Mostly we've chosen a nomadic life and our agriculture has been concentrated on nurturing the fruits of nature rather than creating old-fashioned farms—capitalist or collective alike."

"Where will you stay during rainy season?" Karla asked, her expression both surprised and concerned.

"We'll seek high ground," the southerner said. "In fact, we've already begun to move provisions uphill. We break camp every week to accustom ourselves to life on the move. It's actually rather interesting."

"And you've enough food always picking without planting?"

"We store breadfruit and coconuts."

"You sound like Sioux," Deidra observed. "I prefer the Navajo way of life."

"Back to the topic," Karla said. "Inventory."

Everyone turned to the eastern woman.

"East neighborhood," Karla said, "has built up a three month supply of food, with some delicacies, and has completed a major housing program. We also retain most of our original tools—having broken only a single ax. Our alcohol comes to twenty bottles of hard liquor and we have a six-month marijuana reserve."

"That's impressive," the ponytailed northerner said.

Deidra asked what more the east village needed.

"Well," Karla answered, "we're out of razors and we've been reduced to using flint and clam shells to shave. And we need the usual disposables: toilet paper, tampons, laundry and hygiene supplies."

"The list says that you have a one-month supply of cleaning items."

"Yes," Karla said, "we're processing coconut oil for soap and using salt water to rinse our teeth. Private mouthwash and toothpaste supplies—especially soap—can be conserved for special occasions. Everyone cares for his or her own ration."

"The island capitalists," the southerner said.

"Neo-socialists is how we think of ourselves: unplanned socialism and an unbureaucratic regulated economy. We divided into individual lots as soon as we settled and let every neighbor tend her own backyard first. One-half of harvested wood and food is brought to the communal barn and the other half is kept for personal use. Even meals are private. We try to avoid the mass produced food of the mess hall. Too much waste and insipid taste."

"Do you need anything else?" Deidra asked.

"If it isn't hoarding," Karla said, "we'd like to pick up our share of the spare MREs and rice rations—so we can plan out next year's planting."

No one spoke a word and Karla didn't press her request. Indeed, after a long pause, she said the matter could be discussed at a later date and asked what problems the others might have, particularly the westerners.

Deidra now looked at her own notes.

"As you see," the west villager soon said, "we have enough food, and shelters are being built for the rainy season. I guess we're also out of razors and toiletries, but that's to be expected. The only problem I see is we're a little behind schedule, but that's because we have four children and two teenagers—and a pregnant girl who isn't working very hard: my husband's ex-girlfriend."

"Any needs," Cynthia Fallows raised her hand, "you consider particularly pressing?"

"Probably clothing. If there are ten untorn shirts in the entire village, it's a miracle. We threw too many into the scrap heap for candle wicks and rags early on. Most of us thought needle and thread work was a bit too traditional."

Everyone laughed and Karla asked if the westerners currently needed anything.

Deidra said they didn't.

Only then was the meeting opened to discussion.

"It seems to me," the Nurse Fallows began, "we'll need to keep a central reserve of food and tools and medicine, as originally planned. But we now need to decide how to bring some equality and stability to local economies. Do we let one camp go hungry and another do without wood? Or should we allow for a more charitable flow of property from each according to her means and to each according to his need?"

The delegates nodded.

"I propose," Nurse Fallow continued, "that we all contribute to a central warehouse from which each can take as he or she needs."

"I disagree," the southern delegate said. "We can't afford to give any of our food to other villagers. We've just enough for ourselves."

"So have we," Deidra said.

The northerner raised his hand. "You all," he declared, "were given lands with more fruit than we have. Most of our trees are nothing but wood; only a termite could find enough to eat on the north side of the island."

"Do you fish?" Deidra asked.

"We can't catch anything."

"Have you planted crops?"

"Yeah," the delegate said, "but the corn failed and the rains washed out our beans. Ours isn't very good farmland."

"You've managed to grow dope."

"We threw a few seeds into the forest and they grew."

"You must have magic beans," Karla said with a dour face.

"If magic is a state of mind, then I guess we do."

The discussion continued another hour until the council voted to redistribute all central supplies, except a three-week reserve (since its stores already were scheduled to be restocked with the planned resupply). The northern delegate thought the influx of food would alleviate tensions in the village, though he haggled with the southern delegate over the particulars of the agreement. It also was decided to arrange for cooperative trading between neighborhoods. An obvious imbalance of provisions was growing and needed to be redressed. Even the northerner admitted heavy forests that rendered his district less desirable could be traded for fruit from the southern glades or fish from the western lagoon (though he requested trading partners assume liability for delivery of any logs they acquired and vigorously refused to barter any razor blades). What to do about the obvious shortage of consumer goods—especially toilet paper and razors—was delayed for future consideration, as was a fuller consideration of private property. Everyone agreed that such a fundamental debate required the consensus of the entire island and shouldn't be considered so soon after the changes in marital law.

Finally, there were brief debates regarding the establishment of a central market and the planting of tobacco. The council failed to achieve consensus on a proposal to establish a bazaar where goods and services might be exchanged—fearing that such a market, useful as it might be, smacked too much of capitalism. As for tobacco, while the majority clearly considered tobacco a contraband crop and vigorously opposed establishment of tobacco plantations, consensus was not achieved regarding the treatment of citizens who might surreptitiously harvest tobacco plants hidden in the forest (like California cannabis farmers). While few favored the outright legalization of smoking, no one wanted to criminalize possession of a cigarette. Eventually, it was decided to explore laws in which the tobacco industry would be eradicated while allowing private citizens the right to possess up to an ounce of tobacco without legal repercussion.

The meeting lasted long after supper had been served in New Plymouth and the final piece of new business was to name the recently discovered atoll of natives (until such time as the aboriginal name for the island could be discovered). After suggestions based upon geographical or anthropological topography were rejected, Deidra relayed Sean's quip about the natives being the lost inhabitants of Roanoke Island. Everyone was amused by the joke and the name itself was adopted. Delegates spent the night in New Plymouth to stay for a reception for Dr. Morales. Councilors scheduled to gather taxes made plans for Wednesday morning.

KARLA THROTTLED BACK and the launch slowed as she navigated along the perimeter of the coral reef—the morning light shimmering off the waves while she steered through the surf. Already she saw the tents and huts of the northern village through the indistinct backdrop of the forest as she throttled the engine one last time and angled toward shore, then cut power and tilted the motor forward to prevent the shearing of the propeller shaft pin against sand. After weighing anchor, all three councilors (Karla, Deidra, and the ponytailed northern delegate) jumped into knee-deep water and sloshed ashore. When they reached the beach, the ponytailed northern delegate shouted for his neighbors to come collect their supplies.

None stirred.

The northern village consisted of little more than three walled huts and a dozen tents, most of them sagging. There was a cord of firewood stacked near a fire pit situated just beyond the border of dried algae that demarcated high tide. What remained of a burned barn stood a stone's throw away—its scorched timbers utterly collapsed—and a naked toddler with dried streaks of waste staining her buttocks and sand sticking to wet legs played in the sand. When Deidra talked to her, the girl just picked her nose. Every effort to inspire the child to talk failed and Deidra eventually concluded she had a speech impediment—then told the girl to stay away from the water as Deidra herself hurried to join the other two delegates deeper inland.

"Where are they?" Karla asked the northern councilor just as Deidra neared them.

"Morning siesta," the northerner answered. "It's too hot to work right now."

Deidra and Karla glanced at each other, but said nothing as they followed the ponytailed man to a large tent.

"Here we are," the northerner said, "the storage tent."

The northerner unzipped a canvas tent (military surplus in origin) and led the two women inside. Scores of coconuts were piled in a corner of the tent.

"Take what you need."

Karla picked up a coconut. "How fresh are they?"

"Don't know."

"When did you pick them?"

"We found a lot of these on the ground."

"Get me a machete."

"In the corner," the man said.

Karla fetched the machete and struck the husk several times, then cracked the nut itself with a single blow. No milk spilled and the meat was dry and tough.

"These can't be eaten," Karla declared.

"I guess they are a little dry."

Deidra groaned. "Would you eat them?"

"Suppose not," the northerner said with a frown. "Unless I really had a severe case of the munchies."

"Charity doesn't give away its scraps," Karla said with a scowl, "like a soup kitchen."

"Guess not, though I'm not sure beggars should be choosers. Follow me."

Now the man led Deidra and Karla down a half-cleared trail into the woods, passing an open sewage pit stinking with flies and maggots just before reaching a large tent in which four women and two men (none of them clothed) smoked weed from a water pipe.

One of the men invited Deidra and Karla to join the party, but both women declined. The northern delegate passed on the dope, but told his neighbors he'd return as soon as he could.

Several minutes later, the northerner led Deidra and Karla down a narrow, vine-covered trail deeper into the forest—where they found a small pasture with five well-staked tents and a smoldering fire.

"The Cleavers manage the rest of our supplies," the delegate said as he pointed to a fair-faced brunette, waved goodbye, and hurried toward camp.

As the delegate departed, the brown-haired woman—who wore a buttoned blouse and frayed shorts—put a finger to her lips to signal the two visitors, then pointed to the outskirts of camp.

"My daughter's napping," the woman whispered. "Over here, please."

Karla and Deidra moved as told and the woman picked up three empty mugs and a pot of coffee as she led them across the small camp. All three women took seats on empty supply crates beneath palm trees.

"I'm Sally McNeal," the brunette said, "what is it you need?"

"An explanation to begin with," Karla said.

"He took you through camp?"

"If that's what you call it."

"I call it a ghetto."

"I grew up on a reservation ghetto," Deidra said, "and I never saw such things."

"I grew up in Georgetown," Sally said as she shook her head with a grimace, "and I never even imagined such a mess."

"What's going on?" Karla asked. "We came here to collect charity for the islanders and now we find the need for charity at home."

"It's not charity they need," Sally said, nodding in the direction of the main northern camp. "Not one of them has done a full day's work since we arrived. At first, it was beach parties and MREs. Then they began scouring the land for coconuts and bananas. They picked every green banana in reach—only to find they all got constipated and couldn't eat any more of the things. The whole stack rotted. Then one of the fools cut down all of our grapefruit trees and left the fruit to rot. Now the heathens eat raw breadfruit most of the time, along with whatever nourishment they can get smoking dope. Your buddy Jason lives on marijuana brownies without the brownie. The one I feel sorry for is the girl. She lives like an animal. I guess those two boys are half-starved too—and poorly raised."

"We saw the girl," Deidra said. "Is she normal?"

"There's nothing wrong with her a good mother wouldn't cure, if that's what you mean. She talks when someone listens."

Deidra nodded.

"A few of us had enough," Sally continued, "and broke away."

"Executive Council wasn't told," Karla noted.

"No," Sally said, every word followed ever more quickly by another, "we didn't want to make a scandal and we've not even left the neighborhood, not really. It's just that we moved to this site so we could keep their stench at a distance"—the woman took a deep breath and began to talk a little more slowly—"We have a utility tent, a storage tent, and three residences. We're going to build a barn soon."

Deidra smiled. "And food stores?"

"We've got enough breadfruit and coconuts to last the rainy season. And the men have been salting fish for a couple days. We'll be okay."

"We were told you had no fish."

"To tell the truth, we haven't exactly announced the fish. We're hiding them for winter provisions."

"Do you have enough to share with the natives?"

"I heard about them," the woman said, "and I'd really like to help, but my guess is our own neighbors will be begging handouts soon enough. When our trees stop producing, they're going to be hungry."

"What're they thinking?" Karla said as she shook her head.

"They're not thinking," Sally said. "It's the dope. Not only are they so busy smoking the stuff that they can't think straight, but they've worked up some pipe dream to feed themselves. The idiots cleared three fields and planted marijuana in all of them. Of course, the fields were washed out with the rains and now their hopes are down to a few plants they bartered from Jason. They hope to trade dope for food and didn't plant even one row of corn. I heard they salted the entire stock of seeds and roasted them as snacks."

"Who's going to need that much dope?" Deidra asked. "We're too busy clearing land out west to party. And it's not likely that we'll be exporting the stuff anytime soon."

The woman nodded as she refilled cups of coffee.

"How many of you live here?" Karla asked.

"The Murphy's and their baby. My little girl and I. And a single guy named Roberto."

"So you live as a separate neighborhood?" Deidra said.

"Almost. Roberto heads back now and then. He takes food with him and brings smiles back. I'm guessing a trade is made."

Deidra looked puzzled. "Pot?"

"Not that kind of a smile. The kind that comes from a woman."

"Oh," Deidra said, "does that concern you?"

"Well," the woman said, "it's not ideal, but he works like a fiend. We wouldn't have made it this far without him. How he spends his share of the profits is between him and God."

Deidra and Karla nodded as the woman walked to a tent, then returned with a small crate that she placed before the two visitors.

"It's not much," Sally explained, "only a couple dozen lemons. But the tree is really fruitful and we'll lose some of the lemons before we can use them. They might be good for those islanders. In case they have the rickets."

Karla and Deidra thanked Sally for the donation and said they'd ask the Executive Council to investigate the northern village. On the return to the beach, they passed the tent of unclothed northerners. The ponytailed delegate sat naked, pinching a joint in one hand and stroking a middle-aged woman's thighs with the other. When he motioned for Karla and Deidra to take a break, the visitors just picked up their pace back to the boat. Once they cleared the woods, Karla observed that some people couldn't comprehend the difference between civilized sex and animal instincts. Deidra agreed.

After loading up the box of lemons and requisitioning several bundles of wood stacked near the beach, the women planned the rest of their day. They hoped to gather provisions from the other villages before supper—as well as to spend a few hours at New Plymouth preparing the goods for shipment to the natives. Some supplies would be bagged and others boxed, but the entire load needed to be tarped and tied before they retired for the night (since the trip was planned for the morning). Work plans drawn, Karla and Deidra set out to accomplish their purposes.

LINH SAT on a stump in front of the medical tent at New Plymouth where she watched a middle-aged male African-Islander stroll into the dispensary and quickly depart with a bottle of pills in hand before heading north. A moment later, a skinny and hairy-legged white woman emerged from a south-leading trail while carrying a bawling boy of two. Snot crusted across the boy's lip and his nose was swollen. The woman's hair was flat, her lips pale, and her eyes circled with dark rings. She looked straight at the medical tent and told the child to enter. When the boy balked, she dragged him in.

Linh listened to the subsequent commotion as the doctor shouted for the boy to sit still and winced when she remembered the trouble of taking young children to the doctor—especially for shots. Even as the boy's screaming grew louder, Ursula stepped from the tent, rolling her eyes.

"Am I pregnant," Ursula asked Linh, "with one of those?"

"They all have their moments."

"No one told me."

"How'd it go?"

"I listened to the heartbeat. I've put on three pounds."

"Really?"

"Do I look like I've gained more?"

"You look as thin as before, but maybe starting to show a bit."

"Only in the belly," Ursula said. "When is my chest supposed to swell?"

"Mine never did. It just hurt for nine months."

"I know the pain."

"How far along are you?"

"Beginning my third month."

"It passes so fast."

"It felt like an eternity vomiting in that tent."

"I remember."

Now Ursula tapped her abdomen. "I need to pee."

"Is this," Linh said with a smile, "just an excuse to use the good toilet?"

"I really have to go."

"So do I."

Both women walked behind the hospital tent where an eight-foot-tall plastic outhouse stood. The portable toilet was anchored with steel chains attached to concrete blocks buried deep in the ground and it didn't shake when Ursula pulled the door shut and snapped the handle. A few minutes later, she emerged from the portable toilet sporting a big smile.

"No flies," the pregnant woman announced, "and no stink and no urine on the seat. I sat down the whole time. There're even wet wipes and disinfectant spray. Heaven on earth."

"I can't wait," Linh said.

When Linh too emerged with a wide smile on her face, Ursula laughed out loud. "I told you," she said, "it was heaven on earth."

"Cleanliness, if I remember, is next to godliness."

"We need to get one of these for our village."

"Lisa calls them the crappings of capitalism."

"Then we should steal toilet paper as a good proletariat."

"The lords would hang us for poaching."

"We," Ursula said, "could argue it damages the environment to tear palm leaves off the trees to wipe ourselves."

"It's not me you need to convince," Linh said. "Talk to Lisa."

"Right. She thinks squatting in the woods is the best invention since ... well, since bran flakes."

"Circle of life and all that."

"And all that."

The women found a bit of fresh fruit at the base camp and sat to eat before starting west. As they left New Plymouth, Ursula picked up a bag of vitamins and an assortment of pain relievers from the dispensary. They walked fast and arrived home midafternoon—just in time to sort scraps saved from boxed lunches and prepare a late supper. Linh insisted on making a pot of fish and rice soup and Ursula didn't have the heart to object, so the latter baked flatbread to supplement what promised to be another uneaten dinner—and was careful to double the number of loaves.

An hour later, buckets of fish and rice still steamed in the pot while every crumb of bread was gone, along with two buckets of fresh fruit and three-dozen roasted breadfruit. Only Viet, sitting before the watchful eyes of s wife, scooped a second helping of soup into his bowl—though even he was careful not to let the ladle scrape the bottom of the pot.

28

COMING OF AGE IN PARADISE

An alarm rang from Kit's tent shortly before dawn. After dressing, the former actress hurried to a nearby tent— where she called out until Tiffany emerged from the dwelling and accompanied her to the mess hall. Kit prepared a pot of creamed breadfruit and Tiffany mixed muffins while they talked.

"Did I tell you," Kit asked, "Ryan started work on our house?"

"I saw the poles," Tiffany said.

"He said it'd be done in a few days. At least the frame."

"Brent said ours will take a month or so. I told him I'd find a better contractor if he keeps delaying."

"I'm looking forward to the move," Kit said. "Ryan and I were accustomed to a seven-bedroom mansion. We're not made for a one-room tent. It's just too confined."

"Is Ryan back home?" Tiffany asked.

"Not yet," Kit said. "I mean when he returns."

"Tell me about it. Brent snores and the kids kick."

"I guess I shouldn't complain."

Now Tiffany took a turn stirring the creamed breadfruit for a couple minutes. Only after a long pause did she speak.

"I don't want to be too intrusive," Tiffany said, "but ... is everything okay with you and Ryan?"

"Why do you ask?"

"You seemed so in love at our interview. And even a few weeks ago."

"We were."

"Do you spend any time together now?"

"I guess," Kit said, "it's hard to date after you've been married. We grew so accustomed to seeing each other we hardly needed to make an effort. Now we're so busy and so far apart, it seems."

"Do you still love him?"

"I've never stopped," Kit said as she dropped her eyes, "but it's different ... I guess I'm just tired."

"I'm glad to hear that's all it is."

"The question is whether he still loves me."

Tiffany took a drink from her coffee and Kit looked away.

"Even though we can remarry a week from Sunday," Kit continued after a long pause, "he hasn't said a word."

"Like you said, we're busy."

"Would you take that from Brent?"

Tiffany admitted she wouldn't take it very well at all.

"I won't make him marry me," Kit continued. "Can you imagine a shotgun wedding where the bride can't get pregnant?"

"I made Brent marry me and I'm not pregnant."

"You were at one time."

"Even so," Tiffany said, "I made him marry me the first time too."

"Maybe," Kit said with a shrug, "I should've made Ryan marry me right away. It's changed us so much to be single. It's easier to be married than to marry."

"You're slender, blond, and a philosopher," Tiffany faked a scowl. "Now I'm really jealous."

"I'm the jealous one," Kit said without a smile. "You have a great husband and two wonderful boys. Your life is what I really long for."

The cream of breadfruit came to a boil just as a mechanical timer rang for the muffins (which baked in a Dutch oven). Both women worked the next several minutes without talking. Only after chopped bits of sugar cane were added to the creamed breadfruit and a second pan of biscuits set in the oven did they rekindle their discussion.

"There's no privacy here," Kit said, "and no leisure. Ryan and I don't have the chance to talk like we used to."

"Brent and I go without sleep to talk."

"That's where that decree hurt us. It's hard not living with your own husband. Or whatever Ryan has become."

Tiffany dropped more cane into the pot. "Like you said," she observed, "you'll have privacy in another week or so."

When Kit dropped her voice and said the wedding needed to come soon, Tiffany asked what was wrong.

"It's just that," Kit whispered, "I've kept apart from him and he's not making much effort either. I went to him once and felt cheap afterwards."

"With your husband?"

"That's the point," Kit said, "he's not my husband and he's not a boyfriend or a fiancée or anything at all."

"In a way," Tiffany said, "I guess he isn't."

"It's odd not being married to your own husband," Kit said. "Especially when he's in no hurry to remarry."

"Kit," Tiffany said, "you've overlooked something important. He's building a house for you. Maybe he plans to elope."

"A new house and a second marriage," Kit said as she raised her eyebrows and forced a smile. "What more could I want?"

"You're on your first of both as far as most of us are concerned."

"Not according to the law."

"Marriage isn't a law; it's a relationship."

"I thought so once," Kit said as she folded her arms against her breasts, "but I've come to see Ryan changed the moment our marriage was annulled. It's as if the formality made him faithful. As if he stopped being a husband when we were no longer considered married."

"You made him faithful," Tiffany said.

"Not faithful enough."

"Has he ever cheated?"

"His eyes wander."

"They'll wander," Tiffany said, "back to you if he doesn't go blind first. The dissolution caught both of you at a low point. I suppose we all have a bit of wanderlust."

"I won't make him marry me."

"It worked well with Brent."

"Ryan is a different sort."

"They're all the same."

"Ryan is childless," Kit said, "and Brent's a father. Brent made choices; Ryan still feels for his freedom."

As the smell of hot muffins began to fill the hall, Kit pulled the pan of rolls from the oven and set them on the table while other villagers hurried toward the aroma of fresh pastry. Linh was the first to enter the room and to heap her plate high with muffins for her whole family. After she served her family (and ate three herself), she helped with cleanup so Kit could take a break.

It was Dr. Morales and Steve Lovejoy who woke to make final preparations for the overseas voyage. Karla and Deidra soon joined them—only to find the boat already fueled and loaded. The two men pushed it into the surf as Deidra started its motor and Karla manned the wheel. After climbing aboard, Dr. Morales opened a nautical chart and plotted vectors while Karla held the course. Steve and Deidra just enjoyed the dawn of a new day. No one talked, with each of the four islanders enjoying the rush of the breeze and the spray of the salt. Indeed, no one had moved faster than a downhill run for months and they now enjoyed the thrill of speed: of automobiles and airplanes and subways and ships. Even the smell of fuel drifting from a reserve container caused reminiscing. In any case, the boat covered the open sea in good time—the calm waters accommodating the day's travel. None of the voyagers fell ill.

Visibility was good and it didn't take long to find the atoll. Deidra spotted it with binoculars where it was marked on the chart and Dr.

Morales navigated a safe course through a gap in the reef. Soon they motored in the still waters of the lagoon, the boat's wake pushing to a V-shaped wedge of sea water. Anxious natives who emerged from grass huts were noticeably agitated by their first encounter with an internal combustion engine and the unusual waves following the boat, so Karla cut the engine and coasted to the shallows.

After weighing anchor, Steve guarded the boat while the others waded ashore and moved toward several children pushed forward as human shields by older brothers and sisters. No native spoke or moved for several minutes, excepting some whispering from the older children. It was only after Dr. Morales pulled slices of sugar cane from a canvas bag and dangled them at arm's length that the youngest natives inched forward. When he showed them how to eat the slivers of sweet, they followed his example and ate from the cane strips that he tossed to them.

Almost immediately, squeals of laughter rang across the beach as children tasted sugar for the first time. Indeed, their shouts drew mothers and fathers from the cover of the forest and soon even old women wrestled bits of cane from children and sucked stalks without sharing. Everyone buzzed with excitement and sugar: shouting and dancing at the godsend. Only after stalks of cane were chewed to tasteless splinters did the natives congregate around their benefactors.

Now the anthropologist used a few words, several gestures, and a couple nods to explain his mission to the wary natives—who posted stout men with long-shanked spears as a guard between the foreigners and the trail leading inland. After bits of food and trinkets were exchanged, the islanders reached into their boat for larger tools. Though native guards initially were startled by the shovels and axes and posed their weapons for self-defense, Dr. Morales settled their nerves by swearing peace in the name of the goddess and demonstrating how the tools were useful for digging holes and chopping wood.

Following the demonstration, a weathered patriarch with a thin beard and wiry arms eyed the women of Paradise—approaching

Karla to sniff her arm after some hesitation and several false starts. He squeezed her bicep and then a thigh. Even as Morales tried to distract the old man by digging a hole even deeper, the native lifted Karla's shirt to weigh one of her breasts—which were fuller and rounder than the spindly teats of the indigenous women (though not nearly as long)—in the palm of a hand. After failing to divert the old patriarch, the anthropologist advised Karla to accept the ritual greeting. The chief (as the patriarch turned out to be) clearly was pleased with the shape and size of the strange woman and jabbered something to his clan that Morales was unable to translate. Though Karla quickly pulled away and let her shirt fall over her chest, the native wasn't to be ignored, but spun the fair-skinned woman by the shoulders and squeezed both buttocks. The other islanders hopped and jumped in excitement, even the women. The young guards struck their spears into the sand in loud approval. Some licked their lips.

Dr. Morales drew attention away from a red-faced Karla by pulling a string of salted fish from the boat and throwing it to the villagers. The natives mobbed the prize as thirty salted perch were reduced to bits of bone before the anthropologist could explain that the fish were best broiled before eating.

Meanwhile, Steve unloaded crates of food and bundles of wood and Deidra started a fire. As the fire began to blaze, Steve and Deidra pried open a crate and showed the aboriginal women how to roast breadfruit while the anthropologist tutored aboriginal men (including the old patriarch) in the use of shovel and ax. Both the chief and the anthropologist soon expanded on the rudimentary vocabulary they'd passed during the previous visit of Dr. Morales.

The chief kept the shovel and ax for himself, but divided the food crates among his people, each man allotted an equal share. The natives tucked their food into leather pouches tied around their waists—cut from the dried skin of some small mammal. The food was well received and Morales was nearly mobbed when he tried to drag unopened crates back to the boat for transport to families watching from across the atoll. Only with considerable difficulty did he convince the natives that he wanted to deliver the food by boat and had no intention of Indian giving. Even then, the natives stepped back only on orders from their chief.

The packages were delivered as Steve delivered fresh fruits and salted fishes to the beaches of the various motu while Karla handed bits of chocolate to the children (over Deidra's strident objections). Their gift-giving completed, the visitors returned to the main island and feasted with locals on raw panandu and half-broiled gull. The fowl was undercooked, so the islanders didn't eat much—though their native hosts didn't hesitate to devour every scrap left by their finicky guests. When the natives had finished, only a few of the larger bones remained.

After dinner, Dr. Morales and Steve were offered women as expressions of gratitude. The anthropologist tried to convince the chief they preferred to take a carved tortoise shell sitting near a tall palm tree, but the old man wouldn't allow this breach of custom, so Morales slipped into a hut with a fair-faced girl whose breasts were unstretched and teeth mostly in place. Meanwhile, when a wrinkled woman missing her front teeth tried to pull Steve into the woods, the latter objected that he was a married man and sprinted back to the boat—which Karla and Deidra had anchored further offshore from fear of the old chief.

It didn't take Morales long to demonstrate his cultural awareness and subsequently seek out the chief for further negotiations. When he returned to the boat, he carried a magnificent tortoise shell on which was carved an elaborate series of images and petroglyphs.

"The chief didn't want to give it up," Dr. Morales explained as he loaded the native handiwork in the back of the boat, "but I swore on faith with the gods to return it before the next full moon. In return for its use, I promised to bring more food. And wood, too. The natives cook their food only on special occasions since they have only a few trees for firewood since no one is allowed to harvest trees growing in the sacred groves of the goddess."

"What about their cultural integrity?" Deidra said as she looked at the anthropologist. "I thought we weren't going to make them wards of the state."

"It's odd," Dr. Morales said, "but they expected us to come someday. They tell stories of great men who bring food from across the waters and fill their bellies with meat and their fires with wood."

"I thought they didn't know any outsiders."

"They don't, but they believe the gods sometimes send gifts from beyond the waters."

"If we're the fulfillment of their prophecy," Karla joined in, "then we aren't intruders. We fulfill the essence of their faith."

"That's how I see it too," Morales said. "They're some type of cargo cult and we're ... we're bringing the cargo."

Even Deidra was pleased with this turn of events and said so. She and the anthropologist continued to talk as Steve pushed the boat into deep water and Karla started the engine with a single pull of its cord. A minute later, the boat was cruising home at fifteen knots. As all four islanders reminisced about the places, people, and customs they'd observed, the trip passed quickly—reaching the shores of the State of Paradise an hour before dusk.

HEATHER SAT ALONE on the bridge. The evening shadows already stretched to their limit as the sun slipped behind the horizon. She used a steel-tipped brush to untangle the wet strands of her long hair and water poured from a halved coconut shell to rinse away the soap. Soon she turned to the sound of footsteps coming from the village and saw her parents emerging from the dusk.

"There she is," Charles called out.

"Clean of body, clean of mind," Joan said as she looked at her daughter. "That's our Heather."

Heather didn't laugh.

"Lighten up, daughter," Joan said. "You are undoubtedly the most serious girl I've ever met."

"What do you need, mother?"

"Your father and I need to talk to you."

"Now what's happened?" Heather asked. "You've decided on sex change operations? Maybe a his and her deal for married couples.

Complete with matching monographed towels—this week only. Maybe I can save some money by just calling mom dad and calling dad mom and treating you like cross-dressers. Of course, since sex changers can't bear children, you'll have to tell everyone I'm adopted."

Charles laughed.

"Very funny, Heather," Joan said. "You're not too far off the mark."

Heather scowled.

"As you know," Joan continued, "your father and I have an open marriage. That said, our affairs aren't working out very well on this island."

Heather shrugged.

"The problem is ... how can I say this nicely?" Joan paused for several seconds. "I'll just be frank, Heather. The problem is you."

Heather glared at her mother.

"Don't get me wrong," Joan continued. "We love you and mostly we're very proud of you. Especially your good grades and good manners. But young people around here see us more as parents than as sexual beings in our own right. Sometimes we even have to limit our appetites to protect you. Not to mention you sneaking in my tent, you naughty girl."

"Even kinky," Charles added.

Heather's face went pale.

"Tell her about that girl, Charles."

"Last week," Charles explained, "I could've enjoyed one of the choicest young women from the south. I saw in her eyes she was interested in what I had to offer. Until, that is, she said I looked like Heather's dad. When I admitted I was the culprit, she gasped, giggled, and got away. I suffered a great deal of frustration on your account after almost having that bird in hand."

Heather opened her mouth but no words came out.

"And it's the same in our neighborhood," Charles said. "I have no doubt the least interest would get me Olivia. And I'd like to try her once or twice—she has nice hips. But I just can't motivate myself in front of you."

"We never could," Joan said. "I guess that's why we hid ourselves from you for so long. It's one of our hang-ups."

"Rather like the incest taboo," Charles said. "It may be nothing more than a meaningless custom, but a custom it remains and we feel bound by it."

"To be honest, Heather," Joan continued, "we expected you to set yourself free here. We thought to free you from the dictates of patriarchy. However, we now find conservatism is entrenched in you and you in it."

Heather's lips curled and her cheeks went taut.

"And that's why," Charles concluded, "we'd like a divorce."

"You ... just married," Heather said, her voice cracking.

"Not from each other," Joan said, "but from you. We'd like to end our parental association."

Heather's knees buckled. "I'm not ..."

"I've already checked with the staff," Charles said, "and it's perfectly legal. And we're confident it's for your good. Even birds push unwilling chicks from the nest."

"You can't stop being my parents."

"Now that's an interesting point," Charles said, "especially since it's accepted law in every nation that a child can be unparented. Essentially, that's what adoption does. It removes one set of parents and replaces them with another set. What we propose is simply to perform the first half of an adoption."

Neither Heather nor her parents spoke for a long time. Heather's face was pale and her hands trembled while her parents just appeared embarrassed.

"Will she be an orphan?" Joan asked after a time.

"I don't think so," Charles said. "We haven't died."

"I'm glad," Joan noted. "I'd hate to make her an orphan. It's so sad."

"Who are you people?" Heather said with a shake of her head. "Has the sun bleached your brains?"

"No," Charles said, "but we're finally free to live in total freedom here and to live without constraint or restraint or any other hypocrisy."

"My name is Heather," Heather snarled, "I'm a seventeen-year old hypocrisy."

"That's an interesting observation," Joan said as she touched her ex-daughter on the arm, "Understand that we still love you, but it's best for us not to be your parents any longer. You're ready to fly on your own and we're tired of being objectified as parents rather than accepted as sexual beings in our own right."

"You can't do this to me," Heather declared as tears now washed her cheeks. "It's not right for you or me or anyone else. It's horrible and you're horrible parents. The worst ones in the whole world and I wish I'd never been born."

Joan forced a smile.

"That's a profound metaphysical question," Joan said, "that we could discuss for ..."

"For goodness sake," Heather shouted, "stop your damned philosophizing."

"Listen to me young lady," Joan growled with squared jaw and steeled eyes. "It's not your place to lecture the woman whose choice brought you into the world. Show a little respect."

Heather dropped her head and Charles stepped between the quarreling mother and daughter.

"By the way," Charles said, "we'd really appreciate it if you called us by our proper names from now on. Charlie or Charles will do for me. Your choice."

"You know I prefer Joan," Heather's mother said, "but you can call me Joanie for old time's sake."

"No more mom and dad or mother and father," Charles said.

"I'll try to remember, Pa," Heather said with a hollow tone.

"We don't hear you," Joan replied, clapping both hands over her ears as she and her ex-daughter's ex-father turned for camp, strolling hand in hand.

Heather dropped her bag of toiletries to the ground and folded her arms across her chest, digging fingernails into her forearms until they bled. She waded into the Pishon River, muttering to herself as she splashed through the darkness. When she reached the first bend, she broke into sobs.

RYAN THREW the core of a half-eaten mango into the fire. It sizzled and burst into flame as he watched it steam and smoke until it burned to a blackened crisp. He wondered how many trees wouldn't grow and how many birds wouldn't be nested in its limbs and began to count the number of seeds in a second mango when two slender hands reached from behind his shoulders and clasped over his chest.

"Hi, Ryan."

Ryan said nothing as he took the woman's hands in his own, rubbing thumb to thumb and palm to palm as he allowed the woman to nuzzle her cheek to his own.

"You seem somber," Maria whispered.

"We burn up so many chances," Ryan said as he closed his eyes. "Love. Happiness. The future is just fuel for our passions. Burn, baby, burn."

"I've never seen you so full of thought."

Ryan looked toward the fire.

"Men are thinking animals," Ryan said after a long pause. "Or maybe just animals."

"You've become quite the philosopher tonight," Maria answered as she squeezed Ryan's hand.

"I don't know myself, let alone philosophy."

"How many chances have you burned up?"

"Too many," Ryan said. "I really did love her. She was everything to me once and now I'm throwing her away like a mango core. And her children with her."

"She doesn't have children."

"She might have."

"People grow apart," Maria said. "Over time."

Ryan nodded and Maria looked at her own slender legs, warmed by the fire and glowing in its light. She stretched them as far as she could, toes pointed toward the horizon and thighs parted a little.

"Maybe they don't have to," Maria whispered. "Maybe we don't have to."

Ryan looked away. "We eat the fruit," he said, "and throw away the seed. We taste the pleasure and dispose of love."

"Did you tell her?"

"We burn life up."

"Did," Maria spoke a little louder, "you tell Kit about us?"

Ryan said nothing.

"Did you tell her?"

"It wasn't the right time."

"Why not?"

"She's been depressed."

"So have I," Maria lay her head on Ryan's shoulder as she let him stroke her hand. "I dream of us building our own house someday and of being known as yours."

"Kit once said the same."

"Love's not static," Maria said as she lay her hand on Ryan's knee, "or eternal or absolute. People love and people change. You don't love her any longer and it's not fair to hide it from her. Duty isn't love. Pity isn't love."

Ryan didn't reply.

"Would you make her stay," Maria asked, "if she no longer loved you?"

Ryan shook his head.

"No," Maria said, "you'd never make such a hateful demand. You'd never ask Kit to live a lonely and loveless life for your sake."

"I wouldn't."

"Then why ask it of yourself?"

"I hadn't thought of it like that," Ryan said as he straightened up.

"Do unto others," Maria said. "Isn't that the law of love?"

"Spare me the sermon," Ryan said as he moved one hand down Maria's thighs and the other across her chest. "What I need is a kiss."

When Maria unbuttoned her shirt and dropped it to the earth, Ryan jumped back.

"Not here, for goodness sake," Ryan protested.

Without a word, Maria took his hand as Ryan followed without protest to his tent—their love muted and quick. After they finished, the couple kissed goodnight and Maria returned home without retrieving her blouse.

29

THE INCIDENT ON TURTLE BEACH

Heather rose before dawn, her eyes blackened by dark rings of sleeplessness and bad dreams. She found a blouse near the cold ashes of the fire pit and placed it beside Maria's tent, then sat in the darkness as the sun rose. When Kit woke a few minutes later, both women worked for an hour, though Heather remained pensive despite Kit's efforts to humor her. Only a quip about Linh-inspired fish gut pancakes finally brought a smile to the teenager's face. Thereafter, the two women stirred pancake batter and cooked until the aroma of breakfast awoke the camp and a line queued for flapjacks—a line that dispersed only after everyone finished seconds and some took thirds before the batter ran dry. Only Lisa missed out, having gone to inspect the beaches for pollution and litter. Despite her absence at breakfast, lots were drawn during an impromptu meeting to select new officers: with Hilary being made Chief Neighbor and John chosen to serve on the Executive Council.

Following breakfast, Heather and Kit spent an hour cleaning before taking a seat in the mess tent to talk over tea as they watched Linh's daughters sunbathe and the twins shower themselves with dirt.

Heather pointed at the boys. "Do you," she asked, "want to clean them?"

"Not me," Kit laughed. "I scrubbed the griddle."

"I know. But they're filthy today."

"They're little boys."

"I was never one of those."

"A warm bath," Kit said with a laugh, "would make it so much easier. And a bar of soap."

"I'd give my virginity for a hot shower," Heather said before quickly blushing at her own quip. "I mean, I'd marry the man who bought me a shower."

Kit fell silent for a time.

"I've known," Kit said after a long pause, "women to give it for less."

"Give what?"

"Their virginity. You said you'd give it up for a hot shower."

"I didn't mean it."

"Still, I know women who married—as you say—for a lot less."

"I've had friends who first gave themselves up," Heather said, "for cheap beer and bad lies from skinny boys."

"You're not like the others your age," Kit said. "You're like the girls I knew when I was young."

"My ex-parents call me old-fashioned."

"Your parents are very modern."

"Ex-parents."

"They're just a little confused," Kit said. "Like teenagers. Give them time and they'll come home."

"No," Heather said, "they meant what they said. Their words were chosen with care. Whatever else they are, they're truth tellers—as best as they can see. It was they who always taught me to lift the veil, expose the lie, tell the truth."

"Your choices aren't theirs."

"We have different ends."

"I don't know," Kit said with a little smile, "whether you and your parents will have different ends, but certainly you've had different beginnings."

"Philosophy," Heather said, "teaches that an end isn't just what follows a beginning. It's also an aim or an aspiration."

"What exactly," Kit asked as she lowered her voice, "are you aiming for in your life?"

"Not cheap beer and lies. Or skinny boys either."

"My grandma told me to make a man swear his love with his hand on a Bible. She said nothing else cures them of themselves."

"Do you believe in the old-time religion?"

"I like what it brought."

"What's that?"

"Honor and loyalty. And love."

"You think so?"

"I can remember it. Though I was only a girl, I remember my pious aunt as a bride—so pure and innocent. It's a wedding I've never forgotten."

"Were all weddings like that?"

"No, but they were closer than today. Love itself seemed deeper and more demanding."

"What was love like when you were young?"

"William Shakespeare," Kit said with evident glee, "and Cotton Mather used to tell me ..."

Heather rolled her eyes. "I'm serious," she said. "What was dating like when you were young?"

"You've read the books and seen the movies."

"I'm sorry to say," Heather explained, "I don't get my history from Hollywood, even if you and Ryan made the film. Can you tell me what you saw? I've always wondered."

Kit leaned back and took a deep breath and thought about the question for a long while.

"Well," she finally said, "I guess that always depended on the girl."

"For nice girls," Heather said.

"I had several high school friends who married before they got pregnant."

"I know a girl who has two babies by three men."

Kit looked confused, her cheeks scrunched and nose wrinkled.

"The girl couldn't identify one of the dads," Heather explained, "and the courts didn't demand a blood test."

"Which of them paid support?"

"Neither."

"She supports herself?"

"No," Heather answered, "her uncle provides for her and the children."

"That doesn't seem right."

"Her Uncle Sam is very generous."

Kit laughed out loud. "He must be—to help promiscuous nieces. My uncles would've have called me a tramp and sent me packing."

"That's horrible."

"You asked what it was like when I was a girl. Though we'd given up believing in witches and ghosts by my day, we still believed in illegitimate births. At least when I was a girl. A few people still believed in virgins."

"And unicorns?" Heather asked as she blushed.

Kit said she wasn't quite that old.

"Today," Heather said, "they tell us to live and let live."

"That's what men say."

"Women do too."

"I don't."

"Why not?"

"When Ryan swore loyalty to me, I knew he'd be faithful. Not because he was all that reconciled to monogamy or so utterly devoted to me. I knew it because Ryan is a man of his word. You realize he gave up his career and brought us to this island because he felt compelled to uphold his public pronouncement to leave the United States if the Republicans won the election?"

Heather looked down. "You expect him," she whispered, "to live his whole life as a perfect husband because of a single promise?"

"I'm not that naive," Kit answered, "and our vows weren't foolish. Ryan scripted the ceremony himself; he promised to love me as long as he was able and to honor me with truth if he wasn't."

"That's not very romantic."

"No, it isn't. But it's true."

"Still, it'd be hard to hear at your wedding."

"It wasn't stated quite so crassly," Kit said. "Ryan is good with words and made it part of the joy of our special day."

"I don't want just a special day," Heather said as she looked up, "I want love that'll last an eternity. I want a man who will love me forever."

"A Mormon?"

"I like my cola," Heather said with a smile.

"You may have to give it up," Kit said, "to get the man of your dreams."

"I'm not sure which I'd prefer."

"I know exactly what you mean. A bottle of cola can be as satisfying as a husband. And I've haven't much of either for a long time."

"I can't really compare them."

"Someday," Kit said with a grimace, "you'll find the right guy. Or at least the right soda."

"I think I may be diet soda," Heather whispered after a loud laugh. "Every guy I've ever gone out with has wanted to fool around the first date. I won't and they don't call back. Not one of them."

"It's their loss."

"I'm not gaining much myself."

"You've kept your self-respect."

"How much happiness does that bring?" Heather's face slumped forward as hair veiled her face.

"You'd be surprised," Kit said as she closed her eyes tight.

"It's not like," Heather said, "I'm some pious miss wanting to wait a week after the honeymoon. All I want is to love the first man who touches me. To really love him and to have him really love me. And to be really sure. Is that asking so much?"

Kit poured hot water from a pot into her cup, dipped a tea bag, and stirred two sugar cubes while Heather waited for an answer.

"It's funny," Kit said after a time, "but once upon a time I remember hearing that songs of sex before marriage seemed scandalous—even for couples in love."

"Now," Heather said, "there'd be a scandal if they demanded love before sex."

"It's what we wanted, I guess."

"Not me," Heather said. "I want a man who'll die to other women and live to me alone. Who will love the children I give him and stay at my side when I'm old and gray. I want a man who won't run off with some girl when he turns forty and who won't flirt or look around. Ever."

"There never was such a man," Kit said. "What you want is a husband without eyes or hands or even a ..." Now she paused.

"I understand."

"I'm not so sure you do. Even Ryan looks and flirts, though he's a completely faithful husband."

"Until now," Heather blurted out.

Kit looked Heather in the eyes and asked what the teenager meant.

Heather looked away until she found the right words. Only after a long pause did she speak. "He's not," she whispered, "your husband now."

"I wonder," Kit said with a frown, "if he realizes it?"

Heather said nothing.

A moment later they rinsed their cups and Heather told all four children to search the village for litter while she prepared their lunch —though she gave larger disposal bags to Linh's daughters than to the twins. The sun already was beginning to climb to its midday heights when the children left the village.

By MIDMORNING, Lisa reached the waterfall where the Pishon River poured into the bay, collecting litter as she hiked downstream. At the falls, she removed lab equipment from her backpack: eyedroppers, test tubes, and petri dishes. Filling three of the glass tubes with fresh water, she measured drops of testing solution into each. One tube turned blood red and another light blue. She observed no reaction in the third beyond the dilution of the earth-colored chemical. Lisa rinsed the equipment and returned it to the storage case. The stream remained unpolluted, with the exception of the occasional plastic bottle or torn garment tangled along the banks.

The young woman's next task was to pick up litter strewn around the bay. She made two passes, one along the shore and the other several yards inland—filling a trash bag with biodegradable materials like banana peels, coconut husks, dead fish, a worn shirt, and even a frayed bra draped over a rock. The other bag remained empty except for a plastic wrapper and two dirty condoms. Lisa picked up the prophylactics with a stick since she didn't know who they belonged to and didn't want to find out. After securing the litter, she walked toward the beach and turned north.

As soon as she reached Turtle Beach, Lisa knew something was wrong. Fresh footprints stamped into the sand indicated trespassers had entered western territory. When Lisa saw that they led to dozens of shallow holes, she dropped her backpack and sprinted to the turtle nesting grounds, kneeling at the first hole she saw. There, a crushed shell was abandoned to the sand, its inch-long occupant dead in its own yolk. Every footprint led north, so Lisa followed them, quickly reaching a full run. When sand filled her shoes, she kicked them off —and her socks with them—and even when sand turned to soft mud and wet grass, Lisa continued to track the steps of the robbers. Only when she came to rocks did she move more carefully.

When she heard laughter ahead, Lisa redoubled her pace and found the poachers smoking a joint at the next bend, a little south of their own village. There were four of them—three northerners and Jason—and two wooden crates were stacked between them.

When the men saw Lisa coming, they greeted the young woman who now approached them—breathless and red-faced from her hard run.

"What's going on, Lisa?" Jason asked.

"You've poached our eggs," Lisa said as she caught her breath.

"You can cook yours however you like."

The others laughed.

"Take them back," Lisa said.

"We're hungry," one of the northern men said.

"You have to take them back. It's illegal to hunt sea turtles."

"Not by our laws," the hungry man said, "and not by the law of necessity either."

"They belong to our district. Your territory ends this side of Turtle Beach."

The man shrugged his shoulders. "Waste not, want not. You weren't using them."

"The turtles were."

"And we thank them for guarding our breakfast."

"That's our territory."

"From each according to his means. To each according to his ability," the man said as he motioned to the others it was time to leave.

As he turned away, Lisa jumped forward and pulled at the crates —which tipped and spilled their eggs. Several eggs were dashed against rocks and all of them cracked. Sticky gobs of yolk and tiny fetal turtles oozed on the ground—wasted to no apparent good.

"You bitch," the northern man growled. "We haven't eaten a good breakfast for two months."

The hungry northerner stepped forward. Though Jason grabbed his shoulder, the man broke free and lunged for Lisa—who stood her ground. Only after he came within arm's reach did the attacker stop before the young woman who stared him in the face, her fists clenched and back stiff.

"Eco-chick," the man said with a sneer, "plans to whip me."

The other men also laughed.

"Don't hurt her, Chuck," Jason said, "or you'll get a week time out. On a tropical island. With food and stash. And no work detail. It was hell, I tell you. Absolute hell."

When Lisa looked down to see a tiny turtle waving its delicate flippers atop a rock, sbe dropped to a knee to extend a hand to the tiny creature. Before, however, she could take the fetal turtle between her forefinger and thumb, the northerner dropped the heel of his boot on the animal and twisted his foot until green guts oozed. Afterwards, he shook bits of fetal turtle from the sole of his boot, sprinkling Lisa with blood and bile.

Just for a moment, Lisa froze before the blood-soaked rock. Then, without looking up, she drove from her legs as hard as she could and smashed her shoulders into the man's chest. Stunned by the ferocity of the attack, the northerner staggered backwards and Lisa pushed as hard as she could as the man grabbed her wrists. Both tumbled to the ground, Lisa landing atop her foe as she thrust a knee into his groin —though the northerner blocked the attack with a thigh as both cried out from the shock of collision. Lisa had lost the advantage of surprise and now her much larger foe rolled over, pinning the young woman and laughing hard as he held her down.

"She loves me," Chuck said. "She loves me not. Which is it?"

"I hate you," Lisa yelled as she clawed for his wrists.

Chuck forced Lisa's hands to the ground.

"Let's go," Jason said, still standing several feet away. "We've still got enough eggs. I'm hungry."

"But she loves me."

Lisa tried to throw the northerner off, but couldn't move and her hips only rocked him a bit rather than dislodging him.

Now Jason tugged at Chuck's collar. "It's your choice," he said, "if you want a rash of shit. All I want is some grub."

As the others picked up the second crate of eggs, Jason followed them and the northerner finally rolled away from Lisa—who sat in the dirt breathing hard and sobbing soft. After several minutes, she wrapped the dead turtle in her torn shirt and took it to the shore for burial at sea before she limped home, taking a half-hour to cover ground crossed in a sprint just a few minutes earlier.

SOON AFTER LISA limped into camp with bloodstained elbows and a swollen knee, Jose stood before the neighborhood—his face flush and pitch high. He waved his arms as he talked.

"Can't you see?" Jose protested. "Violence begets violence. They assault her and you attack them. It'll end in more fighting. The better way is to turn the other cheek and resist not an aggressor. Meekness will inherit the earth."

Deidra stood up, her back turned at Jose.

"To begin with," Deidra said, "to roll over and take the rape is old advice—and bad advice come to find out. You'd be singing a different tune if you were a woman."

Jose shook his head in disagreement, but Deidra paid no heed.

"Second," Deidra continued, "we're not Christians and the Sermon on the Mount has no place here. Even I know enough theology to realize the scheme works only if the Christian God actually exists as the protector and avenger of innocent people. It's not meekness but the meek themselves who are supposed to inherit the earth. We need to keep church and state separated."

Jose shook his head more vigorously in protest this time, but Deidra still paid no heed.

"Third," Deidra aid, "they've done enough harm. We need to teach them a lesson. Especially that Judas, Jason."

Hilary and Joan applauded and Ryan stood, getting Jose's attention with a wave of his arm.

"No one is attacking anyone," Ryan said. "We'll send a delegation to talk with them. Maybe we can resolve this peacefully. If that doesn't work, we'll go to the General Will."

Olivia jeered from the crowd even as Ryan ignored her.

"We'd gain little by fighting," Ryan continued, "since someone might get hurt and the problem still will exist."

"The General Will of the People will pass resolutions," Deidra said, "but what's needed is action. The northerners hurt one of our own and it's our duty to protect her. She's our people."

"That's the line of militarists," Jose said.

"Those who live by cowardice will die by cowardice," Deidra said. "The northerners poached our land and struck our neighbor. Can we pretend it didn't happen? Should the Sioux have lined up at Little Bighorn to be butchered by Custer's cavalry?"

"No one's asking," Ryan replied, "that we surrender to anyone. We just need to operate by the laws. Let's send representatives to investigate and negotiate."

"To negotiate with criminals?" Deidra responded. "Is that really sensible?"

"It makes more sense," Ryan said, "than asking innocent people to risk life and limb."

"I want a vote," Hilary shouted from the crowd.

A vote was taken and Ryan's position won out. Kit, John, Linh, Viet, Tiffany, Charles, Maria, Ursula, and Heather wanted to give peace another chance while Hilary, Brent, Sean, Olivia, Ilyana, Joan, and Deidra preferred immediate detention of the aggressors. Lisa remained in her tent and Jose boycotted the vote, believing both approaches equally motivated by revenge. Ryan was appointed head of the delegation while Sean and John were made his assistants. Deidra volunteered to accompany them and Hilary was sent to request an emergency meeting of the General Will of the People. As the west villagers assembled for the march north, the sun remained high overhead.

IT TOOK the four delegates thirty minutes to reach the northern village, where they found a dozen people—seven men and five women—circled around a low-burning fire. Turtle shells—some of them a foot wide—littered the area and the northerners barely acknowledged the arrival of the westerners. A square-shouldered youth walked from the fire pit to a pile of wood stacked twenty feet away and sat on it.

"Greetings, neighbors," Ryan said.

No one answered.

"Greetings," Ryan said louder.

Still no one replied, so Ryan walked near the fire to speak. "We have a complaint."

A teenaged boy stood. "So do we."

"What's that?" Ryan stammered.

"One of your women destroyed our property and attacked our

men," the teenaged boy said as he pointed at the man standing near the woodpile, "and knocked Chuck into the rocks. It could've given him a concussion."

"She had good reason," Ryan said.

"He stepped on a turtle, accidentally. It's no cause for violence."

Deidra stepped forward.

"We," Deidra said, "didn't hear of any accidents."

"We've got," the teenaged boy said, "three men—including one of your own—who tell it that way."

Ryan kicked at the sand.

"We've got," Ryan declared, "a woman with cuts and bruises which say otherwise."

"Tell her not to roll in the rocks."

John pushed Deidra aside and took the front place.

"The eggs are ours," John said.

"Yours?" one of the northern women sneered. "I cooked them myself; they come from turtle nests on the north point."

"Liars!" Deidra screamed.

"Get lost," the northern woman responded, "you damned bourgeois moralists."

Someone threw a banana peel which struck Deidra in the cheek. Laughter rang out and a second piece of rotted fruit sailed toward her. In a breath, fish bones and rotted fruit filled the air. As fruit flew faster and jeers grew louder, the westerners retreated ignominiously toward the trail—though Deidra stopped to shout that further poaching would be considered an act of war against man and god alike. As she turned away, a well-aimed breadfruit struck her in the back of the head and she staggered several steps before buckling at the knees. Sean and John grabbed her by the shoulders and helped her down the trail until she regained her footing.

Hilary returned later that night with news the southern and eastern districts were too busy to summon a General Will until the end of the week. An emergency meeting of the Executive Council, however, had been called for the next day. No one was heartened by the news.

30

SKIRMISHES AND RETREATS

Deidra opened her eyes. She wiped the inside of her thigh with a single finger and groaned out loud; her fingers wet from the flow of menstruation. When she snapped her wrist and flung blood across the tent, droplets splattered Sean's face.

"Ohhh," Sean said as he wiped the moisture away without knowing what it was, "is that dew?"

"A lot of good you've done," Deidra snapped as she crawled out of bed toward a stack of clean clothes across the tent.

Sean rolled over and looked toward his wife. "What'd I do?" he asked.

"Absolutely nothing."

"I suppose that's good," Sean said as he yawned.

Deidra glared at him. "My period started," she said.

"As they say," Sean said as he stretched and sat up, "the first rule is to do no harm."

"What do you think you're doing in my bed?"

"Sleeping. Till a minute ago."

"I didn't bring you here for fun and games."

"You were faking it?" Sean said. "You're a better actress than Kit."

"You've done her too?"

"I w ..." Sean paused. "I've seen her movies."

"You're such a boy."

"I'm man enough to make you squirm and shout."

"But not man enough to give me a son. Or a daughter."

"You want to get pregnant?"

Deidra looked at her groom for a long while. "I want," she eventually said, "to have a baby."

"That's news to me."

"I told you the first time."

"When?"

"When I prayed for the blessing of the great tiki."

"I thought it was a figure of speech for good sex."

Deidra said nothing.

"You mean," Sean said as he turned red, "you used me for my ... sperm?"

Deidra laughed out loud. "I'm not saying," she replied, "you don't have soft hands, but it's conception that really sticks inside a woman."

"I thought you wanted me."

"Why wouldn't I?" Deidra said with a shrug. "But I'm no tramp who does every man she likes. I bed a man for my reasons. Not his."

"You used me for a sperm donor?"

"You enjoyed donating."

"Well, I'm not giving any more blessing, as you call it."

"They say it's more blessed to give than receive."

"I don't want another baby," Sean said, his voice deep and raw. "I've already got one kid on the way and I don't intend to populate the new world by myself."

Deidra turned around, her face hard and voice uncompromising. "You," she scowled, "can conceive or you can leave. Doesn't matter to me which."

When Sean just stared without speaking, Deidra threw an empty backpack toward him.

"Pack up," she said, "and be out of here before breakfast."

"You're serious?"

"If your things are here in an hour, I'll throw them in the dirt. You weren't much help this month and now you don't want to do anything at all."

"But we're married," Sean said with a smirk.

"I want a divorce."

"You can't just end a marriage on your word."

"I just did," Deidra said, "so get out of here before I have you charged with stalking."

"I want alimony," Sean turned red.

"I'll tell you what," Deidra said, "we'll split fifty-fifty. You get the kids and I'll keep everything else. Now get out of my tent."

"You're crazy."

"Only to think the gods would bless the seed of a white man. It was poorly conceived theology."

"I'm damned if I do and damned if I don't," Sean growled. "Babies are ruining sex."

Deidra no longer looked at her ex-husband, but turned to a stack of clothing until she came to a worn towel—which she ripped into three long strips before folding one of them into a small rectangle that she inserted between her legs as a menstrual cloth. After making herself comfortable, she pulled a cotton shirt over her shoulders and a pair of knee-long khaki shorts around her hips. Only then did she leave the tent—carrying a pair of sandals in one hand and her tiki in the other. It was time for morning prayers.

Sean didn't take long to pack. In a few minutes, he carried his over-stuffed backpack to Jose's tent and threw it inside. Jose was just returning from breakfast and laughed hard when told of Deidra's behavior, but invited Sean to stay—as long as he didn't bring any babies. Two women overheard their banter and it wasn't long before the entire village knew Sean had been jilted.

EXECUTIVE COUNCIL DELEGATES reached the west village before noon, assembling at the new dinning hall. Steve Lovejoy was the first delegate to arrive and two women came thirty minutes later: a petite African-Islander from the south named Heidi and light-skinned

Nurse Fallows from New Plymouth. The northerners sent no delegate at all while Deidra represented the westerners. Formalities were skipped and old business ignored as the meeting moved straight to the point. To avoid a conflict of interest, it was decided Lisa should present her case directly rather than through an advocate. The rest of the westerners waited at the back of the mess hall—impatient for the administration of justice. Only Linh and Tiffany, who tended the children, remained absent.

"Before we begin," Heidi said, "I need to make a sad announcement. We lost a southern child yesterday. A baby died from influenza: Belinda's little girl."

Several neighbors gasped and others turned stone-faced. Two women wept.

"We buried her last night," Heidi said. "Her neighborhood is meeting today to resolve the housing issue. Three children have the flu, and two adults. We have to figure out how to avoid the spread of germs as well as how to keep our young ones warm while we're living as nomads. The rains have been much tougher than we anticipated."

Kit raised her hand. "Do you need provisions?" she asked.

"No," Heidi said, "we have firewood and food. Our tents are just too wet. We'll figure something out. I just thought you should be told one of our children died."

A moment of silence was observed. Five minutes later, the neighborhood's grief was set aside for the hard business at hand as Lisa recounted the events of Thursday—the poaching and pushing by northerners.

"What do you want us to do?" Nurse Fallows asked after events were recounted.

"You're the government," Lisa replied. "You tell us."

"We can talk with them."

Several westerners groaned.

"That won't do," John said. "We restrained our response expecting Small Council would make satisfaction."

"That's all very well," Nurse Fallows said, "but we can't administer punishment by our own authority. Only the General Will of the People can do so."

"When?" John asked.

"I can't say. The south is tied up with sick children."

"And the east village," Steve added, "is busy for the next few days putting a roof on a new theater. I have no problem calling a meeting, but I'm not sure everyone will come. The roof has to be raised before the wood gets wet and warps."

The westerners groaned again.

"Then we'll make matters right ourselves," Hilary protested. "If the state can't protect us, we retain the right to defend ourselves."

"And just where," Heidi asked, "would you get that right?"

"Through Madison and Locke."

"Just a pair of dead white males."

"No," Hilary said, "they revealed to us our right to freedom and self-defense. You do remember We the People?"

"I remember the failed Constitution of the Old World and I remember we're moved to Paradise."

"We emigrated to Paradise in the spirit of the Declaration of Independence and its author. At least I did."

"I'm not Sally Hemings," Heidi declared, "and you're not Thomas Jefferson. The Founding Fathers are no more your forefathers politically than they were mine genetically."

"We want justice," Hilary said.

"We must be patient."

Hilary stamped her foot. "And we want it now."

"No slogans here," Heidi scowled. "Justice takes time."

"How much time?"

"Enough to wait for."

"Fine," Hilary said, "we'll wait—if you'll detain the accused so he can't do any more harm. Even the United States detains criminals."

Heidi conferred with her fellow councilors.

"That's fair enough," Heidi announced a minute later, "the man will be arrested ... I mean, held for trial. Lisa will need to come with us to make a positive identification. We'll need escorts."

All of the western men except Jose volunteered to help. So did Hilary, Lisa, Deidra, and Joan.

"I protest," Jose objected, "this is worse than militarism—it's militiaism. It's not free government and it's certainly not progressive. Coercion is unfit for the citizens of Paradise."

No one applauded his short speech.

"Don't be a little pu"—Sean cut himself short—"Peace-nik."

"Pacifism brought me here," Jose protested.

"Peace brought all of us," Sean said, "but we're not talking about fighting for oil or killing for Unified Fruit. We want to protect our own community. Hopefully, the jerk will surrender. But if not, we have the duty to drag him to justice."

"Only by persuasion."

"Then come help us persuade him. Maybe you can make a difference."

"I'll go talk," Jose said. "To make peace."

Within the hour, Nurse Fallows hurried toward New Plymouth to brief developments to the professional staff while the newly organized company of militia began its march north. Hilary and Sean took point and moved without weapons. At the rear, John and Ryan picked up thick walking sticks in case of trouble. A contingent of eleven neighbors and councilpersons otherwise armed with nothing heavier than water bottles moved between them. The company moved in single file, their pace far from steady and their ranks irregular; some marched stone-faced while others joked and laughed. Jose wept for the entire thirty minutes that he followed the column to the north village.

"I DON'T LIKE THE NORTH."

It was Heather who talked as she stirred a boiling pot of diced pineapple whose tangy aroma filled the dining hall.

"It is hard," Kit said after a long pause, "to say anything nice about them. As a village, that is."

"Do you think there'll be trouble?"

"I hope not."

"I have a bad feeling," Heather said.

"I feel like a traitor," Kit said.

"Or a draft dodger."

Kit threw another handful of pineapple into the pot. "Is it thick enough?" she asked.

Heather stirred the pot with a long wooden spoon several times before tasting a spoonful and telling Kit to add more gelatin.

Kit did so.

"I'm no fighter," Kit said after a time. "I couldn't beat a rug. Still, it doesn't seem right for us to stay here in safety while the other women march with the men."

"Especially," Heather said, "after Sean practically drafted Jose."

"I know."

The pineapple continued to thicken as Heather moved the wooden spoon in a wide circle. Several minutes later she announced it was ready and the two women used potholders to grab the pot's handles as they pulled it from the fire—and soon ladled hot jelly into sterilized glass jars.

"I'm no pacifist," Kit said, "but I've always thought war man's work. Grandpa fought the Nazis while Grandma stayed at home and raised their children. That always seemed natural."

Heather agreed.

"I suppose," Kit continued, "Betty Grable did more for the war painted on tanks than driving one."

"Spoken like a true veteran of the silver screen."

"I've mustered out of Hollywood now."

"Maybe we should've sent along some pinup posters of you in your hula skirt. Linh tells stories."

Kit blushed.

"It'd give Sean," Heather said, "something to fight for."

"I don't think those posters would inspire your mother."

"Heaven only knows," Heather said, "but we can hope not. Heather doesn't want two moms."

Kit shook her head before returning the discussion to the current crisis.

"I just hope they don't fight," Kit said.

"So do I."

Both women poured the hot jelly. After a dozen jars were filled, Kit smiled and Heather asked what she was thinking about.

"I remember Grandma," Kit explained, "making homemade marmalade when I was a girl."

"I remember Joan," Heather said with a scowl, "shopping for kosher jam at a Manhattan deli. For observant neighbors."

Kit laughed, then picked up a small pan of hot melted wax from the edge of the stove and poured it over a jar filled with jelly. The wax spread over the jelly, congealing as it stuck to the glass and quickly thickening—leaving a sealed quart of jelly preserved for future use. Kit set the jelly beside twenty others like it before choosing another jar from thirty that remained empty. She ladled jelly into jars as Heather poured wax.

Both women continued to talk.

"Linh and Viet finish the mango jam?" Heather asked.

Kit nodded.

"Then all we have left is the banana?"

"And a little kiwi too," Kit said. "We'll have two hundred jars. That ought to keep us for a while."

"We won't finish today."

"I meant it ought to supply the village for a few months."

Heather shook her head. "Sean," she noted, "can eat a whole jar in a single sitting."

"Maybe," Kit said, "we should put him on limited rations?"

"I like that," Heather said, "we can give half of his share to Ursula. She's the one eating for two."

Both women laughed as Kit filled the last jars and dumped the final pint into a polished coconut husk for the evening meal. After using a spatula to scrape the pan clean, she flicked the last bit of jelly into the husk and set the pan aside for soaking. Heather retrieved a plastic crate for stacking of the jars. They finished work long before their friends returned from the north.

THE MILITIA CLOSED ranks as it entered the village. The afternoon sun blazed above the treetops and a thin waft of smoke circled overhead. Two women—a blond girl in her mid-twenties wearing a bikini and a brown-haired woman in her mid-thirties wearing nothing at all—watched the strangers march into their village. The older woman ran to the longhouse to summon help and soon five men in various levels of undress filed into the commons, followed by three women.

Heidi led the militia toward the assembled northerners. "Small Council," she announced, "wishes to speak with you."

"No one told us you were coming," Father Donovan said as he moved to the front of his fellow northerners.

"We couldn't exactly announce the meeting," Heidi said, "since you're the cause of it."

"I'm also a member of Small Council."

"Then join with us in securing justice."

"I'd rather join with my friends."

Heidi groaned.

"What do you need here?" Father Donovan demanded. "We've no extra food for the foreigners if that's what you want."

Heidi didn't flinch. "What we want is justice."

"Don't we all?"

"And we want it now."

"Don't we all?"

"This citizen," Heidi said, pointing at Lisa, "claims she was assaulted."

A chorus of hisses broke from the northerners.

"Don't we all?" Donovan said as the northerners laughed.

Lisa stepped forward and pointed to a square-faced man standing behind two others—accusing him of being the man who'd killed the turtle and attacked her.

"What do you have to say about this, Chuck?" Father Donovan asked the man.

"I say she's a liar."

"We'll let the people decide," Heidi said, "who's telling the truth."

"Fine by me," Donovan said. "We can also let the people decide what to do with thieves and mobs. This is the second time these capitalist pigs have marched into our village just because we don't share their bourgeois lifestyle."

John stepped forward. "We came," he said, "to keep the peace."

"Armed with clubs?" Donovan said, pointing at John's walking stick. "Or are those just ceremonial peacemakers?"

"We're not here to fight."

"We're not talking to anyone who brings weapons in our camp," Donovan declared. "We won't be intimidated."

Heidi looked at John and Ryan. "Get rid of those clubs."

Ryan flung his stick into the woods, watching it spin until it struck a tree and cracked, but John dropped his only after Heidi gave him a long look.

"Now we can talk in peace," Father Donovan announced as two northerners stepped beside him and all five women moved behind him.

Heidi took a position before the northerners, with her supporters from the Executive Council and the west village situated only a few steps to her rear—even as additional northerners arrived.

"Apparently," Heidi declared, "there was a fight over eggs."

"There was," Donovan said.

"And they were western district eggs."

"That's not true," the naked woman now shouted as she stepped in front of the priest.

"I'm not going to argue the case out here," Heidi said, "like I said, both sides will have their day in court."

"I'll be there with witnesses," the priest said.

"With perjurers," John scoffed, "is more like it."

"She attacked us," Donovan said as he rolled his eyes, "and she fell. She needs to be a little more careful with her step. As well as with the truth."

"I said we're not going to argue it out here," Heidi said. "Chuck can return with me to New Plymouth until we can sort this thing out."

"Not likely," Father Donovan replied.

"This is a serious charge," Heidi said, "and we can't let accused criminals roam free."

"No grand jury has indicted him."

"West village did."

"They don't exercise authority over us."

"Small Council does."

"Then indict her," Donovan pointed at Lisa, "for assault and destruction of property. And the rest of these fools for trespassing."

"Be reasonable," Heidi said as she took a step toward Donovan. "We just want him to come with us."

But the naked woman wasn't going to allow Heidi to make an arrest and now rushed forward and shoved Heidi hard. Heidi caught the woman's hair as both women tumbled to the ground—where the northern woman's forehead struck a rock. The crowd stilled, except for the loud gasp of another northern woman at the sight of gushing blood.

Before anyone could speak, all hell broke loose.

Donovan sprang upon his opponents, knocking Sean to one side and punching Lisa in the chest. His compatriots did the same and nearly every westerner went down, except Sean and John. Sean kept to his feet after Donovan's push, parrying the blows of a burly white man and immediately dropping his attacker with a hard blow that flattened the man's nose against his face and loosened his front teeth. Meanwhile, John grabbed an assailant by the wrists and flung him into a tree. The northerner didn't get up and John jumped into the melee, fighting beside Sean to aid fallen comrades—pulling the naked woman off Heidi and freeing Lisa from the weight of a broad-hipped woman who'd pinned her.

As the brawl continued, Sean knocked the wind from a wiry

Asian-Islander pulling Ryan's hair—felling the man with three quick punches to the stomach—then whirling about and telling John to charge Donovan himself (who was helping three northern compatriots wrestle Charles to the ground). All four northerners fell under the impact of the well-timed charge and the two westerners immediately pulled Charles away, dragging him to the protection of an improvised skirmish line organized by Steve. From the rear, Jose sobbed and asked why they couldn't live in peace.

Just as he reached the protection of his compatriots, Sean screamed from pain. The naked woman had struck him hard in a knee with John's discarded walking stick. He collapsed and stayed down, though John grabbed the woman before she could swing the weapon a second time and twisted her arm until she dropped the weapon—pulling her hair backwards so her throat was laid bare and her eyes welled with tears, then pushing the woman toward Donovan.

"Enough of this nonsense," John shouted.

"Let her go," Donovan screamed.

"We came in peace and you started war. We fought with fists and she used a weapon."

Donovan and his fellows slowly circled the westerners with an enveloping move, so John pulled the woman's hair until she cried out.

"That's close enough. You want to fight man-to-man, it's fine with me. Let our women go in peace and send your women home. Then we can fight it out."

"No one goes anywhere till she's free," Donovan said.

"That's fine with me," John answered as he pushed the woman toward Donovan, causing two men to jump back for fear of being knocked over. As they jumped away, John darted forward and grabbed the walking stick lying before them and raised it over his shoulder.

"This battle is over."

When two northerners sprang forward, John swung the stick hard. The weapon brushed just past the face of one man and over the ducked head of the other. Both men retreated.

"Get out of our camp," Donovan shouted.

The westerners and councilors backed from the north village until they reached the safety of the woods. Only then did they walk single-file back home—with John and Steve comprising a rear guard. Jose helped Ryan with Sean (whose knee already was swollen and stiff) by providing a shoulder to share the burden of weight. Hilary sprinted ahead to post a warning and Lisa ran to New Plymouth to summon help.

Before dark fell, the sound of an emergency siren wailed from atop Mount Zion even as the westerners recovered in the sanctuary of their village—where they made plans and treated wounds. Within half an hour, Sean's knee was immobilized with an air cast to await further medical attention and a cold rag was packed against Charles's loose tooth. Nothing could be done beyond some cleaning for John's torn knuckles, Ryan's bruised cheek, Steve's swollen eye, and Heidi's bruised scalp. Triage was administered and coffee brewed.

Lisa returned three hours after dark and announced that an emergency meeting was planned for the next morning. In fact, the entire state had been mobilized and every islander summoned, regardless of circumstance. Only the very sick would be excused from duty (with labor fines to be levied on villages with absent members). The first emergency session of the General Will of the People had been called. Viet and Brent were posted as guards that night—both men armed with clubs in case the northsmen attempted further violence.

31

PROTESTS, RIGHTS, AND WRONGS

B y midmorning, thirty-five islanders assembled at the west village and another dozen straggled in a short time later. Members of the Executive Council established a staging area near the beach where unopened cases of MREs, wool blankets, and food supplies were motored in by boat. By noon, half of the citizenry was congregated, many of them sullen or shocked from yesterday's violence and others nervous with excitement. Some also grieved the dead child.

Kit and Heather prepared a kettle of vegetable soup for lunch while Tiffany and Linh served flatbread loaves baked earlier that morning. Ursula mixed a vat of fruit punch and Heather arranged trays of sliced citrus. Jars of jam were unsealed and a cask of red wine was cracked open. Less than an hour into the afternoon, lunch was finished and dishes cleaned. Only then did sixty-five (mostly) silent citizens of the state of Paradise vote by clear majority to restore law and order. Since both popular sentiment and the lease with Russia precluded organizing a military force, the militia was mustered as the Gendarme of the General Will of the People.

Half of the fighters, among them most of the men and some of the tougher women, armed themselves with hastily sharpened spears and thick-handled clubs. Others—excepting only war protesters like Jose—filled bags of rocks with stone missiles, though several citizens contented themselves with carrying emergency medical supplies. Six women (including Heather and Kit) volunteered to tend children and prepare food at the west camp and Sean was assigned guard duty when he proved unable to walk without a staff. Though Sean protested his assignment to rear duty, Viet and Brent convinced him that the column needed to move fast to catch the north village napping and that an effective guard really was required at the west village.

Soon, the militia counted off and divided into two columns for the march north, moving two abreast along the trail until they arrived at the outskirts of the northern village—where the columns wheeled apart and encircled the village before northern resistance could be organized. Since the northsmen hadn't posted pickets, they were caught completely unawares, most of them napping. Only a few exiles living in the woods realized what was occurring and they neither resisted nor sounded the alarm. In fact, two men among them fell in with the militia. It was only when the first volley of stones crashed into the longhouse that the northsmen realized their predicament, surrendered their weapons, and permitted themselves to be separated into small groups for the march south. None dared resist.

By late afternoon, ninety-five citizens of Paradise were seated by district in the great tent pitched at New Plymouth—western plaintiffs and northern defendants sitting to the front and only a handful of citizens excused from attendance. The Executive Council and professional staff faced the citizenry and a platform was raised from which Heidi spoke. The tent soon warmed, but no one murmured—and the entire assembly remained subdued while oaths were sworn and the charter proclaimed as the General Will of the People reconstituted itself for the second time in a day, now with its full complement of citizens. Children were kept in place with sharp words and short tugs of ears while babies were quieted with goat milk and bits of broken bread. Rumors circulated with whispers and gasps.

Heidi surveyed her audience until every citizen stilled.

"Let's not beat around the bush," Heidi declared. "We have issues that require immediate resolution."

No one objected.

"The south neighborhood," Heidi said, "requires assistance. Many of you know we lost a child this week; Peregrine White died of the flu. What you might not know is we nearly lost two others. Doctor Graves says our tents are killing our young ones and we don't have enough time to build houses. We're asking the east village for its help."

An east villager stood. "What can we do?"

"We'd like to move our children," Heidi answered, "into some of your buildings till the flu passes."

A collective groan rang from the east village.

"We understand it'll be inconvenient," Heidi said, "but our children are dying and someone needs to help. What did we come here for except to help one another?"

It was Alan who had stood.

"We've built our homes," Alan said, "while your people roamed the forest like animals. And now you want to bring your children into our houses with vomit and diarrhea and germs? How fair is that? Should we suffer for your poor planning?"

Now the groans came from the south.

"All we need," a southern man said, "are a couple buildings. Even your barn would work."

"Just one building," Heidi begged, "until we can build our own."

Alan folded his arms across his chest. "How long," he asked, "will that take?"

"A week or two."

"We can raise a house in less than three days."

When Heidi asked Alan if he was volunteering, Alan conferred with his neighbors for several minutes before answering.

"We'll loan you," Alan said, "a warm barn for your children and send a dozen workers to build a house. We can frame a simple building large enough to hold six children and six adults in a day or two—complete with a thatched roof and walls. That's more than

enough space and we can't afford anything more if our own schedules are to be met. We have plans for rainy season."

Heidi asked if the children could be sent immediately and Alan
consented. Scattered applause greeted the compromise and Heidi
expressed her gratitude before announcing it time to discuss the
main item—a dispute between the west and north neighborhoods.
Heated protests sounded from the northerners and cold silence from
the west neighborhood as she began discussion.

"Yesterday," Heidi said, "there was fighting between the north and
west villages. Several people were injured."

Father Donovan jumped to his feet.

"Let me speak," the priest said, not waiting for permission to
speak as he pushed his way through the crowd. "Some of you know
me and others may not. My name is Father Gerald Killian Donovan
and I've been selected to represent my neighborhood in this dispute."

"You are the dispute," Hilary shouted from the crowd.

Donovan signaled for quiet with the sweep of a hand.

"Our neighborhood," Father Donovan said, "was given the worst
territory on this whole island. We have less land and fewer trees than
anyone else. Our creek isn't enough to piss in and our beach is fish-
less. We're out of coconuts and breadfruit and reduced to eating flour
mash twice a day. Mind you, we don't resent the affluence of the west
neighborhood—with its rich fishing grounds and ripe fruit orchards
—but we don't have those things and can't have them where we're at."

"Let them eat dope," a woman shouted from the west.

"In any case," Donovan continued, "we're making it, even though
we have to spend more time scavenging food than any other village
on this island—which, I might add, is fouling up our own building
plans. I've known Nicaraguan peasants who had an easier go of it
than we do. And that under the tyrant Somoza."

Someone shouted that they'd been given food reserves and Father
Donovan turned red.

"To tell the truth," the priest explained as his face reddened a
little, "we stacked ours on the beach, but the tide came in further
than we expected and everything washed to sea. Our entire supply

was on that beach. It'll likely wash up on Christmas Island, or there-abouts, in a few months."

"How much dope did you lose?"

"We were lucky," Father Donovan replied, even redder in the face than before, "it was stored in the barn."

Some in the crowd jeered while others just shook their heads.

"Two days ago," Father Donovan continued, "my neighbors and friends were gathering food. We're hungry and we need protein badly, so they decided to collect a few eggs. Not that anyone wanted to, but necessity required it."

Sean laughed out loud and Olivia cursed—though a southern woman shouted for them to mind their manners.

"My friends tell me they went to Turtle Beach," Donovan said, "where they found two dozen eggs on our side of the border, which is why some of my neighbors mistakenly said we collected them from the tip of the island. I can't discount one or two nests might have straddled the border or been a few feet across it, but I guess Chuck thought of the west more as good neighbors than trade rivals. None of us ever expected them to be so territorial. So possessive. We're just hoping they don't want to set up checkpoints and border guards. Or issue passports and make us fill out visas and work permits."

A few settlers laughed, mostly from the south.

"Lisa," Donovan continued, "called them poachers and knocked the food from their hands. Chuck says he stepped on a broken egg while trying to avoid an uncracked one when she slammed into him. He still has a knot on his head from the rock he struck. The next thing we know, a mob of westerners arrive at our camp threatening us. We were scared and when they came with reinforcements yester-day, what were we to think? Everyone knows they're prejudiced against our lifestyle. We thought they were coming to destroy our village—which they call a tropical slum. We don't have much, but we have the right to keep what little we possess. And we're not ashamed to say we'd fight for it."

"We're sorry about the injuries," Donovan said as he stepped forward and spoke a little less loud, though everyone who listened heard. "Things got out of hand, but I'm still not sure who started the fighting. Do with me what you think best, but give my village justice. All we need is a piece of good land and a few decent trees."

Heidi stepped forward. "The northsmen," she declared, "attacked Small Council without warning or reason. All we intended to do was bring Chuck here for your judgment."

"Armed men marched on our village," Donovan shouted. "What were we to think? You weren't there a day earlier when we were threatened by your western compatriots. It felt like a death squad coming for us."

After Ryan stood and asked to speak, Heidi gave him the floor and the former actor wasted no time with formalities or frivolities.

"To begin with," Ryan said, "the northsmen raided our land. They were told to keep from Turtle Beach. Jason—who was with them— knew perfectly well the beach was ours and the turtles under our protection."

Applause erupted from the west neighborhood.

"Second," Ryan continued, "Lisa admits she attacked Chuck, but only under provocation. He refused to return the turtle eggs to their nests and deliberately crushed a protected fetal turtle with his bare foot."

No one stirred, neither west nor north.

"Third," Ryan said, "we were on a peaceful mission and didn't hold weapons when we were attacked yesterday. We even threw our walking sticks away—only to be clubbed with them. As Heidi noted, our goal was to detain the aggressor for trial. We were public servants on official business and the northsmen attacked us."

A couple northerners hooted, though most remained quiet.

"The fact is we've reached a crisis in this enterprise," Ryan continued, "and violent men are using intimidation to force themselves over us. They've become lazy and lethargic and their bellies are hungry. As for their complaints about land, I was the one who laid out the districts. To be sure, there are minute differences between the neighborhoods since we're living on a tropical island rather than in a suburban subdivision; but this island can support three or four times the present population without serious cultivation. If the northsmen planted just a little corn or wheat with their dope or fished at dawn, they'd be able to satisfy their hunger."

Catcalls came from the north neighborhood as Ryan turned to the entire General Will of the People—now projecting his voice as loud as he could.

"Today you have a choice," Ryan shouted. "It's up to each of you to decide whether we'll tolerate northern fascism or whether the rule of law will prevail."

Scattered applause greeted the conclusion of Ryan's speech and he returned to his own people as Heidi stood to ask who wished to speak next and several people raised their hands. One woman seconded Ryan's motion and another sided with Donovan. Two men declared themselves to be unable to sort out the facts of the case and Jose declared he'd vote only for a peaceful solution. A gray-haired feminist reminded the assembly not to overstate the value of a fetal turtle only a minute removed from its shell.

The staff sociologist then took the podium.

"We sound like conservatives," Dr. Law said, "fixing blame, advocating law, and judging morality. How can we forget our principles? Are we a mob of gossips judging and condemning our neighbors? I should hope not."

The crowd stilled as the sociologist continued.

"What we have here," Dr. Law explained, "is a classic case of policy-driven human conflict: two competing cultures are clashing over the press of resources and respect. On one hand, the northerners who emigrated to this place came looking for the fullest possible expression of liberty. And that freedom is represented to them in the legal cultivation and enjoyment of marijuana. On the other hand, the west neighborhood values material progress and success—a more bourgeois form of secularity. Everyone knows how adept they've become in the cultivation of crops and the gathering of the fruits of the earth."

The sociologist took a breath before continuing.

"Turtle Beach," Dr. Law explained, "represents the point where these two cultures clash. To the northerners, it represents freedom from bourgeois values and middle-class careerism. The beach is a place to find food and to eat it so that free living might be enjoyed. For the westerners, though, the beach represents a place of refuge from the cares and labors that consume them as they toil through their days. The turtles of the beach were an exempt species and their home a natural sanctuary—one spot where the desires of the belly and the needs of the market might be checked."

The crowd grew more attentive. Eyes were fixed forward and ears cocked to the podium.

"There's been a clash," Dr. Law continued, "and while it's difficult to sort out the details, I agree we ought not spend all afternoon fixing blame. It'd be far better to fix the problem."

"Blame is the problem," Ryan said as he stood. "The northerners are lazy and violent and they're going to be our ruin if we don't stop them."

"See what I mean," the sociologist said, "even Ryan has been driven to legal conservatism; he's preaching conservative fictions of crime and punishment."

Ryan threw up his hands and sat down as a murmur worked through the west neighborhood.

The sociologist stood his ground.

"We don't have time," Dr. Law declared, "to discuss the theory of the matter. I'll present a paper in a few weeks. All we can do now is to address the problem as we are confronted with two possible courses of action: either we can hold a trial and mete out punishment like silent majority and moral majority conservatives or we can take progressive steps to alleviate the problem."

Heads nodded throughout the crowd.

"I propose," the sociologist said, "we help the northerners help themselves. What they need is shelter and food. We can build them a longhouse and fill their empty barns with gifts of food just as we're doing with the southerners."

"Do you actually mean," Ryan asked, red-faced in anger, "we should reward them for being sociopaths?"

"What I mean to say," the sociologist's words came out slow and deliberate as his hands moved in perfect cadence to his speech, "is that we need to fix the underlying causes of their behavior. To address root causes. Our choice is between a war on people or a war on poverty. I choose compassion."

Ryan turned to the assembly.

"And how often," Ryan asked, "will we need to repeat this gesture? If we give in to their violence, not only will we never escape threats but they themselves will be destroyed in a vicious cycle of dependency upon the public dole."

An Asian woman from the south camp jumped to her feet. "Oh lord," she cried out, "Ryan has morphed into Newt Gingrich."

"Gingrich," Ryan shouted, "wanted to starve the poor. I only want to stop thuggery."

Another woman's voice rang out, this one from the northern village. "The new Newt."

A third voice repeated her words. "The new Newt."

A moment later, hecklers from the south and north neighborhoods were chanting, "New Newt. New Newt."

Ryan seethed with anger and humiliation, but sat when Heidi returned to the podium. It took her several minutes to settle the crowd.

"Ryan is no Newt Gingrich," she said, "but it's clear there are two distinct paths before us. Do we wish to make an inquiry into this incident to punish it or initiate relief efforts? Or do we wish to do both? Or neither? I suggest we take motions for formal consideration."

Heidi's proposal was seconded and carried.

The next motion was made by a black-haired man, perhaps thirty years old, from the south—who handed a baby to a nearby woman before standing to speak.

"I wanted to say," the black-haired man said, "while I don't agree with their violence, I understand the desperation that motivated the northerners. I've heard men and women of my own neighborhood speak harsh words against other islanders since our lives took a turn for the worse. I recommend we forgive them for a bad solution to an even worse problem."

A couple neighbors applauded and a tall Latino from the south village stood.

"I agree with Jon," the southern Latino said. "Let's make a clean start."

"That's easy for you to say," a man from the east village shouted as he too stood.

Everyone looked to the speaker from the east village.

"That's easy for you to say," Alan repeated himself, "because you're no better than they are. Some men steal with guns; others use the law. You've just confiscated our property and our labor, so it doesn't bother you at all to see laziness rewarded. You people chose the life of nomads, so sleep in the rain. And they chose dope, so let them eat marijuana brownies."

A dozen east villagers laughed and a few gave Alan high fives.

A blonde in her thirties sitting with the delegation from New Plymouth now stood. She wore ragged clothes and showed thin hair chopped unevenly around her shoulders. It was Janine Erikson, the staff psychologist, who now spoke.

"There are two sides to charity," Dr. Erikson said. "One is the need of those who receive public assistance. All of us can agree that there is such a need even if we disagree about the causes of the crisis. The hungrier the northerners become, the more likely they are to erupt into violence. Why else do you think the elder Bush sent food to Somalia? It sure wasn't compassion. He didn't care about Afro-Americans, let alone Afro-Africans. Still, we also need to consider the effects of charity on what used to be called our own souls. As a materialist and a scientific psychologist, I'm not much of a believer in eternal souls, but I do have faith that generosity makes an impact upon our own lives. What drew me to the political left was its ability to make me a better person. I grew up trick-or-treating for UNICEF and sponsoring walk-a-thons for breast cancer and AIDS research. For the last few months, none of us have lacked for anything truly necessary and already it seems that our love grows cold. We who willingly endured heaps of bureaucratic waste and corruption in the United States hoping against hope that the smallest sliver of our taxes —months of labor, I hasten to add—might reach those in need now are quarreling over a day's work to help our immediate neighbors. We've proven ourselves worse than the Amish—who pay federal taxes without collecting benefits and still sweat willingly for their kith and kin."

Everyone listened, some with teary eyes and others with burning cheeks.

"We need," the psychologist continued, "to help our neighbors whether or not they've made their own mess. None of us really believed welfare mothers and drug addicts were completely without blame, no matter what we were forced to declare in public. We simply insisted on forgiveness and a new start rather than starvation or jail or workhouses. Mistakes have been made and crimes committed, but I don't see why we can't assist needy neighbors to stop this cancer before it grows. I propose that ..."

Here the psychologist took a minute to choose her words. "I propose," she said, "we both build a barn for the northerners and fill it with food and at the same time punish anyone who instigated violence and terror, of whatever camp he or she might be."

Heads nodded and hands clapped as the slight-framed woman finished speaking. Within seconds, a dozen settlers seconded her motion, cast their votes, and accepted the final proposal by a margin of fifty votes. Even a few northerners voted for it.

"Now we're showing the world how to live," the psychologist told the crowd after the votes were tallied. "I'd like to propose we build the house tomorrow. If everyone helps, we can finish it in a day or two and have this problem solved."

"Does," Dr. Erikson asked, "the west neighborhood object?"

"We accept your proposal," Ryan announced after a short consultation with west villagers, "to keep the entire island involved in this matter and we volunteer a month's rations. We also suggest another month's stores be taken from the central reserves for our neighbors to the north. All we ask is that the assault on Lisa be treated seriously and northerners respect our territorial limits and environmental protections."

"They say good fences make good neighbors," the psychologist said. "I propose we accept your proposal and request that members of the Small Council confirm border markings between the two territories while the rest of the assembly builds the longhouse."

The crowd voiced its approval with scattered applause and words of encouragement as Ryan signaled for the floor.

"I'd also like to suggest," Ryan said, "we establish a clear procedure for dealing with poaching. Maybe set up a Department of Natural Resources."

"Good point," Dr. Erikson said, "but let's take this one issue at a time. First, let's vote on the rations. How many of you vote to stock the north neighborhood with one month's rations and to accept the west neighborhood's offer of one month's food?"

The vote was unanimous in favor of the proposal.

"Now I need a vote on setting up territorial lines in the north. All those in favor say yea."

The crowd thundered its yea.

"Nay?"

A couple voices protested.

Dr. Erikson gave a thumbs up.

"Very good," the psychologist said, "help is on the way. Now for the criminal matters. I'd like to say I'm personally offended by the behavior of Father Donovan and some of his camp followers. According to Lisa's testimony, they assaulted a woman, destroyed a protected species, and poached from their neighbor's property. And we know from the Small Council's own testimony they attacked a peaceful delegation in defiance of public authority. I propose we punish Donovan with a month's exile for inciting a riot and Chuck a month for assaulting a woman. The other two should be given a week for poaching."

Donovan jumped to his feet.

"Slander and lies," the priest shouted, "there are no witnesses and there is no proof."

"You admit," Heidi looked straight at him, "you ate turtle eggs, right?"

"From our beaches."

"Then I suggest we go to your side of the beach to find one of the empty nests. If it's there, we'll commute your sentence to time served. If not, we'll double it."

Donovan said nothing.

"I know the place," the psychologist testified, "where the nests were robbed and I guarantee they were within the western district. In fact, the only turtle nests on the entire island belong to the west neighborhood."

A dozen settlers clapped hard and Donovan sat down.

"Poaching isn't a crime," Jason said as he stood. "You can't punish us ex post facto. It's unconstitutional."

"What constitution are you speaking of?" Heidi asked. "We know no law but this people's will. We're not slaves to the political ideals and legal fictions of Puritan fanatics, Yankee traders, and Southern slavers. This assembly is the law and the constitution and the king and the sovereign. What we do is good and right and legal."

"We came," Jason shouted, "to preserve more rights than Americans, not fewer."

"We also came for love and harmony," Charles said as he stood to speak, "but you've proven yourselves exploiters rather than idealists, wreckers rather than builders. Do what you wish with your free time, but you need to support yourselves. We don't have infinite reserves or indefinite patience."

Jason sat down.

"The northerners," Charles continued, "have turned a tropical paradise into a slum which we westerners now must support by our own sweat—not with the taxes of the idle rich, mind you, but the sweat and work of honest liberals. We're glad to help once again, but this island is under no obligation to support its lumpenproletariat forever. Even Marx and Lenin understood that. Burn your marijuana till the smoke steams out your ass for all I care, but make sure you've provided for the munchies to follow."

Now a cascade of voices and hands were raised. Half the island spoke their mind and almost all agreed the northerners had crossed the line. While some talked of peace and love and others of class obligation, everyone agreed Donovan and his compatriots merited discipline both for their own benefit and as a public example. However, a number of voices from south and north protested that the proposed punishment was too severe and justice needed to be tempered with mercy. Ryan and Charles protested clemency, but were outvoted and eventually it was decided Donovan should be sent to temporary exile (or timeout, as some preferred to call the punishment) to Big Motu Island for three weeks with no more than dried food, fresh water, and a few tools. The priest was to be denied recreational drugs for the first week of his sentence. Chuck was warned not to break the law again on pain of similar punishment while Jason was judged a little more harshly given the fact he was a repeat offender and betrayer of former neighbors: he was sentenced to two weeks on a small motu with minimal rations and no drugs and fined three ounces of marijuana (to be handed over for medicinal use).

However, when weather experts objected that even a light squall might wash Jason to sea, his sentence was commuted to a seven-day timeout at New Plymouth with his ration reduced to coconut and breadfruit for the full week. In addition, he was to be tied to a public bench with a loose rope and draped with a placard declaring him a thief. In light of Jason's reduced sentence, it also was decided to exonerate Lisa for her defense of nature against Chuck's eco-violence (though the assembly explicitly rejected the young woman's misbegotten and heretical belief that fetal life of any species whatsoever might possess intrinsic value). Lisa was warned to submit future complaints to public authority for litigation, no matter how serious any particular concern might seem.

Once sentences were ratified, the assembly broke into quiet murmuring and scattered applause. Then the charter was recited as prescribed and Heidi spent several minutes reminding everyone to gather at the north camp early in the morning, as well as to bring provisions and tools sufficient for the task. As soon as the meeting ended, Jason was taken to New Plymouth for detention and Father Donovan was ferried across the lagoon in a motorized launch. Jason was provided an empty tent and a wool blanket while Donovan was allowed a sleeping bag, a pup tent, a hand ax, and a tin of matches—as well as appropriate supplies of food and water. Neither man required a guard and the detail sent to deliver Donovan to the motu returned home shortly after dusk.

32

AN INDIAN SUMMER OF LOVE

Most islanders arrived at the north village by midmorning, soon after the LCVP landed with a quarter-ton of construction materials and food supplies—though the first westerners arrived before breakfast, only to find northerners still sleeping off a late night party. Sean woke the slow-rising northerners while Jose prepared something to eat. In the meantime, Ryan directed west villagers to organize a construction site in a meadow close to shore. The westerners worked fast under his command, locating and cataloguing every tool and common supply they could find in the district—from saws found rusting in fruit orchards to vegetable seeds discovered rotting in damp packets. Tools were cleaned and blades sharpened—despite gibes from westerners that northerners might more seriously hurt themselves (or others) with sharpened axes and knives.

When the staff from New Plymouth arrived in the landing craft, the professional staff took charge of the day's work and reassigned Ryan to manual labor. Throughout the morning, construction materials were hauled from the landing craft and carried to the meadow. Postholes were dug and the ground between them smoothed while fast-drying concrete was mixed and poured around fifteen-foot poles positioned in deep holes. Meanwhile, while some islanders raised the barn's frame, others cut a trail toward a distant fruit grove and dug a drainage ditch in the vicinity of a bog. When the day drew to a close, the islanders divided into small groups for dinner and later found places to sleep under the stars. Only a few returned home.

The second day, even more progress was made. The barn's frame was finished early—and walls subsequently nailed to the timber poles. By noon, thatched grass cut the previous day was hung from the roof and banana leaves picked that very morning were lined in freshly dug food cellars. After lunch, workers filled the barn with crates of dried foods brought by LCVP and sacks of fresh fruit picked from district orchards. Mangos, limes, kiwi, papayas, pineapple, and sugar cane were brought in burlap bags and set on shelves while bags of coconuts and breadfruit were dumped into food bins. Several watermelons were rolled to a corner and strips of salted shark (donated by the professional staff) were hung from the ceiling. Even the stock of seeds was replenished. A month's supply of firewood was stacked neatly in the barn and a temporary latrine was dug near the swamp.

As the barn filled, several workers were reassigned to decontaminate a maggot-infested cesspool only a few feet from the camp's sole freshwater stream. The pit was covered with heaps of clean dirt and marked as a toxic waste site (slated for future cleanup) and a narrow canal was dug to divert the stream further from the toxic cesspool—to prevent underground seepage and pollution. Other detoxification efforts included: the pulling down of two filthy shacks, the burning of a mold-filled shed, and the scrubbing of the longhouse with saltwater and sand until it no longer stank. By late afternoon, work was finished and dinner drawn from individual rations while Kit and a southern woman mixed vats of tea sweetened with lemon squeezings and sugar cane.

Shortly before dusk, a dedication was offered for the new barn, with the vast majority of the islanders participating in the formalities. Ryan himself sloshed a little champagne over the barn before passing the bottle for drinking. After taking a sip, Heidi climbed atop a stump to deliver a speech.

"Once again," Heidi said, "we've risen beyond adversity to accomplish a great thing. We've united north and south and rich and poor. Thank all of you so very much. Do we want to do this for the south neighborhood too?"

A few cheers rang out.

A southern woman raised her hand.

"Thanks just the same," the southern woman said, "but we have our food and we need only a building to house our children. Adults can make do in our temporary quarters for a few days."

"Any objections?" Heidi said as she looked to the east villagers.

"Can we delay that new construction for a week or so?" Alan asked. "We've lost three days already and need to catch up at home."

"You'll let the children stay with you till the south's new building is ready?"

Alan sighed loud.

"Fine," Alan said, "we'll raise one building as soon as possible—for the children. But then we need to be left alone to work our own projects. Does that work?"

The southern woman said it worked well and Heidi looked to the assembly for concurrence. Most heads nodded, so she approved the request and announced a return to normalcy as the islanders broke into spontaneous applause and Dr. Morales climbed atop the stump.

"I have another proposal," the anthropologist said. "As you know, I've made some effort at establishing contact with our indigenous friends at Roanoke Island. Well, I've finally decoded some of their turtle shell carvings and discovered their harvest feast comes several days after the coming new moon—which is less than two weeks away as I reckon the calendar. The feast is devoted to their goddess of life and is celebrated by a great banquet. I'd like to send emissaries to observe the feast so we can learn their religion."

"Learn what?" John shouted from the crowd. "To worship their gods?"

"When in Rome," the anthropologist nodded, "is the anthropologist's first commandment."

"I'm not bowing to any damned idols," John said a bit too loud as he looked at Deidra. Several people standing close to him inched away.

"Of course not," Dr. Morales replied, "no one can be made to do anything. We'll take only volunteers to the island. But I need to tell you up front that I've not only been required to venerate idols, but even to induce hallucinogens to enhance my cultural studies. I had a mentor who ate the ground bones of Yanomami tribesmen from the Amazon forests."

"I'd like to volunteer," Deidra shouted as she glared at her former husband.

"I'll need to make plans," Dr. Morales said, "before we can finalize arrangements. Tomorrow I sail for Roanoke Island to speak with the chief. Who knows ..."

"Eeeehhh."

The anthropologist's sentence was cut short by a commotion as a middle-aged woman—who stood near the open door of the long-house—turned red-faced from embarrassment.

"I'm sorry," the middle-aged woman explained. "A couple of teenagers in there are ..."

Everyone laughed as word circulated through the assembly what had occurred. Every neck stretched to see who was involved and an awkward silence fell over the crowd as a blond-haired and blue-eyed boy of fifteen (with narrow shoulders and skinny arms) emerged from the building grinning—soon followed by a girl his age who also had blond hair and blue eyes. The girl's face was flush and she held a torn shirt across her smooth chest and narrow shoulders. Both teenagers showed the same big-toothed smile.

"Oh lord," a woman's voice cried out, "it's the Epstein twins."

The crowd hushed and the girl blushed as the boy pulled her close with an arm held around her back—his fingers cradled beneath her breast.

"C'mon sis," the youth said, "forget her. She's a bigot."

Another voice bellowed through the crowds, this one a deep and fierce one belonging to an older man. "Get your hands off your sister!"

"It's a free country, pops," the boy said. "We can do as we please."

Now the youth leaned into the girl and kissed her lips as the older man pushed his way through the crowd until he reached the skinny-armed boy and pulled him away from the girl.

"You're as free," the man shouted, "as your father lets you be and I told you to keep your paws off your sister."

The boy squirmed free. "She may be your daughter," he declared, speaking with a loud, clear voice, "but she's going to be my wife."

"You can't marry your own sister," the father screamed, fury in his face and rage in his voice.

"It's not against the rules," the boy yelled back, now turning his face toward the assembly, "and we love each other. So in the presence of these witnesses, I declare my sister is my wife."

"And I declare before these people," the girl vowed, "my brother is my husband."

"To hell with both of you," their father stammered, "take her and be damned. You're almost adults and I can't stop you from doing what you please, but not under my roof. Never under my roof. Your mother and I have suffered enough from your shenanigans."

Then the man turned to his fellow islanders.

"Their mother and I," the man declared with an exasperated tone, "have tried to keep them from each other since we came here, but we can't do anything about this mess since the law on marriage was passed. They insist they have rights. I want you to transfer them to another neighborhood since I'm not about to watch my own children make out. Not without wringing their scrawny necks like chickens. How the hell did I become father-in-law to my own son and daughter?"

The crowd was stunned and no one spoke—though several young people giggled before being stared down by their elders. After a long pause, Heidi climbed back to the podium and assessed the situation.

"Uhhh ... we can arrange a transfer," Heidi said as she looked around until her eyes fixed on those of Ryan. "Would the west neighborhood work?"

Before Ryan could answer, Linh and Tiffany jumped to their feet shouting—with Kit following their lead.

"Not with us," Linh yelled.

"No way," Tiffany said.

"It's wicked," Kit shouted.

When someone from the east village shouted that the western women were bigots, Kit turned toward the voice.

"Not one of you," Kit declared, "can accuse me of being a bigot. Hollywood's leading gays were among my friends and I never held it against a man the number of women he slept with. Consenting adults was my mantra even when my own personal choices seemed a bit more straight-laced. Nevertheless, there has to be a line drawn somewhere, even if it's only in the sand. These children—and I mean children—are brother and sister. If we won't stop them from marrying, then we won't stop anyone or anything at anytime. No civilization has ever allowed incest. It's the one universal taboo and we are in danger of scandalizing the entire world and becoming the absolute relativists the religious right accused us of being. We'll disgrace our cause forever."

"Actually," Dr. Morales declared as he beckoned for the assembly to listen, "it's not perfectly clear that incest is a universal taboo—only that nineteenth-century scholars thought it so. However, we now know that earlier thinkers were merely attempting to defend cultural relativism against charges it would invite moral anarchy stemming from the dismantlement of religious mores. For that reason, they posited that human society has its own internal logic which regulates relationships far more effectively than legal codes or natural law or transcendent ideals."

"So," Kit said with an angry frown, "we shouldn't have rules against perversion?"

"Exactly," Dr. Morales said, "we all know that Nancy Reagan's 'Just Say No' approach to drugs and sex is a waste of time."

"Every culture forbids incest," Kit said.

"In fact," Dr. Morales continued, "the taboo against incest isn't universal: Egyptian pharaohs married their sisters and were considered all the more godlike for doing so."

"So," Kit asked, with noticeable sarcasm to her voice, "we should practice incest as religious piety?"

"It is ironic."

"And," Kit continued, "this marriage represents some kind of great spiritual awakening?"

"I didn't say I accept the legitimacy of pious incest. Only it occurs."

"I don't understand. Is incest acceptable or not?"

"Look at it this way," the anthropologist replied. "Human animals have a biological imperative to mate. So do birds and bees and bats and bears. Now, dogs and cats sometimes mate with siblings or parents. Nature doesn't stop them."

A collective groan came from the islanders.

"That's probably," Kit said, "because they don't know what a mother or a father is."

"That's not true. Even a kitten knows whose teat to suck."

"Exactly," Kit said, "it goes to its own mother. Not to a father or a sister or a brother. Nature understands right relationships."

"A chimpanzee," Dr. Morales explained, "mates with any fertile female in its troop—mother or sister or daughter."

"So parents should mate with their children?"

"Not before sexual maturity."

"What if a father really desired his teenaged daughter? What should he do? What should we do?"

"That's not likely to happen."

"But if it did? What then?"

"Well," Dr. Morales said after a short pause, "I guess he'd need to deny those particular urges."

"You mean he should just say no?"

The anthropologist blushed.

"On what grounds," Kit said, "should a man—or woman, for that matter—just say no to incest?"

"On social grounds."

"Meaning what?"

"Meaning," Dr. Morales said, "anti-social behavior that is contrary to progressive mores."

"It sounds like you want us just to keep from openly scandalous behavior?" Kit said.

"That's one way of putting it."

"What if there was no scandal in incest?"

"In that case," the anthropologist said, "there'd be no reason to deny the expression of natural biological impulses."

"So," Kit paused to think through her words, "you're saying that biology is destiny? That every sexual desire is acceptable?"

"We are biological creatures—made by sex and for sex. The logic of biology provides no reason to shackle our sexual impulses."

"Are you," Kit asked, "saying every perverse itch ought to be scratched?"

"What I'm saying," the anthropologist said, his tone clearly exasperated, "is there are no divine laws or transcendent ethics that restrict human behavior. No rules of any sort exist and we have no right to tell others what to do. That's the path of public stockades and private suffering. It's the way of the Puritans and pilgrims and ..."

"Everyone who hates indecency."

"You still don't understand. Each person must make his or her own values. That's what it means to be human. What's inhuman is to force one person's preference on others—unless it can be objectively verified as true or real or natural. And the prohibition against incest fails on all three grounds: there's no final truth that condemns it; it certainly exists among real people; and nature doesn't stop it."

"Nature doesn't stop a lot of gross, disgusting things," Kit said. "That doesn't mean we should sit in our own ... excrement."

"I don't consider gross a precise term of the social sciences."

"And I don't consider incest a good custom. It's both wrong and unhealthy."

"There's no real difference between right and wrong," Dr. Morales explained, "and there's nothing unhealthy about sleeping with an aunt or sister or mother."

"Wait a minute," Dr. Graves said as he joined the discussion. "This is where you and I part company since there are real genetic consequences to the pairing of close relatives. We're all educated and I need not belabor the point. On eugenic grounds, I'd request that this marriage be forbidden."

A round of light applause broke out and the anthropologist thought about the problem before answering.

"I agree with you," Dr. Morales said, "regarding the genetic risks; but what if the boy will accept a vasectomy? Would there be any health risks to the couple themselves?"

"That's," the doctor said as he shook his head, "a rather permanent solution for such a young man."

"So is celibacy."

"It's not quite so permanent."

"I don't care to stand here all night," a woman shouted, "while you people debate ethical niceties. It's getting late. Give us something to vote upon so we can leave."

"I agree," Heidi said. "The issues are clear and we need to make some decisions. First, we need to determine whether or not brothers and sisters will be allowed to marry and then we can decide what to do with this particular problem. The stakes are the following: if we outlaw sibling marriages we'll need to dissolve this marriage and force this couple apart. That means they live in different villages and we'll need to punish them if they defy our vote by sneaking into the forest to engage in carnal relations. On the other hand, if we permit sibling marriages, these teenagers must be absolutely allowed to live as husband and wife—as legitimate as any other. I move we vote on the legality of sibling marriage. All those in favor say yea."

A loud yea came from the crowd.

"All those against say nay."

An equally loud nay was muttered.

Heidi lost no time in moving to the next stage. "We'll vote by hands," she announced. "Those in favor of permitting sibling marriages raise your right hand."

Hands went up and a count was made. Thirty residents cast votes for sibling marriage, mostly from the east and north neighborhoods.

"All those for outlawing sibling marriages raise your right hand."

This time only twenty-six hands were raised, mostly westerners and southerners. Many residents didn't vote.

"Sibling marriage is legalized."

Groans of dismay came from the west neighborhood while cheering rang from the east. The northerners showed little reaction and the southerners were divided.

"Since sibling marriage," Heidi declared, "will be permitted, I suggest we require genetic counseling for relatives who wish to marry."

Heidi's proposal was adopted and the assembly decided the young newlyweds should live with the northerners—though they were told that their marriage would be legally recognized only after they had received birth control guidance and genetic counseling from Dr. Graves. The assembly awarded them a supply of condoms for a wedding gift.

Following the vote, the father to both bride and groom alike walked home in dismay while his distraught wife scavenged a bottle of scotch and drank herself into a few hours of anguished bliss.

LATER IN THE EVENING, several women of the west neighborhood sat around the campfire as they drank rum and pineapple juice. Only Ursula abstained from alcohol.

"It's a scandal," Kit said. "Can't we stand for anything?"

"Only," Heather said with a shrug, "when we're not against something else."

"Like a child who can't be told no."

"It's all politics," Linh said. "The east villagers were afraid a moral stand would turn against their lifestyle and the northerners feared we someday might outlaw their dope."

"If word leaks out," Kit said, "we'll be shamed before the entire world."

"I'm ashamed already," Heather whispered.

"Brent and I are leaving," Tiffany said, "our boys aren't going to be exposed to open incest."

"Viet says the same," Linh added, "he said we're taking the next boat home."

"I just hope I'm not carrying twins," Ursula joked.

"With my parents," Heather said, "it makes me glad to be an only child."

"At least," Kit said, "you've kept your sense of humor."

"We foundlings are scrappers and survivors."

Now the other women laughed.

"Speaking of losing and finding," Heather said, "do you realize I've managed utterly to lose my innocence without finding a man? Some tropical paradise this has proved to be."

"You've done well," Ursula said, "much better than I have."

"If you leave," Heather said as she looked to Tiffany and Linh, "so will I. This is the nicest neighborhood on the island. I can't bear the thought of living with any of the others."

"We have our own problems," Kit said.

"But most of you are nice."

"So are many of the others," Kit added. "The quiet ones."

"A toast to nice neighbors," Linh said as the women raised their drinks.

"Speaking of neighbors," Heather said, "did I tell you Dr. Morales invited me to visit the natives?"

"I'll bet," Kit said with a bitter sneer to her voice, "they don't marry brothers and sisters."

Everyone laughed.

"Of course not," Tiffany said, "they have children and no parent would ever permit such an indecency. It's the childless who have such harebrained ideas."

Kit looked away.

"I'm sorry," Tiffany apologized. "You spoke well today. For all of us."

Kit said nothing.

"I'm serious," Tiffany blushed. "Brent and I would want you to raise our children if anything happened to us."

"Ryan wouldn't want children."

"That's his loss," Tiffany said, "you'd make a great mom. You're sweet and strong—and kids love you. If anything happened to us on this island, we hope you'd be the one to raise our children. To get them back home."

Kit looked into her drink. "That's kind of you to say."

"Viet and I feel the same," Linh added, "and sometimes I think my kids like you better than me. They even ask me to dress more like you."

"Mine," Tiffany said, "ask me to pretend to be her. They call me Aunt Kit."

"I like those kids," Kit whispered.

"I just hope they don't abandon us for you," Tiffany said.

"In Paradise," Heather quipped, "such things have been known to happen."

"I feel the same way," Ursula joined in, "when my baby takes his first look at Kit's chest, I'm afraid he'll prefer hill country over flat lands."

All five women roared with laughter.

"It's all show," Kit said. "I'd give anything to nurse a baby just once."

"When's Ryan going to marry you?" Ursula asked after a time.

"I'm not sure he will. We've drifted apart."

"Don't you want him to?"

"I suppose," Kit said, "but I'm tired of waiting for a proposal from my own husband."

"If I were you," Tiffany said, "I'd just ask him."

"If you were her," Ursula said, "you'd just tell him."

"Don't ask," Kit said, "don't tell. That's my motto."

The banter continued several minutes more as the women

finished their drinks and the fire burned down. Linh and Tiffany were the first to retire, followed by Ursula and Heather. Kit remained at the fire another hour and only after its coals were covered with gray ash and the night air had chilled did she stumble through the dark toward her tent. Though she retired late, she was restless and easily distracted by the noises of the forest.

IT WAS STILL DARK when the fly unzipped on Ryan's tent and Maria crawled in. Ryan opened his eyes and smiled—love was coming before the first glint of dawn. It would be a good day.

"It's nice to see you so early," Ryan whispered.

Maria put a finger to her lips and told Ryan to be still while she lit a candle. She pointed to her grass skirt. "You like it?"

"The same one?"

"I sewed this one myself. For you."

"I like it."

"This is my best shirt," Maria said.

Ryan looked at the shirt. Even through the flickering candlelight he saw the round lift of her breasts and the glow of golden skin through thin cotton.

"I like that even better."

"I'm glad," Maria said. "It's my wedding ensemble."

Ryan grinned. "Who are you marrying?"

"You."

"And when are you marrying me?"

"Now."

"I haven't told Kit."

"I was patient," Maria said, "when you couldn't marry her, but I won't be while you can. Today ends the waiting period and tomorrow she'll be available, so you must choose today. Not tomorrow. Not tonight. Now."

As she spoke, Maria unbuttoned her shirt and crawled forward. When Ryan wrapped an arm around her back and tried to pull her close, she arched her spine and kept him at bay.

"Not before marriage," Maria said.

Ryan again tried to pull her close, but this time the young woman locked her elbows against his chest and said he'd have to choose. Now Ryan looked at Maria's eyes, then at her uncovered breasts which contrasted with the bleached white cotton of her unbuttoned blouse. The woman's auburn hair fell to her shoulders and her smooth body sparkled in the flickering candlelight.

Ryan twitched. "I'll tell her this week."

"Now."

"Let me break it to her softly."

Maria smiled and moved closer. Her lips touched Ryan's as he pulled her so close that her breasts pressed against his chest as she lay hands on him until desire stirred—then she pushed him away.

"Only a taste."

"Be nice," Ryan groaned.

"One good turn deserves another."

"I've tried to tell her. To tell the truth, she half expects me not to marry her. I just can't get the words out."

"You need to be a man."

Ryan tried to grab Maria by the waist. "I'll show you a man," he declared.

Maria blocked his hands. "I told you before," she said, "I'd make you beg for my baby."

"I'll tell her today."

"Before breakfast."

"You won't touch me again until we're married."

"We never spoke of marriage."

"And we didn't speak of duplicity either," Maria said. "I know you slept with her on the beach."

Ryan started to object.

"No lies," Maria said. "We've not confessed everything, but we've never lied."

Ryan nodded.

"Also," Maria said, "I like Kit and it's only fair to her. It's not right to string her along."

Ryan said nothing.

"You're in love with me," Maria said, "and I with you. Do you want us to continue or not?"

"Of course I do."

"Then you've already made your choice. It only remains to announce it."

"I suppose so," Ryan said as he moved toward the young woman, taking both of her hands in his as he glanced at her breasts and hips. "Maria, will you marry me?"

"Now?"

Ryan nodded.

"I do," Maria said.

"Then I now pronounce us man and wife."

Maria threw her arms around Ryan's neck and told him to kiss the bride as Ryan blew out the light and they tumbled on his grass-filled mattress, making little effort to remove their clothes quietly. When they fell apart twenty minutes later, Ryan rolled over to sleep while Maria picked up a half-clean shirt and stepped outside to wash.

33

CONCEIVED IN SORROW

Kit opened her eyes. Someone was making love not far away and it was hard to sleep despite the fact that the couple kept it quiet. She pulled a pillow over her ears until the rustling of the couple faded away, then closed her eyes as the first glimmer of dawn began to light the east sky and birds sang love songs from the forest.

Now Kit reached to touch Ryan, but he wasn't there. She sat up and pulled a blanket over her legs as she leaned forward, her chin resting atop a knee and her hands clasped around her legs. She thought of Ryan; it seemed so long since his touch had stirred passion—except when she was drunk earlier that month. Kit blushed and put the memory out of mind. Quarrels and tiredness had dulled love and the dissolution of her marriage was harder than she expected—as if the invalidation of paperwork also had annulled their love. Even after the tryst on the beach, Ryan seemed uninterested and unaffected. How else to explain he hadn't proposed? Or hadn't come to bed for so long?

Baby birds chirped from a nearby tree and Kit wondered how many chicks had hatched even as she remembered her own empty nest. Ryan was wrong to deny her a child and to have talked her into a tubal ligation and he was wrong to be so hard-hearted. Tiffany and Linh understood and so did Ursula. Even Deidra knew the desire for a child. Kit slipped a hand under her nightshirt to touch the tiny incision on her belly—which felt lumpier and longer than ever. However, when she measured it against a fingernail, it remained unchanged.

"He was no more foolish than I was," Kit reminded herself, "it was my body and I should've taken care."

Kit closed her eyes and remembered Ryan. They had been through so much together, good and bad. She wondered whether she ought to ask him about remarrying to get their life back to normal.

"Even old flames," Kit told herself, "can be rekindled and I suppose I'd better start burning before Ryan warms himself somewhere else."

Now the nearby couple began to talk a little too loud for this hour and Kit wondered who it was. The woman's voice was too young to be Joan or Olivia and too high-pitched to be Deidra. Nor was it Hilary or Lisa—their tents were pitched too far away. Since Tiffany and Linh always showed a rather maternal modesty, the only neighbors left to count were Heather and ...

Kit stiffened and her stomach turned when she remembered that Ryan was the only man Maria had shown any interest in. Quickly dressing even as her stomach knotted, Kit hurried toward Maria's tent just as the latter emerged through her front flap. As Kit ducked beside a neighboring tent, Maria sauntered toward the Pishon River, clutching her toiletry bag and wearing a wrinkled shirt. Only one man on the island owned a shirt like it: its Italian cut and pastel pattern being a handmade original—a shirt Kit herself had designed for Ryan during a film shoot in Milan.

Kit waited until Maria was gone before she hurried home, already sobbing and covering her eyes. She didn't emerge from her tent for breakfast and continued to weep when Ryan came to declare their marriage over, explaining that he'd just married Maria and planned to register the marriage in New Plymouth before taking a honeymoon. Ryan hoped a short absence would help Kit recover from the shock and apologized for handling his new relationship so poorly—

reminding Kit she'd never done anything to cause the loss of his love and that he'd kept his vows for as long as they were married. He gave Kit the half-built house and wished her happiness. For her part, Kit listened red-eyed and ash-faced from the tent floor without speaking a word until Ryan tried to comfort her with a hug. After she pushed him away and told him to leave, Ryan collected his belongings without further discussion.

The next three days were hard. Though Kit didn't grieve publicly, her shock was evident. Linh and Tiffany helped talk through the pain while Ursula and Heather tried to comfort her with an array of distractions and desserts. John offered his assistance, but remained circumspect and cautious in everything he said. Mostly, however, Kit was consoled by the presence of the children: the twin boys playing with her on the beach and the older girls begging to learn card games late into the night.

As for Ryan and Maria, the newlyweds enjoyed a honeymoon of surfing, sunning, and swimming at one of the larger motu. After three days, they returned home and slipped into their own tent following a few words with Charles and Deidra. A short time later, Ryan pulled stakes and moved his nylon home further from the main village, beyond earshot of Kit's tent—a move most villagers thought for the best. Throughout the ordeal, Hilary spent considerable effort reminding villagers they needed to keep schedule regardless of recent troubles since the village was missing its quotas.

THE MORNING after the newlyweds returned to Paradise, Tiffany and Linh journeyed north, carrying bags of live birds and buckets of crabs as they hiked up the coast. It took the women nearly an hour to reach the site where Lisa had been assaulted (the deceased turtles now memorialized with wooden crosses) as the women walked barefoot and burdened through the rocks.

Soon they took a break.

"My arms hurt," Linh said, "these birds keep jumping around. It's hard to hold the basket."

Tiffany looked into her buckets of crabs. "I feel like I'm carrying a whole sea of these crabs."

Linh took a drink from her canteen, then offered it to Tiffany—who emptied it and pointed to Linh's blouse.

"That shirt is due for the rag pile," Tiffany said.

"It's my best one."

"Do you realize it's torn across the back?"

"That's the least of its problems," Linh replied. "Look how thin it's worn. And I don't own a bra to my name."

"At least you're trying to maintain respectability. I haven't seen Lisa in a blouse for two days."

"Viet is very private."

"At least," Tiffany said, "we've discovered why Polynesians were topless. They lacked long-wearing wool."

"Wool?" Linh said. "Wood wouldn't wear well around here."

It took the women another twenty minutes to complete their journey and they soon arrived at a village that looked abandoned; the previous night's fish dinner hadn't been cleaned and two gulls fought over the scraps as a small girl—a blond toddler with uncombed hair and a dirty face—played by herself on the beach.

While Linh started for the longhouse, Tiffany approached the child and asked the girl where her parents were.

The little girl dug in the sand with a stick.

"Do you know where your mom and dad are at?" Tiffany asked a second time.

Still, the child said nothing.

"Do they always let you play at the beach by yourself?"

The girl let a handful of sand slip through her fingers.

"Did you know," Tiffany asked, "the water's very dangerous?"

"Fish," the girl said as she pointed to the surf.

"Can I play with you?"

The little girl sat down and dug into the sand and Tiffany did likewise, digging a trench toward the surf as the child scooped handfuls of sand. Before their efforts had made much headway, Linh returned.

"Those people," Linh said, "are filthy and disgusting."

When Tiffany motioned toward the girl, Linh lowered her voice.

"They're heaped," Linh whispered, "inside that building like swine. There's food rotting everywhere—it already reeks. Someone vomited in a corner and someone else urinated all over a wall. They don't care. Anyone not passed out is too stoned to move. We're supposed to subsidize this crap?"

Tiffany pointed at the girl. "She's as skinny as a skeleton," she said. "Who knows what she eats? I'm not leaving her here to be washed out to sea. Of course, that's the only washing she'd get with these filthy people."

"Let's take her home."

"I'll ask first," Tiffany said, "we don't need more trouble."

"Don't bother," Linh said with disdain to her voice. "They'll neither notice nor care."

"It's best to ask."

Now Tiffany walked to the longhouse, glaring as she looked inside and realized Linh hadn't told her everything. Not one person in the building was clothed. Men lay astride women and women atop men. Two women lay arm in arm and one man displayed himself indecently as he slept. The room was hot and humid and the stench boiled outwards. A young man lay near the door, his eyes rolled back and his mouth open. Tiffany kicked him in the ribs.

"Oww," the young man yelled, "what d'you want?"

"The little girl belongs to you, right?"

"Sort of," the young man said, "what's wrong with her now?"

"Wake up," Tiffany said as she kicked the man a second time. "She can't babysit herself."

"Then put her to bed."

"Do you want me to watch her for the day?"

"Ask her mother."

"Do you know who I am?"

"Who gives a shit?"

"I give a shit."

"What's she to you?"

"I'm Tiffany. From the west. Tell your wife—who I might add is asleep in that boy's arms—I have her daughter."

"Whatever. She ain't my wife and it ain't my kid."

"By the way, what's her name?"

"Who?"

"The little girl."

"Brittany," the man said as he rubbed his ribs, "but you can call her Shittany for all I care."

Tiffany turned to leave. "We're leaving," she said, "birds and crabs for your dinner. We'll set them in a tent so they don't overheat."

No one responded.

Tiffany and Linh started home as the little girl walked between them. It wasn't long until they brought Brittany to Kit—who was very excited to spend the day with the child, telling stories and playing in the park. When no one came to get the girl by dusk, Kit decided to watch her for the night and the two played dress up late into the night. Brittany was so happy to have a friend that she jabbered until she talked herself to sleep. Only then did Kit slip from the tent to tend her chores.

URSULA SAT ALONE near the fire. She wore an oversized tee shirt and tight-fitting shorts traded from a southern woman (who'd lost ten pounds since arriving) and nibbled slowly at a piece of stale bread. When Sean sat a few feet away to take his supper, she turned her back until she heard him move closer to her.

After several minutes, Sean broke the silence.

"Does it move yet?"

Even under the loose shirt, a slight bulge in Ursula's belly could be seen over which the pregnant woman now placed her hand.

"I think," Ursula replied, "I felt a quiver once. It's hard to say this early. Maybe it was indigestion."

"A quickening," Sean said, "is what Thomas Aquinas called it, if I remember my Ethics of Reproduction class readings."

Ursula said nothing.

"Can I touch it?"

"It's yours too, whether you want it or not."

"That wasn't nice."

"You and Deidra weren't nice."

"She was the one who ..."

"Since," Ursula interrupted, "you're a father, try to be a man."

Sean placed his hand on Ursula's belly. "It's hard," he whispered, "to imagine a baby in there."

"You don't need to imagine anything. It's real enough."

"And that I'm a father."

"Of sorts."

"C'mon Ursula," Sean protested. "Give me a break. Just for tonight."

"For tonight," Ursula grimaced, "so I can enjoy some peace too."

Neither spoke as they watched the fire burn and neighbors move about—Kit slipping into her tent where the northern child slept and Brent romping in the dark with his sons while Tiffany prepared herself dessert.

"You need something to eat?" Sean asked.

"I already fed myself. I'm learning to be a single mother."

"I'm a jerk," Sean said as he twisted the palm of his hand into his face, "and I know I've hurt you. I know we're done as a couple; but I've been thinking about the baby and I don't want to be a bad father. My brother's never even seen his son. I don't want to be like that."

Ursula looked up.

"Need," the pregnant woman said with a scowl, "a little female company since you were tossed out of Deidra's tent?"

"I've tried," Sean said as stomped his foot and stood to leave, "I've done my ..."

"Sit down and take it. I deserve some payback."

Sean slumped a little, then sat down.

"But I won't cheat my child," Ursula said, "of her father—even if he is a pig. But remember this: you're welcome as the father of my child. Not as the man who shares my bed."

"Okay," Sean whispered before he returned his hand to Ursula's belly.

After a time, Ursula asked whether Sean preferred a son or daughter. Though visibly confused by the sudden mood change, Sean said he'd like a son.

"Me too," Ursula said as tears formed in her eyes.

Ursula didn't explain why she was weeping and Sean didn't ask, but just offered to fetch more juice—though wincing as he put weight on his still-swollen knee. After limping a few steps, Sean looked back toward Ursula, his voice quiet and quivering.

"Ursula," he said, "I really am sorry. You were the best girl I ever had and I threw it away for sex with a crazy woman."

Ursula's eyes glistened.

"The irony," Sean said, "is Deidra's driving herself insane to conceive the baby we made by accident."

Ursula just sobbed.

"I really screwed up," Sean said.

Ursula nodded.

Sean limped away to get juice. After serving Ursula, he helped her to bed, then lay near the fire and watched the coals burn down until he fell asleep. Only when the fire burned out and the chill of the night cut through his clothes did he stagger to Jose's tent—not long before the first stirring of islanders in their tents could be heard as a new day began.

"RYAN, COME CLOSER."

Ryan rolled over and looked at his new wife. Maria lay beside him, her hips draped with a sheet. The tent was bright since they'd slept in late.

"You wear me out," Ryan said. "Wasn't last night enough?"

"Not now," Maria said, her face drawn and taut. "We need to talk."

"What's wrong?" Ryan asked, propping himself up at the elbows with a long yawn.

"I'm pregnant."

Ryan snapped his jaw shut and threw his hand over his mouth, but his yawn hadn't ended and his tongue was still extended. As a result, he bit his tongue and uttered a muffled cry.

"Thamn," he said rubbing his tongue with his fingertips. "Thut thu thu theen pregnanth?"

Maria stared into Ryan's eyes. She spoke her next words very slow and deliberate. "It's medical slang for having your baby."

After a pause, Ryan found his tongue again. "How pregnant?"

"A month."

"You've been pregnant for a month and this is the first time you've decided to mention ..."

Maria's glare cut Ryan short. "Didn't you take health class?" she growled. "I've just missed my period and didn't suspect until a couple days ago."

"It was nice of you to mention the possibility."

"I knew how you feel about babies and I had no intention of worrying you unnecessarily."

"I appreciate the concern."

"Don't be so sarcastic."

"Don't be so pregnant."

Maria shook her head and Ryan sat upright for a moment before he dropped his jaw again.

"Did you know it," Ryan asked, "when you made me marry you?"

"When I what?"

"When you"—Ryan decided not to repeat his previous words —"when we married."

"I didn't know until last night, I told you. It was the first time I used a pregnancy test."

"Did you have an inkling?"

Maria dropped her eyes an instant, but then lifted them and stared straight at Ryan.

"Honestly?" Maria said. "I wondered. But my period's not regular, so I wasn't sure. It always was a possibility, I suppose."

"How many pills did you miss?"

"All of them."

"You weren't on birth control?"

"There isn't any."

"I thought you had a supply."

"They gave me condoms."

"Did you ever think of using one?"

"Not when on the first night and afterwards would've been too late."

"How can you be so stupid?"

"I wasn't the only one," Maria answered as she glared at her husband.

"Shit," Ryan said. "This is a mess."

"How's that?"

"I wanted some time for us, for ..."

"Give me respect, not clichés. I'm your wife."

"It's just that we should enjoy our freedom for a while."

"Love isn't free and I'm not cheap."

Ryan clenched his forehead between his hands. "What's wrong with a little innocent fun?" he groaned. "I bring beautiful women to a tropical paradise and all they can think about are babies"

"You do realize how they're made?"

"I know how they're made; I just don't get why."

"Someone," Maria said, "needs to explain to you the facts about life: about women and making life. The whole Eve thing."

"You're keeping it, aren't you?"

"The baby is us. He—or she, for the matter—is the fruit of our love."

"Now what am I supposed to do?"

"Lemaze, I expect."

"I'm not ready for fatherhood."

"I heard my dad say the same thing when mom was pregnant with my little brother—their fifth."

"Why didn't you tell me that you weren't on the pill?"

"Why didn't you ask?"

"It's the woman's ..."

"Don't go there," Maria warned. "We made our choices and now we're going to be parents. You're not going to leave me the way Sean did Ursula. She sold herself too cheap and I won't make her mistake. I played by the rules and left you alone as long as you were married. And now the rules declare you're obligated to honor your wife and child. Do well and everything will be good between us. Treat me like a whore and I'll leave you broken and bruised. And it starts with your attitude. Like it or not, you're going to be a happy father. You'll not humiliate me the way Sean did Ursula."

Ryan bowed his head. "I won't embarrass you," he promised. "Maybe you're right about Sean. Just give me a few days to think about it. I've never even imagined being a father. Not once."

"You think too much," Maria said, "What you need to do now is learn to live with life. I'm going to announce my pregnancy to the neighborhood and you'll be at my side with a smile. Heather saw me getting the kit last night and word could already be out. She's not usually a gossip, but we're not neighborhood favorites right now."

A few minutes later, Ryan and Maria walked straight to the dining hall where they announced the pregnancy to Deidra and Heather. They also told Jose and Linh (who were eating outside the mess). Ryan remained cheerful the entire time—though he said he hadn't thought about the child's sex (and didn't care) when asked by Jose if he preferred a boy or a girl.

34

THE HARVEST FESTIVAL

The last week in July passed without further incident, though it took Brittany's mother three days to fetch her daughter. The easterners were more diligent: building a barn (near the south tip of the island) dry enough to protect southern children from winter rains and sending for the children even before the last door was hung late on Friday afternoon. While most east villagers were just relieved to see the children depart, Alan grumbled and griped that they hadn't left soon enough—and that they'd stained walls with muddy finger prints and floors with tropical juice stains. In any event, he and other inhabitants of the east village worked nights to clean the mess and then raise a roof over the new theater, as well as to plane timber for the latter's interior walls. New Plymouth staff also monitored overdue west village elections during which Linh was made Chief Neighbor and her husband was appointed to Executive Council.

Only Dr. Morales didn't assist with the belated elections—though he did sail west to invite Heather to visit Roanoke Island to help prepare the harvest feast. Indeed, anthropologist and intern arrived together on foreign soil early Thursday morning and worked all day learning local customs. After hours of negotiation over broken sentences and uncertain translations, Morales decided Heather should remain with the natives to finalize preparations while he sailed home to gather guests and gifts. Morales returned to Paradise on Friday evening, asking his compatriots to make preparations for a Sunday banquet and offering Charles and Joan the first invitations to attend the festival.

Everyone was pleased with the news, especially Deidra—who thought it fitting that Western civilization played the role of Squanto. On Saturday, the LCVP was loaded with food drawn from central reserves and village levies: bundles of wood, salted fish, jars of jelly, baked breadfruit, fresh lemons, ground sugarcane, live crabs, and the last bag of popcorn on the island. Deidra, Lisa, Jose, Ryan, Maria, Charles, and Joan spent the night at New Plymouth in anticipation of an early start, along with three volunteers from the north village and two from the east and south districts. Dr. Morales himself represented the professional staff of New Plymouth. Outsiders brought sleeping rolls to New Plymouth and either settled into empty tents or found quiet places beneath the open sky. Joan shared a hospital bed with a northerner while her husband slept under the stars beside Karla from the east village. Ryan and Maria stayed in an unoccupied supply tent.

A festival also was planned for the island of Paradise. Two plump chickens (large speckled hens nearly the size of wild turkeys) were fated for butchering and there was talk of slaughtering a troublesome goat belonging to the southern village—though the animal was spared for the sake of Lisa and several southern children who had befriended it. A southerner also protested against moral cannibalism by chanting "a goat is a man is a bird" and two young mothers begged for the animal's life on grounds that their children needed as much fresh milk as possible. Salted ham (the only one on the entire island) was accepted as a substitute, along with a vat of instant potatoes and several large cans of creamed corn. Packaged foods were supplemented with hand-churned butter, stream-cooled milk, bread, biscuits, cakes, and bowls of fruit. Crabs and fish also were planned. It was decided to hold the festival at the west village—which had the best beach on the island, as well as the most convenient location. Only the northerners complained about the walk.

ON SUNDAY MORNING, Kit rose before dawn. After raising her ax several times over one of two condemned chickens, she called for John to take care of the unfortunate fowl. John beheaded the larger hen with a single stroke, then held the bird fast while its headless torso convulsed as its blood drained. A moment later, the second bird also was dead and John was gutting dinner while Kit plucked feathers. After cleaning, the birds were smothered with spices and butter and cooked inside a cast iron pot—smoldering over a thick layer of hot coals. Periodically, logs were added to the fire to keep the birds baking. While the chickens cooked, John retrieved crabs from live traps and Kit kneaded dough. When Linh and Tiffany joined them, work went still faster yet. By midmorning, the chefs were joined by neighbor and stranger alike (a slim majority of them women) as they cleaned food and cooked.

When the noon meal was ready, John asked permission to say a traditional grace, but only he and Kit closed their eyes to give thanks while the others continued conversation and passed plates. Nevertheless, despite the awkward beginning, the meal brought satisfaction as dish after dish was served. Both chickens were picked clean and every trace of the twenty-pound ham also disappeared. Likewise, twenty crabs were eaten, as well as six seagulls netted by the southerners—and even some smoked fish. Indeed, the hunger for meat proved so insatiable it led to the butchering of the previously reprieved goat—which soon was broiling over an open spit with a mango stuffed in its mouth.

As word of the feast spread, those few islanders who hadn't planned to come arrived with empty plates and growling stomachs. Several men picked at the goat as it cooked, though Ursula diligently chased them away with a wooden spoon. Even so, a fifth part of the goat disappeared before the roasted animal was removed from the spit.

While the goat cooked, islanders played volleyball at the beach. This time nearly everyone stripped their shirts—the fear of ripping their few remaining clothes being far greater than private embarrassment. A couple women wore bikinis and one even played in shirt and shorts, but most islanders removed their shirts and applied what remained of their sun lotion to the more tender parts of their bodies or covered themselves in coconut oil as a precaution. By now, a majority of citizens had acclimatized themselves to the increasing exposed mores of Paradise, being both physically tanned and socially inured to the radiance of light. Those who didn't look upon the nakedness of neighbor or friend seldom noticed those who did and generally didn't care, except for several parents who cloistered their children farther down the beach.

In a like manner, John and Kit took a sailboat into the open seas. Though John's previous sailing had been restricted to a reservoir near Phoenix, Kit showed him a few tricks for steering in open seas as they spent the afternoon circumnavigating Paradise and reminiscing about their former lives. Both expressed concern that rain might ruin the day after they saw dark clouds skirting along the horizon, but their good fortune held and the storms kept at a safe distance. Kit teased that John's earlier blessing had brought the favor of heaven, though John pointed to his fellow citizens at the beach and quipped that prayer more likely would bring damnation to the whole island— maybe a volcanic eruption or some other fire direct from hell.

Nevertheless, the volcanoes of the Pacific Rim remained inactive and the only thing broiled was the goat served at dusk. By the time John and Kit had secured the sailboat and arrived with empty plates at the table, they found that the goat was gone—a bit of gristle and a few bones were all that testified to the life that had been taken.

Wind blew into their faces as the voyagers sailed through open water at six knots and it took them longer than expected to reach their destination. Though they couldn't know it, their compatriots were eating broiled chicken even as Dr. Morales and his unconquistadors (as they deemed themselves) steered through a gap in the coral and landed at the main island—where locals greeted them on the beach. There, the aroma of cooked meat flavored the shore and stirred hunger pangs in the citizens of Paradise—who dropped the LCVP's loading ramp into two foot of water and waded ashore, each visitor bringing baskets of food and gifts as if from the gods. Dr. Morales returned the carved tortoise shell to the chief before joining his compatriots (who waited to be summoned in order not to disturb the solemnity of the religious ceremony). The unconquistadors were glad to do so, lest they be mistaken for Columbus and Cortés by ruining civilizations more ancient than their own in pursuit of piety and plunder.

The chief emerged from the woods after several minutes, flanked by two sons—each man armed with a ceremonial lance. He welcomed his guests in the name of the goddess before leading them deeper into the island. Several citizens of Paradise looked in disbelief as they passed poorly constructed huts and worn-out hammocks, as well as heaps of fish bones and bird's claws littering the ground in every direction; others tried not to pass judgment by their stares. Soon, the entourage came to a grass meadow with lines of turtle shells and a table set before a decorated palm trunk: a twelve-foot swayed pole decorated with geometric shapes, grotesque human images, and symbolic animal forms. The twisted torso of a fierce goddess crowned the totem, her legs crouched for birth and breasts hanging nearly to her hips. Her face was contorted in unchanging anguish—lips stretched and tongue extended—as the foreign guests paid homage. Deidra worshipped with genuine American Indian chanting.

The chief motioned his guests to sit before turtle shell bowls arranged near the back of the field—each one overflowing with slices of breadfruit, pieces of fish, and polished coconut husks filled with water. As guests took seats after offering their own gifts of fish, jelly, and fruits to the goddess, the chief's sons moved the visitor's gifts to their father's table for portioning and distribution. Only when spoils were divided did the chief bless the meal and call his people to feast —now eating foods never before imagined.

Eyes grew wide as natives tasted for the first time fruit jelly and tuna steaks (caught the previous day and simmered overnight). Their children squealed with delight as they tasted watermelon and nearly sucked their cheeks down their throats when they bit into lemon— and grew rambunctious and unruly after chewing sugar cane to pulp. All the while, the citizens of Paradise whispered among themselves how good it was to be of help to such a downtrodden people; even Deidra expressed pleasure at the cultural benefits of profit sharing.

The old chief grinned as he watched his clan eat and an hour passed until children licked the last bits of cane and adults sucked the bones of salted fish. When the chief raised his hands to the heavens, native and guest alike fell silent as he motioned for a teenaged girl to come forth and she did so: her back stiff and eyes dropped. She wasn't much more than sixteen—short, skinny, and underfed—but the girl had passed puberty; her breasts were swollen, her hips carried a hint of fertility, and her fleshy belly protruded several inches over the ragged grass skirt that covered her hips. She looked to be a few months preg- nant or at least showing a stretched belly not yet contracted following birth. The chief said a few words before blessing the girl with a kiss to the forehead and the girl bowed before the totem to worship.

"Fascinating," Dr. Morales whispered. "A real fertility ritual. She's being inducted into the cult of the goddess at the phallic-shaped totem. I think the girl is the chief's daughter or wife. Possibly both from the looks of her. They only have one word for female and it covers all ages and relations—and it's similar to their word for goddess and life and feast. There's another argument against universal taboos."

Deidra observed that the totem showed a woman in labor and everyone was pleased to observe that it was a matriarch who was honored as the primary tribal deity. Then the citizens of Paradise watched as several native women and every man in the tribe danced in a wide circle before the teenaged girl while the chief led a grotesque drama in which the men used sticks and gestures to simulate the making of a human baby. The latter rocked three-foot rods back and forth while the women tried to grab the logs whenever they came close. Whenever a woman succeeded, she left the dance—until the final girl seized the totem and fell prostrate as the chief blessed her in the name of the goddess. A moment later, the tribe broke into frenzied celebration. Only then did the chief speak with Dr. Morales.

"They honor," Dr. Morales explained after returning to his own table, "the goddess as the life-giver by dedicating this girl to her. As near as I can tell, she'll be made the chief's wife and her child dedicated to the glory of the goddess. Now comes the feast of the goddess. This is solemn and we're not allowed to talk during such a holy time. Not one word. From what I deciphered from the carvings, they believe a goddess came to this island from another world and nearly perished in the sea. The story is she washed up on a turtle or something—I couldn't understand—and gave birth to this tribe. Now she's said to provide both daily bread and new life: the word is the same. It wouldn't surprise me if all these people were descended from one pregnant woman and her offspring. She must have given birth to a boy and slept with him later. Maybe she was lost at sea or set ashore, typically for infidelity or some other crime. This is incredible. Perhaps the most important anthropological find of our century."

"It's also a beautiful service," Deidra said. "Very meaningful."

"But what does it mean?" Karla asked. "I wish we spoke their language."

"Soon enough," Dr. Morales said. "Heather'll pick it up quickly. She's a bright girl."

Joan looked at Charles.

"Where is our ex-daughter?" Joan asked.

"I hope she's busy with a native boy," Charles said. "Bringing about a little intercultural unity."

"You've always had," Joan said, "such high aspirations for her."

"Maybe," Dr. Morales continued without comment, "she's preparing food. Or doing daycare. The children aren't here yet and these tribespersons do have rather stereotypical gender roles."

"No doubt," Joan said with a frown, "she's helping somewhere. That girl's going to end up in the streets of Calcutta with the Sisters of Charity if she doesn't watch out. Probably christened Mother Heather Theresa. Charity and children and celibacy—how did we fail her? I can imagine her reciting the rosary and kneeling for the eucharist if she had the chance."

"I can imagine," Charles said with a laugh, "her becoming the eucharist if the job wasn't already taken."

"Shhhh," Jose said. "It's beginning."

The islanders hushed as the chief raised a decorated coconut husk and smashed it against the totem. The coconut shattered and blood splashed across the base of the pole. Then the old patriarch fell to his knees and prayed aloud—his arms outstretched and eyes opened. When he was finished, he turned to his people and gave a blessing. The natives broke into shouting and laughter as two middle-aged women emerged from the trees: each one carrying a decorated turtle shell wider than her own spindly hips. One woman presented her shell at the chief's table and another walked to the visitors—where she dumped shredded meat on their shell tables and motioned to eat. As the guests ate, she disappeared down the path, only to return a couple minutes later with more food. In this way, the women served ceremonial meat until everyone on the island ate. Only then did the women feed themselves.

The aroma of the meat was strong. Several of the islanders hadn't eaten anything but fish or an occasional bird since arriving and the scent of roasted flesh came on strong. They tore at the slices of meat with their fingers and swallowed them almost without chewing. Only Lisa didn't eat.

"This is really good," Dr. Morales said. "You have to try it."

Lisa shook her head.

"I haven't eaten animal flesh," the young woman said, "since high school. I won't judge your lifestyle, but I'm no carnivore. I don't even eat hamburgers."

"Still," Charles said, "I hadn't realized how much I missed a good steak."

"Me too," Joan added. "Heather's going to miss out."

"Don't worry about her," Dr. Morales observed, "the helpers are always given a double portion. She'll get more than any of us."

"I'm her ex-father and I claim her share as payback," Charles said as he grabbed the last piece of meat.

"Divide that with me," Joan said, "if you know what's good for you, since I'm the one who endured labor. Don't try to expropriate the excess value of my labor for your own profit. Don't be such a capitalist pig."

Charles laughed as he tore the meat into thirds and shared portions with Joan and Karla. A moment later, he finished eating and wiped greasy fingers on his shirt as he reclined.

"That was tasty," Charles said. "What was it? Goat?"

"No," the anthropologist said, "I've had kid before. This didn't taste the same and the strips were too long. Besides, the natives don't have goats."

"Beef?" Jose joked and everyone feigned a scowl.

"It wasn't very strong," Karla said. "I'd guess a sea mammal. Maybe dolphin or whale?"

Everyone nodded.

"I'd harpoon Moby Dick myself," Jose said with a loud laugh, "to have another taste of this."

Lisa punched him on the arm. "Some pacifist you turned out to be," she scowled.

"Only with my own species."

"Look at that," Joan said, pointing to the chief's table. "They've got more."

"That isn't a dolphin," Jose said.

"It looks like a pig."

"There can't be boars here," the anthropologist looked perplexed as he spoke. "The island's too small."

The others paid no attention. Ryan licked his fingers and Maria gnawed a bone into which the taste of the meat was deep cooked as the chief spoke out loud and pointed at his table while motioning for his guests to approach.

"He wants some of us to come forward," Dr. Morales explained. "As guests, we're allowed to feast from the goddess's own plate. He says a plate has been prepared to honor us as gifts come from the gods and asks us to taste first to see that his people are worthy of their goddess."

Deidra's eyes welled with tears.

"This is just ..." She couldn't find the words to express her joy and her sentence died unfinished.

Several islanders started forward, with Dr. Morales in front and Charles and Joan at his heels. Jose and Lisa came behind them, followed by Deidra, Karla, Ryan, and Maria. The others waited at their shells, too full to eat another bite. Only when the entourage moved within fifteen feet of the chief's table did the anthropologist stop dead in his tracks—Joan and Charles running into him, their jaws dropped and eyes wide. Karla let out a squeal and Jose gasped. Lisa turned white. Ryan and Maria were at the end of the line and couldn't see.

"The gods be damned," Deidra shouted, "it's a baby."

And so it was. A roasted baby of a month or two lay on the table: its skin seared from burning and its joints swollen from cooking. The chief twisted an arm and the well-cooked limb snapped like a dry stick. When the old chief handed it to Dr. Morales, the anthropologist neither moved nor spoke. Lisa wept and Jose backed away. Karla stared at the cooked child and Deidra fell to her knees in horror. The others froze where they stood.

Joan found her voice first. "Oh lord," she screamed, "where's my baby? Where's my little girl?"

As soon as Joan looked at the chief's table, she saw a tightly bound wrap of brown hair—still sporting Heather's scarlet ribbon—draped over a side. She screamed from horror, her eyes wide and hands covering her mouth.

"Damn me," Charles cried out, staring wild-eyed at the grease stains on his clothes. "Damn me. I've wiped Heather on my shirt."

As Charles ripped his shirt off and flung it away, the bewildered chief jumped to his feet—his eyes offended and confused. Just as he began to protest this grave insult, Charles sprang forward and landed a blow to his jaw and both men tumbled from the impact. As the chief fell into the bloodstained totem pole with Charles atop him, one of the chief's sons thrust a lance into the white man's back—near a kidney. Charles gasped and the man struck a second time, now driving the spear into the base of the attacker's skull.

Charles moved no more.

By the time the mortal wound had been inflicted, the meadow broke into a brawl as the second son heaved his spear into Joan's back and she fell writhing in pain. Dr. Morales kicked the youth in the groin and pushed him into the table—which crashed upon the chief even as screams and shouts came from every direction and the deep alarm of a conch bellowed. Almost immediately, rock and coral flew at the visitors and Deidra was struck in the head—falling to the ground, mute and unmoving as blood pooled around her shoulders. The remaining citizens of Paradise raced for the boat as stones flew fast and fear grew strong.

Indeed, they fled without reflection or hesitation—with those nearest the danger running the fastest. Jose was the first to leap into the landing craft and immediately fired its engines while others dove into the boat and began to raise its ramp. By the time the slow-running Dr. Morales clamored breathless into the boat, natives were swarming the beach—rocks and spears in hand. Wood and stone pinged with harmless noise into the sides of a landing craft built to shield rifle fire. As the boat started to sea, a spear flew over the closed ramp and struck Karla in the neck.

She bled out a few miles east of Paradise.

35
___

REACTIONS AND READINESS

Sirens wailed from Mount Zion soon after dark. News of the disaster crossed the island within the hour and everyone marched for New Plymouth at the double time. The motorized launch was sent to pick up Ursula and Sean, as well as others from the west and north districts who tended children or couldn't walk fast. Afterwards, Jason borrowed the boat to retrieve Father Donovan from exile. As the crowds assembled, there was neither laughter among adults nor play by children. Fear gripped the grownups and shock disseminated even to the youngest among them as citizens gathered in small groups of distraught idealists. Whenever too many people came together, someone walked away of his or her own accord, unable to bear too much human companionship.

Less than two hours after the alarm first sounded, emergency generators were fired to power two floodlights that illuminated the main tent and it wasn't long before everyone, including the previously exiled Father Donovan, took a seat. Ryan addressed the citizenry from the lectern, wasting no time with formalities or frivolities.

"The facts are these," Ryan announced. "Karla was hit in the neck with a spear and died on the trip home. Charles was left wounded on the island, presumed dead. Deidra and Joan also were left wounded.

The doctors can't even guess whether their injuries were mortal. Heather apparently was served as dinner. We're also missing Ashley from the north and Stuart from the east village."

Steve stood. "Let's go get 'em."

Several men gave a hurrah until Ryan raised his hand to request the floor to silence them.

"Charles," Ryan said, "struck their chief and Morales hurt one of his sons. We're not going to be greeted with handshakes."

"Stuart's my next door neighbor," Steve declared. "I'm going to get him and the others."

More shouts echoed through the hall.

"We don't even know if they're alive," Ryan replied.

"I'm not," Steve's voice boomed, "going to give the damned heathens time to cook my friend."

Ryan said nothing as Steve walked forward.

"My motto always has been to live and let live," Steve said with clenched teeth and rolled fists, "not surrender and be eaten. We need to save our friends. If we won't do it, who the hell will?"

Jose raised his hand.

"You're talking war," Jose shouted. "Let's solve this peacefully. Let's send a delegation."

"Fine," Steve said, "and let's paste them with relish."

"That's not funny."

"We don't have time to debate," Steve said. "There's barely enough time for action."

"And so begins every war," Jose shouted, "every first strike. Every act of violence. There's never time to reflect. Not until everyone's sobbing over tombstones."

"There really isn't time tonight."

"We'd better make time," Jose said as he shook his head in dismay, "or we'll end up as dead imperialists."

"If," Steve snarled as his face exploded with rage, "you want to take the launch to negotiate for the lives of our people, do it. We'll applaud your bravery and bury your bones when we get there—that is, any left uneaten. We're loading the ship and bringing our friends home. I ask the assembly for the right to lead an expedition to save our people. As some of you know, I've seen war before."

The motion was seconded by at least fifty hands even before Ryan could submit the proposal for review. Debate was entertained.

Jose was the first to object.

"I amend," Jose said, "the motion to request that a peace delegation be sent instead. In keeping with our principles. We're becoming the militarists we hate. The Americans also claimed a right to redress the sinking of the Lusitania and the bombing of Pearl Harbor. Look where that led."

"To Parisians singing La Marseillaise," someone shouted, "rather than Deutschland über alles and Hawaiians speaking English instead of Japanese?"

Jose's motion was voted upon, but received only five votes, so he tried again.

"I vote," Jose said, "we amend the motion to rescue our people, but not to hurt any indigenous peoples. Don't we believe every culture is equal and there are no taboos? We have the right to save our skin, but not to punish someone else's bad taste."

Shouts and threats rang through the assembly hall until Steve raised his hand to signal the crowd.

"We don't have the time," Steve shouted, "to debate this. Let's vote and move on."

Jose's second motion also failed.

"Now let's vote upon the original motion," Steve said.

"I amend," Jose said as he again took the floor, "the original motion placing Steve in charge. I'd like to form a committee to screen applicants for an officer corps. We need ethical men and women in charge of our soldiers."

"Damn it, Jose," Steve growled, "you're deliberately stalling. We need to vote and move on. No more amendments. Voice vote. All of those in favor of sending a rescue party, say yea."

A loud yea thundered through the assembly hall.

"Nay?"

Several half-hearted votes were cast.

"The LCVP," Steve said, "will hold a platoon. That's two from the staff and eight from each neighborhood. Volunteers to the front."

Sixteen men and eight women stepped forward. Among them were Ryan, John, Sean, Viet, Brent, and Hilary. Steve counted off the volunteers before turning to his fellow islanders.

"I'm going too," Steve said, "so we need nine more volunteers."

One man and one woman from the north stepped forward.

"Very good," Steve said. "Seven more. If it comes to fighting, we can't let ourselves be outnumbered by the enemy. We need to fill that boat with every fighter it can carry."

No one stepped forward, so Steve told the volunteers to assemble by neighborhood. When they had done so, he took a quick count.

"We need," Steve said, "two westerners, two southerners, and three east villagers to even out the levies."

When no one volunteered, Steve implemented a draft—starting with his own people.

"The east village," Steve declared, "volunteered four men and one woman. I need three women to fill its quota. Cast the lot."

The women who drew short sticks moved to the front and Steve next turned to the southerners—drafting two women. Only after the northern village had fulfilled its quota did Steve turn to the west village and observe that the western quota remained short two persons.

"We've lost," John stepped forward to explain, "one man and three women already. We have no one else to give. We can't have mothers fight alongside their husbands or Olivia leave her daughter. Kit's no warrior and Ursula's pregnant. Heck, Sean's fighting with an injured leg. That leaves Lisa and Jose—and they're both avowed pacifists."

"So am I," a voice from the mass of volunteers said.

Lisa dropped her eyes and blushed.

"A fair-weather pacifist," Jose shouted out for everyone to hear.

"I'm sorry," Steve said, "but we need two people. We can let the mothers stay. Give us Kit and Ursula."

Though both women stepped forward, Kit grasped the younger

woman by the arm and patted her friend's pregnant belly before stepping further forward alone.

"She counts for two," Kit said, "so we'd be over our quota."

"We need one more," Steve said.

"Draft Jason," a westerner shouted. "Let the criminal fight."

"I can live with that," Steve answered. "He's close enough."

"You can't draft Jason," Jose shouted, "or anyone else. The charter protects every citizen from compulsory military service and can't be abridged. We've all sworn it many times."

Steve faced the assembly.

"First," Steve declared, "the same assembly that ratified the charter can amend it, including any anti-abridgement clause. Second, we were thinking only of an organized military force, not an emergency situation to save our own citizens. So let's get back to business. Can someone second the motion to draft Jason to fulfill the west village quota?"

Several voices seconded the motion and a voice vote was taken. After Jason's name was added to the rolls, Steve turned to the assembly and asked if there were any final considerations.

"I won't fight with drafted women," John said as he stepped forward and spoke with disgust in his face and anger in his voice, "when there are men in this assembly who need to join our ranks. You know as well as I do half of these women will freeze if it comes to real fighting and most will prove too weak. It's not like we have time to broaden their shoulders and harden their chests. As it is, we'll double casualties for man and woman alike if we take them. Kit couldn't hit a softball hard, let alone a human being. I won't fight beside her."

Several other voices joined in.

"It's chicken shit," one man said, "my wife stays at home."

"Wussies," another grumbled.

Two women were pushed toward their chairs by irate husbands and three others walked away on their own; Kit sat down after John told her to.

"We need to leave now," Steve threw his arms in despair. "What do you propose?"

"A draft for the vacant positions," John said, "a draft of men. We keep only women who really want to fight—and can do so. This isn't high-tech combat. It'll be cracking skulls with axes and clubs, not pushing fingers to buttons or pulling triggers."

Several men and most women among the volunteers groaned.

"Who's eligible?" Steve asked.

"Every man among us," John answered. "We have no 4Fs."

Jose jumped up in protest. "That's not fair," he shouted. "I don't want to fight. It's militaristic, it's sexist, and it's a macho stereotype. Hell no, I won't go."

"Fair enough," Steve said, looking straight at John. "We'll count off and draw numbers. Those picked go. No debates."

John nodded. "Anyone object?"

Several voices did object, so a vote by hands was ordered. Only eighteen people voted against the proposal. The vast majority approved and every man then counted off. Lottery numbers subsequently were written on a slip of paper and dropped into an empty knapsack—from which Steve selected draftees. To his dismay, Jose was the first man chosen and found no support for his complaint that compulsory military service violated the charter. His continued protests were ignored as the majority turned against him.

Indeed, draftees and volunteers alike were given two hours to draw supplies, complete training, and report for duty. The supply shed at New Plymouth was opened as an armory and its tools offered as weapons: axes, shovels, hoes, machetes, and knives. Steve told every soldier to sharpen two wooden spears and collect one large stone and several smaller ones. Rudimentary combat techniques and self-defense moves were demonstrated by former soldiers and martial arts students before the four squads elected officers to lead them into battle, if necessary.

While weapons were selected, training conducted, and farewells said, Steve and John drafted a battle plan—with Dr. Morales providing geographical and cultural intelligence. It soon became evident a night attack would be futile since tides and reefs made navigation perilous. If the landing craft were grounded, they might be butchered on the beach or otherwise stranded on the island. It was decided to wait for daylight to clear the reefs safely and land as an organized force under a functioning command. A dawn attack was planned and word sent that the LCVP would depart at two o'clock in the morning.

Using a sketch of the atoll drawn by Dr. Morales as a basis for operational planning, Steve and John decided to deploy and fight as neighborhoods, both to facilitate a fighting spirit and foster effective communications. The basic plan was to send three squads forward to secure the beach and reconnoiter the island while holding a fourth section in reserve to defend the boat. Once the plan was drafted, Father Donovan and other leaders suggested several useful changes. After modifications were approved, Steve drew an army surplus blanket from the stores and found a quiet place to rest while John searched for a bite to eat. Lights out was ordered four hours before scheduled departure, though one fire was permitted for islanders suffering the night's chill. Couples stole into the woods for private embraces or caressed near the flickering flames of burning wood. Alarm clocks were set for two o'clock in the morning.

The state of Paradise was at war.

"HEATHER WAS A NICE GIRL."

Kit sat beside John, her head propped against his shoulder. A dim fire burned through some trees as she talked through the dead of night. A piece of dried bread had been tossed aside.

"It's horrible," Kit whispered. "They're horrible."

"I'll give her remains a Christian burial, if I can."

Tears rolled down Kit's cheeks. "Her parents too," she whispered. "For her sake. If they're dead."

"She once asked me to adopt her," John said after a pause. "If I'd been her father, I wouldn't have let her go."

Kit touched his cheek. "Don't blame yourself," she whispered.

"She had parents whether they wanted to be or not. No one could have replaced them."

"They didn't deserve her."

"She was our counterculture."

Kit sobbed and John's eyes misted as he wiped her cheeks. Neither talked for several minutes.

"I feel like a coward," Kit said.

John gently grasped Kit's chin with his hand and turned the woman's eyes to his own.

"Swear to me," John said with a stern voice, "you won't tolerate such nonsense—not even from yourself. None of us are made to hack enemies with axes, especially women. If Hilary wants to fight, let her. But someone gentle and sweet like you isn't made for war. You're not a man."

Kit's breasts heaved as she sobbed, soft flesh rising and falling with each breath. Her hands quivered even as John's forearm tightened his grip on her wrist.

"You're not a man," John said a second time, with an even gruffer voice, "but a woman. I see it with my eyes and I feel it with my heart. Don't ever think of yourself as anything else."

As Kit's sobbing slowed, John dropped his voice.

"Your place," John whispered, "is with Linh and Tiffany. They'll need help if things turn out poorly. Understand?"

Now Kit wrapped her ankle around John's foot and John reached his arm around Kit's waist to pull her close. Neither of them slept before John gave Kit a kiss to the cheek and walked to the designated assembly area.

RYAN LAY beside Maria on his wool blanket, beyond earshot of the camp. Both lay naked beneath a sheet.

Ryan was red in the face.

Maria wasn't.

"I'm sorry," Ryan said. "I've never failed before."

"Too bad we don't have one of those little booster pills."

"There's some at the dispensary," Ryan said as he sat up.

Maria pulled him down.

"It's all right," the young woman said. "I'd be nervous too."

"I avoided," Ryan said, "the draft for Vietnam and now I've volunteered to fight cannibals. Some paradise."

"Take care of yourself and don't be a hero."

"You can bank on that."

"They'll see," Maria said, "that they're outnumbered and outgunned and you'll pick up our wounded without a fight."

"We can hope. We can hope."

Maria lowered her voice. "Ryan?"

"What?"

"I'm not sure I want to stay here any longer."

"You want to admit failure?"

"We're spiraling downward."

"We'll talk when I return."

Now a shout came from the dark that there remained only fifteen minutes before departure.

"I'm sorry," Ryan said, "but I wanted to give you something to remember me by."

Maria patted her belly. "You've already done that."

"I'm glad my name won't die with me," Ryan said. "I'd never even thought of it before now."

Maria squeezed her husband's hand.

"If something happens," Ryan continued, "tell my son about me. Or my daughter."

"I'll tell her everything."

"Just the good."

"What would you want me to remember?"

"Talk to my publicist," Ryan said as he stood to dress.

"You can tell her yourself," Maria whispered. "I expect to see you come home tomorrow night. To finish what we started a few minutes ago. I'm not done with you quite yet."

"I'll do what I can," Ryan said.

Maria slipped into her clothes and wrapped a blanket around her shoulders before walking with Ryan to the beach.

STEVE WOKE an hour before the alarms were set to ring, so he stacked logs on the fire to kill time. After filling a pot of coffee and breaking open a box of rations, he called out the time and ordered the militia to assemble—asking John to load the LCVP with one MRE and two jugs of water for each soldier. This army wouldn't march on empty stomachs. Meanwhile, family and friends carried tins of coffee and spare blankets to the ship, as well as two medical kits and bundles of hastily sharpened spears. At the last minute, it was decided to substitute the camp veterinarian for the camp physician (who had volunteered to deploy) and to instruct the New Plymouth staff to ready the hospital for casualties—as well as to keep the emergency radio on standby in the event it proved necessary to seek outside assistance. Final plans were drafted, mournful tears were shed, and wishful hopes were shared—and a few islanders even gathered for prayer during which a east villager named Dillon petitioned God to help their side.

Four conscripts and two volunteers failed to report for duty, so Steve delayed the departure—sounding a loud horn three times to call those who were absent without official leave to station. After fifteen minutes passed and they hadn't arrived, the decision was made to proceed without them—and two southern men present for farewells were pressed into service. Islanders gathered at the shore pushed the loaded landing craft to sea and it wasn't long before the boat was navigating through the lagoon toward the dark horizon. John and an eastern volunteer sailed the motorized launch before the landing craft, hauling rope and tackle in the unlikely occurrence that the larger boat faltered in the open seas. No one wanted the men and women of Paradise to drift into danger or death.

Both boats crossed the coral barrier and disappeared into the dark no more than thirty minutes after Steve called assembly. On board, officers were elected and orders given. Nerves were raw and voices snapped as the LCVP approached its destination and several men and a couple women vomited against the high walls of the craft while others used long ropes to retrieve seawater to wash down the worst of the foul mess. Indeed, rinsing was just finished when the boat came within sight of Roanoke Island—the dark outline of the island lighted by the early morning sun. Gestures and shouts were used between the two craft to coordinate the final leg of the voyage over the roar of their engines.

When they reached Roanoke Island, John motored ahead to reconnoiter the atoll while Steve and the militia readied themselves for battle. Water was sipped and bits of chocolate eaten. Bootlaces were tied and weapons shouldered. After straws were drawn, the northsmen were assigned a reserve position at the rear of the boat while the other squads lined single file to disembark as soon as the boat struck sand.

They didn't have long to wait.

36

WAR IN HEAVEN

"We've passed the coral. Weapons ready."

After shouting his warning, Sean crouched beside Brent against the ramp gate. Behind them stood Viet, Ryan, Hilary, and Jose. Jason decided to fight with northern friends and was stationed with Donovan's war party and medical staff to the rear. The landing craft dipped in the surf and several of the militia groaned. Sean looked over the top of the steel gate and turned white. When he turned around, he shouted as loud as he could over the diminishing whine of the engine—which already was throttling down.

"They're waiting," Sean shouted. "So haul ass after I drop the gate. West village left. East village right. Southerners forward. Northsmen to the rear. Don't lose this boat, boys and girls. It's our ride home."

Three men cracked weak smiles. Two others vomited and one pissed his pants. A woman stood in the urine trembling without attempting to move her feet. A few seconds later, the shallow-draught boat slowed to a halt in waist-deep water—where Sean dropped the gate with a pull of the lever as the citizen-soldiers of Paradise jumped into battle.

The first spear struck immediately. Brent hadn't taken two steps before a scrawny native hurled a bone-tipped spear straight at his chest. The spear struck in the sternum and Brent collapsed, blood spurting from his mouth and nose. Ryan tripped over him and fell forward as a second spear flew waist-high into the boat, missing his head by inches. A southern woman gasped, then howled in pain and clutched the spear lodged in her side. Meanwhile, Sean jumped into the surf to pull Brent's head above water as everyone else sprang from the boat in frenzied terror. As a northsman pulled Brent into the craft, Sean shouted for the nurse—who already tended the wounded woman—then told the northsman to do what he could while he himself limped to join his compatriots (having reinjured his knee during his jump).

By the time Sean limped into line, the first volley of native spears had ended. Brent and the southern woman were down, and two other islanders staggered back to the LCVP with gaping wounds—one in the leg and the other in a shoulder. Steve used the lull to direct islanders into formation against what appeared to be an irregular line of twelve men and several boys. Spears were passed to the northerners and the advancing neighborhoods moved forward as the northerners volleyed missiles in an effort to drive the natives back to shore. Only if the islanders advanced to dry land could they effectively bring their superior numbers to bear.

The natives, however, didn't retreat from the missiles, but darted in front of falling spears while raising high their short, sharpened lances. Closing the gap with the southerners in a matter of moments (and having the advantage of surprise and maneuverability against opponents still waist deep in the surf), the cannibals struck the center with deadly effect. Five southerners went down without the loss of a single native. The younger cannibals finished off fallen opponents using shards of sharpened shell while older tribesmen retreated and regrouped for a second attack. Two southern men dragged a wounded friend to the safety of the rear.

As the islander's attack stalled in confused horror, the cannibals eluded a volley of northern spears and sprinted through ankle-deep water to flank the western line—all the while screaming with a demonic intensity as they gained speed. The chief's two sons led the charge of twelve warriors against a squad of five westerners. Seeing the threat, Jose swam for deep water and Ryan shouted for help—though he didn't wait to hear the response of those still in the LCVP before joining a shoulder-to-shoulder defensive line hastily organized by his fellow westerners. When the natives attacked the loose formation, Hilary deflected the thrust of the foremost warrior with a poke of her spade and Sean hurled a javelin that struck the man in the ribs. Blood gushed from the cannibal's mouth as he slipped into the sea. No one tried to save him, though he was the son of a chief. Rather, the others pressed their attack over his sinking body. The second son of the chief lunged at Viet with an American-made ax, but slipped in the surf as he approached. Viet lifted his own ax high and drove it into the native's back so that the chief's son never moved again, his spine severed between the shoulder blades.

Meanwhile, Hilary and a skinny native grabbed each other by the throat as they spun about in a grim-faced dance of death, but the man had a stronger grip and soon pushed Hilary underwater. Hilary was on her knees with the surf splashing across her face when Ryan hurled his spear and struck her attacker in the buttocks, breaking his death grip and forcing the man to limp away. Viet sprinted to help the fallen woman, but arrived too late to prevent a stocky native from grabbing Hilary by the hair and snapping her neck over his knee. Her bones cracked and she let out a short grunt as her eyes rolled to the back of her head and she sank beneath the sea. Then the native turned toward Viet—who called to Sean and Ryan for help as he retreated to deeper water.

Indeed, all three westerners backed into waist-deep water as a ragged line of nine warriors moved to encircle them. Five natives prodded with their lances to pin the westerners while four others fanned behind their foe in an enveloping move. In addition, four boys followed their elders, bloody shells in hand as they waited to finish kills with a slash of the throat. The westerners pulled stones from their pockets and prepared to throw, trying to keep the natives at bay, but it didn't work. Within seconds they were cut off and a high-pitched command of the stocky native made it evident the end was near.

That end never came.

No one noticed that the motorized launch had circled behind the LCVP and it was without warning that John gunned the boat for the natives who had flanked his friends. The boat struck hard and two natives crumpled under the impact of fiberglass and disappeared under water, the engine whining for an instant as its blades shredded flesh and bone before stalling. But even before the sound of the engine had died, John and the southerner leaped from the boat—axes in hand—and charged the foe. Utterly shocked by the sight of seawater turned blood red, the cannibals turned to face this new threat just as a volley of spears was hurled at them—striking the old chief in the arm and a bloodthirsty boy in the face. The chief grabbed his arm and ran for land while the young boy flipped into the sea and didn't get up. A second volley was hurled, then a third. Three more natives were wounded, two of them (including another boy) seriously enough to leave the battle. The northsmen had aimed well.

Reduced to five men and two boys before a reinforced enemy, the natives backed away as the tide of battle turned. The westerners advanced under John's commands to maintain contact with the foe as east villagers to their right marched at double time toward the beach. Under Steve's direction, the militia from the east village fanned into a firing line as they reached sand and blocked the only path of retreat. The cannibals turned to the new foe, only to be flanked by a third column—Father Donovan's northsmen had grabbed axes and shovels after hurling their last volley of missiles and now closed with the natives on the dead run. The natives didn't see them until the first northsman came crashing into their line swinging a double-edged ax into the back of a thick-armed cannibal. Others went utterly berserk and tackled natives to the ground as they poked eyes and chewed ears. In the short-lived melee, two easterners fell and one northsman was slashed across the face, but all of the natives were struck down or killed outright. Some were hacked to death with hoes and shovels and others pierced with spears. One was beheaded with a clean swing of an ax.

The fight was over in a breath.

Casualties were severe; the citizens of Paradise lost seven dead and seven wounded—two in critical condition. The natives lost eight dead, six wounded, and one missing—not counting one throat-cutting boy captured uninjured. The northerners posted guards around captives as the other villages reformed their ranks, though southern numbers were so decimated that it fell to the east and west villages to sweep enemy territory since the full complement of northerners was needed to guard the boats, watch prisoners, and tend wounded compatriots. Steve loaded two lightly injured southerners on the launch before taking it to search the smaller islands for stragglers and civilians.

It was still early morning when John led his men into the native village—little more than a scattering of hammocks and lean-to tents—where women and children wailing from anguish and apprehension were driven at spearpoint to the beach. A second sweep netted four more refugees: two women, a small child, and the wounded chief. These were marched back to the beach to take their place with prisoners being interrogated by Dr. Morales. The old chief, however, wouldn't talk and even threats couldn't open his tongue. As a result, a third expedition was launched. This time John was told to keep moving until he found the lost citizens of Paradise and to simply tie up captives and stragglers until they could be properly processed. Late in the morning, six well-armed citizens of Paradise marched into the heart of the island. All of the westerners were among them, except Sean and Jose; the former proved unable to walk and the latter remained unwilling to fight.

Moving first to the totem pole, John collected the remains of Heather's scalp. After looking for every strand of hair he could find, he removed his shirt and covered her remains for later burial. Meanwhile, Viet piled wood around the totem pole and placed the bones of the devoured baby atop the wood and set them ablaze after John commended the child's soul to God. Then the search party moved toward the far side of the island.

As they neared the beach, the sickening and sweet stench of burned flesh filled the nostrils of the rescue party, so they hurried toward the odor and found what remained of the missing citizens of Paradise. Charles and Joan were unclothed (with long strips of flesh sliced from their arms and legs and rolled in salt for jerky) while Deidra remained clothed and mostly intact (excepting only several fingers chewed to the knuckle). Ashley was no more. She had been eaten raw and little more than a gnawed skeleton remained, though a few pieces of unpicked ligament also stuck to her joints. It was even worse for Stuart—who was smoked over a fire that still smoldered, his once-white skin cooked golden brown and a spit run from his anus to his mouth. It was clear he'd suffered terrible agony—the anguish of death evident from his contorted face and wild-staring eyes.

It took the search party an hour to bury their dead. After graves were dug and bodies buried, Viet watched as John performed a Christian burial service as best as he could remember. Both men wept.

JOHN AND VIET returned to the beach by early afternoon, forced to detour from the main path after the burning totem toppled and set the woods aflame. The grass was still burning when the two men came to a smoldering field, where thick smoke forced them to thread their way through the brush. There, they captured two more natives —a young mother with stretched teats (no wider than her wrist and hanging past her ribs) and a young child. Caught hiding in tall grass, the woman jumped away but was grabbed by the quick-footed Viet. While John tied the native's feet with nylon cord, Viet investigated a noise in nearby brush—which proved to be a whimpering baby boy. Viet attempted to return the child to its mother, but the woman refused the child until Viet compelled her with sharp words and pointed gestures.

After marching the captured mother and child to the beach, John and Viet were greeted by utter horror: the throat-cutting boy was hanging from a palm tree, his broken neck stretched and his eyes bulged out. An eastern guard explained that the boy had been caught nibbling the fingers of a dead southerner. The easterner also pointed to a young woman and old man dangling in a nearby grove and noted that the woman had killed a northern guard with a knife thrust to the back and the old man was the tribal chief. Moreover, every one of the captured warriors lay on the beach dead—the spears driven deep into their chests still standing upright and the eyes of the executed heathens opened in unblinking terror. The easterner didn't know why those prisoners had been put to death and didn't really care.

John turned pale when he saw the line of bodies. When he saw Viet sprint toward a band of northsmen gathered near the treeline, he followed his friend—shouldering a spade as his weapon. As the two westerners approached jeering northsmen, they saw Father Donovan using a sharpened spear to tear open the pregnant belly of a dead native.

"What the hell are you doing?" John screamed as he pointed first to the hanged prisoners and then to the disfigured corpse.

"They," Father Donovan answered, "need to be taught a lesson."

John's face turned almost purple. "Murdering prisoners is a lesson? What kind of lessons do the dead learn?"

"Were we supposed to set them free?"

"We were supposed to decide justice at the Assembly."

"Why burden others," Donovan said without hesitation, "with this bloody business? Let's get it over with here and now. Justice is in our hands."

"Murder is justice?"

"Capital punishment is the proper term."

"On what grounds were they executed?" John whispered, his anger evident in the clenching of his teeth and trembling of his voice.

"The girl," Donovan said with a glib tone, "murdered Roberto and the boy ate Serina. This one tried to escape. And the chief ... well, let's just say the others needed to be taught to fear us. Sometimes it's better to be feared than loved."

"What others? They're all dead."

"Only the men."

"Why couldn't you wait for the General Will of the People to assemble? What was the hurry?"

"I guess," Donovan said with a smirk, "they tried to escape or something. They're damned cannibals. We can't talk to them and they're not going to make peace. What else could we do?"

Chuck and Jason moved beside the radical priest.

"Kill them all," Jason said, "and let the worms sort them out."

"You'll give an accounting," John now waved his arms and clenched his fists as he screamed, "to the assembly for this butchery. I swear it. This is no different than the cannibalism I saw on the other side of the island."

"No?" Father Donovan yelled back. "Maybe we ought to plan a barbecue. I'd kill them all again if I could. No regrets for me."

Now Steve returned from patrol and joined the conversation. His voice carried rage, though his fury was controlled and subdued.

"This isn't combat," Steve said through gritted teeth. "It's murder."

"Your first war?" Donovan taunted as he laughed out loud. "Or did you earn a Boy Scouts merit badge in strategy and tactics?"

"We took plenty of prisoners during the Gulf War."

"That wasn't war," Father Donovan said. "It was a live-fire exercise. Nicaragua was war."

At that moment, a muffled scream sounded from the trees and the three westerners hurried into the woods—where they discovered a teenaged native lying on her back, her wrists bound and mouth now gagged. The girl's nose was bloody and eyes bruised, and she watched in terror as two northsmen (and one of their women) determined her fate.

"Mind your manners," the northern woman told the arriving westerners. "They cast lots to see who'd do her first. You'll have to wait your turn."

One of the men started to unbuckle his belt, but immediately howled in pain when John swung the flat edge of his spade into the side of the man's leg. A knee buckled and the man collapsed. His partner jumped back and the woman raised her own ax as John thrust his shovel forward—ready to brawl.

But there was no fight, for two more fighters quickly reinforced Steve and his compatriots when Ryan and a southern man hurried to the scene—the former actor now wielding two spears and his associate brandishing a large knife. Even after Donovan and two confederates arrived a few moments later, the balance of power continued to favor Steve and his allies.

"Put the weapons down," Steve ordered the northerners.

"She's war booty," a northsman said.

"That's a bit literal," Father Donovan said with a grin as he joined his companions, "but I do like the pun."

"No one touches the girl," John said as he stepped closer to the girl and aimed the sharp of his spade at the chest of the northern man with an unbuckled belt.

"I'm with John," Steve said. "There's been too much butchery already."

"They're not real women," a northsman said, "only cannibals. They won't even care."

"They're human beings," John said, "and they have rights."

"They ate our neighbors."

"Is she worth your life?" John said with a scowl. "I tell you this girl won't be touched while I live."

"You westerners," Father Donovan scowled, "are nothing but damned bourgeois moralists. Like Russian liberals, you have no idea what it takes to make a proletariat revolution; and like American academics, you gave up on the socialist triumph too soon. Do you think politics is a debating society? Do you think we fought the Contras with ideas? Do you think we terrorized Reagan's gunmen with quotes from The Communist Manifesto?"

"You won't terrorize this girl with anything."

"Suit yourself," Donovan said, "and take her with my blessing. I've known monks who were less fastidious than you people."

Viet lifted the girl to her feet and escorted her toward the LCVP—which had been moved closer to shore—with the help of Ryan while Steve and John argued with Donovan over the fate of the prisoners. After some banter, Donovan said that the math alone dictated a policy of extermination.

Steve asked him to explain what he meant.

"We brought thirty-something soldiers with us," Donovan said, "and we have room only for our own missing neighbors."

"One man," John now dropped his chin and whispered, "was cooked and another eaten raw. Some were being smoked for preservation. No one else needed to see that gruesome mess, so we buried them."

"There's nothing to eat on this god-forsaken island," Father Donovan said, "except human flesh. They'll eat their own children if we give them the chance. You two are the humanitarians. Tell us what to do."

"How many are there?" Steve said as he made his own quick count.

The other waited for his numbers.

"Eleven women and thirteen children," Steve announced. "If we bury our dead on this island, the weight should balance out. These natives are skin and bones. And the sea is calm."

"I'd bring," Donovan said with a scowl, "our dead home and leave the heathen to eat themselves. There's not a boy over ten still alive and they'd all be gone before they can reproduce. Problem solved."

Now Dr. Morales pushed his way into the conversation. "That's genocide," he declared.

"Genocide of three dozen cannibals? I don't think so."

"A whole people group would be exterminated."

"And good riddance."

Steve put a hand on Dr. Morales's shoulder.

"We'll take them with us," Steve declared. "It's the only decent thing to do. It's all women and children."

"See," Father Donovan said, "how things manage to work themselves out? If the men still lived, we'd have had to leave them all behind to eat or be eaten. As it's said, God works in mysterious ways."

The northerners walked away while Steve and the westerners returned to the battle site and spent the next hour burying those killed in battle (with Brent and Hilary numbered among them). John recited the Lord's Prayer over their graves and Steve ordered a military salute at their funerals—during which Father Donovan conducted final sweeps of nearby islets. Though screams were heard from one islet, Donovan and his raiders returned with no prisoners and answered no questions. Afterwards, captives were loaded into the landing craft and guarded by the bloodstained veterans of Paradise. By midafternoon, John steered the motorized launch through the coral reef as the LCVP followed close.

It was a choppy return to New Plymouth, broken several times by the sobs and sickness of terrified natives—whose taboo against crossing the sea was being violated and whose untested stomachs churned. The soldiers of Paradise, however, showed little regard for the suffering of cannibals vomiting out the remains of family and friend and turned cold shoulders to the natives and their crying children, though one ill-tempered northerner knocked a wild-eyed and screaming girl to the deck and kicked her in the ribs. The hysterical native wept and wallowed in a pool of half-digested flesh for an hour. Only when the landing craft came within sight of Paradise did an eastern woman splash her with a bucket of seawater.

37

HYSTERIA AND HUMANITARIANS

John motored the launch into the murky waters of Paradise late in the afternoon. As soon as the dark-shadowed island was in distant sight, he abandoned escort duty and gunned for port—where loved ones awaited news of the expedition. There, he told a fleet-footed girl to sound the alarm atop Mount Zion as he briefed everyone close about the destruction of southern manhood and slaughter of his own friends—as well as the fate of those initially captured by the cannibals. He also explained that the General Will of the People was needed to deal with captured civilians. No one who listened uttered a word and only after his account was finished did villagers individually approach him with fear and trembling, asking if he knew the fate of loved ones. Some islanders soon wept from grief while others sobbed from relief. Young children wandered aimless, unable to absorb the shock of death and grief. A southern boy who had lost both parents wept inconsolably, but there was no one to comfort him and eventually he wandered into the forest.

The siren already wailed atop Mount Zion when the LCVP lumbered aground. Medical assistants brought stretchers to transport the wounded to the infirmary while the living embraced with unashamed hugs and kisses. John ran to base camp—where he learned that contact had been made with a yacht whose captain promised to relay any requests for medical assistance. On his own authority, John instructed radio operators to request immediate medical assistance, then returned to the beach to deal with the captives. Meanwhile, native women who deboarded the landing craft were contained to the beach by armed guards—where they and their children wailed, tore flesh, and pulled hair at the sight of an enemy so numerous and strong. Some trembled as they eyed roasting spits built on the beach while others watched a polyglot of races—every black or white or red or yellow or brown face fixed on them—stare in unforgiving hatred or inconsolable grief.

Some natives tried to make amends. A sharp-toothed woman in her twenties, visibly quaking in fear, stepped forward with her head bowed as she dragged a toddler through the sand and carried a baby at her hip—placing both before the citizens of Paradise before scampering back to her own people. The toddler ran as fast as he could toward his own people and even managed to slip past his mother by diving between her legs, but the baby just thrashed in the sand and cried. The mother pointed at him, cried out shrill sounds and unintelligible words, and motioned for her enemy to take the child.

"Oh lord," Dr. Morales said, "she's offering her child for dinner so we'll spare her."

Though the anthropologist returned the child to its mother with a few curt words, the woman backed away, pointing at the child and shouting to the people of Paradise. When none responded, she rolled the baby into the sand a second time and stepped away.

As the baby cried, a battle-tested northsman pushed the anthropologist from his path and approached the child—pointing with one hand and holding a hoe with the other.

"Pick it up, you damned heathen!" the northsman screamed.

The woman didn't move.

"Pick up your baby!" The northerner aimed the weapon at the mother. "Pick it up now!"

Now the woman became hysterical, babbling with such speed

that Dr. Morales didn't even try to translate. As the baby cried still louder yet, the northsman grew even more agitated.

"Someone," the man screamed, "better shut the little heathen up."

When no one responded, the northsman became utterly enraged —now screaming and threatening the woman as he motioned toward the child in a dozen different ways. Still, the woman wouldn't go to her child and the baby screamed ever louder until the northsman finally raised his hoe above the baby's chest.

"This is its last chance," the northsman threatened.

"I'll take him!"

It was Kit who called out for the child's life as she pushed through a crowd of onlookers and threw herself between the raging northsman and the crying baby. Only as she moved the child into the forest (where the baby's cries were muffled) did the warrior lower his weapon. Only then did the native woman stop her pleading and protesting.

A few minutes later, the captive cannibals were driven inland and placed under guard in a meadow. When several islanders set food and water before them, the women scrambled to eat. Boys and girls who threaded between the feet of old women and young mothers alike (to grab a share of the food) received kicks and blows for their pains, though one of them occasionally would run off with a handful of food—fighting off his peers to keep everything for himself. Few, however, succeeded and only after all adults had satisfied their own hunger did the young secure a few scraps to eat. Even babies weren't fed until their mothers first quenched their own thirst by lapping milk pumped into their cupped hands or suckling the teats of other nursing mothers (who soon received the same favor in turn).

Guards looked on the spectacle with evident disgust, cursing some natives and poking others with sharpened sticks to stop the worst abuses. Some of the women scurried from their sticks and others hissed in anger, but no matter how hard they poked and prodded, the guards couldn't inspire the cannibals to a single act of Christian charity, human kindness, or maternal love.

. . .

THREE HOURS after the militia's return, a moment of silence was observed for the dead and wounded as the General Will of the People was called to order inside the large tent—the assembly dimly lit with lanterns. Steve briefed the assembly on the day's fighting and asked for citations of bravery for several men. He singled out John, in particular, for several acts of heroism and humanity throughout the long day and commended the southern soldiers who'd suffered the brunt of the initial attack without breaking ranks. Upon his recommendation, the assembly awarded the fallen southerners a unit citation for valor and authorized combat ribbons for all veterans of the short war.

Only then did talk turn to even more difficult matters.

"There's also bad conduct to deal with," Steve said, "and I wish I wasn't the man standing here."

The assembly hushed.

"Several men," Steve said as the kerosene ran dry in a flickering lantern and a shadow subsequently covered his face, "and one woman went AWOL this morning and one man deserted in the face of the enemy. They let others die in their place and exposed our people to greater risk."

No one stirred as Steve continued.

"Not one of us," Steve said, "came here to wage war. But we all voted—the democracy voted and the people willed—to fight. Can some of us be exempt from the draft because we have high-minded principles or weak stomachs? Will we let the sons of senators stay home while others risk defilement and death?"

Now Tiffany stood, her sons clinging to their mother's legs as she spoke slow and deliberate, her eyes puffed and bloodshot and her face stained with tears. Her voice quivered.

"My children lost their father," Tiffany said, "while other men ran away: men who left no children behind. Or wives or husbands. Or anyone at all. Punish them all. Unless they can bring Brent back."

Other voices seconded her proposal.

Lisa also stood.

"I lost," Lisa said, "my best friend Hilary. They say she might've had a chance if one of her neighbors ... her own neighbor, I say ... hadn't run away in battle. I've always been a pacifist and I still respect a refusal to kill. But refusing to die is different. Let those who dodged the draft live with their own consciences, but anyone who ran away in battle has no place among us. He could have stood beside her without killing. Or even stepped between her and the savage. That's good enough."

Several northsmen holding flaming torches spoke next, most of them veterans of the one-day war. One wanted to brand draft dodgers with hot irons and flog Jose while others preferred to send cowards into permanent exile. One northsman even advocated capital punishment—though his proposal was greeted with silence by most villagers and caused Ryan to rise in protest.

"I might have died for Jose's cowardice," Ryan said, "while you were held in reserve. But hanging him, even if he deserves it, is no solution. It's just more killing."

The northsmen hissed.

"I know we must do something," Ryan continued, "since no one can be allowed to spurn the will of the community or to send someone to die in his place. I respect pacifism like any other man, but I had a cousin who was a conscientious objector—and who died in Vietnam as a medic saving another soldier's life. Jose should have tended our wounded on the battlefield. Others might have survived. All I ask is that we stop the killing."

"This isn't the place to debate ethics," Jose said as tears streamed down his cheeks, "nor the day. But I had the right to refuse to be part of a military machine. Today I watched boys cut the throats of grown men and saw children hanged. There was butchery and mayhem and I was right to refuse to participate in it. I'm not ashamed of my actions. I ran away from genocide, not from duty. I'm the one who deserves a medal."

Jose sat down and a dozen red-eyed women stood up. A Latino woman from the south spoke first.

"I'm not debating the coward," the Latino woman said. "I propose every draft dodger lose his citizenship and every deserter be exiled. Why should they enjoy rights they won't fight to preserve?"

Several voices seconded her motion and the woman sat without further talk as Steve opened the floor to discuss what forfeiture of citizenship entailed. After several minutes, it was agreed non-citizens would be denied the right to serve in public office and vote in elections—island or village. It also was decided that the restoration of citizenship could be granted only by the General Will of the People. Though most conscientious objectors said little, Jose protested a great deal.

"This is too much," Jose argued. "Even Nixon didn't go this far. He let protestors go to Canada in peace. It's tyranny and oppression and I refuse to accept it."

"You won't have to," Father Donovan shouted from the shadows, "because you'll be gone."

"Don't waste a boat on him," a southern woman shouted. "Let him swim to Canada."

"Cut it out," Steve said. "We aren't barbarians."

"We are," a burly northsman shouted, but no one laughed.

"We can put him on one of the motu permanently," Steve said, "or we can send him home on our rescue ship."

The audience fell silent at the unexpected news.

"Some of you haven't heard," Steve explained, "we've made contact with a yacht. Its captain has offered to evacuate our wounded. Probably to Hawaii. It'll be here by tomorrow."

The audience buzzed and Steve waited until the excitement faded before he continued.

"Let's vote on Jose's punishment," Steve said. "Exile on one of our motu or exile to America?"

Though Jose begged to be returned to America (protesting that even the United States afforded more freedom than Paradise), it was decided by a margin of two votes that he should be exiled to an island —with southern widows arguing that banishment to America would be a reward rather than punishment. Afterwards, Father Donovan pointed at Jose as he projected his voice over the crowd.

"I propose," the priest declared, "he be exiled to Roanoke Island where he can live with the memory of his cowardice."

Several amens saluted this proposal and it was accepted. A few minutes later, Jose was bound with ropes to await execution of his sentence—openly sobbing as he was led away.

"There's one final issue," Steve announced a moment later, "and it's the most serious yet. We nearly came to a fight over the fate of captives."

"Why'd we bring the cannibals here?" a northsman said. "They'll eat us in our sleep. Or they'll eat their children on our own tables."

Heads nodded and shouts sounded as Dr. Morales stood.

"These people are a living cultural artifact," the anthropologist said. "We've never encountered anyone like them before and it's important for future scholarship they not be compromised by modern society. We must respect their way of life and not stand as cultural imperialists. Though we've already killed almost every hope for the unadulterated continuation of their culture, if we return some boys and girls, perhaps they have at least a remote chance of reproduction and survival as a bastardized cultural legacy."

Catcalls erupted.

"You killed my husband."

"You murdered Heather."

"Let them eat anthropologist."

Dr. Morales sat down—his scholarship repudiated—and Father Donovan stood.

"We're forgetting one thing," Father Donovan said. "Our own charter guarantees citizenship to every person living among us. If they stay, they vote—and we'll bring a neighborhood of cannibals into the political process. I don't see how our ideals can survive it."

"We can't send them back," Ryan said, "or they'll eat our dead and their living. And Jose."

"Then we execute them," Donovan said with a shrug.

"For what crime?" Ryan shouted, red-faced and angry.

"Not crime, but crimes."

"Name one."

"Crimes against humanity."

"Cannibalism isn't a crime against humanity."

"That's only because Hitler," Father Donovan said, "was a vegetarian, so the Nuremburg Tribunal didn't have to address the issue."

"So what?" Ryan said. "We still have no authority. What laws could we use?"

"The laws of war."

"The war is over."

"Then we use military tribunals to mete our justice," Donovan said. "I've seen them used more than once."

"I'm no anthropologist," Ryan said, "but even I can't see executing the natives for breaking our standards of civilized conduct."

"Then what was today about?"

"Trying to save our own neighbors."

"Which," Father Donovan said, "required us to fight the natives for living according to their own laws and customs."

"No," Ryan said, "it was our neighbors who they ate."

"We handed Heather to them," Father Donovan said, "like a lamb to wolves. They only took the others after we attacked their chief."

Ryan said nothing.

"They did no more to us," Donovan continued, "than they've done to their own people. Hell, the more I think about it, the more I think they breed just to make food. How else could a few dozen people survive on those god-forsaken little islands? Where else could they get a little protein? They played Morales for manna from heaven and now we've lost our comrades."

"We have two choices," Steve said as a light flickered out and a corner of the assembly tent went dark. "Either we send them home to eat each other or we civilize them here. Executing them is out of the question."

The northsman scoffed.

"They're just hungry," Ryan said, "that's all. Food will break the cycle of cannibalism. There's plenty of room on this island for us to live together in peace. Who knows but we'll save them by our good example? Sure, they'll become citizens over time, but we can amend the constitution to allow only children born on our island itself to possess full voting rights. The others can be admitted into active citizenship on an individual basis."

"Brent died," Tiffany asked as tears streamed down her face, "so cannibals could be made citizens? To live with his children?"

Several other widows and widowers agreed and it wasn't long before even Ryan acknowledged that his proposal wouldn't pass.

"I accept the judgment of the people," Ryan said, "but we can't send the children away since the women will eat their babies in a heartbeat. We can't aid and abet cannibalism. If not for their good, then for our own sake, we have to let the children remain."

This proposal was far more acceptable and the majority nodded their heads, if only slightly.

"How old?" Father Donovan.

"I'd give the teenagers a chance," Ryan said.

"No," Donovan said, "they've the taste for human flesh already. It'll never stop. The babies are harmless enough and probably children under ten. Teenagers will have to fend for themselves."

Dozens of voices seconded this proposal.

"There are children," Father Donovan said as he stood and raised his voice from the shadows to silence the assembly, "who haven't yet reached puberty. How can we support or even look after them?"

The audience let the priest answer his own question.

"If they're kept under supervision," Donovan continued, "they can be made to help with crops and harvests—and help earn their own keep. Why should our own people be forced to work twice as hard to replace losses while those who are responsible escape all accountability?"

"Made to help?" Viet snapped as he stood up. "Under supervision? We're talking forced labor. Be clear."

"I'll be perfectly clear," Father Donovan said. "No euphemisms. I'll say the very word—reeducation camps. It's the only way that these people will escape cannibalism. They can go home to eat each other or they can stay here and be taught what they need to learn. In fact, we can be humane enough to let even the adults stay if we use camps. In just a few months, the younger ones will pick up enough English to communicate our ideals to the older generation."

"Do you mean to say temporary slavery?" Viet asked.

"I wrote my thesis at Marquette against the theology of Southern racism and slavery," Father Donovan replied, "and I believe in freedom more than any person here. We'll let the natives choose their own lifestyles, sleep with their own loves, and worship as they please as long as they give up cannibalism and work their quota."

Viet pressed the point. "Which is?"

"The same as ours," the priest replied. "The same as ours. Of course, some of us will have to oversee their efforts and guard them from each other."

"Ours will be happy slaves."

"I don't like forced labor," Ryan now joined the discussion, "but we've forced some of our own people to work for a living, so why not these people? We're no better than them and no worse. Donovan is right; it's the only way to protect us and them alike."

Similar remarks were made by others, though a slim majority seemed to favor deporting the cannibals until Steve reminded them that sending the natives home might lead to cannibalism of the corpses of their loved ones. Consequently, it was voted to reeducate the natives in Paradise. It also was decided the cannibals should be made to help feed themselves—with a food levy to be collected to provide for their guards. Indentured servanthood—or "citizenship training" and "republic education" as some called it—was to last only as long as the savages remained a threat to public safety. Children were given to the childless couples of the east village to perpetuate their own lineage and Kit was allowed to keep the boy she'd saved. In any event, no one else wanted the younger children. The southerners needed mature adults to work their fields and the northerners solicited teenaged girls. Jason explained that his adopted village hoped to bridge the linguistic barrier with the selection of younger women. It was hoped that the girls would learn some English while engaged in intimate relationships and that their subsequent offspring would be raised bilingual. This seemed a good idea to the majority, skepticism from the west village not withstanding.

After the meeting ended, chains and padlocks brought for animal care were drawn from storage and shackled around the fiercer cannibal women's wrists and ankles. Combinations and keys were sent to the respective neighborhoods where cannibals were assigned to work—excepting only the west village (which assessed that slavery was more work than it was worth). The first native accepted her chains without protest, but the next three saw the final state of the former's enslavement and resisted. Only after one of them was whipped with a leather belt for biting a northsman did the others submit. Once adults were secured, all natives were returned to the LCVP as an improvised prison. By the time islanders finally dispersed to their own homes, the dark already was deep.

Several citizens of Paradise didn't go home, but wandered around New Plymouth in grief (some of them sedated by liberal doses of Valium). Others slept near the beach, hoping to beg a ride home as soon as the American yacht arrived. Grieving widows turned to their children for consolation and distraught men did the same (though several stepparents made alternative arrangements for the care of children to whom they weren't deeply attached). It was in this way that Brittany was sent to Kit—with the boyfriend of the girl's dead mother not bothering to say farewell.

KIT CRADLED a dark-skinned baby in her arms as she walked along the pitch-black shore with Linh and her daughters—who helped with Brittany, Tyrone, and Theodore. Viet and Tiffany took the more direct path of Mount Zion, along with Ryan and Maria, while Sean and Ursula hurried ahead. John remained in mourning at New Plymouth, as did Olivia and Ilyana. Lisa stayed with a friend from the south. Everyone else was gone. Six of twenty-four neighbors were killed in two day's time and two others removed from the village.

Now the beach was pitch black as the cloud-obscured moon

provided little light. War-weary islanders watched the movement of flashlights and lanterns atop Mount Zion and Kit twice stubbed her toes on rocks. Both twins skinned their knees and Linh broke the strap of a sandal. Only Brittany didn't receive a scratch. The westerners walked until they came to their own beach, then turned inland. Only then did the cannibal's son fuss such that Kit nursed him with a rag soaked in coconut milk.

"He's finally eating," Kit said.

"I'll have the girls milk a goat when we get home," Linh said.

"Will one bottle get him through the night?"

"He hasn't eaten much. You should fix two."

"And I'll get some cool water for storage."

"Not bad for a first-day mom."

"It's awful," Kit said as she looked toward Brittany, "that she lost her mother."

"Her mother was a drunk and a whore; the girl is better off with you."

Kit said nothing.

"No one watched her," Linh continued, "not even at the beach. She played alone, ate alone, and babysat herself."

Kit didn't disagree.

"If," Linh said, "we had child protection services, she'd already be in foster care."

Only after a long pause did Kit glance at Tiffany's twin boys.

"Do they understand any of this?" Kit asked with a tremor to her voice. "Do they understand their parents are gone?"

"It's a blessing they don't."

"I wonder if they'll ever recover from such a loss," Kit said.

"I did," Linh whispered.

The baby fussed for a few moments in Kit's arms—until she settled him with more juice.

"It's terrible," Kit said, "to think he's a cannibal's son and the northerners wanted to kill him. That these tiny cheeks have been nourished by milk made from human flesh."

"It's the spirit that counts, not the flesh. The child has done no evil and we don't believe in original sin."

"Don't we? I'm not sure what I believe any longer."

Linh gave a weak smile. "What I believe," she said, "is Viet and I are leaving Paradise as soon as we can."

"So am I," Kit said. "Even Hollywood is better than this. They only devoured each other figuratively."

The last leg of the walk passed without further chat and Kit soon moved an exhausted baby into Ursula's crib—which Sean had brought to her tent. Linh's daughters fetched bottles of fresh goat milk and stored them in pails of cool water. The baby woke once, trying to chew through Kit's shirt to suckle from dry breasts until she offered him a bottle instead.

38

THE FIRST COMING OF OFFICERS AND GENTLEMEN

Jose was awakened at dawn and escorted to the motor launch by a delegation consisting of Ryan, Steve, Chuck, and Dr. Erikson. Only the southerners chose not to send a representative since they grieved so many dead family and friends. During the trip, Steve advised the convicted deserter how best to survive and reminded him that President Carter had granted amnesty to draft dodgers just a few years after the war in Vietnam ended—though his words provided little comfort and Jose remained tearful throughout the voyage.

When the launch landed at Roanoke Island, matters were mostly as expected. Bodies hanging from trees were swollen and those left on the beach were stripped to bone by crabs. No signs of cannibalism, however, were detected and it was deemed safe to leave Jose alone. He was provided an assortment of tools and materials, including: shovel, ax, tent, bedroll, rope, hammer, saw, nails, knife, waterproof matches, magnifying glass, seeds, sharpening stone, fishing line and hooks, ten MREs, plastic jugs of fresh water, an emergency medical kit, a crate of canned fruit, and his own backpack including personal effects such as a Mennonite New Testament, an unopened deck of playing cards, and a leather soccer ball. Even after being asked one last time if he'd be willing to serve in the militia, Jose refused. Three of the four delegates expressed their hope that monthly visits would be permitted and asked Jose to care for the graves of the fallen in exchange for any additional support. For emergencies, Ryan left a flare gun and a short-range transmitter, along with a spare battery.

The launch returned before noon to Paradise Island, only to encounter a seventy-foot yacht steering toward shore. Ryan set a course to intercept the yacht and Steve signaled its captain to follow the launch through a break in the coral. The yachtsman did as told and twenty minutes later dropped anchor in the calm of the lagoon, having safely passed through the coral reef. As the yacht secured anchorage, Steve and Chuck returned Dr. Erikson and Steve Lovejoy to the beach near New Plymouth before they themselves motored back to The Spirit of Liberty—where they moored the launch to the yacht and climbed aboard. There, a middle-aged blonde served them sweet tea with real ice as she explained that her husband would be along shortly.

A moment later, a muscular and clean-shaven man emerged from the bridge.

"Captain James ... I'm sorry. It's Jim Strong," the clean-shaven man said. "Sorry to keep you, but we were trying to contact the Fleet."

Ryan extended his hand.

"Really glad you're here," Ryan said, "I'm Ryan Godson."

"On the way in," Captain Strong said, "I was speaking with your people over the radio. They want to evacuate some casualties to Hawaii and they're stabilizing one man for travel. We hope to sail tomorrow."

"They explain what happened?"

"Someone said cannibals."

Ryan nodded.

"I spent," Captain Strong said, "over twenty years as a naval officer sailing the Pacific and never even imagined such tribes lingered hereabouts. What bad luck for you all."

"It's ruined everything."

"We'll get you fixed up," the yachtsman said. "I've been in touch with a couple navy buddies at Pearl Harbor and they said they'd relay the distress call. If any ships are close, we'll have the wounded choppered out as soon as possible."

"That's good news," Ryan said. "We've already lost too many people."

"Now tell me about those cannibals."

Ryan relayed the whole story. He told of the harvest feast and the eating of Heather. He told of the brawl that first day and the pitched battle on the beach. Finally, Ryan explained that the State of Paradise had moved surviving natives to Paradise and punished its own draft dodgers and deserters.

Jim Strong listened without saying a word. Only after Ryan fell silent did he ask a question. "Where's this Roanoke Island?"

"An hour or two east."

Captain Strong pulled a folded map from his shirt pocket and pointed to what appeared to be empty sea along the edge of the map.

"About here?" the yachtsman asked.

"I'm no map expert," Ryan said, "but if you say so."

"I don't want to sound like an international lawyer," Captain Strong said, "but you've made a bit of a mess."

"I'm not sure," Ryan said with a puzzled look, "that I understand."

"What I mean is it sounds like you've committed war crimes."

"I ... I ..." Ryan choked on his own words.

"Not only," the yachtsman said, "did you invade a foreign country without U.N. authorization, but slaughtering those natives clearly was illegal. When word gets back to The Hague, you may very well face a tribunal since that island wasn't part of your territory."

"They were eating our people," Ryan protested.

"I'm not saying," Captain Strong said, "you didn't have the right to defend yourselves as a sovereign nation. Personally, I respect your guts. In fact, you may very well be exonerated for your behavior and you probably deserve a medal, but you will give an accounting—especially for murdered prisoners."

Ryan turned to a northsman. "I warned you people," he growled, "to be more civilized."

Chuck said nothing.

"They were illegal killings by our laws too," Ryan told Captain Strong. "There was no legal authority for them. They were never authorized."

"I'm not your judge," Captain Strong said. "I'm just here to evacuate the wounded. Why don't we take a look?"

Ryan said he'd take Captain Strong to shore via the launch.

"Please," the captain said, "don't sail into open water with me in that boat. You people are suicidal. After years on cruisers and destroyers, even this yacht seems small."

"We took the LCVP to Roanoke Island."

"Suicidal," Captain Strong said with a smile, "was the word I chose and I stand by it. Those things weren't safe during the war and they're museum pieces now."

Now the captain called his wife to the deck bridge. Cynthia Strong was a fortyish woman whose shoulder-length blond hair already showed a few streaks of frosted gray and who dressed in a tank top and shorts that were neither too tight nor too fashionable; it was she who had served the iced tea. Now a second blonde, maybe two or three years older, accompanied her. The younger woman wore loose shorts and a knit blouse—and covered her hair with a bright red cotton scarf. A plain silver cross graced her breast. Both women sported wedding bands.

"Has Jim introduced you to the crew?" Cynthia asked.

Ryan shook his head.

"I swear he lost his manners at sea. This is my sister Jackie and she's married to Steve. He's another retired sailor ..."

"His name is Commander Steven Johnson," Captain Strong said.

"Steve," Cynthia continued, "is below deck. He was up all night navigating."

"Tell him thanks," Ryan said as he glanced at the second blonde.

"I will," Jackie answered.

A minute later, Ryan and Chuck climbed down a rope ladder and boarded the launch. Chuck dropped Ryan at New Plymouth beach before asking permission to use the launch to motor north, claiming that he wanted to bring Father Donovan to New Plymouth to help with evacuation arrangements. Ryan didn't object, asking only that Chuck return the launch as soon as possible since the wounded required transportation to the yacht. The northsman assured Ryan he wouldn't be long.

WITHIN THE HOUR, Chuck talked with men from his village. Father Donovan clenched his fists in rage as he listened to his compatriot describe Captain Strong. Other northsmen also bantered, but it was Donovan who spoke loudest.

"Who the hell," the priest muttered, "does he think he is? He's not our judge."

"Someone will be," Chuck growled, "if he runs his mouth."

"Let 'em," Donovan said, "it's our word against his."

"Really?" Chuck said with a shake of his head. "What about Steve and Ryan and John? What about the bodies we buried?"

"I was an elected officer and what we did was legal."

"And maybe," Chuck said, "they'll try us at Nuremberg to make that point clear. Or we can share cells with Serbs at The Hague."

"We're done for," Donovan growled as he slammed a fist into his own thigh. "Forensics will paint this black and white. No one will ever understand the situation we were stuck with."

"I'm not worried about forensics," Chuck said, "as much as I am about that sailor."

"Maybe," Jason now entered the conversation, "he'll let it drop."

"No chance," Chuck said. "He's spit and polish."

"Then," Father Donovan said, "we need to escape before we hang,"

"Where to?" Jason asked, his voice strained. "How? That launch couldn't sail us to our deaths."

"There's only one way home," Father Donovan whispered.

Everyone looked at him.

"The yacht."

Heads nodded.

"We'd be caught before we hit full throttle," Jason said.

"Not if they weren't looking for us."

Jason asked how it could be done.

"We'll destroy all radios and take the yacht," Father Donovan said.

"And go where?" Jason asked.

"I've got an uncle in Panama," a northsman said.

"In a stolen yacht," Donovan laughed, "we'd never touch a pier. And we don't own passports either. We'll have to reach the U.S. mainland. From there, we can disperse and go home."

"We'll be arrested as pirates," Jason said, the blood drained from his face, "if we steal the boat."

"Only if they catch us," Donovan said.

"We're progressives," another northsman said, "not criminals."

"What do you propose?" Donavan asked.

"Wait for a fair trial," the northsman said, "and a chance to prove our case."

"Every one of us standing here," Father Donavan said, "cut a throat, split a skull, or took an unwilling woman. And even those who stayed behind voted for war. No one believes in international courts more than I do, but I'm telling you a bunch of American colonists wiping out a native population won't play well either in Omaha or The Hague. Even if we avoid prison, we'll be ruined."

When one northsman wept that they had no options and were lost, Donovan pointed east.

"We can leave," the priest declared.

"Won't work," Chuck said.

Father Donovan told him to explain.

"The boat doesn't have enough range," Chuck said, "and we don't have money to refuel. We'd never reach California and we can't chance docking anywhere else."

"You sure about the fuel?"

"I'm positive. Even if she's full, we couldn't make the coast. And she's not full. They've burned fuel since Honolulu. A lot—I would guess—since they got here in a hurry."

Twenty minutes was spent suggesting possible fuel stops before everyone agreed the yacht wouldn't work. Another twenty minutes was spent spinning out additional options and the following thirty minutes was spent discussing possible legal charges and prison sentences—with everyone admitting they'd face several years for killings that U.S. soldiers were permitted. Only after the conversation died did Father Donovan present a fourth option.

"There's only one thing we can do," he said. "We have to get rid of the evidence. Courts can't convict on hearsay."

Chuck asked how it could be done.

"We put out our version of the story."

Jason's jaw dropped. "Wouldn't we have to get rid of the bodies?" he asked.

"Fire and water," Donovan said, "will do the trick. We burn them and throw the bones to sea."

"What about witnesses?" Jason said. "We weren't alone."

"We'd have to quiet them," Chuck said.

"Or discredit them," Father Donovan said. "If we cut radio communications, they'd never get word out. We could stage it so no one could figure anything out or ... I wonder if those damned westerners could be made to take the rap; it's their fault we're in this mess."

"That's cutthroat," Jason said, his voice hoarse and dry.

"It's life or death," Donovan said. "And it's Godson and Lovejoy and Smith who forced this crap on us with their otherworldly ideals."

"It's war," Chuck said.

"It's murder," Jason protested, "of civilians."

"Do you think," Donovan said with another scowl, "Ortega beat the Contras without shedding civilian blood? Every war has its collateral damage and its incidental casualties. We didn't invent war; we're only playing by its rules."

"I don't know about this," Jason said. "I don't want any part of it."

"Every man," Father Donovan stared down every one of his northsmen, "is for me or against me."

"I don't like it either," Chuck declared "but they backed us into a corner. We fought for them and they betrayed us. I'm not going to prison so they can play the innocent heroes. Not after we saved their asses in battle."

"What about the natives?" Jason asked. "What about our women?"

"Here's the bottom line," Father Donovan said. "Almost every man in this villages stuck a spear in a native or tied a rope around a neck. We're all guilty by their sanctimonious rules. So we can either take their punishment like sorrowful boys or we can fight for our rights. If they pull the wounded out of here and repeat any of the stories Ryan told the yachtsman, we're all doomed. Our terms of charter allow the Russians to reclaim the island for violations of international law and, if they do so, we won't control the situation. I dare say every man standing here will be in a world of hurt. And don't think you can plead down charges because I'll see to it that anyone who plea bargains hangs with me—even if I have to confess to more crimes than were committed. Too bad for the Americans, but they aren't our people. They're foreigners inserting themselves into our domestic affairs and it's our duty to fight them. They'd fight if some Russian mixed himself into American politics. If some boat landed in Florida with Cuban sailors? Am I right?"

"A Cuban would be fried for sure," Chuck said.

"You're damned right he would be," another northsman added.

"I'm not sure," Jason said.

"Everyone kills or dies," Donovan said with an anger that twisted his face such that his right eye appeared shut and his left forefinger and middle finger clenched and trembling, both fingers curled almost in a hook, "so we're all in it together. If we burn the bodies and sink the yacht, we'll have a few days before anyone else arrives. We can arrange cooperation from our neighbors or silence them for good. Dead men tell no tales. Who's with me?"

"I can't do it," Jason said.

"Can you trust American justice?" Donovan said. "Against progressives?"

Jason shook his head.

"Besides," Donovan said, "we only need to silence those on the beach at the time. The rest are speaking hearsay. That's just a few men. We can live in peace with everyone else."

"What about the yacht?"

"It's in our territory," Donovan said, "and under our jurisdiction. We can board her and take the radios. We'll claim that ... let's say, that the westerners are stirring up civil war and planning to maroon us."

"That's lame," Jason said, "they'll never believe it."

"We only have to prove we believe it."

Jason dropped his eyes and said he didn't want to face prison.

"You will," Donovan said, "go to jail if they dig up those bodies. We need to buy enough time to burn them properly. The worst that can happen is they add a few years to a life sentence for genocide. I'm not bloodthirsty, but it was Morales who stirred this up and the others with him. We were forced to fight for the very reasons Americans justify their wars, but they'll never recognize it. So it's their own hypocrisy that makes us fight them."

Now all of the others nodded, except Jason.

"Also," Donovan continued, "the natives didn't see their husbands die and they can't speak English, so they can live. When this is over, we'll let you pick out a girl for your own."

"How about the tall teenager with straight teeth?" Jason asked.

"Tall?" Donovan said, "she's not even five foot."

"That's three inches taller than any of the others."

"She's yours to keep, but we get a turn too."

"Share and share alike," Jason replied, smiling at his own quip.

Now the mood relaxed as Donovan put his arm around Jason's shoulder. "Can we count on ya, buddy?"

Jason nodded.

"Everyone fights," Donovan said, "and, if necessary, everyone kills. We conquer together or we hang together. Anyone who shirks, dies."

Jason gave his assent and the desperate men drew up plans to seize the yacht—passing a flask of rum to steady nerves while they schemed.

It was late in the afternoon when the motorized launch pulled beside the yacht. Donovan shouted for assistance and both women peered over the rails to see a northsman stretched across two seats of the boat—his leg in a splint and blood dried around his ears. Jason and Chuck sat beside him.

"He fell from a tree picking coconuts," Donovan shouted. "Doc Graves told us to evacuate him."

"No one's boarded yet," one of the women said, "my husband's still ashore."

Donovan cut the engine as a fellow northsman grabbed the ladder extending down the boat's hull and secured the launch.

"The doctor said to bring him straight here," Donovan shouted.

The women looked at the four northsmen, then whispered between themselves. Finally, Jackie nodded and Cynthia waved to the men waiting for permission to board.

"I guess we're all Americans," Cynthia said, "bring him aboard."

"Do you have a backboard? He shouldn't move."

Cynthia moved toward the cabin and shouted something inside and soon a man's voice asked what was needed.

"A back board to pull him up," Donovan replied.

Commander Johnson now appeared on deck, shaking his head. "We have everything but that," he explained.

"I have an idea," Father Donovan said as he pointed at Jason. "You stay with him. We'll be right back."

Donovan and Chuck climbed aboard the yacht as Commander Johnson helped them over the rail and waved his hand across the boat.

"Take anything you need," the retired sailor said.

"Let's take a look at the mattresses down below," Father Donovan replied.

"They're too flimsy."

"Let's take a look," Donovan replied as he stepped toward the hold. "Maybe we can shore one with some planks."

"It's worth a try."

Commander Johnson and Father Donovan descended into the hold of the boat while Chuck lit a cigarette and stayed atop—where the two women spoke in whispers. A moment later the thud of a distant firework sounded and everyone looked toward New Plymouth to see that a red flare had burst over the beach and slowly fell to earth.

"Something's wrong," Cynthia Strong said as she stood. "What's going on?"

Chuck remained composed, though he did pause before answering. "I'd guess," he said, "they need the launch."

"Why a flare? That's a distress signal."

"We use 'em around here all the time," Chuck said with a shrug, "since we don't have phones or radios."

"That's really odd," Jackie Johnson said.

It was at that moment Donovan emerged from the stairwell alone —a knife in his hand and blood smeared across his shirt.

"God save us," one of the women cried out.

"No one has to get hurt," Donovan shouted, but the women didn't listen. Cynthia Strong sprinted for the helm as Chuck dropped his cigarette and jumped to block her escape, but didn't get far as he tripped over Jackie Johnson's outstretched foot and smashed his face hard into the deck. Before Jackie could make a break, however, Chuck grabbed her by the ankle and pulled her down. When the woman twisted around and drove a knee into his groin, Chuck cried out even as he grabbed her by the hair and drew a knife from his belt— plunging it deep into Jackie's breast as she slammed a fist into his nose. The blonde's eyes rolled backwards and she fell limp as blood soaked through her shirt where an artery had been severed. When Chuck released his grip on the woman's hair, her red scarf fluttered to the deck.

Meanwhile, the dying woman's sister reached the cabin and

fumbled to unlock a desk drawer with Father Donovan hot on her heels. Just as she pulled the drawer open, Donovan lunged over the desk, knocking both the woman and the drawer to the ground. Still, the woman found what she sought and racked a round into the chamber of a black pistol as Donovan grabbed her wrists. Both fought while kneeling—which meant that Donovan was unable to leverage his greater strength against the desperate woman. Four hands struggled for the grip of the gun until a single shot was fired and Cynthia Strong slumped to the floor—blood gushing from a gaping hole in her neck.

Father Donovan looked around. Glass fragments and splattered blood covered the cabin floor and the window was shattered where the bullet had finished its course. He stepped away from the quick-growing pool of blood and took a long look at the middle-aged woman—who still breathed even though she didn't otherwise move —then returned to the deck and told Jason and the decoy (both of whom had climbed aboard) to throw both women overboard.

"Since we're pirates now," Donovan said, tucking the pistol into his belt, "might as well feed them to the sharks."

The two men did as told and dragged the bodies to an opening in the deck rail where the boarding plank attached, several times slipping in the blood trails that followed their crime. A few moments later, one motionless corpse and one shallow-breathing woman slipped beneath the waves. Meanwhile, Donovan used Jackie Johnson's cotton scarf to wipe drops of sweat and blood from his face, then wrapped the bloodstained cloth around his own head as a bandana —with a single tight knot tied behind his skull.

"Now all four of us have killed," Donovan said, as he pointed with a forefinger to his accomplices, "and we're in this to the death. Let's see what goodies they have on board."

The northsmen descended into the hold of the yacht as Chuck fidgeted with his swollen nose and gingerly touched a chipped tooth.

. . .

JIM STRONG SAT with Ryan on a bench near New Plymouth. The yachtsman looked exasperated and the former actor appeared perturbed. Late afternoon shadows already darkened the brush and hid the forest.

"Your people need to be evacuated," Captain Strong said. "That Asian boy is going to die if he isn't in a hospital soon. You can see it in his face."

"Can you get him out?"

"The only chance he has is for us to get medics and doctors here. Pronto."

"Can you call for help from your ship," Ryan said.

"As soon as I return to it," the captain replied. "For the record, it's a yacht."

"Someone's coming," Ryan said as he turned toward a stout Latino coming from the path to New Plymouth. "A northerner."

When Ryan asked the man where the launch was, the northerner pointed toward the sea and said that a neighbor named Mark had broken his leg and was being moved to the yacht.

"We have timetables," Ryan winced. "You should have checked."

"Sorry," the man said, "the bone stuck through his knee. They're going to send for the doctor once he's on board."

"Stick around," Ryan said, "we'll need help ..."

The northerner cut him off. "I'll be back in a minute. I have something to do first."

Before Ryan could object, the man disappeared on a north-leading trail.

"That's a friendly neighbor," Captain Strong said.

"Probably setting up a drug lab," Ryan replied.

Neither man laughed.

"It could be a while before they return," Jim said. "Let's make a call now. You do have long-range transmitters, don't you?"

"Two radios and a cell phone," Ryan said, "only for emergencies."

"Let's fire one up."

Ryan started for the storage tents of New Plymouth and Jim

Strong followed. When the men came to a large tent marked for emergency use only, Ryan unzipped its flap and stepped inside.

"Ouch," Ryan said as he brushed against something jagged and then groped in the dark until he found a large flashlight on a stand just inside the door—which he shined across the nylon floor and gasped. Both radios were in pieces on the ground and the satellite phone was crushed. A sledgehammer had been left near the broken pieces.

Captain Strong used the flashlight to look around. Though nothing else was broken, he appeared concerned.

"There's mischief here," Captain Strong said. "Hand me that flare gun."

Ryan picked up an emergency flare gun and three flares and handed them to the visitor. Captain Strong loaded a flare into the gun as he hurried outside. Aiming the weapon high and in the direction of his yacht, he pulled the trigger. The flare shot upwards and exploded over the beach, like a fireworks celebration exploded out of season.

"My brother-in-law," the yachtsman explained after the flare had fallen into the sea, "will know how to respond to a clear warning."

"What can he do?"

"He can secure the yacht and call for standby assistance."

"The sooner the better," Ryan said. "I don't really know these people any more."

"And he can arm himself."

Ryan looked perplexed as he shook his head. "Guns," he explained after a long pause, "are illegal in Paradise."

Crack.

It was at that very moment that the report of a pistol shot echoed across the lagoon. Shocked by the sound, Captain Strong ran for the beach while Ryan shouted for help and followed at his heels. Once they reached the shore, Captain Strong pushed a kayak into the water and paddled hard toward his yacht while Ryan rallied the men and women of New Plymouth—sending a long-legged girl running toward Mount Zion to sound the alarm and a short boy toward the east village to summon Steve. Dr. Erikson and several others armed themselves with axes and shovels as Ryan picked up a set of binoculars kept near the flagpole and watched Jim Strong paddle.

Ryan watched through binoculars as the yachtsman rose from his kayak and scampered up the ladder. Even the islanders watching without binoculars saw movement against the side of the boat— though only Ryan could see that one of the northsmen held something in his hand as he waited for Captain Strong to draw near.

Crack.

Though Ryan was the first to realize what had happened, even those watching with the naked eye saw the distant form of a man fall into the sea.

"Oh lord," Dr. Erikson said, "they have guns."

"That's illegal," a tall woman said. "They can't keep them."

"What're we going to do?" Dr. Erikson asked. "We aren't armed."

"Shit," the tall woman said as she turned pale. "Only criminals have guns."

The sound of quick steps from the woods startled them and everyone spun around, weapons raised. There was no need since it was Steve and two sturdy compatriots from the east village.

"I heard gunshots," Steve said. "What the hell's going on?"

Ryan handed Steve the binoculars.

"It was the northsmen," he said. "They shot Jim Strong and smashed our radios. Also it looks like they've commandeered the yacht."

"What's this about?" Steve said.

"It's not about anything good," Ryan said as looked Steve in the eyes. "Jim Strong was talking about war crimes when he heard of the trouble with the natives. I wonder if they're trying to escape."

"Or headed," Steve said, "to Columbia for more dope."

"There were," Ryan said, "four people on that yacht and I've heard only two shots. The women may be hostages."

"They have their boat," Steve said. "We can only hope they'll leave."

"I don't think so," Dr. Erikson said. "Look."

Everyone turned seaward. Flames now rose from the deck of the yacht and lit its hull like a torch as the launch shoved off and motored north.

"It's to the death," Steve said. "We need to move everyone inland before they catch us in the open. We need weapons, blankets, tents, food, medicine, and matches from the emergency tents."

No one moved.

"Now!" Steve barked out loud as everyone scampered for supplies.

Within minutes, couriers were sent to brief islanders in the south, east, and west villages—to warn of danger and direct loyal citizens to secure a stronghold in the hills. Ryan and Steve also instructed a runner to sound the emergency alarm.

39

THE SECOND AMENDMENT TO THE
CONSTITUTION

S oon after a distant siren broke the still of the evening, John instructed west villagers to light a bonfire to signal to scouts posted atop Mount Zion that their warning had been received. As Kit soothed her fussing baby near the fire, the rest of the western villagers assembled in the mess tent. Though no one knew what had happened, men sharpened weapons while women and children gathered provisions as speculation ran wild. Some thought the alarm caused by jittery nerves while others guessed a raid by escaped cannibals. No one supposed it was their own kind gone awry.

As dusk darkened, west villagers noticed the bobbing of a flash-light descending Mount Zion and it wasn't long before a winded runner arrived from the trail near the Pishon River. The runner paused to catch breath before explaining the situation—warning westerners of northern treachery. He gave directions to the emergency assembly point before sprinting toward Mount Zion while shouting a final warning for the west village to make haste.

Now John took charge, posting Sean and Olivia as sentries and ordering everyone else to fill backpacks with blankets, tents, clothing, food, and other necessities—and advising everyone to wear boots and to bring enough water and firewood for several days. With preparations soon complete, sentries were recalled and given a few minutes to retrieve personal gear before John led the column of armed refugees toward Mount Zion: an unsheathed ax in his right hand and a dimmed lantern in his left. Olivia and Ilyana tucked hand axes into their belts and helped Lisa carry a medicine chest. Behind them, Kit and Maria herded six children and a goat as Linh coaxed Tiffany forward. None of the mothers possessed weapons except for kitchen knives stored in their backpacks. Ursula walked before Sean and Viet —who shouldered a thick pole from which jars of water and bundles of wood dangled—while Sean carried a long-handled ax and Viet armed himself with the steel helmet originally found on Roanoke Island and a hand ax slipped into his belt.

As the party of westerners inched up the slopes of Mount Zion, their voices became little more than grunts and whispers. When the refugees saw fires burning from the northern end of the island, they knew their enemy didn't sleep and moved even more quietly through the night. When the westerners reached the crest of Mount Zion after a three hour march, they met two armed men who led them to a large ravine and showed the new arrivals where to pitch camp—warning the latter to keep fires small so flames didn't reveal their position.

While Sean and Viet pitched tents, John searched for Ryan and Steve. He found them in a ravine.

"Glad to see you two," John greeted the two men.

"And I'm glad to see you made it," Ryan said. "Is Maria with you?"

John nodded.

"Kit?"

John pointed toward the western refugees and nodded a second time.

"How's Tiffany?" Ryan asked.

"Slipping into shock."

"I'm sorry about Deidra. How're you doing?"

"I don't know," John said. "Just trying to survive."

Ryan swept his hand around the camp.

"We've set up a perimeter," Ryan said. "There are men with spears and axes hidden outside the camp and reserves posted inside.

Tomorrow we'll build walls to block bullets. We have a spring inside the camp and we've sharpened branches and saplings into arrows and spears. Dr. Graves hopes to concoct sedatives and poisons for arrow tips. We'll have a fighting chance up here."

John asked how many guns the northsmen possessed.

"We're not sure," Ryan said. "Steve said he's only heard two pistol shots, probably the same caliber. We're hoping there was just one or two guns on the yacht."

"How many of us are there?"

"Before you arrived," Steve now said, "we had most of the east village, New Plymouth's staff, and what's left of south village. The southerners have left only two men, plus women and children."

"Then we outnumber them?" John asked. "I mean, the northerners."

"They had five children and nine women," Steve replied, "and lost one man in the war. That gives them nine men plus Jason. We figure they'll lose a family or two to desertion. That totals maybe eight men against four westerners, six easterners, a staff member, and one southerner—plus our women. We have five or six women willing and able to fight. The northerners should have the same."

"That's only half our strength. Where are the others?"

"Some are wounded," Steve said, "and others are conscientious objectors who refuse to fight."

"We can't afford," John said, "the luxury of protest."

"What can we do about it?" Ryan said with a shrug.

"I'd vote," Steve said, "that anyone who won't fight doesn't remain in camp."

"We can't make them fight," Ryan answered.

"We don't have food and water for slackers," Steve said.

"Well," Ryan said with a sharp tone, "we can't make anyone fight."

"We'll discuss it in the morning," Steve replied.

It was at this moment that Viet arrived—excited and breathless. "There's a fire to the east," he said.

"Campfire?" Steve asked.

"The east village."

Steve turned pale as Viet led him and the others to a ridge on the eastern side of Mount Zion and pointed toward a bright glow near the east shore. The men watched as the flames grew higher. Even from the heights, the silhouettes of burning buildings could be discerned wherever winds had pushed the smoke seaward.

"That's the whole town," Steve observed.

"At least," John said as he put his hand to Steve's shoulder, "you weren't there."

"I wonder why."

"If I had to guess," Viet said, "I'd say they're forcing us to fight. They probably want to bring us to open battle."

"That's suicide against their guns," Steve said.

"We need," Viet said, "to protect our camp and fight on our terms."

"Guerilla war?" Steve asked.

"Ambushes and traps," Viet said with a nod. "We can make them afraid to move up this hill. Set up an outer perimeter and force them into firing lanes. We can bring supplies to camp as we need them. Till help comes."

"When will that be?" Steve asked.

"God only knows," Viet said. "God only knows."

"There's a sunken yacht," John said, "and four missing Americans. Someone will be coming soon enough."

Soon, all of the men of the camp organized a guard rotation and each one took his turn as sentry while his compatriots rested. Already, the campfire burned down and most women and children lay fast asleep, exhausted by travel and crowded into a handful of tents. Only a few teenagers and adults unrolled their sleeping bags beneath the stars. It was decided to call the General Will of the People into session at first light.

DAWN BROUGHT a cold breakfast since it was judged too risky to kindle a fire. Though the ravine masked firelight, it couldn't conceal the upward spiral of smoke. Consequently, some islanders ate leftover MREs while others satisfied themselves with little more than salted perch. Two goats were milked to fill the bottles of the babies, but no one else drank—not even toddlers. No one was satisfied with small portions and there was considerable grumbling over the paucity of rations until leaders promised to send foraging parties to fetch food reserves from the villages and forests; though it also was decided the risk of danger was such that refugees must endure their hunger until nightfall. Only then could foragers be more safely deployed. No one wanted to die to scavenge a coconut.

Several scouts ordered to locate the enemy returned after two hours and reported that the motorized launch was anchored near New Plymouth—though no attack preparations were observed. Consequently, it was decided to convene a General Will of the People at midmorning to exploit the lull. Two men were sent downhill with flare guns and three women were posted along the hillcrest with binoculars while everyone else assembled in the ravine.

Ryan stood on a mountain swell as he addressed the assembly after passing around the remaining rations in a small bucket—several loaves of stale bread and a couple tins of imported herring—that did little more than stir hunger.

"While certainly it's peacemakers who are most blessed," Ryan declared, "some of us held a war council and drew up defensive plans. We need your ratification."

No one stirred.

"Our intent," Ryan announced, "is to protect our people atop this hill while we send raiding parties to hit the enemy and gather supplies. We'll set up traps on the trails and strike the northerners when they sleep. We'll burn their tents and supplies and set their captives free. There's unpicked food and uncut trees on this hill, so we can survive a month or two if necessary. They have guns but it won't do much good shooting uphill as long as we're over the ridge, so we can exploit the terrain. And if we can find some gasoline and oil, we can even the odds with incendiaries and explosives. Once their ammunition is used up, we'll have the upper hand. All we need to do is make them shoot and miss."

"Just how many guns and bullets," a man's voice called from the crowd, "do they have?"

"Maybe one or two guns. Maybe a hundred bullets. It's hard to say."

"Isn't that worth finding out?" the man pressed his point.

Ryan shrugged.

"And exactly when is help coming?" a woman asked.

"We don't know," Ryan said. "Our best hope is that the yacht will be missed and a search party sent."

"That could take weeks," someone grumbled. "We can't wait that long."

"We're pretty sure Captain Strong was in contact with American military forces. We hope they'll come looking soon."

"That's not much of a hope."

"What do you propose?" Ryan said. "I suppose we could load the LCVP and sail for Roanoke Island—and end up cannibals eating ourselves if no one finds us. Or maybe we could head for the westerly currents and a slow death by starvation if we miss Pitcairn Island. Or maybe just let the northsmen butcher us one at a time."

The man didn't reply.

"Steve Lovejoy," Ryan said, "will help build bunkers on the hill. This isn't his first war. We'll use trees and dirt to make a fortress. Then we can stock it with arrows and rocks, clear a field of fire, and set up traps—hidden holes with sharp spikes. Everyone builds and everyone fights. Anyone who refuses to work or fight leaves right now. Later tonight, we'll send a raiding party to the north and supply details east and south. We plan to save the western reserves for future needs."

A southern woman stood.

"We southerners," the woman said, "have suffered enough. I lost both of my boyfriends and my friends lost their husbands. Why should we give up our food first? Why not the west camp?"

"Because," Ryan replied with a scowl, "yours is safer to bring back to camp until we're better prepared to fight."

"But why don't ..."

"I'm sorry," Ryan said, "but we don't have time to debate. All of us who plan to fight have agreed to this plan, including those on guard duty. We only need authorization to begin."

A black-haired man from the east village stood.

"I'm a pacifist," the black-haired man said, "and it's against my principles to fight or support your war effort."

"Then you can help collect supplies."

"Not if they'll be used by soldiers."

"What do you propose?" Ryan said. "That the water you draw be shared only with non-combatants?"

"That's not a bad idea."

"What about the soldiers who stand guard while you gather food? Don't they deserve a fair share?"

"My conscience won't allow me to give food to armed men."

"Will your conscience defend you?" Ryan asked.

The black-haired man looked down.

Steve now raised his hand to speak. "I vote that everyone who won't fight be expelled from camp," he said with a grim face and a curt tone, "and I mean, this morning. This camp is at war and everyone shares in the risks and dangers and protection. If you can't do the crime, you can't have the time."

"You mean ... you mean," the black-haired man protested, "you'd throw us at their mercy?"

"As you would us," Steve answered. "If you stay, you dig trenches and build earthworks or carry an ax. Or you can leave. It's your choice."

"That's a choice between killing and dying. You can't force that decision on us. It's obscene. It's immoral. It's ..."

"It's the essence of war," Steve said, "and we have no choice."

"We need to vote now," Ryan announced.

No one objected.

"Every wasted minute," Ryan said, "may cost a man his life. Or a woman hers. Traps need to be dug before nightfall. I second this proposal and request a vote."

The crowd assented and a vote was taken—with a majority determining that every citizen must choose fight or flight. Among those in the political minority, only the black-haired man and his wife continued to announce themselves conscientious objectors and declare their intent to depart. Without further discussion, the majority authorized the couple's request for a week's rations and gave permission to take a sailboat to Roanoke Island until hostilities ceased. Farewells were brief and the pair of resolved pacifists broke camp without delay. Meanwhile, Ryan briefed everyone else on specific war plans before fielding a host of questions. While most islanders approved of self-defense plans, a slim majority disliked offensive operations, either from hatred of militarism or fear of casualties. After an hour of debate, a vote was taken and limited defensive operations were approved.

Steve was utterly disgusted by the strategy while Ryan and John were merely dismayed. Viet nearly mutinied at its folly—insisting victory would be given to the army that chose its own field of fire and mobilized its entire citizenry as General Giap did against Americans forces in Vietnam. A majority of his fellow citizens didn't agree and ignored the protests of what was thereafter deemed the War Party.

After the votes were tallied, Steve took charge.

"There's one more thing," Steve said as the people hushed. "The northsmen have a gun. Or guns. The fighting is going to be rough and both men and women likely will die. The northsmen have proven themselves pernicious from the assaulting of Lisa to the murder of the natives to yesterday's treachery. We can't afford to hold too many prisoners and we don't have the means to exile or imprison them. Sad to say, it's kill or be killed. No quarter. There's no way around it. I don't want illegal killings to occur, but they will if we lack the death penalty. Only if we have legalized capital punishment are we going to escape retribution for war crimes when this is over."

A man raised his hand.

"We can't murder prisoners," the man said.

"We can't murder prisoners," Steve agreed, "but we can declare martial law and make illegal possession of a gun a capital crime by constitutional amendment and send word any rebel caught with a gun will die. Maybe that'll put a little fear into them."

No one made the proposal.

"If we don't do this," Steve said, "they'll take potshots till the last of us has dropped. It's us versus them."

A voice from the crowd seconded the motion and after several silent seconds the second amendment to the constitution was enacted without further discussion—unauthorized ownership of a firearm was declared a capital crime. The assembly further decided that unauthorized ownership of a firearm should include persons conspiring with or benefiting from illegal weapons.

AMBUSHES WERE SET on the slopes by nightfall. Sharpened foot-long stakes were embedded into two-foot-deep holes covered with branches, leaves, and dirt. A dozen such traps were set across the trail on the west side of Mount Zion and another three dozen placed along a perimeter defense on the north side of the camp. Laborers also stacked trees along the east edge of the summit and covered them with dirt as a redoubt capable of stopping pistol shots. Extra weapons were prepositioned throughout the camp in case of attack: stones, spears, axes, shovels, hoes, and even coconuts.

Shortly after dusk, two details of armed settlers were deployed. Viet led two easterners to collect intelligence on northern preparations and intentions while Steve led foragers to find fruit on Mount Zion. Everyone else continued to work: digging ditches, felling trees, shoveling dirt, and posting guard. Only children were permitted the leisure of early bed. Not until the perimeter was secured did weary islanders fall into camp, leaving several men posted as guards and a few others sleeping at battle stations.

After being relieved of duty for a time, Ryan found Maria near a fire and sat beside her. The fire was little more than hot coals in a tarp-covered pit of ashes—though it remained warm enough to brew coffee.

"There you are," Ryan said to his pregnant bride when he saw her.

"I want to go home" Maria said, her face stained with tears.

"It's not safe."

"It's safer than here."

"No," Ryan said, "the west village is too close to the northsmen. Too easy for them to raid."

"Home," Maria said. "I want to go home. To the United States."

"Isn't Paradise our home?"

"This isn't my home," Maria said. "I was crazy to come—and now I'm pregnant and scared and hungry. There are madmen making war on us and cannibals want to eat what's left over. I gave up grad school to become a side dish."

"You're safe tonight with me."

"I'd feel a lot safer if you had a gun."

"It's against the law."

"Power," Maria said as she shook her head, "is politics from the barrel of a gun. Haven't you learned that yet?"

"I guess," Ryan said with a shrug, "I'm a hopeless idealist."

"You're right about that: idealism is hopeless. Even in Paradise."

Ryan placed a hand on Maria's thigh.

"You can't live without hope," Ryan said. "If we can't dream of a better world, what will we become? That's the sin of the right."

"Maybe it's their realism," Maria replied, "even their wisdom."

"I won't give in to pessimism," Ryan said. "I won't accept the world as it is. I will uphold my faith in mankind and the promise of a better future. I will work to improve the world."

"You will become fat on the bones of barbarians," Maria said with a weak smile, "and dung in their bowels—if you don't clear your head of idiocy."

Ryan fell silent as Maria threw a few sticks into the fire and lay down on her side, belly toward the warm flames. Only after Maria slept did Ryan return to the perimeter to stand guard at a fortified position—where he looked into the dark until his eyes blurred and his head hurt, straining to see every shift in the shadows and listening for every snap of a stick. It was nearly midnight when he was relieved by a southerner and wrapped a wool blanket around himself as he closed his eyes to rest.

URSULA'S SHIVERING WOKE SEAN. The dark was deep and he couldn't see her face in the shadow of a beech tree—where she lay covered with a single wool blanket. When Sean touched Ursula's cheek and found it wet, he sat up.

"Ursula, what's wrong?"

"I'm cold."

"Our fire went out?"

"Hours ago."

Sean slid from the warmth of his wool blanket and walked to a fire a few feet away and rolled a small log on it. The coals remained hot and it wasn't long before the wood crackled and radiated its warmth outward.

Meanwhile, Sean found a spare blanket in an unoccupied tent and spread both it and his own blanket over Ursula before lying down a couple feet from her. He folded his arms and crossed his legs to draw in his own warmth.

Ursula turned toward Sean. "You're cold too," she said.

"I'm okay."

"Come under the covers with me. It'll keep us both warm."

Sean scooted toward the mother of his unborn child and pulled the blankets over himself.

"That's better," he said as he pressed his hand to Ursula's belly. "Can I touch the baby?"

"That's fine."

"Does it move much?"

"He," Ursula said, "or she, quivers once in a while, I think. Mostly at night. I felt something a few minutes ago."

"I feel like a god—a life maker."

"Then I'm a goddess?"

"You always were."

"I'm still cold," Ursula said after a time, "come closer."

Sean moved closer to the pregnant woman until her breasts flattened against his chest.

"You are cold," Sean said, "I can feel you against me."

"Has it been so long," Ursula whispered, "that you can't tell the difference between hot and cold?"

Sean smiled and moved his hand down the young woman's belly.

Ursula didn't object.

"I'm sorry for being a fool," Sean said.

"You were a jerk," Ursula said, "but I guess I didn't make it easy for you either."

"I wasn't much of a man; at least not a good one. I'm so sorry."

"I can't talk about it anymore," Ursula whispered as she pressed a finger to Sean's lips. "Tend your business here."

"Can you do this?" Sean asked as he stopped his hands where they were. "I mean, being pregnant?"

"I'm not ready to burst quite yet."

"I don't want to hurt the baby."

"Tend your business."

Sean slipped one hand between Ursula's legs as he pulled her close with the other drawn around her waist. After several seconds, he loosened his grip and fell away from the young woman.

"I don't want it," Sean said. "Not like this."

"You don't want me?"

"I mean," Sean said, "no more meaningless sex. Only what's good for you and our baby."

"I don't understand."

"Ursula, I want you more than I want to make love. I want it to be good between us. If I can't have you, I don't need the sex."

Ursula looked at Sean a long while through the dark of the night, then pulled him close and began to sob.

"Now," Ursula said with a quivering voice, "you've become the man I wanted. The man I need. The man my ... the man our baby needs."

"Our child," Sean said, "needs a father, not just a boyfriend for his mom."

"I know."

"Should we marry?"

"That's your choice," Ursula said. "All I want is a man."

"I choose you."

"Now?"

"Ursula Gottlieb-Tate, will you marry me?" Sean whispered.

"Yes."

"Then I pronounce us husband and wife."

A tear fell down Ursula's cheek as she let herself be kissed as a bride for the first time. The fire burned hot for the next several minutes and so did love. When the couple was finished, they tossed blankets aside to cool themselves. Their bodies were so close that they had no need for more than a single blanket, even after the fire burned to ashes.

Early in the morning, Sean rose to rekindle the fire and to prepare a plate of food for his wife.

40

CRIMINALS AND GUNS

S couting parties deployed at dawn. Three pairs of soldiers—
each including a strong fighter and a fast runner—patrolled
along the north, west, and east slopes of Mount Zion while
the south trail was secured by a single picket (with a conch shell)
ready to insure northern raiders didn't infiltrate the south slope
undetected. Behind the scouts came foragers searching for food.
Most stayed close to camp while they collected green bananas and
unripe pecans and dared not deploy to more fertile orchards at the
base of the hill for fear of a northern ambush. Meanwhile, sentries
posted atop Mount Zion as lookouts trained their eyes and binoculars
on a waft of smoke rising from the north and watched northsmen
ferry supplies from New Plymouth to the northern village via the
motorized launch. By noon, foragers had collected enough food for a
couple meals, after which they returned to the refugee camp atop the
mountain and recalled all pickets to camp.

Afternoon was spent shoring defenses as traps were dug and
earthworks built. Every man and several women took weapons training: practicing close quarters combat with spears and axes and
knives. Dulled weapons were used for practice, though one girl
managed to cut herself with a table knife and two men pulled

muscles while sparring. Spears were hurled into a dirt mound and arrows shot into discarded crates. Most of the hastily organized militia showed marked improvement after their rudimentary training.

Late in the afternoon, Viet returned from long-range patrol with disconcerting news: he had watched the northern camp for several hours and observed them preparing for battle. Spears were being sharpened, bows strung, and firebombs stockpiled. The northsmen had gathered provisions and were teaching lethal combat techniques even to their women. Viet claimed to have crept close enough to hear Father Donovan tell fighters the battle might require the liquidation of all opponents and natives; he also reported that two native women had been taken in chains to the northern camp—though he could only guess what they were needed for. In any case, Viet assessed that the northsmen intended to wage war and expected them to commence operations by day's end.

Viet's report secured political power for the War Party. By two votes, it was decided to forego a defensive posture in favor of offensive strikes. The General Will of the People authorized Viet and two volunteers to raid the northern camp—specifically to destroy the launch in order to end the northsmen's decisive mobility along the coast. It also was voted to send a raiding party to New Plymouth to forage for supplies and free the native women. Not only was it considered inhumane to keep the women locked in the LCVP for days on end, but it also was hoped the cannibals would menace northern operations. The War Party assessed that every bullet spent on a heathen was a shot that couldn't be taken at the islanders themselves. Three women and two men objected on grounds that the cannibals were a worse danger than the northsmen, but were outvoted. Lisa and Alan volunteered to free the natives during the night's supply run.

Supper consisted of unripened fruit and overripened vegetables. Linh cooked a pot of breadfruit and salted-perch broth and was pleased to see her soup drained to the last cup for the first time. Babies drank warmed goat milk and toddlers nibbled from crackers and peanut butter. Children were sent to bed early and guards posted for three-hour shifts. Viet marched his team west while Lisa and Alan followed a half-dozen foragers to base camp. Because the sky was clear and the moon nearly full, the foraging party deemed it prudent to avoid the main trails.

THE AMBUSH PARTY threaded single-file through shadows and twists of the trail. Passing through the west neighborhood's abandoned camp, they crept to the coast before turning north. After crossing Turtle Beach, the team moved north so cautiously that it took an hour before the point man saw the light of a northern fire. Viet posted his companions as a rearguard and crept toward his foe—though it took another thirty minutes before he was within earshot. Near the north village, Viet was forced to hide behind a bush when a squad of armed northsmen passed within ten feet, though they looked neither right nor left as they filed south. Viet prayed silently for his family and his companions—recollecting for the first time in decades prayers he'd been taught by the clergy who'd sponsored his family for resettlement from Vietnam.

Several minutes later, Viet raised his head from the brush and took a long look. As best as he could see, only two men and six women remained at the camp: all of them sitting around the fire as they passed a water pipe and laughed loud. Behind them, the motorized launch was tied to a tall palm tree on the beach. After Viet watched the northerners several minutes, he heard muffled cries of suppressed anguish that he considered investigating until he remembered the critical nature of his mission: if the northerners could be slowed to foot speed, the advantage of high ground would be magnified since Mount Zion both provided a natural barrier to protect allied forces scavenging for forage and served as a natural observation post. Viet held his position and endured the cries for what seemed an hour—though he suspected the clock would have shown the passing of no more than a few minutes. Only when the wailing became the piercing screams of a tortured woman did the stoned northsmen stumble toward the far side of their village, leaving behind only a single woman—and she was sprawled nearly motionless in the sand.

Now Viet saw his chance and crawled forward, soon standing and then darting between trees. When the terrorized woman screamed from a distance yet again, Viet stopped for a moment—this time listening to the guffaws of drunken men. Whatever was taking place evidently held their attention.

It was time to make a move.

Viet jumped up and sprinted into the open straight toward the fire, his ax raised high. The woman lying in the sand tried to stand when she saw the approaching enemy, but proved too stoned to do so and fell backwards as the intruder ran toward the motorized launch. Slipping behind the boat's fiberglass hull to catch his breath, Viet reached for the keys to the boat, only to find they weren't in the ignition. With no time to search for the missing keys, Viet climbed into the boat to look for whatever combustible material he could find. He found a blanket, a shirt, and a can of reserve fuel—which he splashed across the boat, careful to pour plenty of the gasoline on the control panel, steering column, and the motor (whose fuel cap was removed to insure it would ignite).

The combustibles readied, Viet climbed from the boat and looked toward the shore. After removing his shirt and swiping it across the fuel-soaked deck of the boat, he wrapped it into a ball and dipped his hands into water to wash away every trace of gasoline. Turning his back to the village and pulling a lighter from his pants pocket, Viet lit the shirt, threw it into the boat, and sprinted for safety moments before the fuel ignited and light flashed across the surf. Indeed, he took only a few steps before the fuel tank exploded—knocking him forward and singeing the hair on his back. Still, Viet kept to his feet as he ran through the surf, sprinted across the beech, and darted into the refuge of the forest.

As for the woman at the beach, though she staggered to her feet and turned toward the intruder as soon as the boat blew up, she chose not to sound the alarm when Viet ran straight toward her waving his ax. Instead, she raised her hands in surrender until the west village raider had disappeared into the cover of the trees from which he had come. Only then did she cry for help as she staggered toward the sea—where the launch was aflame from stern to bow and already beginning to list to its starboard side.

When Viet reached Turtle Beach a few minutes later, his companions were gone, so he jogged south alone. At his home village, he filled a duffle bag with spare clothing for his family and keepsakes treasured by his daughters and also found some food in the barn—which had been looted only haphazardly. The jellies and dried fruit were gone (along with the fish), but plenty of flour remained. Viet grabbed several bags of flour, a tin of sea-salt, and a canister of dry yeast. He also picked up a bag of sugar, a small tub of lard, and several cast iron pots and pans. Only as he reached the bridge over the Pishon River did he notice the bobbing of lights coming down the northern trail toward the village: a northern scouting party. Viet crept into the dark of the forest, slipped off his shoes, and moved slowly uphill, keeping as far as possible from the main trail to escape any war party waiting in ambush.

New Plymouth was sacked. Tents were torn open and poles hacked into kindling. The supply sheds were ransacked and the ground littered with broken pill bottles, opened cartons of gauze, and smashed medical instruments. The library had been burned to the ground and even the toilet was tipped. The foraging party salvaged a box of medical supplies, several articles of loose clothing, and even two crates of packaged food before triggering an emergency beacon overlooked by the northsmen. After the others began their trek toward Mount Zion, Alan and Lisa moved toward a south-leading trail to complete their assigned mission—telling the others they'd be along in a few minutes and not to wait. The foragers wished the pair good luck before disappearing into the trees and it wasn't long before the crunch of grass underfoot no longer sounded.

Alan and Lisa crept toward the beach, watching for northern

patrols and ambushes. Long before they reached the landing craft, they heard the wailing of heathen women pounding fists against wood walls—the clank of chains reverberating across water and sand.

"At least they're still alive," Alan said.

"And inside the boat," Lisa added.

"Probably too frightened to leave. Or still chained."

"Or too short."

"I'll lower the ramp myself," Alan said, "since you don't fight. Just don't be a distraction. I want you to keep watch to the north—looking for northsmen. I can handle these pygmies. What I don't need is a bullet in my back."

"I won't fight," Lisa said. "I'm not a soldier."

"Just scream and run for your own life if the northerners come. I'll see to my own safety."

Lisa nodded.

"I'll be back in five minutes," Alan continued. "Be here."

Lisa said she'd stay put.

Alan then slung his ax over a shoulder and jogged toward the screeching of the natives while Lisa slipped into shadows and turned her face north. Behind her, the shrieks and screams of native women sounded so fierce that Lisa shuddered as she remembered the stretched breasts of the cannibals: elongated from suckling babies whom they had eaten. A shiver ran across her own breasts and she clutched her nipples.

A moment later, the heavy thud of a steel ramp against solid ground reverberated across the lagoon and Lisa stared into the darkness as she imagined what it must have been like to watch hundreds of warships dropping their payloads of armed soldiers into the terrible battles that engulfed the Pacific and brought a man-made hell to so many tropical paradises. She trembled to consider how artillery had destroyed pristine beaches and aircraft had firebombed unspoiled forests.

"No soldier," Lisa said, "will die by my hand."

Lisa looked back again. The noise of the women grew louder and more pitched. They seemed more fevered and maybe a little closer. She wondered how Alan was doing; he seemed to be delayed.

It was then that a scream penetrated the forest—a man's howl of such anguish that Lisa froze from fear. Only when the man screamed a second time did the young woman take a hesitant step toward the pain. A third shriek, even more anguished than the others, finally broke Lisa's trance.

Now Lisa sprinted toward the cries, slowing only when she turned a sharp bend in the path. There, under the pale moonlight, she saw Alan pinned to the ground by four natives while several others fed like dogs from the soft of his belly. He writhed hard and even from a distance Lisa heard his gasps of breathless anguish. She also saw skinny legs slipped from their chains and hands bloodied with fistfuls of bowels—as well as children slapped and kicked whenever they squeezed between the arms and legs of crouching mothers to take a bite for themselves. As she approached the stricken man, Lisa saw that Alan's face was utterly contorted from pain and his eyes wide from trauma and terror, though she heard no words come from his mouth.

Lisa again froze—her heart racing and hands trembling. Tunnel vision obscured every sight but that of her stricken friend and she no longer heard the shrieks of the natives or saw them circling to her side. Her hands and feet felt sluggish and her mouth felt dry and salty. She saw Alan's ax a few feet away and reached for it, almost unthinking, with both hands—though securing it with surprising difficulty. Wishing to chase the natives away, she threw the ax at the feet of a native. But stress and adrenaline proved strong and the ax sailed much further than Lisa had intended, now catching a scampering child in the back. The girl let out a yelp as her legs went limp and she crumpled to the ground.

As cannibals scattered in every direction, Lisa pulled the weapon from the unmoving child and hurried toward her fallen friend—whose stomach was torn open and guts strewn from shoulder to thigh. His eyes were vacant and he breathed slow. Blood drained from his torn throat.

"You're already dead," Lisa cried out. "What I do isn't war and killing, but mercy and peace."

Alan choked out a single breathless word—though Lisa couldn't make it out as she raised the ax high over his chest. When she drove the ax downward with all her might, Alan's eyes went wide with utter horror as the sharp edge of the ax broke his sternum and split his heart. His eyes rolled and a mouthful of frothy blood gushed outward. He was dead before the young woman pulled the ax from his chest. Taking a deep breath that cleared her blurred vision, Lisa turned toward the natives who had begun to circle the now-armed pacifist—their hands filled with stones and sand.

Seeing an opening, Lisa closed her eyes, and charged past an old woman—clumsily brushing the old woman's arm with the sharp edge of her bloody ax as she passed by. The old woman fell to her knees with gasps too anguished to cry out. Though several natives already had returned to feast from Alan—once again lapping blood and chewing organs—their children swarmed the old woman: one slurping blood from the ground as the matriarch writhed in pain and others gnawing at stretched old breasts and tearing off mouthfuls of aged fat and loose skin as fast as they could. The old woman gave a blood-curdling scream when a girl poked a finger into the socket of her eye and popped out an eyeball—severing its cord of veins and nerves with a single bite before running into the woods to enjoy the delicacy. Now the old woman screamed until her voice went hoarse and even then groaned loud until her life finally drained away.

Panicked and sobbing with blurred vision and racing heart, Lisa ran for Mount Zion as fast as she could, making no effort to show caution. She cast aside the bloodied ax after a few steps and tore hair from her own head after a few more. Only when she heard shouting from a north-leading trail did she step into the shadows—stumbling into a ditch and hiding in brush. There, the bloodstained pacifist closed her eyes as she remembered the screaming, cannibalism, and a terrible coup de grâce.

.   .   .

CRACK. Crack. Crack.

The first three shots were too high. Donovan had pulled the trigger too quick to make adjustments and the bullets whizzed harmlessly over the crest of the hill. The northerners beside him weren't pleased.

"Aim! Aim!" Jason screamed as he squared against four islanders wielding raised axes and pointed spears—who now charged toward the northern raiding party that had appeared on the north slope in the dim light of early dawn.

As Jason and the other northsman continued to advance from the forest, Donovan steadied himself against a tree and took aim at one of several islanders who now charged his compatriots—and were armed with six-foot lances tipped with razor-sharp shells.

Donovan squeezed the trigger until the gun jumped.

Crack.

Crack. Crack.

Following a miss, an islander was struck in the shoulder, spun into a tree, and collapsed.

Crack.

A second islander fell—this one from a bullet to the chest. Only two opponents remained. Both of them darted to the left flank of the northerners as Donovan fired at the closer target.

Crack. Crack. The second shot struck the man only a few feet away and the man collapsed without a sound.

Now the last attacking islander retreated into the shadows of the trees as Donovan and his northsmen turned toward the refugee camp.

"Ahhhhhh."

Someone to Donovan's right screamed and the priest spun toward the cry. Jason had stepped into a spike-filled hole and now cried for help as blood spurted from gash to his thigh. When the wounded man tried to disimpale himself from the spike with a violent jerk of his body, he screamed out and then fainted from shock and pain. A northern raider reached to pull Jason from the trap until Father

Donovan shouted that Jason was mortally wounded and must be abandoned to his fate.

Now Donovan—flanked by a single compatriot—hurried toward a ravine at the edge of the encampment, where he saw a dark-skinned woman shouting for help.

"Kill her," Donovan ordered his associate as he himself scanned for other threats.

"Will do," the northerner said as he charged his lance and ran straight at the woman, his weapon directed at her belly.

When the woman turned to run, she slipped in mud and fell to a knee, now screaming as the northsman closed the short distance between them at a dead run.

Ten steps ... eight ... six ...

The northsman never reached his target. The sound of running came from the woods and a terrible shriek sounded from the shadows. The lancer heard the yell and tried to turn his weapon, but moved a step too slow as an islander crashed into him. Both men staggered from the blow—the northsman's lance knocked from his hand.

Thirty feet away, Father Donovan watched in horror as the attacking foe brought his weapon to bear against his northern target with a violent twist of his body: the ax swung shoulder-high. The northsman didn't duck and the ax caught him across the back of the neck. His squeal was cut short as his head flung twenty feet into the forest and blood sprayed the earth. His foe killed, the attacking islander sprinted to the fallen woman—interposing his body between her and Donovan's line of sight.

Crack. Crack.

At least one of Donovan's shots struck the ax-swinging islander. The man fell to his knees, clutching his side.

Crack. Crack.

Donovan fired into the woman's breast and belly and she fell backwards.

Click.

When Donovan tried to finish off the wounded fighter (who

already had staggered to his feet), he found the chamber empty and the gun's slide locked to the rear. As his wounded enemy shouted a war cry and staggered forward with a raised ax, Donovan backpedaled into the forest—fumbling for bullets from his pants pocket, but managing only to drop several of them in tall grass during his panicked retreat. Only after he cleared the ravine did he dare stop to reload his weapon behind the cover of a tall tree.

After reloading, Donovan waited several minutes for a counterattack. When none came, he slipped down the hill and started for home: the sole survivor of the ill-fated raid. The path wasn't as dark now and he made good time back to the north camp, arriving before dawn broke over the eastern horizon.

41

THE GULAG ARCHIPELAGO

T he first hours of the new day were spent burying the dead and planning a stronger defense. It was decided to strengthen and extend the bermed walls around the camp's entire perimeter, as well as to manufacture additional bows and arrows and more bundles of spears. More traps also were authorized and the General Will of the People even ordered women to man the walls, either to fight or pass weapons. The battle had been a close call and it was assessed matters might have ended in utter catastrophe if Donovan had successfully fired even one more bullet—knocking Sean completely out of action and giving himself a chance to reload. A motion was passed to keep more islanders on guard duty since too many fighters were sleeping when the enemy struck. Though the northerners lost two fighters and wasted numerous bullets, the islanders suffered three men and one woman killed and one man wounded. The odds in favor of the allied villages had been reduced and the absence even of three or four militia might cost them both a battle and their lives.

After defensive arrangements were decided, a trial was held of Jason (now pulled from the trap). It was a quick trial and judgment by the rump of the General Will of the People was summary and unforgiving—with Jason accused of treason, war crimes, conspiracy to commit murder, assault with intent to kill, and illegal possession of a firearm. He was convicted within minutes and executed without further adieu, being indulged neither final meal nor last word. Only two citizens voted to commute his sentence to life imprisonment and even his appeal for one last joint was refused before he was hanged from the lowest branch of a tree at the edge of camp. As he slowly strangled a few inches above the bloodstained soil of Paradise, all of his judges turned away, except Olivia—who spit in Jason's face as the condemned man defecated down his own leg.

Kit wept and prayed from a distance.

Hilltop defenses were completed before dinner: bunkers were fortified with cut timber and shoveled earth and bundles of spears placed strategically along the walls—along with slingshots and rocks and bows and arrows. Provisions were stored too. Including the food and medicine brought to camp, it was assessed the camp contained enough supplies to endure a siege of several days at half rations, not counting fruit trees close enough to pick under cover of darkness. Cords of firewood were stacked as a final redoubt and a hundred gallons of fresh water were stockpiled in plastic jugs. Tents were repositioned at the center of camp—several of them pitched in shallow depressions and partially protected by walls composed of whatever rock, wood, and dirt was available.

Everyone agreed the day's work was productive, though no one looked forward to the dangers of the night.

LISA WAS SPOTTED by a day patrol and returned to camp by midafternoon. Now she ate a handful of uncooked oatmeal as she listened to Kit describe the battle for Mount Zion. The former actress cradled the dark-skinned baby forsaken by the natives and held the hand of the light-skinned girl abandoned by the northsmen as she led Lisa to a shallow grave shared by Ursula and Sean—where Lisa lay a few wildflowers on the fresh dirt before stepping away, tears streaming down her face as she embraced Kit.

"Ryan told me Sean died for her," Lisa said.

"That's what she told us," Kit said as she wiped tears from her eyes. "No one saw for sure."

Lisa wept.

"His last words," Kit said after a time, "were to name the baby."

"What name did he give?"

"Only heaven knows. He whispered the name to her before he died. She held him until she passed away a few minutes later. I prayed with both of them as they slipped away."

"I'm so sorry for speaking poorly of him."

"He was very brave in the end."

"And as good as any man."

"Anyone else?"

Kit shook her head.

"Not from our village," Kit said, "except Steve was killed outright and two easterners wounded. One died a few hours ago and the other has a shattered arm. He's out of the fight."

"How many of them?"

"They say one dead and Jason was left on a pongee stick. Donovan and his gun escaped. Our defenses weren't complete."

"Jason fought us?" Lisa asked with a subdued voice.

Kit nodded.

"He's a bastard," Lisa said.

"He atoned his crime."

"How could he ever atone for all the evil he's done?"

"They hanged him outside camp."

"This is all too much," Lisa said as her shoulders sagged and tears formed in her eyes. "What have we done to Paradise?"

Kit looked into the forest for a long while.

"He gave us their plans," Kit eventually said. "They intend to kill Ryan and John and anyone who fights for them. Apparently, they're afraid of facing war crimes charges."

"That makes perfect sense," Lisa whispered, "kill lots of people to escape punishment for killing a few."

"None of this makes sense to me," Kit said with a shrug.

Lisa agreed.

"They hope," Kit continued, "to portray themselves as good men and heroes."

"They couldn't."

"They could if evidence is burned and witnesses buried."

"They'd have to kill us all."

"They will," Kit swallowed hard as she spoke, "if we don't swear loyalty."

"Let's swear it and stop the killing."

"There's a hitch."

Lisa waited for the older woman to speak.

"They'll require a blood oath," Kit said. "Everyone who wishes to live must murder a prisoner: one of the natives. Every northsmen has —except a couple holdouts already sacrificed as victims."

"You don't mean," Lisa said after a long pause, "those nice people who broke away?"

"Jason," Kit said as she nodded her head, "told us the northsmen are bound by blood and will fight to the death."

Lisa dropped to her knees short of breath and fell face first upon the fresh grave, wailing from grief. Her sobs were so loud that Kit left Lisa to grieve alone when the latter's crying woke the cannibal's son from his nap and made Brittany cling in distress to her foster mother.

STREAKS OF FLAME shot from the forest soon after dusk. Viet watched from his foxhole when he saw a flash of light to his left. Three additional arrows followed the first: the burning missiles striking the bermed wall within twenty feet of each other. The flames were dark-smoked and thick and showed the presence of petroleum. Now a flaming ball arched from the dark and landed within the fort; it was a fuel-filled coconut husk that split on impact and sprayed a southern woman with flaming gasoline. Her first scream was from surprise and her second from searing pain as her leg burned. Two men rolled her into the dirt to smother the flames, but were too late to prevent at least some third-degree burns. The woman cried and screamed until Doctor Graves sedated her with morphine.

Several minutes later, a voice cried from the dark—the voice of Father Donovan. John told him to approach under truce and Donovan came near enough to be heard.

"We'll bring a hundred more tomorrow," Father Donovan shouted loud enough for the entire camp to hear. "We can burn your fort or we can burn you. Those who side with us will live; those who don't will die. Choose tomorrow which side you'll take."

"We've," Ryan shouted his reply, "already decided."

"Then you're going to die for the moralizing of Godson and Smith."

"Our morality will kill you too," Viet shouted.

"And what will that get you?"

"A good conscience, at least."

"You may have principles, but we have fifty gallons of gasoline and thirty bullets."

"Liar."

"Send someone to look," Donovan said. "I have the bullets with me and the fuel's in our camp."

"So," View scowled, "you can kill our delegate under a flag of truce. Go to hell."

"Send a woman or a child for all I care. You have to know you can't win this fight."

"We'll take some of you down with us."

"That's why we're giving you this chance," Father Donovan shouted. "We're realists. If we start this battle, it'll be to the death. We'll burn you out and shoot you down. But you'll get a couple of us too. Give us your oath you'll cooperate in our fact-finding investigation of recent events and we'll spare you. No one gets hurt. Not even John or Ryan. Not even Steve."

The northern chief was answered by the firing of two arrows that flew harmlessly over his head and Donovan responded by aiming his pistol and firing once. His bullet struck a bunker, splintering the wood.

An islander yelped.

"Damn," the man shouted, "he hit me."

The wounded man ducked behind the wall and wiped away blood from his face while two women tended his wounds.

"Just splinters," Kit told him. "Not too bad."

"Well, they don't feel all that good," the man said with a wince. "Enough is enough. I'm changing my vote. I'd fight even up, but this is a massacre. As soon as he shows enough sense to climb into a tree to fire down, we won't be able to hide. And that's besides the threat of being burned up and burned out."

"We'd be at their mercy," Kit said.

"We're at their mercy now," the man snapped. "I always said better red than dead."

"They'll kill us all."

"We can make a fair peace."

"They'll make us murder each other."

"That's what we're doing now," the wounded man said, "and maybe it will stop if we just cooperate. They need peace too. It's in everyone's self-interest."

"They'll break it."

"We can ask for guarantees."

Now John joined the conversation from several feet away. "How?"

The man shrugged.

"A truce," John shouted toward the forest, "till morning—to decide how good your word is."

Donovan's voice sounded from a different location. "Fair enough, but no raids tonight from you either."

Soon, the sound of the northsmen retreating downhill made it evident hostilities had ended for the day—though the islanders called a council only after patrols confirmed the enemy had departed. The perimeter was drawn tight so sentries could participate in the public assembly—with a single delegate from every village deployed into the woods for security (after passing voting rights to loved ones who shared the guard's opinions). Then the

General Will of the People was called into emergency session, though the oath of allegiance was skipped for the sake of brevity.

"We must choose," John said as he began the meeting, "whether to defend ourselves or hope for mercy from the merciless. They've slaughtered non-combatants, murdered men who came to help us, and ignited a civil war. I won't depend upon their good graces."

"Then why," a soft-voiced man interrupted, "did we accept a truce?"

"To buy time," John answered, "to test their good will, but also to finish our defenses."

"That's dishonest."

"Prudent is a better word."

Now a middle-aged southerner with shoulder-length hair stepped into the center of the assembly.

"The choice," the southern man declared, "is between war and peace. I believe in peace."

Several neighbors clapped.

Others hooted.

"We don't need to depend on mere promises," the long-haired southerner continued, "we can verify the peace."

"Let them give up that gun if they want peace."

"Would you?"

"Not to those barbarians."

"And," the long-haired man said as he nodded, "neither will they, so we have to decide whether peace and coexistence are worth trying. If we don't, every man will die on this hill and northsmen will take our women and children for their pleasure. That's the ancient law of war; once walls are breached, no quarter is given."

"At least we'd die like men," John said, "and maybe, just maybe, we can drive them away. That's the honorable path."

"Honor?" the long-haired man sneered. "Just who do you suppose will raise a monument to wasted valor? It's our lives we need to save, not our honor."

"I've lost my husband," a southern woman spoke up, "my home, and my friends, but I'm not going to lose my daughter. Not for some tribe of gods-forsaken heathen. Has anyone considered the cannibals are set loose—and by our own hand? They'll roam this island like wild animals until we're all gnawed to the bone. We have to settle this civil war because, unfortunately, the real war is still ahead."

Half the neighborhood nodded and clapped as the woman sat down and a friend near her stood.

"And I'll say something," the woman's friend said, "that came to me while I was lying with my face in the dirt. I'm glad we killed the natives. Otherwise there'd be even more of them to fight."

"I fought them like anyone else," John said, "but they aren't the enemy at our gate."

"They will be," the woman said, "if we don't make peace with the northerners so we can hunt them down."

"We'll deal," John said with a shake of his head, "with the natives as we have to. For now, we're safe in these walls and, hopefully, we'll be delivered from this island before long. The task is to keep the northerners at a distance for a few days."

The long-haired southerner raised his hand to speak. "I want a vote," he said, "regarding whether we should fight or make peace."

This motion was seconded and discussion was entertained.

"If we fight," the long-haired man continued, "all of us could die. If we make peace, all of us could live."

"If could were would," John said, "I suppose we'd build wooden ships from wishes and sail to California."

"What the hell is that supposed to mean?"

"Don't bet on pipe dreams."

"Well," the long-haired man said after a brief pause, "even a slim chance is better than none at all."

"We can't know who will live or die if we fight," John said, "but we do know—for absolute certain—that we can't trust the northsmen to be honest or merciful. They have to be disarmed. Only then can we make peace."

"You mean that we can only make peace on our terms. After we've crushed our own people."

"Not on our terms. On safe terms."

"I see the logic of both arguments," Ryan said as he joined the debate, "but what if we combine them? What if we can bring about a truce without throwing down our weapons?"

"How?" John asked.

"Diplomacy," Ryan said. "We can open a dialogue. Over time, both armies can slowly demobilize and foster good relations. We can negotiate for camp inspections, offensive weapon reductions, and maybe the eventual elimination of that gun once we've settled the causes of the war. From armed conflict we can move to cold war, then to détente and peaceful coexistence. It's been done before."

"We don't have forty years."

"Then we'll need to accelerate negotiations."

"I don't understand how that can be done," John said, "since there's nothing to negotiate. Donovan's marauders murdered natives and we saw it. We can't lie about the crime, can we?"

"We can't lie," Ryan replied, "but a legal fiction may prove useful for all of us. This assembly is the law of the land and it can legitimize what took place. Ex post facto, if necessary. Can't we grant amnesty from prosecution to our own wrongdoers? And if we do, no power on earth can touch them."

"Tell that to the International Tribunal at the Hague."

"If it comes to that, Donovan will have to fend for himself."

"That's exactly why," John cried out, "he can't give up the fight till all the witnesses are dead."

"Talk about a conspiracy theory," the long-haired southerner sneered. "Sounds like Ken Star and his right-wing chorus."

"Let's not go there," John said, "but let's ask ourselves this: what if Jason told the truth and the northsmen are going to make us kill natives to prove ourselves? Can you kill one?"

"Jason was a liar."

"What if he wasn't lying?"

"He probably hallucinated that little nightmare."

"He was straight sober and you know it."

"I don't know anything of the sort."

"Let's assume for a moment," John said, "that he spoke the truth. Would you kill to save yourself?"

"Isn't that war?"

"The slaughter of innocents?"

"They're not innocent. They ate our neighbors. Every one of them with teeth took a bite."

Several voices cried out in agreement as neighbors claimed the cannibals were guilty of terrible sins.

"Yeah," one man shouted, "let The Hague try them for cannibalism and war crimes. They started it."

"They broke the law first," a woman said.

"If the truth is known," Ryan said, "the men we ... I mean, the men the northerners put to death broke international law and were punished rightly."

"And what of Captain Strong and his family?" John asked. "By whose laws were they killed?"

The long-haired man from the south said nothing.

"Do you think American authorities," John continued, "will let that murder stand? Do you think they'll be bamboozled by sophistry?"

John looked around and saw that no one disagreed.

"We all know better," John continued. "There will be a trial and every one of us will be called as a witness. Donovan knows it and he has to silence every voice. He'll make every one of you prove yourself loyal to him through some terrible crime."

"We can deal with that," the long-haired southerner said, "when the time comes. For now, all we want is to stop the fighting. If we can just make a truce, we'll be safe enough for a while. This fort will protect us and a truce will let us collect supplies."

"Listen," John replied, "if we lay down the sword, we won't pick it up again. Right now, they're trying to divide and conquer us. If we don't hang together, we'll hang separately for sure."

"I call for a vote," the long-haired southerner said.

After this man's motion was seconded, John stood up and straightened his shoulders.

"Either we fight," John declared, "or I leave. I won't surrender myself to Donovan. Who'll fight with me?"

Though thirteen hands were raised, John's proposal fell short of a majority.

"Fight or die," John said. "Who wants to live?"

Now, only twelve hands remained raised.

"One last time," John said, his eyes red and shoulders stooped, "who will stand against the northsmen?"

Several hands dropped. Only a handful of westerners continued to favor armed resistance.

"We'll make peace in the morning," the long-haired man said as he stared at John, "and no one breaks the truce tonight. I propose we make sedition a capital offense. Anyone who starts fighting dies like Jason. We've already made a truce. Why should we all be killed for old-fashioned notions of honor?"

The assembly enacted his proposal, with even Ryan and Olivia breaking from their home village in showing willingness to give Donovan a chance to prove his intentions were peaceful. The majority also thought a few days without fighting might allow time to bolster defenses and gather provisions for a long siege. Guards were posted on the perimeter and reserve troops lay down to rest. For the first time in two days, there was no immediate fear of battle.

42

DETENTE AND DEATH

Rain fell at dawn. Winds picked up first and showers followed a few minutes later, falling so fast that fires were extinguished and wood soaked before coverings could be raised. Consequently, breakfast brought only cold coffee served with a spoonful of sugar and a few drops of goat milk, along with withered fruit and shriveled vegetables. After eating, the refugees squeezed themselves into their tents, seven or eight people pressed into dwellings designed for four. Only sentries remained at their posts—without tarp, poncho, or raincoat. Suffering was great and many parents went hungry to provide extra food to famished children. Even so, work started midmorning amidst rain and mud: trees were knocked down to clear the perimeter, logs set into the bermed wall, and water jugs were filled to capacity with rainwater.

It was noon when Father Donovan's emissary arrived. The man brought a scribbled note and met with refugee leaders in a nylon tent from which everyone else was excluded—most of them sent into the rain. Demanding an immediate cessation of hostilities, the northsman required Viet and John to make a separate peace and promised that any man or woman (even those singled out for special treatment) who swore allegiance and proved loyalty would be spared since every available fighter was needed to hunt cannibals. Furthermore, the emissary threatened anyone who continued to fight with death and also warned that their families would be denied protection from the heathen. The messenger smirked when told Steve was dead.

After several westerners insisted on proof of Donovan's trustworthiness by removal of the firing pin of the pistol or the surrendering of bullets, the emissary made a counterproposal—suggesting an exchange of hostages as a better way of securing peace. He argued that removal of the gun alone wouldn't reduce tensions if evil motives and sharp sticks remained. Though Viet and John were appalled by the proposal, their compatriots weren't. Many even applauded the suggestion, claiming that mutual vulnerability was the safest course of action. The northern messenger claimed the idea of a hostage exchange was his own and requested permission to confirm the plan with Father Donovan and the northern war council. Despite objections from several westerners that they didn't trust the northern emissary, the majority of refugees voted to send the ambassador back to his own people for further guidance while the allied villages voted whether to proceed.

Soon after the northerner left, the refugees gathered to consider the exchange of hostages, assembling atop Mount Zion under dark skies as Ryan called the General Will of the People into session. Though the rain drove hard and everyone soon was drenched—shivering from the cold and embittered by the situation—no one objected to the meeting.

"We have to vote yea or nay on exchanging hostages," Ryan said, "and decide how to choose them. I need a motion."

"I propose," the long-haired southerner stood as he spoke, "we exchange hostages with the north camp to make peace."

Ryan asked for a motion to second the proposal and received one before calling for discussion.

"If we fight," a southern woman said, "they win. Every one of us knows we can't beat them as long as they have that gun. One effective attack and we're dead and our families and friends left to their mercy."

"If we exchange hostages," John objected, "our loved ones are at their mercy. Our only chance is to fight to get that gun. We still outnumber them and they know it. A few traps and a good ambush and that gun won't mean anything. Donovan will find himself at our disposal. Alone."

Dr. Graves lowered his umbrella and raised a hand. "How many of us," he asked, "would live to see such a victory? A pyrrhic victory is a total loss, medically speaking."

Several voices agreed.

Viet raised his voice over the chorus of assent.

"We're not," Viet shouted, his tone angry and agitated, "just talking about survival. This island is finished. Our camps are burned and our people dead. A yacht is sunk in our harbor and innocent people murdered—four according to Ryan, two of them women. There'll be an investigation and the deaths of cannibals will come out. Father Donovan is a veteran of the Nicaraguan wars and knows it —and so should we. The criminals want to separate those of us who saw the atrocities from those who didn't and we'll either go along with the evil or be liquidated. Their own representative said everyone has to help hunt cannibals. What do you think he meant? He meant we all kill so every hand is stained and every mouth silenced. That will insure friendly witnesses at The Hague."

Viet was catcalled.

"He didn't say that."

"You just want to save yourself."

"What did happen on Roanoke Island?"

"I don't really care," the long-haired southerner said, "what happens to the savages. What I do care about is my own child. Only God knows what will happen to her out here if I'm killed and, since there isn't a God, a truce is our ... is her ... only chance."

"I've got two daughters," Viet said, "and my worry is twice yours. But I won't become a liar or a butcher in front of them to save my skin. Nor to save theirs."

"I love my daughter enough to do anything for her."

Viet stared at the man. "Anything?"

The man nodded.

"Will you murder a native child?" Viet asked.

"If it's my child or a cannibal," the man replied, "I would. Those children chewed our people. They're not so innocent."

"Murdering children is plain evil."

"Not," the gray-haired man declared, "as evil as sending your own child to the butcher when you have it in your power to save her. Would you leave your daughters without help in a foreign land? So they're eaten alive by pagans or abused by Donovan's thugs? That's child abuse."

"Don't you see?" Viet cried out. "That's why we fight."

"You're both right," Ryan now joined the discussion. "If we fight and lose, we're lost and so are our loved ones. On the other hand, if we surrender, we're at their mercy and I don't trust them any more than Viet does."

Everyone waited for Ryan to split the difference of opinion.

"That's why we have to exchange hostages," Ryan said. "If they hurt our loved ones, we'll take an eye for an eye. Mutually assured destruction does have its advantages. I don't like the idea, but there'll be less killing than war and hopefully none at all. Besides, have any of you stopped to realize it raises our odds to get some of their people off the battlefield? We can set terms so they lose a couple fighting men."

"It's mad," Viet said. "Our odds may increase, but our ability to conduct operations doesn't. Every spare man will be stuck with guard duty. And it makes the gun all the more lethal."

"How's that?" the southern man with long hair asked.

"Because they'll have more bullets per fighter and can afford to miss more often. And because we won't be able to overwhelm them with a concentration of forces. That's the one thing they fear: that one of our people can break through and take the gun from them. It's the one risk they can't take."

"But," the southern man said, "if they surrender two or three prisoners, they'll have fewer men to post guard, to flank us, or to protect Donovan while he reloads."

"Check and mate!" someone shouted and several islanders clapped.

"Everyone knows the issues," the southern man said as he panned the crowd. "I move we vote."

The call for a vote was seconded and, a few minutes later, the poll was tabulated. Subsequently, it was decided by a two to one margin to exchange hostages. After the vote, Ryan stood before the rump of a people he had brought to the new world.

"All right," Ryan asked, "any volunteers?"

No one volunteered.

"Then how do we draft—by vote or lottery?"

Viet moved that they choose hostages by lottery and his proposal was seconded. The poll was close, but a single vote determined the lottery would be used rather than nominations. After discussion, it also was decided every neighborhood should surrender a citizen as a hostage. Several southerners objected that this method put each of them at greater individual risk given their low numbers, but the westerners pointed out that they too had suffered massive casualties and blocked a revote. The various neighborhoods assembled in the rain and selected hostages. The gray-haired man was picked from the south and a muscular youth from the east. Ilyana drew the short stick from the west and Nurse Fallows was taken from New Plymouth village. Hostages were told to pack their personal effects and prepare to move.

Two hours later, the envoy returned. He brought with him four people: a tall northerner named Jake with a bandaged face, Father Donovan's half-dressed girlfriend, a disconsolate Sally McNeal, and a terrified Bryan Murphy. The islanders confirmed they'd exchange two women and two men, but when their hostages were summoned, Ilyana was missing. So was her mother. Leaders immediately decided to draft another westerner and this time Maria drew the short stick. Within minutes, the northern envoy—assisted by the eastern and southern hostages—dragged her screaming from the camp.

The departing southerner begged everyone to keep the peace or he himself might die and the northern emissary warned the islanders to be sure they heeded the man's advice. After the enemy left, the two northern men were bound with ropes at the center of the camp and their women placed under armed guard several feet away.

Rain continued to fall.

THIRTY MINUTES after she was brought to camp, Sally told her guard she needed to use the latrine. She was escorted to the edge of the woods by Viet and did her business while the latter stood guard (careful to keep the woman within reach even as he respected her privacy). Afterwards, Sally asked to speak with her captor.

"It's Viet, right?"

"Yeah."

"I need to tell you something, but you must swear to be discreet."

"What is it?"

"Swear."

"I can't promise until you tell me why."

"Because," Sally explained, "they'll kill my daughter if I betray them and they'll kill you if I don't."

"I'll be discreet," Viet said with a frown.

The woman stared into his face. "You're a father?" she asked, her voice cracking as she spoke.

"I have two daughters."

"I have to trust you," Sally said after a long pause.

"Go ahead."

"I don't know how, but this a trap. For sure. Don't trust the other two northerners. Only me and Bryan."

"Why do you say that?"

"Donovan's girlfriend volunteered to come and so did the guy. And they told us—I mean, me and Bryan—they'd feed our kids to cannibals if we resisted."

"The northerners have cannibals?"

"A couple are tied up like animals."

Viet looked bewildered as Sally continued.

"They let the beasts eat Andrea alive," Sally said as she began to sob. "They tied her up and made Bryan watch his own wife die. It was horrible. Those women ate her like wild dogs. She screamed for hours while the northsmen smoked dope and laughed. Bryan broke free and pushed a cannibal into the fire, but Donovan tied him again and slit Andrea's throat while they held Bryan's eyes open. It was horrible."

Sally's voice cracked as she finished.

"Andrea," she said with a tremor to her voice, "was the best friend I ever had."

"What else do you know?"

"Only," Sally said, "that they told me and Bryan to cooperate or they'd feed our children to the other one. They're going to get all of us. Don't tell them I said anything. Please, I beg you."

Viet hugged the distraught woman, then dried her tears before leading her back to the other prisoners—where he ordered both Sally and Donovan's blond girlfriend tied with cords before he called his fellow refugees to emergency session at the edge of camp. Only there did he repeat what he'd learned.

"We've traded four fighters," Viet said after relaying facts, "for a warrior, a woman, and two prisoners. Plus we lost Ilyana and Olivia."

"Exactly," John said, "they've flanked us in the truce."

Dr. Erikson stepped forward.

"This can't be true," the psychologist said with a tone both exasperated and anxious. "Donovan gave us his own lover."

"Are you crazy?" John snapped. "He doesn't love anyone or anything. He uses. He lies. He hates."

"No one only hates," the psychologist replied. "That's pure abstraction. And I don't believe it anyway. I've seen them together; he loves her."

"You better hope so," Viet said, "because you've staked your life on it."

The blood drained from Dr. Erikson's face.

"Sally spoke of a trap," Viet continued, "so I had both women tied up. That way it won't be so evident she clued us in. Plus it'll keep that other woman under wraps."

"So," a woman's trembling voice came from the back of the group, "what do we do?"

"To begin with," John said, "we need to interrogate the prisoners."

"What if they won't talk?"

"We'll see that they do."

"How?"

"We'll find a way," John said with a grim look.

"Do you mean torture them?" the woman asked.

"I didn't say that," John growled. "We need to question them—to elicit information from them. We especially need to find out how many bullets they really have left. We can count shots and make them waste ammunition with hit and run attacks. Hurried shots miss more often."

"You're talking about another war."

"Do we have a choice?"

"We need to keep our word," Dr. Erikson said.

"We all know it's a trap," John said. "Why walk into it?"

"How do we really know it?"

"Sally told us."

"How could she know? Did they tell someone who hates them?"

"She endangered her own child to warn us."

"It's all spying and sneaking and I don't trust her."

"It's like the Cold War," Doctor Graves now spoke. "You have to expect even your enemy to be rational."

"We trusted the Soviets," Viet said, "only as far as our tanks in Germany could shoot and our spies could report."

"You were a Cold Warrior?"

"I was," Viet said, "still in college when the Berlin Wall fell."

"You sound like Ronald Reagan."

"Then Reagan," Viet said, "had more sense than I gave him credit for. I'm not going to allow these people to kill us one by one with subterfuge and traps. We have to rescue our hostages immediately. If we move quick, we'll hit them completely unprepared. Probably stoned and celebrating."

"You're not going to make war," Dr. Graves turned red as he spoke, "on your own authority. It's illegal. We've made our peace with the north. Now we must let it stand. Every day we can go without fighting creates momentum to end this crisis."

"We're gullible fools," Viet said to John, "letting the enemy bide his time to crush us. Your name is on their list too. Get these people to listen."

"So that's what this is all about," Dr. Erikson said, "your own fears and phobias."

"Damned right," Viet said, "I'm afraid of those people. They're evil."

"There's no reason to use pejorative terms ..."

"Tell it to the Marines. I haven't got the time."

Dr. Erikson looked perplexed, but before she could ask Viet what he meant, a shriek sounded across the camp—the pained scream of a woman.

Viet and John raced to the noise as the others followed at their heels. When they arrived at the center of the makeshift refugee camp, they found an eastern guard lying on his back, gasping for breath as blood seeped from the corners of his mouth and a gaping wound on his shirtless chest spewed blood just below the ribs. He had been stabbed in a lung.

Several yards away, Bryan Murphy was slumped over from the tree to which he was tied, blood seeping from the severed aorta where his throat was cut. His opened eyes didn't blink as they stared ahead at nothing in particular. Sally kicked in the mud, not far from the dead hostage: her face bloodless, her lips blue, and her eyes yellow. Blood and bile flowed from her lower back—behind a kidney. Viet unfastened buttons and bindings as she turned the woman on her stomach while Dr. Graves tore strips from his shirt and stuffed them into the wound.

As the injured woman stopped thrashing, Viet stroked her hair and otherwise spoke to Sally with soothing words.

"Sally, what happened?" Viet asked.

Sally's legs quivered and her eyes were wild from pain as she choked out her reply through terrible anguish. "Save my daughter."

"What happened?"

"Swear it."

"What happened?"

"Swear."

"I'll do what I can," Viet said, "I promise."

"Take her ... to my sister ... in Michigan."

Viet said he would try.

"God have mercy ... on my little girl," Sally whispered with a hoarse and weak voice, "and forgive us ... this foolishness."

"Tell me what happened."

"The woman ... I warned you about ... told your guard ... she had to use the latrine ... so he untied her ... but she had a knife ... She cut him down ... told us shut up ... or die."

Sally paused to take a breath. Her eyes started to roll to the back of her head before she snapped her head and awakened herself.

"She cut Jake free," Sally said. "When she stabbed Bryan ... I screamed ... I tried to roll away ... but Bryan never had a chance ... He was tied up ... They ran ... when they heard ... you coming."

Sally choked from pain and Viet wiped her cheeks and looked to Dr. Graves—who gave a grim shake of the head to answer the unspoken question.

Viet whispered a few final words into Sally's ear before calling several men to follow him to a gully beyond earshot while Kit and others comforted the dying woman with promises and prayers.

At the gully, Viet explained there was a time for war and a time for peace as he tucked a knife into his belt, slipped a lighter in his pocket, and picked up a long-handled ax. After giving instructions to his wife and kissing his daughters, Viet spoke privately with John, strapped on the gunner's helmet found on Roanoke Island, and marched into the woods. Early evening shadows already were long as dusk descended to cover the mud and blood of a terrible day.

Dr. Erikson stood in a light rain before every remaining member of the camp, except three teenagers posted as pickets. Her clothes were soaked and she stood before the citizens of Paradise with fallen hair and unshaven legs. Her shorts were ragged and her face gaunt. No fire was lit and most of her features were obscured in the gloom of a dark night. Only those standing near the psychologist saw her dirt and despair.

"Viet has gone to make war," Dr. Erikson said, "and our truce will be broken. We're all going to die for his sin if we don't make peace now. We don't have any more time. We need to figure out the root causes of this war and resolve them in a hurry. Before it's too late."

"It's the natives," a thin-faced easterner said, "and our refusal to admit the northerners might have been right about them all along."'

"Right about war crimes?" John stood to protest, his voice angry and pained alike.

"Not war crimes," the eastern man replied, his voice just as angry, "but war itself."

"I was there," John said. "We're talking about rape and murder after the battle was over."

"What could anyone do with such people?"

"We could have brought our people home and left the natives as they were."

"That's unrealistic."

"And we could've distinguished the good from the bad."

"They're all bad."

"Or at least separated their leaders from their followers."

"This is going nowhere," Dr. Erikson interrupted. "We're talking in terms of good and evil, absolutes and universals. That's not our way."

Everyone quieted down as Dr. Erikson continued.

"The fact is," the psychologist said, "they did what they thought expedient and we'll do what we think best. It's insane to talk of right and wrong or justice and injustice. I don't know whether there are such things or not. But I do know this: we need to look at this situation logically and rationally before it destroys us all. We haven't much time."

Still, no one else spoke.

"Life is choices," the psychologist continued, "and we need to choose now. There's no use hashing out history when the future is imperiled. Agreed?"

Several voices assented.

"The northsmen," Dr. Erikson said, "have their own choices to make and they'll do as they want. What we have to do is present alternatives that secure our needs."

Everyone waited to hear Dr. Erikson's plan.

"Viet's going to war," the psychologist said, "and we can't stop him. He's already gone and will be an outlaw in the sight of Donovan. So we must choose whether to join him—and he could be dead already for all we know—or to break from him openly so we don't go down with him."

Murmurs sounded from the assembly.

"Personally," Dr. Erikson continued, "I don't like what's been done to the natives, but none of us are under any obligation to die for some gods-forsaken cannibals. I'm not judging them or their lifestyle, but they're not allowed to judge mine either. Cannibalism or vegetarianism are choices. So is war or peace. And charity or self-interest. I don't want to sound heartless, but those people will have to defend themselves just as we're fending for ourselves."

Several women clapped.

"I'm fighting with Viet," John declared.

"Then you'll die with Viet."

"At least we'll die with honor."

"There's no honor here," Dr. Erikson said. "That's a quaint concept used to motivate draftees and subalterns."

"If you make peace with them," John said, "they'll make you do things you'll regret the rest of your life."

"Not nearly as much as I'll regret having my throat cut and having no life to despair. I don't see much glory in Sally's death, do you?"

"Maybe not," John said, "but there's certainly no honor in scurrying into the dark like a cockroach."

Dr. Erikson dropped here eyes, but said nothing.

"You've all forgotten," Ryan now spoke, "they have Maria and the others. Unless we can kill them in one raid, we can't fight at all or four more of us die. We have to sue for peace and hope for the best."

"I agree," Dr. Erikson said, "but what about Viet?"

"We have to warn Donovan he's on the march," Ryan said with a low voice as he stared at the ground.

"That's treachery," John turned to Ryan, his face red with anger.

"Viet," Ryan said with a subdued tone, "committed treason when he went to fight on his own authority."

"After they killed three people by a ruse."

"Who's to say what happened?" Dr. Erikson shouted.

Now Linh broke into tears and ran from the meeting while John tried to rally the islanders to war.

"By a show of hands," John cried out, "how many of you will fight? How many of you want to save yourselves?"

Only a few hands raised—all of them from the west village.

"All right," John conceded, "you win. I can't fight without you. All I ask is we don't disarm ourselves until we've got an agreement. When Donovan comes in the morning, I'll talk to him and see what we can work out. If he'll at least talk, I'll do what I can to get our hostages back and make peace."

"That's reasonable," Dr. Erikson said, "all any of us are saying is to give coexistence a chance."

Ryan also agreed to delay offering reconciliation terms until morning and Dr. Graves suggested sworn affidavits be drafted regarding the legality of the killing at Roanoke Island—with Ryan and Donovan being authorized to draft a legal deposition that both preserved the integrity of allied villagers and secured the interests of the northsmen as much as possible. When John observed that they'd be forced to lie, Dr. Erikson argued truth was a relative concept and a far greater good would be served by progressive legal fictions than absolutist moral truths. She pointed out not only northsmen and islanders, but even the cannibals themselves might be spared additional casualties by a single lie.

Public opinion swung to her side and the majority voted that Ryan should draft a document that could be ratified by the entire community—a document that would protect everyone in case of legal repercussions. It was believed such a legal framework might allow the natives to be returned to their ancestral home and the exiles to the state of Paradise. Donovan was to be allowed to do as he wished with the bodies of the dead cannibals as long as he promised to stop the killing and free all hostages. The proposal was signed by everyone in the camp except western holdouts and underage children—and even Ryan voted to ratify it as the only way to save Maria's life.

The rains ended with the meeting and Dr. Erikson immediately ventured into the forest waving a white flag and shouting for a northern picket. In time, a tall Asian girl emerged from the forest and received the offered terms. She was warned that Viet had left without legal authorization and might pose a threat to the northern village. When Dr. Erikson asked that Viet be spared for the sake of the day's truce, the northern girl just cursed the psychologist and sprinted north.

43

REFUGEES AND REPUBLICANS

A s Kit dozed under open sky—covered with a wool blanket that she shared with the baby boy cradled against her side —a hand cupped her mouth and pressed so hard that Kit barely could breathe.

"Shhhh," John whispered. "I've got the girl. In five minutes, bring the baby south. If he cries, say he has colic or something. Bring everything he needs. We aren't coming back. Five minutes."

Without waiting for a reply, John slipped past a dimming fire and hurried toward the south perimeter while Kit stared at the moon—which remained nearly full and whose reflected radiance would endure several hours more before vanishing into the light of day. Kit pulled back the wool army blanket and embraced the baby who slept beside her, an empty bottle of goat milk dangling from his lips. She stroked the dark hair of the cannibal's son and he smiled through his sleep so that Kit saw his toothless gums. Afterwards, Kit counted to one hundred and sat up. The child was limp from exhaustion and hardly stirred as his adopted mother swaddled him in the blanket. Kit stepped into a nearby tent where she searched for one nearly empty and two full canisters of baby formula that she threw into a canvas bag along with her last bottle of goat milk, a spare baby bottle, and an extra pair of rubber pants—pressing the bag between breast and the blanket-wrapped baby as she stepped back into the night.

Kit walked south as she threaded through tents and bedrolls of sleeping refugees while holding the child to her bosom. One man opened his eyes and looked straight at her, but she put a finger to her lips and pointed to the baby. The man dropped his head back to earth as Kit feigned disinterest and pretended to be an exhausted mother fussing with an infant. She was an accomplished actress and the ruse succeeded.

A moment later, Kit reached the perimeter bunker where Linh waited to help her neighbor climb the wall—with Kit delivering the child to Linh when the latter was atop the berm. Both women slipped outside the perimeter and neither made much noise as Linh led Kit through a field of booby traps that guarded the camp: each hidden pit marked with a tall stick that Linh removed as soon as she passed the trap. Soon, the women followed a narrow streambed down the east side of Mt. Zion.

Only after several minutes did Kit dare whisper to her rescuer. "Who? What? Where?"

Linh placed a finger to her lips and they walked another five minutes until they came to others hidden at the base of a treeless crop of rock. John carried a full backpack and held an unsheathed ax as he watched for danger while Tiffany stood guard near the children —who shared wool blankets as they rested. Kit noticed for the first time that Linh carried a sharpened lance.

"We're leaving the island," Linh said. "It's your choice."

"Anywhere," Kit said, "away from these savages."

"Donovan or the cannibals?"

"Does it matter?"

Linh said that it didn't and Kit agreed with her.

A short time later, the children were roused from sleep and John led the small party further down Mount Zion. After a while, they came upon an overgrown trail and followed it east. No lantern was lit, no flashlight was carried—not even a match was struck as they moved along the dark trail, communicating via whispers to keep their column close. Kit carried the baby and Linh shepherded Brittany while each of Linh's daughters took a twin by the hand and Lisa helped Tiffany stumble through the dark. The column of refugees spent hours descending the hill, taking a break only when the baby finally fussed.

"We're safe here for a few minutes," John said.

After Kit prepared a bottle of goat milk, John sat beside her to watch while she gently nudged the bottle into the child's mouth until the baby began to suck on the rubber nipple.

"Good job with the baby," John said. "I didn't hear a peep."

"He slept."

"I was afraid to bring him, but ashamed to leave him behind."

"Where's Viet?"

"He's making preparations."

"What's the plan?"

"We'll take the LCVP and a boatload of supplies to Roanoke Island. Jose has an emergency transmitter and batteries to signal for help. We'll try to extend the antenna range and fix the broken radios, if we can."

"You were the picket up there?"

"Yeah," John said. "I volunteered."

"Then we left the others defenseless?"

"For a while," John said. "It's Viet's job to confirm the northerners stay in their beds tonight. When we get to the boat, we'll raise the alarm. I was off duty a few minutes ago and set a clock to awaken my replacement. He should be on duty by now. Probably cursing me as a deserter."

"They'll be," Kit said as she dropped her eyes, "completely at the mercy of the northsmen."

"That's what they wanted," John said. "Besides, their best hope is that Donovan will realize he can't reach us, so getting rid of witnesses won't help him. It'll just make his guilt greater."

"Where's Ryan?" Kit asked as she sat up, her eyes wide and mouth open.

"We couldn't find him."

"He's not in camp?"

"They said he left after dark."

"Where?"

"I suppose to get Maria."

"We should've waited for him."

"Linh spent hours searching."

"I can't leave him," Kit said. "He was my husband."

"Don't worry," John told her. "I left a note in his sleeping bag. If he wants to leave, I've given him a rendezvous point and a signal. I'll return tomorrow night to get him."

"That's good," Kit said as she wiped her eyes.

"I told him to bring Maria."

"If they release her."

"Yeah," John nodded, "if they release her."

As the baby stopped feeding, Kit set him over her shoulder—patting his back until he burped. Even in the dark, she could see his head bob and eyes roll in a determined effort to stay awake. The child failed to do so and soon was nestled in a sling that pulled him to the underside of Kit's breasts.

A few minutes later, John returned to his place at the head of the column and led the band of escapees through the forest.

VIET HALF-CARRIED and half-dragged four large jugs of fresh water across the beach. Several crates of food and two containers of medical supplies sat near the LCVP and two goats with snouts tied fast and bells removed were tied to the handle of the largest crate. Three shovels, two full-size axes, three hand-axes, a machete, three tins of matches, two large tents, a stack of wool blankets, several steel pots, a fishing net, fishing tackle, folded visqueen, spare clothing, and even a small sailboat were collected nearby. Viet lined up the water jugs and dropped a backpack beside them before jogging up the beach—reaching his destination a few minutes later.

When he reached New Plymouth, Viet turned on a flashlight and entered a supply tent where he collected three broken radios, four spare batteries, an emergency transmitter, two lanterns, spare flashlights, a large antenna, a coil of wire, and an electronics tool kit. The equipment was secured in a waterproof bag and placed in a canvas sack before Viet switched off his flashlight and left the tent. His hair now soaked with sweat and his neck sore and stiff, Viet removed the steel helmet that protected his head—dropping it along the trail as he hurried for the main beach.

At the beach, he collected two five-gallon cans of diesel fuel, carrying one in each hand after slinging the canvas bag across his back and dragging his load past a charred hut, a burned-out shed, and litter scattered across the main trail. Discarded goods marked the path to the flagpole that once denoted Paradise—a pole now toppled and obstructing the road to New Plymouth. Viet saw the charred remnants of the flag of Paradise (burned out in the center and singed along its frayed edges), but made no effort to walk around it as he passed. Rather, he trampled the flag into the mud as he carried one five-gallon can of diesel to top off the LCV and a second as a spare.

After fueling the landing craft, the western scout sat down, having decided not to drop the gate until the others arrived. The loud reverberation of the door might alert northern patrols to the escape attempt and Viet wanted to give no more notice than absolutely necessary. When he last spied on the northern camp, the northsmen were still partying and there'd been no torchlight on the hill since that time. Still, it wouldn't do to be careless with the lives of family and friends staked on his every move. Viet opened a water jug and drank straight from the canister, careful not to spill any. If the boat sailed off course, they might need every drop to survive. After quenching his thirst, he jogged back to the base camp where he found four additional five-gallon jugs, filled them from a nearby stream, and lined them near the other supplies.

Now Viet was prepared to escape.

It wasn't long before Viet heard sounds coming from the forest. Slipping a long knife into his belt and picking up a sharpened machete, he crept toward the noise. When he reached the trail, he crouched into the shadows and began to crawl forward, closing the distance in a matter of moments.

After a few seconds, Viet sighed from relief and showed himself.

"Daddy! Daddy!"

Both of his daughters raced from the column of refugees. The dark was ending and the girls recognized their father even through the murky dawn.

"Not so loud, girls," Viet said. "It's not safe yet."

John stepped forward and greeted Viet with a handshake. "Everything ready?"

"Everything's here," Viet said. "I've got Molotov cocktails and arrows soaked with kerosene inside the boat. We can fight them off."

"I'd rather not. Let's just get out of here. You got lanterns?"

"Both oil and battery—and three working flashlights."

John nodded his approval before signaling the others to move closer and pay attention. "We're going to load the ship, then we can ..."

Crack.

John froze mid-sentence as every head spun toward Mount Zion. The unmistakable sound of a gunshot had echoed from the summit. A second shot was fired, then a third as John spun toward Viet, fear in his face.

"We don't have much time," John cried out. "Fire it up."

The deep echo of a conch shell sounded from Mount Zion even as John herded the refugees toward the supplies and Viet ran toward the landing craft. It took both men a minute to get into position. While they moved, sporadic gunfire continued atop Mount Zion—though it wasn't clear whether a battle was being fought or prisoners massacred. In either event, everyone hurried to the boat.

"Nuts," Viet said after he jumped into the driver's seat and turned the key to no effect. After a second unsuccessful attempt, he lit a match and looked under the panel—only to see that every wire had been cut.

"God help us," Viet shouted, "they've cut the wires."

"You said you checked them," John said, his tone exasperated and confused. "You said they were good."

"They were fine yesterday, but now they're spaghetti. Donovan must've cut them when he raised the ramp. The ramp was dropped too, but you can see that someone lifted it back up."

John looked up the hill and saw that several lanterns had started down the slope. "We've got to leave," he said out loud.

"This boat's not going anywhere," Viet shouted.

"We can't fight them here."

"We can't stay."

"What about the motu?" Kit asked, fear evident in her voice. "Can we get to one of them?"

"That'll work," Viet said. "It has to work. It buys some time."

"They'll come after us," John said.

"We can fight them on the beaches. At least we'll have a chance."

Now Viet dashed for the large rope that anchored the LCVP to a wide palm tree standing perhaps thirty yards inland. With a single swing of his machete, he severed the rope, then ran toward the water.

"Get the sailboats," Viet shouted. "Load what you can. One boat for the children and the other for supplies."

John did as told and Kit followed his lead while Lisa kept the children huddled together and Linh ran to help her husband. Together, the couple tried to push the LCVP into deeper water, their backs straining against the boat and their legs pushing hard against shifting sand. The craft moved just a few inches with every push and pull of the waves until it spun to one side after several minutes—its ramp finally positioned over waist deep water. Only then did Viet order Linh to stand aside as he climbed into the hold. A moment later, the steel door crashed before the waves and the hold flooded as Viet stumbled out of the boat and waded to the shore.

Meanwhile, John and Kit dragged two sailboats (including the craft near the supplies) to shallow water and began to fill the larger one—with Lisa's help—with previously stacked supplies. After Viet reached the sailboats, he insured that the most critical items were packed on one boat while Linh helped Kit load the children aboard the other. Already, twenty minutes had passed since the last gunshot was heard and the bobbing of lights down the slopes of Mount Zion was closer.

"They're half-way down the mountain," John said. "This is packed the best we can. Everything else can be replaced or picked up later."

"What about our people?" Viet asked. "It's going to take two trips and we don't have much time."

"Here's what we'll do," John said. "You and Linh take the kids and Tiffany. Kit and Lisa can come with me to the west village. We'll pick up more supplies and meet you at the beach later this morning."

"I can't sail," Viet objected, "but I can fight. And I've got my weapons and traps in place. I can hurt them worse than you can."

"You also have children."

"That's why I have to fight," Viet explained. "For the lives of my own children. They'll be slaughtered if the northsmen get near them. I'm a father and I intend to keep Donovan's marauders from my daughters."

When John started to protest, Linh waved him off.

"Viet's right," Linh said. "You and Kit need to take care of our children if anything happens. We trust you. Meet us at our old beach as soon as you can. We'll decoy the northsmen while you make your escape."

"John and I," Kit said as she stepped forward, "should ..."

"You," Linh interrupted, "have a baby and a toddler to care for. Your place is with them. My daughters are older. They can survive without me."

"Only in body," Kit said.

"It was their bodies I gave birth to and right now that's enough for me. There's no other choice."

"I'm expendable. You're not."

"Listen," Linh said with a stern voice as her eyes moved between John and Kit, "I can't sail and neither can Viet. Both of you have spent years sailing and can get these children—all of them—to safety. Now's the time to act."

Kit no longer objected.

"I'm staying too," Tiffany said, finally awakened from her stupor and despair. "That'll make room for more water and supplies for my boys. Besides, I can't sail and that boat will only hold one adult with all these kids."

"Me too," Lisa said.

"We can't leave all of you here," John protested. "Let's dump the supplies and go."

"You're clutching straws," Viet said, "and you know it. We'll starve on the motu without the supplies. They're our only real chance. They're the only chance for our children."

"Northsmen will be here in twenty minutes," Viet said as he pointed to the lanterns, now just above the tree line as they neared the base of the slope, "and we need you to guard our daughters. Get them to safety while we lead the northsmen south. God willing, they'll never see where you went if we can keep them off that mountain for a few minutes. All you need to do is land on the far side of the motu. As long as we keep moving, they'll never catch us. Bring the boat back at noon to pick us up—if we're standing in the clear."

"They'll see us and follow."

"They won't follow," Viet said, "without boats."

"Make sure you destroy all of them," John said. "Beyond any chance of repair."

A moment later, neighbors said farewell with hugs and kisses. Viet and Linh gave tearful final instructions to their children and Tiffany sobbed as she hugged her twins—pleading with them to remember the courage of their father. All three parents begged John and Kit to take good care of their children if anything happened, then pushed the two sailboats into the surf: Kit sailing one boat and John the other. The three women on the beach found hand axes and ran toward the line of boats moored just beyond the reach of high tide while Viet picked up a can of gasoline and waded toward the half-sunken landing craft.

As their sails lifted with wind and pulled the heavy-laden boats south, John and Kit watched the women hack through the thin fiberglass skins and aluminum frames of two overturned kayaks and one large fishing boat. They also watched Viet set ablaze the half-sunken cab of the LCVP and two overturned wooden rowboats already shattered by ax blows. By the time their sailboats turned west along the south perimeter of the island, Lisa already had fastened her long hair into a loose ponytail and now remained on the edge the beach—waiting to be noticed—as gulls circled over the path to New Plymouth where Viet and two women marched north.

A blood red sun rose from the east.

44

RESISTANCE AND REPENTANCE

Lisa waited no more than five minutes before she heard shouting from the main trail. She inspected her backpack one last time, checking its canteen of water, box of raisins, chocolate bar, rye crackers, and peanut butter. Sufficient calories and water existed to run for hours, if necessary. Then she tightened her shoelaces and adjusted the elastic-banded jogging shorts that hung loose on her hips. She pulled a green tee shirt over her head and stuffed it into her backpack—which she dropped behind a bush. Finally, she flipped her watch for an easier read and slipped into a shadow. There, she scratched her naked chest and tugged at tangled underarm hairs while she waited for her pursuers to arrive.

She didn't have to wait long.

In less than a minute, Father Donovan came from the forest with a man to each side. Two women followed them. One was buxom and short while the other was broad-hipped and tall and neither looked to compete in a foot race—which meant the contest was between Lisa and the men. Lisa remained crouched behind brush until the northerners were beyond tree cover, then sprang from the shadows to grab her pack. Once she jumped, she moved fast—stirring as much brush and sand as possible. Two nearby gulls squawked and flew away as the young woman grabbed her bag and turned south.

By the time she was at a full run, Lisa knew the ruse had worked. Donovan and his comrades sprinted toward her, shouting and waving weapons as Lisa ran into the woods—careful to run at a pace that would neither wind her nor deter her pursuers. Her legs were strong and breath deep and she couldn't lose this race if she ran it smart. She deliberately splashed mud and broke branches to keep her foe on her trail. If the enemy really had a chance of catching her, the run might have been considered reckless or brave. As matters stood, it was only clever—for the young woman kept her lead without breaking a sweat.

Lisa jumped rocks and scampered over fallen trees nimble as a doe. Only when she came to the strewn bones of Alan—which someone had dragged a hundred yards down the trail (either to hide the body or feast alone)—did Lisa momentarily lose focus, slowing to turn her head and keep her stomach from exploding. The crash of a man's steps through the woods and his shouts for a gun brought renewed focus. Now Lisa sprinted down the trail until she turned a bend where the cover of brush was thick.

After this, Lisa made no more mistakes. She slowed when the northsmen lagged and sprinted when they ran. She led her pursuers past Alan's remains, down a wide lane, and toward the southernmost tip of the island. There, Lisa ran faster to avoid being cut off by a quick-thinking northsmen who might bisect the circle she was running—though she remained confident she'd brought the foe far enough south to allow Viet to move against the northern side of the island as planned. If John and Kit were fortunate enough to have rounded the tip of the island without being observed by any northern scouts, the west village might yet escape. Lisa had decoyed the enemy and now it remained only to save herself.

Lisa's strides soon grew long and the splash of mud less noticeable. Branches no longer broke when she passed and the occasional cobweb was left threaded across the trail. After she took a long drink and a short meal, Lisa removed her shoes so the very sound of her step softened. When she put an ear to the wind, she heard only distant shouts and eventually nothing at all. Only then did Lisa slow to drink water and eat an energy bar. Even if her foes guessed her destination, it'd take the winded northerners at least an hour to make the hike—if they were cautious. If they were careless, Viet would insure some never finished their journey.

Lisa's eyes filled with tears when she saw smoke atop Mount Zion. The refugee camp was destroyed and scavenger birds already circled the smoke in search of carrion. She thought of searching for survivors, but changed her mind when she remembered the distance of the climb and the danger of cannibals, reminding herself that the village had made its choice and must now live or die by what had been decided—just as the west villagers would live or die based on their decision to flee.

The young woman kept near the shoreline and under cover of trees whenever possible. Gulls squawked overhead and sea turtles lumbered across the beach as she jogged north, but she saw no northerners or other islanders. Once she reached the western beach, Lisa looked toward the motu where John and Kit planned to sail and now remained hidden, but decided against an attempt to swim the short distance for fear of exposing the location of her friends and endangering her assigned mission. Instead, she dug out a shallow hole in the shadows of a glade of ironwood trees and covered the hole with a bit of brush. Here was a safe spot to wait for the return of the others.

MORNING BROKE BEFORE VIET, Linh, and Tiffany marched through New Plymouth, destroying two supply tents and one supply building as they passed—dumping and scattering all food in order not to leave anything useful to the enemy. Though occasionally slowing to listen for movement to their rear, Viet kept the pace steady and used a compass to navigate the northern slope of Mount Zion. It took three hours to cover the short distance as they moved off-trail through the forest, frequently doubling back, setting traps, and trying to cover tracks. When they finally arrived at the outskirts of their own village, Viet scouted the looted and burned tents and barn for intruders before helping the women gather some of the abandoned provisions and finding a hiding place near the recycling area. He gave Linh his watch and told her to move to the beach precisely at noon, whether or not he himself had returned, explaining that John had promised to return precisely on the hour.

Viet himself marched north at the double time since less than two hours remained to complete the work he'd been assigned. He moved quickly past Turtle Beach and up the west coast until he came to the northern camp. There, Viet slipped into trees and looked for guards. During a final check to his rear, he noticed that a curtain of smoke now hung over the peak of Mount Zion, obscuring whatever horrors had occurred. Viet shuddered and refocused full attention to his mission. Dropping to his hands and knees, he crawled through the brush until he came within twenty yards of the camp.

The village looked empty.

Yesterday, it was full and Viet could do nothing for Sally's daughter—who sat disconsolate near the half-eaten body of her mother's friend. Now the camp seemed deserted as Viet peeked around the corner of the barn only to see two dead cannibals: their eyes open and bodies swarmed with flies. The bruised face of one native woman was splattered with dried blood and the throat of the other was cut.

Viet soft-toed into the camp, his weapon posed to strike. When he heard a cough from the longhouse, he moved to it. Reaching into his pack, he grabbed a Molotov cocktail, pulled a lighter from his pocket, and jogged toward the longhouse—hands trembling and breath short. He lit an oil-soaked rag stuffed into the bottle and nudged the door with his shoulder as greasy smoke burned from the bomb he carried.

A man slept on the far side of the room and two women lay near the door beside a young girl with uncombed hair and a mud-stained face. One of the women—a tall woman in her mid-twenties with matted blond hair—bolted upright as soon as Viet entered the building.

"A fanatic," the tall woman cried out.

As the man rolled for the spear at his side, Viet threw the Molotov cocktail at the wall. It shattered close to the northerner and sprayed the man's back and legs with burning gasoline. The man screamed and dropped his weapon as he sprang to his feet and bolted toward the door, where Viet slashed his arm with a machete as the northsman stumbled outside. Meanwhile, both women also jumped to their feet—only to find themselves trapped between fire and a hard-faced enemy who blocked the sole exit. They begged for quarter as the flames spread.

Near them, the little girl cried.

"Give me the girl," Viet shouted.

Though her compatriot clenched teeth and said nothing, the blond woman started to push the child toward Viet until the second woman—a thirtyish woman with wide hips and dark hair unevenly cut at her shoulders—seized the girl and pushed her near flames that already engulfed the rear wall and fanned across the ceiling. Smoke filled the room and the eyes of both women welled from tears as their throats choked and the girl cried.

"Let us out or she burns too," the dark-haired woman screamed.

Viet motioned for the child and also let the women pass. But as the first woman hurried through the door, he caught her ankle with his foot; the woman fell hard and her compatriot tripped over her as they stumbled through the door while Viet pulled the girl from the burning building.

Once the girl was safely outside, Viet turned back to the women —his weapon raised to strike.

"Where are our hostages?"

"Donovan took them," the blonde replied.

"Where?"

"To negotiate."

"All of them?"

"All of them still alive."

"Who's dead?"

"The men."

"How?"

"Chuck cut their throats."

"What about the women?"

"I don't know."

Viet clenched his teeth as he postured his weapon even higher. The woman talked faster.

"Donovan," the woman said, "wanted to keep Maria for himself but she escaped. And Chuck caught Jason's whore and her mother hiding in your village. I don't know what happened to them."

"I won't kill you," Viet said as his face darkened, "but I'll disfigure you for the rest of your days if you tell another lie."

Viet dropped the blade of his machete so it rested atop the nose of the dark-haired woman—who raised her hands in submission and talked.

"They were torturing them," the dark-haired woman said, "outside camp. I heard some screaming for a while. Chuck told me that they were dead."

"When?"

"A night or two ago."

"Where's Ryan?"

"I don't know. I thought he was on your side."

"What about the other girl? The Murphy's daughter?"

"She's dead."

"How?"

"She was fed to the cannibals."

"Son of a ... Why? Why would you do that?"

"Chuck said they were hungry."

Now the wounded northsman moaned as shock receded and his pain intensified. Both his clothes and skin still smoldered as he writhed and groaned just a few feet from the longhouse. Viet decided the man wasn't a threat and faced his prisoners, both of whom turned pale as they watched the burned man crawl toward the sea.

"Give me your feet," Viet ordered.

The women didn't move.

"Your word's worthless and I can't let you run to Donovan."

The women didn't move, so Viet raised his machete.

"One cut," he said, "across your heel and you won't run anywhere. If it was just me, I'd take my chances. But I have this child to protect and I gave her mother my word."

The women didn't move.

"Your last chance," Viet said, "I can make the cut small and clean or I can slash. Your choice."

Now the women turned on their bellies and straightened their legs. Neither woman cried out as Viet cut their right heels just enough to hobble them for a few days. As the women clutched their wounds, Viet used his lighter to set aflame every building in the village. Tools and weapons were thrown into torched huts—along with food packets and supply crates. Water jugs and fuel barrels were sliced open and dumped to the ground. Though some tents were left intact, one caught fire from a spark and two others were slashed to pieces. Viet even scooped sand into a pot of soup.

Ten minutes later, Viet stuffed medical kits into his backpack, picked up Sally's orphaned daughter, and jogged for the west coast of Paradise—where his rendezvous point south of Turtle Beach was located. Looking to the sun, he realized that little time remained.

JOHN AND KIT steered their sailboats toward the west side of a large motu and landed on a sandy beach. After hiding the children behind trees, John collected firewood and fruit while Kit pitched tents. Linh's daughters milked a goat and warmed a bottle over a low fire, careful to follow Kit's instructions not to burn green wood or smoky leaves. When the bottle was warm, the girls fed the baby while Kit prepared a late breakfast of coconuts and bananas—with Kit reminding everyone to be judicious with the fruit of the motu since their stay might last longer than anticipated. For that reason, John had picked only one coconut and three breadfruit for lunch, leaving most fruit hanging on the tree. After reviewing emergency escape plans with

Kit, John pushed one of the two sailboats into the lagoon while Kit prayed for his safety.

The wind blew against his sails until John paddled past the south edge of the motu, where the breeze filled the canvas and sent the boat sailing through the lagoon. As he sailed, John looked to his watch and calculated he'd arrive just a few minutes early, then scoured the coast for activity—where he saw pillars of smoke spiraling from the north and dark clouds of dissipated smoke hanging over Mount Zion. As the smoke rose heavenward, John offered a silent prayer for Viet. When he finally neared the rendezvous point near Turtle Beach, he saw smoke begin to billow above his own village. Someone was near, likely Viet pursuing a scorched-earth strategy.

John tacked toward the beach.

It was as he neared the beach that John saw a woman come from the woods, observing through his binoculars it was a half-naked white woman who waved to him. Probably Lisa. She jogged toward the rendezvous point where the main trail came from the western village. Much further south, two men hurrying along the beach pointed toward his boat, but John didn't care since they'd never close the distance in the little time that remained. As the woman approached, John noticed she had a child with her and prayed to reach shore fast.

Crack.

The muffled sound of gunfire came from the forest near the west village. A pause was followed by more shots.

Crack. Crack.

Crack. Crack. Crack.

Crack.

The last shot seemed to echo several seconds. John shuddered for his friends and sailed straight toward shore while fingering his ax. If anything happened, he would need to chop large holes in the boat. Better he perish than the northsmen be given an easy chance to capture Kit and the children. Kit would require a day or two to prepare their escape on the other boat. Or maybe help would come before the northsmen could build a raft to cross the lagoon.

The water grew shallow and the boat pitched in the small waves. The woman on the beach waved frantically as John raced into shore at full sail, turning the rudder hard and dropping his sails at the last minute to prevent the craft from running aground. As Lisa dragged a young child into the lagoon, John jumped into the water and lifted the little girl into the boat before pushing Lisa aboard and telling her to leave if she saw anyone else approach. John then grabbed his ax and started inland just as Linh came running from the woods, followed by two men—one of them waving a pistol.

John raced back to the boat.

Linh ran hard until she reached the surf and high-stepped into the waves—where John hoisted her into the boat even as the enemy fighters closed their distance at a dead run. As Linh rolled into the boat, John shoved the sailboat seaward, jumped aboard, and turned the sails to catch wind.

Lisa pushed both Sally's daughter and Linh to the floor even as the shouting from the beach was complemented with gunfire.

Crack.

Crack. Crack.

"Eeeeehhh," Linh screamed as a bullet pierced the fiberglass hull and struck her in the side.

John shouted for the women and girl to cover their heads—though Lisa ignored him as she plugged a hole in the boat with one hand and the wound in Linh's side with the other. They waited for more gunfire, but none came as Donovan fumbled to reload, then stooped to recover several bullets he dropped. By the time the priest was ready to fire, the sailboat had moved beyond pistol range.

John took the little girl under arm as he steered straight across the lagoon while Lisa nursed Linh. The stricken woman didn't complain even when Lisa stuffed a strip of cloth ripped from John's shirt into her gaping wound and pressed hard with her right hand to stem the flow of blood. Fortunately, winds were strong and it didn't take long to reach the islet, though the journey was slowed by the sluggishness of the sinking craft as water filled the hull despite Lisa's efforts to plug it with her left thumb.

With six inches of water sloshing in the hull, John ran the boat aground at the first suitable strip of sand—where he struck hidden coral and tore an unrepairable gash into the hull. With little concern for the sailboat, John jumped into ankle-deep water and lifted Linh from the craft, carrying her toward the shade of a tall palm tree as he shouted for Kit to bring a medical kit. But even though they packed gauze in the wound and wrapped it tight, the bandages soaked through as blood seeped from the bullet hole and color drained from Linh's face.

Despite her pain, Linh refused morphine and asked that her daughters fetch a bit of food before telling John to come close. Through gasps and groans, she explained how the west villagers had met at the rendezvous point and then decided to burn their own village. Lisa stayed with the northern child while Viet led Tiffany and herself inland. Just after they set fires, the westerners were ambushed by northsmen; Tiffany was stabbed in the neck while Viet countered the enemy with gasoline bombs and a machete—burning one northsman and slashing another before he and Linh fled. When Donovan pursued them, screaming threats and firing shots, Viet ordered his wife to flee while he made a last stand. Linh heard the firing of shots and then the cries of her husband. A moment later, she heard the coup de grâce.

It was then that Linh had reached the beach.

Taking a moment to catch breath, Linh told John that she knew she'd die soon and made him promise to care for her daughters since neither she nor Viet had suitable family. She begged him to stay with the girls wherever they might go until he promised to do so.

After John went to summon the two girls, Linh called Kit to her side for a few private words. Only when Kit swore to do everything asked of her (just as John had) did Linh close her eyes and fall silent, trying to endure without complaint what were increasingly sharp swells of pain as she waited for her children.

Upon their return, Linh's daughters wept and apologized that they'd found so little food, but their mother thanked them for their efforts and explained their father was dead, begging forgiveness for the foolish decision to leave the United States. Both girls forgave their mother with tears and touches as the latter explained she'd provided for their future—then prayed God to forgive her sins and protect her daughters. Later that day, John buried Linh in a shallow grave marked with a rough-hewn cross and tropical wildflowers.

45

COMING DOWN FROM A BAD TRIP

Tomas Morales cowered in a thicket of nearly impenetrable brush on the south slopes of Mount Zion. He was one of the few to escape after the northsmen fell on the camp and survived only because he was the southern lookout. Once the first shots were fired, Morales sounded the conch alarm and fled into the forest—taking with him nothing more than a machete—which he had used to cut through vines until he rested near a shallow stream in the south-central forests of Paradise. Exhaustion and anguish took their toll and the anthropologist didn't awaken until late in the day: thirsty, hungry, and sore. He crawled from the bush and lapped water from the stream like a dog. His thirst satisfied, he looked for fruit or edible leaves, but found nothing and now reclined against a tree to ponder his predicament. He was friendless and foodless, abandoned to a tropical hell, and caught between cannibals and criminals. It wasn't a situation he'd studied and he couldn't recollect any guidance from his dissertation committee.

After an hour, Dr. Morales heard the rustling of grass and the slosh of someone walking upstream. As the noise moved closer, Morales raised his machete to defend himself—though he remained hidden in the brush in hope the danger would pass him by. Soon enough, a half-starved teenager approached wearing nothing more than waist-length hair and wielding a stone knife in one hand and a piece of food in the other. She gasped at seeing Morales, but relaxed when he lowered his weapon upon realizing it was the girl with whom he had shared a bed on Roanoke Island. They looked at each other for what seemed minutes before Morales stood tall and the young native bowed in submission as she offered herself for the anthropologist's pleasure.

Morales refused her. Instead, he uttered the native word for food and rubbed his belly. The girl surrendered a half-eaten breadfruit which the scholar devoured in a bite, though the fruit served only to awaken hunger. He'd eaten half-rations for several days and the taste of starch stirred a ravenous appetite he'd never known before, so he requested another helping. When the girl said nothing, Morales repeated himself—this time with evident irritation. The native motioned for him to follow and he did so, watching for trouble and posed for self-defense. He stayed several paces behind the girl as he watched for traps and ambushes, careful to keep his eyes open and weapon ready.

After several minutes, they reached a small clearing south of Mount Zion where two other natives rested: a gaunt-faced woman shivering from fever and a bleary-eyed woman who appeared exhausted. The girl signaled her elders and they discussed some point of protocol among themselves before turning toward Morales and bowing to their new chief.

"When in Rome," Morales said as he accepted their homage, "worship Mars."

One of the women crawled close and rolled upon her back, pointing to her belly and motioning for the stranger to enter. The anthropologist didn't do so. Instead, he told her he was hungry and requested more food. The woman crossed the makeshift camp and brought back roasted meat. Upon inspection, Morales determined the meat was human, probably broiled over the fires of the east village and clear proof the natives could cook. It also was evidence the tribesmen ate flesh that didn't come from their own loins: a radical cultural shift that already threatened to compromise their customary rites of cannibalism. The anthropologist groaned at his role, albeit unwitting, in cultural desecration as he returned the meat to the woman—who ate without hesitation.

Cannibalism no longer shocked. Too much had taken place during the past few days for horror to stir and Morales rubbed his growling stomach as the sweet smell of the meat filled his senses. His belly gnawed and now his face contorted as he felt his stomach chewing through itself; the anthropologist grew hungrier with every bite the woman took.

"It looks like liver," Dr. Morales said, "and what's really the difference between a pig and a man? We eat pig's hearts and we implant them in men. We transplant men's hearts and we ..."

Morales stepped toward the woman.

"I've got to be consistent," the anthropologist explained to the cannibal women, though they didn't understand a word of what he said, "with my profession of cultural relativism. This is the true test—the final examination. If I can do this, I'll crush Western stereotypes for good. Shock scholarship fleshed out."

When Morales opened his palm, the woman placed the half-eaten liver in it and the anthropologist took the meat, smelled it, licked it, and finally took a big bite that he swallowed almost without chewing. The second bite went easier and he chewed a bit without gagging. Then a third bite was eaten and a fourth. By the time the liver was gone, the new chief was licking his fingers and enjoying the aftertaste of his rare-cooked dinner.

Now the anthropologist told the woman to fetch more meat. As she ran to do as told, he examined the two women who remained. The older one—who had a runny nose and a cough—was in her mid-twenties: wide-jawed, emaciated, and short. She offered herself to the anthropologist, but he passed over the sick woman for a roll with the teenager who'd brought him to the clearing. Morales was strong from the taste of human flesh and the reception of homage, so he also took the other woman after she returned with more food. She accepted him willingly, begging Morales to bless the seed in her belly so it might grow strong as a tree and bear meat for their tribe—which he did.

Afterwards, they collected their weapons and retired into the dark of the forest. Though Dr. Tomas Morales was a chief and god, his subjects were no less savage for being ruled by a renowned scholar.

THERE NO LONGER REMAINED A REASON FOR the refugees to hide since Donovan knew their position by the return of the sailboat. John strung fishing line tasseled with shells across strategic entry points, hoping invaders might trigger the line into sounding an alarm. While Kit wondered whether the shells worked more as wind chimes than an alert, even she agreed the alarm was necessary. In any case, the immediate advantage remained with John since attackers would both tire themselves and risk sharks by swimming across the lagoon while John could sail to any point of the main island at will. Assessing that it'd take the northsmen several days to fashion a boat, John decided to start the tasks of building a fort and manufacturing weapons only after a good night's rest. In the meantime, he kept several of Viet's firebombs and a butane lighter close at hand.

All seven children now rested in a tent, the older girls having cried themselves to sleep grieving for their dead parents. The twins slept noiselessly beside them, two little girls were paired in a bedroll, and the baby was swaddled in a blanket near Lisa—who was covered with a bit of canvas sail for the sake of decency and warmth.

John and Kit now sat on a blanket near a small fire. Both showed tear-stained and dirty faces from weeping over their loss: the death of Deidra and the disappearance of Ryan. They also mourned Brent and Tiffany—and many others. This was the first time since the outbreak of hostilities against the cannibals that they'd had sufficient time to reflect upon the catastrophe that had befallen Paradise and only now did they feel the depth of their sorrow. No longer consumed with food and fighting, they mourned and wept for those who had been lost until tears would no longer flow. Hours passed while they comforted each other without word.

Kit's shorts were torn to the hip and her blouse also was ruined. It had no buttons and was tied with a knot at the waist, the left side of the shirt little more than a tattered rag. She wore no bra and her breasts hung loose. Her legs were bronzed from three months of sun and her hair bleached blonder than before—falling flat and unwashed down her back. She sat upright, legs together, and toes toward the fire as she wiped away tears.

"I'm cold."

John—who wore a dirty, sleeveless tee shirt that mismatched his khaki shorts and dark boots—moved closer, rubbing his leg against Kit's thigh as she nuzzled her shoulder to John's chest and crossed her second leg over his, wrapping her ankle around his foot and laying a hand on his side. Only when John unintentionally brushed fingers against Kit's breast did she pull back.

Kit said nothing for a long time.

"Linh made me," Kit eventually said with a somber voice, "promise to raise her children."

"She made me," John looked surprised as he spoke, "swear the same thing: never to leave them. No matter what."

"She must have been delirious from pain."

"She was dying and she knew it," John replied, "but she wasn't irrational and she even refused morphine to keep her mind clear."

"I suppose you're right."

"Did she make you promise to raise them here?"

"Not here," Kit said, "but in America. She wanted me to get them back home."

"The same with me."

"We've both promised to raise them."

"I can see how we'd raise them together here," John said, "but if we get back, your home is Hollywood. I think I'm going to Nebraska to work for my brother."

"My place," Kit said as she looked at John, "is with these children."

"So is mine."

"And," Kit said, "I'm keeping the baby boy, if I can ... and any others who need a home."

"How can you raise all those children by yourself? And from Hollywood at that?"

"I can't," Kit whispered. "The only role I'll ever play again is mother."

"You may earn an Oscar."

"You really think so?"

"You'll have my vote."

Kit leaned on John's shoulder as he pushed a log into the fire with his food. They watched the flames rise and felt the heat.

"How shrewd," Kit said after a time. "She wanted us together."

"I think so."

"I mean, she wanted to fix us up."

"I just lost Deidra and you Ryan. I hope he's not hurt."

"I'm not saying," Kit said, "she was right, because it's too early for both of us. But it is what she wanted."

"I suppose."

"And we promised."

"People," John said, "would think it perverse."

"We've done nothing wrong—unless we betray a dying friend."

"These children will need two parents: both mom and dad."

"So what do we do?"

"We could raise them together, I guess."

"Not from the same house. I promised my grandmother."

"I guess we could marry."

"Is that," Kit asked, "a proposition or a proposal?"

John looked straight at the middle-aged blonde, who nodded once to make her intention clear.

"Will you be my wife?" John asked.

"Now?"

"Do you see any reason to delay?"

"No."

"Neither do I."

Now John looked into Kit's eyes and took her hands into his own. "Will you marry me?" he asked.

Kit nodded.

"Do you," John whispered, "take me as your husband before God?"

"I do."

"Then with God as our witness, I pronounce us husband and wife. Till death do us part."

John kissed his bride and gently squeezed her hands.

"Not here," Kit whispered, "not so near the children."

"You're right," John said, "but at least you can come closer and let me sleep beside my bride."

Kit nestled herself to her groom, their legs intertwined and bodies held fast. They talked a few minutes before contenting themselves with the quiet of touch. As the fire flamed and flickered into coals and ash, Kit looked toward the heavens and silently prayed—asking whether anything good could come from such a sin-stained world. Her prayers finished, Kit clasped the hand of her now slumbering husband.

On her honeymoon night, Kit twice rose to feed the baby.

THE DARK REMAINED deep as Ryan heard voices. He lay on his stomach, perhaps thirty feet from the trail to the immediate north of New Plymouth, in a shallow ditch he had dug with his hands and where he now was hidden beneath a dark blanket and piled foliage. Mud was smeared on his face and he didn't move at all—overwhelmed with regret that he'd failed to find Maria at the north camp during a day-long wait outside the camp in hope she might escape. By dusk, he had returned to New Plymouth and salvaged stale crackers from a discarded MRE, then found a wool blanket and looked for a safe bed down site. He chose a spot overlooking the main trail from behind thick brush—from which he could watch for his wife without exposing himself to northsmen or natives. After all, it'd do Maria no good if he were shot. Or eaten.

Earlier, Ryan thought he saw native children running through the forest, but he couldn't be sure and they didn't return. Now he fell asleep, cheek pressed to the grass and arms tucked beneath the warmth of a wool blanket. He was careful not to snore and occasionally startled himself awake from fear of too much noise. But no one heard him. The birds had quieted for the evening and only tropical insects made their presence known. A few bats circled above.

It was whispering from the trail that awoke Ryan. When he raised his head ever so slightly and squinted toward two shadows, he saw that the taller one resembled Father Donovan. When he cocked his ear toward the men, he decided that the man also sounded like the renegade priest.

"Chuck, you catch her?"

"I lost her tracks in the river."

"Where?"

"A stone's throw down the trail."

"We'll get her tomorrow, unless the heathens eat her first."

"That'd be a waste of a good woman."

"I agree," the man who sounded like Donovan laughed. "Some bodies are made for better things than buffet."

"Shhhh," the shorter man said as he raised his hand. "Someone's coming down the trail."

Ryan watched as the men crouched, then slipped into the shadows as someone approached. He listened as they whispered, but couldn't make out their words. Only when the stranger walked past the brush did Ryan see the men spring on the unknown person—the taller man striking at the stranger's shoulders and the shorter one at the knees.

A woman's scream sounded as the stranger fell. The shorter man raised a spear and drove it into a small woman who had been knocked to the ground and died without another sound. The spear was pulled and blood wiped in the grass as the two men discussed the kill.

"Nice hunting," the taller man said. "I didn't have to fire a shot."

"Don't waste them on the natives. It's your last magazine and we still have armed islanders to hunt down. We can take care of the cannibals with spears and knives. And the women."

"How many are left?"

"Let's see ... John ... a couple western women and their brats ... Ryan and Maria ... two eastern men and three southern women ... and Morales. Plus we have the nurse. And there's the deserter on Roanoke Island. Maybe a few more. Hell, I never knew half these people."

"That's at least a dozen," the taller man said. "Plus kids. Probably more."

"With six bullets."

"But if you take out John, we win. Morales is a scholar and Godson didn't even do his own stunts. He shouldn't be too much trouble."

"What about the cannibals?"

"We can arrange a heathen hunt when the real enemy is gone. They're not very smart about leaving tracks."

"We shouldn't have any trouble with them," the shorter man said. "Just string up Godson by the thumbs and they'll come sniffing for dinner. He'd make great bait."

"The performance of a lifetime."

"Good manners might require us to let the heathen have a few bites before we kill them. Last meal of the condemned and all that."

The men laughed before moving toward the beach while Ryan wiped sweat from his forehead and pressed his face into the dirt—hoping help would come soon.

THE DAY HADN'T YET dawned when Lisa sailed from the motu. She left a note saying she didn't want to take food from the mouths of children whom she couldn't in good conscience fight to defend—and so left Paradise with a sailboat, two day's rations, a box of matches, a blanket, two gallons of fresh water, and a compass. The note explained that the boat would be of no further use to John since he couldn't fit all the children and necessary supplies in the small craft for a voyage into open seas. The note also indicated that Lisa herself would return once she'd retrieved more food and an emergency radio from Roanoke Island. She thanked John and Kit for their kindness and reiterated that she really was the most expendable member of the party.

Kit wept when she read the note while John commended Lisa's courage, not only for this current mission but also for decoying the northsmen while Viet and the women freed captives and attempted their escape. After a time, Kit fixed a sparse breakfast and John fished until he hooked a meal-sized perch and speared a small crab, both of which Kit cleaned and cooked as John collected a dozen clams (which he threw into a bucket of water for future use). Meanwhile, one of Linh's daughters wept while thatching grass and her sister listlessly milked a goat until she filled a baby bottle. The four younger children cried for more food until Kit fed them stale flatbread. Only then were they satisfied enough to play along the beach: Theodore and Tyrone building sand castles while Sally's daughter and Brittany splashed water. Kit kept the cannibal's son in the shade since she was unwilling to risk sunburning such a young child.

It was noon when John heard the distant thumping of rotary blades. He immediately shouted that helicopters were coming and told Kit to pile brush and wood into three piles that he set ablaze using his gasoline bombs. They threw every stick they could find into the fires and the smoke rose high even before the helicopter reached the archipelago. By the time the reconnaissance helicopter approached from the east side of the main island—its reverberations only partially muffled by Mount Zion—John was calling for the children to find more wood while he broke off the branches of a dead tree and Kit threw sailcloth, oars, and even an empty backpack into the fires. The smoke soon grew thick and dark and it wasn't long before the signal drew the attention of the helicopter's pilots—who turned from Mount Zion for the west motu, banking hard as they reconnoitered the small band of refugees.

As John waved and Kit hugged the children, the pilot hovered a short distance offshore and gave a thumbs-up. When an emergency medical kit and food rations dropped from the sky like manna from the heavens just before the aircraft flew toward the horizon, John and Kit fell to their knees and thanked God for the United States Marine Corps.

46

A SWORD EAST OF EDEN

Prevailing winds were southerly and Lisa struggled to hold a course to Roanoke Island. She was miles further south than planned and was trying to tack north when she heard the distant whine of turbines. Though the helicopters were mere specks on the northern horizon, she knew American military forces had come. If she tacked northwest, she'd reach Paradise by nightfall—and with it both salvation and civilization. Lisa stared beyond the seas as she lowered her main sail and drifted in the swells of the sea—her face buried in her hands as she weighed options.

There was no good alternative: life in the United States was corrupt and the tropical paradise was a veritable hell. Pollution, militarism, racism and moralism plagued the old order while cruelty, lawlessness, poverty and oppression ravaged the new world—and the land itself was scarred after several days fighting. Lisa remembered the bodies and burning, the hatred and hysteria. She shuddered to think how many animals had lost homes: how many birds were driven from nests and how many insects were no more. It seemed everything human brought evil and exploitation in old world or new society alike. Their hopes had proved baseless and their idealism had been exposed as a childish fantasy. As she drifted in the warm water of the Pacific, the young woman wept until her tears dried and throat hurt. After a time, she took a drink of water and ate raw breadfruit as her boat continued to drift in the open seas.

Lisa looked south and wondered how far it was to Easter Island. They didn't eat people there. It was bad luck to have encountered cannibals—who'd ruined everything with the help of the northern druggies. Remembrance of the first weeks came to Lisa's mind: mornings of gentle rain, afternoons of caressing sunshine, and hours of natural love. Lisa felt her skin flush from the memory and her breasts warm. It'd been long time since pleasure stirred and she threw her tattered green shirt into the sea, then slipped from her shorts and tossed them overboard too—unmindful she'd polluted the ocean. The sun rained its warmth on bare thighs as cool breezes massaged warm breasts and long hairs on tanned legs tingled; and it wasn't long before her eyes grew heavy and she slept to the whispers of the wind.

When she awoke, the sound of military machinery was no more and the sun neared the horizon, so Lisa hoisted her sails and steered south, having decided to let the wind take her where it would.

A COUPLE HOURS after she first heard helicopters fly above the island of Paradise, Maria startled at the sound of a pistol shot and a burst of automatic gunfire that followed it. The young woman cleared the brush from her face and looked to the trail, hopeful that help was on the way. She couldn't be sure who was close and didn't want to be the last victim of Chuck's spear or Donovan's gun, so she remained hidden in the thickets.

Fifteen minutes later she heard a second burst of automatic weapon fire, this one followed by the shouting of a man who sounded like Ryan. When the shouting ended, she crawled from the brush and stretched: her legs cramped from confinement and skin sore from scratches.

She hadn't moved from the briars all night.

Maria looked at herself and frowned. Two days of captivity and hiding had left their mark: her arms and legs were bruised, her skin scratched, her shorts dirtied, her shirt bloodied, and her hair matted with twigs and leaves. She was filthy, but she was alive. She waited another twenty minutes before creeping down the path and it wasn't long before she heard the giving of orders and the sounds of shouting—and more helicopters buzzing over Mount Zion. Maria listened as one of the aircraft hovered for a moment over the forest, then continued toward the main beach. Just as she began to run, the young woman encountered pickets posted on either side of the path.

"Halt."

Maria stopped as a man in desert camouflage and carrying a rifle (pointed down) emerged from the brush.

"Go slow, ma'am," the man said, "and raise your hands."

Maria did so.

"You have any weapons?"

Maria shook her head.

"Stay there while we get the sergeant," the Marine said as two compatriots also emerged from the brush, one of them bolting toward the beach while calling for help. The other two men just watched Maria.

Sergeant Abbott soon approached at the double-time, accompanied by the picket and two additional Marines. When they arrived, two guards were standing in the clear as they eyed the captured woman.

Their sergeant wasn't amused. "What are you two idiots doing?" he barked.

"Keeping an eye on the prisoner," one of the two Marines said. "Should we frisk her?"

Sergeant Abbott sent two privates who arrived with him to scout ahead before dealing with the wayward pickets.

"Sergeant Abbott, what's wrong?" one of the pickets asked.

"You two are fools. What if she was a decoy? You'd both be dead."

"But ..."

"But, we already took one round and one shooter is dead. Not everyone is going to be as helpless and hapless as the last fool we captured."

"I didn't think ..." one of the Marines started to say.

"You didn't think," Sergeant Abbott said louder yet, "because you're a dead Marine and dead Marines don't think about anything at all. Now get your sorry asses back to the rear, both of you, and write your mothers letters of apology for being stupid and for being dead. I'll mail them tomorrow."

"But Sarge ..."

Sergeant Abbott snapped. "Move!"

The men ran to the rear and Sergeant Abbott ordered the remaining picket to find a forward post. Only then did he turn to Maria.

"I'm sorry for the bad language," the sergeant said, "but those boys are punishment for my sins."

Maria said nothing.

"I'll," Sergeant Abbott said, glancing at his boots, "have to check you before you can enter camp."

When Maria consented with a nod, the sergeant patted her down. Since she didn't wear much clothing, the procedure didn't take long and the Marine wasn't too intrusive. Afterwards, Sergeant Abbott radioed Lieutenant Howard for orders and subsequently repositioned his men on the perimeter before he himself escorted Maria to base camp—taking several minutes to reach the collection of field packs and supplies that delineated the furthest reach of American diplomacy and military power.

There, at an improvised base camp, Sergeant Abbott suggested Maria wash herself at the beach as he sent a Marine to fetch toiletries and rations. Soon, a squad of Marines gathered to watch as Maria submerged into the lagoon—snickering and oogling as they stared at the wet shirt clinging to her breasts and the dripping shorts sticking to her thighs.

"What're you boys doing?" Sergeant Abbott's drawl came from nowhere and the men turned around.

"Taking a break, Sarge," one of them replied, "till we get orders."

"I'll give you Marines some orders," Sergeant Abbott said. "I want you to move the sand from the left side of the beach to the right side and the sand on the right side of the beach to the left side."

The men stared at him.

"Do you Marines know your left from your right?" Sergeant Abbott snapped.

The men said nothing.

"Move the sand from left to right and right to left. Is that clear?"

"I don't see," one of the Marines replied, "no left or right here, Sergeant Abbott."

Sergeant Abbott used the heel of his boot to dig a straight line several feet across the sand. "This," he explained as he pointed across the line, "is the left side and there is the right."

Two Marines smirked.

"Move now!" the sergeant shouted and the men scampered for spades and shovels.

Within minutes, the Marines dug fast and furious into the sand while Maria watched red-faced, not knowing what to say as Sergeant Abbott removed his shirt and placed it around the young woman's shoulders—the shirt's tail falling to her thighs as Maria turned away to fasten the garment and the sergeant looked into the woods until she was done.

Only when Maria was dressed did Sergeant Abbott speak.

"I'm really sorry," the sergeant said. "Here, I found you a bite to eat. It's all warmed up. The best the Marine Corps has to offer right now."

Maria took the heated MRE and ate—and the sergeant with her. When she was full, she thanked him for his kindness and boarded a helicopter that ferried her to a ship cruising less than thirty minutes north. After receiving dry clothing, she returned Sergeant Abbott's shirt, along with a note expressing her gratitude for his graciousness and good manners. When she boarded the helicopter, Maria saw Ryan sitting at the foremost seat, so she moved to a rear seat and stared out a window. She didn't speak a single word to her husband during the short flight and requested separate quarters on the troop transport after they landed.

Ryan didn't object.

I\ was Sergeant Abbott who entered the bunker atop Mount Zion the second day of Marine operations, having jumped the four-foot berm and rolled to a firing position. He saw no enemy to engage—only a dozen bodies on the ground: lifeless, contorted, and buzzing with flies. Every race and gender was represented. The sergeant called for help and three Marines rolled over the berm, one of them with vomit dripping down his chin.

"Check these bodies," the sergeant said. "Make sure they're dead."

"What if they're alive, Sergeant Abbott?"

Sergeant Abbott thumped the Marine on the head.

Even through a kevlar helmet designed to stop a bullet, the man winced. "What was that for?" the Marine snapped.

"If they're alive, they're not dead. Call a medic. Execute your training."

The chastened Marine—indeed, all three of the young men —hesitated.

"Move!" the sergeant barked and the riflemen moved.

While his men checked for survivors, Sergeant Abbott scanned the camp for traps, then jumped the berm and began to scour the woods. In a matter of moments, he'd shouted loud enough for every Marine in the platoon to hear his command.

"Halt!"

Every Marine recognized the sergeant's voice and stopped—even the lieutenant nominally in command of the platoon.

"What's up, Sergeant Abbott?" the lieutenant yelled.

"I want every man," the sergeant answered, his commands both loud and clear, "to fix bayonet and prod the ground where he steps. I see patches of dead grass. Looks like traps."

A moment later, a corporal poked into a circle of yellowed leaves and found a hollow pit beneath. When he brushed away the camouflage, he saw a sharpened stake.

"Lieutenant Howard," the corporal shouted. "There's a pongee stick."

"We advance slow," Lieutenant Howard yelled. "Anyone who gets hurt answers to Sergeant Abbott."

The men moved through the woods searching for survivors and corpses—and found plenty. One man lay on the ground in rigor mortis, a noose tightened around his broken neck. Others had gun wounds or cut throats. Most bodies were fresh, dead only a couple days. In any case, it wasn't long before the corpses were collected and laid out in a long line. A quick count revealed twenty-five, plus four unmarked graves. The death count rose to thirty when one of the graves was found to contain a young couple buried arm in arm.

These weren't the only bodies discovered. Others were found along trails as the platoon swept inland, guarded by reconnaissance squads moving along its flanks. Survivors were far fewer in number. Beyond the man who had surrendered the first day and the Latino woman detained soon after, only a couple dozen survivors were located on the main island: three middle-aged women and a bag of rotted fruit were found in a cave on the south side of the island; a pair of fraternal twins was discovered clutching each other on the north slope; and three Polynesian women with bad teeth and an anthropologist were captured in a forest (one of the women suffered fever that might have killed her without medication and another nearly died from food poisoning caused by eating spoiled meat). In addition, a gray-haired woman in her fifties was found unconscious from a blow to the head and a petite Asian girl was discovered cowering behind a waterfall to the north of Mount Zion.

More ominously, three men in their twenties were captured with spears in hand—their bodies painted with dried blood—and accompanied by four women and five captive Polynesians, including three children. Two of the women walked with limps and assisted an unarmed compatriot who was badly burned. The spear bearers insisted on talking with an officer and subsequently told Lieutenant

Howard they'd survived a mutiny. Howard had them tied up as a precaution, apologizing in advance for any injustice. Sergeant Abbott told his men to treat them like American citizens, but didn't bother to apologize for the binding of hands with plastic ties and tape.

By day's end, the island was combed, infrared sensors were set up for night operations, and another dozen survivors located. Seven people came forward claiming American citizenship and five natives were captured as they hid in the brush (including two children). Every refugee or captive was provided rations and medical examinations before being sent to the beach for processing; names were checked against rolls of U.S. citizens and survivors offered a return to the United States. Not one of them opted to stay in Paradise. Shortly after dusk, survivors were choppered to a troop carrier—where most slept late into the next morning and begged seconds at breakfast.

The following day, the Marines rose at dawn and by midmorning several refugees had been returned to the island as village representatives to identify the dead while the Marines secured bodies in bags: the process taking the better part of the day. After a Sea King transport helicopter was used to airlift the dead to the carrier group for transport to Hawaii, refugees were returned to shipboard quarters and Marines to the tropical island—where Captain Bradford declared the island secure and gave permission for a cookout.

That evening, Marines feasted on fried fish and baked clams and drank palm wine, expensive champagne, and Russian vodka—drawing from food reserves discovered on the island. Some set rifles aside to scrimmage in the sand with a hollowed coconut while others found discarded fishing tackle and tried their luck in the sea. Officers mostly talked among themselves—though several eyed the enlisted men with noticeable envy since they themselves weren't permitted to fraternize with their subordinates or participate in the games. One particularly gung-ho squad of Marines even stripped to their shorts and jogged the perimeter of the island (though carrying loaded weapons per the orders of Captain Bradford). Meanwhile, officers discussed the terrible battles of the Pacific during which some of their own grandfathers suffered grisly combat and malaria-ridden campaigns on long-forgotten islands. Long past dark, Marines lounged on the beach, enjoying tropical fruit and talking about girl-friends, families, cars, bars, dogs, drink, and even a few churches.

Not one Marine failed to enjoy his (or her) night off ship since everyone, enlisted and commissioned alike, understood that a few pleasant hours in the South Pacific enjoyed at government expense wouldn't come again and soon they'd return to the close quarters of their troop carrier to continue a tedious voyage to Egypt for several grueling weeks of live-fire exercises planned in the desert for mid-September. Most insisted the gruesome task of digging up the dead was worth a couple days on a tropical paradise. Many younger men thought the island as close to paradise as a man might find in this world—though several sergeants insisted the island wasn't worth much to them without their wives and children.

CAPTAIN BRADFORD STIRRED a cup of hot coffee as he tried to remember the events of the sleepless days he'd endured. It was diffi-cult to sort out the fragments of memory and momentary glimpses of information as his eyes burned and thoughts drifted. He was still stir-ring his coffee and his memory when a soft-bellied naval officer with a star on his shoulder and a square-shouldered Marine with an eagle on his collar entered the briefing room. Each man was accompanied by an executive officer.

It was the admiral who told Bradford to begin.

"This is the down and dirty, sir," Captain Bradford explained. "Nothing prepared."

The admiral nodded.

"We've interrogated the refugees," Captain Bradford said. "I've had civil affairs and intelligence teams debrief them. What seems to have taken place, as best we can piece it together, is the island experi-enced civil unrest starting a couple weeks ago, possibly from a lack of food. It broke into civil war after they battled a tribe of cannibals who inflicted heavy casualties on the liberals ... I mean, citizens of Paradise. The north villagers claim they killed a dozen or so natives in open combat while others say some of the killing was done in cold blood. We exhumed the bodies and found a number of wounds consistent with the murder of prisoners. What a mess that was. There was one body that ..."

The admiral frowned.

"Captain," the senior officer said, "you can skip the gory details. Just put them in the report."

"Yes, sir," Bradford continued. "Anyway, the day after the battle with the cannibals, Captain Strong came to help, but was murdered —along with his family. Probably by some of the northerners. It was then that a full-scale civil war began: the northerners against everyone else. When the outlaws captured Strong's pistol, they gained the advantage."

Captain Bradford sipped his coffee.

"As best we can tell," the captain said, "an exile at what they call Roanoke Island escaped the fighting and a few refugees unwilling to accept a truce escaped to the western motu fearing ... what's his name again? Oh, Father Donovan. Sorry, sir, I'm so tired I can't think straight."

"Donovan?" the admiral raised his hand. "Wasn't he the crazy with the gun?"

Bradford said he was.

"Who was that first prisoner?"

"Ryan Godson."

"The actor?"

"The same."

The admiral looked perplexed. "I thought," he said, "Godson was the guy on the motu with Kit Fairchild. They said she was rescued with her husband and some children."

"Godson," Captain Bradford said as he shook his head, "left her for another woman, so she divorced him and married John Smith."

"Where's Godson's new wife? Dead or alive?"

"On the ship. No thanks to her husband."

The admiral leaned back and waited for an explanation.

"Her name is Maria," Captain Bradford said, "and she was taken hostage. The only thing that saved her was Donovan's ill will; her throat was too pretty to cut."

"Say no more."

"Don't worry, sir. She escaped before he could touch her, but she loathes Godson now. She's upset he never came to save her."

"He abandoned his own wife?"

"It's even worse than that—she's pregnant."

"Remember," the admiral said as he shook his head from disgust, "the accounts of Tutsi men deserting pregnant wives during the Rwanda massacres?"

"We're not," Captain Bradford said with a grimace, "supposed to judge others, sir."

"To hell with political correctness if you can't judge a coward by the yellow of his belly."

Everyone in the room laughed.

"Anyway," Captain Bradford continued, "when the refugees surrendered, the northsmen slaughtered them, except those who fled to the woods. They tracked down a few of them, but luckily we landed before they could find them all. We were briefed one hundred and two Americans came to this island and we found forty-eight survivors—with fourteen of them being natives. That includes those taken on the motu and the exile to Roanoke Island. Including Captain Strong and his family, we have sixty-five former Americans confirmed dead and seven still missing. We're told one woman sailed to Roanoke Island, but never arrived. We sent helicopters to search for her, but she's nowhere close—if she's still alive. Two of the missing were ordered to leave the fortified camp after they refused to fight and disappeared. No one has any idea what happened to them. There's also a toddler who probably wandered into the forest after his parents were killed during the battle with the natives; he hasn't been seen for more than a week."

"What's the chance he's alive? Or the others?"

"Not on this island. If they're alive, they aren't approaching our men and they've remained undetected by our patrols. Given how thoroughly we've searched this island and posted lookouts, I just don't see any more survivors being found. All of the missing should be presumed dead. Even the woman lost at sea."

The Marine colonel whispered a few words to the admiral and the latter nodded in response.

"Tell me about Captain Strong," the admiral asked. "Did you find his remains?"

"No, sir. The yacht was sunk in the lagoon, but not entirely submerged. Divers retrieved Commander Johnson's remains from within, but Captain Strong is gone. We did find some bones washed ashore that may belong to him or one of his crew. There wasn't much left after the crabs and birds took what the fish hadn't eaten."

"You've saved them for DNA testing?"

"Yes, sir."

"And you've confirmed both women are dead?"

"A shot," Captain Bradford said, "was heard and there's second-hand reporting from the north villagers—and no one saw either woman ashore."

"How many dead cannibals?" the colonel asked.

"Half of those brought to the island," Captain Bradford answered. "We found several others hunted down like animals and a couple eaten by their own tribe. But if we hadn't come when we did, the whole lot of them would have died of colds. One of them with Dr. Morales was just about gone."

"Why didn't he treat her?"

"He's not a real doctor," Bradford said, "only a sociologist or something."

"Did you get proper medical attention taken care of?"

"Yes, sir. A navy corpsman saw to them—and a baby with Kit Fairchild. He had the sniffles, but he'd never been exposed to any of our diseases before, so a corpsman put him on antibiotics and fluids."

"What about the dead soldier?"

Bradford's face went blank. "We didn't lose anyone, sir."

"I mean the sailor from the Second World War."

"Sorry, sir. We couldn't find a grave. We're guessing he met an ugly end."

"Any tags?"

"No, sir. Only a steel helmet."

"I'm sure," the colonel concluded, "the Pentagon will send a team to search for remains."

"It was his bad luck," Captain Bradford observed, "to end up in this area after being sunk. We guess he had blue eyes and left some progeny behind. Those who still survive, that is. The cannibals seem to confuse lineage with lunch. In any case, they thought the gods were sending more of his kind—which explains their willing reception of the liberals. They thought their prayers for food were being answered."

"So what do you propose that we do, Captain Bradford?" the admiral asked.

"That's above my pay grade, sir. I guess I'd call the Department of State."

"I talked to Secretary Powell not an hour ago," the admiral said, "and it seems we have an international incident on our hands. By landing U.S. troops on this island, its sovereignty returns to Russia: especially since the paperwork for transfer of possession and citizenship remains in process. This was still Russian territory. Technically, you conducted military operations on foreign soil. You killed a man on Russian territory."

Captain Bradford turned white. "Oh shit," he muttered before snapping to attention with an apology.

His superiors weren't offended.

"I said a lot worse to General ... I mean Secretary Powell," the admiral noted, a tight-lipped grin to his face.

"What do we do now?" the Marine colonel asked.

"We can't gather trial evidence," Captain Bradford said, "without further trespassing."

"That's a good catch," the admiral said.

"And we can't court martial them since we weren't at war," the Marine colonel added.

"Another good point."

"We have to let them go?" Bradford's words trailed off at the end of the last sentence, disappointment evident in his voice.

"What would you say if I told you a Russian trawler was headed this way to claim Russian rights?"

"I'd say we need to clear the island's territorial water."

"We're going to make you a sailor yet," the naval captain said while the Marine colonel faked a scowl.

"Oh," Captain Bradford said suddenly. "I see. These people committed crimes on Russian soil."

"That's right. They're not our problem. We don't even have to waste fuel choppering them back to Hawaii."

"Captain, your orders," the Marine colonel now said with a tone that allowed no disagreement, "are to transfer anyone you suspect guilty of war crimes or treaty violations to Russian custody. It's their jurisdiction, so they make the call."

"Aren't they U.S. citizens?" Captain Bradford asked.

"Not necessarily," the colonel said, "most surrendered citizenship when they swore loyalty to this new country. State says they'll tear up the paperwork on the guiltless, but process the forms of anyone we give to the Russians. These people aren't worth an international incident."

"When, sir?"

"We'll send a launch to the trawler when it arrives. Hand over any prisoners and have civil affairs prepare a report to share with the Russians. We'll need to let Washington take a look at it. Lawyers at State say they can interview witnesses back home."

"Yes, sir."

"Now tell me who we should send to the Russians," the colonel said.

"The north villagers," Captain Bradford answered, "we caught with weapons should be handed over and two of the northern women are suspected of torture. They had blood under their fingernails. I'd hand them over too. On the other hand, I think the draft dodger exiled to Roanoke Island was innocent enough and the clan we found on the motu were good people. Godson and his wife didn't do anything wrong, nor did most of the others we picked up—at least not as far as we have good evidence."

Both commanders accepted Bradford's judgment and the next morning five handcuffed northerners were transferred to a Russian fishing boat. Captain Bradford spent an hour explaining the situation to a neatly dressed Russian sailor who spoke flawless English. Both the translator and his captain were pleased with American cooperation and expressed little interest in returning additional prisoners to Russia— deferring to Captain Bradford's judgment regarding their innocence. The translator even permitted the U.S. Navy to return the native women to their own island, as long as they were given sufficient food to survive until their plight could be considered by international authorities.

On the other hand, the Russian insisted Ryan Godson sign paperwork admitting all relevant facts of the case and confessing a breach of contract so that Russian claims on the island and retention of initial payment alike would be guaranteed. Moscow, the civilian-dressed officer explained, had spent the surety and was anxious to nullify reimbursement claims against government officials who had profited from the sale. For that reason, the Russian civilian requested that Ryan sign a waiver forfeiting all rights in Russian, American, or international courts alike. The people of Russia, the well-dressed sailor explained, would pay no more bills for misbegotten socialism.

Though Ryan at first sidestepped the request by protesting that he had rights as an American citizen, he was warned by the Russian official that further protest would mean a slow boat to Vladivostok and by Captain Bradford that his citizenship remained in question per Department of State guidance. Still, it was only after the trawler's captain elaborated on the slowness of Russian justice, the cold of Russian jails, and the length of Siberian winters that Ryan decided not to quibble points or press his case.

Several hours later, the American fleet conducted burials at sea of dead natives and returned survivors (and the remains of their compatriots) to Hawaii. Thereafter, the Russian trawler transferred its flag to the island of Paradise and rechristened the archipelago Novi Mir.

Male prisoners were locked in the ship's hold while the crew (except a single guard found drunk at post the previous week) went ashore to party. Occupying torn tents discovered at New Plymouth, the Russians drank, smoked, danced and made friends of the captured women.

In fact, when the trawler finally weighed anchor, the women were no longer shackled and had sworn affidavits regarding the guilt of their male compatriots. In exchange for cooperation and companionship, the women were released in Anchorage—their purses stuffed with Russian rubles. As soon as the women cleared customs, they hurried to a medical clinic that screened for STDs.

Once they reached Russian territory, the northern men were warned that the Ministry of Justice had indicted them for war crimes and planned to impose ten-year sentences—advising the accused not to expect any surprises at their trial since Russian retention of the island depended upon their conviction.

The northsmen's appeals fell on deaf ears.

47

WHENCE? WHITHER? WHEREFORE?

Two nights had passed since Lisa turned south. She retained a week's rations and water supply, having filled her canteen from a cloudburst. Her freckled skin was tanned dark—except for her buttocks (which were so burned she couldn't sit). The winds pushed south and the boat sailed where it was sent. Lisa shuddered to think of missing Easter Island and ending up in the Antarctic—especially since she hadn't kept a single strip of clothing. That, however, was a problem hundreds of miles away. For now, she rummaged through her knapsack and found her last bottle of tanning lotion, dabbing just enough to block the sun. She didn't waste a drop. If the ointment ran dry, she'd suffer for sure. Lisa crouched to keep sore skin from the bright sunlight reflected from the sea.

It was high noon when the young woman noticed the indistinct rise of a distant island and sailed straight toward it, reaching the outcrop by midafternoon. As she drew near, she realized the island wasn't large—being no more than several acres of high slopes and narrow beaches perched over the sea and encased by a barrier of heavy surf. Waves broke hard across the windward side of the isle until they rejoined on the leeward side. After twice circumnavigating the island, Lisa knew there was no return from a landing. There'd be one chance to get in and none to leave since her boat would be wrecked in the rough surf.

Lisa looked south, seeing no other sign of land—or anything human—and sighed as she thought about her fallen world, old and new alike. She remembered the pollution and urbanization of America: the wasted energy and the redundant industry, the encroachment and exploitation of everything good. She reminisced over the gentle rains of Mount Zion and the soft sun of the old forest. She warmed with thoughts of nature's sweet ways and recoiled from the terrible recollection of murderous wars, barbarous cannibals, evil northsmen, and a turtle taken too young from the thin protection of its shell. She remembered Donovan and Jason, as well as Tiffany and Linh. She wept for Alan and the natives she had injured—and for butchered bodies and burned villages, forest fires and burning oil. She sobbed aloud for Hilary and realized the sunken yacht was probably leaking fuel into the white sands of the South Pacific: Paradise was polluted and spoiled. Lisa wept for generations of fish cut off, innocent birds killed, and needless suffering imposed on nature.

"Never again," Lisa declared as she wiped her eyes and strained to see the uninhabited and untended garden that would become her private sanctuary, "will I mistake nurture for nature and work for freedom. I'll not plant an Eden to be shaped by human hands but enjoy what springs from the earth itself. No planting, no tilling, no cultivation."

Now Lisa opened the sail to the full strength of the wind as she reached full speed and tacked for the island. The breeze was strong and her increased skill in sailing (after three days at sea) was evident as she hit the waves at a right angle—and the sailboat was flipped by a five-foot breaker just as Lisa pushed herself free. She heard the thunder of the surf and the snap of fiberglass as she was pushed underwater, striking sand and cutting her left hand on shards of coral before breaking to the surface and gasping for breath.

As a second wave broke over her, Lisa swallowed water as she swam for shore. After the wave passed, Lisa staggered to her feet and limped into the shallows where the froth of the foam washed her feet while she spit out water, caught her breath, and looked for her boat. All she saw were bits of fiberglass washed across the sand—along with cans of supplies and torn canvas. Everything else was gone.

The beach was perfect.

A narrow strip of sand circled the slopes of the hill and craggy rocks insured this was no place for human habitation. The island was large enough to support one or two people at most, but never a city, village, or even a family. There would be no factories, no villages, no pollution. Only those few things Lisa herself brought would make an impact on the environment and the young woman swore to bury them within the week. Neither she nor anyone else would ruin this paradise. There would be neither northsmen seeking plunder nor westerners seeking comfort. No yachtsman would bring guns and no helicopter would bring rescue. She herself would feast from the fruits of this natural paradise and recycle every nutrient her own body didn't require. If she were careful never to build a fire or raise a shelter, she'd always be housed by a perfect canopy of nature—its luscious innocence unspoiled by human greed or need.

Lisa smiled as she watched two gulls circle. Their nests would be safe with her and she hoped the birds might soon be her friends, living with her in a true symbiotic friendship. Now a large turtle lumbered down the beach and Lisa watched it slip into the sea without giving chase. It too might soon be her companion. No human malice had harmed the birds and beasts of this place and she expected—or at least hoped—to befriend them all.

A few minutes later, the young woman shimmied up a banana tree to pick two brown-spotted bananas—and ate the larger of the two without wasting the slightest strand of fiber or bit of fruit before returning the peel to its place below the tree that grew it—careful not to rob the ox of its grain—and saving the second banana for supper. Afterwards, she found water seeping from a crack in the rocks and drank from it until her thirst was quenched. Later that evening, she picked large banana leaves from a tree and lay them across her unclothed body as she beheld the glimmering of the stars on a clear night. Even in sleep, her pleasure didn't end. Visions of love fulfilled came many times and she slept late the next morning—worn from dreams and desire.

Indeed, Lisa woke only when the warm of the sun stroked her face, the first moment of her new life—life without hours or days, clocks or calendars. She didn't open her eyes right away, but enjoyed the caress of dawn on her face, the dew of the grass soothing her sunburned buttocks, and the gentle massage of her breasts at the soft hands of ...

Lisa startled as she opened her eyes. Her jump was reflexive when she saw an egg-sized spider perched on her nipple, hanging by an indiscernible thread spun into the heavens. The spider bit Lisa once before scurrying back to the treetops. The young woman groaned when she saw a drop of blood pool on her naked breast. Within minutes, her groans were repeated and her breast was swollen. At first, she had thought to kill her attacker, but almost immediately returned to her senses—knowing she was the interloper into the spider's kingdom. It lived here before she came; she was the trespasser. Now Lisa decided to find a coconut tree to collect oil to salve her wound.

She didn't go far.

Not fifty steps uphill, she came to dozens of webs—many of them several feet wide—strung between trees and bushes and rocks. Most were filled with the carcasses of dead insects, though larger ones contained the bones of birds and one even held fast the carcass of a rare fruit bat. Lisa shuddered when she saw the withered remains of an endangered species; she also quivered from pain since her left breast already had swollen to twice its normal size—the infected nipple bright from poison—and her chest itched and ached.

Knowing she needed to act fast, she took a deep breath as she squeezed poison from the wound until blood ran clean, then pressed harder to drain the infection as her chest throbbed and nipple stung. When she screamed from pain, a startled flock of birds flew away. Lisa lay down and nursed the wound until the swelling slowed and the pain ceased several hours later—knowing that the tenderness would last for days and wishing there was someone to assist and comfort her.

The spiders didn't care.

RYAN FLASHED a smile at the stylish reporter across the table. His hair was short and teeth polished and he wore a summer jacket with matching Italian shoes and tinted sunglasses. Cameras rolled and microphones recorded as a producer signaled they were live.

"I'm Marla Landover," the reported announced, "on the beaches of Waikiki with Ryan Godson—who has just returned from his mysterious quest."

The reporter flashed a smile at the camera. Her high cheekbones were perfectly framed by silky blond hair that brushed her collar and her lips were covered with a coat of ruby gloss that framed an ultra-white smile. Diamond earrings flashed from her earlobes, sparkling bright against the contrast of her dark tan.

"Ryan," Marla said, "today agreed to a multimillion dollar contract with an undisclosed motion picture company to tell the true story of his adventure in the South Pacific. The deal is one of the largest in Hollywood history and gives the studio rights to the story, as well as to Ryan's acting and directing skills. Ryan will even play, believe it or not, himself. Filming is scheduled to begin before the holidays and Ryan hopes to release the picture as a summer blockbuster."

The reporter brushed her blond locks behind an ear and held a cordless microphone. "Tell us," she cooed, "about your adventure. The world is waiting to hear."

"You'll have to wait for the movie, Marla," Ryan said after shaking his head. "It's going to be the true account of life in a tropical paradise."

"You have thousands of fans who can't wait, Ryan. And I'm one of them. You have to tell us something."

"Since even movies have trailers, I suppose I can tell you a few things."

"We're ready."

"I'm a father now."

The reporter blushed. "R-really? Boy or girl?"

"Actually, my wife's still pregnant and we haven't done an ultrasound. I guess I should say I'll be a father soon."

"Did Kit ever hope to get pregnant at her age? I'll bet she's surprised."

Now it was Ryan who looked embarrassed. "I don't think so," he said with a subdued tone. "Kit's not pregnant that I know of and she's no longer my wife."

"That is a surprise."

Ryan stopped smiling. "Kit and I," he explained, "parted company. We've both remarried."

"Who's the lucky girl? Will you introduce her to Hollywood?"

"Probably not," Ryan said, "since she's decided to return to graduate school and I'm not going to stand in her way."

"You'll support her and the baby while she attends school?"

"However I can."

"That's very sensitive. Women could use more guys like you."

"I do what I can."

The reporter tossed her head, to clear the bangs from her eyes as she asked whether Kit planned to star as herself in the film.

"Well, to be honest"—this question caught Ryan by surprise and now he stumbled for an answer—"I really hadn't ... I mean to say I never asked, but it's my impression she's given up acting."

"Kit Fairchild has given up acting? That is news."

"It is. All of us were changed profoundly by our stay in Paradise; some for the better and others for the worse. I don't think Kit's up to the challenge of acting any longer and—to tell the truth—I respect her for understanding her limits."

"You mentioned problems?" the reporter asked with a smile. "What happened on your island?"

"We learned a valuable lesson," Ryan said after a pause, "that even the most careful screening can't weed out every trace of fascism and conservatism and authoritarianism."

The blond reporter looked confused.

"The movie will give the details," Ryan explained, "but it's enough to say we suffered violence at the hands of militarists who joined us like wolves in sheep's clothing. When we were faced with a crisis, some of them turned to violence and oppression: right-wing violence and conservative solutions. Violence begat violence and brought war to heaven itself."

"That sounds horrible? Are you alright?"

"It was close," Ryan said. "I led one battle against armed warriors from a cannibal tribe and helped organize resistance to those who thought to mistreat native peoples."

"Real fighting? Like war?"

"I hated it," Ryan said, "but it was like a horror film—or maybe a suspense drama or historical epic. We fought for survival. They even took my wife hostage."

The reporter's eyes grew wide. "Your wife was taken hostage? Was she hurt?"

"She already sounds better."

"She's not with you?" the woman now chose her words carefully. "She's not here?"

"No," Ryan said. "Her mother is helping Maria through the pregnancy. I spoke with her yesterday over the phone."

"And she'll join you after the baby's born?"

"We'll have to see what's best," Ryan said, "my lawyer's still confirming whether we're officially married. The Russians possess our state archives and there's some question regarding the legality of our vows. To tell the truth, I'm not absolutely certain I'm properly divorced from Kit."

"When will you return? I'd love ... I mean, we'd like to send a reporter to watch you film."

"We won't be going back. We hope to film in Hawaii or maybe Tahiti. The Russian government claims we broke our contract by allowing Marines to land on the island. What were we supposed to do? Fight them? My agent is considering a lawsuit to recover our damages."

"Against?"

"Against the U.S. government."

"What about the Russians?"

"Probably not," Ryan explained. "They were within their legal rights given the illegal U.S. attack on a foreign state. That's why we signed off on the paperwork. That, and intimidation by the U.S. military."

Now a producer working behind camera waved until he caught the reporter's eyes—who then looked into Ryan's face.

"We have time for one last question," Marla announced.

Ryan told her to continue.

"Tell us one important lesson," the reporter said, "you learned from this experience and hope to communicate in your film."

"I suppose," Ryan said after a pause, "I've learned how fragile tolerance and diversity really are. The intolerance of our world is so difficult to escape. It takes education and deep social consciousness to make a transition from the old way of life to a new one. A few of our people weren't up to the challenge and ruined things for everyone else. It's the same problem we face here in the United States. And I guess I've also come to realize the best way for me to effect change isn't to live with a few dozen like-minded people on a tropical island, but to use the platform of stardom to reach as many people as possible. It's my obligation to produce movies that entertain and raise social awareness. That's how I can help to make America a better place to live. That's where my audience is."

When the interview was finished, Ryan invited Marla to dinner. Off-camera, he told stories of life in a tropical paradise: of the battle with the cannibals and his effort to save Maria from the northsmen. He also told how Maria had threatened to sue for child support and how he would stand by his child with whatever it took to insure the best schools and career opportunities—even though Maria trapped him into fatherhood, wasn't entitled to child support by the laws of Paradise (where the child was conceived), and had repaid his loyalty by corresponding with a Marine sergeant deployed to Egypt.

Marla was impressed with Ryan's decency and spoke of it throughout the night. The next day, she ordered breakfast in bed— believing it the very least Ryan deserved—then stayed over for the weekend after sending resort staff to purchase bikinis, bras, and women's boxers at a nearby boutique.

KIT DRESSED in a sleeveless cotton shirt with the top buttons unfastened and sweats that hung loose from her hips and bunched at the ankles. Her arms remained slender and strong (still a little tanned from the hard sun of Paradise) and her shoulder-length blond hair was wrapped in a loose bun atop her head, only a few missed strands falling behind her ears. She stood beside an ironing board, pressing wrinkles from a stack of clothing—her breasts dancing and hips swaying to the rhythm of her work. What was soft rippled with every bend of the knee and trembled with every twist of the waist—though Kit paid heed only to the task at hand, determined to smooth every shirt with hot steel and scalding steam. She worked fast and it wasn't long before several folded shirts were stacked on a nearby table. As she finished the last shirt, the telephone sounded.

Kit answered on the third ring and smiled.

"Hi, John."

"Just ironing a little."

"I do too," Kit laughed.

"Your church shirt."

"You need to look nice for the baptism of the children."

"God might not care, but I do."

"A pressed shirt isn't a vanity. I should know."

"This coming weekend."

"He said the second Sunday of the month."

"I'm sure he meant September, but I'll call to confirm."

"I think it's September 10 or 11. No, that's wrong. Sunday is September 9."

A moment later, Kit grew serious. "We don't have a choice," she said. "No one knows his given name."

"Morales doesn't know their language very well and I doubt he paid any attention to children's names—except maybe a few of the girls. Besides, I like Jonathan Augustine Smith. It sounds very ... reasonable."

"It's not like he'll want to use the whole thing."

Kit listened for several seconds.

"Just a short one. Right after lunch. The girls watched Brittany and the baby while I slept."

Again Kit listened before talking.

"Oh, I figured out why he was so restless last night."

"Not that," Kit said. "He's cutting his first tooth. Cindy says he'll be cranky for a few days."

"Just baby Tylenol."

"Maybe some numbing paste if he fusses at night."

"No. She stopped by a few minutes ago to get the girls. We talked over tea. I like Cindy. She's a nice neighbor. And a big help since she's already raised four children. At least to puberty."

Now Kit grew serious and she pressed both hands to the cordless telephone as she spoke. "Yes, I watched him."

Kit listened for a couple minutes with unspeaking nods. "Believe me," she eventually said, "I worked in Hollywood. You don't have to tell me what they're going to do with the truth."

"Not at all. John, you have to listen to me. I swear to you ... I swear to you on the grave of my grandmother I'm content here. You didn't make me turn down the role. I didn't want it. Besides that, Ryan never asked."

Kit grew more serious yet.

"I promise."

"Yes."

"Listen," the former actress finally said with a touch of irritation to her voice, "I'm telling the truth. From my heart. This is what I want. This is what I wanted in the beginning. Nothing more. Hollywood was a fantasy, a dream. No, a nightmare. But it's over now and the less said of lost years, the better. I have the husband I desire, the children I love, and the home I need."

Kit fell silent for nearly a minute.

"No. I love Omaha. I don't want to move."

"The people are nice, it's affordable, and I like Cindy."

"So do the girls. Right now they're in the backyard with Cindy's daughter and that Jones boy."

"No. He's a nice boy from a good family. I think they're Presbyterian too."

"Really? He'd do that for us?"

"If your brother will sell to us, we should stay here. I love this house."

"It's big enough."

"I like being so close to the children."

"Even if we could afford something that size, I don't want empty rooms. They're too cold."

"Not that kind of cold. I mean, lifeless. They'd just remind me of what I was."

"Ryan can keep it. I like this house—our home."

Now Kit spoke with an unbending tone. "You're full of worries today," she said. "I'm here for good. You're stuck with me. In case you didn't notice, Ryan left me. I committed to him for good if he'd have given me the chance. I've never left a man in my life."

Kit laughed out loud.

"Is that what this is about?"

"No, I'm not still married to him. The lawyer told us in Honolulu."

"He'll pipe down when I swear off alimony."

"John," Kit finally said, "we married before God and before God we are married. Even the minister says so. The paperwork will sort itself out. It's only been a few weeks. Since we followed the law of the land where we lived, like it or not, you're my husband and I'm your wife. And you're also the legal father of the children to whom I am the legal mother. All the lawyers admit that much. And since the state no longer exists, neither you nor I can even think about leaving each other. There's simply no way to do so."

"We have enough. I don't want his money."

"Besides, someone would just sue us for it. Everyone else will want a share and it was Ryan's name on the paperwork, not mine. I'd be really surprised if he doesn't face dozens of lawsuits before it's all over."

"Breach of contract. Wrongful death. Reckless endangerment."

"And foolish idealism too."

"I guess we were all guilty of it."

Kit moved the receiver to her other ear. "It's not just Ryan on television, is it?"

Kit's voice softened. "What's bothering you, John?"

After a moment, Kit laughed a little.

"Oh, for goodness sake."

"For you or for me?"

"You promise?"

"If you're just worried about me, stop. I don't need any more children. Mind you, if we have another, I wouldn't object. But I don't need to have the ligation reversed."

"Because four is enough. Linh's daughters are really hurting and I'm learning to be a mother at the worst time for them. Brittany never stops talking and the baby does nothing but eat. Can you imagine what it'd be like if Sally's sister and Tiffany and Brent's parents hadn't wanted their children? I'd be having a nervous breakdown."

"I'm fine. It was good to get a full night's sleep. The bags under my eyes even cleared a little."

"No," Kit protested, "I'm really not against another child."

This time she fell silent for a long while.

"He'd take monthly payments?"

"No, I don't think so."

"It's just that ... well, it sounds silly, but I'll tell you the truth. It just seems spending the time and money to reverse it when I have four kids to take care of would be even more frivolous than getting them tied in the first place. I've had enough of self-indulgence. God willing, I want to consider someone else's needs for a while."

"Really?" Kit batted her eyes. "Me too."

"Come home early and I'll give you proof of my happiness."

"Cindy already offered to babysit."

"I'll be dressed in an hour."

"Of course, I have to dress. We're going out first."

"Dinner's enough. No movies."

"Because I've seen enough of what Hollywood has to offer."

"John, stop talking like that. I hope there's no one around your desk."

"The only reason I'd check into a hotel would be to sleep. We can do everything else in the privacy of our own home. For a lot less money, too."

"Yes, I'll see if Cindy can keep the older children for the night. We can have the others in bed by eight."

Kit listened for a long while. "I realized something when Ryan was interviewing," she finally said. "Do you know what our big mistake was?"

"Not just Dr. Morales."

"No," Kit said, "I realized I can't change the whole world and it was chasing the wind to try. What I can do is make a new world—a nice home—for a few loved ones and maybe a couple strangers. Do you think that's enough from one human life?"

"I hope so too."

A moment later, Kit said goodbye, then switched the phone off and returned to her ironing (where only two dresses and a white blouse remained in the basket). Soon, short bursts of steam and the hard press of a hot iron removed every wrinkle from the white blouse. As Kit folded the blouse, she looked at the pressed garment and her eyes misted as she remembered that one like it was to have been the centerpiece of her bridal ensemble. Then she remembered how she married John wearing nothing more than rags and decided to dress formal for their evening together.

Looking out the kitchen window, Kit saw Linh's daughters playing with their friends—then heard the footsteps of a toddler upstairs, followed by the cries of a baby. Kit unplugged the iron and fetched a bottle of milk from the refrigerator, hurrying upstairs to feed the baby and change his diaper. She needed to collect the children's overnight things and change clothes, as well as to prepare a quick supper for the children. Both girls had inherited their mother's skill in the kitchen and required further instruction before they could be trusted to prepare real food.

Kit hurried up the stairs, hoping to finish her work before John returned home—he was due within the hour.